THE DEATH OF KINGS

RENNIE AIRTH was born in South Africa and has worked as a foreign correspondent for Reuters. The first novel in his John Madden series, *River of Darkness*, published in 1999 to huge critical acclaim, was shortlisted for four crime fiction awards and won the Grand Prix de Littérature Policière in France. *River of Darkness* was followed by *The Blood-Dimmed Tide*, the CWA Ellis Peters Award shortlisted *The Dead of Winter* and *The Reckoning*. *The Death of Kings* is the fifth novel in the John Madden series.

Also by Rennie Airth

RIVER OF DARKNESS

THE BLOOD-DIMMED TIDE

THE DEAD OF WINTER

THE RECKONING

RENNIE AIRTH

THE DEATH
OF KINGS

PAN BOOKS

First published 2017 by Mantle

This paperback edition first published 2017 by Pan Books
an imprint of Pan Macmillan
20 New Wharf Road, London N1 9RR
Associated companies throughout the world
www.panmacmillan.com

ISBN 978-1-5098-1733-7

1 3 5 7 9 8 6 4 2

A CIP catalogue record for this book is available from the British Library.

Typeset by Ellipsis, Glasgow
Printed and bound by CPI Group (UK) Ltd, Croydon, CR0 4YY

Visit ww
and to buy
news of
so tha

For Ronald Vance

For God's sake, let us sit upon the ground
And tell sad stories of the death of kings

William Shakespeare, *Richard II*

THE DEATH OF KINGS

PROLOGUE

Kent, August 1938

WHEN SHE HEARD the stair creak beneath her foot, Portia stopped and stood frozen. Her heartbeat quickened with excitement.

She didn't want to be seen. She planned to slip out and then return to her room in time to appear for tea as though nothing had happened; as though she had been resting, which was what she had told the others she would be doing when she had left them in the drawing room after lunch.

But there was always the danger that he might be spying on her; keeping a watch on her movements. She knew that he didn't trust her any longer. He suspected that she might be trying to take matters into her own hands.

'What is this game you're playing?' He had come to her room the night before after the household had gone to bed. 'Are you out of your mind?' His face, which so seldom showed any feeling, had been stiff with rage. 'Do you think you're on the stage? Must you always be the . . . *actress?*' He had spat the word out as though it left a bad taste in his mouth. 'Leave this to me. Just do as you are told.'

She had tried to calm him, telling him not to worry. 'They're in a safe place,' she had assured him. But she had resented the tone of his angry accusations and the evident scorn he felt for her. As if *he* wasn't the one playing his own

1

game! She still didn't know what he was up to – what his scheme involved – only that she had a part in it and would be rewarded in due course.

Or so he had said. But she no more trusted him than she did any other man. And as it happened, his suspicions were justified. Unknown to him she had already put her own plan into action and he was helpless to stop it. The stage had been set; all that was required was for the curtain to go up.

She knew her lines – she had written them herself – and before leaving she had stood before the full-length mirror in her room taking in not only her appearance but also the expressions on her face as she rehearsed the scene she was about to play.

She had dressed with care, choosing a simple skirt and blouse, and covered her red hair with a silk scarf. Although the occasion hardly called for a display of jewellery, she had put on the pair of earrings she had been lent for the weekend and then, unable to resist the temptation, had slipped the pendant around her neck as well. Carved in the shape of the Buddha, it was made of jade and deep green in colour – the shade most valued by Chinese emperors, she had been told. She had already removed the paint she had put on her nails the night before – that had been purely for show, and to draw attention to her hands as she played with the pendant – and having examined her reflection in the mirror she went one step further, wiping the lipstick off her mouth. She meant to display a new image of herself, one about which there could be no mistake: that of a woman with a serious purpose, not a plaything to be used and then cast aside at will. As if by reflex she reached for the small leather handbag that was hanging by a strap from her shoulder. Searching for the clasp, she opened it and slipped her fingers inside. Yes . . . everything she needed was there.

Now, with the house as silent as a tomb around her, she resumed her descent of the stairs, reaching the empty hall below with its echoing paved floor and then crossing it on tiptoe, padding softly as a cat. Her goal was a long corridor that ran the length of the house and when she came to it she turned right and made for a door that gave onto the garden.

She had almost reached the end of the passage when a figure appeared from one of the doorways ahead of her and she slowed her pace, unsettled at being discovered. But it was only one of the maids, who stood aside, bobbing her head as Portia went by. The door was a few paces further on and as she opened it and slipped out into the blazing hot afternoon a wave of relief washed over her.

Although she didn't want to admit it – even to herself – she was afraid of him. The men she had known in her life, and there were many – too many – had been mostly of a type and she had learned what to expect of them, which was little enough. But *he* was different – unreadable, unknowable – and she had sensed that his silent presence and cold, ever-watchful eye signalled a more dangerous and less predictable nature than any other she had encountered in the past.

The door she had come through gave onto a path that stretched the length of the garden. Walled on either side by high yew hedges whose topmost branches had been trained to meet overhead, it offered a shield against prying eyes – even those who might be watching from the bedroom windows above – and once she had entered the long, cool tunnel she was able to relax and focus her mind on the business ahead. She was already a good ten minutes late for her appointment (deliberately so – she would not be the one kept waiting) and when she came to a wooden gate in the high brick wall at the bottom of the garden and saw a party of a dozen or more people, both men and women, strolling along a path that crossed the expanse of common land beyond it, she paused and waited while they made their slow way towards the tree-covered knoll which was visible from the terrace of the house behind her and which she had been told bore the name of Holly Hill. She assumed that the casually dressed group were hop-pickers; the harvest was in full swing and driving down from London the day before she had seen the fields surrounding the village busy with pickers. But since today was Sunday she knew they wouldn't be working and didn't want the rendezvous to which she was heading disturbed by passers-by.

As soon as the last of the party had disappeared into the wood she went through the gate and made her way swiftly across the field on a path less trodden than the one they had used. The two paths met on the far side of the meadow just short of the wood and when Portia got there she glanced over her shoulder to make sure she was not being followed before continuing in the wake of the group whose voices she could hear in the distance ahead of her; plunging into the gloom of the wood whose deep shadow was in stark contrast to the bright sunshine she had just stepped out of.

She was treading unfamiliar ground. She had never been invited to the house where she was a guest before, so its surroundings were new to her. But she had been given directions easy enough to follow: some way into the wood, near the top of the slight rise she was ascending now, was the ruin of an old hermit's hut. It was situated a little way off the path, but easy to spot. They were to meet there. As she neared the top of the knoll she began to scan the surrounding trees and presently caught sight of the stone structure. Overhung by a towering beech, it was without a roof; only the walls still stood.

She stopped to peer at it and as she did she heard the sound of movement behind her. It might have been no more than a twig breaking, but she stood still for long seconds peering into the shadowy depths of the wood, waiting until she was sure no one was there. Only when satisfied did she turn back to peer at the ruined hut again and almost at once caught sight of a figure moving about inside. One moment it appeared at the single window, the next it was standing in the doorway, barely visible in the deep shade cast by the branches overhead.

Poised to move forward now, she hesitated. Was she going too far? Had she overreached herself? She knew what *he* would say; it was why she had kept it a secret from him. Still she felt a tremor of doubt, and for a moment her nerve faltered.

Then anger came to her rescue, the deep rage that had been building inside her – for years it seemed. She had been used once too often; humiliated in a way she was no longer prepared to tolerate. It was time someone paid the price.

An actress, *he* had called her, and standing there motionless in the wood, she couldn't help but picture herself as a character in a play, or perhaps a film: a woman of mystery, a woman with a secret. It was the sort of part she had always longed for, and while there were no cameras, no lights adjusted so as to catch her face half in shadow as she waited, she could still comfort herself with the knowledge that hers was the leading role in the drama that was about to unfold.

Her moment had arrived, the one she had dreamed of, and her only regret was that there was no one to record it, no director standing hidden in the shadows somewhere behind her ready to shout the magic word.

'*Action!*'

PART ONE

1

London, August 1949

'I'M SORRY TO BE the one to tell you, John, but it's no go. Not on the available evidence. Cradock won't go along with it, and I see his point.'

Sitting at ease in his shirt sleeves, with his tie loosened and his cuffs rolled up, Detective Chief Superintendent Chubb settled back in his chair with a sigh. A man whose drooping jowls and moist, dog-like eyes had earned him comparison with a bloodhound in his younger days together with the nickname Cheerful Charlie, the chief super's naturally mournful expression was well suited to the role forced on him that morning as the bearer of bad news.

'He even went so far as to refer to a can of worms, which is not like him at all.' Chubb shook his head regretfully. 'For one thing, there's no proof as yet that these two pendants are one and the same, and even if they are that doesn't necessarily mean that a mistake was made in the original investigation.'

'How's that, Charlie?'

Madden cocked an eye at him. Old colleagues in the distant past, they were sitting facing each other across a desk in the chief superintendent's sun-filled office at Scotland Yard. For nearly a week now London had been sweltering in a heatwave and with August not even half done and no sign of a change in the weather, it seemed likely the capital would continue to suffer for a while yet.

'Come on, John.' Chubb looked discomfited. 'You know as well as I do that there are nearly always loose ends in any inquiry; it's rare that all of them are tied up. Just glancing through the file it seems to me there are any number of ways that pendant might have gone missing. For one thing someone else may have picked it up and simply pocketed it; for another it may still be lying around somewhere in the wood. We've only the word of this anonymous correspondent that the one he sent to Derry once belonged to Portia Blake.'

He awaited the other's reaction. Madden was considering his response.

'Well, I'll pass on what you say to Angus,' he said finally. 'But he won't like it.'

'I'm sure he won't.' Chubb winced. The man they were speaking of, Angus Sinclair, formerly a chief inspector, now retired, had once been their superior, and while Chubb was willing to admit that he had learned all he knew under Sinclair's stern tutelage he was also wont to claim, only half humorously, that the experience had left him scarred for life.

'He's very upset about this, Charlie.' Although Madden, too, had suffered on occasion from the chief inspector's acid tongue during his time as a detective with the Metropolitan Police, now long past, the two men had become friends during the years they had worked together and on retiring Sinclair had chosen to settle in the same Surrey village of Highfield where Madden and his wife lived. 'He thinks there may have been a miscarriage of justice. As you're aware, the man they arrested was eventually hanged. And we all know how Angus feels about capital punishment.'

Chubb grunted. 'I never shared his views, mind. If you take a life, you deserve to swing. That's my opinion.'

'Yes, but what's bothering Angus now is whether this man, Norris, was in fact guilty. Or was the wrong man sent to the gallows? He won't rest easy until he's satisfied on that point.'

The chief super's sigh sounded a long-suffering note. Fanning his face with a sheet of paper taken from the file in front of him, he turned to the third person present at their meeting.

'What's your opinion, Inspector? You've read this.'

Billy Styles hesitated. A detective for close on a quarter of a century now, he owed his early opportunities not only to John Madden, under whom he had cut his teeth in a still-famous murder case, but also to Sinclair, the senior officer in charge of the investigation, who had overlooked his inexperience at the time and given him a chance to show his worth. He would have preferred to take their part, but like the chief super he had his misgivings.

'I agree that initially we'd have to show that these two pendants are one and the same – at least as far as the AC is concerned.' Assistant Commissioner, Crime, Eustace Cradock was their immediate superior and a man with whom Charlie Chubb had never enjoyed the easiest of relationships. 'He won't budge otherwise. But actually, after thinking it over, I feel there are one or two other questions that need answering.'

'Do you?' Chubb eyed the younger man in feigned astonishment. 'This is the first I've heard of it.'

'Well, for one thing, why did she go for a walk, this Portia Blake? There didn't seem any good reason for it; not right after lunch in the heat of the afternoon. And why did she go alone?'

'Why shouldn't she?'

'I just thought it strange, her being an actress and all, and a good-looking young woman, too.' Billy scratched his head.

'I must be slow, Inspector.' Chubb's gaze was stony. 'You'll have to explain that to me.'

'I think what Billy's saying is that it seemed out of character,' Madden intervened. 'I thought the same when Angus told me about the case: and so did he, apparently – at the time.'

'Then why didn't he do something about it?' The chief super was losing patience.

Madden rubbed his chin.

'The whole trouble with the investigation – and Angus is quite ready to acknowledge that now – is that it was resolved too quickly; too easily. This man Norris was arrested almost at once; all the evidence seemed to indicate he was guilty.'

'It still does. And correct me if I'm wrong – but didn't he confess to the murder?'

'He did; although he later retracted his confession. But that was part of the problem, you see.' Madden strove to clarify the issue. 'Once the Kent police were persuaded they had their man, there seemed no need to continue with the inquiry and the investigation was wound up, leaving certain questions, as Billy says, unanswered.'

Clearly unhappy with what he was hearing, Chubb growled.

'All right. Let's say I accept that for the moment. What about this actress? What was so strange about her behaviour?'

'Well, as Billy said, for a start it was a very hot day, yet she chose to go out shortly after two o'clock without telling anyone and when her hosts and the other guests were either resting or otherwise occupied in their rooms. If she hadn't been spotted by a maid she would have slipped out without anyone noticing. It could be argued that was her intention.'

Madden frowned.

'She was an attractive young woman with no shortage of admirers and one can't help but wonder whether she wasn't on her way to meet one of them. Why go out in the blazing heat of the afternoon otherwise? It might not have been so surprising if she had stayed in the garden. But she left it to walk across a field and into a wood, which was where her body was found.'

'And just who might she have been going to meet?' Chubb cocked an eye at Madden. 'Has Angus any ideas about that?'

'Not that I'm aware of. But if she was headed for a rendezvous it was most likely with a man.'

'And you – or rather Angus – now think this imaginary bloke could be the real murderer?'

'It's possible.'

The chief super shook his head again. A rumble of discontent issued from his lips.

'Possible maybe, but not good enough, John, and you know it. It's guesswork. Don't blame Cradock. For once I agree with him. We all know what will happen if he consents to reopen the case. All hell will break loose. It was bad enough the first time round, what with an actress getting herself topped and the Prince of Wales's name being batted about like a ping-pong ball. We won't want to go through all that again if we can help it.'

He peered at his listener.

'Look, Styles here said you were planning to go down to Kent to have a word with Tom Derry and take a look at this pendant. Fine. I've no problem with that. In fact, if you learn anything interesting you might pass it on to us. But if you're going to ask any more questions, for heaven's sake be discreet. I don't want this thing suddenly blowing up in my face; and neither does Cradock.'

He paused to lend weight to his words.

'As for Angus, he'll just have to swallow it. I'll write him a letter explaining why we can't take it any further; not as things stand.' He cocked an eye at his visitor. 'How is he generally – in good spirits?'

'I wouldn't say that.' Madden prepared to get up. 'His gout's playing up again. I left him growling like a bear in his cave.'

'Then like as not he'll bite your head off when you give him the news.' Chubb chuckled.

'I shouldn't be surprised.' Madden rose to his feet. 'Look, I understand your position, Charlie, and I'll do my best to explain it to Angus. Thank you for giving me your time. Helen sends her regards and says she hopes you'll pay us a visit again soon. I'm sure Angus would like to have a word with you as well.'

'I'll bet he would.' Chubb rose to bid his visitor farewell. 'So he can bite my head off too.'

'I'm sorry it's turned out this way, sir.' Billy Styles walked with his old mentor down the corridor from Chubb's office to the head of the stairs. 'I'd like to have given you more support, but . . .'

'But Mr Sinclair doesn't have a strong case.' Madden patted him on the arm. 'Don't worry, Billy. I knew I'd be batting on a tricky wicket. I told Angus I would try, but I didn't really believe we could persuade either Charlie or Cradock to act. It'll take more than that pendant to get them to reopen the inquiry.'

'Mr Sinclair must know that.' Billy was puzzled. 'I just wonder why he's stirring things up. I know he was in charge of the investigation, but only nominally, to judge by the file. It was almost all over by the time he got down there. The Canterbury police arrested the bloke the next day.'

'Yes, only nominally, as you say, but he was still in charge.' Madden paused at the head of the stairs leading down to the lobby. 'And the man was hanged: that's the point to remember. That's why Mr Sinclair is so upset. If he thinks for a moment that they were wrong – that he played some part, no matter how small, in sending an innocent man to the gallows – it'll go on tormenting him. He's always hated capital punishment. He thinks it's barbaric.'

Billy reflected.

'I'm surprised he didn't come up to London himself.' He grinned. 'Then Charlie would have had to face him. He wouldn't have enjoyed that.'

'Oh, he would have come. You can be sure of that. But he's immobilized at the moment. As I told Charlie, it's his gout. Helen has told him he's not to budge from his cottage until his gout eases a little. Even then, I doubt he could manage a trip to London. He's quite crippled at the moment.'

In her role as Highfield's doctor, Madden's wife had overseen the former chief inspector's health ever since his retirement four years earlier.

'Since I was coming up to town anyway I offered to have a word with Charlie in person. Mr Sinclair wrote to him a week ago. He's still waiting for a reply. I'm sure he'll get it in due course – but it won't be the one he was hoping for. I'll have to ring him this evening and give him the bad news.'

Madden started down the stairs, but paused when he caught the look in Billy's eye.

'I was just wondering.' The younger man scratched his head. 'Isn't there something I could do? I'd like to help Mr Sinclair if I can.'

'No, don't do anything, Billy, not for the moment.' Madden was quick to discourage him. 'Charlie's a good sort, but he won't take kindly to having his orders ignored. And as it happens, it's no inconvenience for me to slip down to Kent. I'll be up in London all this week and probably next week too, but not fully occupied. I'm rather looking forward to seeing Tom Derry again. You remember him, don't you?'

'Of course.' Billy grinned in happy recollection. 'That was when we went down to Maidstone together.'

The visit he was recalling had occurred more than a score of years earlier when he had worked under Madden on an investigation into a series of brutal murders that had begun in Highfield but taken them far afield in search of the killer. Their travels had included a trip to Maidstone where the then local CID chief, Tom Derry, an old friend of Sinclair's, had proved to be of particular help.

'Derry was transferred to Canterbury in the Thirties, which is how he came to be involved in the Portia Blake murder. He's retired now, but it was his letter to Mr Sinclair that got the ball rolling. I rang him yesterday and explained about Angus being laid up at the moment and that I was coming down in his place. Derry's also worried that they may have arrested the wrong man.'

'Well, if both of them feel the same way there may be something to it.' Billy frowned.

'Perhaps. I'll know better when I've talked to him.'

Madden started down the stairs.

'Before then, though, I'm going to have to ring Angus and give him the bad news.'

He glanced back over his shoulder.

'Spare a thought for me, would you?'

2

'Yes, Angus. I see. No, really, I understand. Not at all, Angus – I was happy to be of help. Yes, of course I'll give you a full report when I get back. By the way, are you feeling any better?'

Madden listened with the receiver pressed to his ear; and then, like Chubb earlier in the day, he winced.

'I'm sorry to hear that. Helen did say it might take some time to wear off.'

Again he was silent as he listened to the voice at the other end of the line.

'Quite so. It sounds most unpleasant. We'll talk again very soon. Goodbye for now.'

As he replaced the receiver Madden looked up and saw that his daughter, Lucy, was standing at the bottom of the stairs listening. He hadn't heard her come down from her bedroom upstairs. She was shaking her head.

'Poor Angus.'

'Yes, poor Angus.' Madden scowled. 'But he's certainly making a meal of it.'

'You're being very hard-hearted,' she observed piously.

'Am I?' Madden led the way into the sitting room. 'According to your mother he's the worst patient she's ever had, and I can believe it. I thought he'd be pleased when I told him I was going down to Kent tomorrow. Not a bit of it. He said I should have been more insistent with Chubb, made him see reason.'

'Poor Angus.'

'Will you stop saying that?' Madden caught her eye and she laughed. He stood back to take in her appearance. 'What a lovely dress. Did you make it yourself?'

'Sort of.' Lucy turned slowly about so that he could appreciate the full effect of the tight-waisted, bouffant garment. Cut well below her knees in the so-called New Look – a fashion that like so many had come from Paris (and been much derided by killjoys when it first appeared as a waste of scarce material) – it swirled about her graceful figure in a shimmering blue wave. 'It's an old evening dress of Mummy's which I cut down and made some alterations to. Can you remember her wearing it?'

'Yes, now that you mention it.' Madden's gaze softened. 'You're really very good at this. Are you going to make a career of it?'

It was more than a year now since Lucy had come up to London with the idea of finding a job, and to her parents' surprise had accepted a lowly position in the salon of a well-known dress designer (somewhat to the disappointment of her mother, who still nursed the hope that her unpredictable daughter might eventually realize she had a good mind and try for university).

'But that's what I'm doing, in a way.' Lucy had sought to console her. 'I'm studying, learning things. I'm a bit of a dogsbody at the moment, but that'll change, you'll see.'

'Perhaps I'll have a famous daughter one day.' Madden mused agreeably on the thought. 'We'll all be invited to view the new Lucy Madden collection.'

'You never know. It might happen.' Lucy was busy checking her reflection in the mirror above the mantel. 'I feel I'm abandoning you tonight,' she said. 'Are you sure you'll be all right?'

'I expect I'll manage. I've got Alice to look after me.'

'Dear Alice. She hardly knows what to do with herself now that Aunt Maud's gone. She talks to me about her all the time.'

It was the recent death of Helen's aunt – and Lucy's great-aunt – Maud Collingwood that had brought Madden to London. Surviving well into her nineties, the old lady had passed away peacefully in her bed – as she had always sworn she would – two months earlier and when her will was read Helen and Madden found that she had left them her house in St John's Wood.

'It's not that surprising, I suppose – I was her closest living relative – but what on earth are we going to do with it?'

For a while Helen and her husband had toyed with the idea of letting the house. But the problems of absentee land-lordism had finally persuaded them to sell it.

'We can use the money to buy a flat which Lucy can use,' Helen had pointed out. 'And it can be somewhere for Rob to stay as well when he's in London.' Their son, a naval officer, was presently serving on a cruiser in the Indian Ocean.

The decision having been made, Madden had set himself the task of finding an estate agent to handle the sale and of disposing of such furniture as they did not wish to keep while Lucy, who had been camping with friends in an over-crowded flat in Knightsbridge, had moved to St John's Wood.

'I'd rather not leave Alice in the house on her own,' Helen had explained.

Aunt Maud's long-time maid and companion, Alice Penny had made plans to spend her retirement with her sister and brother-in-law at Hastings, on the south coast, but her move had been delayed by the alterations that would have to be made to their home before they could take her in. In the interim, Helen had insisted that she remain in her late mistress's house and Alice in turn had decided that she would continue to serve as cook and maid there for as long as the Maddens might need her.

Lucy, meanwhile, was busy in front of the mirror putting last-minute touches to her make-up.

'Could you help me with my dress, Daddy? It's those buttons at the back. They're so hard to reach. I don't know how Mummy used to manage. Did she have a maid to help?'

'I should think so. People did in those days.'

Madden came up behind his daughter and began the painstaking job of fitting each small cloth-covered button into its appropriate slit. Glancing at the mirror he saw their faces – Lucy's fresh glowing complexion and his own weathered visage where the lines around his eyes were deeply carved now and his dark hair streaked with grey. As always in summer, when his skin grew tanned, the scar on his forehead – a legacy of the months he had spent in the trenches during the First World War – showed white against the brown skin. She caught his eye in the mirror and smiled.

'When you took me to dinner at Rules the other night we were spotted by a friend of mine, Polly Manners. She rang me next day wanting to know who my madly attractive escort was and did I know any other fascinating-looking older men like him I could introduce her to.'

'Madly attractive!' Madden spluttered. 'What a ridiculous thing to say. And you're much too young to be thinking about older men.'

'Correct me if I'm wrong, but isn't that what's called a contradiction in terms?'

She kissed him on the cheek, and then stood back to examine her reflection in the mirror.

'Don't wait up for me. I won't be back till late.'

'Dancing till dawn again, are you?'

Madden regarded his lovely daughter wistfully. Lucy had inherited not only her mother's looks but also so many of her mannerisms that there were times when he seemed to be seeing Helen in her youth reborn in the golden-haired girl before him.

Lucy shook her head. 'You keep forgetting I've got a job. I have to get up in the morning. You're confusing me with Mummy. It was she and Violet who used to dance the night away. Literally. Violet has told me all about it, how they would gather in Piccadilly at the end of a ball to have breakfast at one of those mobile kitchens. "Ah, the times your mother and I have seen the sun come up over Green Park."'

One of Helen's oldest friends, Lady Violet Tremayne was a fixture of Highfield life.

'Of course, Mummy denies it furiously. She says Violet exaggerates everything. But I know which one of them I believe.'

Lucy put on her stole.

'I wish I were staying in with you tonight. I'd much rather hear about this case of Angus's and what happened at Scotland Yard today. You must promise to tell me all about it when you come back from Kent. I want to know what you find out – every last detail.'

To Madden's surprise, when he had told his daughter about the mission Sinclair had entrusted him with she had reacted instantly to one of the names he had mentioned.

'The Portia Blake murder! Of course I remember that. When I was at St Clare's we used to smuggle copies of the *News of the World* into the dormitory and read it by torch-light under our sheets. She was an actress, wasn't she? She looked lovely in her photographs. It was awful to think of her being strangled that way.'

In the course of her chequered scholastic career Lucy had spent some months at a boarding school in Dorset, one from which her parents had hurriedly removed her when it became apparent from letters sent by the headmistress that she was about to be expelled for persistent misbehaviour.

'We always thought there was more to it than met the eye, the other girls and I. The trouble was the police made an arrest almost at once. It was over so quickly.'

At that moment the bell rang – it was the taxi she had telephoned for earlier – and Madden accompanied his daughter to the front door.

'Oddly enough, that's exactly what Angus says,' he told her as she kissed him goodnight.

3

'IF ONLY SHE hadn't been an *actress*.' Tom Derry scowled at the word. 'It was all Fleet Street needed to start licking its lips. We'd hardly had time to shift the poor woman's body to the mortuary slab in Canterbury when more than a score of them descended on us from London – reporters, photographers . . . the lot. They pretty well laid siege to the house.'

He muttered to himself, as though the memory still had the power to rile him.

'And, of course, it wasn't only that. It was also because of where she was staying: her host, Sir Jack Jessup, was a big name. "Black Jack Jessup" – that's what the newspapers used to call him. Actually he was christened with your name, John. But he was always known as Sir Jack, and preferred to be called that. He'd been quite a lad in his younger days, always in the public eye for one reason or another, and later on he became "one of the Prince of Wales's set", as the press liked to put it then. I don't know how much truth there was in that, though Edward did come down here to stay a couple of times before he abdicated. But it meant the papers could put it all together – actress, Prince of Wales, murder! Well, I don't have to draw a picture for you. It was meat and drink to them.'

He fell silent for a few moments as a flock of sheep materialized on the narrow lane in front of them and he was forced to steer a careful path between their woolly bodies.

'That's also why Angus was sent down from London. As

23

soon as our chief constable heard about the murder – and that was within an hour or two – he was on the blower to the commissioner in London. He could see what lay ahead and wanted any brickbats that might be coming our way from the press or public spread around, with the Yard getting its fair share. At least that's my opinion.

'And the irony was she had never been much of an actress anyway, Miss Portia Blake. I looked into her background and found she'd only been in a handful of West End plays and one or two films, and always in walk-on parts, never as a lead or anything close to it. But the press boys weren't going to let a little thing like that spoil their party.' He snorted.

Madden glanced across at his companion for the day. Not surprisingly, the former Kent detective had aged with the years. Now quite bald, Derry had also shrunk, at least in Madden's memory as he recalled the lanky individual he had first encountered in Maidstone all those years ago. Like Sinclair, he had retired from the force at the end of the war with the rank of superintendent. But he seemed as alert as ever and had greeted Madden warmly when he had arrived at his cottage on the outskirts of Canterbury earlier that morning.

'I remember the day you came down from London as though it were yesterday,' he had told him. 'Whatever happened to that young cub you had with you?'

'He prospered, I'm happy to say. Billy Styles is his name. He's a detective-inspector at the Yard now and he sends his regards.'

Although Madden and his wife had visited Canterbury more than once to stay with a cousin of Helen's who was married to a local solicitor, they had not done so since the end of the war, when the couple had moved away, and Madden had been shocked by what he'd seen as the taxi from the station had borne him through the city. Accustomed as he was to the sight of bombed-out buildings in London, where the snail's pace of post-war reconstruction had left much of the city still in ruins, he had not expected to see damage on a similar scale in the much smaller confines of Canterbury.

'The Germans used us as a target for any bombs they failed to drop on London,' Derry explained to him later. 'Canterbury was on their way home and they just unloaded whatever they were still carrying before they crossed the coast.'

Luckily the famous cathedral, like St Paul's in London, had survived relatively unscathed, and Madden had turned to look at its imposing spire rising above the town as they set off for their destination.

'You might be interested to see the spot where the murder took place,' Derry had suggested. A widower now like Sinclair, he had provided his visitor with a cup of tea on his arrival and handed him a buff-coloured folder.

'That's a copy of the file the Canterbury police have in their records. They were kind enough to make one for me after I raised the issue with them. I put the letter I got in there. I expect you'd like to read it.'

Madden had removed the envelope from the folder and taken out the letter which was typed on cheap notepaper and addressed to 'Chief Inspector Derry'.

I have reason to believe that the jade pendant accompanying this letter is the same one that disappeared from Miss Portia Blake's body in August 1938.

It had started without ceremony.

Rather than tell you why I suspect this I will leave it to you to establish the truth of the allegation. It should not prove difficult. As you may have noticed there is a slight flaw in the stone. That should be sufficient to identify it.

Since the piece could not have been stolen by the man who was hanged for Miss Blake's murder, the question arises: who else could have taken it?

And why?

I leave the rest to you.

The letter was unsigned.

'Chief inspector?' Madden had examined the piece of notepaper closely to see if it had a watermark. 'Was that your rank then?'

Derry nodded. 'Either the writer knows that or he got it from newspaper files.'

'Could I have a look at the pendant?' Madden had asked.

They had been sitting facing each other in armchairs in Derry's small parlour and without replying the former superintendent had reached into his pocket and pulled out a velvet bag tied with a drawstring. Turning it upside down, he had leaned across and emptied the contents into his visitor's hand. He had watched as Madden held the stone up to the light. Deep green in colour and suspended from a gold chain, it was carved in the shape of a seated Buddha.

'Yes, I can see what your letter writer means about it being flawed. Mind you, it's hardly visible. And it doesn't spoil the look of it.' Madden had pointed to a line hardly wider than a hair in the plump stomach and paler than the dark green around it. 'How do you plan to check whether it's the same pendant? Is there someone you can ask?'

'Not really. Both Miss Blake's parents died when she was still quite young and she was brought up by an older sister who lives in Ipswich. It was she who collected Portia's things after she died. I spoke to her on the telephone, but she wasn't able to help. She didn't know anything about any pendant.'

Derry shrugged.

'But there is one other possibility. Miss Blake had a flat-mate called Audrey Cooper; another actress. I found her address and phone number in the file and rang her. Unfortunately, she was out of town, but I managed to get hold of some other woman – a flatmate, I gathered – who told me Miss Cooper was on tour in the provinces with a theatrical company. She'll be back in London next week. I thought I'd wait until then to talk to her.'

'But this pendant resembles the one Portia Blake had?'

'Oh, yes. We were given a description of it. She was wearing it at dinner the night before she was murdered and the housemaid who saw her as she was leaving the house next day said she had it on. I can confirm it wasn't among her effects when we searched her room later.'

Madden had studied the note again.

'The wording's strange, isn't it?' he remarked. '*I have reason to believe . . . rather than tell you . . . the question arises . . . I leave the rest to you.* If whoever wrote this had any information regarding the case, why not just come forward and say so? What did you make of it?'

Derry shrugged.

'My first thought was that the writer was playing the fool with us. But although the tone is odd he – or she, though I get the impression the writer is a man – seems to know something; or wants us to believe that he does.'

'But to what purpose, I wonder?' Madden frowned. 'It seems clear that the writer wants the case reopened. But if so, why not point a finger at someone? It's far more likely the police would be interested if they were given a name.'

It was at that point that Derry had suggested they drive out to the village of Burnham, near to where the young woman had been killed.

'You'll understand what's bothering Angus and me better when you've seen the actual murder site.'

Derry had assured his visitor their journey wouldn't take long – the village was only a few miles from Canterbury – and soon after they left the outskirts of the city Madden found they were in the midst of open countryside, a gently rolling landscape which in other parts of England might have been covered with wheat or barley but here was planted with field after field of hops. He saw that the plants had turned from green to yellow, a sign that they were ready for harvesting.

'This is the time of year, the same month in fact, when the Blake woman was murdered.' Derry gestured at the land on either side of them. 'The fields around here were full of hop pickers, just as they are now. Owen Norris, the man convicted of the murder, was one of them. He was an itinerant farm worker; he'd come here for the harvest, same as the others. At the time I thought it was a crime that was unpremeditated; that Norris had come on Miss Blake by chance.'

He glanced at Madden.

'Now I'm not so sure.'

'That's where she left the garden.'

Madden followed the direction of Derry's pointing finger and saw a green wooden gate set in a high brick wall overhung with trailing creepers.

'You can't see the house from here. We'll have to wait until we get higher up into the wood.'

They had left the car in the village half a mile away and walked along a narrow road bounded by the same wall until they reached the field they were crossing now on a path that branched off from the road. Ahead of them was a wooded hillock which Derry had already identified as the spot where Portia Blake had met her end.

'There's another path that leads from the gate.' Again Derry pointed. 'It joins with this one further on and it's the one she took. The strange thing is there were people around when she was killed, and quite nearby, too. If there was someone waiting up there in the wood to do her in – and that's only speculation, mind – then he was certainly taking a chance.'

'People?' Madden glanced inquiringly at him.

'Hop pickers. A party of them had walked here from the village. It was a Sunday, not a working day, and they had been having a drink at the pub and must have crossed this field at almost the same time as Portia Blake came out of that gate. They walked up through the wood and out the other side to where they were camping. Norris had also been at the pub, and drunk too much as usual, or so the landlord said. He'd wanted another drink at closing time but been sent on his way after an argument. He followed the same route as the others – the one we've just taken – but they were some way ahead by this time and he never caught up with them.'

Derry paused to lend significance to his last words.

'Might he have seen Portia Blake entering the wood?' Madden asked.

'He might . . . though he said not.' Derry shrugged. 'Let's go on, shall we?'

They continued, crossing the field and passing the point where the path Portia Blake had taken joined the one they were on, and then walking up the slope to the wooded knoll. When they came to the first of the trees Derry stopped and turned round. Madden followed suit.

'There – now you can see it. That's the house. It's called Foxley Hall. It was bought by one of Jessup's forebears in the last century from a family that dated back to the Conquest. Originally it was a Norman manor, one of the oldest in the country, but it was sacked and burned during the Civil War and then rebuilt in the Dutch style; or so my architecturally minded friends tell me.'

Madden shaded his eyes. It was after midday and the overhead sun was bright. It glinted on the many windows at the front of the house and brought a glow to the red brickwork which was topped by a line of triangular gables, all clearly visible now above the tall garden wall. They were high enough that he could also see the flagged terrace in front of the house and below it, descending in shallow steps, several other terraces decorated with lawns and flower beds, one of them containing a wide lily pond.

'She went out by a side door – that's where she was seen by the maid – and must have come down that yew alley you can see at the edge of the garden.' Derry's pointing finger had shifted. 'She wouldn't have been spotted walking down – the hedges form a tunnel – so it doesn't look as though anyone in the house could have noticed her.'

'Is the house empty now?' Madden asked. He could see that the ground-floor windows were shuttered.

Derry nodded. 'Sir Jack died here in 'thirty-nine, shortly after the war started. The lady he lived with moved out soon afterwards. He only had one child, a son named Richard – Sir Richard now – and he was away on active service for most of the war. When it was over he decided he didn't want to live here and the house was let to tenants. Lately he's decided to sell it and I'm told it's going to be turned into a school. Apart from a caretaker, no one lives here now. You can see that the garden's been allowed to go.'

Madden nodded. He had divined as much from the untrimmed hedges and empty borders.

'The lady Sir Jack *lived* with, you say?'

'A Mrs Castleton, she was, Adele Castleton.' Derry smiled.

'I wouldn't say she was notorious exactly, but she'd certainly had her name in the papers often enough before she hooked up with Jessup. He was still married, but his wife wouldn't give him a divorce. I believe he and Mrs Castleton had been together for some time, living as man and wife, but not legally hitched. I must say I thought her a damned attractive woman when I met her. Not young any more, but I could understand any man losing his head over her.' He shook his head in rueful memory.

Madden had turned from studying the house to listen to him. 'I'd be interested to know who was staying with them that weekend,' he said. 'Do you still have the names?'

Derry nodded. 'They're in the file. We interviewed them all briefly. Initially, we just wanted to know where they were when the murder took place. We were going to question them again, in detail, but when Norris was arrested – that was only two days after the murder – the investigation was wound up and we never got to do it. They weren't a particularly interesting bunch. But one in particular did catch my eye: a Mr Stanley Wing. I don't mind admitting I didn't like the look of him. He was a business associate of Sir John's, some kind of oriental; not pure Chinese; a half-breed I would say. He certainly had a touch of the chink about him. I don't know if you're aware of it, but the Jessup family fortune was made in Hong Kong.'

Madden nodded. 'Jessup's are one of the great trading companies out there – *hongs* they're called. You were telling me about this man Wing . . . ?'

'There's not much to tell.' Derry shrugged. 'As it happened, I interviewed him myself. He said he had come down from London for the weekend at Sir Jack's invitation and had brought Portia Blake with him. There was nothing to tie him to her murder, no obvious motive. But as I say, I had a feeling about him. He seemed to me the sort of man you wouldn't put anything past.'

'Were they together, he and Portia Blake – as a couple, I mean?' Madden frowned.

'I don't believe so.' Derry shook his head. 'You can check it in the file, but my recollection is he simply said they were acquainted and that he had driven her down from London at Sir Jack's invitation to spend the weekend.'

'Where was he when she was murdered?'

'In his room, resting, he said. So were most of the other guests. As I told you, we never got round to checking their alibis.'

'What was it about him that you didn't like? Was it something he said?'

Again Derry shook his head.

'No, it was the man himself. He didn't seem bothered by Miss Blake's death. In fact, he didn't show any emotion at all. He just stared at me with those black eyes of his.'

He clicked his tongue in irritation.

'The trouble is, this all happened over ten years ago. The people who were in the house that weekend, staff and guests, are mostly scattered; and as you'll see from the file, some of them are dead.

'Here we are, then.'

Derry took off his hat and wiped his bald pate with a handkerchief. Their walk from the village along the road and across the sun-bruised meadow had been warm work.

'This is the spot. She was found lying inside that ruin; so whoever murdered her – whether Norris or some other man – must have either killed her there or else dragged her body inside with the idea of hiding it. But it turned out to be visible from the path; it was spotted through the doorway by these young boys. They were the ones who raised the alarm.'

The former superintendent paused to give his companion time to take in the scene. Madden looked about him. Out of the bright sunlight now, they stood in the dark shadow cast by trees in full summer leaf. Hard beside them was an old stone wall, part of a ruined structure that had once been a small hut, though little remained of it apart from the walls and the uneven brick floor. They had followed the path through the wood until they had reached the crest of the knoll, at which point Derry had veered off it and Madden had spotted the ruin through the trees.

'These lads – there were three of them – had come from the opposite direction; they were on their way to the village and one of them saw something lying just inside the door-way.' Derry pointed to the dark recess. 'He was curious enough to come over and have a look to see what it was. As I say, her body was lying inside the hut but close to the door-way. It must have been her face that he spotted; it was pale enough to show up in the dark.'

'The killer was careless, then.' Madden frowned. 'If he'd taken the trouble to drag the body into a corner it probably wouldn't have been found for hours, not until after a search for her had been made. That sounds more like the man you arrested, more like the act of a casual killer rather than some-one who was lying in wait for her.'

'True.' Derry nodded. 'But it could be that these boys forced the killer's hand. They told us they had been chatting as they came up through the wood, and being young lads they were probably making a racket. The murderer, whoever he was, would have heard them and he may have decided to get moving while he still had a chance to escape unobserved.'

He put his hat back on and then paused to reflect.

'Let's look at this first from the point of view of Norris being the killer,' he said. 'Let me explain how we came to arrest him and charge him so quickly. We knew by calculating how long it would have taken him to walk from the pub that he would have been a few minutes behind Portia Blake when she began walking up the path into the wood. It's possible he could have spotted her from the road and quickened his pace to catch up with her. We also know that Miss Blake got no further than this ruined house; if she had gone on, the boys coming up the hill from the fields on the other side would have seen her. So if Norris killed her it must mean he caught up with her at the top of the hill and probably dragged her off the path and into this hut. We believed that he meant to rape her and was probably trying to silence her by choking her, using her scarf to do it. But he'd overdone it, we reckoned, and killed her by mistake, after which there was nothing he could do but make himself scarce.'

He glanced at Madden, as if to gauge his reaction.

'I expect Angus told you, but the reason we were able to arrest him so quickly – it was only two days after the murder – was because he tried to sell some earrings Miss Blake was wearing to a Canterbury jeweller. They were also made of jade, carved in the shape of dragons, but paler in colour than the pendant, and we knew they were missing from the body because the maid who had spotted her going out remembered she was wearing them. Norris was trying to sell the earrings to the jeweller together with the girl's wristwatch, which was also missing. We'd already put out a description of the earrings and the jeweller simply got his assistant to call the police and kept Norris there long enough for them to turn up and arrest him.'

Madden pondered.

'Am I right in thinking he denied the murder at first?' he asked.

'That's correct.' Derry nodded. 'His story was that he'd spotted her body from the path just as the boys had and simply stolen the stuff off it; nothing more. Well, we didn't believe him for a start, and even less so when we checked with Central Records at the Yard and discovered he'd done time for attempted rape. He'd been caught in the act of assaulting a young woman near Pontypridd, in Wales. There was no doubt about it, either; he'd torn off most of her clothes and was on top of her when her cries were heard by a couple of farm workers who came to her rescue. Norris was given eight years. He'd only been out for a few months when this happened. We reckoned he must have been ready to try again after all that time in stir. But as I say, he denied murdering her or trying to rape her. He would only cough to the theft at first. But after we'd interrogated him for a day or two he changed his mind and signed a confession.'

'In other words, he cracked?' Madden's voice was sharp and Derry caught his eye.

'I know what you're thinking.' He scowled. 'We all know that people can be made to confess to things they didn't do if they're denied sleep and questioned without a break for long enough. But that didn't happen with Norris.' He looked hard at Madden. 'I'm not saying we didn't push him, but I made it clear to the team of detectives I had with me – and Angus can confirm this – that he wasn't to be bullied and browbeaten into saying anything he didn't mean.'

'I accept that.' Madden nodded. 'But it does seem to me he changed his story rather suddenly.'

Derry shrugged.

'The truth is right from the start he seemed ready to give

in; half a dozen times he appeared to be on the point of confessing and that only made us more sure that we'd arrested the right man. I had the impression he didn't want to go on with his denials; that he was tired of the struggle; that he wanted to end it. So when he agreed to sign a confession – this was two days after we'd arrested him – I wasn't surprised. I'd been expecting it.'

'But now you don't feel the same way?'

'I wouldn't go that far; not yet.' Derry grimaced. 'I just wonder now if it wasn't life he was sick of; his own, I mean; if he hadn't had enough of it. His family had disowned him after the attempted rape conviction – I learned that later. They were Chapel – very religious. They didn't want anything to do with him. None of them came to his trial at Maidstone.'

'Yet he went back on his confession later.'

Derry nodded. 'At the trial he did, but the judge wasn't having it – he made that clear in his summing-up – and Norris seemed to accept it. I remember watching his face when the jury returned its verdict. He shut his eyes when he heard the foreman's words. That was all. Then he seemed to sink back into himself. He didn't speak again. He was hanged at Pentonville the following January. Angus and I were both there. It's a nasty business, a hanging. Thank God neither of us has ever had to attend another.'

While he'd been talking Derry's stoop had grown more pronounced and now he moved away from Madden and went to the single window aperture in the wall behind them. Brushing off the ledge he sat down.

'I can't stand for too long these days,' he explained. 'I need to take the weight off my old pins.' He fanned his face with his hat.

'Tell me about the pendant now.' Madden frowned. 'What part did it play in the investigation?'

'Not much, as it turned out.' Derry had given some thought to his answer. 'But one thing I can tell you is that Norris didn't take it. At first we assumed he had, along with the other stuff, but he was adamant; it was the one thing he stuck to. Quite simply, he didn't know what we were talking about. We had to explain to him what it was – a green stone hanging around her neck. He swore he had never seen it and by the end I believed him. He'd confessed to everything else, after all, so why not that? His defence counsel raised the point during his trial. He said the fact that the pendant was missing suggested that someone else might have killed the girl. But the judge wasn't buying it.'

'What did you think had happened to it? At the time, I mean?'

'That it must have been lost, torn off in the struggle she'd most likely had with him. She had a small handbag with her when she left the house; it was hanging from her shoulder by a strap. The maid who saw her told us that. We discovered it lying in a bush near the hut. It looked as though it had fallen or been thrown there. Norris said he couldn't remember seeing it and we were inclined to believe him since there was a gold compact with an enamelled top inside it, a pretty thing that he certainly would have taken and tried to sell if he had seen it.'

'Did he tell you they had fought?'

Derry shook his head. 'The fact is he didn't have much to say, not off his own bat. Once he'd confessed to the killing he seemed to think that was it and he needn't say anything more. We had to keep prodding him. It was mostly a matter of question and answer. We would ask him, for instance, if he had grabbed her from behind and he would nod. Then we'd have to insist he say the word "yes" so that it could be written down for the interview. It was the same with most of the other details. Did he drag her to the hut, and so on? Each time we had to get him to agree it had been so.'

'So in effect you wrote his confession for him?'

'You could put it that way.' Derry looked displeased.

'Go on about the pendant, would you?' Madden spoke after a moment.

'Well, the area around the hut had been searched as a matter of course, but after it became clear that it was missing I widened the area considerably and made sure every inch of ground was gone over, but without result. So we still couldn't explain for certain how the pendant had disappeared. But it wasn't crucial to the inquiry. It was possible she had lost it somewhere else in the wood: perhaps she managed to break free from Norris and he had to chase her and it came off. We thought it might still be lying here somewhere, hidden by dead leaves.'

'Charlie Chubb suggested that might be the explanation.' Madden grunted. 'For what it's worth, he pointed out that it wasn't uncommon for investigations to end with a few questions still unanswered.'

Derry nodded in agreement. 'That was what we told ourselves – Angus and I. And it's what's bothering us now. Did we make a mistake in shrugging it off as just one of those things? If this turns out to be the same pendant' – he tapped his jacket pocket – 'then perhaps we did.'

Madden took off his jacket. He slung it over his shoulder. Derry had put his hat back on but was not yet ready to move from his seat on the window ledge. He sat there gnawing at his lip.

'Let's consider the alternative,' Madden said. He stirred the dead leaves at his feet with the toe of his shoe. 'Supposing it was someone else who murdered her – how could he have managed to do that, given there were so many people about? How is it nobody saw him?'

'I've wondered that myself.' Derry mopped his face. 'You might even say the question has been occupying my mind to the exclusion of all others since I received that note.'

'The suggestion has been made that Miss Blake might have gone out that afternoon to meet someone: that she had a rendezvous arranged in the wood or somewhere near it and that whoever she went to meet might be the person who murdered her.'

'Angus and I discussed that possibility. We spoke on the phone a few days ago. If she was coming here to meet a man he could well have been waiting for her in this hut.'

Madden frowned. 'If Norris was no more than a few minutes behind her, as you say, that wouldn't have left much time for the murderer to act. He must already have had it in mind to kill her.'

'That's a fair assumption.' Derry nodded.

'And that would make him a very different kind of killer.'

The Kent detective shrugged.

Madden continued to stare at the ground; he was lost in thought.

'The next question then is how did he escape?' He looked up. 'What route would he have taken?'

Derry rose from his seat and looked about him.

'Well, he didn't use the path, obviously, or he would have run into either Norris or those young boys who were coming from the opposite direction. He must have made his way through the wood, which would have meant crossing the path and going straight on until he hit the road, which is over there.'

He pointed over Madden's shoulder.

'But he could equally have taken the other direction, slipping out the back of this hut and going on until he came out of the trees into the fields, where he might well have been noticed by some of the hop pickers. On balance, I think he would have headed for the road. But where he went after that is anyone's guess. He might have had a car handy; or he might have strolled into the village. Once he had put some distance between himself and Miss Blake's body he would no longer have been an object of suspicion. Depending on how he was dressed, he could even have passed as just another picker.'

Shrugging, he glanced at his watch.

'But I see it's after twelve. What do you say to a bite of lunch in the pub? We can talk about it some more there.'

'I remember you,' Madden said. 'I saw you fight at the White City before the first war. Nineteen twelve, was it? Your opponent was a Frenchman. You knocked him out in the fourth round. You weren't Mr William Batty then.' He nodded to a wooden board on the wall behind the bar where the legend *Wm. Batty, prop.* was depicted in faded gold lettering. 'You were Kid Cannon.'

The landlord's battered face broke into a broad grin. Though he looked to be in his sixties now, with short grey hair, a crooked nose and a belly that threatened to overflow his trousers, he was still recognizable as the fresh-faced young man pictured in boxing trunks standing with his fists raised in a photograph hanging beside the board.

He slid the pint of bitter he had just pulled across the bar.

'That's for remembering, sir. It's on the house.'

'Thank you, Mr Batty.' Madden raised the glass to his lips, but then paused when he caught the other's eye. The landlord was giving him a strange look. 'What is it?'

'I wouldn't have taken you for a copper,' William Batty said.

Madden smiled. 'Well, you're half right,' he conceded. 'I used to be with the force. But I quit years ago. How did you guess?'

'I recognized that old fellow you came in with.' Batty nodded towards the back of the pub where Derry had wandered off a few moments earlier in search of a lavatory. 'I remember him from when a young woman was murdered here before the war. He took a statement from me.' He paused. 'I was just wondering why he'd turned up again. There's not more trouble, is there?'

Madden shook his head. 'Mr Derry's retired. He was just showing me where that murder happened, taking me over the ground. We worked together on another murder case years ago. That's how we got to know each other. I was down in Canterbury and he offered to drive me out here.'

He thought for a moment.

'Incidentally, do you recall the man they arrested drinking in your pub on the day of the murder?'

'Too right, I do.' The old boxer's friendly grin showed where two of his front teeth were missing. 'He was always the last to leave, always wanting one more beer. That day was no different and since I'd already called time, I told him to hop it.'

'Did he ever give you any trouble?'

'Was he violent, do you mean – up for a fight?' Batty's grin widened. 'Not a chance. Not him. He was the whiny sort. He used to sit in a corner drinking on his own. He never joined in. I thought he looked sorry for himself.' He shrugged. 'Maybe he had reason.'

'Were you surprised when you heard he'd been arrested?'

'Surprised?'

'Did you think it likely he could have killed someone? Did he seem to be the type?'

'Would I have taken him for a murderer, you mean?' The landlord stroked his cropped head thoughtfully. 'No, I don't think so. But then you can never tell, can you? You can never be sure.'

'Sure?'

'You think you know people, but you don't.' Batty shook his head ruefully. 'Not really.'

Derry had reappeared while he was speaking. Madden turned to acknowledge his companion.

'I've been explaining to Mr Batty here that you've been giving me a Cook's tour of the murder site. He's wondering why you're taking the trouble.'

'Is he now?' Tom Derry favoured the landlord with his flat copper's stare. 'Well, let him. And in the meantime he can draw me a pint of whatever it is you're drinking – I seem to recall they serve a good brew here – and put up a plate of sandwiches for us while he's at it.'

They had walked from the wood back to the village, a distance of less than a mile by the road but somewhat longer by the route they had followed after Madden had asked Derry if he could show him where the hop pickers were at work.

'I'm a farmer now. I'm curious. I've never seen a hop harvest in progress.'

Returning to the path, they had continued along it, eventually coming out of the trees to find that on this side of the wood the hop fields stretched into the distance as far as the eye could see. Soon they were walking along a deep lane flanked by long lines of trailing plants where the pickers were busy filling bins with the cone-like flowers that contained the resins and oils used to impart an agreeably bitter taste to ale and beer. The scent of them was overwhelming in the hot summer air.

'It's like a pilgrimage every year.'

Derry gestured at the lines of pickers, many of them wearing straw hats against the hot sun. Men and women seemed equally represented and Madden saw that there were children working there as well, their small fingers nimble and well adapted to picking the flowers.

'Whole families turn up, many of them from London. They do it to escape the heat in the city and although the work's hard it's something of a holiday, for the kids at least. They go swimming in the river when they get the chance. By the end of the summer they're as brown as berries.'

Proof of his words came a few moments later when they reached the end of the field and turned into a much wider avenue where a line of huts with corrugated-iron roofs stood and where a group of younger children, some no more than three or four years old, were playing in a circle under the eyes of a grey-haired woman busy herself at a washing-tub.

'A lot of these kids get conceived down here, too, I've been told.' Derry had grinned. 'Hopkins, they're called. Everything's rough and ready and if the weather's fine like it is now a lot of people sleep out. There's no telling what goes on under the stars.'

'And Norris was a part of all this, was he?' Madden had been curious.

'Hardly. These are families. They stick together. Like I say, he had no one. He probably slept rough, got his food where he could, did his work and then drank his wages away at the pub.'

'After he'd stolen that stuff from the body, where did he go?' Madden had paused to look up and down the long line of huts.

'Not back here. He was never seen again by the team he'd been picking with. When we caught him in Canterbury he was dirty and unshaven and said he had slept out the two nights preceding. His story was he had realized what a fool he had been to take the jewellery off the body and panicked. He knew if he was caught he wouldn't be believed, not with his record. In the end he had decided to try and get rid of the stuff as quickly as he could and scarper. What worries me now is that he may have been telling the truth.'

Madden had been silent at that point. Running the facts as Derry had reported them through his mind he had hit on what he thought was a snag.

'Assuming that Norris wasn't the killer, he must have come on the body *after* the boys found it' – he had finally given voice to his doubts – 'after the sound of their voices had scared off the real murderer. But is that possible?'

'I'm afraid it is.' Derry had looked glum. 'After their discovery the lads ran to the village to alert the local bobby, an officer called Duckworth: he retired a few years ago and went to live in Maidstone. I've spoken to him: there's nothing new he can add to what we know. The boys didn't think to leave one of their number behind to stay by the body and it must have been all of ten minutes before they came back with Duckworth.'

'But if Norris was innocent surely they would have run into him on the way. He was coming *from* the village after all.'

'Not necessarily.' Derry shook his head. 'Before we even got to the question of the murder, while we were still establishing his movements, he told us he had stopped for a leak in the wood on the way back from the pub, which sounded reasonable given the amount of beer he'd put away. Later, when we questioned him about the boys, he said he'd left the path and gone into the bushes to relieve himself and didn't see or hear them when they ran past, and given the fact that he was the worse for wear from drink at the time that may well have been true.'

'That's agreed then, is it? You'll take the pendant back to London with you? It'll be more use there than down here.'

Derry weighed the velvet bag in his hand.

'If you can find the time to show it to that woman Portia Blake shared a flat with you'd be doing Angus and me a favour, and saving me a trip to London. As I said, she'll be back next week, and her phone number is in the file.'

He handed the bag to Madden, who loosened the drawstring and drew out the pendant. Their conversation inside the pub had been interrupted by the arrival of a party of pickers, a noisy group eager to down as much beer as they could in the short lunch break allowed them. At Batty's suggestion the two men had taken their glasses and the sandwiches he had made for them outside into a small courtyard where tables and chairs were set.

Derry watched now as Madden held the pendant up before his eyes. The green stone glinted in the sunlight.

'The fellow who sent that to me – could he be the killer, do you think?'

Surprised by the question, Madden stared at him.

'It's the teasing tone of the letter. I can't get it out of my mind. It's almost as though he wants to play games with us.'

'Now . . . after all this time?'

'Maybe he's bored,' Derry suggested. 'Perhaps he thinks he's so far separated from the murder in time that he can afford to have some fun at our expense.'

Madden weighed the question.

'But would he really take such a chance simply to amuse himself?' he asked. 'Surely it would be better to let sleeping dogs lie.' Pondering the question, he chewed his lip. 'But he's playing some sort of game, isn't he?'

Derry snorted. 'In that case, I wish he'd be kind enough to tell us the rules.'

Madden glanced at his watch.

'We'd better be getting back to Canterbury. My train leaves in half an hour.'

He put the pendant back in its bag.

'I will take this with me if you like. I'll ring that woman Portia Blake shared a flat with next week and try and arrange to show it to her. There's no point in us racking our brains until we know whether it's the same pendant. Let's hope she can help.'

'And take this, too, while you're at it.'

Derry pushed the file across the table.

'I've done all I can from this end.'

4

BILLY STYLES SAT BACK from the table with a sigh. He rubbed his stomach appreciatively.

'My word that was good, sir! Pheasant, you say?'

'But only out of a tin.' Madden was apologetic.

'Still . . .' Billy sighed again. 'The truth is I can't remember what the real thing tastes like. It's been so long,' he reflected. 'You keep thinking it's going to end, don't you, the rationing and the queuing and the shortages, but it just goes on and on. It's like the war never ended. At least, that's what Elsie says.'

He was referring to his wife, whose complaint was one heard often these days. Towards the end of the preceding year the government had suddenly relaxed controls on a wide range of products, prompting hopes that the corner had at last been turned: that the relentless burden of economic austerity which a war-weary Britain had borne since the end of hostilities in 1945 would finally be lifted. And so it had seemed – for a while. Then, in March of that year, the meat ration, pitiful though it was, had been cut yet again, and while sweets had come off the ration the following month, to the delight of millions of children, they had gone back on the restricted list almost at once thanks to the huge demand for them. In the circumstances, Madden couldn't help but feel guilty over the relatively sumptuous meal he had been able to offer his old protégé whom he had invited to dinner at St John's Wood after learning that he was living a bachelor life, Elsie having taken their three children up to Bedford to spend a fortnight of the summer holidays with their grand-mother.

'It's time I confessed to knowledge of a grave offence which I've kept silent about for years,' he said now as they rose from the table. 'I'm sorry to say Aunt Maud was a shameless exploiter of the black market. There's a cupboard in the kitchen full of questionable items. I've never had the nerve to tell you. You might have felt obliged to arrest her. I did raise the issue with her several times, but to no effect. She seemed to take the view that at her age she was safe from the clutches of the law.'

'She was probably right.' Billy chuckled. 'I can't see anyone having the nerve to haul an old lady like her into court. Mind you, it's turned into something of a joke now, rationing; a bad joke, that is. It's not only spivs who break the law; regular grocers do the same if they think they can get away with it. Elsie says she's seen them slip stuff under the counter to favoured customers. It used to be that every-one was prepared to go without – it was the patriotic thing to do. Not any longer.'

Madden sighed. 'Be that as it may, I must get rid of this stuff before the estate agents start showing the house. I'm going to put it in the hands of a couple of them starting at the end of the month. You wouldn't care for a tin or two of caviar, would you?'

'I don't think so, sir.' Billy's grin widened. 'For one thing, I've never tasted the stuff; for another, Elsie would want to know where it came from and next thing the neighbours would be talking about it and then the whole street would know.'

'I see your point. But there's a fine Stilton sitting in there which I hope you'll take home with you when you go. Elsie won't object to that, I'm sure. And I can offer you a glass of good cognac now. Aunt Maud bought only the best.'

Madden led the way into the sitting room and having seated his guest in one of the two armchairs that still remained – the process of getting rid of the furniture was already under way – busied himself at the drinks tray.

'I must say Lucy's looking lovelier than ever.' Billy smothered a yawn. 'She's what the Yanks call a knockout.'

Madden's daughter had joined them earlier for a quickly swallowed meal before going out. She had been collected by a young man driving a sports car.

'Is that the boyfriend?' Billy had asked. Treated since time immemorial as one of the family by the Maddens – he had held their baby daughter in his arms – he felt entitled to ask the question.

'Oh, I don't think so.' Madden had dismissed the notion. 'He's not special so far as I know. None of them seem to be.' He mused on his words. 'Just between us I think she takes after her mother. According to Lady Violet, Helen had a string of admirers when she was Lucy's age; all full of hope, all doomed to disappointment.'

'She was waiting for the right man then, was she?'

Billy caught his old chief's eye and smiled. Madden handed him his glass. Billy sniffed the rich fumes.

'Before I go, sir, can we have a last word about this Portia Blake business? I'm still not sure what you think. Do you agree with Mr Sinclair and Mr Derry that the investigation should be reviewed?'

Although they had talked about the case at length over dinner Billy felt he still hadn't plumbed the depths of Madden's mind on the subject. His old chief had been open enough about the former superintendent's misgivings following his return from Canterbury, but had given little indication of his own views.

'I'm quite ready to raise the matter again with Mr Chubb if you think that's on the cards. But I should warn you he'll need something more than that pendant if he's going to change the AC's mind.'

Madden picked up the object from a low table beside him and held it up to the light. Earlier he had shown the small jade Buddha to Billy and pointed out the faint flaw in the dark green stone.

'I realize that,' he said, 'and to answer your question, I'm still not sure. Derry seems to feel that, if we can show it's the one that belonged to Portia Blake, that should be enough to get the wheels of the law moving again. But I don't agree. It doesn't necessarily follow that they arrested the wrong man. It all depends on who sent the pendant to Derry and how the sender acquired it in the first place. One can't rule out the possibility that whoever is behind this has no connection to the original police investigation: that having come into possession of the pendant in some way and being familiar with the details of the case, he has either seen a way of using it to his advantage or is simply bent on making mischief. But let's stick to the facts.'

He put down the pendant and picked up the folder Derry had given him.

'Assuming we can establish that this is Miss Blake's pendant, the next step would be to look at the guests who were staying at the house that weekend. Their names are all in this file. I imagine you'll find them in your own records. If Cradock changes his mind and gives the go-ahead for the investigation to be reopened I can hand it all over to the Yard. But it might be as well in the meantime if we try to ascertain now just who these people are and where they are living.'

'I could help,' Billy said. 'It wouldn't be going against orders just to locate them, and we can do that a lot more easily than you can.'

'Most of them should be easy enough to find.' Madden had the file open. 'They include a Lord and Lady Cairns and a Mr Rex Garner. I don't know who they are but Derry said they were all society figures. Garner's wife was there with him, but she died during the war. Sir Jack's son, Richard Jessup, was present at dinner on the Saturday night. He had come down from London, but he didn't stay the weekend. He left directly after lunch the next day; at that point Portia Blake was still alive. The local vicar and his wife were dinner guests, but he passed away during the war according to Derry. Sir Jack himself died in 1939, but the lady he lived with – a Mrs Castleton – is still with us. She might be worth talking to, and the son as well, Sir Richard as he is now. He took over the chairmanship of Jessup's before his father died. They've got an office in the City.'

He looked up.

'As I said, if Cradock has a change of heart I'll leave it all to you. But if he keeps digging in his heels I might have a word with one or two of them myself, particularly if they're here in London. Angus will expect it of me. I hope Charlie won't take offence.'

'I'm sure he won't.' Billy tossed off the last of his cognac. 'He hasn't said so, but I get the feeling he'd like to move on this. He just needs a good reason.'

About to rise, he paused. He saw that Madden had something more to say.

'There's one more name in here and I've left it till last.' He tapped the folder again. 'He's going to present the biggest problem, but unfortunately he may turn out to be the most important from your point of view. His name is Stanley Wing.

He was a business associate of Sir Jack Jessup's, an oriental, part Chinese. Derry took against him. He didn't like his manner. While that might simply have been a reaction to the fact that he was foreign and had "a touch of the chink about him", as Derry rather indelicately put it, I think there was more to it than that. Tom Derry had a lifetime of experience in dealing with criminal types. If he felt there was something off about this man Wing, I'd be inclined to take him seriously. The trouble is, the Jessup family's business is based in Hong Kong and I suspect that's where Wing is most likely to be found. That might involve sending an inquiry to the police there. You'd have to check with Charlie before you could do that.'

'Did Mr Derry have any reason to suspect him?'

'Not that I'm aware of. But he brought Miss Blake down from London with him. What's not clear is how well they knew each other. Derry was shocked by how little reaction he showed to her death. But that may just have been his way.'

'The inscrutable oriental, you mean?' Billy grinned.

'Something of the sort.' Madden's tone was dry. 'Anyway, if this inquiry is reopened he's bound to figure in it one way or another so we'd better try and locate him. As Derry pointed out, there's been a war since Miss Blake was murdered and, among other things, Hong Kong was occupied by the Japanese. Most of the Europeans living there were interned in camps; a number of them didn't survive the experience and there's no telling what might have happened to Wing, where he might have ended up. He was closely associated with them.'

He put down the file.

'There's no evidence he was involved in Portia Blake's death. But it was he who brought her down to Kent and one has to wonder why. She wasn't well known as an actress; not a name to conjure with. And it's unlikely that she knew Jessup personally; she wouldn't have been part of his set.'

He looked at Billy.

'So what was she doing there? Perhaps Wing can supply the answer. But you'll have to find him first.'

5

'YOU DIDN'T WASTE any time, did you, George?'

Madden's voice held a wistful note. He cast a regretful glance over the scene before him.

'You've certainly been busy in my absence.'

When last he had stood where he was, beneath the arched entrance to his stable yard, the surrounding fields had been gold with ripened corn. Now harvested, but not yet ploughed for next year's crop, the bare, stubbled acres wore a desolate look.

'We couldn't wait, sir.' George Burrows, his farm manager, was apologetic. 'There was no telling how long the fine weather would last. We didn't want the harvest spoiled.'

'I understand. And you were quite right. I was stuck in London. I couldn't get away.'

'It was a better year than last, sir.' Burrows sought to cheer his employer. 'And we'll be getting a good price for it.'

That much at least was true. With food subsidies still high up on the government's list of post-war priorities, farmers remained a pampered segment of the population. But Madden's personal satisfaction derived from humbler roots. Like a boy with a new toy, he had been looking forward to watching the Deere harvester they had bought in the spring, an American machine shipped to England during the war, second-hand but with relatively little wear and tear on it, go about its work. Now he would have to wait for another year.

He glanced at his watch. Although it was only mid-afternoon, too early to think of going home, he felt the prick of conscience. He had returned from London the previous day and with the excuse of having much to catch up with both at home and here at the farm had managed so far to avoid dropping in on Angus Sinclair, who he knew would be waiting anxiously for any news he might have brought back.

'I've really nothing to pass on to him that he doesn't know already,' Madden had told his wife. Helen had been at the station to meet him and Lucy when they had returned home for the weekend. 'He's bound to be disappointed.'

Later that evening, at supper, he had brought them both up to date on the inquiries he had been making on the chief inspector's behalf.

'Did you ever know Jack Jessup?' he had asked Helen. 'He must have been a figure in society before and after the First World War. I was thinking you might have run into him.'

'Daddy's being diplomatic,' Lucy had interrupted. 'He means when you were going to all those parties with Violet.'

'Thank you, my dear. I'd never have guessed.' Helen smiled sweetly. She turned to her husband. 'No, I don't think I did. He would have been quite a lot older than the people we went around with. But I remember what they called him: Black Jack Jessup. He was supposed to cut rather a dashing figure.'

'And you wouldn't have known his son, of course?'

'He would have been too young. He can't be much more than forty now. Why do you ask?'

'I may have to go and see him, though I want to talk to Angus about it first. As things stand there's really nothing more than that pendant to indicate that they might have arrested the wrong man, and it's not enough in itself. The Yard won't move on this unless something more turns up.'

'Then why are Angus and Mr Derry pushing so hard to get the case reopened?' Helen had put the same question that Billy had asked earlier. 'They must know that.'

'I'm sure they do.'

'Then *why*?' Lucy had persisted with the query.

Madden had hesitated before replying. It was a question he had asked himself, and he was still not sure he had the right answer.

'It's not that easy to explain,' he said, 'and I may be wrong. But it's to do with the feeling they both have that they may have made a mistake. Bear in mind these were two very experienced detectives who had every reason to believe at the time that they were dealing with an open-and-shut case. Norris wasn't just the obvious suspect: he almost begged to be arrested and charged. He was close to the scene of the crime; he admitted to stealing jewellery from the victim's body; he had a record that appeared to single him out as precisely the kind of violent criminal they were looking for; and to cap it all, he confessed. In the circumstances there can't be many detectives who wouldn't have come to the same conclusion as they did. I know I would.'

'Even though this man Norris tried to retract his confession?'

'Even so. Remember that only happened when he came to trial, and as every policeman knows – and judges too – it's a ploy criminals often try. That wouldn't have been enough to sway me.'

'Then what's behind it?'

'Something they both find hard to put into words, though Derry gave me a clue to it when we talked. It's Norris's confession – not the fact of it, but the way in which it came about. He wasn't bullied into talking. Derry assured me of that and, even if he hadn't, I worked with Angus long enough to know he would never have permitted such a thing to happen. Derry was convinced Norris *wanted* to confess – that he was just waiting for an opportunity to do so. Now he wonders – and perhaps Angus does too – what brought that on? Was it simple guilt, as they assumed at the time, or something more complex? His life was in ruins, after all. His family had disowned him. Had he come to the end of himself? That's what Derry wondered. Had he had enough?'

Madden paused to let his words sink in.

'What I think is that Norris's behaviour may have left a seed of doubt in both of them, something they weren't really aware of at the time, something subconscious. It's been lying there all these years and the pendant turning up this way has reawakened it. Now they both want the investigation reviewed, and if it turns out they were wrong it can only do harm to their reputations. Yet they still insist on it. That fact alone speaks louder than words.'

He shrugged.

'But it's only a supposition, and I'm not going to put it to Angus. For all I know I may be wide of the mark and I don't want to upset him even more. All I can tell him at present is that Chubb and Cradock are both aware of the situation, and that Charlie at least is open to any suggestions. However, I doubt that will be enough to improve Angus's mood and I expect to be hauled over the coals when I pluck up the courage to go and see him.'

'Don't be too sure. You may be in for a surprise.' Helen smiled. 'I'm hoping you'll find him chastened. I told him this morning he had to stop behaving like a bear with a sore head, snapping at me every time I looked in on him. That I had no magic wand I could wave to make him feel better. He would just have to be patient.'

Not altogether encouraged by her words – patience had never been his old friend's strong suit – Madden had contrived to avoid passing by his cottage on his way to the farm that morning. But now, with no further reason to delay, he waved goodbye to Burrows and set off down the winding road that led to the bottom of the valley where there was a stream with a path running alongside it that passed by the chief inspector's abode.

'Wing, you say? The oriental gentleman? I didn't speak to him myself, but Derry took a dislike to him, I recall. He was planning to question him again, and in more detail. But then Norris was arrested.'

Seated in the shade of an apple tree, with his right foot, encased in a loose felt slipper, resting on a well-cushioned stool, Angus Sinclair frowned.

'We had nothing on him. Other than the fact that he'd brought the Blake woman down to Kent with him, there was no reason to connect him to the murder. Has Derry got some new information?'

Madden shook his head. 'It was just a feeling he had at the time. He thought Wing was a dubious character. And he didn't like the way he reacted to Miss Blake's death; or rather that he didn't react. He seemed unmoved by it.'

'The Kent police had already done the preliminary interviews by the time I got down there,' the chief inspector explained. 'The guests had all been questioned. I did have a word with Sir Jack Jessup, but he wasn't able to help. He was too upset. He seemed to take the view that he was personally responsible for the safety and well-being of anyone staying under his roof. I felt sorry for the man.'

Shifting in his chair, Sinclair grimaced with pain. Madden waited for the explosion he was sure would follow. Instead, to his surprise, a pained grin appeared on the chief inspector's face.

'I can see you're holding your breath. Have no fear. I'm a reformed character.'

He resettled himself carefully.

'I got a fearful wigging from Helen yesterday. She said I was behaving like one of those gout-ridden colonels in a *Punch* cartoon whose toe has just been stepped on. I was reduced to shamefaced silence.'

Madden had already noted that his old colleague seemed in better spirits that day and had attributed the change to the presence of his daughter – a great favourite of the chief inspector's – whom he had found setting the garden table for tea when he arrived. Lucy had walked down from the house with a plate of freshly baked scones and accompanied by the Maddens' basset hound, Hamish, another welcome visitor and one with whom Sinclair was wont to claim a special tie, though admittedly only on the basis of the dog's name.

'You will admit,' he had said to Helen once, 'that while he never ceases to dig holes in your garden, he has always left mine untouched. It's clear he accords me special dispensation as a fellow Scot.'

The chief inspector was especially proud of his roses, now at the height of their full-blown summer beauty, and before Madden sat down to have tea with them both, he had spent ten minutes watering the beds under the approving eye of their temporarily stricken owner.

Her duty done, Lucy had departed, rousing Hamish from his deep sleep on the grass beside Sinclair's chair so that he could accompany her. Before leaving she had warned both of them that she expected to be kept fully informed on the progress of their inquiries.

'You're not to keep this case to yourselves,' she had told them sternly. 'It's much too interesting. If two heads are better than one, then three are better than two. I'm sure if you let me put my mind to it I'll come up with some good ideas.'

Seated in a cane chair now, with the sun lower in the sky, but the day still warm, Madden ran through the main points of the meeting he had had with Chubb at Scotland Yard.

'He's not dead set against reopening the case, Angus. But as Billy Styles says, he needs a good reason to do it. Cradock may be more of a problem. He's afraid of raking it all up again; he dreads what the papers will make of the story. We'll have to tread carefully. I promised Charlie I'd be discreet.'

'What have you got in mind?' The chief inspector had listened patiently while he made his report.

'Well, first off, I'm going to ring this woman Portia Blake shared a flat with, an actress called Audrey Cooper. We need to know if she can identify the pendant.'

Madden had brought the jade figurine with him and Sinclair had been examining it while he listened, holding it up to the sunlight and tracing the faint flaw in the green stone with the tip of his finger.

'If she confirms that it's the same one, we need to decide what to do next. My own feeling is I probably ought to talk to some of the other people who were staying at the house at the time of the murder. But that carries a danger with it.'

'What danger?'

'I don't want the fact that we're looking into this case to get out. It wouldn't be fair to Charlie Chubb. He's being as cooperative as he can be. He's ready to consider anything new we come up with. It would seem like a stab in the back if he were to find the story suddenly splashed across the front page of a newspaper. We should think carefully about who we approach.'

While he was speaking, Sinclair had made another cautious move in his chair.

'Have you any suggestions?' he asked, having completed the manoeuvre successfully.

Madden nodded: 'Since his father's no longer with us, I thought Sir Richard Jessup would be the best person to approach. He didn't stay the whole weekend, but he was present at dinner the night before Miss Blake was murdered. He could tell us something about the other guests and where they are to be found now. And, most important, he would have a strong interest in keeping this business out of the newspapers, from the point of view of both his family and his company. If you agree, I thought I'd write him a note and request an interview. He can always refuse, of course. But my guess is he would want to know what's afoot. How the note is worded will be important: this is not an official inquiry, after all. I'll draft something over the weekend and show it to you before I go back to London.'

He reflected for a moment.

'And I'll have to cook up some sort of story to tell Audrey Cooper, as well. I don't want her thinking that the police are about to open a new investigation.'

The chief inspector looked troubled.

'I'm starting to feel guilty about this, John. You've already done too much. The truth is this case has become something of an obsession of mine since Derry wrote me that letter. It troubles me.'

'And it never did before?' Madden probed cautiously.

'What do you mean?' Rather as he'd feared, Sinclair responded sharply.

'This particular investigation, it never bothered you?'

'Did I ever wonder if we'd sent the wrong man to the gallows? Is that what you're asking?'

The chief inspector had arrived all too quickly at the question which Madden had asked himself, and which he had decided it might be best to avoid.

'The way Derry described it to me made me wonder if there had been any uncertainty in your mind at the time about the way Norris's confession came about. How he suddenly caved in. Derry said he had had the feeling all along that Norris wanted to confess, and had taken it as a sign of his guilt, but that now he wondered if there hadn't been some other reason behind it.'

He waited for the other's reaction. Sinclair's frown had stayed fixed. But he was biting his lip now, seemingly uncertain of his reply.

'Not at the time.' When he spoke finally, it was in a decisive tone. 'I was satisfied we had the right man. As for the speed with which the whole business was wrapped up, there was nothing unusual about that. As you well know, most murder inquiries are resolved quickly; they seldom drag on. The identity of the killer is usually clear from the start, and it certainly seemed to be the case with Miss Blake's murder. I will say this, though: I was disturbed by Norris's manner. There was something about it that didn't seem to fit the circumstances. It was almost as though he was no longer concerned with the questions being put to him; as though he had withdrawn into some private part of his mind. Then again, murderers behave in all sorts of ways when they're arrested. Over the years I've witnessed everything from defiance to abject grovelling. I was convinced of Norris's guilt. But it left me troubled, mainly because I'm so opposed to capital punishment. I thought he was a weak-minded man who had almost certainly killed Portia Blake in a moment of panic, and probably by mistake when she tried to cry out. His execution, at which I was obliged to be present, was far closer to cold-blooded murder than any act of his. So if you're asking whether it bothered me over the years – yes, it did. And when I received Derry's letter with the news about this pendant I felt instinctively that I wanted to get to the bottom of it. If we made a mistake, let the world know about it. If nothing else, it might make people question whether hanging is a just and civilized punishment, or merely society's way of exacting a brutal revenge; and beyond that to the moral problem posed by executions that turn out to be mistaken, as this one may well do.'

He stopped. Observing his old friend's flushed and angry face, Madden kept his peace. It was left to the chief inspector finally to break the silence between them.

'But to go back to what I was saying before, I don't want to drag you any further into this business. If you can get Miss Cooper to confirm that the pendant is the one Portia Blake owned, that would be a great help. It might even be enough to persuade Cradock to reopen the inquiry.'

Madden shook his head. 'I'm afraid not, Angus. Charlie has already made that clear. The assumption we've been working on – the one the sender of this letter to Derry is trying to sell us – is that if Norris wasn't the killer, then the pendant must have been removed from Miss Blake's body by the real murderer, presumably because he thought it might incriminate him. But as Charlie said, there are other possible explanations for its disappearance. I think he was echoing what Cradock had said to him, trying to break the bad news to me gently: telling me we were going to need more than that.'

Sinclair's growl on learning this came as no surprise, and Madden quickly went on.

'Let me do as I suggest. First, I'll speak to Miss Cooper and, depending on what she tells me, try and see Sir Richard after that. To tell the truth, after spending a morning with Derry going over the ground I've become rather fascinated with the case. Quite apart from the question of the pendant, there are other aspects that make me think it might be worth persevering with: the character of Portia Blake, for one. We really know very little about her, other than that she was an actress of no great distinction. Before going any further we ought to try and find out more. Miss Cooper could be of help there.'

'You think there might be a reason she was killed?'

'There might. And that's reason enough to go on, at least for the time being.' Madden smiled. 'Besides, Lucy would never forgive me if I dropped out now.'

'Well, if you're determined . . .' The chief inspector tried unsuccessfully to mask his satisfaction. 'Is there anyone besides Jessup you feel you should speak to?'

'Yes. Mrs Castleton. I take it you know who I mean?'

'Of course.' Sinclair seemed mildly surprised. 'Jack Jessup's companion – or should I say, mistress? But why her, in particular?'

'She can probably give a better account of the guests than anyone else. She was the lady of the house, after all. And women are generally more observant than men.'

'*Are* they?'

The chief inspector's feigned astonishment was a sign that his good humour had been restored.

'You've waited all these years to tell me that?'

6

'So you think this might have belonged to the fair Portia?'

Audrey Cooper picked up the pendant. Gaunt, with cropped, greying hair and deep grooves along either side of her mouth, the actress's raddled cheeks, untouched by rouge or powder, showed the scourges of time. Dressed carelessly in slacks and a stained and crumpled blouse, she had clearly made little effort over her appearance. But her glance was sharp enough.

'That's what I'd like to find out,' Madden said.

He had rung her the day before, and having explained why he wanted to see her had been invited to call the following morning at her flat, which proved to be situated on the top floor of a house at the bottom of the King's Road in Chelsea. Sunlight pouring through a grimy picture window illuminated an untidy sitting room cluttered with books and what looked like scripts piled on tables – with a dirty plate here or there resting on top of them – and hung with framed posters and photographs of faces, most of them well known and belonging to the theatrical profession. They were sitting facing each other, Miss Cooper on a chaise longue upholstered in some faded rose-coloured material shiny with age and wear, Madden on a straight-backed chair that creaked each time he moved.

'Or rather, Mr Derry would.' He went on, 'He was one of the detectives who oversaw the investigation. He's retired now. He lives in Canterbury and since he knew I would be in London for a week or two he asked if I could help. I'm a farmer, but I used to be with the police. That's how we come to know each other.'

'You said on the phone you were just helping to tie up loose ends.' Miss Cooper spoke in a hoarse voice that Madden had fancifully associated with the cigarette burning in her fingers – it was the third she had lit since his arrival – until she apologized for her croaking and explained that she had all but lost her voice as a result of appearing recently as Lady Bracknell in a production of *The Importance of Being Earnest*.

'I'm afraid my dulcet tones and Oscar's deathless wit were lost on the cloth-eared worthies of Scarborough. They like their comedy more earthy oop north.'

Although Madden had handed her the pendant some minutes before, she had not yet done more than glance at it. It was as though she wished to examine his credentials first before giving serious attention to the matter that had brought him to her door.

'What do you mean by loose ends?' she asked, eyes narrowing. 'As I recall it, a man was hanged for Portia's murder. Is there some question about that now? And if so, why are you making this inquiry, and not the police?'

'Well, to answer your last question first, the police are aware of the existence of the pendant, but they don't feel it's significant in itself. Even supposing it is the same one, there could be various explanations for its turning up like this. They certainly don't think that it justifies reopening the investigation.'

'But your friend, Mr Derry, feels differently?' Miss Cooper expelled a lungful of smoke.

'Not at all. He was surprised to receive it, of course. It arrived out of the blue along with a note saying the sender believed it might have belonged to Miss Blake. Now it was known that she had a pendant similar to this one – she was seen wearing it during that weekend – but it disappeared when she was murdered, and what Mr Derry wants to know is whether it's the same piece of jewellery.'

'And that would be what you call "tying up a loose end"?' Extinguishing her cigarette, she reached for another.

'In effect. It's the sort of thing old detectives obsess about. Mr Derry thinks what might have happened was that the pendant was torn off Miss Blake's neck when she was assaulted and has been lying in the wood ever since. It's possible someone picked it up and sent it to him; someone who thought it might interest the police, but doesn't want to get involved.'

'And Mr Derry won't rest easy until he knows the truth?' Her tone was disbelieving. 'That's what you're telling me?'

'I wouldn't go that far.' Madden shifted uneasily on his creaking chair. The fiction he was offering Portia Blake's old flatmate had been concocted by none other than Lucy, who continued to take a lively interest in the inquiries he was making, and the longer he went on with it the less convincing it sounded to his ears. 'What really concerns him is that if the pendant did belong to Miss Blake, then it ought to be returned to her family. I'm told she has a sister living in Ipswich.'

'Has she? I wouldn't know.' Miss Cooper shrugged. 'Portia never talked about her family: she made no bones about wanting to leave her past behind.'

'You must have met the sister, though, surely. Didn't she come by to collect Portia's things?'

The actress stared at him.

'Yes, of course she did.' It had taken her a second or two to collect herself. She clicked her tongue in irritation. 'I remember now. I helped her clear out Portia's room. But that was the only time I ever set eyes on her.'

She had recovered well enough, but just for a moment Madden thought he'd detected a false note in her voice, and he wondered what had prompted it. Now, however, as though deciding on a change of strategy, the frown of suspicion creasing Miss Cooper's brow faded. She looked thoughtful as she picked up the pendant and held it to the light. He was startled to see her put down her cigarette in an ashtray and pick up a monocle from the table beside her. She fixed it to her right eye.

'This is not an affectation, I assure you,' she said, as though reading his mind. 'I'm as blind as a bat in one eye and long-sighted in the other. It's made for some uncomfortable moments on the boards, I can tell you.'

She studied the green stone carefully, turning it this way and that to catch the light until it seemed she had found the right angle, at which point she held the pendant still and peered hard at it.

'Well, I can't swear that it's the same piece.' She lowered the stone. 'But it is very like the one Portia had. I can see it has a slight flaw and the same was true of hers. I happen to know that because she kicked up a fuss about it.'

'A fuss?'

'She thought she'd been short-changed by the gentleman who gave it to her.' Miss Cooper's smile was scornful. 'She was sensitive about things like that; though not much else.'

Madden weighed the remark. It seemed he was being invited to probe further.

'It was a present from a man, was it?'

'Like most other things Portia possessed. She was – how shall I put it – *acquisitive*.' Miss Cooper's smile had turned wintry. 'Her other outstanding quality was ambition, which is a terrible thing to be burdened with when it's not allied to talent.'

'I take it you didn't care for her.'

'Is it that obvious?'

She handed the pendant back to him. Madden slipped it into his pocket.

'I just wonder why you had her as a flatmate.'

'Do you, indeed?' Miss Cooper removed her monocle. 'Well, I don't mind telling you. I was rather taken with her charms, and being a shrewd little minx, at least where that area of life was concerned, she led me to believe that she wasn't wholly opposed to the idea.'

She regarded him quizzically.

'Are you shocked?'

'Not at all.'

'What she actually needed at the time was a place to stay, and she probably also thought that I might be of some help to her in the business. She still harboured ambitions as an actress at that stage in her career.'

'At that stage? Did her ambitions change while she was staying with you? Was she looking to make her mark some other way?'

The question seemed to intrigue Miss Cooper. She drew back to study her visitor.

'For someone who is just doing a favour for an old colleague you seem remarkably interested in the late Miss Blake; and better informed about this business than I would have thought possible.'

'I spent a fascinating day with Mr Derry down in Kent.' Madden contrived to look apologetic. 'Although I wasn't expecting it, he showed me over the ground where the murder took place and explained how it came about. I wondered what Miss Blake was doing there; why she was included in Sir Jack Jessup's house party.'

'A nobody like her – is that what you mean?'

'I wouldn't put it that way. She just seemed out of place. According to Mr Derry she had been brought down from London by a business associate of Jessup's. But they don't seem to have been a couple in any sense.'

'You're referring to Fu Manchu?'

Seeing the look on his face, she laughed.

'Or should I say, Mr Stanley Wing?'

'Did you know him?' Madden spoke after a pause.

'Hardly.' She shrugged. 'I only saw him once when he came here to pick her up. My Chink, Portia called him. Once she actually did refer to him as Fu Manchu and said he was a wily oriental and she didn't trust him an inch. As far as I could gather they had some sort of business arrangement.'

'Do you know what that was?'

She shook her head. 'Only that it had to do with jade. Portia had been wearing various bits of jewellery for some weeks, but they didn't belong to her. They had been lent her by Mr Wing. He took her to some parties and functions. She was showing them off for him.'

'Was the pendant one of those pieces? I thought it belonged to her.'

'So it did.' She lit a fresh cigarette.

'Do you know who gave it to her?'

Miss Cooper shook her head again. 'We didn't share confidences. In fact we were never really on friendly terms, and after a few months I told her she ought to start looking for other lodgings.'

'Could it have been Mr Wing?'

'Possibly. Although he didn't sound like the sort of man who gave girls presents. The other kind were more Portia's cup of tea and she had no scruples when it came to making them cough up.'

Her laugh had a cruel edge.

'Early on in our brief acquaintance she admitted that she'd put it over on one of her swains by telling him she was pregnant. He gave her not only money to take care of the problem, which was wholly fictional, but also a lovely wristwatch from Cartier by way of consolation.'

She was watching his expression as she spoke.

'Just because Portia was a rotten actress didn't mean she wasn't gifted in other areas. It's true her fair limbs never graced my sheets, but they certainly found their way into other beds; or so I deduced from the hours she kept. She'd had a brief liaison with some lordling before I met her and managed to claw her way into society. She got invited to parties, and when we were still on speaking terms she would drop names like confetti, the sort you might see in the gossip columns. Little idiot!'

Miss Cooper spat out the words in disgust.

'She thought she was one of them. But the men were just passing her around.'

'Did you ever meet any of them?' Madden asked.

'Why? Does it matter?' Her glance had sharpened.

'Not really. I just wondered.'

'Did any of them spend the night here? Is that what you're asking?' She laughed. 'Not to my knowledge, though there were times when I was away in the provinces. As far as I know her assignations took place elsewhere and didn't always last all night. I used to hear her coming in at three or four in the morning, so I imagine it was often a case of, "Thank you, my dear, that was delightful and here's five pounds for the taxi."'

'They were not what you'd call affairs, then?'

'Affairs . . . ?'

'They didn't last long?'

'About as long as the average mayfly's earthly existence.

Poor little Portia. She was out of her depth. One moment she'd be riding high, talking about Buffy, or darling Ferdie, and telling me how they were about to take her to Paris, or to go skiing in the Alps; the next she'd be dropped like a hot potato and retire to her bed in tears.'

'Still, when you said she had other ambitions, is that what you meant?'

She picked up the monocle again and fixed it to her eye.

'How quick you are, Mr Madden.' She studied him. 'Not *quite* the farmer, are we, or not altogether? Are you sure you're not with the police still?'

'Quite sure.' He held her gaze.

'Yes, Portia's ambitions had shifted from the stage by then. I think she saw herself as married to one of these sprigs of the aristocracy she met at the parties she went to; she began to picture herself in tweeds managing a great country house; Lady Muck in all but name. I told her she was losing touch with reality, but I don't think she listened. She would have hated to hear me say it, but underneath it all she was still little Sadie Mott from Ipswich.' She caught her questioner's eye. 'Yes, that was her real name, but she ditched it early on. She must have found it hard to picture in lights.'

Madden was silent. He was thinking about what she had told him.

'Do you remember when she was given the pendant?' he asked, after a pause. 'Was it around the time she met Wing?'

'I really couldn't say.' Miss Cooper stifled a yawn. 'The only time I saw it was just before she went off to Kent with him. She was wearing it. I hadn't noticed it before and she showed it to me. That's when she complained about the flaw. "You'd think he could have afforded something better," she said. She was quite put out.'

'But you don't know who "he" was?'

This time she didn't bother to hide her yawn.

'I've already told you I don't. By that time I was simply putting up with her presence until she found new digs. We seldom exchanged more than a few words.'

She put out her cigarette and removed the monocle from her eye.

'So? Is that it? Have you tied up your loose end?'

'I believe so.' Madden made to leave.

'What are you going to do now?'

'Return the pendant to Mr Derry and tell him what you've told me: that it could be the one that belonged to Portia Blake. It'll be up to him to decide what to do with it.'

'And you're sure there's nothing more you require of me?' Her tone was mocking.

Madden hesitated.

'There is one thing I'm curious about,' he said. 'How did Portia come to meet Stanley Wing?'

'I'm afraid I can't help you there. I never asked her. Does it matter?'

'Can you describe him for me? What was your impression of him that time when he came to collect her?'

'Now that *is* an interesting question.'

She reached again for her cigarettes.

'He was here when I got back from wherever I had gone that afternoon. I found him waiting while Portia got ready. They were going somewhere together. She had mentioned him before so I wasn't surprised when he introduced himself. From what Portia said I had thought he was pure Chinese; but it was obvious from his features that he had European blood in him. His eyes were very dark, almost black. He made little effort to converse with me. He wasn't rude exactly, but his manner was dismissive. My presence was an irritation to him. He kept looking at his watch as though every moment he was forced to spend in my company was tedious and distasteful to him. It was a memorable few minutes.'

Her laugh was hollow.

'There I was in my own sitting room being quietly despised by a male of dubious origin. I had half a mind to ask him to leave, but he hadn't *quite* given me cause. Then Portia appeared with a flurry of excuses and apologies. She'd been delayed somewhere and had been late getting back to change. It was plain she was nervous in his presence.'

'Nervous . . . ?'

'I'd never seen her like that with anyone before. On the whole she tended to hide whatever insecurities she felt behind a mask of pretended confidence and she certainly thought that she knew how to deal with men – the kind she mixed with, anyway – flirting with them one moment and scolding them the next. But it was plain Mr Wing was a horse of another colour. He didn't respond to any of her chatter. He simply looked at his watch and said: "You are late." And with that they left.'

She drew thoughtfully on her cigarette.

'I say "nervous", but I think I'm being overly generous to Portia. I had the distinct impression that underneath it all she was just the teeniest bit afraid of him.'

Audrey Cooper stood on the landing listening to the footsteps of her visitor as he went down the stairs. After she had heard the street door open and close she went back inside. Lighting another cigarette, she stretched out on the chaise longue and stared at the ceiling.

'I *wonder* . . .' she mused aloud.

Just then the door at the rear of the sitting room opened and a young woman stuck her head in.

'Has he gone, Aud?'

'Like the wind, my sweet. Were you listening?'

'No, of course not.'

The young woman came in. Pretty in a doll-like way, with blonde curls and bee-stung lips, she wore a blue cocktail dress cut lower than was customary, showing the rounded tops of her breasts.

'Who was he?'

'A farmer, he said, though I found that hard to swallow.' Miss Cooper drew thoughtfully on her cigarette.

'What did he want?'

'I'm not sure. I didn't know what to make of him: a bit of a dark horse, our Mr Madden. Very polite on the surface; but I can't help feeling there was more to him than met the eye. And more he could have told me, as well.'

Miss Cooper expelled a long plume of tobacco smoke into the air. The girl came around the chaise longue and stood in front of her. Born Gladys Wainwright, she now went by the name of Pixie du Pre and until its recent demise had been dancing in the chorus of a West End musical.

'Good God!' Audrey Cooper's eyebrows went up. 'Why are you dressed that way? You look like a tart.'

'I told you. I'm going to Bobby Bishop's party. Hugh Grantham will be there. He's casting *Fortune's Child* next week and it'll be a chance to meet him.'

'Well, you won't catch his eye in that get-up, darling. Hugh dances at the other end of the ballroom. I know whereof I speak. And take some of that lipstick off, for heaven's sake, or he'll think you're auditioning for a corner on Curzon Street. Here – you can use my handkerchief.'

She drew the somewhat soiled object from her shirt pocket and held it up. The girl snatched it from her.

'Ooh, you can be nasty.'

She went to a mirror hanging on the wall at the side of room and set to work on her face.

'And just because dear Hugh's eye will be occupied elsewhere, don't imagine for a moment that there won't be other men on the prowl, or women come to that, with quite different thoughts in mind. Behave yourself.'

'You know I will.' The girl glanced over her shoulder. 'You can trust me.'

'Can I, my little Pixie?' Miss Cooper yawned. 'Funny how that word always brings betrayal to mind.'

Without warning she got up suddenly and went to a writing-desk in a corner of the room. Sitting down in front of it she began to go through the small drawers, pulling them out one at a time and scrabbling through the contents.

'I'm sure I put them here,' she muttered to herself. 'I couldn't have thrown them out.'

'What are you looking for?' The girl was examining her reflection in the mirror.

'Nothing you need bother your pretty little head about.' Miss Cooper slammed the last drawer shut.

'Damn!'

She sat scowling at the wall. Then her face changed.

'Hang on, though . . . !'

Springing to her feet, she strode across the room and disappeared through the door which Pixie had left open. The girl, meantime, had finished with her face. After a last glance in the mirror she took a light coat from a hook by the front door and slipped it on.

'I'm going now, Aud,' she called out.

Miss Cooper reappeared. She had a small wooden box in her hands. Clearing a space on the table in the middle of the room where the scripts lay piled she emptied the contents on to it. They proved to be an assortment of costume jewellery – rings, bangles, necklaces – plus some odds and ends in the shape of loose beads, a broken wristwatch and a bunch of keys. She stared at them for a long moment.

'I don't *believe* it.'

Unsure what she was supposed do, Pixie hovered by the door. 'Aud, I have to go . . .'

'Shhh . . . !'

Miss Cooper's frown came back, fiercer than before.

'Let me think.'

She lifted her gaze from the table and stared out of the window. Then with a gesture that might have been rehearsed for the stage she slapped her forehead audibly.

'But of course . . . you *idiot*, Audrey!'

She picked up the box, an ornate object whose lid was decorated with a leafy intaglio design, and searched with her fingertips along its bottom edge until she found what she was looking for. There was a pause, and then, like magic, a shallow drawer slid out of the box. Miss Cooper stared at its contents for a long moment. A smile came to her lips.

'Bingo!' she said.

Late getting back from Chelsea – at that hour, near the end of the working day, taxis were hard to come by – Madden returned to St John's Wood to find the pavement outside Aunt Maud's house crowded with pieces of furniture which were being loaded by three men into a removal van bearing the name of an auction house painted on its panelled sides. Alice stood on the doorstep with her arms folded watching them with an eagle eye.

'This is the first lot from upstairs, sir,' she told Madden when he had picked his way through the clutter and joined her. 'They'll be back next week for the heavy stuff. I've told them to leave our beds until last.'

His daughter was already home from work and impatiently awaiting his return.

'What did she have to say? *Is* it Portia's pendant? Are we on the right track?'

Busy in the kitchen choosing a supper for them from among Aunt Maud's hoard of contraband delicacies, Lucy paused in her examination of the tins she had lined up on the table to interrogate her father.

'Did she swallow your story about Mr Derry wanting to send the pendant back to Portia's family?'

'As I remember, that was *your* story,' Madden replied stiffly. 'And I thought for a moment she'd seen through it. It would have served me right for telling fibs.'

'Well . . . ?' Lucy waited impatiently. Her father had disappeared into the larder. 'Did you like her? Miss Cooper, I mean? Was she another glamorous actress, like Portia Blake?'

'Far from it.' He reappeared with a bottle of beer in his hand. 'She was spiteful and mean-spirited . . . and dressed like a scarecrow to boot.'

'Oh, dear . . . !' Downcast for a moment, Lucy bit her lip. 'But what did she have to say? What did she tell you?'

'Oh, I can't go into that.' Frowning, Madden removed the cap from his beer. He searched for a glass. 'It wouldn't be proper.'

'Not *proper* . . . ?'

'It was too squalid for your tender ears.' Smiling, he took a glass from the cupboard and began to fill it with beer.

'Daddy . . . !' There was a warning note in her voice.

'You don't want to know about the seamy side of life. Not yet.'

'For heaven's sake!' Lucy exploded. 'What makes you think I don't know about it already?'

Madden drew back. 'I'm glad your mother didn't hear you say that.'

'Daddy, *stop it.*' She circled the table to get closer to him.

'Well, all right.' He held up a hand to check her advance. 'But you must promise to be discreet.'

'I'm always discreet.'

'I'm sorry to have to tell you, but it seems Portia Blake was no better than she ought to have been.'

'What does that mean?'

'She had a lot of men friends.'

'What's wrong with that?' Lucy bridled.

'They gave her presents . . . jewellery and the like.'

'Oh . . . I see.' Her face cleared. 'Was the pendant a present?'

'Apparently. But Miss Cooper doesn't know who gave it to her. She knows something, though . . .'

Madden took a sip from his glass of beer. He reflected on his words.

'What do you mean . . . something?' Lucy fought to curb her impatience.

'I don't know . . . she didn't say.'

He was remembering the actress's slight hesitation.

'But all at once she changed note and started telling me all sorts of malicious stories about Portia – and before I'd even asked. I think she was trying to distract me.'

'From what?'

'That's what I'm not sure about. I must have missed something.'

Madden shrugged.

'I also heard a lot about this Chinese fellow, or part

Chinese, Mr Wing, and the more I learn about him, the more mysterious he seems to be. I can't make him out. I still don't understand what role, if any, he played in this business.'

'What are you going to do now?' Lucy asked.

'Have a word with Angus. I'll ring him later. This is his affair. I don't want to do anything without consulting him first.'

'What do you think you *ought* to do?'

Madden pondered.

'Well, although I haven't managed positively to identify the pendant – all Miss Cooper could tell me was that it looked like the stone Portia had – I think it's probably the same one. She remembered it had a flaw. So the best thing now might be if I sent Sir Richard Jessup that letter Angus and I worked up requesting an interview with him.'

'And then?'

'Wait and see if he's willing to talk to me.'

7

'RICHARD JESSUP? Well, if you have any problem there, let me know, John.'

Ian Tremayne beamed from his place at the head of the table. A rumpled looking figure, Lady Violet's husband was given to wearing torn sweaters and old jackets patched at the elbows on the weekend; as a relief, perhaps, from the more formal garb required by his position as a senior official at the Foreign Office. Though a rare visitor to Highfield in the early years of their marriage – he'd been frequently posted abroad – he had lately been occupying a desk in London, and he and his wife had been dividing their time between their flat in town and Lady Violet's ancestral home of Stratton Hall.

'I see him at the club quite often. He's very approachable.'

'Yes, but he may not want all this dragged up again.'

Still awaiting a reply to the note he had sent Jessup, Madden would not have chosen to discuss the matter at the lunch to which he and Helen had been invited that Sunday along with their daughter had not Lucy taken it into her head to air it.

'Daddy's got involved in a fascinating old murder case,' she had announced as they sat down at the table. 'It was one of Angus's and what everyone's wondering now is whether they hanged the wrong man. Angus would be looking into it himself if he wasn't immobilized, poor thing, so Daddy's doing it for him. And I'm helping.'

The subject having been raised, there was nothing Madden

could do but direct a scowl of disapproval at his daughter in the vain hope that she might be persuaded to curb her tongue; a wasted endeavour, since Lucy had contrived to avoid his glance while treating the company to a colourful review of the case as she saw it together with a full account of the dramatis personae involved.

The name Jessup – when he heard it uttered – had done more than ring a bell with Ian Tremayne.

'I know him quite well,' he told Madden, 'and not just from seeing him at the club. We spent a few months in Hong Kong after the war, Violet and I. Richard was there for some of that time getting the company back on its feet after the Japanese occupation. I was very impressed with him. The old boy, Jack Jessup, left it in bad shape. I was told they nearly went under. But Richard seems to have done a good job and I'm given to understand that the business is prospering now.'

'That's perfectly true.' Lady Violet had been paying close attention to what her husband was saying. 'But you're leaving out the most important part,' she said.

As slender as a reed in her youth, Helen's childhood friend had acquired over the years a figure more in keeping with mature middle age; without, however, losing any of her taste for mischievous gossip.

'It's what made all the difference, really.'

'I expect you're referring to his marriage.' Ian turned to his wife with a faint, but detectable sigh.

'Of course I am. You can't pretend it didn't have any effect on the company's fortunes. Sarah Temple was a very wealthy young woman. Marrying her was one of the cleverest things Richard ever did.'

This time her husband's sigh was more audible; it bore a long-suffering note.

'One could put it that way,' he said. 'Except you make it

sound calculated and cold-blooded when it was nothing of the sort. By all accounts they were smitten with each other. And just to put the record straight, it wasn't Sarah's money that went into Jessup's: it was her family's – her father's, to be precise – and he made a business decision. Richard had already begun negotiations with the investment group Temple headed before he and Sarah ever met.'

'If you say so, dear.' Violet's smile suggested she knew better.

'They were married shortly before the war started.' Ian turned back to Madden. 'Richard was away a lot of the time, on active service, but Sarah stuck it out in London throughout the Blitz. We met her in Hong Kong when they came out. She immediately got involved in relief work with refugees. She's a woman of strong principles. The Temples are a Quaker family.'

'You make her sound rather formidable.' Helen's interest had been roused.

'Then I've given you the wrong impression.' He turned to her. 'She's not like that at all – at least, not in my opinion – just . . . just *upright*. And very attractive. Richard's devoted to her.'

'And there's someone else you *must* talk to, John.' Lady Violet was just warming to her subject. 'You'll have heard the name Adele Castleton, I'm sure?'

'It's been mentioned.' Madden frowned. His reluctance to pursue the topic seemed to have escaped their hostess.

'La Belle Dame Sans Merci!'

'The *what* . . . ?'

'That's what she was called in her heyday.' Violet's eyes sparkled. 'Men used to go mad over her. They would lose their senses, poor things, and when she was done with them, which was soon enough, they'd be found alone and palely loitering, like that poor man in Keats's poem.'

'Honestly, Violet.' Helen was laughing. 'What nonsense you talk.'

'It isn't nonsense at all. It's perfectly true. In fact, if I were you I wouldn't let John go anywhere near her unescorted.'

'What was she like?' Lucy was enthralled.

'Well, whenever she arrived at a party a hush would fall.' Violet turned to her. 'Then the whispering would start. Was it true she'd been having an affair with the Duke of so-and-so? Had she actually abandoned him in Deauville, like they said, and run off with a jockey?'

'What did she look like? Was she lovely?'

'Not beautiful exactly, but striking: dark-haired, dark-eyed, and with a doomed air.'

'A doomed air . . . !' Lucy echoed the words with a sigh. 'Is that something you can cultivate . . . with practice, I mean?'

'No, and don't let me catch you trying.' Helen fixed her daughter with a stern parental eye. 'And don't listen to Violet either. She's exaggerating, as usual. It's true a lot of men fell for Adele Castleton, but she wasn't like her reputation. I met her once – properly, I mean, not just to be introduced. It was at one of those parties. We happened to find ourselves alone and we sat down and talked. All I can tell you is she couldn't have been nicer.'

'Don't spoil my story,' Violet pleaded.

Madden saw Tremayne roll his eyes in despair. For his own part he had given up any hope of diverting the conversation into other channels.

'I spent a morning down in Kent last week talking to the detective who worked on the case with Angus, a man called Derry.' He addressed the remark to Ian. 'I was surprised to hear that Sir Richard was selling his father's house, particularly since it's been in the family for generations.'

'So was I,' Ian agreed. 'In fact, I asked him about it once. We dine together at the club now and then. The answer was quite simple. He's never thought of it as home.'

'Why is that?'

'Well, I don't know if you're aware of it, but his parents separated when he was very young and he was brought up by his mother.'

'Derry said something of the sort.'

'She lived in Hampshire, not far from Petersfield, and Richard always loved their house. When he took Sarah there she said at once it was where she wanted to live. Jack Jessup was very ill at the time, and Richard kept their decision from him. But once the war was over he let the house in Kent to tenants and then, later, decided to get rid of it. The last I heard there was a plan afoot to turn it into a school. Richard's mother died only a year or so after Jack passed away and he and Sarah settled in Hampshire when the war was over. From what he's told me they seem to be very happy there.'

He reflected on his words.

'He's an impressive fellow in all sorts of ways, Richard Jessup. He had an outstanding record in the war, as well. He started with a commission in the Guards, but he got himself transferred to the Parachute Regiment and was highly decorated. I didn't get that from him, incidentally. He never talks about it. But I know for a fact that he jumped at Arnhem and managed to get what was left of his company back across the Rhine when the Germans had our chaps surrounded. I hope you manage to talk to him. It'll be well worth your while.'

*

'I know, I know – I shouldn't have done it. I can't imagine what came over me.'

Lucy buried her face in her hands.

'I suddenly realized when I saw you scowling at me. Is it that serious?'

'That all depends.' Sitting in the front seat of the car beside Helen, Madden had to twist his body round to look at his daughter, who was seated in the back. 'You've just blurted out the whole story to one of the biggest gossips in England. Before we left I had to ask Ian – *beg* him – to speak to Violet: to make sure she understood that she simply mustn't talk about this case to anyone. The last thing we want is to see it plastered all over the newspapers. But if Violet has her way that's exactly what will happen.'

Madden fixed her with what he hoped was his fiercest scowl.

'And only the other day you were telling me how discreet you were.'

'I just thought it was something we could talk about at lunch.' Lucy appeared genuinely stricken. 'Have I really done something terrible?'

'We'll have to wait and see. Ian will try his hardest, I know, but one can't trust Violet an inch. She's incapable of keeping anything to herself.'

'Oh, dear . . .' Lucy covered her face again.

Helen brought the car to a stop. She cleared her throat.

'Here we are,' she announced brightly. They had stopped in front of one of the cottages on the outskirts of Highfield village. 'Oh look – there's Mrs Tomkins waving from the window.'

She turned to her husband.

'Lucy's going to make a dress for her,' she explained. 'She has to measure her up first.'

'Mrs Tomkins . . .' Madden's laugh was bitter. 'There's another chatterbox.' He glared at his daughter. 'Try and restrain yourself this time. Keep your mouth full of pins, or whatever it is you do when you measure someone up.'

Lucy dropped her hands.

'That's a *horrible* thing to say,' she said. 'You're being sarcastic. You're *never* sarcastic. Not with me.'

'Yes, all right, I'm sorry.' Knocked off balance by the unexpected angle of attack, Madden was momentarily robbed of words. 'But you see what you've driven me to.'

He watched as she opened the car door.

'And from now on we're not going to talk about this case any longer; we're not going to discuss it. I'll do what I can for Angus, and that'll be the end of it.'

Choosing not to reply, his daughter climbed out of the car. Head held high, she walked down the short path to the front door of the cottage, which opened as she reached it. In a moment she had disappeared inside.

'Oh, Lord . . . !' Madden groaned. 'I've upset her.'

Helen's face was a study.

'Are you trying not to laugh?'

'I'm sorry, my dear.' She put a hand to her mouth. 'I'm just wondering how long that particular resolution will last.'

'What resolution . . . ? Oh . . . I see.' He scowled. 'You mean you think she'll talk me out of it?'

'Heaven forbid.'

'That's what you're implying, though, isn't it?'

Helen was mute.

'You think I'm putty in her fingers.'

'Have I ever said that?'

'Yes, as a matter of fact you have. I remember the occasion distinctly.'

Madden had given up trying not to laugh himself.

'You said Lucy had always known how to handle me, and when I protested and said that wasn't true, you corrected yourself. Not *always*, you agreed. That wasn't fair. She hadn't really got the hang of it until she was six.'

'So you think this man Wing may be the key to the problem. But is there a problem? You've been at it now for a while, John. What's your feeling?'

Angus Sinclair shifted in his chair. Given the warmth of the day, Madden had expected to find his old friend outside. He had come prepared to help with any chores that might need doing only to discover that another of the chief inspector's willing helpers had anticipated him.

'I thought I'd give the hedge a trim,' Will Stackpole announced from the top of the ladder where Madden had found him perched when he came in through the garden gate.

Clad in rough trousers and a flannel shirt, rather than his customary blue – it being a Sunday – Highfield's bobby had ascended a set of rickety steps to a point where he was able to ply the shears he was wielding to and fro along the top of the tall laurel hedge flanking the small garden. Madden had paused to talk to him – and to inquire as to the chief inspector's whereabouts.

'He was sitting out here until ten minutes ago.' Will nodded at the cane chair positioned under an apple tree. 'But he said it was getting too warm for him, so he went inside.'

'How is he moving now?'

'Better, I reckon.' The constable's tone was judicious. 'He's still not walking as such. More like hobbling, I should say. But don't tell him I said that.' He grinned.

'Helen says it'll likely be a couple of weeks before he's properly back on his feet.'

'Ah, well, she would know.' Will accepted the verdict with a solemn nod. His lifelong admiration for Madden's wife, dating as it did from the time when they had played together as children, had never wavered. His face brightened. 'I bumped into Lucy in the village yesterday. She tells me she's helping you with these inquiries you're making for Mr Sinclair.'

'Gave you a rundown on the case, did she?'

'I wouldn't call it that, exactly.' Will scratched his head. 'But she said you were learning some interesting things, the pair of you.'

'The pair of us . . .' Madden growled. 'Listen, Will, I've told her she's not to go around chattering about this business. If the papers get wind of it they'll turn it into a story in no time. Some of the people involved are well known to the public. If Lucy so much as mentions it to you again you're to speak sternly to her. Tell her she's meddling in what could be official police business. Be firm.'

'With *Lucy*?' Stackpole appeared to find the prospect unnerving. 'Well, if you say so, sir . . .'

'I do, Will. I do.'

Leaving the constable suitably awed (or so he hoped), Madden had gone inside then to find Sinclair seated in an armchair with his foot resting, as before, on a cushioned stool. A pile of books stood on the low table beside him and he had one open on his lap.

'I'm finally acquainting myself with the crimes and follies of mankind,' he announced, as Madden made his entry. 'A little late in the day for a retired chief inspector, you might think. But I persevere. This is Gibbon's *Decline and Fall of the Roman Empire*.' He patted the tall pile beside him. 'I'm barely into the second century AD and already I'm appalled by the depths to which human depravity can sink. Speaking of which, have you anything new to report?'

Madden had earlier given his old colleague a brief account by phone of his meeting with Audrey Cooper and they had decided there was reason enough for him to send the letter the two of them had already composed to Richard Jessup requesting an interview. Now he enlarged on what the actress had told him during their talk, with particular reference to what she had had to say about Stanley Wing.

'Is there a problem?' He echoed the chief inspector's question. 'Do you know, Angus, I still can't make up my mind. I think that pendant is probably Portia Blake's. But was it found in the wood some time later: was it a chance discovery? Or was it taken from her body by someone other than Norris – by the real killer in fact? That's what the person who sent that note to Derry would like us to believe. But how did it fall into his hands? And if he's trying to incriminate someone else, why not point a finger? Why not say who the alleged guilty party is?'

Madden paused to let his words sink in.

'Because either there is no guilty party – he's making this up – or he knows something but doesn't want to reveal it.' He answered his own question.

'So what's his motive then?' The chief inspector frowned.

'I don't know.' Madden shook his head. 'We'll have to wait and see. Somehow I don't think we've heard the last of him.'

Sinclair grunted. 'You're saying the pendant and the letter to Derry are only his opening gambits.'

'That's how it looks to me.' Madden shrugged. 'But to get back to Wing, I still don't understand what he was doing in England at that time, what he was up to. I can't place him in any recognizable context. We're told he was an associate of Jack Jessup's. But what does that mean? And then there's the effect he had on people.'

'What effect?'

'Look at Tom Derry, for example. He took against Wing the moment they met, and for no good reason other than that he didn't care for his manner. Miss Cooper had a similar reaction. She positively disliked him – and on very short acquaintance. Yet there he was, an invited guest at Jack Jessup's dinner table. It doesn't add up. At the very least it needs explaining. As does Portia Blake's presence in the house that weekend. There's also their relationship to consider – if you can call it that. Audrey Cooper said they had a "business arrangement". What did that involve, I wonder?'

'What you require, then, is someone to explain all these mysteries to you.' Sinclair eased a stiff muscle in his back.

'In a nutshell.'

'Someone like Sir Richard Jessup. I take it you haven't heard from him yet?'

Madden shook his head. He rose from his chair.

'I gave him my London address in the note I sent him, and the phone number, too. But there's been no reaction from him so far. I rather thought he'd want to see me. By rights he ought to be curious, human nature being what it is.'

'Human nature?'

With a sigh the chief inspector resettled himself in his chair. He opened the book on his lap.

'Well, as to that, I feel bound to tell you that Mr Gibbon, for one, had a very low opinion of it.'

8

'Here now, watch what you're doing. You'll take a piece out of the wall if you're not careful. There's no rush.'

Alice stood at the bottom of the stairs, her stern gaze fixed on the two workmen who were manhandling a large oak wardrobe down the stairway. They were moving very slowly, only a few inches at a time, but still too quickly for Alice's disapproving eye.

'Miss Collingwood wouldn't want to see any damage done,' she confided to Madden, who was standing in the hall a little way off ready to offer help if it was needed. 'She was very particular about marks on the walls and suchlike.'

Since there was little he could say, other than to point out that having quit this world for the hereafter, Alice's late employer was unlikely to be taking any further interest in earthly matters, least of all the state of her walls, Madden restricted his response to a grunt. The workmen were employed by the firm of auctioneers assigned to dispose of the furniture not wanted by Helen or by Alice, who had been told to take her pick of any of the pieces she wished to retain for her own use when she decamped to Hastings. Alice had opted for a pair of bedside tables, two standing lamps and a painting of Westminster Bridge at sunset which hung in the hall above the telephone and which she confessed to having a particular liking for.

'I always stop when I'm dusting to look at it.'

Nearly a week had passed since Madden had posted his

letter to Sir Richard Jessup and, with no response to it received as yet, he was starting to wonder whether he ought to consider advancing the inquiry in some other way, though the prospect was hardly appealing. While it might be perfectly possible to track down the other guests who had been present that weekend, it would be difficult to approach them without some kind of introduction, which Madden had hoped Sir Richard might supply him with. There was no reason to think they would be willing to respond to questions put to them about a long-ago murder by someone with no official backing; one who could not even claim to be a licensed private detective.

'If he decides not to reply to my note, or turns me down,' we may have to think again,' he had told Sinclair. They had spoken on the phone the previous evening. 'The trouble is, Richard Jessup is the one person who can smooth the way for us. If he's willing to cooperate then presumably any of the others I might want to speak to will find it hard to refuse.'

'Let's wait until the end of the week,' the chief inspector had advised. 'Let's see where we stand then.'

The wardrobe, meanwhile, had descended to the foot of the stairs and was making its slow way down the short passage to the hall and the front door beyond it. Alice was backing away before it, keeping an eye on the object and obliging Madden to retreat in the same manner until he was forced outside and on to the pavement. The rest of the procession followed at its own snail-like pace until finally the operation was completed and the wardrobe stood by the side of the road, ready for loading into a van parked nearby.

Leaving Alice to oversee its final disposition, Madden went back inside. Earlier that morning the telephone had been unplugged and, together with the table on which it stood, had been removed from the hall to the sitting room to give the men leeway as they shifted the various pieces of heavy furniture brought from upstairs. Now Madden retrieved the instrument and plugged it back into its socket. As he did so – and at almost the same instant – it rang. He picked up the receiver.

'Excuse me, sir.' It was a woman's voice. 'Have I got the right number?' She read it out.

'That's correct.'

'And am I speaking to Mr Madden?'

'You are.'

'Oh, I'm so glad. I've been trying to get you all morning, but there seemed to be something wrong with the line. I'm Sir Richard Jessup's secretary. Miss Harmon is my name. He has asked me to apologize for not responding to your letter sooner, but he's been in America for the past fortnight and only got back to London yesterday. He'd be happy to see you, he says, and wonders if you would be free to call on him at our offices in the City this afternoon. He realizes that it's short notice, but since he'll be away again next week he thought you might like to take this opportunity of talking to him.'

'I would.' Madden didn't hesitate. 'And it's very thoughtful of him. Would you thank him for me?'

'Certainly, sir.' She sounded relieved. 'Our offices are on Cheapside, quite close to the Mansion House tube station. Would two o'clock suit you?'

'The building was in Watling Street. You can see the place from here. It was destroyed during the war.'

Sir Richard Jessup pointed.

'It was during the Blitz and luckily it happened at night

when there was no one in the place. I managed to rent these offices from one of the big insurance companies but we're going to rebuild our old headquarters. It's just a bomb site now, as you can see, but I'm hoping we can get construction started in the New Year.'

With a full head of dark hair and blue eyes that seemed to carry an electric charge, Jessup had been at the window in his office looking out when Madden entered and had turned at once to shake his hand and draw him over to the spot where he was standing. They were on the fifth floor of an office block on Cheapside and the view that Madden found himself looking at took in the great dome of St Paul's Cathedral on one side and the distant silhouette of Tower Bridge on the other. The site Jessup was indicating, one of many in that part of the City damaged or destroyed by bombs, was situated directly in front of them. It was only a little way off, and by chance Madden had walked up that way from the tube station, passing through narrow streets lined with gaping pits like empty tooth sockets. Small enterprises had once flourished in these lanes, rubbing shoulders with the great banks and financial institutions: jewellers, hatters, glove makers, suppliers of stationery. All were gone now, blown to oblivion.

'Come and sit down.'

Sir Richard led his guest away from the window to a low table a little apart from his desk and surrounded by easy chairs.

'Let's make ourselves comfortable. I'll get Miss Harmon to bring us some coffee.'

In spite of his distinguished appearance – he was wearing a well-cut suit with a silk handkerchief showing at his lapel pocket and a Brigade of Guards tie – Jessup still managed to project an air of informality, and given what he already knew about his host it came as no surprise to Madden to find himself warming to the man. Although clearly at ease with his lofty position as head of a great international concern, Sir Richard seemed disinclined to make much of it and from the outset his manner had been open and friendly. Almost as tall as his visitor, his good looks were enhanced by high cheekbones that lent his face a hawk-like aspect; but if there was something of the fierce predator in the swift glance he had shot Madden's way as he was shown in, he had nevertheless crossed the office without a moment's delay to shake his hand warmly, moving with the long, easy strides of an athlete.

'It was good of you to come on such short notice,' he said now as they sat down. 'As you might imagine, I found your letter intriguing and I'm more than curious to discover what this "informal inquiry" you are making involves. To say that I have qualms at the thought that the investigation might be reopened would be an understatement.' He grinned. 'Neither my family nor my board of directors would welcome it. I can still recall the fuss the papers made ten years ago, and I don't imagine they would be any more discreet second time around. But you'll have guessed that already, and what I want to say is if it turns out there is more to this business than met the eye at the time you can count on me not to put any obstruction in your way. I would rather know the truth.' He looked directly at Madden. 'As my dear wife would say, "let the chips fall where they may".' He smiled again. 'Sarah is American. But perhaps you already know that.'

'I do, as it happens.' Madden returned his smile. 'We have an acquaintance in common – Ian Tremayne. He's married to one of my wife's oldest friends.'

'Imagine that.' Jessup's face lit up. 'I first met Ian in Hong Kong just after the war. Did he tell you—?'

He broke off as the door opened and his secretary entered

carrying a tray with the coffee things on it. During the short interval that followed Madden had an opportunity to take in the spacious office and to admire the handsome Persian carpet underfoot which gave the room a sense of intimacy it might not otherwise have had. His eye was caught by a number of framed portraits hanging on the walls; all were of men, some bewigged and garbed in the clothes of an earlier age, others dressed in more up-to-date apparel. Leaving it to his secretary to pour their coffee, Jessup had been observing him.

'The gentleman you see in that painting behind the desk is our firm's founder,' he said, 'and as ambitious and fly a young scoundrel as ever took ship for the Orient. Jeremiah Jessup was his name. He worked for the East India Company originally and was one of their agents in China when it became apparent in the early nineteenth century that the company was about to lose its monopoly on trade with India and the Far East. Along with some other bright young fellows, he struck out on his own and like most of them made his first money in the opium trade. When that came to an end he branched out into other fields and began trading in cotton, tea and silk. Later on the company expanded – into shipping and cotton mills and construction – all of which we are still actively engaged in. The faces you see up on the wall are of the men who have managed the firm's fortunes since. Nearly all of them are Jessups. That's my father over there: as you see, he's the only one with a smile on his face.'

The painting he was indicating had already caught Madden's eye: the features of the man it portrayed were so like Sir Richard's that he had assumed they must be closely related. Sir Jack was pictured sitting at ease behind a wide desk. The smile his son had referred to seemed somewhat rueful, boyish even, though to judge from the older Jessup's grey hair and lined face he must have been well into middle age when it was painted.

'We had a curious relationship. At first it was distant – my parents separated quite soon after they were married and my mother wanted nothing to do with him or his set – but later it improved and by the end, when he died, we'd become very close. He was a man of enormous charm, but quite unpredictable, a gambler at heart. People who knew him all thought he was wonderful company, my mother excepted, but as a businessman he was quite hopeless. His tenure at the helm of Jessup's alternated between periods when he would take off on one of his many jaunts – to Africa, South America, Alaska; to wherever his fancy beckoned – and other times when he would focus all his energies on the company. And it was a toss-up as to which of the two was more perilous. One way or another, he very nearly did for the firm.'

He laughed without restraint.

'But you didn't come here to listen to me going on about my forebears. Before you put any questions to me – and I'm sure you have a few – could you tell me briefly how this all came about? You mentioned that pendant in your letter and explained that you were acting on behalf of one of the two detectives who had charge of the case. But could you be a little more explicit? And take all the time you need. I've cleared my afternoon of appointments.'

In reply, Madden spoke for the next twenty minutes without interruption, explaining first about the anonymous letter Tom Derry had received and then describing his visit to Kent and his subsequent interview with Audrey Cooper. At that point he paused to take the pendant from his pocket along with the letter and passed both across the table to Sir Richard.

'As you can see from the flaw, we've established that that's probably the same stone as the one Portia Blake owned.'

Jessup held up the piece to the light. He examined it closely, turning it this way and that.

'Fascinating,' he said.

'But there's still no explanation for how it came into the hands of whoever sent the note to Derry. Or what his motive was for doing so. Always supposing it was a man. It could equally have been sent by a woman.'

There was no immediate response from Jessup, who was now studying the note Madden had just handed him.

'The wording's peculiar, isn't it?' he said. *I leave it to you to establish the truth* . . . Does that mean he doesn't know himself if the pendant has any significance? He's just trying it on – seeing if he can stir up some trouble?'

'That's one possibility,' Madden agreed. 'As things stand, the officers I've spoken to at Scotland Yard have no intention of reopening the investigation, and I see their point. There simply isn't enough to go on. I might add that I have no personal stake in this. I used to be a police officer, but that was a long time ago. I'm acting purely on Mr Sinclair's behalf. He's unable to get about at the moment. But he's an old friend and I'd like to help him if I can.'

'And his reason for wanting this matter looked into again – is it only because of the pendant turning up in this way?' Jessup put the letter down. 'Or has he got other doubts as well?'

'Of a sort.' Madden considered his words before replying. 'It's my opinion that both Mr Sinclair and Derry were left puzzled by Owen Norris's behaviour during his interrogation. He was the man arrested and ultimately convicted. They felt they had never got to the bottom of him – they were never sure what was in his mind when he first confessed to the murder and then denied it later on at his trial. On top of that, Angus Sinclair is strongly opposed to capital

punishment and the thought now, even though it's only a suspicion, that he may have been party to sending the wrong
man to the gallows has been enough to spur him into action.
And before you ask, I've formed no conclusions myself about
this case. It's quite possible Norris was guilty as charged. But
I've come to agree with Angus that there's still a question
hanging over it.'

'Why?'

The question was shot at him like a bullet, and the hawk-
like glance that accompanied it was Madden's first intimation
of the searching intelligence that lay behind his host's engaging personality. Once again he had to ponder his reply.

'I can't give you a simple answer,' he said finally. 'I can
only say that I suspect it wasn't by chance that Miss Blake
found herself at your father's house that weekend: that in all
likelihood her visit was arranged, though I don't know how,
for a reason, and that the person behind it was Stanley Wing.'

'Ah . . . !' Jessup expelled his breath in a long sigh. His
piercing gaze remained fixed on his visitor. 'I've been sitting
here listening to you, Mr Madden, and wondering why you
had come to see *me*. What it was you thought I could tell
you that might help with your inquiry. Now I understand.'

A smile played about his lips.

'Stanley Wing . . .' His tone was thoughtful. 'What can I
say? Only that I'm not surprised.'

Without warning he stood up and strode to a table in the
corner of the office where a collection of framed photographs stood. Selecting one of them, he brought it back and
handed it to Madden.

'That was taken in 1935. My father's there in the middle
of the group. The men on either side of him were the senior
staff in our Hong Kong office at the time. It was his birthday.
He'd invited them to his house. Wing is on the right at the

edge of the picture. You can see he's not really one of them. He's standing apart. But that was Stanley Wing all over. He was always the fly on the wall, the lizard on the rock . . . always watching . . . waiting his opportunity . . .'

Madden studied the photograph.

The men, all Europeans apart from Wing, and all dressed informally in shirt sleeves and straw hats, stood in a loose group on a lawn in front of a sprawling house painted white and fronted by a long veranda. Wing, wearing a black suit and tie, stood a little away from them and, as Jessup had said, at the very edge of the photograph. Slim in build, with black hair plastered so close to his head that it resembled a skull cap, he was observing the group through narrowed eyes. The other men, conscious that they were posing for a snapshot, were smiling.

Madden handed the picture back.

'All I've been told so far was that Wing was a business associate of your father's,' he said. 'That doesn't sound as though he was an employee. But if he didn't work directly for Jessup's, what was his position exactly?'

'A good question.' Sir Richard laid the photograph down. 'And to tell the truth I was never entirely sure myself. He and my father went back a long way. Officially he was one of our consultants. But even that doesn't begin to cover his many . . . activities.'

He had hesitated over the word – as though he might have chosen another – and then continued, shrugging as he did so.

'Look, there's a great deal I could tell you about Stanley Wing. But I'm not sure it has any bearing on this business. He was never a suspect, was he?'

'Not that I'm aware of,' Madden replied. 'But then neither was anyone else who was staying at the house that weekend. What I mean is none of them was ever questioned in any detail by the police. Norris was arrested almost at once and confessed soon afterwards. What bothers both Mr Sinclair and Derry now is that the case might have been wrapped up too quickly.'

'Are you saying one of *them* might be under suspicion?' Jessup reacted sharply.

'I wouldn't go that far.'

Surprised by his host's response, Madden sought to reassure him. Up till that moment Sir Richard had seemed relaxed and at ease with the conversation they were having.

'It's more a matter of widening the original investigation. I've mentioned Wing's name. But there were other people staying as your father's guests, weren't there? I was wondering if you could tell me something about them, including where they are now, in case I need to get in touch with any of them. And also whether you could give me a picture of that weekend, what impression you had of it.'

'That's an odd request.' Jessup seemed intrigued by the question. 'Have you asked anyone else about it, anyone who was there?'

Madden shook his head.

'Well, first of all you should know that, properly speaking, I wasn't one of the guests. I had been coming down to Kent from London to see Father nearly every weekend that year. He hadn't been well for some time – he had a heart complaint – and he'd been in the process of handing over the company's reins to me. Although I wasn't due to take over as managing director until the following year, I was already acting in that capacity, and we had a great deal of business to get through. And there was a further complication, if you can call it that.' He smiled. 'My marriage to Sarah was set for September. The wedding was to take place in America, and we had agreed to take a full month's honeymoon afterwards. So there was the pressure of time, and since my father couldn't come to town – he simply wasn't well enough – I had got into the habit of going down to see him regularly, and the fact that he and Adele had guests that weekend was neither here nor there. We simply got on with our business, which was detailed and burdensome.'

He paused. 'I take it you know who I mean by Adele?'

'Mrs Castleton?'

Jessup nodded. 'I must say when I arrived shortly after lunch and she told me who was there I was taken aback. I couldn't imagine what had possessed my father to invite Wing. The previous year I had spent some months in Hong Kong going through the company's books and looking into all its business dealings, and among the conclusions I came to – the most important in many ways – was that we had to sever our ties with him. I'd prefer not to say anything more about that. It doesn't concern the inquiries you're making. But the upshot was that I finally persuaded my father that we had to cut him loose and he wrote to Wing informing him of our decision and also gave appropriate instructions to our management in Hong Kong. They were to have no more dealings with him. You can imagine my surprise then at discovering that he was one of the guests that weekend.'

'Did you know that he was in England?' Madden asked.

'Oh, yes. I'd heard that he was in London, and happened to bump into him at a party earlier that summer. Our encounter was cool, as you might imagine, but he told me he was over here on private business and I guessed it was linked to his interest in jade. I happened to know that he had been active in that area for some time.'

'Selling jade jewellery?' Madden asked. 'Is that what you mean?'

'Not exactly; no.' Jessup eyed his listener. 'Though he let

me think he was. One of the things I discovered when I went out to Hong Kong – it was more in the nature of confirming a long-held suspicion – was that Wing had been dealing on his own in the procurement and sale of jade antiques from the mainland, objects of historical interest and value that had almost certainly been pilfered from graves. The trade was illegal and, although our company hadn't profited from these dealings, Wing had had no scruples about using Jessup's name and his own connection to the firm to further his business.'

He laughed.

'I hadn't intended to tell you that, but you might as well know. And it was only one of the areas he'd been active in, using Jessup's name whenever it was useful to him, and only one of the reasons I had for getting rid of him. When I met him in London he claimed to have gone into the jewellery business and said he was trying to interest local dealers in buying jade pieces from him. I didn't believe a word of it. I thought it very likely he was renewing old contacts with collectors, people to whom he had sold antiques in the past in order to reassure them that the fact he was no longer connected with Jessup's made no difference: that he was still in business.'

He shrugged.

'I hasten to say I've no evidence of that. It was only a guess. But I certainly didn't credit his story about selling jewellery. Jade has never been a particularly popular stone here and the prices it commands are relatively low. He was up to something else, I'm convinced, but I doubt it ever got off the ground, given that the war started the following year and probably put a stop to any scheme he had.'

Jessup frowned.

'I'm sorry. I'm digressing. You don't want to hear all this.

What I meant to tell you was that when I ran into Wing at that party he had Miss Blake with him. She was wearing various pieces of jade and Wing gave me to understand that she was working for him, displaying the pieces at parties and functions to which he'd been invited, stirring up interest in them.'

He rolled his eyes.

'Well, if you could believe that, you would believe anything. I certainly didn't. But since we were no longer affected by what he was doing I didn't give much thought to it. I heard later on that he'd appeared at several social functions during the summer and each time he had had Miss Blake with him.'

'What was their connection, exactly?' Madden asked. 'They weren't a couple, were they?'

'Good heavens no.' Jessup laughed. 'It's quite impossible to imagine Wing in that role. I don't know if one can ever truly say of anyone that they're sexless, but Stanley Wing certainly came closest to it. He seemed to belong to another species. I had no idea then or now what stirred his blood, what might have set his pulses racing. He was an enigma to the last.'

'You've not seen him again?'

'Not since that weekend, in fact. I heard later that he had gone back to Hong Kong. Then, as I say, the war came. And when I finally got out there later – I mean after the Japanese occupation was ended – he was already in prison.'

He saw Madden's startled look.

'You didn't know? I assumed the police here must have told you. But perhaps *they* don't know. After all, why should they?'

He mused on the thought for a moment; then he shrugged.

'He was arrested soon after the Japanese occupation

ended. He was charged with collaborating with the enemy and pleaded guilty. I gathered he'd been up to his old tricks, selling jade art to the occupiers, but also assisting them in other areas, some of which were regarded as vital to the war effort. He was sentenced to six years in prison. He's still inside.'

Jessup smiled wryly.

'Forgive me. I've gone off on a tangent again. You wanted to know about that weekend. I didn't see any of the other guests when I arrived, which was shortly after lunch. My father and I settled down to work in his study. But I already knew from Adele that Wing was there and after I'd changed for dinner I sought him out and we had a brief conversation alone, out on the terrace. I was blunt with him. I asked him what the devil he was doing there. He was smoothness itself. He said he had simply come down to pay his respects to my father. There was no question of any recriminations. He accepted that he was no longer a part of Jessup's and only wanted to express his thanks to the man who done so much for him. It was very much the sort of act I had come to expect from him over the years and I decided to take it at face value. No more was said and we went inside to join the others.'

He paused to collect his thoughts.

'You'll want to know about the other guests, I expect. Besides Wing and Miss Blake they were Lord and Lady Cairns, old friends of Father's, and a younger couple called Rex and Margaret Garner. Harry Cairns died in 1946. I don't think they can be of any interest to you. Rex Garner I've known since boyhood. He and Margaret had got married a couple of years earlier. The local vicar and his wife were also dinner guests. I'm afraid I can't remember his name, but he was quite an elderly man and I was told he passed away during the war.'

He took a deep breath.

'And now we come to the dinner itself, which I imagine is what you've been waiting so patiently to hear about.'

'Have I?' Madden laughed. 'I wasn't aware of that.'

'Do you mean you know nothing about it?' Jessup looked startled. 'I thought you were bound to ask me about it. No one's mentioned it to you?'

'I've only spoken to the two detectives I've told you about – Derry and Mr Sinclair – and to Miss Cooper. She couldn't have known anything about that weekend.'

'No, of course not . . . I hadn't realized.' Jessup bit his lip. 'Well, then I'd better set you straight. Not to beat about the bush, it was a nightmare; hideously embarrassing; and the cause of it all was Portia Blake. Earlier she had appeared in the most extraordinary dress. Not just revealing: the degree of *décolleté* was breath-taking. She was a pretty girl with a good figure and the effect, on all the men, at least – and I won't exclude myself – was deplorable. We simply goggled at her. What's more she was wearing that infernal pendant, and when we sat down at the table she proceeded to play with it throughout the meal, leaning over the table, revealing even more of herself, dangling the thing between her breasts.'

He shook his head in wonderment.

'As I say, I'd only encountered her briefly before, when I met Wing at that party, but I remembered she had been a little too loud then, a bit too sure of herself, talking too much and acting as though she were one of us, which she wasn't.' He grimaced. 'That's a cruel thing to say. But you know what the English are like. You either belong or you don't, and even though she seemed to know a number of people there, particularly the men, she was obviously a fish out of water; and the same was true of that evening at Foxley Hall. She was all wrong, and the sad thing was she hadn't the faintest idea of the effect she was creating.'

He bit his lip.

'The dinner seemed to last an age, and the person who bore the brunt of it was Rex. He was seated opposite Miss Blake and she spent a good part of the meal flirting with him in a rather clumsy way and dangling that pendant in front of his eyes like a hypnotist's toy. By the end he actually did seem mesmerized. His wife, meanwhile, had got more and more angry with the way Miss Blake was carrying on, and heaven only knows what Harry Cairns and his wife made of it, never mind the vicar. I think the only person who enjoyed the performance was my wicked old father. I could see him chuckling.'

He spread his hands.

'So, there you have it. That was the prelude to the poor young woman's death, her last performance you might say, though I can't imagine it had anything to do with her murder.'

'Nor can I,' Madden agreed. 'But I'm interested by your choice of word. A *performance*, you say. Is that how it struck you?'

'Not at the time: not in the sense you mean.' Jessup cocked an eye at his visitor. 'You're wondering if she was deliberately putting on an act.'

'Yes, and was Stanley Wing behind it? He was the one who brought her down there, after all. That's something that's puzzled me from the start. She seemed out of place. What was she doing there?'

Madden's question hung in the air between them. Jessup had fallen silent. He seemed to have drifted off for a moment.

'Do you know, I asked my father that same question the following day.' He collected his thoughts. 'He simply laughed it off. He said Wing had rung him a few weeks earlier and asked if he could come down and see him. He confirmed what Stanley had told me the day before. He had simply wanted to pay his respects to my father before he returned to Hong Kong. They had set a date for the visit, but then a week before Wing was due to come down he had called Father again and asked if he could bring a young lady with him. My father, like me, had never associated Stanley with a woman and he was so intrigued by the notion that he immediately agreed and said she would be welcome. Quite simply, he was curious. He couldn't wait to see what Wing would produce in the shape of a female companion, and he allowed that he'd been well entertained by the goings on at dinner the previous evening.'

Jessup's smile was rueful.

'But that, I'm sorry to say, was my dear old parent all over. He had a mischievous side.'

'Did you see her the next day – Miss Blake?'

'Only briefly. I had spent the morning with Father – we still had some business to get through – and I'd intended leaving immediately to drive back to London. I didn't fancy witnessing a repeat of the previous night's antics and in any case I had an engagement in town. But Adele begged me to stay for lunch. She thought my presence would help to keep a lid on things. But as it turned out Rex had had a similar reaction. He had left the house soon after breakfast to drive into Canterbury, telling Adele that he was going to look up an old friend. Just before we were due to sit down he rang to say he wouldn't be back. He was lunching with his friend. I think our American cousins call it "chickening out".' Jessup smiled bleakly. 'So lunch passed off peacefully and I left as soon as it was over without waiting for coffee to be served. I got back to London in mid-afternoon. I had a place at the Albany then and when I arrived I found that the hall porter was holding a message for me. It was from Adele. I was to ring her at once. When I did she told me about Miss Blake's murder, and I turned round and drove all the way back. The house was full of police. They were taking statements from everyone – guests and staff – with the aim of finding out where each and every one of them had been during the afternoon. I gave my statement to one of the officers – it was brief, obviously – and then went in search of my father. I found him in bed, quite broken up, shattered. He was appalled by what had happened to the poor girl and felt he had somehow failed her. She had been under his roof, after all. It was very like him.'

Jessup bowed his head.

'I spent the night there and the following two days, mainly to comfort Father and do what I could for Adele, who had to cope with everything. I did have a brief word with Wing, but he professed to know nothing about what had happened. He had last seen Miss Blake at lunch, he said, after which he had gone to his room to rest.'

'Did he show any emotion?' Madden asked.

'Good heavens, no.' Jessup's laugh was harsh. 'But then I'm not sure I ever saw Stanley Wing display feeling of any kind. His face was like a mask. You never knew what he was thinking.'

'You said he and your father went back a long way: what did you mean by that?'

Jessup hesitated. For the first time he seemed reluctant to reply.

'It wasn't something my father liked to talk about, and I've tried to respect his wishes,' he said at last. 'What's more,

I'm sure it has no bearing on this case. Do you really want to hear it?'

'Please.'

'Well, if you insist . . .' He paused, gathering his thoughts, it seemed; or perhaps choosing his words. 'They met when Wing broke into my father's house in Hong Kong.'

'Good heavens!' Madden was astounded.

'It was, as I say, years ago. Stanley was just a boy, no more than twelve or thirteen. He'd been living on the streets, keeping himself alive through petty thieving. My father caught him as he was forcing a window, and then had to hold him at gunpoint, because Stanley was armed with a knife and seemed quite ready to use it. "He was as quick as a cobra and twice as dangerous," was how Father put it when he described the incident to me. Any other man would have called the police, but Father always did things his own way. He made Stanley sit down and he began to question him. To his amazement he discovered that the boy spoke fluent English, and when he learned the reason why he was as good as hooked.' Jessup smiled bleakly. 'Stanley's mother had been an English governess employed by a wealthy Chinese businessman to raise his children. Unfortunately for her she caught the eye of his younger brother and their affair, if you can call it that, ended when she became pregnant, at which point her employer dismissed her and she was left to fend for herself. For whatever reason the prospect of returning home didn't appeal to her and she had her baby in Hong Kong. My father never discovered precisely how she survived after that but it seems that both communities – British and Chinese – turned their backs on her and eventually she was forced into prostitution. Still, somehow she contrived to raise her son until she died quite suddenly of what sounded like typhus and Stanley was cast adrift. With no home any longer he was forced to take to the streets, and from then on he lived by his wits.'

Jessup caught Madden's eye.

'My father was a very lovable man,' he said. 'He had a big heart and a bottomless well of generosity which could be extended to almost anyone, but particularly to those he felt were in need. Without any further consideration, and starting that same night, he took Stanley under his wing. Although he didn't formally adopt him, he found a Chinese family for him to lodge with – needless to say they were well rewarded – and sent him to a good school. And although he was away from Hong Kong for long periods, he took care to keep in touch with the boy and when Stanley turned eighteen he took him into Jessup's as a trainee. He probably saw this as just another act of charity, but it came to seem like shrewd judgement on his part.' Sir Richard smiled. 'Stanley turned out to be very bright. Perhaps his earlier life on the streets had taught him things you can't learn at school, but he soon proved adept at dealing with the local administration where he developed the kind of relationships that were invaluable when it came to steering lucrative contracts our way.'

He stroked his cheek; pensive now.

'I have to be careful here,' he said. 'Doing business out East has always involved a certain amount of what we might call corruption, but can also be seen as simply acts of gratitude in return for favours granted. There are times when one simply has to turn a blind eye to whatever's going on. It would be fair to say that the management at the time – and I include my father – were well aware that we were sailing close to the wind and must have decided that the risk was worth it. In the event, we ran into trouble eventually with the authorities and had to pay some heavy fines. The reputation of the firm suffered and in the years leading up to the war it got into serious difficulties, though none of that affected Stanley Wing, who had managed to feather his own nest quite successfully by then and had already moved on to the next stage in his career, leaving the mess he had been partly responsible for behind him.'

'The next stage . . . ?'

'He'd been working for Jessup's for a dozen years or so when he decided to branch out on his own, and proceeded to do so with my father's blessing, which went so far as to grant him official status as a consultant of Jessup's and allow him to put that on his business cards; a grave mistake, in my opinion. It wasn't easy convincing Father later on that his protégé had turned out to be no better than a crook and right to the end he continued to harbour the illusion that Wing had simply been unlucky. He died in 1939, so he never knew about the Japanese occupation of Hong Kong. But he continued to worry about Stanley and asked often if I had any news of him.'

'And did you?'

'Not at that stage, no.' Jessup shook his head. 'I was called up early when war broke out. Earlier I had toyed with the idea of a military career. I had a commission in the Guards and was on the reserve list. The management of the company passed into other hands. Of course I kept in touch with them as much as I could, but I had more than enough to worry about without inquiring after Wing.'

He fell silent again, and this time Madden took the opportunity to put a question he'd been waiting to ask.

'I can't quite square the picture you've given me of Stanley Wing with this person who seems to have been quite at home in London society. You say you bumped into him earlier that summer at a party. How did that come about?'

'I should have explained.' Jessup acknowledged the

question with a nod. 'During the years when Stanley seemed to be doing so well for the firm – gaining us contracts and helping to expand the business – Father took him back to Europe with him on several occasions and introduced him to some of his business colleagues and friends in London. Knowing Father, I believe it was out of genuine goodwill towards Stanley. He meant to treat him as he would any promising young man regardless of his background. Unfortunately Wing took advantage of it in the worst possible way: it was during those early visits that he made the contacts he was able to exploit later.'

'You're referring to the sale of pilfered antiques?'

Jessup nodded. 'They were mostly rich men, collectors and antique dealers, and it was through them that Stanley gained access to society in a more general way; it was how he got invited to people's homes, and even to some of their parties. But from what I heard he was never remotely at ease at them; I knew from others that he was regarded as an oddity.'

He grimaced.

'I realize you're curious about him. But do you really believe he might have had a hand in Miss Blake's death?'

'Oh, no.' Madden shook his head. 'Or rather, I have absolutely no opinion on the subject one way or the other. I still think the man they arrested was the most likely killer. But Wing seems to be a dubious character at best, and we still don't know why he took Miss Blake down to Kent with him.'

He hesitated.

'Are you sure he's still in prison?'

'I've no reason to believe otherwise.' Jessup shrugged. 'My people out there have standing orders to let me know the moment he's released. I don't fancy the idea of Stanley Wing running around free without my knowing what he's up to. But why do you ask?'

'Based on what you've told me about him, I'd say he's the most likely person to have sent that pendant and the letter to Derry: the one most likely to have cooked up a scheme like this.'

'I see what you mean.' Jessup ruminated in silence. He caught his visitor's eye. 'I take it the British police won't be making any inquiries about Wing?'

'Would they get in touch with the Hong Kong authorities, do you mean? Would they try to have him interviewed in prison?' Madden shook his head. 'I very much doubt it. They have no reason to. Of course it would be different if the investigation were reopened.'

'That's what I thought.' Jessup nodded. 'Look, if you feel it's worthwhile I can ask my people in Hong Kong if they have any news of him.'

'That might be helpful.' Madden bowed his head in thanks. 'And while we're on the subject of Stanley Wing, do you happen to know if it was he who gave the pendant to Miss Blake?'

'No, I don't.' Jessup shook his head. 'I mean I've no idea. But I rather assumed it was, given that it's jade. Are you sure it belonged to her? Couldn't it have been one of the pieces she was showing on Wing's behalf?'

'Miss Cooper seemed certain it was Portia's. She didn't know who had given it to her, though.'

'Then I'm sorry – I can't help you.' He spread his hands.

Madden glanced at his watch.

'I've only one other question,' he said. 'I hope you won't take it amiss.'

'I'm sure I won't.' Jessup smiled. 'And may I say that all in all this has been a fascinating afternoon. You've forced me to delve into my memory. These are things I haven't thought about for years.'

'I was wondering if Wing and your friend Rex Garner were acquainted. Had they met before that weekend?'

'Is that what's bothering you?' His host seemed amused by the question. 'Yes, they had. Rex worked briefly for Jessup's when he was a young man. We were friends from our days at Eton and Father knew him well. He was sent out to Hong Kong as a trainee and spent a year there. I remember him talking about Stanley when he came back. "That Wing fellow of yours," he said, "he's an odd bird, but useful."'

'What did he mean by that?'

'I didn't care to inquire.' Jessup's tone was dry. 'I knew enough about Stanley Wing to assume it was probably disreputable.'

He saw the look in Madden's eye.

'Yes, all right. I'll be more explicit. The key to Stanley's success has always been his ability to acquire whatever it is that his customers want. He's by nature a *procurer*, and since I also knew that Rex liked to have a girl on hand and wasn't too particular in that respect, I didn't care to delve too deeply into whatever sort of relationship they might have struck up. But I had a pretty good idea what it involved.'

'Garner only stayed there for a year, you say.' Madden had taken a moment or two to digest the other's reply. 'Why was that?'

'Well, to put it bluntly, he was no good. Rex has never been one to put his shoulder to the wheel. He rather expects things to fall into his lap. The management out there said they couldn't rely on him for anything: that quite often he didn't even bother to turn up for work. In the end it was gently suggested to him that he might seek his future elsewhere.' Jessup smiled. 'Why are you asking me about him?'

'It occurred to me that if Portia Blake was putting on a

performance that evening, it seems to have been directed at him. I was also going to ask, too, whether *they* knew each other?'

'Rex and Miss Blake? You mean, was there anything between them?' Jessup bit his lip. He seemed unhappy with the question. Madden watched as he sat frowning and rubbing his chin. Finally, he spoke. 'Not that I'm aware of: though I admit I did wonder at the time. Margaret had been away in Scotland for a few weeks during the summer and I knew how Rex's eye tended to stray when she was out of town. I even asked him about it, but he swore to me that he only knew Miss Blake casually. He'd run into her once or twice at parties; that was all. He said he'd been embarrassed by the way she had gone at him over dinner. He had no idea why she'd done it, but he'd decided to make himself scarce the following day. He didn't want a repeat performance at lunch. I told you about him driving into Canterbury.'

'What time did he get back?' Madden asked.

'Around mid-afternoon, I gathered. By then Miss Blake's body had been discovered. You're not thinking . . .'

His expression changed.

'No, that's absurd. People don't go around murdering other people just because they're put out. Rex was cross with her, certainly, but that was all.'

His bright gaze stayed fixed on Madden's face. It was as though he were trying to read his thoughts.

'Given the way Miss Blake behaved at dinner, might Garner's wife have suspected that they had had an affair?' Madden asked.

'I can't answer that. I've no idea. But it wouldn't have surprised her . . . not eventually, anyway.'

'Eventually . . . ?'

'The marriage was always troubled. Rex was a rotten husband. He only married Margaret for her money and he was never faithful to her for long. She was very unhappy. Rumour had it she was going to divorce him, but then she died suddenly. That was in 1944. Rex was home on leave and they had a flaming row – or so he said – and she ended up taking an accidental overdose of sleeping pills.'

He was silent for a moment.

'People were surprised when they got married. Margaret was a shy girl, and quite plain. But if you knew Rex as well as I did then I'm sorry to say it made perfect sense. He was on the look-out for a rich wife. It was as simple as that. We were great friends when we were boys, but all that's past I'm afraid. Sarah can't abide him, and I can understand why. Truth to tell, we don't see much of each other now. And when we do, it's usually because Rex wants to borrow money from me. He's managed to go through most of what Margaret left him – and it was a lot – but he still tries to keep up appearances, play the part of a rich man about town. It's all a front, though.'

'Does he live in London?' Madden asked.

'He's got a house near Shepherd Market; heavily mortgaged, I believe. Are you planning to talk to him?'

'I might. It rather depends on whether Mr Sinclair thinks this inquiry is worth pursuing.'

'You're welcome to mention my name if you do,' Jessup said. 'I'll get Miss Harmon to give you his address and telephone number.'

He rose to his feet. Madden did the same.

'I'd like to thank you for being so frank with me,' he said. 'I've got a much clearer picture now of that weekend.'

'I'm glad to have been of help,' Jessup responded, with the open smile that Madden had come to expect from him.

'And please feel free to get in touch with me again if you need to.'

About to move to the door, he checked his stride. He saw that his visitor had something further to say.

'There is one more favour I'd like to ask of you.' Madden had hesitated before making the request. 'Could you possibly put me in touch with Mrs Castleton? She's someone I'd like to talk to.'

'But of course. I should have thought of that myself.' Jessup's smile broadened. 'Nothing could be simpler. She lives near Kew Gardens. She'd been staying at our house in Hampshire taking care of the children while Sarah and I were in the United States, but she's home again now. I could have spent another hour talking to you about Adele. She's a wonderful woman – and far and away the best thing that ever happened to my father. In the few years they were together she made him happier than he'd ever been in his life and I'm glad to say she's still very much a part of our family. Sarah thinks the world of her, and so do the children. As far as they're concerned she's their real grandmother, and I dread the day when I'll have to tell them that she's not.'

He chuckled.

'Unfortunately I'll be away on the Continent for the next fortnight on business. But I'll write her a note before I go telling her who you are and that I fully support the inquiries you're making. I'll give you her address and telephone number, too, so that you can get in touch with her. I'm sure you'll find her helpful.'

'It wasn't just that I liked him, Angus. I was impressed by him. It must be a huge responsibility, running a concern like Jessup's. Yet he carries it all so lightly.'

'And you don't feel he was keeping anything back?'

'About Rex Garner? No, I don't. He doesn't believe Garner could have had anything to do with Miss Blake's death. He made that clear. But he was quite open about his womanizing.'

They were speaking on the telephone. Madden had rung the chief inspector when he got back from the City and was standing now in a hall stripped of all furniture save for the small table where the phone rested. Even the painting that had hung on the wall above – and which Madden was accustomed to gaze at whenever he used the instrument – had disappeared. It was the study of Westminster Bridge which Alice had claimed for her own, and it appeared that she had already taken possession of the object. In its place now there was only the ghostly outline left by the frame on the wallpaper behind it.

'I was interested to learn that Garner also knew Wing,' Madden went on. 'That might be a line of inquiry worth pursuing.'

'Why?'

'We still don't know why Wing brought Portia Blake down to Kent with him. But bearing in mind that scene at dinner, and the way Miss Blake carried on, it's possible it was somehow linked to Rex Garner being there at the same time.'

'Would Wing have known that: before he got there, I mean?'

'I don't know. But it's something I can ask Mrs Castleton when I see her. And I've a lot more to tell you about Mr Wing . . .'

Madden broke off at the sound of footsteps above. Looking up he saw Lucy coming down the stairs.

'Yes, go on.' Sinclair's voice sounded in his ear. 'What about him?'

'Look, if you don't mind, I'd rather not talk about it now,' Madden replied after a moment. 'I'm a bit caught up at present. Let's discuss it at the weekend. We'll have plenty of time then.'

'Was that Angus?' Lucy asked when she had reached the bottom of the stairs and Madden had replaced the receiver. 'I'm sorry. I wasn't listening in.'

'Listening in . . . ?'

'Only I wouldn't want you to think I was eavesdropping.' Lucy's blue eyes were the image of her mother's and at that moment her gaze was guilt-ridden and apologetic. 'I know you don't want to talk about this case in front of me any more and I understand why. I shouldn't have babbled on in that way.'

'My darling, I don't want you to feel shut out . . .'

Madden was at a loss for words. In the wake of the events of the previous Sunday he had been suffering from an attack of guilt: he felt he had been too harsh with his daughter and Lucy's uncharacteristic meekness since then, the burden of sackcloth and ashes she wore, her penitent's expression, had only added to his feeling of remorse.

'It's just that . . . that . . . I prattle on without thinking, I know. I *must* be more careful in future. This has been a good lesson for me.'

She took his arm.

'I've given Alice the evening off. I'm going to make you dinner. You probably don't know, but she managed to squeeze two pork chops out of the butcher this morning. Such riches! Let's go into the kitchen and decide what we're going to do with them.'

She paused when she saw the look on his face.

'Don't worry, Daddy. We're going to have a lovely evening. And I don't want you to think you have to say a *word* about Angus's case. We've lots of other things to talk about.'

'So you see if Rex Garner and Portia did have an affair in the past, it would change things. Of course, it may not be important – she seems to have had a lot of men friends – but he also knew Stanley Wing from years back. Angus and Tom Derry didn't know that: they never had a chance to find out. There may be some significance to it.'

'It's a triangle, isn't it?' Lucy's face lit up. 'A love triangle!'

'Oh, I doubt that.' Madden dismissed the notion. 'Wing wasn't one of her lovers: that's for certain. No, the question is, was Portia just flirting with Garner to amuse herself, or was there some meaning behind the performance she put on with that pendant, dangling it in front of his eyes? By the end of dinner Garner looked quite mesmerized, or so Sir Richard said.'

'I think it meant something.' Lucy was reluctant to abandon her suspicions. 'Otherwise why was the pendant taken from her body?'

'You could look at it that way.'

As though prompted by his own words, Madden paused to study the wine in his glass. The remains of their meal lay about them on the kitchen table. His daughter was a surprisingly good cook – surprising only because she had the gift of never seeming to take pains over anything, yet somehow managing to achieve a level of skill beyond mere competence; and all that with flair and style. Despite having observed her closely throughout her life, he still didn't know how she managed it, any more than he understood why he was talking so freely about the inquiry to her now. It wasn't as though Lucy had raised the subject herself. It was he who had chosen to refer in a casual way to the call he had received from Jessup's secretary earlier that day, a remark that had led with seeming inevitability to the conversation they were having now.

'But it still depends on the two factors being linked.' He dragged his mind back to the present. 'I mean Portia's performance the night before and the disappearance of the pendant. But if someone just happened to find the pendant – if it was torn off her neck in the struggle and picked up later in the wood – then the whole idea of a connection between them falls away.'

'So it could be just a red herring?' Clearly unhappy with the notion, Lucy frowned.

'Yes, and there might be nothing to any of this,' Madden felt bound to point out. 'We have to bear that in mind. All these interviews I'm having – they may be a waste of time. It could be that we'll decide at a certain moment that they were right all along, Angus and Derry. That there's no need to reopen the investigation.'

'Oh, I hope not.' No longer able to restrain herself, his daughter gave vent to her frustration. 'It would be such a damp squib.'

'I'd hardly call it that.'

'Well, you know what I mean.' Catching his eye, she smiled; and then stretched. 'I must get these things washed up before I go to bed.'

'No, don't worry. I'll clear the table.' Madden returned her smile. 'I'll put the dishes in the sink. Alice will see to them in the morning. And thank you for dinner, my dear. It was delicious.'

He watched as she rose and came around the table.

'I'm so glad we talked.' She bent to kiss him goodnight.

'I hated everything being so stiff and formal between us. It made me so unhappy. You don't realize how important it is for me to know that you're always there and that I can say anything I want to you and you'll understand.'

She kissed him again and then went to the door; pausing to glance back at him.

'Why are you looking at me that way?'

'It's something your mother said. She seems to think I'm putty in your fingers. I can't think why.'

'Well, it's not true.' Her smile dazzled him.

'I'm relieved to hear it. Goodnight, my darling. And sleep well.'

9

'THAT TIME YOU met her at a party – what did you talk about?' Madden asked.

'Me, mostly. Of course, I knew who she was and I was rather in awe of her: we all were. But as I said, she turned out to be quite different: not at all what I expected.'

Helen turned to smile at him, her face bright in the morning sunlight. They were sitting on a bench on the platform at Highfield station waiting for the train that would take Madden to London, where he had an appointment to meet Adele Castleton later that day. Wanting to form some sort of picture of a woman about whom he had heard just enough to make him curious, he had asked Helen to describe her and she had been doing her best to recall the details of their brief encounter.

'It was one of those parties in London that Violet and I went to that autumn; there seem to have been dozens, though there can't have been that many. All I remember is that I was starting to get tired of them: the same faces, the same partners, the same dance bands. I had gone to the bathroom and was on my way out when I caught sight of Adele sitting on her own in a small room off the passage. She was smoking a cigarette. I was going to walk by, but she called out to me. "Come and sit down," she said. "Helen, is it?"'

She told me she had noticed me dancing earlier and asked who I was. I felt tremendously flattered. She was older than I was, of course, and a figure in society: not beautiful exactly, but tremendously attractive, with dark hair and pale skin. And something more: it was in her manner, the way she carried herself. I suppose you would call it "presence". She only had to enter a room and all eyes would be drawn to her. That was partly because of her reputation, of course. There were endless stories about her and although half of them probably weren't true, you could tell just by looking at her that she was different; and that she didn't care what people thought of her. I was nervous – I couldn't think what I was going to say to her – but I needn't have worried. As soon as I sat down she began asking me questions. She wanted to know who I was and where I came from and what I was doing with my life. They were quite intimate questions, but I didn't mind because I could see she was really interested, and so I told her that I was getting tired of the social life we were all caught up in, the never-ending parties, and that I'd applied to study medicine at London University, but I wasn't sure whether I'd get in, being a woman. I thought it might sound pretentious to her, but I couldn't have been more mistaken. She said it was a wonderful idea and I should do it. And then she said something I've never forgotten. "Don't be like me and find yourself sitting on your own at a party one night wondering what to do next, and whether it even matters."'

Helen sighed.

'We were going to meet again. She said she would get in touch with me once she had sorted out a few things in her life – that was how she put it – and we could have lunch together and talk more; but I never saw her again. She went to America soon afterwards. I read about it in a gossip column. She was with some man. But I got into university, as you know, and I always hoped that the news might have reached her wherever she was. Will you give her a message from me? Say I remember meeting her and that I'm sorry we lost touch after that.'

A whistle from down the track alerted them to the approach of Madden's train. He had not been up to London that week, preferring to stay at home and attend to work at the farm, leaving his daughter to see to the gradual disposal of Aunt Maud's furniture. Lucy had decided to remain in the house at least until the end of the month while she looked about for a suitable flat for them to buy.

'I'm glad you two have patched things up,' Helen said as they rose from the bench.

'Just as you predicted, you mean?' Madden drew her to him. 'And you're quite right. I won't deny it any longer. I am putty in her fingers. And yours, too, I suspect.'

'Nonsense. Whatever gave you that idea?'

Laughing, she kissed him on the lips. Then she drew back. 'You won't forget my message, will you?'

'Of course not.'

'I wonder if *she'll* remember . . .'

Acting on Jessup's advice, Madden had waited for a few days after their meeting before ringing Adele Castleton.

The interval had also given him an opportunity to discuss the case further with Sinclair, whom he had found in notably better spirits and moving about gingerly with the help of a cane. They had spent an hour together after lunch on Sunday sitting in the shade of the chief inspector's apple tree while Madden gave his old friend an account of his conversation with Sir Richard Jessup; in particular what he had learned about the fateful weekend when Portia Blake had lost her life.

'There was certainly something going on,' he said.

'Whatever the reason behind it, her behaviour at dinner sounds artificial to me. So was she put up to it, and if so, by whom? Stanley Wing would seem to be the obvious candidate. But even if that's true, what possible motive could he have had for stirring things up? And let's not forget there's still no reason to suppose that that scene had anything to do with her murder the next day. That still looks to me more like a chance killing than anything else.'

Sinclair's muttered growl in response had suggested he was not yet ready to accept the proposition, and his next words lent force to that impression.

'But we still haven't heard what Mrs Castleton has to say, have we? Let's suspend judgement until then.'

The lady in question had received Madden's telephone call in what had sounded like a friendly spirit – it was clear that Sir Richard Jessup had been in touch with her – and they had fixed to meet at her house.

'I live near Kew Gardens,' she had told him. 'You can come down by tube if you like, or there's a bus that will drop you at the Victoria Gate. I'm only five minutes' walk from there.'

Of the two alternatives offered him, it was the train Madden chose, and having been deposited at Kew station a little after four o'clock he made his way through leafy suburban streets to the address given him, which proved on arrival to be a small, neat-looking villa standing in its own patch of garden and shielded from the street by an ivy-clad wall.

'I was in love with Kew when I was a child,' his hostess told him later. 'My father was an amateur botanist. Plants were his passion; he seized every opportunity to visit the gardens, and once he discovered that I shared his interest he used to take me with him. We would wander through the park and the greenhouses hand-in-hand. My happiest memories of childhood all have to do with the hours we spent together. When Jack died and I knew I would have to leave Foxley Hall there was only one place I could think of living; which is why you find me here.'

Madden's ring on the doorbell had been answered by a maid of similar vintage to Alice – they were becoming a rarity in post-war England – who had led him through the house to the garden behind it where Mrs Castleton awaited him. Dressed simply in a tweed skirt and workaday blouse, she had been kneeling on the grass, digging in a border with a trowel when he was ushered through a pair of French windows on to a small paved patio, and had risen at once to greet her visitor.

'I've been so looking forward to meeting you, Mr Madden.'

Removing the gardening gloves she was wearing, she had offered him a hand bare of rings to shake. Slight of figure and with short grey hair now – no trace remained of the dark locks that Helen remembered – she appeared to be in her late sixties with a delicate bone structure that gave more than a hint of the looks that must once have drawn men to her; and might still have done so had she wished it. But it was the intense quality of her gaze that seized Madden's attention – her eyes were deep and dark; that and the sense she gave at once of being at ease in his company while not caring what impression he might have of her. He guessed this was what Helen had meant by the word 'presence'.

'You made a great impression on Richard. He wanted to know more about you, he said, but was obliged to spend the time you had together answering *your* questions.'

She had let a few moments go by before speaking again.

It was as though she wished to give each of them the opportunity to appraise the other.

'I felt it was the other way round,' Madden replied. 'I'm still in awe at the thought of what it must take to run a concern like Jessup's. I know that the war interrupted Sir Richard's business career, but if I understood him right he must have felt ready to take on the responsibility when he was still in his early thirties.'

'When Jack had to relinquish control of the company, you mean?' She nodded. 'Of course, he wasn't well, but even so he felt it was time he handed over the reins to someone younger.' She smiled. 'Poor darling, he really was no sort of businessman, and he knew it. And as you say, Richard was more than ready to take command.'

There was a table with some chairs standing in a corner of the patio and she led him to it, turning to her maid as she did so.

'You can bring us our tea now, Agnes.'

She waited until they were alone again before continuing.

'Richard has told me why you went to see him. I do find it extraordinary that this dreadful business should be brought up again after all this time. But he explained about the pendant to me and said all he wanted was to see the matter cleared up once and for all. He asked me to help you in any way I could, which, of course, I'll do, though I doubt there's much I can add to what he's already told you.'

'It's very generous of you both.' Madden bowed his head in thanks. 'But before we begin, I've a message for you. It's from my wife. She wants me to tell you that she went ahead and did what she said she would do. She studied medicine and became a doctor. She wonders if you remember her telling you that. It was a long time ago.'

Plainly astonished, Mrs Castleton stared at him open-mouthed. They sat like that for several seconds, neither saying a word. Then, without warning, she tossed her head back and laughed.

'*Helen!*' she said. 'Is that her name? It *must* be.'

Madden nodded.

'Of course I remember. I can see her now. She was such a lovely young woman, so open and engaging. It was at a party in London. We sat and talked. I was so envious, hearing what she wanted to do with her life. I remember wishing I had done the same; not studying medicine, but something I really cared about . . . botany for instance; or natural history. We were going to meet again, but then . . . oh, let's not talk of that. It depresses me just to think of it.'

She shuddered.

'Helen . . .' She murmured the name again. Then, still clearly struck by the memory he had stirred, she drew back a little in her chair as though to underline the importance of what she was about to say next.

'Tell me, Mr Madden, when you married her did you feel you had won some great and undeserved prize in life?'

He looked at her in wonder.

'How on earth did you know that?'

'I told you – I *remember* her.' Her dark eyes held him captive. 'But tell me more, please. When did you meet?'

'It was after the war – the first war. I was a police officer then, a detective, and I was assigned to a murder investigation in the village where Helen lived. I had served in the army and when it was over I returned to my old job at Scotland Yard. But it wasn't the same: *I* wasn't the same. I hadn't recovered from my time in the trenches.'

'And did you fall in love with her at once?' Mrs Castleton checked herself. She put a hand to her cheek. 'Forgive me,

Mr Madden. It's none of my business. My friends are always telling me I'm too direct. Don't answer if you'd rather not.'

'I'm sure that I did.' Madden had no hesitation in replying. 'Although I wasn't aware of it at first.'

Even as he spoke, he was struck by the extraordinary sense of intimacy she had created between them in the space of only a few minutes. He saw, too, that it was this same gift that must have been at the very heart of the fascination she had held for so many people.

'Quite simply the thought seemed impossible. I couldn't imagine I might ever mean anything to her.'

'Why was that?'

'It was the war. I thought something had broken inside me. I couldn't feel any more. I was numb. A lot of men who came back from the trenches had the same experience. I couldn't see any future for myself. I felt I was damaged goods.'

He had never talked this way to anyone but Helen, yet the words seemed to flow naturally, as though from a hidden source.

'But she saw through all that? Is that what you're saying?'

'As if it were in plain sight.'

The memory of those days – so precious to him – was still fresh in his mind. It was as if he were speaking of yesterday.

'I didn't have to tell her anything. It was as though she already knew. It still seems like a miracle to me.'

'Dear Mr Madden . . .' There were tears in Adele Castleton's eyes. 'I do believe you and I are two of a kind. Jack Jessup was my saviour. I met him in Kenya in 1930.'

She was interrupted by the rattle of crockery behind her, signalling the arrival of the tea trolley, and for a while she was occupied with pouring their tea while her maid hovered over the table, first handing Madden his cup and then offering him a choice of biscuits or cake, both of which were carried on a stand. Only when she had left them did Mrs Castleton resume speaking.

'I was there with friends and we were invited to visit a farm in the highlands. I was already wishing I hadn't come – to Africa, I mean. It seemed like just another pointless holiday: and a holiday from what? I'd been drifting for so long that I'd lost all sense of direction. Jack was staying with the family on the farm. I knew who he was, of course. Black Jack Jessup, the papers called him. He was said to be a friend of the Prince of Wales. He was about to go off on safari the next day and was only there, at the farm, for that one night. I was feeling ghastly.' She put a hand to her cheek. 'Not unwell, but simply despairing. I lost my husband not long after we were married. He was quite rich, but he wanted to be a racing driver and was killed in a crash. After that I seemed to lose my bearings and went from one man to another until I reached the point where I couldn't see any way of escaping from the mess I had made of my life. I sat up late on my own in front of the fire – it was the end of summer and the nights were getting cold – and Jack found me there. He had come down in his dressing-gown and pyjamas to look for a book, but instead he sat down beside me and asked me what the trouble was.'

She smiled.

'I didn't want to talk to him. I didn't want to talk to anyone. I was too miserable. But he wouldn't be put off. He said he wasn't going to leave me. He would sit there all night if necessary. And so after a while we began to talk: that is, I began to talk and he to listen. We sat there until nearly dawn and then he said I had to go to bed. I needed to get some sleep, he said, but since he was leaving later that morning

I would have to be up and ready to go by ten o'clock at the latest.'

She laughed.

'I told him he was mad, but he was absolutely insistent. There was no way he was going to leave me behind. I had to go with him on his safari. He would show me Africa – the real Africa – and we could continue talking. "Don't you see?" he said, as though it were the simplest thing in the world and how could I not understand it. "We've so much to say to each other. And we've hardly begun."'

She smiled again.

'I'll spare you the details – my protestations and so on. Suffice to say when the moment came for the lorry that was carrying Jack and his gear to leave I was on it. I remember waving goodbye to my friends and thinking what an addition this would make to the catalogue of scandalous behaviour that had attached itself to my name over the years.

'I told myself I was setting out on another of my foolish adventures – Lord knows there'd been enough of those – but all the same I had a feeling that this time it would be different. I had already sensed a quality in Jack Jessup that I wasn't used to finding in the men I'd known: a deep strain of kindness. It was what had kept him sitting up with me all night. He had seen that I was in pain and had set out to heal me if he could. Of course, he had no way of knowing that what he was about to show me – the wildness of Africa, the animals, the wonderful unspoilt country – was a dream I had carried in my heart since childhood. I don't know what Dr Freud would have made of the attraction I felt for this man who reminded me in so many ways of my father and who had appeared as if from nowhere to take me by the hand. But we didn't become lovers for some time: not on the safari, and not when we returned to Nairobi. It was only on the voyage back to England. But by then I knew we weren't going to part.'

She was silent for a moment, lost in memory.

'Jack had told me from the very beginning that he couldn't marry me. His wife wouldn't give him a divorce – it was her last way of punishing him – and he was too much the English gentleman to divorce her on grounds of desertion. I told him it didn't matter; and truly it didn't. I had long since lost any desire for respectability. All I wanted was to remain with him for the rest of my life; or his, as it turned out.'

She shifted her glance away from Madden to the sun-dappled lawn beside them and they sat in silence. Then she faced him again.

'We settled down at Foxley Hall and from that moment on we were seldom separated for more than a day or two. I soon realized that, like me, he was also trapped in a way of life he had neither sought nor wanted. I mean the company – Jessup's. It was something he had inherited, something he couldn't get rid of: until Richard grew up, that is, and was able to take it off his hands.'

'He told me he didn't see much of his father when he was young.' Madden was absorbed by the tale he was hearing. 'Was that because of his mother?'

Mrs Castleton nodded. 'As I say, she wanted to punish Jack, and keeping his son away from him was the best way of doing that. But when he got older Richard wanted to know him better, and by the end they had developed a close bond. It made an enormous difference to Jack's last years: not only because of the personal link, but also because Richard proved to be such a strong ally when it came to dealing with the company. He seemed born to take over the business and Jack came to lean on him more and more.

'They were alike in so many ways. I don't know how I

would have coped with the loss of Jack if Richard hadn't made it plain from the outset that as far as he and Sarah were concerned I was as much a part of the family as if we had been married. It's been a great blessing to me, and one I hardly feel I deserve, given my disreputable past. I seem to spend almost as much time in Hampshire with them and their children as I do here. I can never thank them enough.'

Her expression had changed while she was talking. She looked thoughtful now.

'But although they were so similar – both kind and generous – there was one great difference between them. Underneath it all, Richard has a core of steel. I often wonder if he inherited it from his mother. I never met her, but by all accounts she was a woman of iron will, and absolutely unforgiving where Jack was concerned. When Richard began the process of taking over from his father, of gathering the reins of Jessup's into his hands, he realized that some heads were going to have to roll, especially in Hong Kong. Over the years Jack had let things slide to an alarming degree – his heart was never in the business – and Richard told me later he'd been appalled to discover the true state of affairs and how close the company was to bankruptcy. He had had to act quickly. The firings were wholesale and some of the people involved were old friends of Jack's; they had been with Jessup's for years. There was no question that radical action was needed; but it was something Jack could never have brought himself to do. It simply wasn't in him. But Richard sees things with a cooler eye. He's never been one to be blinded by sentiment. He can do what has to be done. I don't know about you, Mr Madden, but it's a quality I've come to admire and value.'

'But not one all of us possess.' Madden's smile was rueful.

'He gave me a hint of it when we talked about Stanley Wing. He said he had had to get rid of him.'

'Ah yes . . . Stanley Wing.'

Her gaze had clouded.

'Richard said you would want to ask me about him. Well, I wasn't altogether surprised when Jack told me he'd invited Stanley down to Foxley Hall for that weekend. He had always felt bad about him after Richard had insisted that the tie between Wing and Jessup's had to be broken. He didn't disagree with the decision – I think he knew in his heart that Stanley was a rotten apple – but having been moved to rescue him when he was a boy he had always felt some sort of responsibility for him. Of course I knew the whole story – how they came to meet, what Stanley's background was – before we went out to Hong Kong for the first time. But it still came as a shock when I realized that under all his surface politeness and formal good manners he obviously detested us.'

'*Detested* you?' Madden was brought up short by the word. 'What do you mean? And how could you know that if he didn't show it?'

'Oh, my instincts are seldom wrong: especially when it comes to men.' She caught his eye and smiled. 'I could see that he hated all of us, the British community as a whole, including the senior staff at Jessup's, even if he tried to keep it hidden. I'm afraid Jack was wrong about him. He believed that Stanley was grateful and even felt some affection for him. But I sensed he was cold, without what we think of as human feeling; cold and watchful. I don't know what his early life did to him; perhaps the damage he suffered was irreparable. But I felt instinctively that he was a dangerous man and it worried me that Jack was so attached to him.'

She paused, frowning.

'Mind you, Stanley had much to be bitter about. We British have such an ingrained sense of what we like to think of as our superiority to other races that we sometimes forget the effect it has on them; and Stanley being of mixed blood had the added misfortune of not being accepted by either community – British or Chinese. Wing isn't his real name, you know. His father was called Liang, and his mother gave him that name, partly out of defiance, Jack told me. Not that it did any good: the family turned their back on her. They refused to acknowledge any connection with Stanley. After Jack took him up he changed his name to Wing, which isn't a Chinese name, properly speaking. Perhaps Stanley wanted to distance himself from his father's people. But he found no great welcome from the British either, I'm afraid.'

'A touch of the chink . . .' Madden grimaced. 'I heard someone use those words about him recently, quite casually, and without thinking. I imagine it's the sort of thing he had to put up with.'

'You can be sure of it.' Mrs Castleton frowned. 'Mind you, Richard wasn't like that. He would never have spoken in that way. He took after his father. But he saw quite early on that Stanley was using the company for his own purposes, some of them illegal, and he was determined to get shot of him. It was a painful decision as far as Jack was concerned; but he knew Richard was right. Still, nothing would have made him turn his back on the boy he had saved from the streets, and when Stanley called that summer and asked if he could come and see us Jack agreed at once. I know that Stanley ended up in prison finally. I'm just thankful it didn't happen while Jack was alive.'

In the silence that followed her words the fluting warble of a thrush sounded from the shrubbery at the foot of the garden. Another of the species had been busy on the lawn for some time, stabbing at the grass with its beak in a ceaseless search for insect prey. Mrs Castleton watched it for a moment. Then she turned back to her visitor.

'Forgive me. I've spent all this time telling you about my wicked past when what you want to know about is that weekend. But is it really likely that the police will reopen the investigation into the poor girl's death? Richard seemed uncertain.'

'And so am I,' Madden said. 'I haven't come across anything yet that would justify it. As he may have told you, I'm only doing this for a friend, a man I worked under at the Yard years ago, and I know from experience that once you start probing into people's lives and their behaviour, which is what happens in a police investigation, all sorts of odd and sometimes embarrassing things come to light which have nothing to do with the inquiry you're making.'

'Dear me. That does sound ominous.'

'I hope it won't be that bad.' Madden smiled. 'But from what I've been told it seems that even before Miss Blake's murder, that weekend wasn't entirely without incident. There was something in the air . . .'

'You're alluding to what happened at dinner the night before: that extraordinary performance of hers.' Mrs Castleton shook her head. 'I'd never seen anything like it. And the dress she was wearing – it would have turned heads in a Soho dive. We were all spellbound when she appeared downstairs; and from that point on, rather like grand opera, things only got worse.'

'According to Sir Richard, she seemed to make a point of tormenting Rex Garner. Was that your impression?'

'Yes, I suppose so.' Mrs Castleton took a moment to think before responding to the question. 'Mind you, she was sitting across the table from him, so in a sense he was her natural audience for all the byplay that was going on with the pendant. I felt she was quite aware that the rest of us were watching her, too, and rather enjoying the effect she was having on the party. Stanley, for one, was positively glaring.'

'The pendant – it was very much part of her act, was it?'

'It was quite central to it, I would say. She kept playing with it, swinging it from side to side like a pendulum. I couldn't think what she was up to.'

'Sir Richard said the effect was hypnotic: on Garner, at least.'

'Did he?' She smiled bleakly. 'I would have said he looked more dazed. He had his wife sitting almost beside him. I think that upset him more than anything. He kept glancing at her as if to reassure her; or at least suggest that he didn't know why Miss Blake was behaving in that way.'

'I asked Sir Richard if there had been anything between them in the past. He said that Garner had sworn to him that there hadn't; though he admitted to knowing the girl, or at least having met her.'

'So I gathered. Richard told me later they knew each other. If I'd known, I would never have invited the two of them down to Kent at the same time. But Miss Blake was a complete stranger to me. I heard her name for the first time when Jack told me that Stanley had asked if he could bring someone with him.'

'I have another question, though I don't know whether you can answer it.' Madden hesitated. 'Did Miss Blake know that Rex Garner would be there that weekend?'

Taken aback, she hesitated before replying. 'You're wondering whether she planned that scene with him.'

'That, and whether Wing might have put her up to it. He seemed to have some kind of hold over her. That's according to the woman she shared a flat with.'

'What a disagreeable thought.' Mrs Castleton brooded on the notion. 'Well, I can't answer your first question except to say that the invitation to Stanley Wing was extended *before* I decided to invite the Garners, so neither he nor Miss Blake could have known that Rex would be here at that point. However, Stanley and Rex had been acquainted for a number of years and if they had run into each other in London, which I believe they did, it's quite possible that Rex might have mentioned he would be in Kent on those dates.'

'It could have been after that that Wing got in touch with Sir Jack again.' He saw that his meaning escaped her. 'Sir Richard told me that Wing rang his father a second time only a week before he was due to come down to ask if he could bring Miss Blake with him.'

'I'd forgotten that.' She frowned. 'But you're right. Jack was captivated by the idea. He told me he'd never associated Stanley with a girlfriend and couldn't wait to see who he would bring with him. In the event Miss Blake, when she appeared, was quite a shock. She was a very pretty girl, and Jack simply couldn't get his mind around the fact that it was Stanley of all people who had brought her down.'

She paused.

'But as far as Wing being perhaps behind that display she put on during dinner, I think you're mistaken. After everyone had gone to bed I went to check on something upstairs and when I walked past Miss Blake's room I heard the two of them arguing – she and Wing. Only they weren't quarrelling exactly: it was more a case of Stanley reading her the riot act. I didn't pause to eavesdrop, but I heard enough to convince me that he was simply furious with her over the way she had behaved. That in itself was unusual; he so seldom showed emotion of any kind. But he was seething, fairly hissing with rage. "What is this game you're playing?" I heard him say. A few minutes later, when I came back, I heard her laughing. "Don't worry. They're in a safe place," she said. Then he muttered something which I didn't catch. But he sounded furious.'

She sighed then.

'It was a terrible shock for all of us when we heard what had happened to Miss Blake the next day; but particularly for darling Jack. He had a very traditional view of his role as host. That one of his guests – even if it was someone he barely knew – should come to such an awful end was a dreadful shock. As it was, he hadn't been well for some time – he had a degenerative heart condition – and the blow seemed to affect his health. He never really recovered after that and, as you probably know, he died the following year.'

'Then I can only say how sorry I am to have brought it all back.' Seeing the sadness in her eyes, Madden regretted the inadequacy of his apology. 'I should have realized.'

'You're not to think that.' She spoke firmly. 'Both Richard and I want this business cleared up. If there's anything more you need to ask me, please don't hesitate.'

'Then I've only one other question, but it's a delicate one.'

'Be brave, Mr Madden.' Her tone was teasing.

'It has to do with the Garners. How would you character- ize their marriage?'

'Oh, dear!' The smile that had come to her lips vanished in an instant. 'Must I? Can it really have anything to do with Miss Blake's death?'

'It's possible.' Madden had to consider his reply. 'But only just. I'll admit I'm clutching at straws here. I gather she was a rich woman.'

'Yes, she came from a wealthy Scottish family. She was an only child.'

'And that Garner very likely married her for her money.'

'That was generally thought to be the case. There seemed no other reason for it. Rex is good looking, and a lot of women find him attractive. Personally, I've never cared for him, but Margaret was immensely flattered by his attentions. They made an odd-looking couple: the handsome pheasant cock and his dowdy hen. We could see the way things were going, Jack and I, but we were powerless to prevent it. Rex had her under his thumb from the start, and I know that as time went by she suffered more and more from the way he behaved.'

'Sir Richard told me how she died. Is it possible she took her own life?'

'Not according to the coroner.' Mrs Castleton shrugged. 'He ruled it a case of accidental death. I had my doubts, however; and so did others. Margaret was in the depths of depression. She seemed unable to face the prospect of what would certainly have been a squalid divorce case. I wasn't alone among her friends, though, in wishing she had grasped the nettle, if only to deprive Rex of what he eventually acquired.'

She caught Madden's questioning glance.

'He was left a lot of money in her will, though I'm told he's gone through most of it already. It meant he didn't have to look for a job, something he's never really had. However, I still don't see what his marriage to Margaret might have had to do with Miss Blake's death.'

'Probably nothing,' Madden agreed. 'In fact, this is what I meant by saying that inquiries of this sort have a way of delving into people's private lives, and not always appropriately.' He paused. 'And on that note I think I should take my leave. Thank you for all your help. You've been very patient with me.'

He prepared to rise to his feet, but checked his movement

when he saw that his hostess was distracted. She had looked away at that moment, frowning. He waited for her to say something, but she remained silent, and in the end it was he who spoke.

'I'm looking forward to telling Helen about our meeting. She was eager to have news of you.'

Mrs Castleton's face cleared at once. She turned to him.

'Will you tell her how very happy I am to hear that she did all she set out to do? And say I'd love to see her again.'

'I'm sure it can be arranged.' Madden smiled. 'In fact, I've a feeling she'll be writing to you very soon. If I know Helen she'll want you to come down to Highfield and spend a weekend with us.'

'Nothing would make me happier.'

She rose then and led him through the house, pausing in the sitting room to point out a framed photograph resting on a table by a window. It showed a man dressed in white duck trousers and a striped vest standing at the wheel of a yacht with a wide expanse of ocean behind him. Madden recognized his face from the painting and the snapshot he had seen in Richard Jessup's office.

'That's Jack,' Mrs Castleton said. 'We used to go sailing every summer. And there's Richard, with Sarah.' She pointed to another photograph. 'That was taken at their wedding.'

The couple stood arm-in-arm, Sir Richard in morning dress and his bride in a dazzling white gown. Slender, with fair hair that was cut short, Sarah Jessup, as she must just have become, faced the camera with a serious expression that was lightened by the hint of a smile playing about her lips. Although good looking enough in a conventional way, it was more the stamp of character that Madden fancied he saw in her face that impressed him.

'You'll hear people say that Richard, too, married her for

her money.' Mrs Castleton, standing at his shoulder, had noticed the direction of his glance. 'Jessup's was still in a bad financial state when they met and Richard was negotiating with the financial group headed by her father, Saul Temple. The war put a temporary stop to that, but later, when it ended, they made a substantial investment in the firm. It's what pulled Jessup's round in the end. You would have to know both Richard and Sarah to know how stupid and wrong those stories are. Richard fell head over heels in love with her and I fancy Sarah did the same. She's a wonderful partner for him; every bit his match.'

Having seen him out of the front door, Mrs Castleton accompanied her guest to the garden gate down a gravelled path bordered by flower beds and shaded, now that the sun was declining, by a tall box hedge. Reaching out to open the gate, she paused with her hand on the latch. Her expression was troubled. Madden recalled her distracted look earlier.

'I'm still thinking of what we were talking about a moment ago,' she confessed. 'I feel I can't let you go until I've unburdened myself. You hinted that if Rex had, in fact, had an affair with that young woman it could have had something to do with her death. Did you mean that Miss Blake might have been threatening to tell Margaret about it? That flirting with him in that theatrical manner was her way of warning him?'

'It was just a thought,' Madden responded cautiously. 'It might explain why she was dangling the pendant in front of his eyes in that way. He may have given it to her when their affair ended. But that's only a guess.'

'I see . . .' She bit her lip. 'So what you're wondering is whether Rex Garner might have been sufficiently disturbed by the thought of his infidelity being revealed to his wife to take drastic action.'

Madden hesitated. He was on delicate ground.

'It's something I've had to consider,' he admitted. 'Maybe I should explain. There are two possibilities: either Miss Blake had the bad luck to fall victim to a man who had already served time for attempted rape, and who in all likelihood was half drunk when they met by chance in that wood. In that case his conviction for murder stands and everything else falls away. But if there *was* a miscarriage of justice, as the two detectives who were in charge of the investigation now believe is possible, then there must be another explanation for her death, and it may well have something to do with her strange behaviour that weekend.'

Mrs Castleton nodded, understanding.

'Then what I can tell you is that Rex would certainly have been upset at that stage in their marriage to have Margaret made aware of his failings,' she said. 'She was very much his meal ticket, if I can put it crudely – she gave him a large allowance – and while he may well have strayed during the two years they had been married he'd been very careful up till then to keep his philandering a secret from her.'

She hesitated. Madden was silent. He sensed she had more to say.

'I didn't want to tell you this,' she went on after a moment. 'But since you're going to find out anyway you might as well hear it from me. Rex spent some time in Hong Kong when he was a young man. Jack sent him out there as a trainee.'

'I know about that. Sir Richard told me. He said Garner came back after only a year. Apparently it didn't work out.'

'That's true. But there was another reason.' She looked him in the eye. 'Rex was caught up in a scandal. Actually it was worse than that – he beat up a woman: quite savagely, I was told. She was Chinese, possibly a prostitute. The story was, he was drunk. I never knew the details – Jack didn't want to talk about it – and I don't know what happened to the woman, whether she ever recovered from the beating. But what I do know is that it was Stanley Wing who got him out of trouble. Somehow matters were smoothed over and Rex was put on the next boat back to England.'

'Did Sir Richard know that?' Madden asked.

'Of course, but he wouldn't have told you about it. He's like Jack was. He has old-fashioned notions of loyalty. He and Rex have known each other since boyhood. And although Richard finds their friendship a burden now – I think I can say that – he would still try to protect him if he could.'

She held his gaze.

'I feel no such loyalty to Rex,' she said. 'He's a selfish, calculating man who has always managed to live off others, mainly women. He's a sponger at heart. I don't wish him ill, but if he did have anything to do with that poor girl's death, he ought to answer for it.

10

'SO YOU THINK it's a toss-up at best, do you, John? But surely there's still a chance the Yard might go for it?'

Angus Sinclair shifted uncomfortably in his chair. He had been immobile for some time sitting under the apple tree in his garden listening to Madden, and although his gout-ridden foot no longer rested on a cushioned stool as before, it was still encased in its padded felt slipper; still tender.

'They might.' Madden scowled. 'There's enough doubt now to make Charlie Chubb think again. I'm not so sure about Cradock, though. He's the one who'll make the final decision and he'll probably need more convincing.'

'But he can't deny that Garner's a possible suspect.'

'Possible being the operative word.'

Madden rose to stretch his legs and to move the hosepipe that had been playing on one end of the rose bed behind where he was sitting. It was the day following his meeting with Adele Castleton and he had stopped at the chief inspector's cottage on his way back from the farm to give him an account of their conversation. Not surprisingly, it was Mrs Castleton's opinion of Rex Garner's character and how he might have reacted to any threat to his marriage that had aroused Sinclair's suspicion.

'If the case were to be reopened, he could certainly be questioned about how well he knew Portia Blake.'

Madden returned to his chair and sat down.

'But whether that's enough in itself to prod the Yard into

action I can't say. There's nothing you could point to as evidence as yet. Garner's disappearance on the day following that dinner and the fact that he didn't show his face at the house again until after Portia Blake's body was discovered is open to question. But he told Mrs Castleton he was going into Canterbury to meet a friend and if he can back that up – if the friend, whoever it was, can give him an alibi – then presumably he's off the hook.'

The chief inspector growled.

'There's no avoiding the mistakes we made in the original investigation,' he admitted. 'We should have checked his alibi at the time; and we would have if Norris hadn't been arrested with Miss Blake's jewellery in his possession and if he hadn't confessed to the murder so soon afterwards.'

He shot a glance at Madden.

'Still, never mind – even if it was eleven years ago it's not too late. Garner can still be asked to name the friend he went to see.'

'But not by me.'

Madden had assumed they would get to this point and was ready with his response.

'I can't do that, Angus: checking alibis is a matter for the police; as would be tracking down the other members of the household – I'm thinking of the staff – which would probably be necessary if this turned into a full-blown investigation.'

'Oh, I can see that.' The chief inspector grunted. 'And as I think I mentioned before, you've already done enough. I'm more than grateful. But I'm sorry to see you so pessimistic. Surely even Cradock will be forced to recognize that there was a lot more going on among Jessup's guests that weekend than met the eye.'

'Yes, but does that add up to one of them having a guilty

secret? We've still no evidence of that. And if you're thinking of Garner as the possible killer, there could be a problem with that. Once you put the actual murder under a microscope it becomes difficult to imagine how Portia Blake could have been killed other than by the man who was sent to the gallows for it.'

'Explain, would you?' Sinclair frowned.

'It's a question of opportunity. How much time would someone other than Norris have had, first to kill her and then to make his escape? Not long, is the answer. Since Norris himself was already entering the wood and the young boys who found the body were coming up the hill from the other side, the murderer would have had at best only minutes to do what he did.'

'But it was still possible.' The chief inspector was insistent.

'I agree – though only barely. But that's not really the issue. The question is, could Rex Garner have done it?'

'I'm not sure I follow you.' Sinclair's frown deepened.

'I'm quite willing to believe he's a bad lot – grasping and dishonest, and quite possibly violent when drunk or angry. But his assault on that woman in Hong Kong sounds to me more like the act of a brutal bully than a cool-headed killer. Not the kind of man who could have strangled Portia in the few minutes he had available to him and then quietly made his escape without being seen. However, I haven't met Garner, so all this is theorizing. He doesn't sound the type, that's all. But he might be.'

'And if not, then there was someone else staying at Foxley Hall that weekend who would fit the bill even better.'

'You're thinking of Stanley Wing.'

Sinclair shrugged.

'Well, whether or not *he* murdered Portia Blake, he's certainly someone I'd look at carefully,' Madden agreed. 'If there was some plan afoot – some idea of blackmailing Garner – then it's likely he was involved in it. From what Jessup told me about him, there doesn't seem much he would have stopped at. But whether that can be *proved* against him is another question. Assuming he's still in prison, he can certainly be interrogated; but how willing he'd be to cooperate with a British police inquiry into a murder he might be involved in remains to be seen.' He glanced at the chief inspector. 'You're right, Angus. I'm not very optimistic.'

Sinclair's growl suggested he was none too sanguine himself.

'And there's something else we've lost sight of,' Madden went on. 'The note that was sent to Derry: the one that started this off. We've still no idea who was behind it, whether he or she actually discovered Miss Blake's pendant still lying in the wood, or came across it in some other way: whether in fact they really know something about the murder or are simply making mischief. I can't claim to have made any progress in that direction. It's still a mystery.'

Madden studied his old friend's face.

'What I'm trying to say is I think I've done all I can.'

'Poor old Angus. He was doing his best to put on a brave face, thanking me for the help I've given him. But I think he was secretly hoping I'd keep going; keep asking questions.'

Madden lowered himself into an armchair. He had a glass of whisky in his hand and he took a sip of it before sitting back with a sigh. Hamish, who was lying on the hearth rug, lifted his heavy head at the sound and surveyed his master for a long moment as though estimating his chances of being taken out for a walk, before lowering his head again and shutting his pouched eyes.

'I had to tell him I'd reached the end of the road.'

'But you haven't spoken to Rex Garner yet. Couldn't you go and see him?'

Lucy looked up from the dress she was working on, her darting needle still for a moment. She was sitting on the sofa beside Helen, who was occupied with her weekly accounts, running her pencil up and down the columns, frowning. Recently she had taken to wearing spectacles for reading and it was a source of wonder to Madden to see how a pair of simple horn-rimmed glasses perched on the end of her nose somehow added a new dimension to a face that had never ceased to hold him in thrall.

'I've thought about that and decided against it. If the Yard does move to reopen the investigation they'll want to tackle him cold. If I went to see him – and if he was involved in Portia Blake's murder – it would put him on his guard, and he'd have time to cook up a story.'

'Aren't you afraid that Sir Richard Jessup might warn him?'

'No, I'm not. I don't believe for a moment that he'd deliberately try to undermine a police investigation if one got under way.'

'But you don't think it will, do you?'

'Not as things stand.'

'Well, then . . .' Lucy's disappointment was plain. 'It's all been rather a waste of time, hasn't it?'

'Oh, I wouldn't say that.' Madden sipped his whisky. 'I've met some very interesting people, two of whom I really liked, which reminds me . . .' He glanced at Helen, who looked up at that moment. 'Have you written to Mrs Castleton?'

'I posted the letter today. I've asked her to come and stay

with us for a weekend next month. I left it up to her to choose the dates.'

'Was she like Violet said she was?' Lucy asked. She bit through the thread of cotton she was using and laid her sewing down. 'Doomed-looking?'

'Not that I noticed.' Madden chuckled. 'But I could see how fascinating she must have been to men. There's a quality of mystery about her.' He paused. 'No, that's the wrong word: it's a sense of depth, rather. She's someone you almost immediately want to know better.'

'But you escaped from your encounter unscathed?'

Madden eyed his daughter. She giggled.

'According to Violet, she used to leave all the men she cast a spell on . . . how did Violet put it, Mummy?'

'Alone and palely loitering.' Helen's gaze remained fixed on her columns of figures.

'You don't *look* pale, Daddy.' Lucy peered at her father. 'But I shall be keeping a close watch on you.'

'Watch all you want.' Madden downed the last of his whisky and stood up. 'I'm going to take Hamish for a walk before supper and see which trees in the orchard need pruning.'

'But are you really going to give up on Angus's case?' Lucy made a final appeal. 'It doesn't seem right just to drop it this way. What if something comes up . . . something new and unexpected?'

'Then Charlie Chubb will be ideally placed to spring into action. I'm going to see him when I go up to London next week. I'll tell him what I've learned about Garner and Wing and everything that went on during that weekend. After that it will be up to him and Cradock to decide what to do. I wash my hands of it.'

Whistling to Hamish he made for the door to the terrace, but paused when he heard his daughter mutter something.

'What was that?' he asked.

'Nothing, Daddy.' She offered him one of her brilliant smiles.

'What did she say?' he asked Helen.

She glanced up over her glasses.

'Like Pontius Pilate.'

Sundays began slowly in the Madden household. Early risers on every other day of the week, Madden and his wife seldom went downstairs for breakfast before nine o'clock, while Lucy, when she was staying with them, was capable of spending the entire morning in bed (to recover, she said, from the rigours of her London life). Thereafter the day was devoted to the enjoyable pursuits of leisure: to reading under the trellised vine that gave shade to part of the terrace or attending to small and undemanding tasks in the house and garden. Although strictly speaking on call as the village's only doctor, Helen rarely stirred from the house except in an emergency, while Madden went to the farm only when he felt his presence there was necessary; as it seldom seemed to be these days.

'The truth is, George can manage perfectly well on his own,' he had lamented, with a sigh, only the night before when Helen and he were preparing for bed. He was speaking of his farm manager, George Burrows. 'I'd like to think I was missed, spending all this time up in London seeing to Aunt Maud's house and trying to soothe Angus's fevered brow. But everything seems to be running quite smoothly without me. If things go on this way I'm going to find myself turning into what I've always dreaded most becoming: a gentleman farmer.'

Spurred on by these guilty thoughts, Madden armed himself with a saw next morning and walked down to the orchard at the bottom of the garden. He had marked out several branches on the older trees the evening before and was engaged in the agreeable business of removing them (and covering himself with sweet-smelling sawdust in the process) when he heard Helen calling to him from the terrace.

'John . . . John . . . you'd better come up.'

'What it is?' He shouted back to her.

'Just come up. There's something you have to see.'

Baffled, he lay down his saw and walked up the long lawn to the terrace. Helen was at the table under the trellis and when he got there he found that she had the Sunday newspapers on the table in front of her. Delivered by the Highfield newsagent's son, who made a leisurely tour of the houses outside the village on his bicycle, they included not only the *Sunday Times* for Madden and Helen but also the *News of the World*, ordered at the request of Helen's maid of many years, Mary Morris, who had taken up residence with them following the death of her mother two years previously and occupied a sunny room on the upper floor of the old, half-timbered house with a view of the long wooded ridge called Upton Hanger that rose like a green wave beyond the stream at the bottom of the garden. It was this last journal that Helen was looking at and as Madden approached she pointed to a story displayed on the front page.

Madden bent over her shoulder to peer at it.

'Oh, Lord!'

He stared aghast at the headline.

Murder of Actress Called into Question – Missing Pendant Found – Was the Wrong Man Hanged?

Further down, and in slightly smaller type, were the words *Society figures involved*.

A photograph of Portia Blake accompanied the story, which gave a full account of the murder and the trial that had followed as well as the names of all the guests who had been present at Foxley Hall that weekend. Clearly a picture taken for publicity purposes, it showed her in an off-the-shoulder dress sitting in a chair with her legs crossed and her hands laced about one knee. Her smile was suggestive.

'I can't believe Violet has been talking about it,' Helen said. 'She promised me she wouldn't.'

She glanced up at her husband. Madden's eyes were still glued to the page.

'Could it have been one of the people you've been speaking to: Sir Richard Jessup, perhaps? All it would take for the story to get out is one careless remark.'

'No, I don't think it was Jessup. It's the last thing he'd want to see happen.' Madden went on with his reading.

'What about that actress, Audrey Cooper?'

'I thought of her at once. She's spiteful enough to take pleasure in starting a rumour of this kind. But if it was she, I can't help feeling she'd make sure that her own name cropped up in the story somehow, if only for the publicity it would give her. And I was careful to tell her that the police weren't interested in reopening the case.'

'Tell me it wasn't Lucy,' Helen pleaded.

Madden shook his head, laughing.

'No, it's not Lucy.' His smile faded. 'I think it's the same person who sent Derry that note.'

'Why? I mean, why do you think that?'

'It's the language the reporter uses.' He pointed a finger at the page. '*Confidential sources have revealed that the jade pendant sent to the police is the same one that disappeared from Portia Blake's body in August 1938.*' Madden quoted from the article. '*There is a slight flaw in the figure that enabled it to be identified.*'

He looked up.

'That's almost word for word what was in Derry's letter: except now it's being stated as an established fact that the two pendants are one and the same. Whoever sent it to him hasn't got the reaction he was hoping for. There's been no sign of any renewal of police interest in the case. He's decided to take the bull by the horns and drag the press in. It's easy to see what he's up to. He wants to force the issue. But what is he *really* after?'

Madden's scowl had returned.

'And who the devil is he?'

11

'WELL, ANGUS HAS got his way.' Charlie Chubb eased himself into his chair. 'Cradock's had to accept that the case must be looked at again. I've just been speaking to him. Or been spoken *to*, I should say. He'd come from seeing the commissioner and if the way he talked to *me* was anything to go by I reckon he'd just had a bollocking. Oh, and he had a few words for you, too.'

The chief super pointed a finger at Madden, who had arrived only a few minutes before and was sitting in front of his desk beside Billy Styles, who had also been summoned to the meeting and who had greeted his old mentor with a smile and a warm handshake.

'"Tell Madden to keep his nose out of police business," he said. "This is not the first time he's interfered. But it had better be the last. And tell him to hand over that pendant as well."'

'Surely he doesn't think I had anything to do with leaking the story.'

Stung by the words, Madden pulled the object from his pocket and passed it across the desk to Chubb. He had intended paying a visit to Scotland Yard later in the week. But the story that had appeared in the *News of the World* had spurred him into ringing the chief super as soon as he got up to London that Monday morning. Chubb had asked if he could come down to the Yard right away.

'It looks to me as though the newspaper received the same

sort of letter as Derry did,' Madden went on. 'The language is similar. And it's equally obvious it was sent by the same person. Whoever he or she is, they want the case reopened.'

'It's partly my fault,' Chubb admitted. He held up the pendant to the light and peered at it. 'I told Cradock that at least we wouldn't be starting cold: that you'd been speaking to some of the people involved as a favour to Angus. That set him off. He said it must have been you that caused the leak to the press. I tried to explain about the note Derry had received and how some of the wording in the newspaper report was the same, but I don't think he was listening. Mind you, his mood wasn't improved by the way the dailies have taken the story up. Have you looked at them, John?'

He gestured to the newspapers spread out on his desk, two or three of which Madden had already glanced at on his journey up to London by train.

'The *Daily Mail*'s the one that really got him going. *Is there a murderer still at large among us? Yard tight-lipped.*'

The chief super chortled.

'One of their reporters rang up yesterday and got hold of the CID duty officer, who said he couldn't comment on the story in the *News of the World* and they'd have to wait till today for any reaction. That's being tight-lipped for you. I'll be issuing a statement later saying the investigation is under review.'

He shrugged.

'Anyway, the word from on high now is that we have to get this business cleared up once and for all. Styles has already told me about your visit to Kent and what Derry had to say. But you've seen a few more people since then, I gather, so if you wouldn't mind telling us what you've learned, and whether you think it amounts to anything, I'd be more than grateful.'

'I'll do my best, Charlie. But tell Cradock that if he's got any more remarks to make about me he can say them to my face.'

His words brought a chuckle from Chubb. He cocked his head on one side and peered at his visitor's scowling visage.

'I don't think he'd dare.'

Chubb settled himself in his chair.

'So if anyone's in the frame, it looks like being Garner. But does the fact that he might have had an affair with Miss Blake really constitute a motive? What's your view, John?'

'It could do, I suppose – if he thought his future was at stake.' Madden tugged unhappily at an earlobe. 'He was upset by the act Portia Blake put on at dinner the night before. You've got both Jessup and Mrs Castleton as witnesses to that. If, in fact, he did arrange to meet Miss Blake the following day so that he could have it out with her in private, I suppose you could argue that she might have pushed him even further; taunted him, and perhaps driven him to an act of violence. Both Derry and Angus thought at the time that Norris had probably killed the girl by mistake: that he'd tried to choke her into submission and gone too far.'

'Grabbed hold of her scarf in a fit of anger, you're saying, and killed her almost before he knew it?'

'Something of the sort.' Madden shrugged. 'But according to Mrs Castleton, Garner also displayed that kind of anger, that lack of control, before – when he assaulted the woman in Hong Kong. The same thing might have happened with Portia Blake, and if, in fact, Garner killed her – and if the pendant was a present he gave her – then it's easy to understand why he might have taken it from her body. But how could it have turned up again in this way? That's another unanswered question. Did he lose it? Did it fall into someone else's hands? Surely he would have wanted to get rid of it as soon as possible.'

The chief super stirred uneasily in his chair. He cleared his throat.

'But on balance, don't you agree that Garner is the most likely suspect?' he asked.

'Other than Norris, you mean?' Madden frowned. 'Yes, I suppose so. Although we still haven't dealt with the problem of opportunity: how little time there was for him to have committed the murder before Norris arrived on the scene. That's assuming *he* wasn't the killer. Either Garner's spurt of homicidal rage happened at just the right moment to allow him to escape unseen, or we may have to look for another explanation.'

'Or at someone else who was in the vicinity,' Chubb suggested. He cocked an eye at his visitor.

'You mean Stanley Wing.' Madden nodded. 'Angus said the same thing. Yes, I can picture him killing Portia in cold blood. But why should he do such a thing? We're still stuck for a motive there. And as I told Angus, if he is the man you're after I doubt you'll get him to admit it, no matter how hard he's pushed.'

Chubb muttered unintelligibly. He and Billy had listened to Madden for close on an hour while he gave them a detailed account of his interviews with Richard Jessup, Audrey Cooper and, finally, Adele Castleton. Now and then one or other had put a question. But for the most part they had stayed silent. Finally, at the conclusion of his long recital, Madden had taken a sheaf of folded foolscap paper from his jacket pocket and handed it to the chief super.

'This is a summary of the various conversations I've had. It includes all the points I think are significant, though you can make your own judgement as far as that's concerned.'

The chief super turned to his younger colleague.

'What's your opinion?' he asked. 'How do we go about this?'

'We should look at both Garner and Wing.' Billy had his answer ready. 'We can question Garner about any prior connection he might have had with Miss Blake now that this is out in the open. We can certainly ask him to confirm his alibi for that afternoon. As for Wing, I reckon we'd better get in touch with the Hong Kong police about having him questioned. Sending a detective all the way from London would be an expensive business. I can't see Cradock authorizing it.'

'While we're at it we can ask them about that business between Garner and the woman he beat up,' Chubb observed. 'It'd be interesting to find out if it's on their books, or if Wing was able to arrange things so that the police weren't involved.'

'As far as Wing is concerned, Jessup has offered to help,' Madden interrupted them. 'He said he would ask his people out there if they had any news of him.'

'Should we question him, do you think? Jessup, I mean.' Chubb asked the question. It brought a shake of the head from Madden.

'I don't think that's necessary: at least, not at present. He wasn't one of the guests that weekend. He was down there to talk business with his father, and he left well before Miss Blake was murdered. He's been very cooperative so far, with me at least. I noticed from the papers that his name has already come up, but only in passing, as it were. They still seem to be fixated on his father and the people he mixed with. Black Jack Jessup has a ring to it, after all; not to mention the Prince of Wales. I'm planning to ring him to explain how this business became public – how I believe the newspapers came to learn of it. I wouldn't want him to think I had anything to do with it; not after he was so helpful. He's still away from London on business, but he should be back by the end of the week.'

The chief super ruminated. He had been making notes on a pad while Madden spoke earlier and he glanced at his jottings now.

'What about this actress – Miss Cooper? Has she got anything more to tell us?'

'She might have,' Madden said, after a moment's thought. 'I'm not sure she was altogether truthful with me. There was a moment when I thought she might be keeping something back, though I'm not sure what. It was only a feeling, mind you.'

'How about Mrs Castleton?'

'I've told you what she told me. I doubt she has anything to add. But she might know what became of the staff at Foxley Hall after Jack Jessup died and she moved out. I imagine you'll want to track them down, if you can.'

The chief super made another note.

'Any other thoughts?' he asked.

Madden hesitated. 'Mrs Castleton said she doubted that Wing was behind the display Portia Blake put on at dinner and she instanced the remarks she overheard him make when she walked by Portia's room later. "What is this game you're playing?" she heard him say. He sounded very angry.'

'Yes . . . and?'

'I think she was right, but only up to a point. What seems to have angered Wing was that Portia took matters into her own hands: it sounds as though her performance at dinner was her own idea, one she hadn't consulted him about. But I think he was pulling the strings, just the same. I think he had a plan hatching. There's still no explanation for why he brought her down to Kent with him.'

'Unless it was what we've been talking about,' Chubb pointed out. 'Unless it was to blackmail Rex Garner in front of his wife: to put pressure on him. I know Garner wasn't rich in his own right, but he was married to a wealthy woman. Wing might have reckoned he could get his hands on a hefty sum if he needed to.'

Madden was slow in responding. Finally, he spoke.

'Look, there's a bigger problem here – for me, at any rate. I can't quite see what Wing was supposed to have been threatening him with. Even if Garner had been forced to admit to his wife that he'd had a fling with Miss Blake, would it really have been so serious? Granted, it might have made things sticky between them for a while, but he could have claimed quite reasonably that their liaison was brief and that he'd recognized his error and corrected it. He'd broken off with the girl. I just can't see that it's the basis for any serious blackmail threat.'

He looked questioningly at his two listeners.

'You're saying there must be more to the whole business?' It was Billy who spoke.

'Or nothing at all, and we've been making too much of it.' Madden shrugged. 'I just feel there's a large hole in the theory as it stands.'

Chubb's growl signalled his displeasure.

'What about that girl in Hong Kong, though? We don't know what happened to her. Could Garner have killed her? Was that something else Wing had over him?'

'It's possible, I suppose.' Madden scowled. 'But the only people who might be able to help you there are the Hong Kong police, and as far as we know they never took any action over the matter.'

*

'Well, at least it'll bring a smile to Mr Sinclair's face.'

Billy Styles lifted his glass of beer in a silent toast to the absent chief inspector. A grin accompanied his words.

'But I gathered from what you were saying, sir, that you don't think we've got much chance of overturning the original verdict.'

'Not as things stand, Billy.' Madden sampled his beer. 'You'll need more than a suspicion that Garner may have had a part in Portia Blake's death. The same goes for Stanley Wing. And the fact that all this happened eleven years ago only adds to the difficulty. Short of a confession by one or other, I can't see you making much progress.'

Following their meeting with Chubb – and since it was the lunch hour, and Billy was free to take a break – the two men had repaired to a nearby pub to exchange last thoughts on the problem that had occupied Madden's mind for the past fortnight and was now the CID's responsibility.

'But what will matter to Angus is that the effort is being made,' Madden continued. 'Once the Yard has announced that it's looking at the case again, he'll feel better.'

'Even if it changes nothing? Even if we decide that the right man went to the gallows after all?'

Madden shrugged. 'Norris is still the most likely culprit. Angus knows that. Nothing I've turned up points decisively to anyone else. It's possible that whatever scheme Wing was hatching was somehow connected to Portia's murder. But it may have had nothing to do with it.'

He looked at his watch.

'I must be off,' he said. 'I've got a couple of estate agents coming to look at the house later this afternoon. We're putting it on the market at the end of the month and they want to inspect it first.'

Billy emptied his glass.

'Well, you can give Mr Sinclair another piece of good news,' he said. 'I've already started putting a team together and Lily Poole's name is on the list.'

The young woman he was referring to, a detective-constable in the CID, had been one of the first of her sex admitted to the Met's plain-clothes division at the end of the war. A protégée of Angus Sinclair, she had quickly made her mark at the Yard and the chief inspector continued to take a lively interest in her career.

'So Charlie has finally come round to her, has he?' Madden smiled. 'Angus will be pleased to hear that.'

Like many of his colleagues, Chief Superintendent Chubb had long harboured doubts about the wisdom of employing women in the force, and not even Lily Poole's accomplishments to date – they had already earned her three commendations – had brought about a change of heart. Until now, it seemed.

'I wouldn't say he's come round exactly.' Billy grinned. 'Lil took the sergeant's exam recently and she's still waiting to hear the result. Charlie's digging in his heels. He told me the other day he's afraid it might have a "disturbing effect" on some of our longer-serving DCs if she was promoted over their heads. I said that short of putting a stick or two of dynamite under them, I couldn't think of a better way of getting them to move off their lazy backsides and do some work.'

12

No matter how many times he visited Rotterdam – and his duties brought him to the great port quite frequently – the sight of the devastation wrought by the German bombers in 1940 never ceased to impress Chen Yi.

This was the purest expression of violence he had ever seen – greater even than the damage wrought by the Japanese on the city of Nanking, where he had been born twenty-six years earlier. This was the iron fist made manifest.

The entire heart of the city had been flattened; obliterated.

They had to invent a new term to describe it. Carpet-bombing was the phrase used. A carpet of bombs had been laid on the old city, and with the work of restoration hardly begun, all that remained of its medieval heart was a ruined church; that and some other half-wrecked structures.

It was towards one of these last that Chen was making his way that evening through the grid of streets that remained like the bones of a skeleton, fleshless, devoid of the houses and shops that had once stood there, in the company of an older man whose name was Huang Wei. Coarse-featured, and boasting a crooked nose that had been broken more than once to judge by appearances, Huang was a famous street fighter and Chen treated him with all the deference due a Red Pole – for such was Huang's position in the family, an enforcer in the language employed by the brotherhood of which they were both members – while privately finding him somewhat comical. But that was true of most of the old ones, the long-standing members, with their quaint titles and arcane ceremonies dating from centuries back. Sometimes Chen wondered if they knew they were living in a new world now: that everything had changed since the war.

The building in question was near the edge of the devastated region and might in its day have been a warehouse of modest proportions. Still with its walls mostly standing, it lacked only a roof, and on reaching it Chen paused to look about him. The deserted street down which they had walked was empty, as was the intersection at which they had paused. However, as they stood there a young man with jet-black hair cut close to his scalp appeared in the doorway of the ruined warehouse. He bowed his head on seeing them.

'All is ready,' he said.

With a glance at his companion, Chen walked past the youth, who stepped to one side and then followed him in, staying a pace or two behind so that Chen could speak to him over his shoulder.

'Is everyone here?'

The question was superfluous. Not one of the score of men he saw standing in a circle near the centre of the warehouse would have dared to stay away. They were 49s – ordinary members only – but they had taken the oaths.

'All are present.'

Again the young man made a slight bow. Chen turned his attention to the scene before him. Although littered with debris, the floor of the warehouse had been cleared in one area and it was there that the group awaiting him had gathered around a man stripped to the waist who was kneeling on the floor with his head bowed and his hands tied behind his back. His flabby body was marked by several tattoos of an exotic nature which included a dragon that wound its scaly tail about his slumped back.

No words were necessary. All knew why they had been summoned there, and if what was to follow bore something of the nature of a ritual it was designed to deliver a message. No one who witnessed it would forget what he had seen. The guilty man had stolen from the family. Money received in payment for the precious white powder they trafficked in had been held back. The betrayal of sworn oaths was gross and unforgivable. Each of the spectators knew that he, too, might one day find himself in the same fatal predicament and it was with this in mind that Chen spoke once more, though only in an undertone.

'We don't believe that Liu was working alone. One or two others might have had a hand in his scheme. Watch their faces. See which ones sweat the most.'

The youth acknowledged the words with the faintest of nods.

'Let us begin.'

Chen turned and went back to the doorway where Huang had been waiting. The older man took off his jacket and handed it to Chen. His shirt and tie followed. Stripped to the waist, his stocky, well-muscled body bore tattoos similar to the ones marking the body of the bound man as well as two scars, one across his chest, the other close to his navel, both the result of knife slashes. Chen folded the clothes and carried them to a block of concrete which had been well dusted. Laying the garments down carefully, he picked up a woodsman's axe which was leaning against the block and brought it to Huang. Although the evening was well advanced there was still enough light in the sky to bring a gleam from the polished head as Huang swung it easily from side to side, testing the weight and balance. A murmur came from the lips of the men standing in the circle. It died as

Huang moved forward, approaching the kneeling man from behind, and then stepping to one side.

Measuring the distance with his eye, he lifted the weapon with both hands and then brought the edge down in one swift stroke on the neck of the kneeling man. The body bucked convulsively as his head was separated from his body and sent rolling across the cement floor. Blood spurted from the neck like a fountain. It continued to flow as the body slumped to the floor, spreading in a dark puddle that shone faintly in the last of the light. A sigh came from the lips of the watching men.

Huang handed the axe to Chen, who walked to where the head was lying. Affecting an indifference he was far from feeling – it was the first such execution he had witnessed – he picked it up by the hair and carried it to the door of the warehouse where another cube of cement stood ready. Laying the axe aside, he settled the head firmly on the block so that the face with its lips drawn back in a last rictus of pain and shock was clearly visible.

Huang, meanwhile, had retrieved his clothes. Taking his time, he put on his shirt and tie and donned his jacket.

Only then did he turn to the circle of men, none of whom had moved.

'Go,' he said. They were his first words. 'And remember.'

'The Deng brothers looked away when you struck the blow. I noticed they were sweating.'

Chen spoke in a toneless voice. Though careful not to show it, he had found the preceding spectacle somewhat absurd (or so he told himself, now that the initial shock had worn off) and the bloody finale overdone. Wouldn't a bullet in the back of Liu's head have done just as well? Couldn't they simply have cut his throat? These old men lived in a fantasy . . . a dream of the past.

Huang shrugged. 'I will arrange for them to be watched,' he said.

After the departure of the others the two of them had waited alone in the warehouse for the cleaning crew to arrive. Not required to attend the execution, they were only aspirant members, Blue Lanterns, not yet initiated into the family. Chen had given them their orders. The body was to be cut up and disposed of: all except the head, which was to remain where he had placed it. All traces of blood were to be washed from the floor, which was to be liberally sprinkled with dust afterwards. They were to keep silent about what they had seen and done on pain of death.

The orders having been issued, Huang had led his assistant outside. Darkness had fallen finally, but the summer night was warm.

'I have received instructions from Hong Kong,' he said, speaking in English. Up till then both men had used only Cantonese. 'There is more work to be done. I shall need an assistant. Is your passport in order?'

'It is.'

'Be at Amsterdam Centraal station on Tuesday, no later than a quarter to two. Bring clothes for at least a fortnight. Make sure they are suitable.'

Unsure what was meant by these last words, Chen simply bowed. The older man regarded him.

'You are not curious to know where we are being sent?'

'Does it matter?' Chen knew well how to frame his reply. 'We follow orders.'

'A good answer.' Huang's slate-coloured eyes were

unreadable: it was impossible to tell what he was thinking. 'But then you are a clever young man . . . or so people say. I will tell you anyway. We are going to London.'

PART TWO

PART TWO

13

'Go on – a *detective*?'

Arms folded, Annie Potter eyed her visitor suspiciously. She was standing on her doorstep barring the way in, and to judge by the work-stained apron tied to her waist and the white flecks of soap suds attached to her tanned forearms it looked as though she was in the middle of her housework (and not best pleased with the interruption).

'Are you having me on? I've seen one or two women in uniform, but I haven't met one in plain-clothes yet. You got a warrant card and all?'

Though slightly built, she looked to have the lean strength of a whippet – or so it seemed to Lily Poole – and thus far she was showing no sign of being willing to admit a stranger through the front door of her small terraced house.

'Course I have,' Lily replied. 'She fished out her card demonstrating that she was indeed what she said she was, a bona fide detective-constable with the Metropolitan Police, and held it out for the other woman's inspection. 'I would have rung you in advance to say I was coming, but I couldn't find your number in the phone book.'

'That's because we haven't got one.'

Despite the sharpness of her tone, she seemed satisfied by the sight of Lily's card and she stepped aside.

'Come on in, then. But keep it down, will you? My youngest is upstairs, sleeping, and I'm warning you now he's a holy terror when he's awake.'

She led the way down a short passage covered with linoleum into a cramped kitchen where a small girl whose dark curls matched her mother's was sitting at the table with a colouring book open in front of her and a box of crayons beside it.

'This is Winnie for Winifred,' she announced. 'And this is Detective-Constable Poole,' she added, turning to the little girl. 'Believe it or not she's a copper, so mind your manners.'

The little girl giggled. Having examined Lily for a moment or two, she went back to her colouring.

'Fancy a cuppa?' Annie Potter asked her visitor. 'I was about to put the kettle on. Then we can sit down and you can tell me what brings you down this way. It wouldn't be about that story I read in the paper the other day, I suppose?'

Her glance had sharpened.

'It's not about that young lady that got herself strangled all those years ago?'

Truth to tell, Lily wasn't best pleased with the assignment she'd drawn. She had hoped for something a little more testing after learning that Billy Styles had been given the job of looking into an old murder case, one she remembered reading about before the war, and had chosen her to be part of his team. She'd been hoping he would make her his number two, but when she answered the summons to his office she had found that Joe Grace, one of the most experienced detective-sergeants on the Met's strength, was already there and waiting to receive his orders.

'The chief super wants this business cleared up quickly,' Billy had told them both. 'Read this file first.' He had tapped a hefty looking folder on his desk. 'There's a lot of detail you'll have to get clear in your minds. Some of the witnesses are dead now, and others may be hard to track down, but we'll be talking to as many of them as we can get hold of. It's pretty straightforward. Either the bloke that was hanged got what he deserved – his name's Norris – or there's been a miscarriage of justice. It's up to us to find out which. And, like I say, we've been told not to hang about.'

The case was a tantalizing puzzle – or so Lily had thought after a day's hard study of the evidence collected at the time and the additional information gathered since, mainly by Mr Madden, whom she happened to know personally, thanks to his connection with the man she was more indebted to than any other: former Chief Inspector Angus Sinclair. It was Sinclair who, on Billy Styles's recommendation, had overseen her transfer from the uniform branch to the CID shortly before his retirement some years earlier. Lily had never ceased to be grateful to them both and it was the favour that Styles had shown her since then – he had taken pains to include her in a number of important investigations, cases from which she might have been excluded on account of her sex – that had given her hope of taking a further step up the ladder at the Yard with this new inquiry that was about to be launched.

Thanks to her careful reading of the file she could see that the man they ought to be focusing on first was this Rex Garner bloke. The fact that he might have had an affair with the murdered woman and never owned up to it was reason enough to look hard at him; and then there was the question of his so-called alibi. Had he really driven into Canterbury that morning to see an old friend? Or had he arranged to meet Portia Blake in private later, after lunch? Was he the one who had strangled her?

Armed with this idea, she had gone to see Styles to suggest that they pay him a visit at his flat.

'You've got the right idea, Lil,' he had told her. 'But he's not in London at present. I've been making some phone calls and I've learned that he went up north a couple of weeks ago. You've heard of the Glorious Twelfth?'

'The glorious *what*?' Lily asked.

'It's the day the grouse-shooting season starts, mainly in Yorkshire and Scotland. The nobs go out with their guns, and I suppose Garner counts as one of them. His late wife had an estate up there. He went up to Scotland a fortnight ago – I got that from his daily – but he's due back in London any day now, so instead of us chasing up there after him I thought we'd just wait until he gets back.'

Styles had tapped the file on his desk.

'Meanwhile, there are some other people we can talk to. I've managed to run down some of the staff who were employed at the house. The butler was a man called Hargreaves. He's retired now and lives in Bournemouth. I'm sending Joe down there tomorrow morning to talk to him. I'm going to slip down to Canterbury myself. It'll give me a chance to talk to Tom Derry and I've learned that one of the maids called Daisy Davenport is working in a dress shop there. I'll have a word with her too. What I'd like you to do is go and have a chat with a woman called Annie Potter. She was another maid, the only one we've been able to track down who lives in London. I've got an address for her from Mrs Castleton. Ask her what she remembers about that weekend. See what you can get out of her. Servants tend to fade into the background – people forget they're there – and sometimes they notice things others don't.'

He'd been trying to encourage her, Lily supposed. (She liked Billy Styles. He had always stood up for her and was one of the few at the Yard who treated her like a copper rather than a butt for one of their pathetic jokes about women in the force.) But talking to a former maid about what she might or might not have seen eleven years ago didn't strike her as much of a challenge and she had made her way down to Whitechapel, where this Potter person lived, with little hope of a fruitful outcome to the interview.

'That's right,' she said now, having accepted the offer of a cup of tea and taken a seat at the table alongside Winnie, who remained bent over her book, busy with her colouring. 'It's the Portia Blake case. We're taking another look at it. The pendant she was wearing at the time of her murder and which was lost has turned up unexpectedly. Do you remember her wearing it, Mrs Potter?'

'Call me Annie.' She turned to glance at Lily from the cupboard where she was fishing around for cups and saucers. 'You're from down this way, aren't you?'

'Not that far off,' Lily admitted. 'I was born in Stepney. My dad was killed in the first war and when my mum died of the flu I went to live with my aunt and uncle. He was a copper stationed at Paddington nick.'

She returned Annie's smile, feeling easier now. Although she was proud of her Cockney roots, Lily knew her accent had faded somewhat with the years due to her living away from the East End; yet Annie Potter hadn't been fooled and Lily hoped that she would prove to be just as observant in other respects.

'Basically, we're looking to see if anything was missed in the investigation,' she said. 'How well do you remember that weekend?'

'Well enough.' Annie shrugged. She put the crockery on the table and turned to attend to the kettle, which had just begun to boil. 'We weren't all that busy: it wasn't a big party. There was all that hoo-ha at dinner, though. You know about that, do you?'

She glanced over her shoulder again, this time with raised eyebrows.

'The way Miss Blake carried on, you mean?'

Annie nodded. 'Danny O'Grady said it was better than a floor show. He was one of the footmen.' She grinned. 'I never saw her in that dress, but Danny said it was so low-cut you could practically see her navel. It was all he could do not to spill the soup when he bent to serve her. He said it was like looking down the Grand Canyon.'

Lily waited until her hostess had filled the teapot with boiling water and brought it to the table.

'What was your job?' she asked.

'I was an upstairs maid. I did the bedrooms and cleaning with Mary Keen. Mary was sweet on Danny. They got married later and went back to live in Ireland. She's got two nippers herself now, like me.'

Annie settled herself at the table. Her brown eyes shone.

'I got hitched myself during the war. I was working in a factory up in Birmingham. We had an anti-aircraft unit stationed only a couple of streets away. Bert was one of the gunners. That's how we met. You married?' she asked.

Lily shook her head. 'Still looking.' She could see from her hostess's animated expression that she was enjoying the chance to reminisce and that the best way to proceed would be to keep chatting to her in a relaxed way. It was a trick she had learned from working with Billy Styles who himself had picked up the technique from Mr Madden (or so he said), the man who had taught him his trade. Except – according to Styles – it hadn't been a technique with his old chief. It was just the way he was; different from other coppers.

'How long did you work at Foxley Hall?' she asked.

'Seven years.' Annie lifted the lid of the teapot to check

the state of the brew and then filled their cups. She handed Lily the milk jug. 'I started when I was just a girl, doing the rough work: laying the fires, cleaning the oven, polishing the shoes. Later I got to be a proper maid.'

'And when did you leave?'

'At the same time Mrs Castleton did. That was in 1939, after Sir Jack died. She couldn't stay there any longer. I don't mean anyone was pushing her out. As far as Sir Richard was concerned she was as good as married to his father and Foxley Hall was her home for as long as she wanted it to be. But she couldn't stand to be there without Sir Jack, so the house was shut up and the staff went their way.' She sipped her tea. 'With the war on, I was ready to leave. I'd had enough of service. But all the same I felt sad. We were lucky to have worked there, all of us, and we knew it. It wasn't like being in service elsewhere; more like being part of a family. But I understood how Mrs Castleton felt. It could never have been the same without Sir Jack.'

She smiled to herself.

'The day I arrived to work there – I was all of fifteen – he had me brought to his study and he said, "I want you to be happy here, Annie. I want you to think of it as your home. If you have any problems, bring them to me. We'll sort them out." And he meant it too. I remember how he used to make a point of praising us and paying us compliments. It wasn't what you'd get in most places, I can tell you. "Oh, I like the way you've done your hair, Annie," he would say. That sort of thing: it was meant to make you feel better. When Mrs Castleton came to stay we thought things would change. But we needn't have worried. She just made everything run better in the house, like you'd expect a woman to, but quietly, with just a word here and there. And when the house was finally shut up she did her best to find jobs for everyone who wanted to stay in service. We're still in touch, her and me.'

Annie's smile blossomed.

'She gave us a lovely wedding present, Bert and me: a full set of cutlery. And she sends us a card every Christmas, and never forgets the kids' birthdays. That colouring book and those crayons are a present from her. Isn't that so, Winnie?'

The little girl looked up shyly, nodded, and then bent to her task again.

Annie added more hot water to the teapot. Lily handed over her cup for a refill.

'To get back to that weekend,' she said. 'The dinner apart, do you remember anything unusual happening? Anything to do with the guests, I mean: in particular Miss Blake, Mr Garner and that Chinese, or half-Chinese bloke, Mr Wing?'

'Oh, him?' Annie rolled her eyes. 'He was a strange one, all right. He'd look at you with those black eyes of his and you'd wonder what was going on in his mind. He gave Mary and me the creeps.'

'Were you surprised when he showed up with Miss Blake? They don't sound like the kind of guests you'd expect to find at a house like Foxley Hall.'

'Oh, well, as to that . . .' Annie Potter's tone was philo-sophical. 'I can tell you we had our share of rum ones over the years, people Sir Jack picked up on his travels. We had a bullfighter once, I remember. He used to chase Mary and me around his room if he caught one of us up there alone. Sir Jack had to turf him out in the end.' She laughed. 'But you're right – Wing and that Miss Blake didn't exactly fit in. Though she thought she did.'

'Oh . . . ?' Lily raised an eyebrow.

'She was trying to play the lady, making out she was at home, putting on airs.' Annie was scornful. 'It wasn't too bad the first evening they were there – Friday it would have been. From what I heard she didn't create at dinner that night; she saved it all for the next day. But I didn't take to her. You can always tell a real lady from the way they treat servants. But she didn't know how. She thought she was better than us, but I could see through her.'

'What about Mr Garner?' Lily realized she'd come across a shrewd judge of character. 'What did you think of him?'

'He was all right, I suppose.' Annie wrinkled her nose. 'He'd been a guest at the house often. When he first came down he was still single and he used to give us the eye – me and Mary, and Daisy Davenport, too; she was one of the downstairs maids. You could see he fancied the girls; but I reckon he was afraid of doing anything to upset Sir Jack. Then he got married and that stopped; he behaved better.'

'What did you think of him, though? Did you like him?'

Raising her cup to her lips, Annie considered the question.

'No,' she said finally. 'Not really. He was charming enough, and good looking, too. But it was all on the surface. Not like Sir Jack. You always knew where you stood with him. He never hid his feelings, never pretended. Everything about him was real. Like when that girl was murdered – you could see how terrible he felt. She was his guest, staying under his roof, and he couldn't forgive himself for allowing it to happen. Except, of course, he didn't: *allow* it, I mean.'

She paused to make sure that Lily understood her meaning.

'He hardly knew her. But that didn't make any difference in his mind. He thought he'd failed her in some way, and he took to his bed shortly after that. He wasn't well anyway – we all knew that – but it really hurt to see him getting worse by the day. I think it broke Mrs Castleton's heart. But there was nothing to be done and he died in less than a year, soon after the war started.'

Lily swallowed the last of her tea.

'So other than what happened at dinner, there was nothing special that you can remember?'

Annie shook her head. She gathered the cups off the table, placing them, with their saucers, one on top of the other. She looked questioningly at Lily. It was clear she wanted to get back to her work.

'Just one more thing, and then I'll leave you in peace. Think back to the day Miss Blake was murdered. I know Mr Garner went out in the morning and didn't return until after her body was found. But where was Mr Wing: what did he do after lunch?'

'Went up to his room to rest, most likely.' She shrugged. 'They all did. Except Miss Blake, of course: she went out.'

'One of the maids saw her leaving, didn't she?'

'That was Daisy. She'd been dusting downstairs and she saw Miss Blake leave by the side door and go into the garden.'

'Where did she go then – Daisy, I mean?'

'To the kitchen, where the rest of us were, having a break; chatting. Lunch had been cleared away and there wasn't much for us to do until tea time.'

'So if someone else – I mean one of the guests – had come downstairs and followed Miss Blake out, no one would have seen them?'

'You mean Mr Wing, don't you?' Annie eyed her shrewdly.

Lily shrugged. 'I'm not saying that. I'm just trying to get the lie of the land.' She paused, considering her next question. 'When did you first hear about the murder? What time was it?'

Annie thought. 'It was close to four o'clock,' she said, 'or maybe a bit earlier. They were starting to get things ready for tea in the kitchen. Old Pat Duckworth, the village bobby, rang the doorbell and Mr Hargreaves went to answer it. He didn't come back for nearly ten minutes, and when he did he told us what had happened. He had had to break the news to Sir Jack, who was still upstairs in his room, resting. He came down to talk to Pat and quite soon afterwards the other guests appeared from upstairs. Apart from Mr Garner, that is – he hadn't got back yet. Sir Jack got them together in the library and told them what had happened.'

'And Mr Wing was among them?'

Annie nodded.

'So as far as you knew he hadn't left his room?'

'That's right.' Annie squinted at her. 'But what you're thinking is he *might* have?'

'If he had, was there anyone else who would have seen him? What about the rooms upstairs, the bedrooms? Could he have been spotted from a window up there?'

Annie shook her head. 'If he went out of the garden the same way Miss Blake did he would have gone down the yew alley, and he couldn't have been seen in there. The branches grew together at the top; it was like a tunnel. It went all the way to the gate at the bottom.'

She studied Lily's face, as though expecting to see some change in her expression.

'When was the first time you saw him?' Lily continued to speak in a neutral tone. 'After lunch, I mean.'

'When the guests came down from their rooms and Sir Jack got us all together in the library – guests and staff – and told us about the murder. He looked terrible. He was that cut up.'

'How did Mr Wing take the news?'

'I don't know. I wasn't looking at him. I was looking at Sir Jack and at Mrs Castleton and wondering if there was anything we could do for them. I didn't take any notice of Mr Wing. In fact, I don't remember seeing him until a few minutes later when I went upstairs with a pile of clean linen and towels to put in the airing cupboard. Mr Hargreaves had told us we had to carry on as normal until the police arrived. He didn't want us sitting around in the kitchen gossiping.'

'You say you saw Mr Wing upstairs? Where was that, exactly?'

'In the passage. The guests' rooms were off it. He was coming towards me and we passed by one another. He didn't say anything. Just nodded as he went by.'

She sat back. Lily smiled.

'Thanks, Annie,' she said. 'You've been a great help. Sorry to have bothered you. I know you've got work to do.'

She glanced down.

'And it was nice to meet you, Winnie. I can see you're really good at colouring.'

The little girl blushed with pleasure. Lily prepared to rise, but then checked her movement when she saw that the look on her hostess's face had changed. Annie was staring out of the window at the back of the kitchen, where there was only the empty yard.

'Annie . . . ?'

She turned slowly towards Lily. Her face wore a puzzled look.

'I've just remembered something,' she said. 'He shouldn't have been there.'

'Who?'

'Mr Wing. It never struck me at the time. But I've just realized . . .' She stared at Lily. 'You see, the upstairs linen cupboard was at the end of the corridor, and Mr Wing came walking towards me from that direction. But he had no business being there . . .'

'No business . . . ?'

'*His* room was at the other end of the passage – his and Mr and Mrs Garner's. Sir Jack's other guests were a couple called Lord and Lady Cairns. Their room was near the cupboard and Miss Blake's was across the passage from theirs.'

She went on staring at Lily.

'So . . . so where could he have been coming from? That's what you're wondering?'

Annie nodded mutely.

'It couldn't have been from this Lord and Lady Whatsit's room?' Lily wanted to be sure she'd got it straight. 'He'd have had no business in there?'

'That's right. And anyway, they were still downstairs.'

'So there was only one other room he could have been coming from?'

Annie nodded mutely.

'He must have been in Miss Blake's room,' she said. 'But what was he doing *there*?'

14

'So THE ASSUMPTION IS Wing went into the Blake woman's room to look for something?'

Angus Sinclair added a question mark to his statement.

'But it couldn't have been the pendant. She was wearing that when she went out.'

'Wing wouldn't necessarily have known that,' Madden pointed out. Having received a full report on Lily Poole's visit to Whitechapel from Billy Styles before he returned home from London for the weekend, he had walked down from the house to give his old friend an account of the latest developments in the reopened investigation. 'But I agree it's quite possible he was looking for something else.'

'But what, I wonder?'

The chief inspector snipped a blood-red rose off one of his bushes and added it to the stems lying on the grass behind him. Whether his gout was truly in remission – he was still moving about gingerly – or whether the Yard's decision to reopen the Portia Blake inquiry had sent a dose of adrenalin through his system, the chief inspector was looking more like his old self, alert and energetic.

'What else could he have wanted to get his hands on?'

'We discussed that,' Madden said. 'Mrs Castleton over-heard Miss Blake tell Wing she had put something "in a safe place". Billy was going to get in touch with Portia's sister. It was she who collected Portia's effects from the flat she was sharing with Audrey Cooper. There might be something among them that will shed light on the mystery.'

'Unless Mr Wing found what he was looking for and pocketed it.'

The chief inspector ran his eye along the line of roses, searching for another victim.

'You say some of those originally involved have been spoken to again? Did they offer anything new?'

'Not really, and Billy also talked to Tom Derry in Canterbury, but he had nothing to add to what he had already told me, and he also saw the downstairs maid, Daisy Davenport. But she could only confirm what she said at the time about Portia leaving the house after lunch. The butler, a man called Hargreaves, retired to Bournemouth. Joe Grace has spoken to him, but other than giving an account of that dinner that accords with Richard Jessup's, the only thing he had to say of any interest was that he thought Rex Garner was more disturbed than he let on by the way Miss Blake was behaving. He was trying to ignore it, Hargreaves said, but actually he was furious. At least that's what Hargreaves thought.'

'But Garner himself hasn't been approached yet?'

'He went up to Scotland for the grouse shooting. He'll be back in London next week. Billy plans to interview him then.'

The chief inspector snipped off a last rose. Bending to collect the others that were lying on the grass, holding the prickly stems in his gloved hands, he led the way up the short path to the front door of his cottage. Madden followed. The roses were for Helen and he assumed that the chief inspector was going in search of some paper to wrap them in.

'And what of Mr Stanley Wing?' Sinclair paused at the door. 'Have you anything more on him?'

Madden shook his head.

'But I'm wondering whether Richard Jessup might have something to tell me on that score. He's only just returned from his business trip; but according to the message Helen took he wants to see me as soon as possible. I'll know more by tomorrow.'

It was Mrs Castleton who had relayed the invitation. She had telephoned the previous evening to say that Jessup hoped both Madden and his wife would lunch with them that Sunday at his house near Petersfield. Helen had taken the call, and when she joined Madden in the drawing room he had seen from her expression that she was pleased.

'That was Adele,' she said. 'She hasn't received my letter yet, but that's because she's been down in Hampshire looking after the Jessup children. His wife had to fly back to America at short notice. Her father's unwell and her mother had asked her to return. Why Adele rang was to ask us both to drive down there on Sunday. She said Sir Richard was anxious to see you. The way she said it made me think it might be important. He'll be home later tonight – he's been away on business – but he wanted Adele to ring us as soon as possible so that we'd have time to decide. I accepted at once and told her I would only ring back if you felt we couldn't make it for some reason.'

There being no such reason – Madden had been as eager as she to accept the invitation – they set off in mid-morning with Sinclair's roses wrapped in newspaper lying on the back seat of the car, knowing that the journey would take the better part of two hours. Jessup's house lay beyond the bounds of Surrey, in the county of Hampshire, near a village called Hawkley, a famous beauty spot and one that the Maddens had visited more than once before the war, when weekend drives in the country had been commonplace: a time distant in memory now. Although the government had finally taken pity on the long-suffering population and re-instated the modest wartime petrol ration, there was little of the precious fuel to spare. As a doctor, Helen had always been able to obtain a supply for her work, but she was reluctant to use it for private purposes, so it had been down to Madden to provide the coupons for their trip. And since his own car, a venerable Humber which had spent the war years sitting on blocks in the family garage like a beached whale, was no longer regarded as reliable for a journey of any distance (it needed a thorough overhaul and new parts that were not presently available), it was Helen's Morris Minor that they took.

New on the market, the car had been heralded by its makers as the answer to the German Volkswagen and its distinctive jelly-mould shape and superior performance had made it an instant favourite with the public. Not many were to be seen on the roads as yet – most vehicles coming off the assembly lines were earmarked for the export market – and Helen's cream-coloured model drew more than one envious glance as they made their leisurely way southwards along the A3 until they were a few miles short of Petersfield, at which point Madden, who was acting as navigator, spotted the signpost for Hawkley. Ten minutes later, still following the minutely detailed directions Adele Castleton had given them, they turned into a pair of wrought-iron gates and up a long avenue flanked by elms that led to the house.

Late Victorian in design, it was fronted by a circular driveway with a lily pond at its centre. The high brick wall of a kitchen garden was visible on one side of the house and it was from that direction that a man wearing work clothes approached them. Short and ruddy-faced, his close-cropped hair seemed to mark him out as an old soldier and he strode briskly towards them, in spite of having a slight limp.

'Mr and Mrs Madden, is it? How do you do, sir – and you, ma'am?' He dipped his head to Helen. 'Lennox is my name. I'm Sir Richard's chauffeur. He's over on the other side of the house with the children, but he told me to keep an eye out for you. Mrs Castleton's hereabouts. I think she's in the kitchen garden. I'll just go and see.'

About to leave them, he paused as his eye fell on Helen's car.

'Oh, you've got one of those have you, ma'am?' His face lit up. 'Is it true they do forty miles to the gallon?'

'Quite true.' Helen was complacent.

'And the independent front wheel suspension . . . does it really make cornering easier?'

'Much easier.'

'I must say she's a beauty.'

He laid a reverent hand on the machine's bonnet.

'Don't encourage him, Helen.'

Turning, Madden saw Adele Castleton approaching. She had a basket on her arm.

'Ted's one dream is to drive in the Monte Carlo Rally. If you're not careful he'll be asking you if he can borrow it next.'

Garbed in a loose silk dress with a flowered pattern, she wore a wide straw hat that kept the sun off her face but did nothing to hide the warmth of her smile.

'Are those roses for me?' Laying down the basket, she enveloped Helen in a warm embrace. 'How lovely to see you again, my dear: it's such a long time. Do you know, you haven't changed a bit?'

She turned to Madden.

'Richard was so pleased to hear you were coming today.

He would have driven up to Highfield himself to see you, but he hadn't set eyes on the children for more than a fortnight and with their mother away he felt he had to spend the weekend at home. Sarah rang from Philadelphia last night. It sounds as though her father has had a slight stroke: not a disabling one, I'm happy to say, but enough to worry them. She's going to stay there for a little while longer. Let's go round to the front and look for Richard. No, wait . . .'

She hesitated.

'Your car will bake sitting in the sun. Would you like to put it under the tree over there?' She pointed to a handsome oak whose spreading branches covered a corner of the drive.

'Perhaps Lennox would like to do that for me.' Helen turned to the chauffeur. 'The keys are in the car.'

'Of course, ma'am.' His face lit up at the prospect.

'But only as far as the tree, Ted.' Mrs Castleton cautioned him. 'No taking it out for a spin.'

'Oh, ma'am . . . you know I wouldn't do that.'

Grinning with pleasure, he opened the car door, and as they went off they heard the motor start.

'Ted served in the war with Richard,' she told them as she led the way up the side of the house. 'He was his company sergeant-major. When it was over Richard offered him a job. Officially he's his chauffeur, but he's far more than that. He does all sorts of things for us. He's a dear man. The children adore him.'

When they came to a door she paused.

'I must just put your lovely roses in water,' she said, relieving Helen of her burden, 'and take this into the kitchen, too.' She indicated the basket she was carrying. 'It's so difficult with rationing still, isn't it? There's a farm attached to the house and we get some stuff from it. But Richard doesn't like to bend the rules, especially when he knows he could do it so easily. But fortunately we've a lovely kitchen garden and I can promise you a good salad to go with our rabbit pie.'

She returned after a few moments and they continued to the front of the house where she paused so that they could take in the view. Before them was a garden boasting a wide, tree-shaded lawn bordered by flower beds and hedged by dense shrubbery, and beyond that a sweeping vista of beech-clad hills stretching for miles into the hazy distance.

At the bottom of the lawn two figures stood facing one another some yards apart. As they watched, the taller of the two moved forward, bringing his arm over in a slow arc. Madden saw it was Jessup, and that he was bowling to a boy who must be his son. The crack of a cricket bat striking a ball reached their ears, and at the same moment another, smaller figure, clad in white, darted like a sprite from the shadows cast by a giant beech and hared after the ball, which had disappeared into the shrubbery.

'Poor Katy.' Mrs Castleton sighed. 'They just use her as a fielder. She hardly ever gets a chance to bat.'

'Hello, there . . . !' Jessup called to them.

Raising his hand in greeting he came up the lawn to meet them, trailed by the children.

'It's so good of you to come all this way.'

He spoke while he was still some way off, and Madden and Helen had time to take in his lithe figure, dressed simply in a pair of shabby corduroy trousers and a flannel shirt with the sleeves rolled up to the elbow.

'Dr Madden . . . ?' He held out his hand.

'Please . . . call me Helen.'

'Adele has told me so much about you.' Jessup looked into her eyes as they shook hands. 'But I want to hear more . . . about both of you,' he added as he turned to greet Madden. 'First, some introductions, though . . .'

He beckoned to his son, who had paused behind him, bat in hand, waiting to be presented.

'This is Jack . . . John, actually, but he prefers Jack, just as his grandfather did. Come and say hello to Mr and Mrs Madden.'

The boy stepped forward. Dark-haired, like his father – and with the same high cheekbones with their promise of good looks – his face was burned brown by the summer sun. Eyes blue as sapphires examined them curiously as they shook hands.

'Now what have you done with your sister?'

Jessup bent to peer into his son's face, ignoring the presence of the little girl, who had held back and was standing some distance off, clutching the cricket ball to her chest and eyeing the visitors doubtfully.

'She's over there, Daddy.' The boy pointed. 'You can see her.'

'So she is . . . !' Jessup drew back in mock surprise. 'Come along, Katy. I want you to say hello.'

The girl approached them, head bowed.

'Shake hands now.'

Still clutching her ball with one hand, she extended the other. It was solemnly accepted, first by Helen, and then by her husband.

'There . . . that wasn't too difficult.' Jessup ran his fingers through her curls, which were fair like her mother's.

'And now I think it's time for your lunch, both of you.'

'It's waiting in the kitchen,' Mrs Castleton announced. She glanced at Helen. 'Shall we take them inside? Then we can settle down on our own. We've a great deal of catching up to do.' She had turned to Jessup. 'And I know you want to speak to Mr Madden. So why don't we all meet in an hour.'

*

'I might have guessed that would catch your eye. She dominates the room, doesn't she? Poor mother – she was afflicted by the worst of all curses: the unshakeable conviction that she was always in the right.'

Jessup spoke from the doorway. He had led Madden to his study, a pleasant book-lined room with a view of the garden and the rolling, wooded countryside beyond, and left him there while he went to wash his hands and put on a jacket. Madden had wandered about, glancing at the books and inspecting the paintings hanging on the walls which included a view of the Hong Kong waterfront busy with shipping, and with the well-known silhouette of Signal Hill rising in the background. He had stopped at a table in one corner covered with framed photographs, one of which had attracted his attention. Larger than the rest, and somehow managing to tower over them, its subject was a handsome dark-haired woman with strong features who gazed back at the camera without even a hint of a smile, seeming to challenge the lens, daring it to find fault with her.

'I never understood how she and Father came to marry. They were young, of course, which may partly explain it. I'm sure Mother was quite inexperienced; my father I'm not so sure. But they very soon found that they couldn't live with each other and parted on the worst of terms; though not before I was sired; obviously.'

Smiling, he came over from the door.

'And there's a snapshot of Rex and me. It was when we were at Eton. We rowed in the same eight.'

The two boys stood side by side, each holding an upraised oar. Easily recognizable in spite of the lock of hair that hung carelessly down over his brow, partly covering one eye, Jessup was half a head taller than his companion, whose hair was brushed back from his forehead. Both were smiling broadly.

'We were great pals in those days.' Jessup's voice was tinged with regret. 'It was only later that we fell out.'

His face brightened.

'And this is Sarah,' he said, picking up a photograph that was standing on his desk and handing it to Madden. 'It was taken on our honeymoon in Paris.'

The young woman whose face Madden recognized from the picture Mrs Castleton had shown him stood with her hands in her coat pockets. A beret tilted at a rakish angle crowned her fair head and a woollen scarf was wound about her neck. The cobbles at her feet shone with rain, but her smile lit up the damp day.

'My mother didn't *quite* approve of her. She didn't think any girl was good enough for her son. But they were starting to get on better when she died. It was soon after Father passed away. Mother had been diagnosed with cancer some time before, but she hung on grimly and managed to be present at our wedding in Philadelphia, something Father was unable to do. It was towards the end of 1938 and he was already too ill to travel. I've always believed that Mother was determined to see him in his grave before she went herself. As I think I told you, I began to spend more time with him as I grew older and she never really forgave me for it.'

Putting the photograph back in its place, he went to a cabinet and opened it.

'Will you join me in a bottle of beer before lunch, John? I've worked up a thirst.'

They had moved easily onto a first-name basis, the transition occurring naturally and without fuss, and Madden had found himself surprised at how quickly a feeling of ease and companionship had grown up between them. Naturally reserved, it was a new experience for him and he put it down to the absence of just that quality in the other man. The openness Jessup had shown him from the first had been like a bridge that they had crossed without effort.

Accepting the glass of beer offered him, he took his seat in a stuffed-leather armchair, one of two set on either side of a low table. Jessup stayed by the window looking out.

'You've been very patient.'

He turned with a smile.

'I was going to ring you when I got back from my trip on Friday and found an express letter from the head of our Hong Kong office waiting for me. It was in reply to the telegram I sent him about Wing. But then something else happened that made me think it would be better to wait until I could speak to you about both in person.'

'If I'd known you were back I would have rung you myself,' Madden said. 'I wanted to explain how this story had got into the newspapers. I think the same person who sent the pendant to Derry also sent a letter to the *News of the World*. Whoever it is seems to want the case reopened.'

Jessup grunted. 'I did wonder about that.'

He came over from the window to join Madden and sat down facing him.

'First let me tell you about Wing. To begin with, he was released from prison two months ago. He'd been inside for four years of a six-year term and there was nothing unusual about his early release, which was for good behaviour. You may wonder why I hadn't heard about it before. I certainly did. But it turns out that Stanley was far from an ordinary prisoner, and the manner of his release was equally unusual. No announcement of it was made by the prison authorities. In fact, it was kept a close secret, which explains why my people didn't find out about it until now. They also learned that he was able to leave the colony immediately, possibly with official help. They were given to understand that he went across the bay to Macau – it's a short ride by boat. But after that he disappeared.'

'What was so special about him?'

'The charge on which he was convicted – of collaborating with the enemy – was real enough. But there was an aspect of it which put him in a different category from others who were charged with the same offence. What he was accused of, in fact, was acting as an intermediary between the Japanese occupying forces and the triad gangs. I take it you know who I'm referring to?'

'They're a criminal society, aren't they?'

Jessup nodded. 'They date from the seventeenth century. Originally they were a secret organization opposed to the Manchu rulers, but later they turned to crime and became involved first in the opium trade and later in all kinds of skulduggery including extortion and drug smuggling; and murder, of course. They spread to Hong Kong a long time ago, but now with the Communists on the point of taking control of the whole of the mainland the colony is their centre of operations. According to police estimates there are upwards of 300,000 triad members active in Hong Kong.'

He saw Madden's look of amazement and shrugged.

'I had always assumed that Wing had triad connections. He could hardly have carried out his business in stolen artefacts without their help. But I hadn't realized until now the full extent of his involvement with them. According to our sources in the Hong Kong police, Wing was recruited by one of the biggest gangs, or families, as they like to call themselves – the Tang – and went through their initiation ceremony which, among other things, requires the sacrifice of a live animal and the drinking of its blood mixed with wine.

Unknown to us, he'd become a fully-fledged member and would have had to swear eternal loyalty to the brotherhood, it being understood that any infringement of the oaths he took carried the penalty of death. The triad gangs are absolutely ruthless when it comes to punishing betrayals, or indeed any perceived affront. Wing, it turns out, had transgressed on both counts, hence the special treatment he received in prison; and the protection he was given when he was released.'

'He became an informer? Is that what you're saying?'

'In effect. The police had evidence that he'd been quick to approach the Japanese when they occupied Hong Kong and point out to them the advantages of using the triads to control the local population and manage the labour force. His actions were treasonable beyond question, and if he hadn't offered to turn King's evidence when he was arrested he would have drawn a much longer prison sentence. But his willingness to cooperate with the police meant he was a marked man from then on: his name was on the Tang's death-list, and almost at once he was the target of an assassination attempt in prison, which led to his being kept in solitary confinement for the remainder of his term. He was still providing the authorities with valuable information about the gangs' activities, so it was worth their while to protect him. And apparently he managed to extract a further concession from them: it was agreed that his eventual release should be kept secret.'

'And now he's disappeared?'

'So it would seem.'

'You're not certain of that?' Madden had caught a slight change in the other's tone.

'This is that other matter I mentioned.' Jessup rubbed his jaw. 'This is what I wanted to speak to you about in person. It's a sensitive issue and it raises difficult questions – for me, at any rate. What I've just told you is information you're welcome to pass on to Scotland Yard. They can discover it for themselves in any case by getting in touch with the Hong Kong police. But this other matter . . . it's put me in a quandary. I'm not sure what to do about it and I'd like your advice, John.'

'Tell me about it. I'll see if I can help.'

'I got back from my trip late on Thursday and when I went into the office the next day I found the letter from Hong Kong waiting for me. I'd barely had time to digest its contents, though, when my secretary told me that an elderly Chinese businessman I'm acquainted with, a Mr Lin Jie, was asking to see me urgently. He had heard that I was back in London and telephoned from his offices in Soho to ask if he could call on me at the earliest possible moment. He'd been unwilling to divulge the reason for his request, except to say that it concerned a matter he could only discuss with me in person.'

Jessup hesitated.

'What I'm about to tell you now is not established fact,' he went on after a moment. 'It's merely a suspicion. But I've reason to believe that Lin was party to the illegal trade in Chinese artefacts I told you about earlier – the ones Wing sold to collectors in this country. Stanley would have needed some sort of cover for his business as well as some means of smuggling the art objects into this country, and Lin was in a position to provide both. He runs a successful import company here in London. I knew that they were acquainted, and from what I was able to learn I felt reasonably certain that they were partners. Given my suspicions, I've always kept Lin at arm's length and we've never done any business together. You can imagine my surprise then when I learned that he wanted to see me. But I was curious to know why and I told my secretary to invite him round. He arrived half an hour later – in some haste, I might add – accompanied by a young man who he introduced as his nephew. I could tell at once from Lin's manner that something unusual was afoot. Normally meetings with Chinese gentlemen of the old school proceed at a snail's pace. Polite inquiries as to one another's health and well-being, not to mention those of one's family, are considered de rigueur before getting down to business. On this occasion all formalities were dispensed with. Lin asked me at once if I happened to know of the whereabouts of Stanley Wing.'

Madden's eyebrows shot up.

'Precisely. I was equally surprised. Before I had a chance to respond, however, he went on to explain that although he was aware that Wing no longer had any connection with Jessup's, he knew that he had once been closely associated with the firm, and with my late father, and for that reason he hoped I might be able to help him in this matter. He was starting to sweat at that point and I noticed that he kept glancing at this young man he said was his nephew, as though seeking his approval. I guessed at once what must have happened: who had put pressure on him.'

'You mean the triads?' Madden frowned. 'I wasn't aware they were active in London.'

'They're not, at least not to any great extent, and not yet. But I've heard rumours that moves are under way to establish a branch here. It's the drug trade: big business for them. But quite apart from that their reach has always been long. Most of our Chinese came from Hong Kong originally. Nearly all of them have families living there. I couldn't ask Lin outright if his had been threatened. But that was how I interpreted the situation. And, of course, it made sense that the triads would come to him for information about Wing. They almost certainly knew of their pre-war connection.'

Madden scowled. 'Tell me about this so-called "nephew" of his. Can you describe him?'

'He was young, very sleek-looking, and wearing what looked like an expensive suit. He didn't speak during our meeting.'

'Could he have come from Hong Kong with orders to hunt Wing down?'

'Possibly.' Jessup frowned. 'But it's more likely he was sent from Amsterdam. There's a big triad presence there. A lot of the heroin that reaches Europe comes through the port of Rotterdam. But he looked too young to me to be an enforcer: a Red Pole in the jargon they use.' He grimaced. 'He's more likely to be his assistant; his jackal, if you like.'

He gnawed his lip.

'There's more,' he went on. 'I haven't finished yet. I thought it rich that Lin should be asking me where Stanley was, given their past association. But I told him the truth: that I had no knowledge of Wing's whereabouts, other than that he had recently been released from prison in Hong Kong; which, incidentally, seemed to come as no surprise to either of them. But then he said something that startled me even more. He asked me if I had any reason to believe that he might be here in London.'

Jessup studied his guest's face.

'You're not surprised?'

'Not really.' Madden shrugged. 'I thought from the start that he was probably the person behind all this. But when you told me he was in prison I had to abandon the idea. Now it's beginning to make sense. But tell me – was Lin fishing, do you think? Was he just trying out the question on you? Or did he have definite information that Wing was in this country?'

'I don't know.'

'It matters, you see.'

'Why?'

'Well, if we knew for certain that he was here, it would tend to support at least one theory the police are working on now.'

Madden stopped. He had forgotten who he was talking to.

'What is that, John?'

Madden hesitated. The ease he had felt in talking to his host had led him astray. But it was too late to back out now. Jessup was listening to him intently, waiting for him to speak.

'It's only a theory, Richard, an attempt to explain some of the facts as we know them. For heaven's sake don't take it as gospel.'

'Go on.' Jessup spoke tersely.

'Let's suppose for a moment that, eleven years ago, Wing tried to set up a blackmail scheme with Garner as its victim. He knew that he had married a wealthy woman and could probably get his hands on a large sum of money if pressed.'

'Why pick on Rex?'

'Well, for one thing, Wing had once done Garner a favour in Hong Kong. Isn't it true he got him out of a bad situation with a woman and put him on a ship back to England?'

Madden paused. Jessup's gaze had dropped.

'I'm sorry, John. My father told me about that. It was years ago. I should have passed it on to you. It was just . . . I didn't think it was relevant.' He looked up.

'No matter.' Madden shrugged it off. 'But the point is – did Garner ever repay the favour? Did he, for example, try and persuade you, his old friend, not to terminate Wing's connection with the firm?'

Jessup shook his head. 'Rex told me Wing had asked him to intercede with my father, but he'd turned him down flat. He said Stanley had made his own bed and could lie on it. He thought it was amusing to see him caught out for once. I always imagined that Rex would have to pay someday for the favour Wing did him. I couldn't see Stanley playing the Good Samaritan, ever. I'm sure he felt that Rex was in his debt.'

'That's what I thought.' Madden had listened closely to his reply. 'Well, if we follow the theory the police are looking at, it goes something like this. In order to make his plan work Wing needed to compromise Garner in some way. That was where Portia Blake came in. Wing was in England that summer and perhaps he found some way to engineer an affair between them. We know that he accompanied Portia to some of those parties you mentioned and he could quickly have seen the possibilities of involving her with Garner, who always had an eye for a pretty face. How he might have managed to persuade Portia to join in the scheme one can't say; but presumably she was going to benefit from it too, financially. So the hook was baited, and once Garner had taken it, Wing could have put the rest of his plan into action. He could have arranged things with your father so that he and the girl were invited to Foxley Hall at the same time as Garner and his wife, whose presence was essential if the plan was to work. Wing probably meant to apply the screw gently . . . delicately. He merely wanted to show Garner the danger he was in. But Portia Blake had other ideas, hence that scene at dinner, which pretty well blew the gaff on Wing's plan, which in any case was finally put paid to the following day when the girl was murdered.'

'I'm sorry, John, but I must interrupt.' Jessup sat forward. 'You keep saying the police think this, the police believe that. What do *you* believe? Does this theory of theirs hold water? Give me your honest opinion.'

Madden considered his reply.

'As I've already made clear to the detectives dealing with the case, I have a problem with it. I find it hard to believe that Wing would have devised such an elaborate plan when the success of it must surely have been in doubt from the start. For all he knew, Garner might simply have thrown it back in his face; he could have told him to do his worst and Wing would have been left helpless. According to Mrs Castleton, Garner had his wife well under his thumb at that stage in their marriage. He could easily have talked his way out of what was only a minor indiscretion. The question is – did Wing have something else on him, some other hold, and was he prepared to use both in an attempt to extort money from his victim? We don't know what happened to that girl Garner assaulted in Hong Kong. It's been suggested he might have killed her and that Wing helped cover up the crime. I take it you can't help with that?'

'Good God, no.' Jessup shook his head angrily. 'If my father had known he would have told me; and he would never have stood by and done nothing.'

'It's pure guesswork at this stage, but without it, or something like it, the theory I've been outlining to you doesn't seem to me to hold up. Mind you, that won't stop the police from considering it, at least.'

Madden paused to empty his glass. He saw that the expression on Jessup's face had changed. A frown had settled on his brow. It was hard to tell what it signified . . . disbelief, perhaps?

'Even if all you've said is true, what has it got to do with the present? There's no point in anyone trying to blackmail Rex now.'

'Not for being unfaithful to his wife – no.'

'What do you mean?'

Madden took a deep breath.

'Richard, I have to remind you again that this is all speculation, and I only bring it up because it's another line of inquiry the police may well decide to pursue. They don't know yet that Wing may be in London and could be the person behind this whole business. But once they do they're likely to reason as follows. Wing is on the run from the triads. Among other things he's short of money. He's never forgotten those months he spent in England, nor his failed attempt to blackmail Rex Garner, and at some point, perhaps when he was in prison, he realizes he can put the same plot, or one very like it, into operation again. Only this time Garner has money of his own, thanks to the legacy left him by his late wife; and the threat Wing can dangle over him now is far more dangerous than the mere disclosure of some piece of marital misbehaviour. By sending that pendant to the police, he's serving notice on Garner that he can tie him to the murder of Portia Blake.'

He stopped. He had seen the look of shock on the other man's face.

'Are you seriously suggesting that Rex might have killed her?' Jessup had turned pale.

'No, I'm merely explaining a line of reasoning that will almost certainly occur to the detectives examining this case.'

'But *how* . . . I mean, even supposing it's true, how could Stanley possibly have known that?'

'Well, for one thing, he might have followed Portia that day when she left the house. He was furious over the way she had behaved at dinner the previous evening. He no longer trusted her and might have felt the need to keep an eye on her. If he did witness the killing, it would have been very much in character for him not to intervene or report what he had seen to the police, but rather look to see how he could profit from it. And it may well have been *he* who took the pendant from Portia's body.'

'Why should he have done that?'

'Perhaps because he knew it was a gift from Garner and something he could use himself if he pressed ahead with his scheme.' Madden shrugged. 'In fact, the possibilities for blackmail must have looked even rosier to him in the wake of Portia's murder until the unexpected arrest of Norris, which happened very soon afterwards, and the even more surprising news that he had confessed to the murder. It left Wing in a quandary. It was too late for him to point the finger at Garner, and in any case there would be no advantage to him in doing so. Unless he could think up some new plan he would have to accept failure. For the time being there was nothing he could do but return to Hong Kong.'

'But if he was unable to move against Garner then, how is it possible he can do so now, more than ten years later?'

'I don't know.' Madden shook his head. 'Perhaps something has happened in the intervening years to change the situation, some new development, or perhaps he's simply desperate, ready to try anything.'

Jessup sat biting his lip.

'Could it really have happened that way?'

'I've no idea. It's only a theory, as I said.' Madden was surprised by the effect his words had had on his host. Although the colour had returned to Jessup's cheeks, his face still showed signs of the shock he had felt on hearing Madden's revelations. 'I'd suspend judgement on it if I were you.'

'I just can't swallow the idea that Rex might be a murderer.'

'Then don't,' Madden urged him. 'There's no *evidence* as yet to suggest that he had anything to do with Portia's death. Because of those stories appearing in the newspapers the police have been forced to look at the case again, and this is just one of the ideas they're playing with. For my money, Norris is still the most likely killer and it may well be that the Yard will come to the same conclusion in the end.'

'But the pendant . . . these letters . . . someone must have sent them. And as you say, Wing could well have had a motive for doing so. And if he *is* in London and he *did* send them, then Rex is bound to come under suspicion.'

A further thought seemed to strike him then and he caught Madden's eye.

'My God, I wonder if he knows about this. He's been up in Scotland for weeks. Is he even aware of what's going on?'

'You haven't heard from him?'

'Not a word. As I told you, we don't see much of each other these days.'

'Well, the police know that he's due back in London soon. They mean to interview him when he returns. It might be best to wait until they've done that before you get in touch with him. And as far as the other matter you raised goes . . .'

'The other matter . . . ?'

'Your meeting with Lin. You said it raised difficult questions for you. What did you mean exactly, Richard?'

Jessup bit his lip. It was clear he was having difficulty answering the question.

Finally, he spoke. 'It's like this, John. I don't mind telling *you* my suspicions about Lin and his past relationship with Wing. But I'm not comfortable about passing them on to the police. They're not proven, as I said, and I wouldn't want to blacken Lin's name without being certain. Is there any way of keeping him out of this?'

Madden shook his head. 'I'm afraid not. Wing's possible presence in London can be inferred from the other information you've given me – I mean his release from prison in Hong Kong and his need to quit the colony in a hurry. The police here will quickly put two and two together, just as I did, and see that it was very likely he who sent the pendant and those letters to Derry and the newspapers. But the fact that triad killers may be actively searching for him here can't be kept from them. They must be told about your meeting with Lin. Why don't you leave it to me to talk to them first? I know the detectives who are working on the case. I can explain the situation to them.'

'Would you, John?' Jessup's relief was plain. 'I'd be more than grateful.'

He shook his head. He seemed at a loss for words. Finally, with a sigh, he glanced at his watch.

'An hour, Adele said. I think we'd better break for lunch.'

'You said Wing had offended against the triad laws in two ways, Richard. What did you mean by that?'

They were walking together along a valley walled by steep, wooded ridges. Madden had paused to put his question, and to glance back along the way they had come towards the house, where he could see in the distance the small figures of Helen and Adele Castleton walking arm in arm on the lawn as they talked. Lunch had been laid in a corner of the garden shaded by the spreading branches of yet another ancient oak and, seemingly relieved by the opportunity offered to switch to a different topic, Jessup had eagerly engaged Helen on the subject of her work.

'I'm all in favour of the National Health Service. In fact, I voted for the Labour Party after the war, much to the horror of my fellow club members, one or two of whom actually threatened to blackball me. But how is it working out in practice? I've heard mixed reports.'

In reply, Helen had outlined the changes the new system of health care had made to her life.

'On the whole it's functioning well enough,' she said, 'except that it tends to encourage people to drop in at their doctor's surgery on the slightest pretext now that it costs them nothing. I've had more than one stubbed toe brought to me for urgent attention. In fact, because of the added workload I've more or less decided to look for a partner to share the practice with me. I've got my eye on a young man who works at Guildford hospital, but would like to move with his wife and baby son to the country.'

The enjoyment which both she and Mrs Castleton were taking in renewing their acquaintance had been plain to see. They had been talking animatedly when the two men had joined them and it was with some reluctance – or so it seemed to Madden – that they had adjusted to the more general conversation that had followed. For his own part, he had listened with pride as Helen spoke in her usual forthright manner about her work. Dressed in a white linen frock – it was one of Lucy's creations – with only a red leather belt to lend a touch of colour, her beauty seemed no less compelling to him now that her hair was starting to grey than when they had first met, and he had taken quiet pleasure in the open admiration he had seen in Richard Jessup's glance as he listened to her.

Lunch done, his host had proposed that they go for a walk, and with Mrs Castleton having decided that she and Helen should remain at the house so as to be there when the children came downstairs from their afternoon rest, the two men had set off through a gate at the bottom of the garden, Jessup carrying a shotgun broken at the breech in the crook of his arm.

'It's more for show than anything else,' he had told Madden with a smile. 'Though I do pot the odd rabbit for the larder.'

The gate through which they passed had given onto a wide field where cows were grazing. Seeing Madden pause to cast an appreciative farmer's eye over the well-fed herd, Jessup, too, had stopped. He had pointed to a row of cottages at the far end of the meadow.

'That's where our farmworkers are housed. One of the first things Sarah did when we settled here for good after the war was to install new plumbing and otherwise bring them up to scratch. Her whole family is strong on social conscience and I've found that it's catching. I've got our management in Hong Kong drawing up plans to improve working conditions in the cotton mills we own. In some cases it'll require complete rebuilding and I've had some opposition to it from my board of directors. But Sarah's father, Saul Temple, came down strongly on my side. He's a very active partner in the business and one I've come to value greatly.'

'He's not seriously ill, I hope.'

'No, the stroke seems to have been a mild one; more of a warning to ease up a little, Sarah says. We spoke last night on the phone. I do wish she had been here to meet you and Helen. We'll have to fix another meeting soon.'

They had walked on, and it was not until they had left the open fields behind them and entered an area where the wooded hangers for which the district was noted rose on either side of the path they were taking that Madden had returned to the subject they had been discussing earlier.

'Wing was guilty of two mortal offences against the triads' code,' Jessup replied to his question. 'One was to turn informer; but the other was more personal, and in some ways graver.'

'More *personal*?'

'He committed the ultimate sin: he caused the triad leader, the head of the Tang, to lose face. The man was an acknowledged Dragon Head, the highest rank in the triad hierarchy.'

'How did he offend?' Madden was fascinated. 'And was he aware of what he was doing?'

'Only too well. But he was caught between . . . between Scylla and Charybdis, if you like. On orders from the triad boss he had managed to get on close terms with one of the most senior Japanese officers stationed in Hong Kong, a general. The man was something of a dilettante, an art collector, and Wing had been providing him with pilfered objects stolen from graves on the mainland and smuggled into Hong Kong in much the same way as he had done with Western collectors before the war. As chance would have it, he had come into possession of an exceptional jade piece, an unusual bas-relief depicting two lovers in a garden. Though carved by an unknown hand, it was clearly the work of a skilled artist. Collectors knew of its existence, but it had been lost to sight for more than a century.'

'Until it fell into Wing's hands?'

Jessup nodded. 'It was promised to the Japanese general, but unfortunately for Wing, the Dragon Head to whom he owed absolute loyalty had got wind of it and wanted the piece for himself. It was left to Stanley to decide which of the two should get it and, not surprisingly, he plumped for the general. The Japanese were in complete control of Hong Kong at the time. If he had reneged on the deal he would more than likely have been executed out of hand. Of course, he was in no less mortal danger from the triad chief, but as long as the Japanese were there he could count on their protection. Once the war ended, however, his days were numbered, and since there was no way he could escape from Hong Kong, he surrendered himself at once to the returning British authorities. Even so, the Tang leader wanted his head.'

Jessup eyed Madden meaningfully.

'I mean *literally*, John. He wanted Stanley's head removed from his body. Apparently it's the trademark of this particular triad boss: his signature, if you like. Where possible the victim's body is destroyed or disposed of, leaving only the head as a warning to others. I told you Wing was attacked in jail. The two prisoners who carried out the assault did their best to decapitate him, but they were attempting to saw his head off with the only weapon available, a makeshift knife, and they were stopped before they could complete the job. Even so it was a near-run thing. They apparently got to within a hair's breadth of Stanley's carotid artery before the guards intervened.'

Jessup stopped to look back.

'I just want to make sure the children aren't following us. Jack will be on our heels as soon as he realizes we've gone for a walk; and Katy won't be far behind him.'

He scanned the valley.

'She must still be resting. Adele's strict about that. She has to stay on her bed for an hour after lunch. They're not allowed to follow where we're about to go now. But there's always the temptation to break the rules.'

Satisfied, he went on, but after only a few steps veered to the right, leaving the path they had been following. Madden quickly caught up with him. Walking side by side, they ascended a grassy rise that formed a saddle dividing the ridge into two wooded hillocks. Although it was late in the afternoon the sun was still hot and both men were sweating by the time they reached the top of the slope, where they paused to take in the view.

'I used to walk these hills when I was a boy,' Jessup said. 'I'd put a piece of bread with a lump of cheese and an apple in a knapsack and disappear for a whole day. I'd take a book with me and lie in the shade for hours, reading. Edward Thomas lived not far from here for a time – at Steep.' He pointed to a distant cluster of red roofs topped by a church spire. 'Have you read his work?'

'I came across his poems after the war,' Madden said. 'The first war, that is.'

'He was one of those who didn't come back. But you did.' He caught his companion's eye. 'I bumped into Ian at the club on Friday evening. He filled me in about your past; or some of it, at any rate.'

'Did he?'

'War's terrible enough, but the worst thing for me, what I found hardest to bear, was the knowledge each time we went into action of how much I had to lose. In the end I had to stop thinking about Sarah and Jack, who was just a baby then, and about this house and these hills, about everything I loved. I had to put them out of my mind. A wise old soldier once told me that the only way to go on and hope to survive was to think of oneself as already dead. Did you ever feel that way?'

'More than once.' Madden smiled grimly. 'And I didn't even have what you had to come back to. Not then.'

'But later, yes . . .' Jessup smiled in turn. 'Adele told me something of what you told her . . . about yourself . . . and Helen. You understand then . . .'

His voice tailed off and he turned his gaze back to the rolling tree-clad country in front of them. Madden waited for a moment before speaking.

'About Thomas's poems, though – I was struck by them. He had a voice all his own.'

'Do you remember the one about the weasel and the gallows?'

'And the gamekeeper . . . ?'

'Who shot the weasel, yes . . . and hung him on a bough.' Jessup's gaze swept the land around them. 'And left him to swing there in the wind and rain, without pleasure or pain. I read it when I was a boy. It was an image I couldn't get out of my mind.'

'Why won't you let the children come this way?' Madden asked.

'I'll show you,' his companion replied. 'It's not much further.'

They continued across the saddle until they came to a straggling line of holly bushes, where they halted.

'There's an old chalk quarry on the other side of this hedge,' Jessup said, 'and I'm always afraid that the children might forget about it one day and go dashing through. A couple of boys from the village who were bird-nesting tried to climb down the side of it last year and one of them lost his footing and was killed in the fall. The drop's all of two hundred feet.'

He picked his way through the tangled branches. Madden followed. The short stretch of turf beyond ended abruptly and he found himself looking down the almost vertical side of an old chalk pit.

'We're at the very edge of the Downs,' Jessup said. 'There are plenty of quarries still active south of here. But this one hasn't been worked for years. I've told the county council they ought to fence it off for safety reasons, but nothing's been done yet, as you can see.'

They retraced their steps, and as they crossed the saddle and came down the slope they saw a figure standing, as if held back by an invisible barrier, rooted to the path below. It was Jessup's son. He was barefoot. Catching sight of his father, he sprang into life and came running up the slope towards them, calling out:

'Daddy, you said you'd tell us when you were going for a walk.'

'Did I? I must have forgotten.' Jessup looked back towards the house. 'Where's your little sister?'

'I don't know.' The boy stood panting.

'Has she fallen down a rabbit hole?'

'No, of course not.' He turned to scan the way he had come. After a few seconds he pointed. 'There she is.'

Madden made out a small figure sitting on the grass beside the path some distance away. Jessup waved to her.

'Come on, Katy,' he called to her.

The little girl showed no sign of having heard. She stayed sitting where she was, head bowed.

'What have I always told you, Jack?' Jessup rumpled his son's dark hair. 'You must look after Katy. I can't be here all the time. You have to keep an eye on her until she's old enough to look after herself.'

'But she's only *five*.' The boy was despairing. 'It'll be *years*.'

'All the same . . .' His father patted him on the head. 'Now run along and see what the trouble is.'

Listening to them, Madden chuckled.

'You'd better not mention it to Jack,' he said as they followed in the boy's footsteps, 'but when our son Rob joined the navy in the last war he told us with a straight face that it was the act of a desperate man. He said if he didn't take the chance to escape then, he knew he'd spend the rest of his life getting his sister out of one scrape after another. Mind you, he had a point. Lucy was particularly trouble-prone.'

'I know all about your beautiful daughter.' Jessup smiled at him. 'I made Ian tell me everything he knew about you and your family. It was the least I could do after burdening you with the history of mine.'

They had reached the spot where the children were. The little girl's cheeks were wet with tears and Madden saw that she was nursing a bloody knee.

'What have we here?' Jessup got down beside her. 'A wounded soldier? Oh, I think we'll need a bandage on that.'

Taking a handkerchief from his pocket, he dabbed her tears dry and kissed her. Then he bound the piece of material about her knee.

'Do we need to call for stretcher-bearers, do you think?' He addressed the question to his son, who shook his head scornfully.

'Of course not. She's all right. She can walk. See . . . !'

The little girl was already on her feet, her tears forgotten.

As Jessup rose, Jack spoke again, this time in an urgent whisper.

'Look, Daddy . . . rabbits! Over there . . . !'

Turning, Madden saw a dozen or so feeding on the grass at the bottom of the ridge not far from where they were.

'Shoot one of them!'

Jessup picked up his shotgun from the ground and slipped a cartridge into the open breech. He fired a shot. The rabbits scattered.

'You missed! Daddy, you're *hopeless*. Lennox is a much better shot than you.'

'You're right, he is.' With a grin Jessup broke the gun and

THE DEATH OF KINGS

extracted the spent cartridge. 'Dead-Eye Dick. That's what we called him. But you don't even like the taste of rabbit, do you?'

Jack shook his head.

'Then why did you want me to kill one?'

Stumped for an answer, the boy was silent. He shuffled under his father's questioning gaze.

'Think about that, and give me your answer tomorrow.' Settling the shotgun in the crook of his arm again, he ran his fingers through his son's hair, pushing it back from his forehead.

'Can I carry it?' Jack looked longingly at the gun.

Jessup shook his head. 'Not until you're older.'

'You always say that.'

'Not until you're this tall.' He held his hand an inch above the boy's head.

'You always say that, too, and you keep moving your hand higher.'

Jessup laughed. 'All right. I promise you can carry it when you're ten.'

'But I've only just turned nine.'

'That means you've only got a year to wait.'

'A *year* . . . !'

The enormity of it left the boy speechless.

'Off you go now, the two of you. Tell Grandma we'll be back in time for tea.'

He watched as the two children set off down the path, Jack in the lead, his sister following at a trot. Then he glanced up at the sky.

'Have you noticed that kestrel?' he asked.

Madden nodded. 'I spotted it earlier. He's been circling for some time.'

'We're old friends.' Jessup watched as the bird glided above them, dipping first one wing, then the other, soaring on the thermals. His face was alight with pleasure. 'He hunts this valley. He won't be best pleased today, though. He probably had his eye on one of those rabbits.'

With their shadows lengthening now, they walked on in companionable silence until Jessup spoke again.

'After you tell the Yard what I've told you they'll start looking for Wing in London, won't they?'

'Unquestionably.'

'Then perhaps I should send them that snapshot I showed you in my office: the one of Wing standing with my father and those others. He was a lot younger than he is now, but it might help.'

'I wish you would, Richard. The more I hear about Wing, the more important I think it is that he should be located as soon as possible.'

'I'll ring Miss Harmon at home this evening,' Jessup said. 'I have to go to Paris for two days, but I'll get her to send it over to the Yard first thing tomorrow.'

Glancing at Madden, he saw that his face had settled into a heavy frown.

'But why are you so concerned about this, John?'

'It comes from something Mrs Castleton said to me when we talked,' Madden replied. 'The only thing she seemed certain of where Stanley Wing was concerned – and I would call her a good judge of men – was that he hated the people he worked with at Jessup's, the British I mean, all of you. We've tended to assume that this whole business has to do with blackmail. But that may be a mistake, or not the whole truth. There may be more to it than that.'

'What are you saying, John?' Jessup had stopped in midstride. He was peering at his companion.

'Wing has spent years in prison, more than enough time to nurse his grievances. He must know that sooner or later the triads will catch up with him. He's living on borrowed time. He did Garner a great service once, and was never repaid. This could be his way of taking revenge. The pendant, the letters to Derry and the newspapers, the implied threat to reveal the true identity of the murderer . . . they're like . . . like . . .'

'The Chinese water torture?' Jessup's smile was bleak. 'The death by a thousand cuts? I take your point.'

'Not altogether, I think.' Madden hesitated. 'I've found it hard to get a picture of the man. Just how dangerous is he?'

The question seemed to disconcert Jessup. He looked away, staring into the distance. Twice he seemed about to speak, but each time thought better of it. But at length he turned to face Madden again.

'There is something else I can tell you about Wing. I ought to have done so before, but didn't because of the feeling of loyalty I have towards my father and the memory of how he always tried to give Stanley the benefit of the doubt. I should add that I have no proof of it. Bear that in mind.'

Madden waited.

'I learned about it when I was investigating his activities – before his ties with the company were severed. I already suspected him of having triad connections, as I told you, and I hired a private inquiry agent to look into his background. He found no evidence of any link to them, which is interesting in view of what we know now. They must have kept it very quiet. But he was told a story about Stanley dating from his earlier life, when he was still on the streets, before he broke into my father's house, which certainly gave me pause. He ran with a gang of boys and one of them told this agent that Stanley had killed a man once.'

'Murdered him, you mean?' Madden's eyes widened.

'Not with forethought – at least not as the tale was recounted to this detective I employed. It wasn't premeditated. But it seems Stanley was lured into the shop of a Kowloon rug merchant, a notorious pederast, on the pretext of being offered work. The man apparently tried to rape him, but Stanley was able to stop him by stabbing him in the ribs with the knife which he carried. Fair enough, you might say. But when he realized the man was still able to cry out for help and could identify him he cut his throat.'

'How old was he then?' Madden was appalled.

'Twelve, I believe.' Jessup's tone was dry. 'You asked how dangerous Wing was, John. I think he's capable of anything.'

'What a lovely day!'

Helen waved for the last time to the group gathered in front of the house: Jessup and Adele Castleton lifted their hands in response; the two children waved back vigorously; Ted Lennox gave them a smart soldier's salute. The chauffeur had a broad grin on his face.

'I do wish Sarah had been here, though. I'd love to meet her. Adele's going to visit us sometime in September. But I'd like to have the whole family over for lunch before then.'

'You two looked as though you'd had a good talk.'

Madden smiled at her as they started off down the long elm-lined drive.

'It was wonderful. I heard her whole life story – what she told you, and more. She still misses Jack Jessup, but all things considered I think she's as happy now as she could be. She loves being a grandmother to the children.'

She glanced at Madden.

'You and Richard really get on, don't you?'

Madden nodded. 'I don't know what it is about him. But it's not charm, though he has that. It's more a sort of grace. He's one of those people unusually blessed by nature, but makes no show of it. I get the impression he'd rather give than receive. I felt it as soon as we met. It seems as though we've known each other for years, but that's thanks to him . . . to his openness. Heaven knows it's not a gift I have.'

'I should say not.' She teased him gently. 'I remember it took me ages to break through the shell.'

Laughing, he touched her hand.

'Did he tell you anything useful?' she asked.

'Rather. I got the full story on Stanley Wing: it turns out he's been a member of a triad gang for years. He's in trouble with them now, deep trouble. They mean to kill him. It seems he may be in London.'

'Oh, Lord!'

'But that wasn't all we talked about. I didn't mean to bring Rex Garner into it, but somehow the conversation turned that way and I ended up by having to tell Richard that he's a suspect; at least as far as Billy and Chubb are concerned.'

'How did he take that?'

'He wasn't happy. In fact, he was more upset than I would have imagined, given that they're not close friends any longer. I tried to explain that there wasn't a strong case against Garner, and that I wasn't altogether persuaded by the theories the police were playing with. But Richard didn't seem to be taking it in. He kept insisting that Garner couldn't possibly have murdered the girl. It wasn't in him.'

He saw Helen's questioning glance.

'But I wonder if he really believes that.'

15

'IT COULD BE HIM, couldn't it?'

Detective-Sergeant Joe Grace peered at the grainy, ill-lit photograph he was holding, which at first glance seemed to show a naked woman sitting alone on the end of a bed. On closer examination, however, the figure of a man lying under the sheets behind her with his face buried in the pillow could just be made out, and it was on this near shapeless form that the sergeant had fastened his gaze.

'The trouble is, it could be anyone.'

Grace clicked his tongue in disapproval. He glanced at Billy. The two of them were sitting in the back of a police car on their way to Rex Garner's Mayfair address. Earlier that morning, knowing that the individual they wanted to interview was due back any day, Billy had rung his number and found he had finally returned from Scotland.

'Still, at least we know who the lady is: Miss Portia Blake in the altogether – and a nice bit of crackling, too. A pity she had to go and get herself topped.' Joe sounded regretful. 'What a waste.'

The photograph, cropped to focus on the two figures – more of the room was shown in the print Grace was looking at – and with Miss Blake's breasts and lap decorously blacked out, had been splashed across the front page of the *Daily Mirror* that morning. According to the story that accompanied it, the snapshot had been received by the editor through the post together with a note, not typed this time but written in printed capitals, stating baldly that the man lying face down on the bed was in a position to reveal 'valuable information' about the young woman's murder. *I will say no more at this stage*, the brief letter had concluded ominously. Both note and photograph had been sent to Scotland Yard at Chubb's insistence.

Coming as it had on the heels of the information about Stanley Wing furnished by Sir Richard Jessup and relayed to the Yard by Madden, this latest development had spurred Chubb to summon the detectives involved to his office for a council of war.

'We've got to put a stop to this nonsense,' he had declared. 'We're being led by the nose and I won't have it. I've sent a telegram to Hong Kong asking for confirmation of what Jessup told Madden, not that I doubt it. I think Wing's here in London all right, and it's odds on he's the one behind this. I want him found, and quick. How's the photo lab doing with that picture Jessup's office sent us this morning?'

'We've got a shot of Wing's face ready to be copied and distributed.' It was Billy who replied. 'I've already put his name out and I've asked for a check on all hotels and boarding houses. But if the triads are after him it's likely he's travelling under a false name. If he is – if he's using a forged passport – that's an offence and we can detain him. Otherwise we've nothing to hold him on for the moment. We could still take his prints, though. We've managed to lift several different sets from the photo. Some of them will belong to whoever handled it at the *Mirror*, but we might find Wing's as well. If so, we can ask him what he's up to. I think we should also get in touch with the Amsterdam police. If Jessup is right about the triads possibly sending a killer from Holland, they might know something about it.'

'I'll see to that.' Chubb had made a note. 'As for the rest, this bloke Garner must be spoken to. I've already asked Hong Kong if they know anything about that woman he's supposed to have beaten up. I'm still waiting for their reply. But I want the question of his alibi cleared up. If he satisfies us on that score we can cross him off the suspects list and Mr Wing may have to work a little harder to get our attention. Find out exactly where Garner is. If he's still in Scotland, one of you will have to go up there and talk to him. I'm not prepared to wait any longer. Neither was the commissioner after he saw that photo in the *Mirror*. He sent word via Cradock this morning that we were to pull our fingers out; only he put it less politely.'

It was following this meeting that Billy had made his call and, having finally located the man they wished to question, he had delayed only long enough to give Lily Poole her orders before setting off with Joe Grace to conduct their interview with Garner.

'Portia's not the only one without any clothes on,' Grace remarked now. He was still peering at the photograph. 'There's a painting of a woman on the wall behind the bed. You can just make it out. She's lying on her back.'

'It's a print of a famous painting by some Spaniard,' Billy said. '*The Nude Someone-or-Other*. Lil told me she'd seen a reproduction of it in a book. Maybe it was put there to lend a little atmosphere to the place. It looks to me like a tart's bedroom.'

'Borrowed for the occasion, you mean?' Joe was intrigued.

'That's my guess.'

'Do you reckon he's seen it?' Grace tapped the photograph with his finger. They were approaching Hyde Park Corner, only minutes away from Garner's house, which was situated in a street off Park Lane bordering on Shepherd Market.

'I shouldn't think so.' Billy grimaced. 'He drove down from Scotland and only got home late last night. Somehow I doubt he has the *Daily Mirror* delivered to his doorstep.'

'You didn't mention it when you called?'

'I think I woke him up. I just told him we wanted to speak to him. He tried to put me off, said he had an engagement this morning, but I told him it was urgent and couldn't wait.'

'Do we hit him hard?' Grace asked. 'We could just shove this under his nose and ask him if the bloke in the bed is him. If he's still half asleep we might catch him off-guard.'

Billy shook his head. 'I'm going to take him back to the day when Portia was killed. I'll tell him we're checking on everyone's movements, and that includes his alibi. Depending on how he answers, we can ask him about that girl in Hong Kong. We'll save the photograph till last.'

Billy glanced at his colleague. Lean, narrow-eyed, and with a pock-marked face that would have sat well on an axe murderer, Joe Grace was one of the Met's most experienced detectives; more to the point, he could also be one of the most disagreeable when it came to dealing with anyone he regarded as a less than truthful witness, which Rex Garner might well prove to be, Billy thought, having already had a sharp exchange with the fellow on the phone a little earlier; especially if it turned out that he had lied about his alibi.

'Let me say at once that I resent this intrusion, Inspector. You've no right to barge in here with hardly a by-your-leave and start firing questions at me for no good reason. I intend to have a word with your superiors. I warn you now I'm not without friends in high places.'

If Rex Garner was trying to present a threatening front,

he was making a poor job of it, Billy thought. Still in his pyjamas and wearing a silk dressing-gown and felt slippers, he looked like a man who had just been dragged from his bed to answer the doorbell; and given that he had probably gone back to sleep after being woken by the call he'd received earlier that might well be the case. His lank dark hair was uncombed and, although he had the kind of good looks that the newspapers liked to compare with a matinee idol's, his bloodshot eyes were bleary and his cheeks unshaven. Nor had he improved the impression he was making on the two detectives when, having led the way into his drawing room, he had poured himself a whisky and then sat down heavily in an armchair. Joe Grace had glanced ostentatiously at his watch. It was barely eleven o'clock.

'I know that the investigation into the murder of Miss Blake is being reviewed. I saw something about it in a newspaper up in Scotland. But I can't imagine why.'

His face set in a belligerent expression, Garner swallowed a mouthful of neat whisky. His gaze moved restlessly about the room, which was large and airy with tall sash windows giving out onto the street, and a ceiling higher than most, which afforded space for a handsome wooden staircase at the back of the room leading up to a gallery lined with books. Despite its elegant appearance, however, there were abundant signs of neglect all about them. Magazines and old newspapers lay strewn around along with ashtrays that must have remained uncleared for weeks, given that Garner had only returned the night before. A thin patina of dust dulled the polished surface of a sun-bathed table near the window.

'There's certainly nothing I can tell you. I was nowhere near Foxley Hall when the girl was murdered. As I told the police at the time, I was in Canterbury for most of that day.'

'Lunching with a friend?' Billy asked. Yet to be invited to

sit down, he and Grace had settled for standing side by side in front of Garner, only a step or two away from him.

'Precisely.'

'Could you give us his name, please?'

'His *name*?' Garner flushed. 'Of course I can give you his name. But I don't see why I should. I was interviewed by the police years ago and they were perfectly satisfied with the answers I gave them then.'

'His name, if you don't mind, sir.' Billy held the other's gaze.

'I do bloody mind. His name was Peter Carrick.'

'And he can confirm that you had lunch together that day?'

'I rather doubt it. Poor old Peter didn't survive the war. His plane was shot down over Germany. He was a bomber pilot.'

Garner's lips twitched in a near smile. He seemed to feel he had scored a point.

'What was he doing down in Kent that weekend?'

The blood returned in a rush to Garner's cheeks.

'How is it you two came to meet for lunch in Canterbury on a Sunday? Is that where he lived?'

'My God, you've got a nerve! Are you accusing me of lying?'

The man seemed intent on working himself up into a fury, but Billy wasn't impressed – and neither, he saw out of the corner of his eye, was Joe Grace. The sergeant's thin lips were drawn back over his teeth. The effect was wolf-like.

'No, I'm simply asking you questions, Mr Garner, the same questions that everyone who was staying at Sir Jack Jessup's house that weekend will be required to answer. We need to trace people's movements that Sunday afternoon.

This is normal police procedure. If Carrick wasn't one of Sir Jack Jessup's house guests, what was he doing down there?'

'His people have a place nearby.' Garner was breathing heavily. 'He was spending the weekend with them and we agreed to meet in Canterbury. I rang Mrs Castleton to tell her I wouldn't be back for lunch. If she hasn't confirmed that yet, I'm sure she will.'

'Thank you.'

Billy took out his pad and made a note in it. Garner watched him with narrowed eyes.

'Will that be all?' he asked.

'Not quite.' Billy put his pad away. 'I've got a more general question for you now. How well did you know Miss Blake?'

'How *well* . . . ?' Like a cartoon character, Garner's face seemed to inflate with renewed rage. 'I barely knew the woman: that's to say I had run into her once or twice during the summer. She was always with that Chinaman, or whatever he is.'

'You're referring to Mr Stanley Wing?'

'You know bloody well I am.'

'With whom you were also acquainted?'

'What of it?'

'Has he been in touch with you recently?'

'The man's in prison, for Christ's sake. Don't you even know that?'

'Are you sure you've had no communication with him?'

'Quite sure.' Garner mopped his sweating brow with the sleeve of his dressing-gown.

Billy took out his pad again and made a further note.

'We've been given an account of the dinner that took place on the evening before Miss Blake was murdered. Can you explain why she behaved in the way she did?'

'Of course I can't bloody *explain*.' The bloodshot eyes bulged. 'She was putting on some kind of act; don't ask me why.'

'An act that was directed at you, it seems. Or so we've been told. According to one account, she appeared to be trying to embarrass you. Would you agree?'

'I don't know what she was doing. And no, I wasn't embarrassed, I was just annoyed. I didn't know what had got into her.'

'Was that why you decided to absent yourself from lunch the next day? Was it because you didn't want to have to sit through the same performance again?'

Garner glared at them, but said nothing.

'Turning to another matter now . . .' Billy consulted his notepad. 'Could you tell us about the incident that took place in Hong Kong some years earlier – it was well before the war – involving you and a Chinese girl? Apparently you assaulted her – so badly that the affair had to be hushed up and you were sent home at once.'

Garner swallowed. He had turned pale.

'We'd like to hear your account of that incident. Also, could you tell us what happened to the girl? Did she recover from the attack?'

'Of all the damned nerve . . . !' Garner found his tongue. But the sudden look of panic Billy saw in his eyes spoke louder than words. 'I want you both out of here. *Now!*'

Billy ignored the outburst.

'And there's one final matter we need to raise with you. Did you see today's *Daily Mirror*? No? It carried a photograph on the front page.'

He nodded to Grace, who produced the snapshot with a flourish and thrust it in front of the seated man's face.

'Recognize anyone?' The sergeant bared his teeth in earnest.

Garner's jaw dropped. Unable to disguise his astonishment he stared transfixed at the photograph.

'That's your friend, Miss Blake, sitting there.' Grace's grin suggested he was enjoying himself. 'But who's the bloke in the bed behind her? That's what we want to know. Any ideas?'

Seemingly struck dumb, Garner's eyes remained fixed on the glossy print. Twice he opened his mouth as though to speak, but each time he closed it without uttering a word. Finally he tore his gaze from the photograph. The two detectives watched as he fumbled for the whisky bottle beside him. He filled his glass with a shaking hand.

'I refuse to answer any more questions.' He sat blinking. His gaze had lost focus. It seemed his thoughts were elsewhere.

Billy cocked his head on one side. He wasn't sure what to make of the man's reaction. He studied the slumped figure in front of him.

'Do you know that room?' he asked.

'What . . . ?' Garner awoke from his reverie. 'No!' He half shouted the word.

'Are you sure you don't recognize it . . . that painting on the wall behind the bed? You can tell us if you were ever there with Miss Blake. You can admit it. It doesn't mean you killed her. We know she had a lot of men friends.'

Swallowing the last of his whisky, Garner grasped the arms of his chair. He rose unsteadily to his feet, forcing them to shuffle backwards.

'I've already told you: I won't answer any more questions.' He stood swaying before them. 'I want you to leave.'

'Fine. But I ought to explain something first. We've been

looking at this case again, going through all the statements, reviewing the evidence. And if we were wrong first time round, if Miss Blake's killer got away with it, then I have to tell you that the facts we're collecting now seem to point to you as a possible suspect. Unless you're willing to answer our questions honestly, unless you're prepared to clear the air, then the next time we question you it will be under caution, and if you refuse to answer you may find yourself facing charges of obstructing the police and perverting the course of justice. Do you understand?'

'Perfectly.'

Garner pointed a quivering finger at the door.

'Now get out.'

'He was scared . . . pissing himself.' Joe Grace snorted, then drew on his cigarette. 'I reckon he was lying, too. He'd been in that room. I'd stake my life on it. The way he stared at the photo . . .'

'He certainly looked stunned,' Billy agreed. He tugged at an earlobe. 'Maybe he realized for the first time what sort of trap he'd walked into back then. But we still can't be sure it was him in the bed, not without more evidence. Mind you, there must be other photos. Whoever's behind this is dragging it out.'

They were standing on the pavement outside Garner's house. Their car with its driver stood waiting, but Billy had paused to mull over the interview they had just conducted.

'My money's on Wing.' Joe nodded. 'He set this up: the room, the snapper. But Portia was in on it too . . . sitting there at the end of the bed, looking so innocent.'

'It seems they were working together,' Billy agreed. 'But what happened to the photographs after she was killed, that's what I want to know? Where have they been all these years? And why has this one suddenly appeared now?'

'Maybe Wing has had them all this time. He went into her room right after she was killed, didn't he? He must have been looking for something. But the war came, and then he went to prison. This may be the first chance he's had to use them.'

'Maybe . . .' Billy gnawed at his lip. 'But I'm still finding it hard to put all this together. It's like Mr Madden says: there are gaps . . . things that need explaining.'

'But it still looks like blackmail.' Grace tossed his cigarette into the gutter. 'And that means Garner's still in the frame. But why was he so bothered? He must know we haven't got the evidence to pin Portia's murder on him. Then again, it was mention of that Chinese girl that really got him going. You scared him. Topping young women who get out of line could be a nasty little habit of his, one that's coming home to roost.'

Billy shrugged. 'As far as that's concerned we'll have to wait to hear from Hong Kong.' He glanced at his watch. 'The person we really need to talk to is Stanley Wing. Let's get back to the Yard and see if Lil has come up with anything. We have to find him before the triads do.'

16

LILY TAPPED ON the door and stuck her head in.

'Excuse me, guv. Can I have a word?'

Lofty Cook looked up from his desk, scowling. When he saw who it was at the door, however, his face cleared.

'Hello, Lil.' He beamed. 'What are you doing up here? Haven't you got enough to keep you busy at the Yard? Don't just stand there looking bashful. Come on in.'

All of six feet and then some, he rose from his chair and reached across the desk to shake her hand.

'Take a pew.'

A chief inspector stationed now at West End Central, Lofty had been a DI at Bow Street, Lily's old stamping ground, when she had first known him, and one of the few officers – she could count them on one hand – who had never held her sex against her. It was he who had paved the way for her move from the uniform branch to the CID, recommending her to Billy Styles when they had worked together on a murder case during the war. Styles in turn had brought her to the attention of Angus Sinclair, who had made it his business before resigning to see her transferred to the Yard's plain-clothes division. Given the task of tracking down Stanley Wing and finding out what she could about any triad presence in London, Lily had decided that Soho was as good a place as any to start. And knowing that the area was now on Cook's patch, she had made the short journey from the Embankment up to Savile Row to pick her old guv'nor's brains.

'You could do worse,' Lofty said, having heard her out. Lily had given him a quick summary of the case and shown him the photograph of Wing that she had in her handbag. 'Though there's been no real Chinatown in London since the war; not since the Blitz. They used to congregate in Limehouse, as you know, but the bombing put an end to that. The community was scattered. Now they're starting to gather again, and Soho is one of the areas where you'll find new Chinese restaurants popping up. If there are any triad visitors in town, word will have spread. You might pick up a whisper there.'

He grinned then. It was as if he knew what she was going to say next.

'You wouldn't have a good snout, would you, guv?'

'A Chink snout? You'd be lucky to find one you could even converse with.' His grin widened. 'Usually it's a case of no spikee English.'

He watched as her face fell.

'I'm just pulling your leg, Lil, though it's not that far from the truth. They don't have much to do with us. They're a close-knit lot and they tend to sort out their own problems. As it happens, I do know someone who might be of help. But it'll be up to her whether she's willing to talk to you or not. And you've got to promise to keep schtum: no passing her name around among those layabouts at the Yard.'

'Word of honour, guv.' Lily grinned.

'I won't come with you.' Lofty hoisted himself to his feet. 'I don't meet her in Soho. They know my face there. But I'll go with you part of the way. I fancy a cuppa.'

*

'She's got a shop off Gerrard Street. She sells silk scarves and trinkets, lacquer-work, that sort of stuff. Anna Wu is the name she goes by. She anglicized it when she came here from Hong Kong. That was before the war.'

Lofty poured some of his tea into a saucer, blew on it, returned the tea to his cup and took a sip. He had led Lily to a cafe near the police station. They were sitting at a table by the counter.

'She's not your run-of-the-mill snout, as you'll see; she's got a mind of her own. But she hates the triads. Her father was a gang member – a low-ranking figure in one of the families. He was killed in a street fight in Hong Kong twenty years ago. She's known to them, of course, and triad couriers use her shop now and then as a meeting place. There's nothing she can do about that, and I turn a blind eye to it. She's too valuable to me.'

'Are they here in numbers, then?' Lily asked. Cook shook his head.

'Not yet. But I reckon they will be. Extortion's one of their dodges. The Chinese restaurants here will soon find themselves paying protection money once a triad branch is established. But drugs are their main business. We can see it coming, but there's not much we can do about it for the present.'

'Does the term Red Pole mean anything to you?' Lily sipped her tea.

Lofty shook his head. 'Should it?'

'That's what they call an enforcer – a killer, if you like. Or so we've been told.'

'And you're wondering if one of them has been sent here from Holland to do this bloke Wing?'

Lily nodded.

'Well, if so, Anna might have heard something about it –

a whisper, as I say. But don't try to push her too hard, Lil. She won't take it.'

Cook was serious now.

'She walks a fine line, and I don't want her put in danger.'

'I understand.'

'And I doubt she'll be able to tell you anything about Wing.'

'Why's that?'

'Because if I was him, Soho is the last place I'd show my face. Once word gets out that the triads are looking for him there'll be any number of people hereabouts ready to shop him. They may not like these thugs, but they know better than to cross them. If I was Wing I'd stay well away from the city centre. I'd stick to the outer suburbs.'

Lofty rose to his feet. Lily followed suit.

'And I'd keep on the move, too.'

The shop, Happy Thoughts, was next to a restaurant named the Jasmine Inn which, like others of its kind nearby, had a row of ducks' carcasses hanging in the window.

'You could do worse than have a bite there afterwards if you feel peckish,' Lofty had told Lily when he'd given her directions. 'I've been getting a taste for Chinese grub since I moved over here from Bow Street.'

As she opened the door a bell tinkled and a woman dressed in a long gown made of black silk decorated with silver flowers and butterflies appeared from behind a curtain at the back of the store. Small in size, her golden cheeks were smooth and Lily could see no hint of a wrinkle around the dark brown eyes that regarded her without expression. According to Lofty, Anna Wu was in her early forties.

'Yes, Miss . . . ?'

Lofty had prepared her in advance for the encounter. He had given her the magic words, as he'd put it, and Lily saw no reason not to plunge right in.

'Your shop was recommended by a friend of mine,' she said. 'He bought a silk scarf from you not long ago.'

'A red scarf?' The yellow face remained blank.

'No, a blue one.'

A crease appeared in the smooth forehead. 'You no detective.' It was an accusation.

'Yes, I am.' Lily had her warrant card ready. She slid it across the glass-topped counter. Miss Wu studied it.

'Who send you here?'

'Mr Cook. He said you might be able to help me.'

'Why he no come?'

'This isn't his case. And he said you two never meet in Soho.'

'Ah . . .' Miss Wu seemed to find these last words reassuring. She glanced at her wristwatch. 'Closing time.'

She came around the counter and went to the glassed door where a sign reading CLOSED hung from a hook. Reversing it so that it faced outwards, she locked the door.

'Come . . .'

She led the way past the curtain at the back of the shop. Lily followed, and found herself in a small storeroom lined with boxes. A brass lamp suspended from the ceiling gave off a faint smell of incense. In the centre of the room were two chairs on either side of a lacquered table. Miss Wu gestured to her to take one. She sat down facing her.

'Why you detective?' She looked hard at Lily, frowning. 'Why you not home?'

'Home . . . ?'

'Young woman stay home, take care of husband.'

'I haven't got one,' Lily said. 'I'm not married.'

'Why not?' Miss Wu's frown had grown fierce.

'I don't know.' Lily scratched her head. 'Maybe because no one's asked me.'

The flicker of a smile crossed Miss Wu's solemn face. 'I have husband. He no good. I throw him out.' The smile vanished. 'Why you detective?'

She seemed determined to find out. Lily shrugged.

'I joined the police when I was eighteen. I always wanted to be a copper. I don't know why.'

'You catch bad men?'

'Sometimes.'

'Good . . . too many bad men.'

Miss Wu studied her hands, first the palms, then the backs. Lily felt she was being weighed in some balance and she waited for the verdict to be delivered. Finally the other woman looked up.

'So . . . ?'

'We're trying to find a man called Stanley Wing. He's from Hong Kong and we think he may be hiding out in London.'

'Why hiding?'

'One of the triad gangs is looking for him.'

'Ah . . .' Miss Wu's glance sharpened. 'Which family?'

'The Tang . . . ?' Lily wasn't sure she'd remembered it correctly, but her questioner showed no surprise on hearing the name. She merely nodded.

'Man's name is Wing, you say . . . Stanley Wing?'

Lily nodded.

'Stanley Wing not Chinese name.'

'He's half Chinese, half English.'

Miss Wu looked thoughtful.

'Someone came to my shop last week,' she said. 'He also

looking for man, but not Wing: man called Lee. This also not Chinese name.'

'Did you know him, the man who came to your shop?'

Miss Wu shook her head. 'He tell me his name is Chen Yi.'

'Was he from Hong Kong?'

Miss Wu shrugged. It appeared that she didn't know.

'Or perhaps from Amsterdam?'

Miss Wu cocked her head on one side. For the first time she looked at Lily with respect.

'Is good guess . . . yes, maybe . . . Amsterdam. Very smooth young man. He show me photograph.'

Lily dug into her handbag and took out the snapshot of Wing she'd brought with her. She handed it to Miss Wu, who nodded after only the briefest glance at it.

'Is same man. Chen Yi say he has scar on his neck now.' She put a hand to her throat. 'I tell him I don't know this man.'

Lily retrieved the photo and put it back in her bag. She was thinking.

'Chen Yi – could he be what they call a Red Pole?'

Miss Wu's eyebrows shot up. She said something in Chinese.

'Where you hear about Red Pole?'

'From someone who knows Wing's background: someone who has been in touch with the Hong Kong police. He said this triad family might send a man to London to kill Wing: a Red Pole.'

Miss Wu brooded in silence.

'Chen Yi not Red Pole.' She sounded positive. 'He man who asks questions.'

'You mean he works for the Red Pole?' Lily wanted to be

clear about this. 'Would *he* be in London too?' They had to know.

'Must be.' Miss Wu shrugged again. 'But you not find him. He waits . . .'

'Until Wing has been located?'

Miss Wu dipped her head in silent acknowledgement.

'And then?'

'You *sure* is Tang family that look for Wing?'

Lily nodded.

'Then they chop head off.' Miss Wu brought the edge of her hand down sharply on the table, making Lily jump. 'Like that. Is Tang way.'

17

'Is THAT IT? Have you got it?'

Chubb grabbed the snapshot Billy was holding out to him.

'Does it tell us anything more?'

The chief super peered at the new photograph.

'Garr . . . !' A growl of disgust issued from his lips. He slapped the print down on his desk where a copy of the *Daily Mirror*, displaying the same picture on its front page, but in cropped form, lay on the blotter. Like the previous one it featured the naked image of Portia Blake, this time seen from behind, but with her buttocks modestly veiled by the now familiar black rectangle, standing beside the bed on which a man was sitting. Bare from the waist up, he was on the other side of the nude woman and leaning forward so that his head was hidden by her body. The picture, which had appeared in that morning's edition, had been sent to the editor through the post as before, but this time without any accompanying note. It had been forwarded at once to the Yard.

Chubb read out the banner headline: '*MYSTERY DEEP-ENS*. They're getting their money's worth, aren't they? The editor must be cock-a-hoop. The commissioner hasn't seen it yet, but Cradock has.' He glared at Billy. 'What's he on about, this bloke? Is he just winding us up?'

'Not us, sir. We're coincidental. It looks to me like he's holding a sword over someone else's head: he's telling him he's got more pictures.'

'Coincidental . . .'

The chief super fumed in silence. Billy coughed.

'We're still working on Garner's alibi. Grace has tracked down the parents of that man Carrick who was killed in the war, the one Garner said he had lunch with in Canterbury, but unfortunately they seem to be away. Apparently they have a house in the South of France. Grace is trying to get hold of the phone number there.'

'Do you seriously believe either one of them will remember what their son was doing that day? It was more than ten years ago.'

Billy could only shrug.

'What about this so-called Red Pole? Do we know that he's in London?'

'We can't be certain, sir, but it's likely. We know that Wing's using the name Lee and that a young Chinese bloke called Chen Yi is looking for him. It's odds on he's working for the Red Pole.'

'Damn silly name.' Chubb glowered.

'I'd be a lot happier if we knew his real one.' Billy grinned. 'Have you had any word back from the Amsterdam police on that?'

Chubb shook his head. 'Only that they're looking into it for us.'

'How about Hong Kong?'

'The same. It's been several days since I sent them a telegram asking about that girl Garner is supposed to have beaten up. My guess is they haven't found anything in their records, which makes me think it wasn't reported at the time.'

'So perhaps only Wing knows what happened to her.' Billy rubbed his chin thoughtfully. 'That could put him in a strong position vis-à-vis Garner.'

Chubb hoisted himself to his feet.

'I'd better go and talk to Cradock. There'll be hell to pay when the commissioner sees today's *Mirror*, and we'd better be prepared. They'll both want to know what we're doing about Garner. Have you spoken to him again?'

Billy shook his head. 'But he knows we'll be back. I told him so. I thought I'd give him a day or so to stew and then call on him again. By then I hope we'll have managed to check his alibi. He's got a meeting fixed with Sir Richard Jessup tomorrow evening.'

'Has he now?' Chubb's eyes lit up.

'I spoke to Mr Madden yesterday. He's up in town again. He'd had a call from Jessup just before he went off to Paris yesterday. Jessup said Garner had rung him and asked if they could meet. He said he wanted to see him urgently. They're having dinner at Jessup's club tomorrow night after he gets back. He told Mr Madden that Garner sounded "agitated".'

'Agitated . . .' The chief super rubbed his hands. 'That's more like it.' He picked up the photograph and newspaper from his desk and tucked them under his arm. Then he cocked an eye at Billy. 'What do you think? Will he crack?'

'He might.' Billy himself had been weighing the same possibility in his mind. 'But it all depends on his alibi. And, like you say, will anyone remember that far back?'

As Billy entered his office he heard a phone being slammed down, followed by a muttered curse. Joe Grace was sitting at the desk across from his, glaring at the instrument.

'What's up?'

'Carrick's parents aren't at their house in France. They were until a few days ago. Now they're driving back to

England. But they're stopping off in Paris and nobody knows what hotel they're staying at.'

'Nobody . . . ?'

'I got hold of the hall porter at the block of flats where they live. They rang him from France a week ago telling him not to forward any more post to them and that they'd be back this week. But they didn't say when. He gave me the name of their daughter, a Mrs Hill. She lives in London.'

'And . . . ?'

'Do you know how many Hills there are in the phone book?'

'No, and I don't want to. Keep trying, Joe.'

Billy himself had a call to make, and as soon as he'd sat down at his desk he dialled the number. The phone rang for some time and he was on the point of hanging up when Madden answered.

'Sorry for the delay, Billy,' he said, after they'd exchanged greetings. 'Alice is moving out today and it's proving to be a wrench. She's lived in this house for thirty years, poor old dear. At this moment she's having a quiet cry in the kitchen. I wish Lucy were here. She'd be better at this than I am.'

'If it's a bad time, sir . . .'

'No, it's not that. But if I have to break off suddenly it'll mean the taxi is here. I'm going to take Alice down to Water-loo and put her on a train for Hastings. It's the least I can do. Tell me – is it something to do with Garner?'

Madden already knew about the meeting Billy and Grace had had with the man the day before. But he was unaware of what Lily Poole had learned in Soho and Billy quickly brought him up to date.

'It sounds as though Sir Richard was right,' he said. 'The triads have got someone here already looking for Wing.'

'And meanwhile the executioner's waiting offstage . . .' Madden hummed thoughtfully to himself.

'We're still in the dark about Garner's alibi. We might hear something later today, but either way I'm going to talk to him again. He's hiding something. Grace and I both felt he wasn't being honest with us.' Billy paused. 'I'd like to be a fly on the wall when he meets Jessup. Why do you think he wants to see him, sir?'

'Probably to ask his advice. Sir Richard's not looking forward to the encounter.'

There was silence between them. Looking across the room at Joe Grace, Billy realized that he, too, had not spoken for some time. The sergeant was sitting with the telephone pressed to his ear. He was writing busily in his notepad.

'What will he do if Garner confesses to the murder and asks for his help?'

'He'll tell him to go to the police.' Madden's response was unhesitating. 'He'll advise him to make a clean breast of it.'

'But what if Garner doesn't take his advice? Will he shop him?'

Madden sighed. 'I can't answer that question, Billy. Only Jessup can. But I don't believe he'd protect him: not if he knew he was a murderer.'

He hesitated.

'Look, he said he'd call me after their meeting tomorrow evening, Jessup, that is. Why don't you come up here and have supper with us? We can wait to hear from him.'

'I don't want to put you to any trouble—' Billy began, but was quickly cut off.

'You won't. We've still got several tins of Aunt Maud's illicit hoard to finish off, and Lucy would love to see you. She'll be here. Why not bring Lily Poole with you, too. Angus is always asking me for news of her.'

'Well, if you're sure, sir.' Billy beamed. 'It'll be a pleasure. Elsie and the kids are still away. But I expect you guessed that.'

As he hung up he caught Grace's eye. The sergeant brandished a clenched fist.

'Yes, Mrs Hill.' He spoke for the first time in a while. 'That's very helpful. And you're sure of that, are you – the dates, I mean?'

He listened in silence.

'Yes, I quite understand. There couldn't be any mistake. We may need a statement from you later. I'll be in touch about that. And thank you again.'

He put down the phone.

'Wouldn't you know it?' Joe's smile was triumphant. 'Alibi, my eye! Garner was lying in his teeth.'

'How could he think he'd ever get away with it?' Chubb shook his head in wonder.

'Well, he did first time around.' Billy settled himself in his chair. He and Grace had hurried down to the chief super's office to give him the news. 'No one was interested in his alibi once Norris was arrested, and especially not after he confessed. Garner had already told Mrs Castleton earlier in the day that he was lunching with a friend in Canterbury and he stuck to the story when the police interviewed him. He was up in Scotland when he learned that the case was being reviewed. He had time to think of who he could name and came up with what he probably thought was the brilliant idea of choosing someone who was dead. I got the impression he wasn't very bright.'

Chubb turned to Grace. 'How could this Mrs Hill be so sure after all this time? Tell me exactly what she said.'

'The whole family was down in France, including Peter Carrick,' Grace replied. 'They've got a house near Nice. They didn't hear anything the Sunday Portia Blake was killed, naturally. But the next day she and her brother went into Nice where they bought the continental edition of the *Daily Mail*. The story was front-page news and since they knew Jack Jessup well – their house in Kent wasn't far from his – they read every line of it. Not only that: Peter Carrick actually knew that Garner was staying there. They'd had lunch together in London shortly before Carrick went off to France and he told his sister he remembered Garner telling him he was going down to Kent that weekend. Carrick was in France the day Portia was killed – there's no doubt of it – and Mrs Hill is prepared to make a statement to that effect.'

'So Garner's put himself right in it.' Chubb still couldn't credit what he'd heard. 'He's practically handed us his head on a platter.'

'We still need more evidence,' Billy responded cautiously. 'But if his face appears in one of these photographs it's going to put him into a near impossible position. He's always denied that there was anything between him and Portia. Wing's the key to this, though. He may be the only person who can prove that Garner was the killer. But will he do that? If it's money he wants, he'll keep us in suspense, at least until Garner coughs up. But if it's revenge he's after, which Mr Madden thinks is possible, he could deliver him into our hands. And if Garner knows that, he might decide to act first and confess. It would look better for him if he did. He could claim he acted in the heat of the moment and killed her by accident.'

Chubb pondered in silence.

'Now that we know his alibi is false, you could arrest him and question him under caution.'

'I know, sir, and I mean to if he sticks to his lies. But it might be wise to let him have this meeting with Sir Richard first. Mr Madden thinks Jessup will press him to come clean about whatever it is he's hiding, and he may have more influence on him than anyone else. It only means waiting another day. We can afford to do that. Meanwhile, we can keep looking for both Wing and this Red Pole bloke and tie up any other loose ends.'

'Loose ends?' the chief super growled. 'I don't want any of those left hanging, not again. What have you got in mind?'

'If you remember, Mr Madden thought that actress Portia shared a flat with, Audrey Cooper, hadn't been entirely frank with him. He had the feeling she was keeping something back. I'm going over to Chelsea with Poole this afternoon to question her again.'

18

BILLY GLANCED AT his watch.

'How did she sound when you rang her?'

'She didn't seem surprised, guv.'

Lily wound down the window. The two of them were sitting in the back of a radio car that must have been standing in the sun all morning. It felt like an oven. The busy traffic in the King's Road had slowed their progress to a crawl.

'In fact, she said she'd been wondering when we'd get around to her.'

'According to Mr Madden she's got a sharp tongue. He didn't care for her. Isn't this the end of the King's Road?' Billy had leaned forward to speak to their driver. 'Are you sure we haven't gone too far, Carter?'

'No, sir, it's next on the right . . . Langton Street.'

Slowing the car as he spoke, he turned across the oncoming traffic, and then braked.

'Crikey! What's going on here?'

The narrow street in front of them was blocked by a small crowd which even as they watched was being added to by people spilling out of doorways on either side of the road. They were gathering around a spot where a blue-clad figure could be seen lying stretched out on the road surface.

'Jesus!' Billy grabbed for the door handle. 'He's one of ours.'

Lily already had the door on her side open. Springing out

of the car, she raced down the street and forced a way through the crowd.

'Stand back . . . police . . . !'

The constable was lying on his back. A young man, his eyes were wide and staring and as Lily went down on her knees beside him she saw his mouth open and close as though he were trying to speak. A man wearing a postman's uniform and cap was kneeling on the other side of the prone body. He was trying to get the buttons of the officer's jacket undone. A stain darker than the blue material surrounding it showed beneath the ribcage.

'I think he's been stabbed.' The postman was out of breath. 'I saw it happen. I was just behind him.'

'Has anyone sent for an ambulance?'

Billy barked out the question. He had arrived on Lily's heels and was crouching down beside her. Lily had taken over the task of undoing the injured man's buttons. When she pulled his blue jacket open they saw the spreading red stain on his white shirt.

'Not as far as I know.' The postman panted his reply.

'Carter . . . !' Billy shouted over his shoulder to their driver. 'Call for an ambulance . . . on the double. And tell dispatch we've got a PC down injured here and we need some officers on the scene.'

Lily was searching through her pockets and her handbag.

'I need a cloth or a scarf . . . anything.'

She called out to the crowd. After a moment a handkerchief was thrust into her hands, then another. Folding them into a pad, she tugged the bloodstained shirt open and pressed the makeshift dressing against the narrow wound oozing blood which she could see in the young man's stomach.

'Anyone here had first-aid training?'

Billy shouted the question, and a voice answered.

'Yes. Me.'

The crowd parted and a woman appeared, elbowing her way forward. Middle-aged and stocky, she wore a confident look.

'I drove an ambulance during the Blitz,' she announced. 'I know what to do.'

Kneeling down beside Lily, she took hold of the make-shift pad from her, keeping it pressed firmly to the wound. 'Edie . . .' she yelled over her shoulder and a young voice answered. 'Run into the house and fetch me two clean hand towels from the linen cupboard; fast as you can.'

Billy rose to his feet. The postman followed suit. His leather satchel had been resting on the ground beside him and he hoisted it on to his shoulder.

'What did you see?' Billy asked him. 'How did it happen?'

'I was walking down from the King's Road a few paces behind this officer when we heard a scream.'

His words brought an answering murmur from the crowd. A voice called out: 'That's right. We all heard it.'

'The officer stopped. He wasn't sure where it had come from; neither was I. Then that door there opened' – he pointed to a nearby house – 'and a man came running out. The constable shouted to him to stop, but the bloke tried to run past him and when the officer grabbed him he hit him in the stomach. At least, that's what it looked like.' The post-man winced. 'But your chap went down at once clutching his gut and the other fellow ran off that way.' He pointed in the opposite direction to the King's Road. 'I don't know what happened to him after that. I saw your man was hurt and I thought I'd better stay and help him.'

'Can you describe the man who stabbed him?'

The postman shook his head. 'I didn't really get a look at

his face. It all happened so quickly. Dark hair – that's all I saw.'

Billy bent down.

'Can he talk?' he asked Lily.

'I wouldn't advise it.' It was the woman tending to the injured man who answered. 'He's in shock. Best to leave him quiet for the moment.'

Billy beckoned to his driver, who was standing by the police car. He came running.

'I got through to dispatch, guv. There's an ambulance on its way. And they're sending more officers. There should be a Flying Squad car here any moment.'

'We're going into that house. Someone in there may be hurt. Wait for the other officers to arrive. Tell them what happened. Lil . . .' He touched her on the shoulder. 'Come on.'

With a last glance at the young constable, Lily got to her feet and followed Billy along the pavement towards the house the postman had indicated. She stopped when the saw the number on the door.

'Guv, look.'

Billy followed the direction of her pointing finger.

'Number 8. This is where she lives: Audrey Cooper. Her flat's on the first floor.'

'Christ!'

Billy was up the steps and through the door, which had been left standing open, in a flash. Lily stayed on his heels. A narrow hallway, empty apart from a bicycle leaning against the wall, led to a flight of stairs. When they reached the first landing they found yet another door standing ajar. Billy stuck his head in.

'Anyone home?' he called out.

There was no reply.

He led the way inside and the two detectives found themselves in an untidy sitting room, carelessly furnished, and with the chairs and settees, most of them showing signs of age, strewn with discarded items of women's clothing. When Lily half stumbled on something and looked down she saw it was a pile of what looked like play scripts. The air was sour with the smell of stale cigarette smoke.

Spotting a door open at the back of the room, Billy hastened to it.

'Miss Cooper . . . ?' He called out her name. When there was no reply, he disappeared through the doorway.

Lily went to the other side of the room where there was a large picture window overlooking the street. A big purple sofa, splitting at the seams and stained with wear, stood away from the wall. Nearby was a small writing-desk. Its drawers had been pulled out; one of them was lying on the threadbare carpet at her feet. As she bent down to pick it up her eye was caught by the sight of a broken vase and some strewn flowers on the floor near the wall. She also spotted something else protruding from behind the sofa.

It took a moment before she realized what she was looking at: it was a bare foot encased in a slipper.

'Guv . . . !' she yelled out. 'In here . . . !'

Billy was back in seconds. He found Lily down on her knees and peering behind the sofa.

'What is it?'

'Miss Cooper, I reckon.' She glanced up at him. 'And there's blood, too . . . lots of it.'

Lily felt a tap on her shoulder. She looked up. A burly PC was standing there holding out a cup of tea. She took it from him with a nod of thanks.

'Drink this.' She offered it to the young woman sitting beside her on the bed. 'You'll feel better.'

The girl showed no sign of having heard. She sat with her blonde head bowed and her arms hugging her chest, sobbing quietly.

'Who'd do a thing like that . . . ?'

Lily barely caught the muttered words.

'Come on, Pixie.' She spoke more sharply this time. 'You can't go on like this. I need to ask you some questions. Have a sip of this tea.'

The girl sniffed. She accepted the cup and saucer offered her, but made no move to drink from it, and after a moment Lily took it back and put it down on the bedside table. Pixie du Pre was the name the young woman had given her, and only after being pressed by Lily had she admitted that she had adopted it for the stage and that her real name was Gladys Wainwright. Escorted upstairs by a bobby posted in the street outside, she had entered the flat almost unnoticed. The forensic squad and fingerprint crew summoned from the Yard had been hard at work for half an hour. They had moved the sofa further away from the wall, giving the pathologist, also called to the scene, room to examine the body, which was stretched out on the floor. The carpet had absorbed a lot of the blood, but there was still a large pool of it standing untouched on the bare boards where the actress's head lay. Pixie's shriek, uttered as she took in the scene from the doorway, had made everyone jump.

Seemingly unable to speak, she had screamed in hysterics for several seconds until Lily had taken hold of her shoulders and shaken her, and when that proved ineffective slapped her on the cheek. Quietened finally, she had allowed herself to be led through the sitting room to one of the two bedrooms at the back of the flat where she had identified herself as Audrey Cooper's flatmate and, like her, an actress. She had gone out that morning, she said, to do some shopping and after lunching with a friend near Covent Garden had taken part in an audition for a new musical. She had no idea what her flatmate's plans for the day were, but as far as she knew she had not been expecting any visitors.

'She's been so strange lately . . .'

A new note sounded in Pixie's voice, and Lily pricked up her ears. Up till then the young woman had been locked in her grief, unable to focus on what had happened. Now it seemed as though she was speaking her thoughts aloud.

'Since when?'

'Since that man came to see her.'

'What man?' Lily reacted quickly. 'What was his name?' And then, as a new thought struck her. 'Was it a Mr Madden?'

'How'd you know that?' The girl turned a teary gaze on her. Lily ignored the question.

'What happened?' she asked. 'What did Miss Cooper say about their meeting?'

'Not much.' Pixie shrugged. 'Only that he was a dark horse and that he wasn't telling her everything. But she began acting funny as soon as he left; she started searching for something, going through the drawers of her desk, talking to herself, saying "Audrey, you idiot!" when she couldn't find it. But then she remembered . . .'

'Remembered . . . ?'

'Where she'd put it. It was in the box where she kept her jewellery. And when she found it there she seemed really pleased. She said bingo!'

'Bingo . . . ?' Lily blinked. 'Yes, but what *was* it?'

'I don't know.' Pixie shook her head. 'She didn't say. She just took the box with her into the bedroom and when she came back she had her handbag with her and said she had to go out. I was going out myself and Aud said she'd walk with me to the bus stop. It's in the King's Road. But she left me there and went on and I saw her go into the chemist. Then the bus arrived and I had to get on so I didn't see where she went after that.'

The words were tumbling from her mouth now.

'But after that she started to behave differently . . .'

'How differently?'

The girl frowned. Her tears had stopped. She seemed to be concentrating now . . . trying to remember.

'You know what it's like when someone knows something you don't know and won't tell you what it is?' Pixie's wide blue eyes were fixed on Lily's face.

'I think so.'

'When they're pleased with themselves about something and can't hide it?'

Lily nodded.

'Well, she was like that. She was up to something, I could tell, but she wouldn't say what it was, and it hurt. I'd thought we were close . . .'

Tears shone afresh in the blue orbs.

'She did say one thing, though . . .'

'What was that?'

'It was after she went off one afternoon and didn't come home till late. When she did, I could see she was even more chuffed. She was like . . . like a cat that had swallowed the cream. "I've been to the far north in search of treasure, Pixie," she said. "I rather think I found it."'

'To the far north . . . ? And back the same afternoon?' Lily was baffled.

'That's how Aud talked,' Pixie explained. 'She had this

flowery way of speaking; theatrical, I suppose. She probably just took the tube somewhere.'

'And what was the treasure?'

'I asked her that, but all she said was, "I speak in metaphors."' Pixie waved her hands helplessly. 'She said the treasure would come later, and with any luck I'd be able to buy myself some fancy new clothes. "We could take a trip to New York together," she said. "Or would you rather have a week in Monte Carlo?" I didn't know what she was on about.'

The far north . . . ? Lily stared at the slumped figure beside her. Pixie's words had started a train of thought in her mind. Pieces were starting to fall into place, like bits of a jigsaw puzzle . . . jewel box . . . chemist . . . treasure. As the picture became clearer Lily pursed her lips in a silent whistle.

Was that it? Had she guessed right?

But before she could take her idea any further there was something she had to do. She touched Pixie's hand.

'You don't want to be here on your own,' she told the disconsolate girl. 'Have you got a friend you could stay with, at least for a day or two? You shouldn't be alone.'

While Pixie made a call on the bedside telephone, Lily went next door to seek Billy's approval for the arrangement she was making.

'They were more than flatmates,' she told him. 'And more than friends, too, I reckon.'

'Aye, aye . . .' Grace, listening in, had winked knowingly, but Billy had simply shrugged.

Her duty done, Lily watched as the police car drove off, and then went back up the stairs. She was ready to share her thoughts with her two male colleagues now.

She just hoped she had it right.

*

'So Miss Cooper found something in her jewel box which she thought was worth a few bob.' Billy scowled. 'But how do we know it had anything to do with Portia Blake?'

'Because she started looking for it the minute Mr Madden left. He must have said something that got her thinking. And all they talked about was Portia and that Wing bloke.'

While she waited for her guv'nor's reaction, Lily looked about her. The sitting room was starting to empty. The work of the specialist squads sent from the Yard was over. The crews were packing up their gear and preparing to leave. Still waiting to do their job, a couple of ambulance men stood by ready to load Audrey Cooper's remains onto a stretcher for transporting to the mortuary at St Mary's Hospital in Paddington where the post mortem would be carried out. Mingled with the musty smell of tobacco and old cigarette butts there was another odour, one Lily had learned to recognize: the metallic scent of blood.

'How's the PC who was stabbed?' Lily asked. She had joined Billy and Joe Grace in the corner where they stood observing the proceedings.

'Stable, according to the ambulance blokes,' Billy told her. 'That lady did a good job tending to him. We ought to send her a note of thanks. You just missed the pathologist,' he went on. 'He confirmed that Miss Cooper had her throat cut. She also had wounds on her hands, which suggest she tried to defend herself. She must have realized he was going to kill her: that could have been when she screamed. Joe and I have been trying to work out whether this was random, or if it's linked to the Portia Blake murder. You're telling us now that it must have been Wing who killed her. Why?'

'Well, for one thing, according to Sir Richard Jessup, he carried a knife in the past. And he wasn't afraid to use it. But mostly because Miss Cooper had something he wanted.'

'Which was . . . ?'

'The photographs . . . or rather the negatives . . . the ones Portia had taken of herself and the bloke in the bed, who we think could have been Garner.'

'Are you sure about that?' Billy's eyes bored into hers. 'Up till now we've been working on the assumption that it was Wing who had possession of those photos.'

'Yes, but what if we've been wrong, guv? What if Portia showed them to Garner in the wood, and when he tried to take them from her they fought and he ended up killing her in a rage? He would have destroyed the pictures, naturally, but there were still the negatives. Maybe Wing didn't find them when he went into her room later because Portia had left them behind in London as insurance. That's how they could have come into Miss Cooper's hands. She could have gone through Portia's things after she heard about the murder. There wasn't much love lost between them. She might have put them aside and forgotten about them until Mr Madden showed up that day.'

The two men stared at her. Grace's narrow features were knotted in a scowl – of disbelief perhaps. But Billy's expression was harder to read. He seemed to be at least considering the idea.

Lily took a deep breath.

'If Wing really had found the photos when he went into Portia's room, why did he go home to Hong Kong? Why didn't he put pressure on Garner right away? Strike while the iron was hot? It doesn't make sense him leaving the country, not if he had evidence pointing to the real killer.'

'What about the pendant?' Grace broke in. 'He had that all right.'

'Did he?' Lily looked at him. 'We don't *know* that it's the same one, Sarge. All we know is it looks like it. Whoever took the photographs off Portia's body must also have taken the pendant. Nothing else makes sense. But how can we know that Wing didn't go back to Hong Kong and have another one made just like it, with the same sort of flaw? Even if he witnessed the murder, even if he knew Garner was the killer, he needed to concoct some evidence before he could put pressure on him. But instead the war came and everything changed, particularly for him. Now he's in deep trouble, near the end of his rope. He's desperate. He comes back to England hoping to put his blackmail scheme into operation again, but he's got precious little to back it up with; only that pendant. He sends it to Mr Derry along with a letter, and when that gets no reaction he writes to the editor of the *News of the World*. He's trying to whip up interest in the case, but he's out of ammunition. Then a miracle occurs – at least from his point of view. That first photograph appears in the *Mirror* – and not with a typed note, by the way; this one was written by hand – and Wing knows instantly who must have sent it. It can only be Audrey Cooper. If Portia didn't have the negatives with her in Kent, she must have left them behind in London and somehow Miss Cooper had got hold of them. So he came calling . . .'

Lily paused for dramatic effect. She could see that what she was saying was finally having an effect on one of her listeners. Billy Styles was rubbing his chin; he looked thoughtful.

'Joe found that jewel box,' he said. 'It was on the floor near her body with some stuff beside it . . . a bracelet and some beads and other odds and ends. I had it dusted in case the killer left his paw prints on it. What happened to it, Joe?'

'It's on the table over there.'

Grace crossed the room and returned with the item in question.

'What I don't see is how she could have missed whatever she was looking for, how she had to go searching for it.' The sergeant's scowl was back. 'All she had to do was open the flipping lid.'

'Yes, but when we found it there was a drawer sticking out of the bottom.' Billy examined the object. 'What happened to that?'

'Search me.' Joe shrugged. 'The fingerprint lads must have shut it. I can't see how it opens.'

'May I, guv?' Lily reached for the box. 'I've seen one of these before.' She ran her fingers along the bottom rim. 'There should be something here . . . yes there it is. There's a spring or something . . .'

She pressed with her two fingers on either side of the box. A shallow drawer slid out.

Grace grunted. 'It's empty.' He frowned. 'There's nothing there.'

'But there might have been,' Lily insisted. 'If it was open when you found it, then maybe Wing took whatever was inside.'

'You couldn't hide much in there.' The sergeant was unimpressed. 'There's no room. A letter maybe . . . ?'

'Or a bunch of photos.' Silent up to now, Billy spoke up. 'But why do you think they were negatives?' He put the question to Lily. 'They could have been another set of prints.'

'That's possible,' she agreed. 'But right after Miss Cooper found what she was looking for she went out. She walked Pixie as far as the bus stop in the King's Road and then carried on down the street. Pixie saw her go into the chemist.'

She paused. The two men were looking at her.

'Well . . . ?' Grace growled.

'Well, apart from buying medicine, what else do you go to a chemist's for?' Lily was grinning.

'To get your negatives developed.' Billy supplied the answer. 'All right, Lil, you've made your point. And we can easily check it. They'll certainly remember handling a set like that. What about the "far north" then? What does that mean?'

'It's only a guess, guv . . .'

'Did you hear that?' A glint had appeared in Joe Grace's eye. 'She's guessing. She must be human after all.'

'Go on, Lil.' Billy smiled.

'Well, Pixie said Miss Cooper was exaggerating the way she always did. She reckoned she'd probably just gone somewhere on the tube – probably to north London. I was trying to think what was there – what might have interested her – and then I remembered the newspaper library at Colindale. That's right near the end of the Northern Line.'

'And what do you think she was doing there? Go on. Tell us.' It was Grace who was egging her on now.

'Again, it's only a guess, but what if she was trying to identify that bloke in the photographs. If she had all the photos, it's odds on his face must appear in some of them. But she probably didn't know who he was. Garner may fancy himself as a ladies' man, but his face isn't known to the general public – at least not to me, and probably not to her. It's possible she wanted to check the newspapers published at the time of Portia's murder. All the guests who were at Jack Jessup's house that weekend were named and most of the papers carried photographs of them. She would have seen Garner's face, and compared it with the photos she had. I'm betting she had the same idea as Wing: to put the squeeze on him for money in return for the photos. She told Pixie they were going to be flush soon. She was talking about them taking a trip to New York.'

Lily went silent. She'd said all she had to say.

Joe was still looking at her – but in unfeigned wonder now.

'Do you know what?' He turned to Billy with a wide grin. 'She's a bleeding marvel.'

19

'JUST TELL ME one thing – are we getting close? That's what I want to know. More to the point, it's what the commissioner wants to know. Are you certain that this latest murder is connected to the case you've been reviewing? It sounds to me as though there's a lot of guesswork involved. Above all, can you assure me that at least we'll be spared the sight of another photograph of Miss Portia Blake with no clothes on splashed across the front page of the *Daily Mirror*?'

Eustace Cradock fixed his two listeners with as fierce a glare as he could muster. A small man with little to mark him out – his most prominent feature was a pointed nose that had a tendency to redden in moments of stress – the assistant commissioner had appeared initially to have grown several inches since their last encounter, and it was only after Billy had stolen a glance beneath his desk and twigged that he was perched on a particularly well-stuffed cushion that morning that the mystery had been resolved.

'Yes, on both counts, sir.' Chubb offered his reply in the blandest of tones. 'We're now certain that this fellow we've been looking for, Stanley Wing – the man connected to the Blake murder – was Audrey Cooper's killer. Confirmation of that was obtained this morning. I'll let Inspector Styles explain.'

The chief super turned to Billy, who was seated beside him in front of Cradock's desk. The two of them had been summoned to appear together, and as luck would have it

Billy had received the information he was seeking only minutes before the call came.

'The Chelsea police have gone door-to-door down Langton Street, where she lived, and also along the street at the bottom of it, which is where the man who stabbed the constable ran off to,' Billy began. 'They found three people – a man and two women – who got a good look at him as he went past, and all of them agreed that he was Chinese, or at least an oriental. I sent DS Grace over there this morning with a copy of that photograph Sir Richard Jessup supplied us with, and one of the women made a positive identification. She saw the man face to face as he ran towards her and she's ready to swear it was Wing.'

'That means we can give his picture to the newspaper now along with his name. We can start a hunt for him. That would be something, at least. Do I need to keep reminding you that the commissioner wants *action*?'

Cradock glared at them both.

Chubb coughed.

'Yes, sir, but doing that would create a new problem – two, in fact. Not only would it tip him off that we're on to him, it would also tell these Chinese gangsters who are out for his blood that he's definitely in London. Wing will be aware of that and it might just be enough to persuade him to drop his blackmail scheme and flee the country. In which case we'd be left with an unsolved murder – Miss Cooper's, I mean – and one of our PCs lying in hospital with a stab wound. I can't see the commissioner being pleased about that. Also, if we keep Wing's name out of the papers for the moment there's a chance the press won't link Audrey Cooper's murder to the Portia Blake case; at least, not at once. I don't recall that anything was made of the fact at the time that they were flatmates. But give the press Wing's name now and we could be letting ourselves in for a three-ring circus.'

Cradock made a noise difficult to interpret: not one of approval, certainly, but possibly a sign of grudging acceptance.

'As for the other point you raised, sir – about the photographs of Miss Blake that have been appearing in the *Mirror* – we're confident that won't happen again. Grace was also able to get confirmation from a chemist near where she lives that Miss Cooper had given them a batch of negatives to be developed. They weren't happy at having to handle them and told her they wouldn't accept any more of the same kind. They included the pictures of Miss Blake and that man that have appeared in the *Mirror* as well as others, some more explicit. There's no doubt that Miss Cooper was the person who sent them to the paper, and since she's dead . . .' He spread his hands in silent explanation.

'But can we be sure that this man Wing won't do the same thing now that he has them in his hands?' Cradock scowled.

'Not a hundred per cent certain, sir. But we're inclined to doubt it. Wing's at the point where he'll have to put pressure on his victim. He's running out of time. The longer this game goes on, the more danger he's in from his triad friends. I'd expect him to get in touch with Garner directly and let him know he has the pictures in his possession. He might even send *him* one or two of the choicer items. I mean those with his face clearly shown in it.'

'And what are *we* going to do in the meantime?' The AC seemed to be spoiling for a fight that morning. 'Just sit on our hands?'

'Not at all, sir.' Chubb's tone remained soothing. 'We're in a position to threaten Garner with arrest now, even if we haven't got enough to charge him as yet. We know that he lied to us about his alibi. Styles and Grace are both of the opinion that he's close to cracking. He's got a meeting set with Sir Richard Jessup this evening, one he asked for. It could be crucial. Jessup's promised to let us know what passes between them.'

'He'll get in touch with you, will he?'

Chubb coughed. 'No, actually it's Mr Madden he's promised to telephone.'

'Madden again!' The tip of the AC's nose turned red. 'I thought he'd agreed to leave this inquiry to those whose job it is to deal with it. Now you tell me he's meddling again—'

'He's not meddling, sir,' Billy broke in hotly. 'He's trying to help. The only reason we are where we are is because of the trouble he's gone to on Mr Sinclair's behalf. He's given us invaluable information, and most of it has come from Sir Richard Jessup, who obviously trusts him. That's what's got us where we are. If it wasn't for the two of them – Sir Richard and Mr Madden – we'd still be floundering.'

'All right, Inspector . . .' Chubb made a calming gesture. 'Keep your hair on.'

Cradock glowered at Billy. For a moment it seemed that he might react. Instead he turned to Chubb.

'What do you plan to do now, Chief Superintendent? The commissioner will want to know.'

'Keep looking for Wing, sir. We've sent copies of his photograph to all the police stations in the Metropolitan area along with the two names, either of which he may be using. I'm hoping we'll have him in custody soon.'

'What about Garner?'

'Depending on what Jessup has to tell us, I plan to call on him first thing tomorrow morning with DS Grace.' It was Billy who replied. He'd had time to cool down. 'He'll

be asked to explain why he gave us a false alibi for the day
Portia Blake was murdered. Unless he can provide a satisfactory answer, we'll bring him in for questioning.'

Cradock muttered something unintelligible. He glared at
them both.

'Well, I only hope you know what you're doing . . . both
of you. But I'm warning you again – I want to see some
action. So does the commissioner. This business has dragged
on long enough.'

'Someone got out of bed on the wrong side this morning.'
Chubb chuckled. 'And someone else has been twisting his
tail . . . the commissioner, I expect. But Cradock's got a point.
Even if we can't charge Garner in the end – we may have to
accept that there simply isn't enough evidence to convict him
– we have to find Wing, and quickly. If the triads get too
close to him he may well throw in the towel and skip the
country.'

Billy's grunt was non-committal. They were walking
down the corridor away from the AC's office and they went
on in silence until they came to the door to Chubb's office.
There the chief super paused.

'I was expecting to hear a little speech from you, Inspector.' He shot a sly glance at Billy. 'I thought we'd get a few
words from you on the subject of Detective-Constable Poole
and her latest contribution to the investigation. Mind you, I
don't mind admitting that was a smart bit of work she did
yesterday, putting it all together after she'd spoken to the
girl.' He shook his head ruefully. 'It's not a gift everyone
has. Most of us have to sweat out the details and then try to
make sense of them. But now and again you come across
someone who seems to sense how the dots are joined up.

John Madden had that gift, I remember.' He peered at Billy. 'Why didn't you say something when you had the chance? You should have spoken up.'

'Not with Cradock in that mood,' Billy growled. 'It would have been a waste of breath. But I mean to see that her work gets recognized. When this is over I'm going to write her up for another commendation. She's already earned it.'

'Good.' Chubb nodded approvingly. 'And while you're at it, you might recommend her for sergeant again. You were right – we've got too many idle DCs around here working out their pensions. It might be time to throw a cat among the pigeons.' He frowned. 'What's she doing now?'

'I sent her out to Brent Cross this afternoon. We had a report from the police there that an oriental answering to Wing's description had been reported staying in a local boarding house. He moved out a few days ago, but he's been seen since in the same general area and I thought we'd better check it. Even if he doesn't know yet that the triads are looking for him here, it's likely he'll stay away from the city centre. I haven't heard from Lil, but I'll be seeing her later this evening. We're having supper with Mr Madden in St John's Wood. Depending on what he hears later from Sir Richard Jessup, I might have some news for you tomorrow.'

Lily checked her wristwatch.

It had just gone nine o'clock. She wondered how much longer they would have to wait. What time did nobs sit down to dinner? (She was thinking of Sir Richard and his guest.) Surely later than she was used to doing. Left to her own devices, Lily usually had something to eat soon after she got home to her flat in St Pancras, which was around six o'clock as a rule, unless she was kept late at the Yard. It was the same when she went over to Paddington to see Aunt Betty and Uncle Fred, the couple who had raised her after she had lost both her parents, one to a bullet in the trenches, the other to the influenza epidemic that had swept the world in the wake of the Great War. Aunt Betty always had them sit down at six-thirty on the dot for what she called either supper or high tea, depending on her mood. Here, as guests of Madden and his daughter, they had eaten at half-past seven. But whether this was the family's normal practice, or done as a favour to their two visitors, it was impossible to say. Nothing about the evening had been familiar to Lily. She had seldom felt more out of her element, but the funny thing was she had enjoyed every moment of it.

It had started when she rang the doorbell . . .

Knowing that she was late – Billy Styles had told her to be at St John's Wood by six – Lily had hurried from the bus stop in the Finchley Road where the ponderous double-decker she had caught at Marble Arch had deposited her. Behind her was a largely wasted afternoon spent in the wilds of Brent Cross, one of the more distant London suburbs, near the end of the Edgware line. It had taken her half an hour to get out there and the same amount of time to get back. In between she had been forced to spend a long after-noon following up a lead which in the end had yielded next to nothing in the way of useful information.

Not that the local plod hadn't been helpful: the station commander, a grey-haired Irishman, had detailed one of his PCs to accompany her to the boarding house where Stanley Wing had, until recently, been staying.

'You were right about him using the name Lee,' he had told her. 'That's how we got on to him. He'd been staying there for a fortnight, according to the landlady. He couldn't produce an identity card, naturally, but he showed her a passport when he registered and gave an address in Hong Kong. She never got a chance to chat with him, she said; he was hardly ever there and took all his meals out. About the only thing he told her was that he was in London on business and wasn't planning to stay long.'

'What about the report that he'd been seen later in the same area?' Lily had asked. 'It might mean he'd just moved to another boarding house. He wouldn't want to remain in one place for too long.'

'I thought of that.' The commander had nodded sagely. 'But we've already checked other boarding houses and hotels and drawn a blank. If he is still hereabouts he's probably found a room to rent. Mostly they're advertised in tobacconists and newsagents, and we're checking those. But there's also word of mouth.' He had shrugged. 'We're doing our best, but the last sighting we had of him, the one you're talking about, happened a week ago and for all we know he may have moved on since then.'

Wing's landlady, when Lily finally spoke to her, had little to add. Sharp-eyed and businesslike – she seemed sure of her facts – she had described her erstwhile lodger as a 'strange one' but 'no trouble at all'.

'He was quiet as a mouse,' she told Lily. 'I can usually hear when anyone's coming down the stairs and going out through the front door, but he used to slip by without a sound. He wouldn't even stop for breakfast, and although I serve supper for them that want it, he was never here. You couldn't tell what he was thinking, either. He'd look at me with those black eyes of his and I wouldn't have the first idea of what was going on in his head.'

She'd had no hesitation, however, in identifying Wing from the photograph she'd been shown and had added a crucial detail about his appearance which disposed of any doubt that might have remained in Lily's mind.

'He had a scar on his throat. I only saw it once. He used to try to hide it by wearing a scarf, which seemed an odd thing to do, given this hot weather we've been having. But one morning he must have forgotten to put it on because when he went past me to the door I saw the mark. It looked like a nasty gash.'

With nothing to show for her afternoon's efforts other than this one small grain of information, and aware that she was a good half-hour late for her evening appointment, Lily had arrived hot and panting at the address she'd been given in St John's Wood. Pausing only to run her fingers through her hair and button the blazer-type jacket she generally wore for work, she had pressed the doorbell . . .

Rapid footsteps sounded from inside, and after only a moment the door was flung open. Expecting to see the tall figure of John Madden, Lily was confronted instead by a young woman about her own age wearing an apron and holding a bowl in the crook of her arm.

'Excuse me, Miss . . .' She had got no further.

'Not Miss . . . Lucy.'

'I'm sorry . . . ?'

'That's my name . . . Lucy. And you're Lily . . . Lily Poole.' A smile had illuminated the young woman's face. 'I know all about you. Angus is forever singing your praises.'

'Angus . . . ?' Lily wasn't sure how to respond. But the young woman, whom she'd guessed must be Madden's daughter, was already stretching out a welcoming hand and she'd allowed herself to be drawn into the house.

'I should have said Chief Inspector Angus Sinclair, formerly of the Metropolitan Police.' Lucy Madden's expression had become grave and her voice had dropped several registers as she intoned the solemn words. 'But, you see, I've called him Angus since I was eighteen. It started when I joined the Wrens during the war. Daddy was shocked. He said I ought to be more respectful to my elders. But Angus insisted. In those days I was stationed at the Admiralty and he used to take me to lunch at the Savoy now and then. I loved it. It was the first time anyone had treated me like a grown-up.'

She led Lily down a short passageway from the bare, uncarpeted hall.

'I'm sorry the house looks so abandoned. It belonged to my great aunt, but she died recently and it's up for sale. Nearly all the furniture has gone. But we've still got chairs and a table in the kitchen. Daddy's gone out with Billy to a pub round the corner. He said they were going to buy some bottles of beer but I expect it was because he wanted to talk to him about this case you're all working on. I read in the paper this morning about that poor woman being murdered in her flat – the one Daddy went to see – and I wanted to hear what Billy had to say about it. But as soon as he arrived they decided they had to go out, and I'm sure it's because they didn't want me to hear what they said. It's *so* frustrating . . .'

They had reached the kitchen, where Lily had her first chance to study the golden-haired girl. She'd been told that Madden's daughter was good looking, but saw now that that was an understatement. 'Stunner' would have been closer to the mark.

'I'm so pleased to meet you at last, Lily.' The radiant smile had returned. 'Can you help me choose something for supper? We've got all these tins' – Lucy waved her hands at the assortment of objects lined up on the kitchen table – 'which we simply have to get rid of before we move out.

Actually, I shouldn't even have mentioned them to you.' She giggled. 'They're terribly illicit. Aunt Maud bought them off a spiv called Sid during the war – poor Sid, he ended up in jail – but never ate any of them except the caviar.' She frowned. 'We could have some of that I suppose . . .'

'Caviar . . . ?' Lily had only ever heard of the stuff.

'Or perhaps not.' Lucy shook her head. 'I think it's dreadfully overrated . . . just, well . . . fishy. But we've got one tin of pheasant left, and some foie gras, which isn't the best thing for one's complexion, but never mind that, and an absolutely delicious Stilton which is sitting in the larder. What do you think?'

She looked inquiringly at her guest. Then her expression changed.

'What lovely eyes you've got, Lily.'

'Me . . . eyes?' Lily was struck dumb again.

'You must do something with them.'

'*Do* . . . ?'

'Come on. This can wait.'

Seizing her visitor by the hand, Lucy pulled her out of the kitchen and up an uncarpeted echoing flight of stairs to the landing above and from there to a bathroom. Positioning Lily in front of the mirror, she rummaged in a cloth bag standing on a table by the basin and brought out a stick of mascara.

'Stand still,' she commanded.

Minutes had gone by. Madden's daughter worked busily. Finished with the mascara, she fished out a compact from the bag. Lily felt the feather-light touch of a powder puff on her cheeks.

'There, now . . . !' Lucy had stood aside. Lily gazed at herself in the mirror.

'Crikey!' she said.

'You see? All it takes is a touch here and there.'

Lucy had put her face beside Lily's and the two of them had gazed at the mirror together.

'Your boyfriend will get a surprise.' Lucy caught Lily's eye in the mirror and smiled. 'Have you got one?'

'There's a young copper stationed at Paddington nick.' Lily couldn't stop herself. She'd never come across anyone quite like Lucy Madden before. 'I met him through my uncle Fred.'

'And is he your boyfriend?'

'He thinks he is.'

'That's the way to handle them.' Lucy was warm in her approval. 'Keep them guessing.'

She cocked an ear.

'I can hear Daddy's voice. They must be back. We'd better go down.'

'So it all depends on what Rex Garner has to say for himself.' Lucy Madden pondered the question. 'He might just decide to confess. It could all be over this evening.'

She turned her eager gaze on Lily.

'But doesn't it seem a little too easy to you?' she asked.

Lily awoke with a start. It had been a long day and after two glasses of wine (which was one more than she was used to drinking at any one time) she was starting to feel drowsy sitting there at the table.

'Easy . . . ? I wouldn't say that.'

'Nor would I.' Billy met Madden's glance and smiled. 'I'll let you into a secret, Lucy. As far as any copper is concerned, the easier the better. But I wouldn't count on Mr Garner coming clean, just like that. Chances are he'll look for a way out. If he's smart, which I don't think he is, he'll realize that we don't have enough to charge him with as yet. Not on the Portia Blake murder, anyway. But there's still that business in Hong Kong. That's hanging fire . . .'

Glancing at his watch, he shrugged.

'Still, I wish they'd get a move on.'

Supper was over and they had been sitting round the kitchen table for some time drinking coffee and sipping wine, waiting for the phone call that Madden was expecting. Initially reluctant – or seemingly so – to discuss the case, Billy had quickly yielded to the pressure which Lucy exerted on him, and which had begun after she witnessed the way her father greeted Lily Poole.

'Billy's been telling me about your work.' Madden had shaken the young policewoman's hand warmly. 'He explained how you put the pieces together yesterday. You were right, of course. That's what Miss Cooper failed to tell me when I spoke to her. She's the one who had those negatives all the time. She must have pocketed them before Miss Blake's sister came to collect her things. Poor woman: look what they brought her to in the end.'

'What did Lily do?' Lucy had pounced on her father's words. 'And why is she blushing like a beetroot?'

'Oh, I can't discuss that.' Madden had adopted a distant air. 'What I really want to do is hear Lily's news.' He had seated their guest at the table beside him. 'Mr Sinclair will demand a full report. He hasn't been able to get about for a while, as you probably know. I've had to be his eyes and ears.'

'Billy . . . !' Lucy had rounded on their other visitor. 'I *insist* on being told. I've seen the *Daily Mirror*. I know all about the photographs.'

'Sorry, luv.' Billy had taken his cue from Madden. He contrived to appear regretful. 'I'm afraid I can't talk about it. Police business, you know . . .'

'Police business! I've never heard anything so ridiculous. You know very well you're going to tell me in the end, so stop teasing me, both of you.'

Catching sight of Lily's expression, she had burst out laughing.

'Don't be shocked. I can say anything I like to Billy. I've known him all my life. He used to take me for long walks in the woods when I was small. I can still remember those afternoons.'

'So can I.' Billy caught Lily's eye and winked. 'I learned a lot, especially about the flora and fauna. You see, when Lucy realized I was a city boy and didn't know a warbler from a water-rat she made up a lot of names to tell me and I went off thinking I had it all sorted out. It came as a bit of a shock later when I learned there was no such thing as a hooter bird and that stoats didn't really build their nests in trees. Or anywhere else, come to think of it. I see she's already been to work on you.' He looked pointedly at Lily's eyes. 'So a word to the wise: mind how you go with this young lady.'

'Billy, you promised!' Lucy's cheeks had turned scarlet. 'You swore you'd never tell anyone about that.'

'No, I didn't. I said I'd think about it.'

He had started to laugh then.

'But I know you're curious about this case – your dad told me – and if you ask me nicely, I might just tell you a little more about it over supper.'

'Billy, Billy . . .'

Madden had shaken his head in despair.

Lily glanced at her watch again, and as she did so the telephone rang.

Madden got to his feet.

'That must be Jessup, he said. 'Do you want to speak to him?' He put the question to Billy, who shook his head.

'I don't think so, sir. You can tell him I'm here, if you like. But he's always been open with you, and he might feel he has to choose his words carefully if he's speaking to a police officer.'

With a non-committal shrug, Madden left them. They heard him pick up the phone in the hall, but his voice was barely audible as he spoke to his caller and he quickly fell silent. A long pause ensued. Then they heard him speak again, and this time they caught the words.

'Thank you, Richard. I'll pass that on.'

He returned to the kitchen looking thoughtful.

'Well, it seems Lucy may be right. It could be over.'

He sat down.

'It sounds as though Garner's in a bad way. According to Sir Richard he was half drunk when he got to the club and in even worse shape when he left a few minutes ago. But he's come to a decision. He's going to get in touch with you tomorrow morning.' He looked at Billy. 'He wants to make a statement, Jessup says. But he'll do it in the presence of a solicitor.'

'Ah . . .' Billy took a deep breath. 'That could be it, then. Did he say anything else – Garner, I mean?'

'Only that he'd heard from Wing.'

Billy pursed his lips in a silent whistle. 'That must have come as a nasty shock.'

'Garner declined to say what had passed between them. But it had clearly upset him. "I thought the bastard was in prison." That was his only comment, according to Jessup. He said Garner was very much the worse for drink by that time and not making much sense. But it was clear he was worried sick.'

'Did they talk about Portia Blake?'

'Her name certainly came up.' Madden frowned. 'But Garner didn't admit to killing her, if that's what you're wondering. What he did say was that he'd given you a false alibi for the day she was murdered. At that point Jessup urged him to make a clean breast of things and told him it would be best if he went to the police on his own initiative and set the record straight. He offered to put him in touch with his solicitor. My guess is you'll hear from Garner in the morning.'

'And if we don't, Joe Grace and I will pay him another visit, like we planned to.' Billy's eyes narrowed. 'I take it there was no reference made to the girl in Hong Kong?'

Madden shook his head. 'Sir Richard didn't mention it.' He paused, frowning. 'I'm just wondering what it was that got Garner so worried. Was it something Wing said to him?'

'He could have told him about the photos,' Billy suggested. 'That would have been enough to send Rex reaching for the bottle.'

'Always supposing the man in the bed is him,' Madden pointed out. 'But it's not *evidence*. It doesn't link him to the killing.'

He pondered the question in silence for a few moments. Then he turned to Lily. 'What do you think?' he asked.

Caught off-guard, Lily collected herself quickly. She hadn't expected to be asked her opinion.

'Well . . . well, we don't know what Wing knows, do we?'

It sounded like a feeble reply to her, but Madden appeared to think otherwise.

'What cards he may be holding, you mean? Yes, that's very true. We shouldn't forget that. For all we know he may be in possession of other evidence incriminating Garner. He may even have enough to tie him to Portia's murder.'

'Or to that girl in Hong Kong,' Lily pointed out.

'Who may or may not have survived the assault she suffered at his hands.' Madden nodded thoughtfully. 'To one or other, you mean?'

'Or both.'

20

'WHERE THE DEVIL is he? He can't just have disappeared.'

Chubb glared at Billy from behind his desk.

'You've tried ringing the house, have you?'

'Several times, sir, but there's no reply. According to Jessup, Garner was going to get in touch with us after he'd spoken to a solicitor. But there's been no word from that quarter either.'

'Could he have changed his mind, do you think?' Chubb's face darkened. 'Sobered up?'

'We'll soon find out. I've asked Lofty Cook at West End Central to send a bobby round to his house to ring the door-bell, and to keep on ringing if he doesn't respond. Of course, he could still be sleeping it off. According to Jessup he was reeling drunk when he left the club last night.'

'Perhaps he never got home,' Chubb suggested. 'But whatever the explanation is, I want answers fast. I've already had a call from Cradock asking if Garner has been brought in for questioning yet. Get cracking.'

Happy enough to obey – answers were what he lacked at the moment – Billy left to return to his own office. He was thinking he might have to take the bull by the horns and ask Richard Jessup for the name of his solicitor. The fact that they hadn't met made it difficult and he wondered whether he could turn to Madden for yet more help. He had still not resolved the question in his mind when he reached his office and found that Lily Poole was on the phone.

'Hang on, guv.' She spoke into the instrument when she saw Billy, and then beckoned to him urgently. 'It's Mr Cook,' she said.

Billy took the phone from her. 'Lofty . . . ?'

'Hello, Billy. I've got news for you. I've just heard from the bobby I sent round to that bloke's house . . . what's his name?'

'Garner . . . Rex Garner.' Billy had caught a note in the other man's voice that alerted him: something was up. 'Did he speak to him?'

'Hardly. If it's the same bloke you want to talk to, he seems to be strung up inside.'

'*Strung up* . . . ?'

'Hanging by his neck.' Cook's tone was dry. 'You'd better let me explain. The constable rang the doorbell, like he was told to, and went on ringing until it was plain no one was going to answer. The curtains at the front of the house overlooking the street were drawn, but there was still a small gap between them. By pressing his nose to the glass the bobby was able to peer inside the room, and what he saw gave him a shock. There was a man hanging from some sort of balustrade at the back of the room. He returned to the front door and tried to break it down with his shoulder, but it wouldn't budge, so he rang the station. I've got a locksmith on his way over to the house now. I'll meet you there.'

With the bell on their police car ringing, Billy and his two colleagues forged a passage through the scattered crowd of onlookers that had gathered in the street outside Rex Garner's house. They drew up in front of the door, which stood ajar. As Billy climbed out of the car a uniformed officer with a sergeant's stripes on his sleeve approached him.

'Mr Cook's inside, sir. He told the rest of us to stay out here.' He pointed to the three other men posted on the pavement. 'He said you'd be the officer in charge. Let me know if there's anything we can do.'

'Just clear the street for now, Sergeant. I'll have a word with you later.'

Followed by Grace and Lily Poole, Billy went into the house. He found Lofty Cook standing just inside the door to the drawing room where he and Joe had interviewed Rex Garner only two days earlier. Beyond him was a grisly sight. The body of a man was suspended by his neck from the balustrade of the book-lined gallery which Billy remembered from his earlier visit. His feet were a foot or so off the floor and his body had twisted slightly away from the door so that his face wasn't visible. Billy had little doubt that it was Garner, and when he walked past Cook to the other side of the room and looked up at the contorted visage he knew for certain.

'It's him, all right, Lofty.' He reached up to touch the black rubber-sheathed wire that had cut so deeply into the man's throat it was only partially visible. 'What did he use, do you reckon?'

'It looks like electrical flex.' Cook had crossed the room to join him. 'And you can see he doubled it.' He pointed higher to where the separation between the two lengths of cable was clearly visible. 'He must have decided that a single strand wouldn't take his weight. Have you any idea why he did it?'

'Quite a few, as it happens. He was our new prime suspect for the Portia Blake killing – and he knew it. I had the feeling he might be close to cracking.'

Lofty whistled.

'Does that mean your case is wrapped up?'

'Not quite. We're still looking for Stanley Wing, the chap Lily talked to you about.'

Cook looked reflective. 'I know this is a Yard case, Billy. I'm not going to stick my nose in. But this is my patch, so if you don't mind I'll stay for a while and see how things work out.'

'Please do, sir.' Billy grinned. They had joined the Met at the same time, right after the end of the First World War, and although initially Billy had led the way in the race for promotions – he had secured his inspectorship earlier than Cook – Lofty had lately inched ahead; he was now a chief inspector. None of which had affected their friendship, which had remained solid over the years. 'By the way, I called Richard Jessup before I left the Yard,' he said. 'He's on his way over here now. He can formally identify Garner for us. And I rang Mr Madden, too. You remember him, don't you?'

'I should say so.'

'He's in London at present and I thought he might want to come down here and see this. He began looking into the Portia Blake murder before we did as a favour to Mr Sinclair. They're neighbours in the country now.'

'Wheels within wheels, eh?' Lofty rubbed his chin thoughtfully. 'Well, it sounds as though you're in luck, Billy. I wouldn't mind having John Madden at my shoulder if I was working a case. He was special, wasn't he? One of those blokes you don't forget.'

'I can't say he was happy when I saw him last, sir. He was muttering to himself in the back of the car all the way from Pall Mall. I couldn't hear what he said, except it seemed to be about some "damned Chinaman", as he put it. And I had a hard time seeing him into the house. He was the worse for drink, but he wouldn't accept any help. Each time I tried to take his arm he pushed me away. But I finally saw him to the door and after some bother with his keys – he couldn't seem to find the right one – he finally let himself in. And that's how I left him.'

Every inch the old soldier, and looking smart in his chauffeur's uniform, Ted Lennox stood to attention as he made his statement. At Billy's request he had been summoned by his employer from the car outside to give an account of Garner's movements the night before, after Jessup himself had revealed that he had detailed his chauffeur to take his dinner guest home.

'I'm afraid Rex was quite drunk and I didn't want to send him home in a cab.'

Sir Richard had arrived a few minutes after Madden, who had caught a taxi down from St John's Wood. Together they had watched in silence as the body of the dead man was lowered gently to the floor. Billy had had to wait for the arrival of the police photographer before the operation could be carried out, but once he had done his work two detectives from the forensic crew who had been standing by had jointly taken hold of the corpse as one of their colleagues loosened the double strand of wire tied to the balustrade above. Clearly appalled by the sight of Garner's livid features, Jessup had looked away.

'I had been planning to return home to Hampshire myself,' he told Billy, 'but it had got so late that I changed my mind and decided to spend the night at my club. My chauffeur was standing by with the car, so I asked him to make sure that Mr Garner got home safely.'

When the pathologist arrived soon afterwards to examine the body – and after Lofty Cook had taken his leave of them

– Billy led both men to a smaller sitting room on the other side of the entrance hall.

'We're going to need a statement from you, sir,' he told Sir Richard. 'The coroner will want to know what Mr Garner's state of mind was when you saw him last night. We can do that later – I'll send a man over to your office – but it would help if you gave me some idea of how he was behaving.'

Jessup had needed a moment to collect himself. Pale and distraught, he had been standing a little apart from them, staring at nothing, hardly aware of what was being said. 'Rex arrived a little after eight,' he said, 'and since it was clear he'd already been drinking I thought it best to go into dinner straight away. He was angry . . . fractious and belligerent . . . we'd hardly sat down when he started complaining about what he said was police harassment.' He caught Billy's eye. 'Don't worry, Inspector, I wasn't taken in by that, but I let him ramble on for a bit, and then I asked him if there was anything he'd like to tell me – anything he wanted to get off his chest. Well, I'm afraid that set him off again, and he turned on me, accusing me of being on "their side" – he meant you, the authorities – and demanding to know why I wouldn't stand by him. I assured him I'd do whatever I could to help, and it was then that he admitted he had given you a false alibi for the afternoon when Miss Blake was murdered. He hadn't met the friend whose name he gave you; he had simply driven into Canterbury and spent the next few hours on his own. He and his wife were due to drive back to London later that afternoon and he timed his return to the house to coincide with their planned departure.'

Jessup rubbed his forehead.

'I was shocked to hear that. I asked him why he'd done it. He said he had told Adele Castleton the same story years ago and thought he'd better stick to it . . .'

'The same story . . . ?' Billy broke in.

'Exactly.' Jessup had spread his hands. 'It was no sort of explanation. I could understand why he concocted an excuse to tell Adele. I'd always thought it was possible that he knew Miss Blake better than he admitted and had simply wanted to avoid seeing her again after her behaviour at dinner the previous evening. But I couldn't believe he'd been so stupid as to tell the police a lie just to cover up what was only a small fib, after all. It was at that point that I began to get worried. I wondered if he had more to conceal.'

'Did he at any point mention the woman he beat up in Hong Kong?' Billy asked. 'I believe you knew about that.'

Jessup nodded. 'Rex didn't refer to it directly, but it might have been on his mind . . .'

'Why did you think that, Richard?' Silent up till then, Madden had interrupted. Jessup turned to him.

'It was when he told me that Wing had been in touch with him. I had asked if he'd seen the photographs published in the *Daily Mirror* and what he made of them. That set him off on another rant. He said the police were trying to frame him. But then he quietened down and admitted that Wing had telephoned him earlier that day and tried to get money out of him.'

'Because of the photographs?'

'I don't know. Rex didn't say. He was cursing Wing as he told me about it. He said he was a leech, a bloodsucker, and he'd never be free of him.'

'And you wondered what he was talking about – whether it was the photographs, or something else?'

'The thought did cross my mind.' Jessup sighed. 'We had left the dining room by then. Fortunately, there weren't too many others there last night, but even so Rex had made something of a spectacle of himself, banging the table with his fist and creating a disturbance. I had managed to get him downstairs where there's a small waiting room by the entrance hall, and after I'd ordered him a brandy – he insisted on it – I told him what I thought he ought to do.'

'Which was to speak to us?' This time it was Billy who put the question.

Jessup nodded. 'I told him there was no way his false alibi would stand up and the wisest thing he could do would be to go to the police at once before they came to him and put the record straight. Then I added that if there was anything else he had to tell you he'd be well advised to take the opportunity to do so and if he wished I could put him in touch with my solicitor.'

Jessup's smile had a bitter edge.

'I was expecting another explosion then, but to my surprise he gave in. He said he would do that. He said he'd had enough.'

'Enough . . . ?' Billy intervened quickly. 'What did he mean by that?'

'I can't say for certain, Inspector. But it sounded as though he'd thrown in the towel. That was my impression. I should tell you that things had been going from bad to worse for some time in Rex's life. He was deeply in debt. This place is mortgaged to the hilt. He owes money left and right. I was just wondering how I was going to get him home when I remembered that Ted was outside with the car. I got him to bring Rex here and to see him inside his front door safely; which I believe he did. But you can ask him that yourself. He's waiting outside.

'What will the police make of this, John?'

Jessup stood on the pavement looking about him. The crowd that had gathered in the street earlier, drawn by the police presence, had largely dispersed and those bystanders still tempted to remain were being gently but firmly moved on by the uniformed officers posted outside.

'What will they read into it? Will they take it as confirmation of their theory that it was probably Rex who killed Miss Blake?'

'They might.' Madden had come outside to accompany the other man to his car, where Lennox stood waiting with the door open. 'They certainly regarded him as a suspect. I told you that. But they were some way from making a case against him. However, there's still that woman in Hong Kong to be considered. They're waiting for word from the police there. So far they've found no trace of her in their records. It's possible she didn't survive the assault she suffered at Garner's hands and somehow her body was disposed of; and it's equally possible that Wing knew that and could pin the crime on him. We don't know what passed between them when they spoke on the phone yesterday.'

Jessup pondered in silence. Although he appeared to have recovered from the shock of seeing Garner's body lowered to the floor, he still seemed troubled.

'Will the question of Miss Blake's murder come up at the inquest?' he asked. 'I expect I'll be summoned to appear as a witness.'

'It may well do.' Madden nodded. 'As Inspector Styles said, the coroner will try to establish Garner's state of mind prior to his suicide, and your testimony will be crucial. He'll want to know why he was so upset. There's no way you can avoid the subject.'

'And what will the police say about it?'

'Not a great deal, I imagine, and not until they have either found Stanley Wing, or are satisfied that he has left the country. At that stage they might issue a statement to the effect that the inquiry remains open, or, if they're satisfied that Garner was Portia's killer, that they're no longer looking into the case.'

'I just hope they tread carefully,' Jessup said. 'I don't like the idea of branding a man as a murderer when he can't defend himself. It's not as though anyone will ever know for sure who killed Miss Blake.'

'Not unless the police catch up with Stanley Wing,' Madden observed. 'He's the one person who might be able to answer these questions.'

Jessup reflected on his words. Then he sighed.

'I can't help feeling I let Rex down. I should have done more for him.'

'Perhaps he was past help, Richard,' Madden said gently. He sensed the other man's distress. 'It looks to me as though he'd backed himself into a corner, and took the only way out.'

Having seen Jessup off, Madden went back inside the house to find that Billy had returned to the drawing room and was standing to one side with Grace and Lily Poole. They were watching the pathologist, who was still busy. On his knees now he was bending over the body and peering closely at the dead man's throat.

'Isn't that Ransom?' Madden asked. It was years since they had met, but he recognized the pathologist's face and recalled that he'd been regarded by the Met's squad of detectives as something of a card.

'It's him all right.' Billy chuckled. 'Do you remember how he used to get the chief inspector's goat? Mr Sinclair couldn't be doing with his shafts of wit. I can't say he's changed all that much. We're wondering what he's going to come up with today.'

As he spoke, the burly figure shifted. Sitting back on his heels, he hoisted himself slowly to his feet and then turned to face them.

'I see business is picking up, Inspector. Am I right in thinking this is your second corpse in . . . how many days? Three, is it? I'm only thankful I was spared the most recent offering: I understand the lady met an unpleasant end.'

His solemn expression changed; his face brightened.

'Isn't that Mr Madden standing beside you? Don't tell me you've returned to the force, sir. I thought you were happily retired.'

'And you were right.' Madden smiled. 'I'm here on behalf of Mr Sinclair, who I'm sure would send you his regards if he could.'

'I very much doubt it. The good chief inspector and I seldom saw eye to eye. But you can give him my best wishes if you like. Now, Inspector, as to your body . . .'

He turned his gaze back on Billy.

'Death was caused by strangulation, as you can see, and I would estimate that it occurred some twelve hours ago: say between eleven o'clock and midnight.'

He bent to buckle the straps on his bag.

'And it was quite straightforward, was it?'

'Straightforward . . . ?' Red in the face from bending over, Dr Ransom stood up. 'Well, that depends on your definition of the word; but yes . . . straightforward . . . after a fashion.'

'Don't be like that, Doctor.' Billy heaved a sigh. 'Just give me the authorized version: did the man hang himself?'

'Once again, I very much doubt it.' The pathologist chortled. He seemed to be enjoying a private joke. 'Seeing as how he was almost certainly dead at the time; strangled, as I said.'

'Strangled . . . ?'

'Prior to being strung up, I mean. And since he could hardly have done it to himself, I'm inclined to think he was murdered.'

'How's it going, Lil? Have you found anything?'

Billy went over to the foot of the staircase leading up to the gallery where Lily Poole was down on her knees.

'Yes, I think so, guv. There are scuff marks at the edge of the carpeting – do you see?'

She pointed. Billy bent over her shoulder to look, and Madden, who was standing on the other side of the young policewoman, followed suit.

'It looks like something was dragged up the stairs.'

'Like a body, you mean?' Billy nodded. He saw where the pile of the carpeting had been brushed back. 'He must have been pulled up by his armpits. He would have been quite a weight.' He glanced at Madden. 'What do you think, sir?'

'I agree. The scuffing could have been caused by the heels of his shoes catching on each step.'

Billy straightened.

'We know that the curtains were drawn, so I don't suppose anyone outside noticed anything.'

Having listened to Ransom's explanation, Billy had directed Joe Grace to organize a house-to-house inquiry using the uniformed officers stationed outside.

'Joe has already spoken to a woman who lives across the street and saw Garner come home last night,' he told Madden. 'She confirmed what Lennox told us: she heard a disturbance in the street and saw Garner, obviously drunk, being shepherded to his front door. But I want people asked about what they might have seen earlier in the evening as well, since whoever killed him may have already been in the house when he got back.'

The pathologist had been succinct in his depiction of how the dead man met his end.

'To put it bluntly, he was strangled twice. There are two separate marks on his throat. They lie at different angles, and are quite easy to spot. I would say that the first one was caused when he was throttled from behind. If Garner was standing or sitting when that happened, the mark would have been more or less parallel to the floor. And it's thinner than the other one, which suggests he was first choked using a single strand of flex. The second mark, the one caused by hanging, lies at a quite different angle – it slants up towards his ears. I think he was either killed or rendered unconscious down here and then taken upstairs to the gallery and hung by a double strand of flex from the balustrade. I will so state at the inquest.'

With the investigation headed in a different direction now, Billy had ordered the fingerprint specialists summoned from the Yard, who up till then had been standing idle, to go over the drawing room inch by inch.

'I want the banisters and the balustrade covered in particular,' he told them. 'Lift all the dabs you can find. Take Garner's prints before the body is removed.'

He glanced at Madden, who was standing beside him, observing, but saying nothing.

'I'd say this was Stanley Wing's work,' he said. 'It's the only thing that makes sense.'

'What I'm wondering is how it came about,' Madden said. 'Why exactly did Wing kill him – and why now?'

Billy pursed his lips. He gave the question serious thought before replying.

'Suppose Garner had already seen the photographs, ones

with his face in, I mean, when he met Jessup last night. The chemist who developed the negatives told us he made two prints of each at Miss Cooper's request. So Wing must have a spare set, and he could have put them in the post right away, that same afternoon, and they would have been delivered next day. We have to remember he's pushed for time. Garner told Jessup that Wing had phoned him. If so, then Wing would almost certainly have demanded money from him and that could explain Garner's state of mind when he met Jessup later.'

Although Madden showed no reaction, Billy saw he was paying close attention.

'And what if Garner told him there wasn't any – money, I mean?' He continued with his train of thought. 'That he was broke? Maybe Wing decided there was only one thing left he wanted to do, and did it.'

At that moment Billy became aware of a figure hovering at his elbow. It was one of the detectives from the forensic squad, a DC named Travis.

'I've got something to show you, guv.' He nodded towards the far end of the room where several armchairs were grouped around a fireplace.

Billy accompanied him to the spot, with Madden at his heels. Travis bent down. He had a pair of tweezers in his hand.

'I noticed there were some ashes in the grate,' he said, 'and that seemed strange. I mean, lighting a fire in this hot weather. So I had a look at them. I reckon they were photos.'

He reached into the grate with his tweezers and extracted a triangular shape, charred along its base. He showed it to Billy, who was bending down, peering over his shoulder.

'That's a piece of a photograph, all right. There's part of a woman's face there . . .' Billy peered closely at the fragment

Travis was holding. 'And a bit of her arm, too. Hang on! I think I've seen this.'

He stood up straight, looking round as he did so.

'Lil . . . !' He called to her across the length of the room. 'Come over here.'

Lily hurried over from where she was standing at the foot of the stairs, watching the fingerprint crew at work on the banisters.

Billy stood aside so that she could see what the detective held in his tweezers.

'Isn't that the same face that was in that painting at the back of Portia's bedroom? You said you recognized it.'

'*The Nude Maja*?' Lily brought her eyes up close to the fragment. 'Yes, that's it, that's her . . . well done, Mike.' She patted Travis on the shoulder.

Billy looked at Madden.

'We can assume it was Garner who burned them,' he said. 'But if Wing rang him like Garner said he did he would have told him that he still had the negatives and there was no way Garner was going to escape this time.'

Madden mused in silence for a moment. 'What I'm wondering is how Wing gained entry to the house last night,' he said.

'I thought about that.' Billy nodded. 'I had the windows checked. They're locked from the inside. They don't seem to have been fiddled with. I reckon he simply knocked on the door and Garner let him in. Granted, he wouldn't have been pleased to see Wing. But he might have thought it worthwhile trying to reason with him: to explain that he couldn't pay up.'

'What about the flex Garner was hanged with, though? That's got me puzzled. Do you think Wing brought it with him?'

Billy scratched his head. He could see that the question was bothering his old chief.

'It's more likely he found it here, in the house,' he said. 'I sent a couple of men downstairs to the basement. They said there was a lot of stuff lying around, including some tools. I think Wing found what he wanted down there.'

'Leaving Garner up here in the drawing room on his own, do you mean?' Madden was still dubious.

'On his own, but most likely passed out, or close to it. That's what we're forgetting. Garner arrived back here dead drunk. It wouldn't have been hard for Wing to deal with him once he'd been let in. He can't have been pleased when he found all his efforts had gone for nothing; that Garner wasn't going to pay. He may not have come here intending to kill him. But he wasn't going to let him off.' Billy shrugged. 'And who knows? Perhaps in the end Wing did him a favour.'

'Meaning what?' Madden frowned.

'If Garner was guilty of Portia's murder – and Wing knew it, and could prove it – then it was odds on Rex was going to end up the same way sooner or later: on the end of a rope.'

21

CHARLIE CHUBB STOOD with his arms folded staring out of the windows of his office. His gaze was fixed on the sky, where a mass of white clouds, tinged with grey, had been gathering in the west all afternoon.

'I keep hoping we'll get a storm,' he said, with a sigh. 'Something to break this heatwave we've been having. The clouds build up, but nothing happens. My lawn's dying of thirst. You're a gardener, aren't you?'

He swung round to face Billy, who was seated in a chair in front of his desk.

'I've got the same problem as you, sir.' Billy looked glum. 'My grass is turning brown. What's more, I saw something in the paper the other day about a hosepipe ban being introduced unless we get some rain.'

Chubb snorted. Two days had passed since the body of Rex Garner had been found hanging in his drawing room and the chief superintendent had summoned the officer assigned to the case to report on the progress of the investigation.

'I've got a meeting fixed with Cradock and the commissioner in half an hour,' he announced as he took his own seat. 'They're not happy with the way things are going, and I can't say I blame them. We've got the press practically accusing us of withholding information from the public, of trying to cover up our mistakes.'

He fumed.

'They know who Garner is – or was. They know his name was linked to the Portia Blake murder and they know we've been looking into the case again. They've put two and two together and think he committed suicide because we were on to him. They want us to admit that the wrong man was sent to the gallows. I'm only grateful that they haven't made the connection to Miss Cooper's murder yet. But they will.'

Billy shrugged. 'They won't be quite so cocky when they learn that Garner didn't kill himself: that he was topped. I wish we could put that out now, but we'll have to wait for the inquest, and that won't be till next week.'

'And what then . . . ?' Chubb glared. 'They'll be jumping up and down, wanting to know who killed him, and I don't fancy the prospect of having to announce that our prime suspect has probably skipped the country. Speaking of which, have we *any* idea where Stanley Wing is?'

'Not for certain, sir. But I doubt he's made any attempt to leave as yet. If he had, I think we'd have heard about it. His photograph and the names he's using are in the hands of the immigration authorities and all ports have been warned to keep an eye out for him.' He paused. 'Of course, there are other, illegal ways of making himself scarce. It could be Wing will try to slip aboard a cargo vessel on the sly. He doesn't know yet that we're after him, but he must suspect that the triads are on his trail and he may feel that that's his best option. But it's not something that can be arranged on the spur of the moment. He'd need time to set it up, and we've warned our snouts on the docks to keep their eyes and ears open.'

Chubb growled unintelligibly. He shifted in his seat.

'I can tell you now – none of this is going to make the commissioner feel any better. He won't accept the idea that a man wanted for two murders might slip through our hands. Perhaps it's time we made his name public and gave his picture to the newspapers.'

'We can if you want to.' Billy weighed the option. 'We still haven't picked up any trace of him beyond the report Poole brought back from Brent Cross. Maybe if we show his picture to the public someone will spot him. But the drawback is it'll tip him off, and that might be enough to persuade him to skip the country while he still can. On balance, I think we should wait a little longer.'

'A few days, then, but no more.' Chubb shook a warning finger.

Billy frowned. 'And we have to think about the future, too. We can certainly arrest him, but can we make a case against him? As of now, the only hard evidence connecting him to Audrey Cooper's murder is the identification provided by that woman who saw him run by her in the street. It was what any defence counsel worth his salt would call a "fleeting glance" and I doubt we could get a conviction on that alone.'

'What about the constable who was stabbed?'

'I'm glad to say he's doing well in hospital, but he can't identify Wing from his picture. It all happened too quickly. He heard the scream, saw the man run out of the house, tried to intercept him and got stabbed in the gut for his pains. He didn't get a clear picture of his face.'

'How about the Garner murder? Can we link Wing to that at least?'

'Not positively. Not as yet. We're still sorting through the fingerprints lifted at the house. Other than Garner's own, there are two other sets that we found in the drawing room that we've been tentatively able to identify . . . One of them belongs to his housekeeper, a Mrs Adams. Ex-housekeeper,

I should say, since she quit her job before he went up to Scotland for the grouse shooting. When she read about his murder in the paper yesterday she rang us. He hadn't paid her wages for a couple of months and she finally got fed up and handed in her notice. Grace went round to see her. Her prints match one of the sets, as I said, and it seems likely that the other one belongs to a maid who was in Garner's employ until a couple of months ago, when he dismissed her. It sounds as though he was having trouble making ends meet. But there were two other sets we found, made by the same person, which remain unidentified, and given where we found them are definitely suspicious.'

'Were they in the drawing room?' Chubb asked.

Billy nodded. 'They were on the banisters, in fact: the only ones we found there. Maybe Garner didn't spend much time with his library. One print was halfway up and the other near the top, and they were both made by a left hand, which was significant.'

'How so?'

'If whoever killed Garner was dragging his body up the stairs, he was most likely holding him under the armpits and leaning back himself as he pulled the body up. It looks to me as though he lost his balance a couple of times, and instinctively grabbed at the banister to steady himself. Both of the prints were left-handed, which fits with that idea: the banisters are on the right going up.'

'Ingenious, Sherlock!' Charlie's doleful visage brightened momentarily. 'You'll make a detective yet.'

'Needless to say, we're hoping these prints will match Wing's. I've sent a copy of them by express mail to the Hong Kong police. They must have his dabs on record. We should hear from them before long, though I'm hoping we'll have caught Wing by then.'

'If he hasn't scarpered, you mean.' The chief super's mood had quickly soured again. 'You do understand what we're facing here? It's not just that we could end up with two unsolved murders and a wounded officer and no suspect to lay the blame on. There's also the Portia Blake case to consider. You can be sure the press will go on pestering us about that. We could always tell them that we stand by the original finding, I suppose, but that's not something I'm willing to do, given what we've learned in recent weeks. And neither, I might add, is the commissioner.'

22

ELEGANT IN HIS silk suit and new Charvet tie – he had bought it at a shop in Bond Street only the day before – Chen Yi strolled down the Mall, enjoying the warm summer weather. He had come from viewing the changing of the guard at Buckingham Palace – a ceremony he had always wanted to see but had only read about – and paused long enough on his way back through St James's Park to feed the ducks in the ornamental pond.

His appointment was for noon and his way took him beneath Admiralty Arch and around Trafalgar Square to St Martin's Lane and Charing Cross Road. It was his first visit to London – but not, he hoped, his last – and he was getting to know the city centre; in particular the area around Soho. It was no secret that the brotherhood would shortly be expanding its operations and with his excellent English and good record to date Chen had hopes of being posted to the capital in a position of responsibility. As yet only an ordinary member – a 49 in the triads' code – he was due for a promotion, or so he believed, and could see himself being named White Paper Fan, or administrator of the newly established branch; or if not that, then perhaps Straw Sandal, which would put him in charge of liaison duties.

Nor did his ambitions end there. The climb to the top could be slippery – and treacherous. But Chen was confident of his abilities and believed that one day he might even ascend to the uttermost pinnacle: he had it in him to be a 489, he believed; a Dragon Head, no less.

His unhurried steps, meanwhile, had taken him past Trafalgar Square and up Charing Cross Road, and presently he turned off it and entered the lower reaches of Soho. He had explored the area several times and called in at a number of shops and restaurants, all run by Chinese, in order to show the photograph he had brought with him from Amsterdam. Up till now his inquiries had met with no success. Nor had the word which Huang had put out among his own contacts borne fruit. But Chen had reason to believe that today would be different. The telephoned message he had received had come as a surprise: he had thought that particular avenue a dead end. Now it seemed that the road to their goal might be open after all. His caller had claimed to be in possession of valuable information.

Soon he had crossed Shaftsbury Avenue, and after walking a short distance up Wardour Street he reached his destination: a building fronted by several windows through which half a dozen young men, all of them Chinese, could be seen working at desks. A glassed door with a board beside it bearing the words NEW CHINA IMPORT COMPANY in gold lettering gave access to the building. Chen went in and crossed the carpeted floor of the lobby to a desk at the rear where the receptionist, a young woman dressed in black, watched his approach without expression.

'I am here to see Mr Lin,' he announced, speaking in Cantonese.

He took a business card from his jacket pocket and slid it across the desk to her.

'He is expecting me.'

*

Chen walked to end of the alleyway, taking care not to step on any of the refuse strewn over the cobbles in front of him. The alley ran past the back of a restaurant and the rubbish bins behind it were, as usual, overflowing with bits of rotting fruit and vegetables which were spread like a minefield across the slippery walkway.

Near the end of the street he came to a door, which he opened using a key. As he started up the narrow stairway the figure of a Chinese woman wearing a soiled dressing-gown emerged from the gloom at the back of the hall. She nodded when she saw him. Chen said nothing. He continued up the stairs.

Though he knew better than to reveal it, he had been shocked by the lodgings to which Huang Wei had led him after they had crossed the Channel by ferry from Ostend and taken the train to Waterloo station. Situated south of the River Thames in a rundown district whose seedy aspect was further marred by numerous unfilled bomb craters overflowing with weeds, the building where they were staying seemed little better than a slum to him, its sour-smelling rooms occupied by the lowest sort of Chinese immigrants, most of them labourers to judge by their clothes and rough manners. Presiding over the establishment was a woman of indeterminate age, who appeared to know Huang. At all events she had greeted him respectfully. But after having shown the two visitors to their respective rooms on the first floor she had left them to their own devices, and Chen at any rate had not had occasion to exchange another word with her.

As he walked down the uncarpeted passage towards Huang's door he heard a high whining sound, steady in note and quickly cut short. After each brief pause, it resumed at the same even pitch. When he knocked on the door, the sound ceased.

'Come.' The terse order was uttered in Cantonese.

Chen entered and saw Huang, barefoot and clad only in trousers and a white vest, sitting in a cane chair by the window. He had a long axe balanced across his knees and held a whetstone in his free hand. His slate-coloured eyes were expressionless as they took in Chen's appearance.

'A handsome piece of neckwear.' He spoke in English. His glance was fastened on the tie Chen was wearing. 'Where did you get it?'

'The tie ... ah ... in a shop.' Chen stumbled over the words.

'Has it not occurred to you yet that we did not come here to be noticed?' Though Huang's tone was mild, his eyes told another story. They had hardened in the last few seconds. 'Why do you think we are staying in this ... ?' He switched back to Cantonese, employing a vulgar term for a lavatory bowl and its likely contents. 'Our purpose is to remain invisible. But you advertise your presence like a ... like a ...' Again he turned to his native tongue, this time using a common term for a male prostitute. 'I blame myself. I should have guessed from the silk suits you wear. I should have known a peacock when I saw one.'

He paused. Chen stood with bowed head.

'Do not take offence at these words of mine. Learn from them. You are a clever young man and you will see that what I say is worth listening to. Appearance is nothing. Let others think less of you. That way you will learn more of them; you will see their weaknesses. In time they will come to fear you. All will follow from that. Keep it in mind and you may rise in the brotherhood. Forget it and you will surely fall.'

'Your words are precious.'

Chen stood with head bowed. Although he was trembling with suppressed rage, he knew better than to show it. He saw now that he had misjudged the enforcer. He had seen him simply as a thug: a man with iron fists and an indifference to physical pain. But there was more to Huang than he had imagined, and he would do well not to forget it.

'I will remember each one.'

Huang returned to the task he had been engaged in, drawing the whetstone along the edge of the axe, setting off the same high, keening note as before. Chen stared at the implement. He knew that Huang hadn't brought it to London with him. His luggage had been confined to a single small suitcase. He had obviously acquired the axe locally, but not from a hardware shop. Although the gleaming head looked new, the handle had been used. It was clear that he had connections here; there must be people he was acquainted with apart from the woman who ran the lodging-house. For all Chen knew the embryo of a new Tang branch already existed. His hopes of attaining a post of importance in the new order had begun to shrivel under the sharp edge of Huang's tongue.

As he stood there another thought came to him, equally disagreeable. Earlier in the day he had allowed himself to indulge in pleasant dreams of the future; he had seen himself rising through the organization, gaining steadily in importance and influence as his talents were recognized, even to the point where one day the leadership might beckon.

But now, watching Huang as he drew the whetstone across the gleaming axe head, Chen was aware for the first time of a flaw in the image he had of himself, a weakness he had not acknowledged before. There was one position in the triad hierarchy that he could never aspire to, and it might be enough to damn his hopes. The cold purpose he sensed in the scarred figure of the enforcer was foreign to his nature. Although the thought was like gall, he knew that the iron that dwelt in some men's souls was not his to command. He would never have it in him to be a Red Pole.

As though reading his thoughts, Huang paused in his labour.

'You looked pleased with yourself when you came in.' His tone was neutral. 'Have you fresh information?'

Swallowing, Chen nodded.

'The old man has news of our bird.'

'Does he know where he is?' Huang showed no reaction. Only his eyes had narrowed slightly.

'No, but he has learned his plans. Wing means to leave the country as soon as possible.' Eager now to placate his superior, Chen ventured a smile. 'With luck we can set a trap for him.'

Huang stroked the head of his axe with a scarred fore-finger. Chen could see that he was thinking.

'This is good.' His eyes bored into the younger man's. 'But how do we know Lin is telling the truth?'

Sweating now, Chen replied.

'He is too afraid to lie.'

Huang nodded with satisfaction.

'You see, I am right. It starts with fear.'

PART THREE

23

'AYE, AYE . . . DO you hear that?'

Hammer raised, George Burrows paused mid-stroke as the rumble of thunder sounded in the distance. Busy shoeing their old mare, he was standing in the stable yard with the animal's foreleg held firmly between his thighs and his hammer raised, ready to drive the nail in.

'We could have a spot of rain later on. The ground could do with it. I'd like to see it softened up a little before we start with the autumn ploughing.'

He bent to his task again. Madden, who was holding the horse's head still, watched as the nail was hammered home, meanwhile musing on the words he had just heard. Aware that the speaker had given no real thought to what he had said, or to who might be listening, he realized that they reflected a simple reality: namely that the farm was coming more and more to be George's responsibility, while his own role was growing increasingly marginal. It was time either to reassert his authority, or to make a graceful retreat. He watched as Burrows took a fresh nail from his mouth and the operation was repeated.

'There – that'll do you for now, old girl.' He stood up, stretching.

The mare, Daisy by name, filled a number of roles on the farm, none of them taxing. Madden used her now and then to ride around his acres, while at other times she was employed to pull a cart carrying vegetables and other produce to the village grocer who was a good customer.

'The autumn ploughing . . . yes, I must give some thought to that.' Madden decided it would be as well to put down a marker at once while the opportunity presented itself. 'I know I've been away a lot lately, George. But it was unavoidable, I'm afraid. Never mind. We'll soon be back to normal.'

'That's good to hear, sir.' As though aware of his employer's unworthy train of thought, Burrows showed every sign of welcoming the news, smiling broadly. 'May was saying only the other day that the place doesn't seem the same without you here.'

May was George's wife, a woman Madden had known since girlhood and believed to be incapable of falsehood. Suitably chastened, he surrendered the bridle he was holding and prepared to leave.

'Well, I only have to go up to London once more,' he announced as he donned his tweed jacket, an ancient garment patched at the elbows, which was draped over the side of a dog cart. 'We'll be clearing out the very last pieces of furniture from the house in the next couple of days. After that it'll be in the hands of an estate agent and ready for viewing. Lucy will stay with friends until we find a flat to buy which she can move into.'

He had not seen fit to mention the other business that had kept him away – George knew nothing of the inquiries he had been making on Angus Sinclair's behalf – but as he made his way along the stream towards the chief inspector's cottage he was only too aware that he wasn't done with it quite yet. Although they had spoken on the phone during the week, his old friend was yet to receive a first-hand report on the latest developments, which included the murder of both

Audrey Cooper and Rex Garner, and as likely as not would be champing at the bit for further details.

'It's as good as over, then, is it? Done with? All wrapped up?'

The chief inspector seemed less than happy with the verdict he had just delivered. Madden had found him where he had so often been these past weeks, sitting in his garden under the apple tree with a book in his hand.

'I can't help thinking it was a pity Garner was murdered. If he had hanged himself as was first thought, Charlie Chubb and his myrmidons could have laid Portia Blake's murder at his door with a clear conscience. Now it's still open to question . . .'

'Not necessarily,' Madden pointed out.

Seated in a garden chair close to Sinclair's, he had spent close on half an hour filling his eager listener's ears with a detailed account of the events of the past few days. The part played by Lily Poole in making sense of Audrey Cooper's actions prior to her death had brought words of warm approval from her old backer. But it was the second murder committed in the course of the week that had evoked the sharpest reaction from him.

'Wing might well have been trying to blackmail him over Miss Blake's murder,' Madden explained. 'He obviously thought those photographs were valuable enough to kill for and he didn't waste any time letting Garner know they were in his hands. But as we've learned, his victim was penniless, or as good as, and he probably told Wing that, which may explain what followed.'

'Still, it's curious about the flex, don't you think?' Sinclair was assailed by the same doubts that had troubled his visitor earlier in the week. 'After all, Wing had a knife, and was only too ready to use it, as we know. Was he trying to disguise the murder, do you think? Make it look like suicide?'

'It's possible. But there could have been another reason. He might have thought that if he used his knife the killing would be linked to Miss Cooper's murder and the police would start putting two and two together.'

Stretching, he sighed.

'But that's been the trouble with this case, Angus. I've never felt easy about it. It's full of unanswered questions, and some of them may never be resolved. For what it's worth, I think they're all tied up in one way or another with the person of Stanley Wing. We've heard a lot about him, but for me he's still a puzzle. Mind you, given his background that's no surprise. None of us can pretend to imagine what it must have been like growing up as he did. While it's true that Jack Jessup rescued him from the streets, I think his character was already formed by then. He saw the world as a jungle; no one was to be trusted, not even his benefactor. I think Mrs Castleton was right. He's driven by hatred. But beyond that there's nothing I can say about him with any certainty. The man's a mystery to me.'

Glancing at his watch, Madden made to rise from his chair.

'I must be getting home. We've got Violet and Ian coming for a drink. I want to be there before they arrive so that I can impress on Lucy the need for discretion. She knows far more about this case than she ought to, which is my fault, and is altogether too eager to talk about it. Luckily we've had some news that might distract her. Rob has written to say he'll be back in England soon and that he's due some leave. Lucy is already organizing several parties in London for his benefit, and with any luck that will keep her mind busy; at least for a while.'

*

As he unlatched the gate at the bottom of the garden, Madden heard the sound of his daughter's voice.

'It's all very well you saying it's a nautical tradition, Mummy, but it simply won't do. If Rob wants me to introduce him to my girlfriends, he'll have to make some sacrifices. I'm going to insist on it. The beard must go.'

Emerging from the orchard, he saw her standing a little way off beside Helen, who was on her knees by a flower bed, busy with a gardening fork. Lucy held a snapshot in her hand. It was one that her brother had sent them when he had written to say that he would soon be back in England. Madden and Helen had admired the photograph, which showed their tall son in full naval uniform and sporting a handsome, bushy beard.

'Daddy, don't you agree . . . ?' Spying her father, Lucy turned to him for support. 'Rob simply can't present himself in decent society looking like a savage.'

'I don't see why not.' Madden went over to join them. 'Your mother and I think he cuts a fine figure. The beard is particularly impressive.'

'Well, I'm sorry to say you're mistaken.' Lucy flushed with annoyance. 'I can't see any of my friends wanting to dance cheek-to-cheek with that great hairy thing.'

'Should this be of concern to Rob?' Madden affected an air of bewilderment. 'Not that your friends aren't charming, I'm sure, but why are you so convinced he'll want to dance cheek-to-cheek with them?'

'Oh for heaven's sake, Daddy!' Lucy lost patience. 'He's been at sea for the last six months. What do you think he'll want to do? I'm going to give him an ultimatum. Either the beard goes, or . . . or . . .'

Unable to think of a suitable threat, she stalked off, heading up the lawn towards the house, with Hamish – her ever-faithful shadow – trotting at her heels. Madden and Helen looked at each other.

'It sounds as though the battle lines have already been drawn.' Madden ventured a comment. 'Lucy seems almost to relish the prospect.'

'Rob will be just the same.' Helen was in no doubt. 'There's nothing they enjoy more. It's a struggle to gain the upper hand, and it started in the nursery, if memory serves. You'd better prepare yourself. We could be in for a lively few weeks.'

Shedding her gloves, and helped by the hand Madden offered her, she rose from the lawn. He collected the tools she had brought.

'How was your talk with Angus?' she asked as they set off up the lawn. 'Is he satisfied with the outcome of this case – or at least resigned to the fact that there's nothing more anyone can do about it?'

'Not entirely,' Madden replied. 'But he knows better than anyone that not all investigations end happily. With Garner dead, I doubt the police will ever know for certain who killed Portia Blake, while if Wing had any hand in her death, that's likely to remain a mystery too unless the authorities can lay hands on him, which seems increasingly unlikely. I wouldn't bet much on his chances of survival with those triad killers after him, so whatever secrets he might harbour will probably die with him. And of course the irony is that in spite of all that has happened in the past few weeks, the police may have got it right first time around. There's still no real evidence to suggest that it wasn't Norris who murdered the poor girl.'

'But your part in this is over?'

'I certainly hope so. There's really nothing more I can do

for Angus. I've asked Billy to keep me abreast of developments so far as the search for Stanley Wing is concerned, but that's for Richard's benefit. Garner's death has hit him hard. They grew up together. He's still trying to cope with the idea that his old friend committed suicide and I'm not in a position to tell him that the police are treating it as a case of murder. They don't want that news released before the inquest.'

They had reached the terrace, and there they parted – Helen to go upstairs and change, Madden to take the gardening tools he was carrying to the potting shed at the side of the lawn. On returning to the house he heard the phone ring in the study and went to answer it.

'Richard . . . ?' He recognized his caller's voice.

'I'm sorry to bother you, John, but will you be up in London next week?'

'Just for a day or two. We're moving out of the house for good on Wednesday. Is there something I can do for you?'

'I was hoping you could join me for dinner at my club.'

Madden hesitated. He had caught an alien note in the other man's voice.

'Is something the matter, Richard?'

'You mean something apart from the frightfulness of this whole sordid business?'

The bitter outburst took Madden by surprise. He was still trying to think of a suitable response when Jessup spoke again.

'No, it's just that I'd like to have your company, John. Would Tuesday suit?'

24

As MADDEN CLIMBED out of the taxi he noticed a man in uniform standing on the pavement; he was looking up at the sky, which was already darkening with the onset of night.

'Hello, Lennox,' he said. 'Are you checking the weather? It looks as though we could have a storm before long.'

'Mr Madden, sir . . .' Jessup's chauffeur turned to him with a smile. He doffed his peaked cap. 'I've just dropped Sir Richard off. He was late getting away from the office. I'll be driving him down to Hampshire later, and I was thinking we'd probably run into some rain.'

As he spoke a flash of lightning showed in the blackness. It was still some distance off and the accompanying rumble of thunder took several seconds to reach their ears.

'Being a farmer, I'll be glad to see it. But I hope for our sake it's not too heavy.'

With a wave Madden went up the shallow steps and through the doors into the club. He found his host standing at the reception counter with his hat in his hand and a rain-coat over his arm.

'There you are, John . . .'

Despite the smile of greeting he offered his guest, Madden noted the dark shadows under his eyes; sure signs of sleep-lessness, he thought. It looked as though the strain of the past few days was taking its toll.

'We appear to have been abandoned. They're building a

new cloakroom downstairs and we're supposed to drop off our things here, but there's no one about.'

As he spoke the sound of laboured footsteps reached their ears. They were coming from a stairwell at the back of the lobby and after a moment the figure of an elderly porter dressed in the customary black garments of his calling came shuffling into view. He was breathing heavily.

'I'm sorry, sir.' Panting, he addressed Jessup, whom he had just caught sight of. 'I was just making sure the back door was locked. What a mess those builders make. They leave everything lying about. The passage to the bathroom is like an obstacle course. I've had complaints from the members. I meant to have a word with them about it this evening, but they slipped out before I had a chance.'

'That's all right, Tom.' Jessup handed him their hats and coats. 'We haven't been waiting long. This is a guest of mine, Mr Madden. Have you got the visitors' book handy? I ought to sign him in.'

As the porter reached beneath the counter for his ledger. Jessup pointed to the row of campaign medals pinned to his jacket.

'Those date from the Boer War, John. Parsons was at the siege of Mafeking.' He was making an effort to sound cheerful. 'Isn't that so, Tom?'

'Quite right, sir.' Still pink in the face, the old man's cheeks flushed a deeper red.

'Mr Madden here was in the first war, and I was in the second. Together we make quite a trio. Someone ought to take our picture.'

The suggestion was well received. Parsons chuckled richly.

'Tom's been at the club longer than anyone.' Jessup bent to sign the book. 'I can recall the first time my father brought me here, when I was still a boy. I can't have been older than fifteen or sixteen. It was to have lunch. You were on duty that day, Tom. Do you remember?'

'Very well, sir.' The porter beamed. 'Sir Jack said he was going to propose you for membership in due course and that I was to keep an eye on you. "See he doesn't get into any mischief," he said.'

'I'd forgotten that.'

As though a magic wand had been waved across it, the strain vanished from Jessup's face in a moment. The smile he offered the old man was full of affection.

'Well, I'm not sure how successful you were, Tom, but you certainly did your best.'

'I've got some news for you, Richard. It'll be welcome in its way, at least I hope so.'

They had paused only briefly in the bar for a glass of sherry before going into the dining room, where Jessup, who seemed more troubled than ever, sat drumming his fingertips on the table while the waiter brought their food and filled their wine glasses.

'I spoke to Billy Styles today,' Madden began. 'The police here have had word from the Hong Kong CID. They've finally tracked down that woman Garner assaulted years ago. She was a prostitute, but she's married now with a family and doesn't want the matter brought up again. The point is, she survived the beating.'

'So Rex didn't kill her.' Jessup's face cleared momentarily. 'Well, thank God for that.'

'It's the first piece of solid information the police have had. So much of this case has been supposition. Unfortunately it tends to strengthen the case against Garner as far as

Miss Blake's murder is concerned. It's the only other thing Wing could have had over him. And we're assuming it was he who sent Garner those photographs. It could hardly have been anyone else.'

Silence fell as Jessup pondered his words.

'Look, John, I realize that the police think Garner killed Miss Blake, but will they take it any further now? Will they make that public? As I said before, it seems hard to condemn a man when he isn't alive to defend himself.'

Madden saw what was troubling him.

'Truthfully, I can't answer that, Richard. It's not for me to say. But I don't believe they will, partly for the reason you give and partly because there are still missing links in the chain of evidence and without them they can't prove that Garner was guilty. It's my belief they'll let the matter drop. At worst they may say that they're not looking into the Portia Blake case any longer and leave the public to draw their own conclusions.'

Jessup sat brooding. He had hardly touched his food.

'I can't tell you how hard I find it, thinking about Rex,' he said at last. 'We were such friends when we were boys. My mother thought he was a bad influence on me, but she was wrong. We both liked breaking the rules and we egged each other on. But there comes a time when you have to grow up, and poor Rex never realized that. He thought he could live life on his terms, bend it to his will. But it broke him in the end and he began to drink more and more. He became a sad figure and people tended to avoid him. I'm ashamed to say I was one of them, and he felt the betrayal keenly. There's a particular pain that comes from shedding old friends. Do you know what I mean, John?'

His glance pleaded for understanding, and Madden dipped his head in silent acknowledgement.

'I'm going to tell you something I shouldn't,' he said, 'but it may help ease any guilt you feel about Garner. He didn't commit suicide, as was thought. He was murdered.'

'Good God!' Jessup was dumbfounded.

'You must keep this to yourself. It can't come out till the inquest. But the pathologist who examined the body is confident that Garner was strangled before he was strung up, and with the same length of flex.'

'But . . . but who by?'

'The betting is on Stanley Wing. He had a motive of sorts. It's clear that Garner wasn't in a position to meet his supposed blackmail demands – we know that from you – and it also seems likely that Wing hated him. There's no proof as yet that Wing was ever in Garner's house, but that may change in the next few days.'

'Change . . . how?'

'There were some fingerprints left on the banisters which don't match Garner's or any of his staff's. It's likely they were left by the killer when he dragged the body up to the gallery to hang it. The police are expecting to receive a copy of Wing's prints from the Hong Kong police any day now. If the two sets match the police will know he was there.'

'And if they don't?'

'Then the police will be faced with another puzzle.' Madden shrugged. 'But that's been a feature of this inquiry from the start. All it's ever done is raise more questions than it answers.'

He caught his host's eye.

'As far as the inquest is concerned, at least you won't have to answer questions about the conversation you had with Garner here at the club before his death. In fact I doubt that the name of Portia Blake will even come up. You'll only be asked to help establish his movements, to say how he got home, which is something Lennox can confirm. You will have to say he was drunk, I'm afraid. That can't be avoided. It may explain why he was unable to defend himself.'

Jessup shook his head hopelessly.

'God, I wish Sarah were here.' The words burst from his lips. 'I miss her terribly.'

'Will she be returning soon?' Madden asked.

'By the end of the week, she says. We talk every evening by telephone, but it's not the same.'

'As soon as she's back and settled you must all come over to Highfield. Helen is counting on it.'

Jessup brightened on hearing the words. The cloud on his face seemed to lift.

'I can't think of anything I'd like more.'

Madden searched his memory to see if there was anything else he could tell his companion that might serve to ease his mind.

'I do have some news about Wing,' he said. 'He was staying in a boarding house in Brent Cross a fortnight ago. The landlady remembers him. But he's disappeared since then. He probably found a room somewhere, the sort that are advertised in tobacconist's windows and don't involve any record being kept.'

'He's a fool to have stayed here so long.' Jessup's tone had turned grim again.

'I believe you're right. It seems certain those triad killers are on his trail. At least one of them – not the enforcer himself, his assistant, the young man who came to your office with Lin – has been asking questions and showing Wing's photograph to members of the Chinese community. They seem to know he's here.'

About to continue, he paused. Jessup's expression had changed. He was looking past him and when Madden turned he saw a black-suited figure standing at the entrance to the dining room. It was Parsons, the porter from downstairs. He was peering about him. When his eye fell on Jessup he hurried across the room to their table.

'I'm sorry to interrupt, sir.' He bent to murmur in Sir Richard's ear. 'There's a phone call for you – it's a Detective-Inspector Styles, of Scotland Yard. I tried to explain that you were having dinner with a guest, but he insisted on speaking to you.'

'Thank you, Tom.'

Jessup rose. He shot a glance at Madden, who shook his head.

'I'm sorry, Richard. I've no idea what it's about.'

'I'd better have a word with him.'

Madden watched as he left the room and then gestured to the waiter, who was standing beside the table with a wine bottle in his hand waiting to fill his glass. He couldn't imagine what might have prompted Billy to call at this hour, but it had to be something important or he would have waited until the morning. Casting his mind back, he recalled the look on Jessup's face when he had watched the body of Rex Garner being lowered to the floor: the pain he must have felt at that moment. All he could hope now was that whatever Billy had to say wouldn't add to his distress.

The sight of Tom Parsons bending to whisper anxiously in his host's ear a moment before reminded him of the scene downstairs, when Jessup had made much of the old man, putting his own cares aside to cheer him and bring a flush of pleasure to his cheeks. It had been the action of a man, as he himself had put it to Helen, who would rather give than receive, and the memory brought a smile to Madden's lips as he sipped his wine. Just then, though, another thought occurred to him, an idea so startling – and unwelcome – that instinctively he thrust it from his mind.

'John . . . !'

Madden looked up with a start.

'Richard . . . what is it?'

Jessup stood beside him. His face had paled in the few seconds he'd been absent from the table.

'They've found Wing.'

'The police . . . where . . . ?' Madden pushed back his chair.

'In the docks . . . that's to say, they think it's him. They want me to go over there.'

'Do you mean they've found his body?'

'Not exactly . . .'

Jessup looked away. For a moment he seemed he might be unable to speak. But then he forced the words from his lips.

'All they have is his head.'

25

A BOLT OF forked lightning split the sky above them. It was followed by a peal of thunder that echoed like a roll of giant drums for long seconds before it died away. The rain that had started to fall in scattered heavy drops a few minutes earlier just as they entered the dock gates turned suddenly into a downpour. The long-awaited storm had finally arrived.

Madden and Jessup had already opened the two umbrellas which Lennox had retrieved from the boot of the car, but Lily Poole, who had been waiting at the dock gates to meet them, had only a raincoat to protect her and Madden drew her into the shelter of his. Leaving car and chauffeur parked at a spot a short distance from the gates, the two men had set off with their guide, but had hardly taken more than a dozen paces when the heavens opened.

'It's only about five minutes from here, sir.'

Lily had to shout into Madden's ear, so loud was the drumming of the rain on their spread umbrellas. She was leading them down a narrow lane walled on either side by darkened buildings, some of them whole, others damaged beyond repair. Lying well downriver on a tongue of land called the Isle of Dogs, which was enclosed on three sides by a great loop in the Thames, the docks had been heavily bombed during the war, as Madden was well aware, and although a programme of reconstruction had been under way since the end of hostilities, with funds in short supply, many sheds and office buildings still stood derelict.

Little had been said during the drive across London. Although Jessup had taken it for granted that his guest would want to accompany him, he had sat silent as they followed the course of the river, past his company's offices on Cheapside and on through the deserted night-time streets of Wapping and Limehouse, heading for the great dock complex. He had already told Madden all he knew before they left the club.

'The murder was reported more than an hour ago, according to Inspector Styles, but it took a while to get a squad of detectives assembled and then to find out what had happened. The best guess seems to be that Stanley was making a run for it, trying to smuggle himself out of the country aboard a freighter, and somehow the triads got wind of it.'

Madden for his part had failed to rid himself of the disturbing notion that had come to him while he was sitting on his own at the table waiting for Sir Richard to return. Although he had tried to dismiss it from his mind – it had been prompted by an incident so trivial it hardly seemed worth thinking about – the thought continued to nag at him.

Lily tugged at his sleeve.

'There we are, sir.' She pointed to a lighted doorway ahead of them. 'You'll find everyone inside.

A few seconds later, ushered out of the rain and relieved of their umbrellas by a waiting constable, they found themselves standing in the shell of a large warehouse empty of goods whose high roof was all but lost to view in the darkness above. What light there was came from a pair of standing lamps whose long cords snaked across the cement floor to an electrical outlet. Like stage spotlights, their beams were trained on an area in the middle of the cement floor where a round object lay. Although they were still too distant from the scene to make out any details, Madden had little doubt that it was a decapitated head they were looking at and his presentiment was confirmed moments later as they approached the spot and he saw the face distorted by a hideous grin and the wide pool of dried blood surrounding it.

Instinctively he glanced at Jessup, who had come to a halt beside him. He was staring at the object with a look of mingled horror and disbelief.

'Sir Richard . . . !'

Billy had just noticed their arrival. He had been standing with a group of detectives at the edge of the illuminated area, watching as a police photographer circled the spot snapping shots from different angles. He hurried over to them.

'I'm sorry to drag you out on a night like this, sir.' He addressed his words to Jessup, though with a quick glance at Madden. 'But we can't be sure it's Wing from the photograph you lent us.' He tapped his breast pocket. 'The features are twisted and . . .'

'It's him.' Jessup's gaze was riveted on the ghastly spectacle in front of them. 'That's Stanley Wing.'

'Ah . . .' Billy let out a sigh. 'It's settled, then. We had to be sure.'

He caught Madden's eye.

'I didn't expect to see you, sir.'

'I was having dinner with Sir Richard when you called. Who found the head, Billy?'

'The river police. They've got a station near the dock gates. A couple of their officers were on a routine patrol around the North Dock. It's where imports are offloaded and the police check the warehouses as a matter of course. This shed we're in is a new one. It's not in use yet. The builders are still putting the finishing touches to it and the officers would probably have walked right past it if one of them hadn't heard faint noises coming from inside. They stopped and shone their torches in. At first they didn't see anything; then one of them spotted something lying on the floor and they went over to investigate.'

Billy shrugged.

'They realized they must have just missed whoever did this.' He gestured towards the head. 'The warehouse was empty. But there was another door on the other side from where they'd come in – that one there.' He pointed. 'They went over to have a look, but they couldn't see anyone out-side. It was dark and the area behind this shed is still pretty much as it was at the end of the war: just a lot of damaged buildings. They decided the best thing to do was to report their find, so one of them stayed here while the other ran back to the station. The news was telephoned to the Yard quick enough and when the duty officer heard about the head he rang me at home and I came over here at once. It seemed likely that the victim was Wing, but I didn't know how to get hold of you, sir.' He looked at Jessup. 'So I rang your number in Hampshire and spoke to Mrs Castleton. She told me to try your club.'

Jessup was silent. He had been standing motionless for long minutes, seemingly unable to tear his eyes from the grisly sight before him.

'We'll have to wait for the pathologist, but it looks like a clean blow to me.' Billy felt he had to say something. 'At a guess, I'd say an axe was used.'

Jessup stirred.

'What about the body?' he asked.

'River police officers are searching the area now, but what with it being dark and a lot of these buildings still in ruins it won't be easy. And the rain isn't helping either.' He beck-oned to Lily. 'Get hold of an umbrella, Lil, and see if you can locate Joe Grace. I want to know if they've found anything.'

He turned back.

'As I understand it, sir, you told Mr Madden that this particular gang gets rid of its victims' bodies.'

'That's correct, Inspector.' Jessup spoke in a dead voice. 'They leave only the head. It's intended to instil fear in their own ranks: to warn backsliders what may lie in wait for them if they break their oaths. Ideally, they like to make a ceremony of it and conduct the execution before a select audience, or so I've been told. I dare say it wasn't possible in this case. They must have felt they had to kill Wing on the spot. But word will get out: the discovery of his head is bound to be reported, and that will be enough to send out a message.'

'On the spot, you say, sir?' Billy frowned. 'So you agree he was probably trying to flee the country?'

'It does look that way, doesn't it?' Jessup shrugged wearily. 'I expect you'll find there's at least one freighter in the docks due to weigh anchor in the next few hours; if it hasn't slipped its moorings already.'

'We thought of that, sir. There's a Chinese vessel, Hong Kong registered, due to cast off in a couple of hours. I sent DS Grace aboard to question the captain, but he swore he knew nothing about it. All his crew were aboard, he said. He brought them up on deck for Grace's inspection and showed him a list of their names. That doesn't mean anything. I doubt Wing's would have been among them, or any other name he might have been using. But what I don't understand was how he could have arranged it. He can't have that many contacts in London.'

'All he needed was one, Inspector.' Jessup's tone was bleak.

Billy studied his face. He shot a questioning glance at Madden.

'Are you saying you know who that might be, sir?'

Jessup opened his mouth to reply, but then seemed to change his mind. He stood biting his lip.

'Sir . . . ?' Billy prompted him.

'This is only a guess, Inspector, and I wouldn't want you to take it as gospel.' Jessup spoke finally. 'I dare say Mr Madden told you about the two Chinese men who called on me recently asking if I had news of Wing. One of them was a businessman called Lin Jie. Although I've no proof of it, I've reason to believe that he and Wing were involved in importing Chinese relics into this country illegally some years ago. And given that it was Lin whom the triads chose to approach when they began searching for Stanley, it does seem likely they had a past connection.'

'So what you're suggesting is it might have been this Lin fellow who arranged for Wing to slip out of the country, and that somehow the triads got wind of it.'

Jessup nodded. 'But don't imagine for a moment that he'll admit to anything. He'll plead complete ignorance and nothing you or I or anyone else might say to him will alter that. He may have been hoping that if the triads learned that Wing had left the country they would leave him alone.'

Billy turned to Madden.

'What do you think, sir?'

Madden came to himself with a start. His mind had been wandering.

'I really can't say, Billy.' He forced himself to concentrate on the moment. 'But I'm wondering how Wing got into the docks.'

'There's a passport control office at the gates,' Billy explained. 'They told us that a number of Chinese came through tonight, all merchant seamen, and their papers were checked. Wing could have been among them. Even if he was travelling on a false passport, it might have been good enough to pass muster.' Billy scratched his head. 'But it's these killers who really puzzle me – how did *they* gain entry? They couldn't have just walked through the gates with the others. And there's a twenty-foot wall around the whole dock complex.'

'I can tell you that, guv.'

Billy swung round to see Joe Grace standing behind him in a puddle of water with Lily at his side. She skipped away smartly as he shook himself like a dog, sending a spray of water from his dripping hair and coat.

'Watch it, Sarge!' she protested. Joe grinned.

'Me and some of the lads have just found a gate at the top of the docks that ought to be locked, but isn't. According to the river police it's open during the day, but locked at night with a chain and padlock. Someone's gone to work with a bolt-cutter. The chain's been cut. That's how they got in, and they left the same way. In fact, they were spotted.'

'By who?'

'A bloke who's got a fish-and-chip shop across the road. He stays open late because of seamen reporting for duty, but he'd closed for the night and gone upstairs to his flat when he saw half a dozen men coming out of that gate which he knew was usually kept locked, which was why he noticed them. They had a bakery van parked there . . .'

'*A bakery van . . . !*' Billy was disbelieving.

'That's what he said.' Joe flashed his wolfish grin. 'But he didn't take a note of the name, more's the pity. Anyway, just before nine, which is when we think Wing was topped, he saw these blokes come out through the gate, and they were carrying something.'

'Like a body?'

'Could have been.' Joe shrugged. 'There were two of them toting it. But it was wrapped in something, cloth or canvas is my guess, and that's all he saw. The men stuck it in the back of the van and off they all went. And before you ask, guv, he couldn't describe them, couldn't even say if they were Chinks, it was too dark. But they were all dressed in black.'

'A bakery van . . .' Billy repeated the words. 'Well, it's a start at least. We'll get on to it right away.'

He looked around him. The photographer had finished his work. The other detectives he had brought with him were standing idle.

'You'd better fetch those officers in out of the rain,' he told Grace. 'There's no point in them searching any longer.'

He turned to Jessup.

'I'm just waiting for the pathologist to arrive before we remove the head, sir. There's no call for you to stay any longer. And again, I'm sorry for having dragged you down here.'

'Don't apologize, Inspector.' Jessup rested his tired gaze on Billy. 'I can't help feeling this was always going to happen – if not here, then some other place.'

'You mean the triads were bound to catch up with him sooner or later?'

'That's always been their reputation. Stanley must have known he was living on borrowed time.'

He turned to Madden.

'John . . . ?'

'Yes, I'm coming, Richard.'

Madden turned, more than ready to leave now, but then paused when he saw that Jessup hadn't moved. Once again he was gazing down at the bloodied object lying on the floor at his feet.

'I can't deny I'd hoped to see this man arrested and stand trial for what he's done.' He lifted his eyes to meet Billy's gaze. 'But I wouldn't wish an end like this on anyone.'

26

Big Ben was chiming the hour as they turned off the Embankment and drove past the Houses of Parliament towards Whitehall. Although the storm had passed, the streets, still wet, shone like mirrors in the lamplight. Looking at his watch, Madden saw that it was midnight.

'At least you won't have to drive me to Hampshire, Ted.' Jessup spoke from the back of the car where they were sitting. 'I'm going to sleep at the club. We'll go down tomorrow.'

He turned to Madden.

'I'm sorry, John. I had no idea the evening would turn out this way.'

Madden was silent. He'd not spoken since they had left the docks. Jessup examined his face.

'You look worried,' he said.

'I've been trying to work out how those men got hold of Wing.'

It wasn't altogether true. His thoughts had been on another track. But the two questions weren't unrelated.

'I'm sorry . . . ?' Jessup didn't understand.

'How did they manage to overpower him and get him to that warehouse? The docks weren't exactly deserted. There were river police stationed there and those merchant seamen who passed through the gates must have walked down the same road Wing would have taken to get to the freighter he was supposed to board. Any sort of rough stuff between him and these triad thugs was bound to have been noticed by someone. At least, you would think so.'

'So what's your conclusion?'

'That it's far more likely he went there of his own accord.'

'To an empty unused warehouse . . . ?' Jessup frowned. 'But why should he have done that?'

'I can only make a guess, Richard.' Madden glanced at him. 'But it could be because he had an appointment there.'

'With Lin, do you mean?'

Madden shrugged.

'He's the most likely person to have set something up. You said so yourself. He might have told Stanley that either he or someone he'd send in his place would be there to ensure that the arrangement with the ship's captain went smoothly. But whatever Wing was told, whatever was arranged, it was almost certainly a blind.'

'A *blind* . . . ?'

'It's only an opinion, mind.' Madden searched the other's face. 'But I doubt that any passage on a freighter was ever fixed for Stanley Wing, no matter what he'd been led to believe. I think the aim was simply to get him to the docks, and then into that warehouse . . .'

'Where the triads would be waiting for him?'

Jessup had understood.

'What you're saying is that he walked into a trap.'

'I'm worried about him, sir, and that's the truth. I haven't seen Sir Richard look this tired since the war.'

Ted Lennox's homely features were a picture of concern as he nursed the big Bentley around Hyde Park Corner.

'Mind you, then he had reason: we were up against it more than once, and he was always worried about us, the men. Is it because of Mr Garner dying that way? Is that what's upset him?'

'Mostly, I think.'

Madden was sitting beside the chauffeur in the front of the car. When they dropped Jessup at the club Lennox had opened the back door for Madden to climb in, but his passenger had declined the offer.

'I'd rather sit up with you, Ted.'

'Sir Richard does the same whenever we go down the country. He likes to chat.'

It was Jessup who had insisted that his guest accept the offer of a lift up to St John's Wood instead of getting the night porter to ring for a taxi, as Madden had suggested.

'The very least I can do is see that you get home safely after what I've put you through tonight.'

Lennox, too, had been quick to add his support to the plan. All three of them had got out of the car and were standing on the pavement.

'I'll be driving up that way in any case, sir,' he had assured Madden with a smile. 'I've got a room in Bayswater for when Sir Richard spends the night in London, and there'll be no traffic this time of night.'

Madden had accompanied Jessup to the doors of the club, which had been locked, and Jessup had rung the bell for the night porter. While they waited he had asked Madden for a favour.

'If the police need to talk to me could you tell them I'll be down in Hampshire? Sarah is due back on Thursday. I'll have to come up to London for the inquest – Rex's that is – but otherwise I'll stay in the country.'

When he heard the porter unlocking the door he had held out his hand.

'Thank you for being there, John. It meant a lot to me. Pray God I never witness another sight like that.'

Madden could see he was exhausted.

'Try and get some sleep, Richard,' he said.

Standing a little way off, Lennox had eyed his employer with concern.

'He'll feel better when his missus gets back,' he confided to Madden now as they drove up Park Lane. 'Don't you think so, sir?'

'I'm sure he will, Ted.' Madden had noticed the chauffeur's worried look. He cast around in his mind for a subject that might distract him. 'I understand you and Sir Richard met during the war?' he said.

'That's right, sir. It happened soon after I'd volunteered for the Parachute Regiment. I was assigned to his company and the first thing he said to me – he was a lieutenant then – was that I should have known better.' Lennox's frown had faded. He was chuckling now. '"Never volunteer for anything," he said. "Didn't they teach you that in basic training?"'

Madden smiled. 'Did you see a lot of action together?'

'Enough to go on with: North Africa, Sicily, Normandy . . . and then Arnhem, of course. By that time I was company sergeant-major and Sir Richard was our captain. We'd been through a lot together by then, and we all felt the same about him. He was one of those officers you'd follow anywhere.'

Lennox glanced at his passenger.

'You were in the first war, weren't you, sir? Sir Richard told me. I reckon you know what I mean.'

'Yes, I know what you mean.' Madden returned his glance. 'Tell me about Arnhem. I've read accounts of the battle, of course, but Sir Richard doesn't talk about the war and I've never spoken to anyone else who was there.'

Lennox sighed.

'Ah, well they tried to make it sound like a victory afterwards, but you could have fooled us. We jumped into a hornets' nest, sir, and that's the truth. It turned out there were a couple of Panzer divisions refitting in the neighbourhood which nobody seemed to know about and we hadn't been long on the ground when all hell broke loose. There was a bridge over the Rhine we were supposed to take so that the troops moving up from the south could cross it, but we never did, and after that things began to fall apart. The weather was bad so we didn't have the air support we were expecting and most of the supplies dropped to us ended up in the Jerries' hands. We'd been there more than a week and were running out of ammunition and taking heavy casualties, too, so in the end the colonel had to call it a day. But word went out to the men that they didn't have to surrender if they could find a way of escaping. There wasn't much left of our company, just a handful of men, but we were posted on the outskirts of Arnhem – we were holding the flank there – and the captain decided it was worth having a go at joining up with other units who were in a neighbouring town.'

He fell silent for a moment as he navigated the turn from Marble Arch into Oxford Street.

'Well, just about then I got hit in the leg by a stray bullet, and I reckoned that was my lot. I'd just have to wait until the Jerries arrived and hope they would take me prisoner and not just shoot me out of hand.' His chuckle had taken on a wry edge. 'I'm not saying anything against them, mind. They were good soldiers, but street-to-street fighting is the worst kind and you don't like to leave any wounded enemy behind you. But the captain took one look at me lying there on the ground and said, "You're not getting out of this that easily, Ted Lennox." Next thing I knew he'd hauled me to my feet and strung my arms around his neck. "Hang on tight," he said, and from then on he carried me.'

He shook his head ruefully.

'We got out of Arnhem all right, and into the next town, but the Jerries were hot on our heels. We could hear them: they were only a few streets away. But I wasn't the only casualty and our wounded were slowing us down. Then, just as we thought we'd be caught, a man appeared in the doorway of a house just ahead of us. He started waving to us and calling out in English: "This way, Tommies, this way!" We'd had a lot of help from the Dutch civilians. They'd taken in our wounded and given us food, so we didn't hang about. We headed straight for his house and he hurried us all inside and told us to go up to the floor above and stay quiet. "The Germans are coming," he said. We could hear them ourselves. It sounded as though they were in the next street. "Don't make any noise. I will say you went past." He spoke good English.

'We went straight up the stairs into a bedroom and waited. We could hear the Jerry soldiers calling out to one another. They were coming closer. The captain had put me down on the bed with another bloke who was also wounded, and while I was lying there I noticed something hanging on the wall. It was a painting of an old-fashioned shield with a funny looking design on it: a sort of hook with a line drawn through the middle. I'd never seen anything like it. I noticed that the captain was looking at it too; staring, I should say. Then suddenly, in a flash, he was gone—'

'Gone . . . ?' Madden cut in.

'He just ran out of the room and we heard his feet on the stairs; then another noise, a sharp cry, more like a yelp, and the sound of a door being slammed. Some of the men went after him, but I had to stay lying there on the bed and only heard later what had happened. This Dutch bloke had been going to shop us to the Jerries and the captain had grabbed him from behind at the front door just in time. It was that shield he had seen . . .'

'It must have been a *Wolfsangel*,' Madden said.

'That's right . . . that's the word.' Ted Lennox looked at him in wonder. 'The captain told us about it afterwards. I was trying to remember the name.'

'It was a simplified design of a wolf trap from German heraldry,' Madden explained. 'The Dutch fascists used it as their symbol before they switched to the swastika. Sir Richard must have recognized it.'

He was riveted by the tale.

'So you all escaped?'

'Only in the nick of time. This chap had a whistle to his lips when the captain grabbed him. I saw it lying there beside his body when we came downstairs. He was about to blow it.'

He shrugged.

'Anyway, we left by the back door double quick, and a short while later we joined up with some of our blokes who were holding positions in the town. There was already a plan in operation to withdraw as many men as possible and that same night we made it back across the Rhine.'

'And was Sir Richard still carrying you?' Madden asked.

'Right up to the moment he dumped me on a raft.' Lennox shook with laughter. 'Later, after we were back in England, he came to see me in hospital. I was up and about by then, but still on crutches. "You'll have to get rid of those," he said, "if you're going to be my chauffeur." I didn't know what he was talking about. "Well, you'll need a job after the war, won't you?" he said. "And I'll need a chauffeur. Think about it and let me know."' Laughing, Lennox shook his head. 'Well, I thought about it,' he said, 'for a few seconds anyway.'

Madden had been so caught up in the tale that he saw with surprise that they had already rounded the top of Regent's Park and were turning up Avenue Road towards Aunt Maud's house.

'The truth is, we all owed him our lives, I reckon.' Lennox's voice had altered. He spoke in a solemn tone. 'All of us who were with him that day.'

The car drew to a halt.

'I can't say for sure what would have happened if the Jerry soldiers had trapped us in that house.' Lennox looked at his passenger. 'But something tells me it wouldn't have ended well. Still, it can't have been easy for the captain, having to grab that Dutch chap from behind and break his neck. But it was him or us. The captain knew that. So it had to be done.'

27

Madden awoke in darkness. Peering at the luminous dial of his watch, he saw that it was just after four o'clock. His brief sleep had been troubled by dreams, none of which he remembered clearly other than the last, in which he had found himself walking down seemingly endless passages which had turned first one way then another and which had ended in a small room where a man was sitting at a table. His face seemed familiar, but it was only after he awoke that Madden realized the features were those of Tom Parsons, the club porter.

Half an hour later, finding that further sleep eluded him, he rose and donning his slippers and dressing-gown went quietly down the uncarpeted wooden stairs to the floor below, where he proceeded to roam about the empty rooms retracing the tangle of thoughts that had kept him awake, a winding maze that called to mind the passages he had stumbled through in his dream.

Finally, worn out by his restless pacing, he sought refuge in the kitchen, where there was still a table with a chair beside it. Settling down there, he sat with his elbows on the table and his chin resting in his cupped palms, staring into the darkness . . .

'What on earth are you doing here, Daddy? Have you been up all night?'

Madden lifted a heavy head. He had fallen asleep in the kitchen. His daughter had found him still sitting at the table with his head resting on his folded arms. He blinked at her.

'This isn't like you at all.'

Looking unusually elegant in a beautifully cut suit which she had acquired in Paris two years before while supposedly studying French, Lucy seemed bent on making the most of her discovery.

'Did you remember to strip your bed? Shall I do it for you? I'm coming back in my lunch hour to collect the bed-clothes and any other odds and ends we've forgotten.'

Madden saw that she had a suitcase with her. It had been their last night in the house. Lucy was moving temporarily into the flat of a friend who was away for a few weeks and whose absence meant that Rob, whose ship was due to dock at Plymouth in a few days, would also be able to stay there with her when he came up to London.

'Thank you. I'll strip my own bed.' Madden clung as best he could to the shreds of his dignity. 'I must get dressed,' he said.

'I don't know what Mummy will say.'

'Nothing, if you don't tell her,' he growled.

'And what were you up to last night? I wanted to hear about your dinner with Sir Richard. I stayed up for ages, but you never came back. Why were you so late?'

'We were busy . . . occupied.' Rubbing his eyes, he dragged himself to his feet.

'Is that all you're going to say?' His daughter was disbelieving. 'After everything we've been through together on this case? I can't believe it . . .'

Madden scowled. Gathering himself, he addressed her in a different tone.

'I've said all I'm going to say, Lucy. I have nothing to add. You're just going to have to accept it. Is that clear?'

She stared at him, open-mouthed.

'You're using your "voice",' she said accusingly.

'My *what* . . . ?'

'That's what Rob and I used to call it. Daddy's speaking in his "voice", we'd say. We'd better do as we're told.'

'I wish I'd known that. I would have used it more often.'

'Well, you're not to take advantage of it now, just because I told you.'

He tried to maintain a serious air, but it was hopeless. All he could do was laugh at her.

'There – that's better.' Satisfied, she kissed him. 'You were looking so sad.'

'Was I?' He put his arms around her and held her close.

'That's my cab,' she said as the doorbell rang. 'I have to go.' She kissed him again. 'But you're not to look sad any more. I forbid it.'

It was true. His spirits had sunk to a point so low he could barely bring himself to attend to the business that had brought him to London. He was faced with a dilemma he didn't know how to resolve. The more he thought about it, the more intractable it seemed, and it stayed with him as he went upstairs to strip his bed and get dressed. When he returned to the kitchen to make himself a cup of tea he was interrupted by another ring at the door. The callers proved to be a pair of removal men and for the next twenty minutes he was occupied watching as they carried the last pieces of Aunt Maud's furniture out of the house.

There being nothing further to do – a set of keys had already been placed in the hands of the estate agent – he was about to call for a taxi to take him to Waterloo station when the phone rang at his feet. It was due to be disconnected at the end of the week. He bent to pick up the receiver.

'Ah, I've got you, John! I was afraid you might have left already. Styles told me you'd be going home today.'

Charlie Chubb's voice sounded loud in his ears. The chief super seemed to be in good spirits.

'What a night you must have had! I've seen a few things in my time, I can tell you, but a severed head all on its own: that's something I've never clapped eyes on, not in forty years on the job. I hope it didn't spoil your sleep.'

'What can I do for you, Charlie?'

'Nothing, really, but if you're heading for Waterloo, as I imagine you are, I thought you might like to drop in here on the way.'

'Why should I want to do that?'

'I'd rather tell you in person. I want to see the look on your face.'

It was clear the chief super was enjoying himself.

'What do you mean, Charlie? What are you talking about?'

'Well, if you insist . . . Wing's body. It's turned up.'

'Good God!' Madden was struck dumb. Seconds passed before he could speak again. 'Where did you find it – in the river? Was it fully clothed?'

'Fully clothed . . . ? That's an odd question. I don't know. But I can tell you it was unearthed in Bow Cemetery. Styles has just called me with the news. But he'll be back here presently, so if you want to hear the full story you'd better look in as I suggested.'

Madden didn't hesitate.

'I'm on my way,' he said.

*

Billy cleared his throat.

'The first I heard about it was just after I arrived for work. I got a call from the police in Tower Hamlets. One of their bobbies had received a report from a bloke who was walking his dog late last night and saw what looked like some men digging in the cemetery there. He was on the other side of the railings, of course, and some way off from where they were.'

He paused to take a sip from his cup of tea. He had arrived in Chubb's office accompanied by Grace and Lily Poole to find Madden already there, and the chief super in the process of pouring out tea from the pot he had had his secretary make for them.

'He didn't think anything of it at the time – he just went home to bed – but when he took out his dog again this morning he bumped into one of the local bobbies and told him what he'd seen. They went to the cemetery, which was open by now, and he showed the bobby where he'd spotted the men. There was a fresh grave there all right, and when the bobby made inquiries he was told that a body had been buried at the same spot a couple of days earlier; it was all above board. But that still didn't explain what this chap with the dog had seen . . .'

Billy paused for another sip.

'. . . so the bobby got hold of the grave diggers who work there and asked them to take a look at it. They said they couldn't be sure, but it looked like it had been messed with. The mound of soil wasn't how they had left it; and it seemed bigger. That was enough for the bobby. He rang the station and a detective-sergeant came over to take a look for himself. He decided to have the grave dug up again and warned the diggers not to disturb the coffin. He knew he'd have to get permission from higher authority if they had to remove it and look underneath. But in the end it wasn't necessary. They hadn't even reached it when they found a body lying in the earth, and when the DS saw it was headless he got on the blower to me. He had read the report I put on the telex the night before. We went over at once. It was Wing all right.'

'How could you be sure?' Chubb asked.

'The body was dressed in seamen's clothes. There was nothing in the pockets, but we found a money belt strapped around the waist under his shirt which the people who buried him must have missed. Along with some cash it also contained a passport in the name of Wing, which meant he must have got into the docks using the other one he had in the name of Lee. That was missing.'

Billy grinned.

'And that wasn't all,' he said, 'though we didn't realize it at first. It was only after we'd got the body to the local mortuary and I had a chance to examine the passport that I found it had a handful of negatives clipped to one of its pages. They'll need to be developed before we can be certain, but even looking at them now there's not much doubt they're the same ones Audrey Cooper had; the ones that got her killed. I've sent them up to the lab.'

'Were there any prints with them?' Chubb asked.

Billy shook his head.

'I reckon Wing must have sent those to Rex Garner,' he said. 'And Rex got rid of them double quick, in his fireplace, if you remember. But that was no skin off Stanley's nose as long as he had the negatives. But when Garner couldn't pay him and he topped him it must have seemed like a lot of trouble for nothing. And I can't see that they're going to be much use to us now, not unless we decide to name Garner as Miss Blake's killer. What's your feeling on that, sir?'

Chubb shrugged.

'I can't see it happening myself,' he said. 'We still can't prove it. But it's not my decision, thank God, and I'm not even sure it'll be Cradock's. The commissioner seems to have his own opinion on the subject. We'll find out soon enough. I've got a meeting fixed with them both for this afternoon.'

He turned to Madden.

'Well, John, I hope you don't feel I dragged you down here for nothing. But after the part you've played in this – for which I'll thank you again, even if Cradock won't – I thought you ought to be in on the final act. And of course Angus will want a full report too. Let's not forget that.'

'Indeed not, Charlie.' Head bowed, Madden had listened in silence to Billy's account. Now he gathered himself to leave.

'We're near enough to lunchtime for me to invite you upstairs to the senior officers' canteen, if you care to stay. I might say the cuisine there has improved somewhat since your day.'

'Tempting as the offer is, Charlie, I'm afraid I must decline.' Madden rose with a heavy sigh.

'I've a train to catch.'

28

THE WIND HAD got up suddenly in the last few minutes and now Madden felt the first drops of rain on his cheek. A change in the seasons was under way. The blue summer skies of the past month had given way to broken cloud, and the weather forecast he had glanced at in the paper coming down to Petersfield had held out the promise of further rain.

Just then a rumble of thunder prompted him to glance up at the sky, and as he did so he caught sight of a kestrel hovering above him, banking against the wind. He wondered if it was the same bird he and Jessup had seen when they had walked up this way together. Lowering his gaze, he saw a figure in the distance. Someone was following him up the path from the house. He recognized Ted Lennox's stocky figure and limping stride. Madden waited for him to catch up.

Although he had given them no warning of his visit he had been warmly greeted by Mrs Castleton when he had arrived by taxi from the station. Shown into the drawing room by one of the maids, he had found her busy arranging flowers in the vases placed there.

'I'm so pleased to see you, John.' She had shaken his hand. 'Richard said you might come down from London today.'

'Did he?' Madden had been surprised.

'He told me you would probably turn up. Do you mean you didn't mention the possibility to him?' Now it was she who looked puzzled.

'It was a last-minute decision.'

Madden had spent some time on the train coming down from London thinking up a plausible excuse for his visit and he offered it to her.

'I was at Waterloo intending to catch a train to Highfield when I changed my mind and decided to come down here instead. There's something I want to discuss with Richard. Has he told you what happened last night?'

'You mean about Stanley Wing?' She winced. 'What a dreadful business! Richard told me about it when he got back this morning. He said he had to go to the docks to identify what was left of the poor creature, but that you were with him, and that made it easier.' She smiled. 'You've been a great support to him, John. Rex Garner's death upset him terribly. But I expect you know that.'

She had paused to place some flowers she was holding in her arms into one of the vases.

'Sarah will be back tomorrow,' she said over her shoulder. 'I want the house to look its best for her.'

Drying her hands on a rag she turned to him again.

'Still it is strange that Richard seemed so sure you would come down today. I don't mean to pry, but is what you have to discuss with him so important?'

Madden hesitated. He wanted to be as frank with her as he could. But there were things he could not say.

'I was at Scotland Yard earlier today and was told they had discovered Wing's body. I felt Richard should know.'

'Oh, that explains it, then.' She seemed relieved. 'Why he thought you might be coming down. He knows, you see.'

'Knows . . . ?'

'A police inspector rang this morning, a Mr Styles from Scotland Yard. Richard came back from London quite exhausted and he'd gone upstairs to rest. But he came down to take the call and afterwards he told me that Stanley's body had been found. I think it was a relief to him.'

'A *relief* . . . ?' Madden was incredulous.

'Of course, it's an awful thing to contemplate, but he did say something that made me think that in some way it was a comfort to him. "At least it's all over now," he said, "nothing more can happen . . . nothing terrible." I thought then that he'd go back to his bedroom to rest, but he decided instead to go out.'

'For a walk, do you mean?' Madden was even more puzzled now.

'He said he wanted to see whether the council had started work on fencing off a piece of land not far from here – it overlooks a disused quarry – which he feels is dangerous.'

'I think I know the spot.' Madden frowned. 'He showed it to me.'

'He said he'd take the children with him. I wish he hadn't. It's going to pour with rain. Anyway, off they went, and so did I. Lennox took me into Petersfield to have my hair done. If only we'd known, I could have delayed my appointment and met you at the station.' She smiled. 'Now, have you had any lunch, John? We can easily fix you a sandwich.'

Madden hesitated. He was baffled by Jessup's behaviour.

'And you're sure he took the children with him?' he asked.

'Without doubt, I'm sorry to say.' Mrs Castleton laughed. 'I'm afraid they're going to get soaked. I was about to go outside to have a look for them. Would you like to come with me?'

She had led the way out through the door onto the flagged terrace where they found Lennox busy with a chore. Dressed in rough clothes, he was down on his knees varnishing a bench. When he heard their voices he looked up.

'Hello, sir.' He greeted Madden with a smile. 'I wasn't expecting to see you today.'

Mrs Castleton was already scanning the field beyond the wall at the bottom of the garden.

'There they are,' she said. 'The children, at any rate. I can't see any sign of Richard.'

Madden followed the direction of her gaze; Lennox, too, paused in his work to look up. Two small figures could be seen making their way across the meadow towards the house.

'Jack's carrying something,' Mrs Castleton said, shading her eyes. The sun had come out for a moment. Lennox followed her example.

'I reckon that's Sir Richard's shotgun,' he said after a moment. 'What's Master Jack doing with it, I wonder?'

Mrs Castleton was already moving towards the steps that led down to the lawn and Madden followed her. Together they walked towards the gate, but before they got there it opened and the children appeared. The little girl ran towards them, calling out.

'Look what I found, Grandma!' She was brandishing a large mushroom.

Mrs Castleton bent to kiss her. 'You mustn't put it in your mouth, Katy darling. It might be poisonous. Where's Daddy?' she asked.

'There . . .' The girl pointed back towards the wooded valley down which they had walked.

Her brother, as though conscious of the importance of the mission he'd been entrusted with, followed at a more sedate pace. He held the shotgun cradled in his arms.

'Daddy told me I could carry it back to the house,' he announced importantly. 'He said I was to give it to you, Lennox.'

The chauffeur had materialized at their side. Solemnly he took possession of the weapon.

'You have to put it in the gun room, Daddy says.'

'Of course, Master Jack – that's where it belongs. We'll do it right away. Would you like to come with me?'

'Just a moment, Jack . . .' Madden checked them. 'Did your father say how long he'd be?'

The boy shook his head. 'He just said he wanted to walk some more, but that we should go back because it was going to rain.' He pointed at the dark clouds that were massing overhead.

Madden turned to Mrs Castleton.

'I think I'll go after him,' he said.

'Must you?' She was unhappy with the idea. 'You'll only get wet yourself. I can't think why Richard didn't come back with them. Just look at the sky.'

'I can't stay long,' Madden said. 'I have to get home. If I don't go now I may miss him.'

Trying not to reveal his growing unease, he turned to leave, but then paused.

'Jack . . . !' He called to the boy, who was already walking away up the lawn with Lennox. They both turned to look at him.

'Did your father say anything else?' he asked.

The boy thought for a moment.

'Only what he's always telling me: that I have to look after Katy and see that she doesn't fall into any rabbit holes.'

Grinning, he gestured at his sister, who was sitting on the grass at Mrs Castleton's feet picking at her mushroom.

'He said I must remember to take care of her.'

*

Heralded by a roll of thunder, the rain arrived all at once, changing without warning from a sprinkling of drops to a sudden downpour that blurred the outlines of the landscape and reduced the approaching figure of Lennox to little more than a shape. Madden pulled up the collar of his raincoat and altered the angle of his hat in an attempt to ward off the lashing drops which were being driven by a high wind.

'What is it, Ted?' He called out to the chauffeur, who had neither a coat nor umbrella and was already drenched from head to foot. 'Is there a problem?'

'Not that I know of, sir.' As he came up to Madden he brushed the water from his face. 'I just thought I'd come with you.'

'You should have brought a coat, man.'

'You're right, sir. But it's a bit late now.' The brief smile he showed flickered and went out. 'The thing is, I'm worried about him, sir, and that's the truth.'

Madden was silent.

'Coming down from London this morning he never said a word. And he didn't sit up in the front with me like he always does. He sat in the back looking out of the window most of the time. I could see he was miles away.'

'He's been under a lot of strain, Ted.'

Madden turned to look up the valley.

'I don't see any sign of him.'

'Maybe he's gone up into the trees for shelter.' Lennox pointed to the wooded ridge above them. He sounded hopeful.

'He'll spot us if he has,' Madden replied. 'I think we should go on. He told Mrs Castleton he was going to the quarry.'

They continued up the valley, Madden walking with head bent against the driving rain, Lennox following in his footsteps. The path they were on had become a rivulet. Water flowed over their shoes as they trudged on. Looking up, Madden saw they had reached a gap in the ridge on their right, a grassy saddle that broke the otherwise uninterrupted march of beech and chestnut.

'We walked up there, I remember.'

He pointed, and heard Lennox's answering grunt behind him.

'That's the spot, all right.'

With one accord they veered off the path and started up the slope. As they neared the top the rain stopped as suddenly as it had begun and the wind died down. The leaden light that had enveloped them like a veil brightened and as they came to the hedge of holly Madden recalled from his earlier visit sunshine broke through the clouds, lending a glint to the dark green foliage.

'We'd better have a look on the other side,' Lennox said.

Stepping past his companion, he picked a way through the spiky leaves. Madden followed.

'Mind your step now, sir,' Lennox cautioned him as they came out on to the strip of turf Madden remembered. It was sodden underfoot. 'You don't want to slip here.'

The drop into the quarry beyond was only a few yards from where they stood.

Both men peered left and right along the empty stretch of grass.

'There's no sign of him.' It was Madden who spoke. The 'thank God' he muttered beneath his breath went unheard by his companion.

Lennox's gaze hadn't shifted. It remained fixed on a point a little way to their left.

'Just a moment, sir.'

When he moved in that direction Madden saw that his

attention had been caught by something on the ground. A strip of mud had been gouged out of the wet turf. It led to the brink of the quarry. Lennox approached it cautiously. Heart thumping now, Madden did the same. Just short of the mark the chauffeur went down on his knees and peered over the edge.

'*Christ, no . . . !*'

His anguished cry brought Madden to his side. Doing what the chauffeur had done, he went down on his knees and leaned forward as far as he dared.

The body was close to the white cliff-side. Richard Jessup lay sprawled on his back with his limbs spread-eagled. Despite the distance between them, Madden could see that his eyes were wide open. They seemed to be staring at the sky, and when he looked up he saw the kestrel hovering above them, motionless in the suddenly still air.

It was late in the afternoon before Madden had a chance to speak to Billy. On returning to the house – and before sending one of the maids upstairs to rouse Mrs Castleton, who was resting in her room – he had rung the police in Petersfield to report the accident, and to tell them that Sir Richard's chauffeur would be waiting by the body of his employer for their arrival.

He had hardly completed the call, made from Jessup's study, when he had heard the door open and saw Adele Castleton. She was in her dressing-gown. She stood in the doorway.

'John . . . ?'

One look at his face had been enough. Even before he spoke he had heard her catch her breath and turn pale. She listened to him in silence, eyes wide, but unseeing. Only when he had finished did she move, and then with a stagger, prompting him to come swiftly to her side. He had taken her arm and led her to one of the armchairs where he had sat with Jessup; there they had talked.

'An accident . . . ? Where . . . how . . . ?'

Like arrows drawn from wounds, the questions had appeared to cause her pain, and Madden had drawn his chair up close to hers so that he could take her hands in his. He had told her all he could.

'It looks as though he slipped. There was a mark in the ground. He must have gone too close to the edge of the quarry.' He paused. 'We must think about the children,' he had added gently.

She had stared at him for long seconds. And then, like a swimmer emerging from a deep dive, she had caught her breath with a gasp and he had seen from the steadiness of her glance that she was in possession of herself again.

'I can't tell them now.' She spoke calmly. 'We must wait until Sarah comes back. Her plane lands tomorrow morning. Richard was planning to drive up to London to meet her. I'll go with Lennox and we'll take the children with us. It's the best way, the only way.'

Her gaze had shifted to the table in the corner where the photograph of the fair-haired young woman wearing a beret and smiling in the rain stood.

'Poor darling,' she had murmured. 'What a homecoming.'

Soon afterwards the police in Petersfield had rung to confirm that they had collected Jessup's body from the quarry and to say that it had been taken to the town's mortuary. Half an hour later Lennox had returned to the house. Pale and still stricken, he had seemed bereft of words and Madden had led him to the kitchen where the cook and housemaids, already apprised of the tragedy, took him into their care. By that time the two children had come down from the nursery where they had been resting after their long walk and Mrs Castleton, who had had time to get dressed before they appeared, had taken them into the drawing room, where a fire had been lit. She had told them that their father would not be home that evening, but that she had a surprise for them. They would both be coming with her and Lennox to welcome their mother when she returned the following day.

'It means a trip to the airport,' she had told them. 'You'll be able to watch the planes landing and taking off.'

While they were together in the drawing room Madden had seized the opportunity to ring Scotland Yard. The news of Jessup's death had not yet reached London and Billy had been dumbfounded when he heard what had occurred.

'You say he fell into a quarry, sir?'

'That's how it looks. He seems to have slipped in the mud.'

'*Seems*, you say . . . ?'

Billy had dangled the question in front of Madden, hoping perhaps that he would take the bait. If so, he was doomed to disappointment.

'You called the house earlier, I believe, Billy?' Madden had responded with a question of his own.

'I wanted to speak to Jessup, sir. He had some questions to answer.'

'I take it you've had those negatives developed.' Madden saw no point in keeping up the charade any longer.

'You mean you know about them, sir?' For the first time in his life, Billy had sounded angry with his old mentor; well put out. 'You knew it was Jessup in that room with Portia Blake?'

'I only guessed. And it never occurred to me until last

night. I'd been trying to decide what to do about it. That's why I came down here. I wanted to speak to Richard: to hear what he had to say. But I never got the chance.' He paused. 'Jessup's wife – widow, I should say – is coming back from America tomorrow. Mrs Castleton is going up to London to meet her plane. I'll return home. Why not come down to Highfield? We can talk about it then.'

'I don't know, sir . . .' Billy had been far from mollified. 'What about this so-called "accident" then? Do you buy that?'

At that moment the door to the study had opened and Lennox appeared.

'Not now, Billy. We'll talk later, I promise.'

Madden had hung up.

29

'IT WAS STARING me in the face all the time, but I never saw it. I didn't want to. It's the only way I can explain it. I was drawn to the man. I admired him. I still do.'

Madden stared into the fire that was burning in the chief inspector's grate. Sinclair watched him closely. Catching Billy's eye, he saw he was about to speak and he held up his hand. *Wait!*

'*He* was the one with everything to lose, not Rex Garner, but somehow I managed to blind myself to the fact. I never could understand why Garner should have killed the girl. Even if he'd been in a rage over the way she had behaved the previous evening – carrying on that way at the dinner table – it still wasn't enough to provoke him into murder; or so I thought. And on top of that there was something that maid, Annie Potter, told Lily Poole that ought to have aroused my suspicions.'

'What was that, John?' The chief inspector was unable to obey his own admonition.

Madden met his gaze.

'She told Lily that Garner and his wife had arrived at the house in Kent on the Friday, as had Wing and Miss Blake. But that evening nothing untoward happened. Dinner went off without incident. It was only on the following evening, when Jessup came down from London, that Portia put on her act with the pendant. And of course it was directed at

Richard, as he very well knew, not at Garner, because it was Jessup who had given it to her.'

'How do you know that, sir?' Billy couldn't contain himself any longer.

'I don't,' Madden said bluntly. 'Most of what I'm telling you is guesswork. I'm simply reading between the lines. You don't have to accept it as fact, Billy.'

They had gathered at the chief inspector's cottage following Madden's return earlier that day from Petersfield. He had rung Helen the night before to tell her what had occurred, but although he had suggested that she might like to join them as soon as Billy came down from London she had decided it would be better if the three of them met on their own.

'Properly speaking, this is police business.'

No less shocked than Madden had been by the tragic end of a man whose worth she had never questioned, brief though their acquaintance had been, she told her husband she would rather hear the full story from him when they were on their own.

Consequently, when Billy arrived in his car soon after four o'clock, Madden had taken him down to Sinclair's cottage at once. One look at Billy's face had been enough to tell him that his erstwhile protégé was far from happy.

'The chief super's getting it in the neck,' he told Madden. 'Both Cradock and the commissioner are saying this would never have happened if he hadn't allowed you such a free hand with the inquiry.'

'An inquiry no one at the Yard was inclined to take up,' Madden reminded him.

'They're all saying you should have informed us the moment you realized that Jessup had been our man all along.'

'I was far from certain, Billy. It was only a suspicion. And what I'm going to say to you now is in confidence. Mr Sinclair already knows and accepts that.'

They had found the chief inspector, fully recovered from his attack of gout now, impatiently awaiting their arrival, and after both had declined the cup of tea he offered them they had all three settled down in front of the fire.

'Jessup told me he met Portia with Wing at a party that summer. He intimated it was a casual encounter, but I suspect it was a meeting Stanley Wing took pains to engineer. Jessup had been engaged for some months, but he hadn't seen much of his fiancée, who lived in America. Wing guessed correctly that he might be ready for a last fling before settling down to marriage and, if so, Portia Blake would have seemed ideally cast for the role: beautiful, and quite clearly available. She was privy to the scheme, too, I'm convinced. That business of showing off his jade jewellery was hogwash, just as Richard supposed, though he didn't know yet what was behind it: that all along Wing had him in his sights. We spent a lot of time wondering whether Wing was bent on making Rex Garner pay for that business with the Chinese woman in Hong Kong when he had got him out of trouble and was never rewarded for his pains. But we should have realized – *I* should have realized – that it was Jessup he really hated. It was Richard who had put an end to his connection with the company, who started him on the downward spiral that would lead to him falling foul of the triads and ending up in prison. And he knew just how vulnerable Jessup was.'

'Vulnerable?' Sinclair was paying close attention.

'Richard was in the process of pulling Jessup's back from the brink. His father had run the company into the ground, but thanks to Saul Temple's decision to invest in the firm he was managing to put things right. I don't believe his engagement to Temple's daughter had anything to do with the deal:

he wasn't that sort of man. But he must have known that if he became involved in a sexual scandal – one that would certainly have made headlines in the press, given his name and position – there was no telling how it would end. Not only could it have led to his engagement being broken off, it would also very likely have put an end to the partnership he was establishing with Temple's investment group. It could have spelt the end of Jessup's.'

'Even so . . .' Sinclair was frowning. 'Could that have prompted him to go so far as to *kill* the girl?'

Madden was silent. He gaze had gone back to the fire. He stared into the flickering flames.

'Mrs Castleton is as good a judge of men as I've ever met. She told me he had a core of steel inside him. She intended it as a compliment, and she was right. But it meant that in the last resort there was nothing he would shrink from, and once I began to think about this case in a different way, what she had said chimed with something that had bothered me earlier about the notion that Garner had murdered the girl in a fit of anger. It simply didn't fit the facts. If, indeed, Norris wasn't the murderer, then whatever happened in that hut must have happened in a very short space of time: minutes only. They would have had to have had a fight, she and Garner; he would have needed time to work himself up into a rage. It seemed to me that whoever killed Portia had decided in advance to commit the act, and that seemed to point to Wing initially. It was something he seemed capable of. But what reason did he have to kill her? I couldn't think of one, and later when it became clear that the murderer had taken not only the pendant she was wearing but probably also the photographs, I was forced to return to our original theory: that she'd been killed by someone she'd been involved with, who seemed to be Garner. But it wasn't he whom she went to meet in the wood that day. It was Jessup, and by that time, though she didn't know it, she had already made her fatal mistake.'

'What was that?' Billy asked.

'She'd decided to tackle him on her own. Up till then Wing had been pulling the strings. I'm sure he'd already been in touch with Richard. He would have told him that he was aware of the affair and might even have mentioned the photographs that had been taken of the two of them together. We'll never know for certain what he wanted: money, perhaps – he had to pay off Portia – but more likely reinstatement as a consultant to the company. It was his entrée into circles that were otherwise closed to him. But he would have applied the pressure gradually: he would have allowed Jessup time to see that his position was hopeless and that his best option was to give in to Wing's demands. Portia ruined all that. She had decided to act independently. It's clear that the performance she gave at that dinner playing with the pendant was her own idea. It was her signal to Jessup that he was dealing with her now. Wing was furious. Mrs Castleton heard him berating Portia afterwards in her room. But she carried on with her plan nevertheless and met Jessup alone the following day with the idea of showing him the pictures. She thought they were her trump card.'

'What did *she* want out of him, do you think – money?'

'That, of course.' Madden shrugged. 'But possibly even more. Audrey Cooper told me she had once tried to frighten one of the men she got involved with by telling him he had made her pregnant. Did she try the same trick on Jessup? Did she perhaps imagine she could force him into marrying her? We'll never know now. Miss Cooper didn't give her high marks for intelligence: she told her she was losing touch with reality. But the thought of the damage Portia could do to him if she went public was probably enough to doom her in Jessup's eyes. He saw with absolute clarity what the stakes were and knew there was only one way to deal with the danger. His chauffeur, Lennox, told me a story the other night of how Jessup had killed a civilian with his own hands during the war, a Dutch fascist. It was necessary; the man had been about to betray them to the Germans. But he did it in an instant. He didn't hesitate. He broke his neck. How many men do you know who could do that? I know I couldn't.'

'Yes . . . yes, but he returned to London after lunch that day.' Billy dragged them back to the issue he was wrestling with. 'Mrs Castleton had to send for him after Portia's body was discovered.'

'He went back, yes, but we don't know what time he arrived. The porter in the Albany who took Mrs Castleton's message was never questioned. Jessup had to wait until after lunch for his date with Portia. Heaven knows what time he got back to London. But thanks to the arrest of Norris none of the guests' alibis was checked, and his subsequent confession must have seemed like a godsend to Richard. He knew what a tightrope he was walking. If his connection with Portia Blake was revealed he would have been high on the list of suspects.'

'How did he keep it secret, though?' This time it was the chief inspector who posed the question.

'Ironically, I think it was Wing who helped there. The room they were photographed in together looked like a tart's bedroom, and may have been used for that same purpose before. I mean as a place where couples could be snapped without their knowing it. It was a world Wing was familiar with, or so I imagine, the sort of thing he was quite capable of arranging, and no doubt Portia went along with the idea. And I expect Jessup was more than happy to meet her in a place where they wouldn't be spotted. It might even have added spice to the sense of illicit adventure. But my point is, the last thing Wing wanted was for their brief affair to attract any attention. It would defeat the whole idea of catching Jessup in a trap of his own making. I'm sure he impressed on Portia the need to keep it to herself, which is why he was so angry over the act she put on later.'

'And after Miss Blake was murdered Wing went to her room to try to recover the negatives of the photographs, but found they weren't there.' Sinclair nodded. 'Do you think he witnessed the murder?' He cocked an eye at Madden. 'Did he know that Jessup was the killer?'

'It's highly likely. He already knew he couldn't trust Portia any longer, not after her display at dinner the night before. He was probably keeping an eye on her and may well have followed her out of the house when she went to meet Jessup. But if he did witness the murder, it's no surprise he didn't report it to the police. What benefit would that have been to him? He wanted to use the fact to his advantage. But when Norris confessed to the murder he must have seen that his chance had slipped by. Now he would have to find some other way of putting the screws on his victim. All he could do for the time being was go back to Hong Kong and think things over – and in the meantime get another pendant made similar to the one Jessup had taken from the girl's body.'

'He knew it was Jessup who'd given it to her?' Billy was intent on getting all the facts straight in his mind.

'Portia would have told him that. It was probably Jessup's farewell gift to her when he ended their affair. And it's more than likely he bought it in Hong Kong – perhaps as a present for his fiancée. Wing might even have known the shop it came from. He could easily have got them to make another like it. But then the war came and everything changed.

Caught between the Japanese occupiers and his triad friends, Wing's life began to fall apart. One can only imagine the bitterness he must have felt towards Jessup. He probably saw him as the author of his misfortunes. And even when he finally came out of prison his problems were far from over. The triads had marked him down for execution. He needed to get away from Hong Kong; he needed to disappear; above all he needed money.'

'And there was only one source he could go to for it?' The chief inspector rubbed his hands together. He was warming to the tale. 'Somehow he had to make Miss Blake's killer pay for what he'd done.'

'It would seem so.' Madden frowned. 'But all he had by way of ammunition at that stage was the false pendant he'd had made, and all he could do with that was send it to Derry along with a note suggesting there'd been more to the murder than met the eye. He was hoping the police would reopen the case so that he could begin to put pressure on Jessup again. But when there was no sign of that he sent a second letter to the *News of the World* saying essentially the same thing – that there'd been a miscarriage of justice – and that had the desired result. The police were finally forced to admit they were reviewing the original investigation.'

'We hadn't much option at that stage,' Billy agreed. 'The press were breathing down our necks.'

'What Wing failed to anticipate was that almost at once the investigation began to focus on the wrong man – Rex Garner.' Madden shook his head. 'That was my fault – or rather Jessup's doing. It was he who told me that story about Portia performing with the pendant at dinner, how she dangled it in front of Garner's eyes and seemed to be taunting him. That's what put us on the wrong track.'

'What about Garner, sir? If he wasn't mixed up in this business at all, how did he come to be murdered?'

Madden was slow in answering. Finally, he shrugged.

'In the end he had only himself to blame,' he said. 'It began when he saw that photograph you and Grace showed him of Portia and the man in the bed. It wasn't him, as we know, it was Jessup, and he either knew that – knew that Jessup had had an affair with her in the past – or he guessed it.'

'You mean he himself was never involved with Miss Blake?'

'Oh, I think he was,' Madden responded forcefully. 'That's to say he'd had the same sort of casual fling with her that Jessup had. He probably gave her name to Richard. As Miss Cooper said, the men were passing her around. He might even have done it at Wing's behest. They were all bumping into each other at parties that summer. We'll never get to the bottom of that. But having given a false alibi to the police at the time of Portia's murder, Garner knew he might be in difficulties, and when you showed him that photo he saw he could at least derive some benefit from it. You thought his reaction was strange, didn't you?'

Billy nodded.

'Joe reckoned it was because he knew it was him in the bed, but I didn't agree. It looked to me as though he was thinking of something else.'

'And you were right. He got in touch with Jessup right away. They had dinner at Richard's club the following night. We'll never know exactly what passed between them. But I suspect Garner told his old friend what he knew, or had guessed, and asked for money in return for keeping his mouth shut. He was broke, as we know. You'll recall that Jessup's account of their conversation was rather different.

He told me Garner was ready to call it quits: that he was going to make a statement to you the following morning in the presence of a solicitor.'

'And an hour or so later Garner himself was topped.' Billy's gaze had hardened. 'I'm beginning to get a nasty feeling,' he said.

Madden caught his eye and nodded. 'I'm afraid it was Jessup who killed him, not Wing, and you may be able to prove that, for your own satisfaction at least. I believe he told Garner he would pay him what he wanted and then got Lennox to drive him home. He knew he could slip out of his club by the back door, the tradesmen's entrance. It was kept locked at night, but I expect Jessup knew where the key was kept. He could have walked up to Shepherd Market. It wouldn't have taken him more than twenty minutes. All he had to do was rouse Garner, who hadn't even gone to bed, as it turned out, and was far too drunk to have put up much of a struggle.'

Madden quelled a shudder.

'Jessup couldn't trust him any longer, you see. Once the blackmail started it would go on. The same was true of Wing. He had to die, too. After he killed Miss Cooper it was Jessup to whom he sent that spare set of prints: care of his club, most likely, and by hand. His blackmail scheme was a lot stronger now that he had the negatives in his hands. But he had to move fast. The triads were hot on his trail. The fragment of the photograph you found in Garner's grate was from one of the prints. Jessup must have left it there to incriminate Rex.'

Sinclair stirred. He'd been silent for some time.

'You say that can be proved?'

'The evidence would be circumstantial.' Madden shrugged. 'It has to do with that length of flex we talked about which was used to strangle Garner and then hang him. It never seemed likely to me that the killer just happened to find what he needed in Rex's basement. I think Jessup brought it with him from his club. They've got workmen in building a new cloakroom downstairs. It seems they're careless with their tools; they leave things lying around. I heard one of the porters say so. A piece of flex that long is bound to have been missed. If the workmen are questioned I expect they'll confirm the theft.'

He saw Billy shake his head.

'Is *that* what put you on to Jessup, sir? You told me yesterday you'd only just twigged to him being the man in the photos. Was it hearing what that porter said?'

Madden nodded. Billy saw the sadness in his eyes.

'We were having dinner together, Richard and I. He'd been telling me how guilty he felt about Garner, how he felt he'd let him down. I think now that he was longing to tell me the truth. He'd been able to cope with the murder of Portia Blake – in his mind, I mean. Perhaps he'd found some way to justify it to himself. But killing a man who'd been his closest friend in boyhood was more than he could stomach. Perhaps he was already thinking of ending it all. The discovery of Wing's body with the negatives on it merely hastened the process.'

'Do you think he arranged for Wing to be killed?' Again it was Sinclair who put the question.

'I'm sure he did, though with the help of that Chinese businessman, Lin Jie. I don't imagine Jessup had any direct contact with the triads, but Lin certainly did, and both of them had good reason to want Wing out of the way. As far as I know Jessup and Wing didn't meet, but they must have spoken on the phone after Jessup received the photographs. Wing would have made his demands then. Since there was no prospect of his ever being linked to the firm again, I imagine what he wanted was money, and a good deal of it. That and safe passage out of the country, which he knew Jessup could arrange through the company's shipping contacts. I expect they were due to meet at the docks, where Jessup would hand over the money. It's possible that Wing promised to give him the negatives in exchange, but I doubt Jessup trusted him to do it. He knew Wing would probably keep back one or two as insurance. He staked his hopes on the triad killers disposing of Wing's body and anything he might have had on him, which would include the negatives. It was all he could do. He was already very close to falling off that tightrope.'

A log crackled in the fire and part of it rolled out of the grate onto the hearth. Madden was on his feet before Sinclair could move. The other two watched as he replaced the burning log and added a fresh one to the blaze.

Billy had been thinking. 'I still don't see why he took his life – Jessup, I mean?'

He hesitated when he saw the look in Madden's eye.

'You're not going to say he fell into that quarry by accident, are you, sir?'

'As far as anyone knows that's exactly what he did.' Madden's altered tone signalled a change in the atmosphere. 'Both Lennox and I saw a mark made in the mud that could have been where he slipped. Richard always said it was dangerous to leave that area unfenced. He wouldn't allow his children anywhere near it. I'll be appearing at the inquest in Petersfield next week, as you know, and if asked my opinion I'll say I believe it was a tragic accident.'

'I don't know, sir . . .' Billy flushed. 'That doesn't seem right to me. Ten years ago a man was hanged for a murder he didn't commit. I understand you might want to protect

Richard Jessup's name. But what about Owen Norris? What about *his* name?'

Madden was slow in answering. Watching him, the younger man saw it was only with difficulty that he brought himself to reply.

'I've no good answer to that, Billy. All I can say is I won't be party to any attempt to lay Miss Blake's murder at Richard Jessup's door; nor Garner's, if it comes to that. You'll have to prove it for yourself.'

He met the other's gaze.

'Remember, everything I've said to you has been in confidence, and I won't repeat it elsewhere. Of course you're free to make your own inquiries and deductions, but before you and Charlie Chubb decide whether you want to take this further, ask yourselves what you'll achieve by it. You can't prove that Jessup committed either of those murders; you can only show he had a brief relationship before he got married with a young woman who later fell victim to a man who was subsequently convicted of her murder and hanged.'

'What about Garner, though, sir? There's that length of flex to consider.' Billy wasn't ready yet to give in.

'Circumstantial, as I said. You'll need more than that to make a case.'

'How about the fingerprints left on the banisters? I'm willing to bet they'll turn out to be Jessup's.'

'I expect they will. But as any barrister would point out, the two men were friends of long standing. What could be more likely than for Jessup's prints to be found in Garner's house? As for Wing's decapitation, in order to prove that Richard had any hand in setting that up you would need Lin Jie's cooperation, and I very much doubt you'll get it. He'll say he has no connection whatsoever with the triads and doesn't know what you're talking about.'

Billy was at a loss. He had never come into conflict before with his old mentor, the man who had taught him his trade and whom he respected above all others. Nor did he appreciate the look of sympathetic understanding which the chief inspector was casting his way just then.

'What do you think, sir?' He turned to Sinclair.

The chief inspector considered his reply.

'All this has come about because I asked John to look into the matter on my behalf.' He spoke after a long pause. 'He's been good enough to share his conclusions with us, though he wasn't obliged to. And, as he says, he can offer next to no proof of what he has said: it's simply how he interprets the facts. In the circumstances I feel it only right to leave any final decision to him.'

Frustrated, Billy turned back to Madden.

'Well, if we couldn't have got a conviction against him, why *did* he go and top himself?'

Madden lifted his gaze from the fire.

'If you want my opinion – and that's all it is – it was because in the last resort he couldn't live with himself any longer. Even before I guessed the truth I sensed there was something eating away at him. And as I said before, he saw things with frightening clarity. Once he learned that Wing's body had been recovered with the negatives on it he knew that the police would launch a new investigation into Portia Blake's murder, one that might result in him being brought to trial. It wasn't just to protect his own reputation that he'd killed the girl. She was threatening to destroy everything he valued: not only his company, but his marriage to a woman he was deeply in love with. The same danger hung over him now; only it was worse. Even if the police couldn't mount a successful prosecution, a murder trial would do terrible damage, both to him and to the people he loved, including his children. It would leave a smear on the name of Jessup and everyone connected to it that would last for years, perhaps for ever. There was only one remedy, and he was ready to accept it.'

Madden looked Billy in the eye.

'He did what had to be done.'

EPILOGUE

'Has Billy forgiven you yet?' Helen took her husband's arm. 'I saw the two of you having a word after the service. I didn't realize he would be there. Was his presence official?'

'No, he came of his own accord,' Madden said. 'He told me he thought he ought to be there. He said he wanted to close the book on the case. And yes, I think he's forgiven me.'

'It's definitely closed then, is it?' She looked at him.

'So Billy said. There was simply no point in pursuing it. Even Charlie Chubb accepts that, though *he* hasn't forgiven me yet. I shall have to make my peace with him. I'll take him out to lunch. That should do the trick.'

The two of them had caught the train up to London that morning to attend a memorial service in honour of Richard Jessup organized by his widow. The occasion, held at St Lawrence Jewry, in Guildhall Yard, had been well attended, not only by City grandees and friends of the dead man, but also by more than a score of men Jessup had served with in the war. A mixed bunch, some of them hard-looking, and most dressed in cheap suits, they had gathered in a group with Lennox at the back of the beautiful Wren church where they stood throughout the service and the speeches that followed. At Mrs Castleton's request, Madden and his wife had kept her company in the row behind where Sarah Jessup sat with her parents and her children. Later, they had been introduced to the widow.

'Adele has told me how close you and Richard became.'

As good-looking in the flesh as she had appeared in the photograph he had seen in Jessup's study, and offering him the same open smile she had shown on that damp day in Paris, her straight glance had carried no hint of unspoken thoughts, nor of any suspicion that her husband's tragic end might have been other than it seemed.

Turning to Helen, she had added: 'I hope we can all get together very soon.'

It was only as they were about to leave that Madden had spotted Billy standing in the courtyard, hat in hand.

'I thought I ought to turn up, sir, just for form's sake.' Billy's handshake had lacked nothing in warmth. 'Quite a gathering, isn't it?' He had nodded at the crowd thronging the courtyard, which included a number of well-known faces.

'The chief super sends his regards. He thought I was bound to find you here and said I was to tell you he still had a bone to pick with you.' Billy chuckled. 'Oh, and by the way, you might be interested to hear that we picked up that fellow, Chen Yi.'

'I remember the name.' Madden was intrigued. 'He was the Red Pole's assistant; his jackal, Jessup called him.'

'He was stopped going through immigration at Ramsgate – he was about to board the Ostend ferry – and brought up to London. I questioned him myself. He was a smooth article.' Billy shook his head ruefully. 'Spoke English beautifully; said he was part owner of a restaurant in Amsterdam and had come over to London to visit a cousin. What cousin? I asked. I thought we might have him there, but blow me if he didn't produce a young Chinese bloke working in a laundry who was ready to swear on a stack of bibles that they were related. So we had to let him go.'

'What about the enforcer himself, Wing's killer?'

'We never saw hide nor hair of him. But then we didn't have either a name or a description.'

Before they parted Madden had put the same question to his former protégé that Helen would ask him later.

'Am I forgiven, then?'

Billy's chuckle had been answer enough. But that hadn't been quite the end of it, as he made plain.

'Still, it might not have turned out this way if he'd been anyone else.'

'Meaning what, Billy?'

'He was too important, Jessup was, too big a name to drag through the mud. The commissioner said as much. It was best to let things lie, he said.'

'And you don't agree?'

'I wouldn't say that exactly.' Billy weighed his hat in his hands. 'But I can't help thinking that all this started because some silly girl got ideas above her station. She wasn't much cop in the brains department, our Portia. You might even say she brought it on herself.'

'And your point is . . . ?' Madden eyed him keenly.

'She didn't deserve to die on that account.' Billy met his gaze.

'No, she didn't.' Madden had put a hand on the younger man's shoulder. 'Hold fast to that,' he said.

He smiled then. 'Oh, and there's one other thing. It's about time you stopped calling me sir, Billy. I'd rather you made it John.'

'So, you had your knuckles rapped?' Helen had enjoyed hearing the story. 'Good for Billy. He's always been a bit too respectful of you.'

Madden laughed. It was early evening and they were

walking arm-in-arm down the lawn to the bottom of the garden.

'Do you think he had a point?' she asked.

'More than ever.' Madden was rueful. 'The trouble was, we became too close, Richard and I. That's something we were always warned about when I was with the police.'

'But you're not any longer, my dear, and you never regarded him as a suspect.'

'True. But I can't help thinking he used our friendship to steer me in the direction he wanted. It almost worked, too.'

'Don't hold that against him.'

Surprised by her words, Madden stopped to look at her.

'Don't think of him that way. He cared for you, John. I could see that. Your friendship meant a lot to him. In the end it was probably what he clung to.'

'I'd like to think so.' Madden sighed. 'But then I find myself remembering something a fellow I met down in Kent said to me. He was an old boxer who ran a pub. He had known Norris, the man they hanged for Portia's murder, and didn't think he had it in him to kill. But then you never know anyone, do you, he said – not really.'

He felt her hand on his shoulder and he turned to face her.

'You know me,' she said.

Madden looked into her blue eyes for a long moment and as he did so felt his heart swell, just as it had years before when he had realized for the first time that she loved him. He took her in his arms.

'Yes, I do. Thank God for that.'

Unknown to them, they were being observed. Standing by the balustrade fronting the stone-flagged terrace, Lucy

Madden and her brother had been watching their parents for some time.

'Look at them!' Rob was scandalized. 'They're just like lovers.'

He shot a glance at his sister.

'What are you giggling at?'

'Nothing . . .'

'Come on.' He knew her too well. 'Spit it out.'

Head cocked on one side, Lucy considered her reply.

'Do you remember that spot down by the stream where we used to go when we didn't want anyone to find us?'

'Where we hid whenever the Mitchell twins came over because we didn't want to play with them?' He scowled at her. 'That patch of grass surrounded by bushes? What about it?'

'When they first met – it was during that big murder case when Daddy was still a detective – Mummy fell in love with him almost at once. She was sure that he felt the same, but he wouldn't say anything. It was because of what happened to him in the war. He was still too locked up in himself. He couldn't talk about his feelings. He thought he wasn't a whole man any more . . .'

She paused.

'So Mummy invited him to lunch. She got Mary to make up a picnic basket and she took him down to the stream, to that same spot, and laid a blanket on the grass . . .'

She fell silent.

'Good God!'

It had taken Rob some moments to find his tongue. He was staring at their parents in disbelief.

'Are you saying she *seduced* him?'

Lucy said nothing.

'How do you know that?' His scowl had turned fierce.

'Mummy told me once . . . woman talk . . .' She smiled.

'Woman . . . *you*?'

'Yes, *me* . . . !' She speared an elbow into his ribs, making him gasp. 'And when are you going to shave that horrible beard off? Poor Annabel was in a terrible state this morning. The whole side of her face has come out in a rash.'

'Annabel . . . ? Which one was she?'

'Which one . . . ?' Lucy aimed for his ribs again, but this time he managed to dodge her flying elbow. 'You spent half the night dancing with her.'

'She loved every moment of it.' Rob was enjoying himself. 'Couldn't get enough of my beard, she said.'

'She did *not*.'

'You're just jealous. You're longing to know what it feels like. Here, let me give you a taste . . .'

He grabbed for her, but she was too quick – 'No, you won't' – eluding his outstretched hand, and then turning and running down the steps from the terrace onto the lawn, pursued by Hamish, who'd been sitting nearby.

Her brother set off after her and caught up after only a few steps. Wrapping his arms around her, he tried to press his cheek against hers, but Lucy resisted, kicking at him with her heels, and when that didn't work, falling to her knees on the ground and tucking her head in her arms.

'You beast . . . !'

'Come on . . . at least try it . . . girls tell me it feels warm and furry.'

Bending down, Rob tried to prise her hands from her cheeks while Hamish, beside himself with excitement now, danced around them in a circle. It was the basset's frantic barking that caused Madden and his wife to break off their embrace and look back.

'Good grief!'

Madden stared open-mouthed at the sight of his two children locked in combat. As he watched they lost their balance
and fell over, still wrestling as they rolled about on the grass.

He turned to Helen for support, but saw no help would
be coming from that quarter. She was laughing helplessly. He
was left to shake his head and say the one thing that seemed
fitting in the circumstances, even if no one was listening.

'Do you think they'll ever grow up?'

extracts reading groups
books new
competitions extracts extracts
discounts extracts discounts
competitions
books new events
reading groups
new extracts
events books
new extracts books
books new titles reading groups
reading groups interviews
books events extracts extracts events
discounts books
reading groups new books events interviews new books extracts
events new events

discounts extracts discounts
www.panmacmillan.com books
extracts events reading groups
competitions books extracts new

VAL McDERMID

Val McDermid grew up in a Scottish mining community then read English at Oxford. She was a journalist for sixteen years, spending the last three years as Northern Bureau Chief of a national Sunday tabloid. Now a full-time writer, she lives in Cheshire.

The Wire in the Blood is Val McDermid's second book featuring criminal profiler, Tony Hill. The first, *The Mermaids Singing*, won the 1995 Gold Dagger Award for Best Crime Novel of the Year. The third, *The Last Temptation*, is now available in paperback.

A Place of Execution, a complex and disturbing stand-alone thriller, was awarded the 2001 LA Times Book of the Year Award (Mystery/Thriller category). Her other stand-alone thriller, *Killing the Shadows*, received critical acclaim on its release in 2000.

She has also written six crime novels featuring Manchester PI Kate Brannigan, and the latest of these, *Star Struck*, won the Grand Prix des Romans d'Aventure in France.

A further five novels feature journalist-sleuth Lindsay Gordon.

From the reviews for *The Wire in the Blood*

'This is a shocking book, stunningly exciting, horrifyingly good. It is so convincing that one fears reality may be like this and these events the awful truth'   RUTH RENDELL

'*The Wire in the Blood* is truly frightening. McDermid's capacity to enter the warped mind of a deviant criminal is shiveringly convincing, and she is equally adept at portraying the interactions, allegiances and petty jealousies that exist among the investigators. Hill, driven and disturbed, is an appealing and original character. This is a writer who just gets better and better'   MARCEL BERLINS, *The Times*

'Terrific chiller from Manchester's answer to Thomas Harris. Val McDermid can do what the Americans do so effortlessly – get inside the mind of a serial killer. Thank God for Dr Tony Hill and psychological profiling'
LUCRETIA STEWART, *Guardian*

'Tension-filled sequel to *The Mermaids Singing* . . . The story, handled with verve, wit and style, never flags'
FRANCES FYFIELD, *Mail on Sunday*

'This is a clever and exciting thriller'
SUSANNA YAGER, *Sunday Telegraph*

'The novel has the same compelling combination of sexual-political mischief and Jacobean psychological intensity that earned the author the crime novel of the year award . . . for *The Mermaids Singing*'

JOHN DUGDALE, *Sunday Times*

VAL McDERMID

THE WIRE IN
THE BLOOD

INDEX

This novel is entirely a work of fiction. The names, characters
and incidents portrayed in it are the work of the author's imagination.
Any resemblance to actual persons living or dead, events or
localities is entirely coincidental.

HarperCollins*Publishers*
77–85 Fulham Palace Road
London, w6 8jb

The HarperCollins website address is:
www.harpercollins.co.uk

This edition published 2004 for Index Books Limited

First published in Great Britain by
HarperCollins*Publishers* in 1997

ISBN 0-00-769755-4

Typeset in Minion by
Palimpsest Book Production Limited,
Polmont, Stirlingshire

Printed and bound in Great Britain by
Bookmarque Ltd, Croydon, Surrey

ACKNOWLEDGEMENTS

It's hard to imagine how I could have written this book without a lot of help from several key people. For their specialist knowledge and willingness to give so freely of their expertise, I'd like to thank Sheila Radford, Dr Mike Berry, Jai Penna, Paula Tyler and Dr Sue Black. I owe an apology to Edwina and Lesley, who ran around like headless chickens researching something that was cut in the rewrites. Without Jim and Simon at Thornton Electronics, Mac and Manda, I would almost certainly have had a complete nervous breakdown when the hard disk crashed. But the perseverance and perspicacity of three women in particular got me through to the end. For that reason, this book is for:

Julia, Lisanne and Brigid
With love

The trilling wire in the blood
Sings below inveterate scars
Appeasing long forgotten wars.
> *Four Quartets,*
> *Burnt Norton*
> T. S. Eliot

PROLOGUE

Murder was like magic, he thought. The quickness of his hand always deceived the eye, and that was how it was going to stay. He was like the postman delivering to a house where afterwards they would swear there had been no callers. This was the knowledge that was lodged in his being like a pacemaker in a heart patient. Without the power of his magic he'd be dead. Or as good as.

He knew just from looking at her that she would be the next. Even before the eye contact, he knew. There had always been a very particular combination that spelled perfection in his thesaurus of the senses. Innocence and ripeness, mink-dark hair, eyes that danced. He'd never been wrong yet. It was an instinct that kept him alive. Or as good as.

He watched her watching him, and under the urgent mutter of the crowd, he heard echoing in his head the music. '*Jack and Jill went up the hill to fetch a pail of water. Jack fell down and broke his crown . . .*' The chiming tune swelled and burst then battered his brain like a spring tide against a breakwater. And Jill? What about Jill? Oh, he knew what happened to Jill. Over and over again, repetitious as the barbaric nursery rhyme. But it was never enough. He had never quite been satisfied that the punishment had fit the crime.

And so there had to be a next one. And there he was,

watching her watching him sending her messages with his eyes. Messages that said, 'I've noticed you. Find your way to me and I'll notice you some more.' And she read him. She read him, loud and clear. She was so obvious; life hadn't scarred her expectations with static yet. A knowing smile quirked the corners of her mouth and she took the first step on the long and, for him, exciting journey of exploration and pain. The pain, as far as he was concerned, was not quite the only necessity but it was certainly one of them.

She worked her way towards him. Their routes varied, he'd noticed. Some direct, bold; some meandering, wary in case they'd misread what they thought his eyes were telling them. This one favoured the spiral path, circling ever inward as if her feet were tracing the inside of a giant nautilus shell, a miniature Guggenheim Gallery compacted into two dimensions. Her step was measured, determined, her eyes never wavering from him, as if there were no one else between, neither obstacle nor distraction. Even when she was behind his back, he could feel her stare, which was precisely how he thought it should be.

It was an approach that told him something about her. She wanted to savour this encounter. She wanted to see him from every possible angle, to imprint him on her memory forever, because she thought this would be her only chance for so detailed a scrutiny. If anyone had told her what the future truly held, she'd have fainted with the thrill of it.

At last, her decaying orbit brought her within his grasp. Only the immediate circle of admirers stood between them, one or two deep. He locked on to her eyes, injected charm into his gaze and, with a polite nod to those around him, he took a step towards her. The bodies parted obediently as he said, 'Delightful to have met you, do excuse me?'

Uncertainty flitted across her face. Was she supposed to

move, like them, or should she stay in the ambit of his mesmerizing stare? It was no contest; it never was. She was captivated, the reality of this evening outstripping her every fantasy. 'Hello,' he said. 'And what's your name?'

She was momentarily speechless, never so close to fame, dazzled by that spectacular dental display all for her benefit. My, what big teeth you've got, he thought. All the better to eat her with.

'Donna,' she finally stuttered. 'Donna Doyle.'

'That's a beautiful name,' he said softly. The smile he won in response was as brilliant as his own. Sometimes, it all felt too easy. People heard what they wanted to hear, especially when what they were hearing sounded like their dream come true. Total suspension of disbelief, that's what he achieved every time. They came to these events expecting Jacko Vance and everyone connected to the great man to be exactly what was projected on TV. By association, anyone who was part of the celebrity's entourage was gilded with the same brush. People were so accustomed to Vance's open sincerity, so familiar with his very public probity, it never crossed their minds to look for the catch. Why should it, when Vance had a popular image that made Good King Wenceslas look like Scrooge? The punters listened to the words and they heard Jack and the Beanstalk – from the little seed Vance or his minions planted, they pictured the burgeoning flower of a life at the top of the tree right alongside his.

In that respect, Donna Doyle was just like all the others. She could have been working from a script he'd written for her. Having moved her strategically into a corner, he made as if to hand her a signed photograph of Vance the megastar. Then he did a double take so exquisitely natural it could have been part of De Niro's repertoire. 'My God,' he breathed. 'Of course. Of course!' The exclamation was the verbal equivalent of smiting himself on the forehead with the heel of his hand.

Caught with her fingers inches from his as she reached out to take what had been so nearly offered, she frowned, not understanding. 'What?'

He made a twisted little *moue* of self-disparagement. 'Ignore me. I'm sorry, I'm sure you've got much more interesting plans for your future than anything we superficial programme makers could come up with.' The first time he'd tried the line, hands sweating, blood thudding in his ears, he'd thought it was so corny it couldn't fool a drunk one sip from catatonia. But he had been right to go with his instincts, even when they had led him down the path of the criminally naff. That first one, just like this next one, had grasped instantly that something was being offered to her that hadn't been on the agenda for the insignificant others he'd been talking to earlier.

'What do you mean?' Breathless, tentative, not wanting to admit she already believed in case she'd misunderstood and left herself open to the hot shaming flush of her misapprehension.

He gave the faintest of shrugs, one that hardly disturbed the smooth fall of his immaculate suiting. 'Forget it,' he said with a slight, almost imperceptible shake of the head, disappointment in the sad cast of his eye, the absence of his gleaming smile.

'No, tell me.' Now there was an edge of desperation, because everybody wanted to be a star, no matter what they said. Was he really going to snatch away that half-glimpsed magic carpet ride that could lift her out of her despised life into his world?

A quick glance to either side, making sure he wasn't overheard, then his voice was both soft and intense. 'A

4

new project we're working on. You've got the look. You'd be perfect. As soon as I looked at you properly, I knew you were the one.' A regretful smile. 'Now, at least I have your image to carry in my head while we interview the hundreds of hopefuls the agents send along to us. Maybe we'll get lucky . . .' His voice trailed off, his eyes liquid and bereft as the puppy left behind in the holiday kennels.

'Couldn't I . . . I mean, well . . .' Donna's face lit up with hope, then amazement at her forwardness, then disappointment as she talked herself out of it without saying another word.

His smile grew indulgent. An adult would have identified it as condescending, but she was too young to recognize when she was being patronized. 'I don't think so. It would be taking an enormous risk. A project like this, at so delicate a stage . . . Just a word in the wrong ear could wreck it commercially. And you've no professional experience, have you?'

That tantalizing peep at what could have been her possible future uncapped a volcano of turbulent hope, words tumbling over each other like rocks in the lava flow. Prizes for karaoke at the youth club, a great dancer according to everybody, the Nurse in her form's reading of *Romeo and Juliet*. He'd imagined schools would have had more sense than to stir the tumultuous waters of adolescent desire with inflammatory drama like that, but he'd been wrong. They'd never learned, teachers. Just like their charges. The kids might assimilate the causes of the First World War but they never grasped that clichés got that way because they reflected reality. Better the devil you know. Don't take sweets from strangers.

Those warnings might never have set Donna Doyle's eardrum vibrating if her present expression of urgent eagerness was anything to go by. He grinned and said, 'All right! You've

5

convinced me!' He lowered his head and held her gaze. Now his voice was conspiratorial. 'But can you keep a secret?'

She nodded as if her life depended on it. She couldn't have known that it did. 'Oh, yes,' Donna said, dark blue eyes sparkling, lips apart, little pink tongue flickering between them. He knew her mouth was growing dry. He also knew that she possessed other orifices where the opposite phenomenon was happening.

He gave her a considering, calculated stare, an obvious appraisal that she met with apprehension and desire mingling like Scotch and water. 'I wonder . . .' he said, his voice almost a sigh. 'Can you meet me tomorrow morning? Nine o'clock?'

A momentary frown, then her face cleared, determination in her eyes. 'Yes,' she said, school dismissed as irrelevant. 'Yes, I can. Whereabout?'

'Do you know the Plaza Hotel?' He had to hurry now. People were starting to move towards him, desperate to recruit his influence to their cause.

She nodded.

'They have an underground car park. You get into it from Beamish Street. I'll be waiting there on level two. And not a word to anyone, is that clear? Not your mum, not your dad, not your best friend, not even the family dog.' She giggled. 'Can you do that?' He gave her the curiously intimate look of the television professional, the one that convinces the mentally troubled that newsreaders are in love with them.

'Level two? Nine o'clock?' Donna checked, determined not to screw up her one chance of escape from the humdrum. She could never have realized that by the end of the week she'd be weeping and screaming and begging for humdrum. She'd be willing to sell what remained of her immortal soul for humdrum. But even if someone had told her that then, she

6

would not have comprehended. Right then, the dazzle and the dream of what he could offer was her complete universe. What could be a finer prospect?

'And not a word, promise?'

'I promise,' she said solemnly. 'Cross my heart and hope to die.'

PART ONE

Tony Hill lay in bed and watched a long strip of cloud slide across a sky the colour of duck eggs. If anything had sold him on this narrow back-to-back terraced house, it was the attic bedroom with its strange angles and the pair of skylights that gave him something to look at when sleep was elusive. A new house, a new city, a new start, but still it was hard to lose consciousness for eight hours at a stretch.

It wasn't surprising that he hadn't slept well. Today was the first day of the rest of his life, he reminded himself with a wry smile that scrunched the skin round his deep-set blue eyes into a nest of wrinkles that not even his best friend could call laughter lines. He'd never laughed enough for that. And making murder his business had made sure he never would.

Work was always the perfect excuse, of course. For two years, he'd been toiling on behalf of the Home Office on a feasibility study to see whether it would be useful or possible to create a national task force of trained psychological profilers, a hit squad capable of moving in on complex cases and working with the investigative teams to improve the rate and speed of clean-up. It had been a job that had required all the clinical and diplomatic skills he'd developed over years of working as a psychologist in secure mental hospitals.

It had kept him off the wards, but it had exposed him to

other dangers. The danger of boredom, for example. Tired of being stuck behind a desk or in endless meetings, he'd allowed himself to be seduced away from the job in hand by the tantalizing offer of involvement in a case that even from a distance had appeared to be something very special. Not in his wildest nightmares could he have imagined just how exceptional it could be. Nor how destructive.

He clenched his eyes momentarily against the memories that always stalked on the edge of his consciousness, waiting for him to drop his guard and let them in. That was another reason why he slept badly. The thought of what his dreams could do to him was no enticement to drift away and hand control over to his subconscious.

The cloud slipped out of sight like a slow-moving fish and Tony rolled out of bed, padding downstairs to the kitchen. He poured water into the bottom section of the coffee pot, filled the mid-section with a darkly fragrant roast from the freezer, screwed on the empty top section and set it on the gas. He thought of Carol Jordan, as he did probably one morning in three when he made the coffee. She'd given him the heavy aluminium Italian pot when he'd come home from hospital after the case was over. 'You're not going to be walking to the café for a while,' she'd said. 'At least this way you can get a decent espresso at home.'

It had been months now since he'd seen Carol. They'd not even taken the opportunity to celebrate her promotion to detective chief inspector, which showed just how far apart they'd grown. Initially, after his release from hospital, she'd come to visit whenever the hectic pace of her job would allow. Gradually, they'd both come to realize that every time they were together, the spectre of the investigation rose between them, obscuring and overshadowing whatever else might be possible for them. He understood that Carol was better equipped than most to interpret what she saw in him. He simply couldn't face the risk of opening up to someone who might reject him when she realized how he had been infected by his work.

If that happened, he doubted his capacity to function. And if he couldn't function, he couldn't do his job. And that was too important to let go. What he did saved people's lives. He was good at it, probably one of the best there had ever been because he truly understood the dark side. To risk the work would be the most irresponsible thing he could ever do, especially now when the whole future of the newly created National Offender Profiling Task Force lay in his hands.

What some people perceived as sacrifices were really dividends, he told himself firmly as he poured out his coffee. He was permitted to do the one thing he did supremely well, and they paid him money for it. A tired smile crossed his face. God, but he was lucky.

Shaz Bowman understood perfectly why people commit murder. The revelation had nothing to do with the move to a new city or the job that had brought her there, but everything to do with the cowboy plumbers who had installed the water supply when the former Victorian mill-owner's mansion had been converted into self-contained apartments. The builders had done a thoughtful job, preserving original features and avoiding partitions that wrecked the fine proportions of the spacious rooms. To the naked eye, Shaz's flat had been perfect, right down to the French windows leading to the back garden that was her exclusive domain.

Years of shared student dives with sticky carpets and scummy bathtubs, followed by a police section house and a preposterously expensive rented bedsit in West London had left Shaz desperate for the opportunity to check out whether house-proud was an adjective she could live with. The move north had provided her first affordable chance. But the idyll had shattered the first morning she had to rise early for work.

Bleary-eyed and semi-conscious, she'd run the shower long enough to get the temperature right. She stepped under the powerful stream of water, lifting her hands above her head in a strangely reverent gesture. Her groan of pleasure turned abruptly to a scream as the water switched from amniotic warmth to a scalding scatter of hypodermic stings. She hurled herself clear of the shower cubicle, twisting her knee as she slipped on the bathroom floor, cursing with a fluency she owed to her three years in the Met.

Speechless, she stared at the plume of steam in the corner of the bathroom where she had stood moments before. Then, as abruptly, the steam dissipated. Cautiously, she extended a hand under the water. The temperature was back where it should be. Inch by tentative inch, she moved under the stream of water. Letting out her unconsciously held breath, she reached for the shampoo. She'd got as far as the halo of white lather when the icy needles of winter rain cascaded on her bare shoulders. This time, her breath went inwards, taking enough shampoo with it to add a coughing retch to the morning's sound effects.

It didn't take much to work out that her ordeal was the result of someone else's synchronous ablutions. She was supposed to be a detective, after all. But understanding didn't make her any happier. The first day of the new job and instead of feeling calm and grounded after a long, soothing shower, she was furious and frustrated, her nerves jangling, the muscles in the nape of her neck tightening with the promise of a headache. 'Great,' she growled, fighting back tears that had more to do with emotion than the shampoo in them.

Shaz advanced on the shower once again and turned it off with a vicious twist of the wrist. Mouth compressed into a thin line, she started running a bath. Tranquillity was no longer an option for the day, but she still had to get the suds out of her hair so she wouldn't arrive in the squad room of the brand new task force looking like something no self-respecting cat would have bothered to drag in. It was going to be unnerving enough without having to worry about what she looked like.

As she crouched in the bath, dunking her head forward into the water, Shaz tried to restore her earlier mood of exhilarated anticipation. 'You're lucky to be here, girl,' she told herself. 'All those dickheads who applied and you didn't even have to fill in the form, you got chosen. Hand-picked, elite. All that shit work paid off, all that taking the crap with a smile. The canteen cowboys going nowhere fast, they're the ones having to swallow the shit now. Not like you, Detective Constable Shaz Bowman. National Offender Profiling Task Force Officer Bowman.' As if that wasn't enough, she'd be working alongside the acknowledged master of that arcane blend of instinct and experience. Dr Tony Hill, BSc (London), DPhil (Oxon), the profiler's profiler, author of the definitive British textbook on serial offenders. If Shaz had been a woman given to hero-worship, Tony Hill would have been right up there in the pantheon of her personal gods. As it was, the opportunity to pick his brains and learn his craft was one that she'd cheerfully have made sacrifices for. But she hadn't had to give up anything. It had been dropped right into her lap.

By the time she was towelling her cap of short dark hair, considering the chance of a lifetime that lay ahead of her had tamed her anger though not her nerves. Shaz forced herself to focus on the day ahead. Dropping the towel carelessly over the side of the bath, she stared into the mirror, ignoring the blurt of freckles across her cheekbones and the bridge of her small soft nose, passing over the straight line of lips too slim to promise much sensuality and focusing on the feature that everyone else noticed first about her.

Her eyes were extraordinary. Dark blue irises were shot through with striations of an intense, paler shade that seemed to catch the light like the facets of a sapphire. In interrogation, they were irresistible. The eyes had it. That intense blue stare fixed people like superglue. Shaz had a feeling that it had made her last boss so uncomfortable he'd been delighted at the prospect of shipping her out in spite of an arrest and conviction record that would have been remarkable in an experienced CID officer, never mind the rookie of the shift.

She'd only met her new boss once. Somehow, she didn't think Tony Hill was going to be quite so much of a pushover. And who knew what he'd see if he slid under those cold blue defences? With a shiver of anxiety, Shaz turned away from the remorseless stare of the mirror and chewed the skin on the side of her thumb.

Detective Chief Inspector Carol Jordan slipped the original out of the photocopier, picked up the copy from the tray and crossed the open-plan CID room to her office with nothing more revelatory than a genial, 'Morning, lads,' to the two early bird detectives already at their desks. She presumed they were only there at this hour because they were trying to make an impression on her. Sad boys.

She shut her door firmly behind her and crossed to her desk. The original crime report went back into the overnight file and onwards into her out tray. The photostat joined four similar previous overnight despatches in a folder that lived in her briefcase when it wasn't sitting on her desk. Five, she decided, was critical mass. Time for action. She glanced at her watch. But not quite yet.

The only other item that cluttered the desk now was a lengthy memo from the Home Office. In the dry civil service language that could render Tarantino dull, it announced the formal launch of the National Offender Profiling Task Force. 'Under the supervision of Commander Paul Bishop, the task force will be led by Home Office clinical psychologist and Senior Profiler Dr Tony Hill. Initially, the task force will consist of a further six experienced detectives seconded to work with Dr Hill and Commander Bishop under Home Office guidelines.'

Carol sighed. 'It could have been me. Oh yeah, it could have been me,' she sang softly. She hadn't been formally invited. But she knew all she'd have had to do was ask. Tony Hill had wanted her on the squad. He'd seen her work at close quarters and he'd told her more than once that she had the right cast of mind to help him make the new task force effective. But it wasn't that simple. The one case they'd worked together had been personally devastating as well as difficult for both of them. And her feelings for Tony Hill were still too complicated for her to relish the prospect of becoming his right-hand woman in other cases that might become as emotionally draining and intellectually challenging as their first encounter.

Nevertheless, she'd been tempted. Then this had come along. Early promotion in a newly created force wasn't an opportunity she felt she could afford to miss. The irony was that this chance had emerged from the same serial killer hunt. John Brandon had been the Assistant Chief Constable at Bradfield who'd had the nerve to bring in Tony Hill and to appoint Carol liaison officer. And when he was promoted to Chief Constable of the new force, he wanted her on board. His timing couldn't have been better, she thought, a faint pang of regret surfacing in spite of herself. She stood up and took the three steps that were all she needed to cross her office and stare down at the docks below where people moved around purposefully doing she knew not what.

Carol had learned the Job first with the Met in London and then with Bradfield Metropolitan Police, both leviathans fuelled by the perpetual adrenaline high of inner city crime. But now she was out on the edge of England with East Yorkshire Police where, as her brother Michael had wryly pointed out, the force's acronym was almost identical to the traditional Yorkshire yokel greeting of 'Ey-up'. Here, the DCI's job didn't involve juggling murder inquiries, drive-by shootings, gang wars, armed robberies and high-profile drug deals.

In the towns and villages of East Yorkshire, there wasn't any shortage of crime. But it was all low-level stuff. Her inspectors and sergeants were more than capable of dealing with it, even in the small cities of Holm and Traskham and the North Sea port of Seaford where she was based. Her junior officers didn't want her running around on their tails. After all, what did a city girl like her know about sheep rustling? Or counterfeit cargo lading bills? Besides which, they all knew perfectly well that when the new DCI turned up on the job, she wasn't so much interested in finding out what was going down as she was in sussing out who was up to scratch and who was busking it, who might be on the sauce and who might be on the take. And they were right. It was taking longer than she'd anticipated, but she was gradually assembling a picture of what her team was like and who was capable of what.

Carol sighed again, rumpling her shaggy blonde hair with the fingers of one hand. It was an uphill struggle, not least because most of the blunt Yorkshiremen she was working with were fighting a lifetime's conditioning to take a woman guv'nor seriously. Not for the first time, she wondered if ambition had shoved her into a drastic mistake and backed her flourishing career into a cul-de-sac.

She shrugged and turned away from the window, then pulled out the file from her briefcase again. She might have opted to turn her back on the profiling task force, but working with Tony Hill had already taught her a few tricks. She knew what a serial offender's signature looked like. She just hoped she didn't need a team of specialists to track one down.

One half of the double doors swung open momentarily ahead of the other. A woman with a face instantly recognizable in 78 per cent of UK homes (according to the latest audience survey) and high heels that shouted the praises of legs which could have modelled pantyhose strode into the make-up department, glancing over her shoulder and saying, '. . . which gives me nothing to work off, so tell Trevor to swap two and four on the running order, OK?'

Betsy Thorne followed her, nodding calmly. She looked far too wholesome to be anything in TV, dark hair with irregular strands of silver swept back in a blue velvet Alice band from a face that was somehow quintessentially English; the intelligent eyes of a sheepdog, the bones of a thoroughbred racehorse and the complexion of a Cox's Orange Pippin. 'No problem,' she said, her voice every degree as warm and caressing as her companion's. She made a note on the clipboard she was carrying.

Micky Morgan, presenter and only permissible star of *Midday with Morgan*, the flagship two-hour lunchtime news magazine programme of the independent networks, carried straight ahead to what was clearly her usual chair. She settled in, pushed her honey blonde hair back and gave her face a quick critical scrutiny in the glass as the make-up artist swathed her in a protective gown. 'Marla, you're back!' Micky exclaimed, delight in her voice and eyes in equal measure. 'Thank God. I'm praying you've been out of the country so you didn't have to look at what they do to me when you're not here. I absolutely forbid you to go on holiday again!'

Marla smiled. 'Still full of shit, Micky.'

'It's what they pay her for,' Betsy said, perching on the counter by the mirror.

'Can't get the staff these days,' Micky said through stiff lips as Marla started to smooth foundation over her skin. 'Zit coming up on the right temple,' she added.

'Premenstrual?' Marla asked.

'I thought I was the only one who could spot that a mile off,' Betsy drawled.

'It's the skin. The elasticity changes,' Marla said absently, completely absorbed in her task.

'*Talking Point*,' Micky said. 'Run it past me again, Bets.' She closed her eyes to concentrate and Marla seized the chance to work on her eyelids.

Betsy consulted her clipboard. 'In the wake of the latest revelations that yet another junior minister has been caught in the wrong bed by the tabloids, we ask, "What makes a woman want to be a mistress?"' She ran through the guests for the item while Micky listened attentively. Betsy came to the final interviewee and smiled. 'You'll enjoy this: Dorien Simmonds, your favourite novelist. The professional mistress, putting the case that actually being a mistress is not only marvellous fun but a positive social service to all those put-upon wives who have to endure marital sex long after he bores them senseless.'

Micky chuckled. 'Brilliant. Good old Dorien. Is there

anything, do you suppose, that Dorien wouldn't do to sell a book?'

'She's just jealous,' Marla said. 'Lips, please, Micky.'

'Jealous?' Betsy asked mildly.

'If Dorien Simmonds had a husband like Micky's, she wouldn't be flying the flag for mistresses,' Marla said firmly. 'She's just pig sick that she'll never land a catch like Jacko. Mind you, who isn't?'

'Mmmm,' Micky purred.

'Mmmm,' Betsy agreed.

It had taken years for the publicity machine to carve the pairing of Micky Morgan and Jacko Vance as firmly into the nation's consciousness as fish and chips or Lennon and McCartney. The celebrity marriage made in ratings heaven, it could never be dissolved. Even the gossip columnists had given up trying.

The irony was that it had been fear of newspaper gossip that had brought them together in the first place. Meeting Betsy had turned Micky's life on its head at a time when her career had started curving towards the heights. To climb as far and as fast as Micky meant collecting an interesting selection of enemies ranging from the poisonously envious to the rivals who'd been edged out of the limelight they thought was theirs of right. Since there was little to fault Micky on professionally, they'd homed in on the personal. Back in the early eighties, lesbian chic hadn't been invented. For women even more than men, being gay was still one of the quickest routes to the P45. Within a few months of abandoning her formerly straight life by falling in love with Betsy, Micky understood what a hunted animal feels like.

Her solution had been radical and extremely successful. Micky had Jacko to thank for that. She had been and still was lucky to have him, she thought as she looked approvingly at her reflection in the make-up mirror.

Perfect.

Tony Hill looked around the room at the team he had hand-picked and felt a moment's pity. They thought they were walking into this grave new world with their eyes open. Coppers never thought of themselves as innocents abroad. They were too streetwise. They'd seen it all, done it all, got pissed and thrown up on the T-shirt. Tony was here to instruct half a dozen cops who already thought they knew it all that there were unimaginable horrors out there that would make them wake up screaming in the night and teach them to pray. Not for forgiveness, but for healing. He knew only too well that whatever they thought, none of them had made a genuinely informed choice when they'd opted for the National Offender Profiling Task Force.

None of them except, perhaps, Paul Bishop. When the Home Office had given the profiling project the green light, Tony had called in every favour he could claim and a few he couldn't to make sure the police figurehead was someone who knew the gravity of what he was taking on. He'd dangled Paul Bishop's name in front of the politicians like a carrot in front of a reluctant mule, reminding them of how well Paul performed in front of the cameras. Even then it had been touch and go till he'd pointed out that even London's cynical hacks showed a bit of respect for the man who'd headed the successful hunts for the predators they'd dubbed the Railcard Rapist and the Metroland Murderer. After those investigations, there was no question in Tony's mind that Paul knew exactly the kind of nightmares that lay ahead.

On the other hand, the rewards were extraordinary. When it worked, when their work actually put someone away, these police officers would know a high unlike any other they'd ever experienced. It was a powerful feeling, to know your endeavours had helped put a killer away. It was even more gratifying to realize how many lives you might have saved because you shone a light down the right path for your colleagues to go down. It was exhilarating, even though it was tempered with the knowledge of what the perpetrator had already done. Somehow, he had to convey that satisfaction to them as well.

Paul Bishop was talking now, welcoming them to the task force and outlining the training programme he and Tony had thrashed out between them. 'We're going to take you through the process of profiling, giving you the background information you need to start developing the skill for yourself,' he said. It was a crash course in psychology, inevitably superficial, but covering the basics. If they'd chosen wisely, their apprentices would go off in their own preferred directions, reading more widely, tracking down other specialists and building up their own expertise in particular areas of the profiling craft that interested them.

Tony looked around at his new colleagues. All CID-trained, all but one a graduate. A sergeant and five constables, two of them women. Eager eyes, notepads open, pens at the ready. They were smart, this lot. They knew that if they did well here and the unit prospered, they could go all the way to the top on the strength of it.

His steady gaze ranged over them. Part of him wished Carol Jordan was among them, sharing her sharp perceptions and shrewd analyses, tossing in the occasional grenade of humour to lighten the grimness. But his sensible head knew there would be more than enough problems ahead without that complication.

If he had to put money on any of them turning into the

kind of star that would stop him missing Carol's abilities, he'd go for the one with the eyes that blazed cold fire. Sharon Bowman. Like all the best hunters, she'd kill if she had to.

Just like he'd done himself.

Tony pushed the thought away and concentrated on Paul's words, waiting for the signal. When Paul nodded, Tony took over smoothly. 'The FBI take two years to train their operatives in offender profiling,' he said, leaning back in his chair in a deliberate attitude of relaxed calm. 'We do things differently over here.' A note of acid in the voice. 'We'll be accepting our first cases in six weeks. In three months' time, the Home Office expects us to be running a full case-load. What you've got to do inside that time frame is assimilate a mountain of theory, learn a series of protocols as long as your arm, develop total familiarity with the computer software we've had specially written for the task force, and cultivate an instinctive understanding of those among us who are, as we clinicians put it, totally fucked up.' He grinned unexpectedly at their serious faces. 'Any questions?'

'Is it too late to resign?' Bowman's electric eyes sparkled humour that was missing from her deadpan tones.

'The only resignations they accept are the ones certified by the pathologist.' The wry response came from Simon McNeill. Psychology graduate from Glasgow, four years' service with Strathclyde Police, Tony reminded himself, reassuring himself that he could recall names and backgrounds without too much effort.

'Correct,' he said.

'What about insanity?' another voice from the group asked.

'Far too useful a tool for us to let you slip from our grasp,' Tony told him. 'I'm glad you brought that up, actually, Sharon. It gives me the perfect lead into what I want to talk about first today.' His eyes moved from face to face, waiting until his seriousness was mirrored in each of their faces. A man accustomed to assuming whatever personality and demeanour would be acceptable, he shouldn't have been surprised at how easy it was to manipulate them, but he was. If he did his job properly, it would be far harder to achieve in a couple of months' time.

Once they were settled and concentrating, he tossed his folder of notes on to the table attached to the arm of his chair and ignored them. 'Isolation,' he said. 'Alienation. The hardest things to deal with. Human beings are gregarious. We're herd animals. We hunt in packs, we celebrate in packs. Take away human contact from someone and their behaviour distorts. You're going to learn a lot about that over the coming months and years.' He had their attention now. Time for the killer blow.

'I'm not talking about serial offenders. I'm talking about you. You're all police officers with CID experience. You're successful cops, you've fitted in, you've made the system work for you. That's why you're here. You're used to the camaraderie of team work, you're accustomed to a support system that backs you up. When you get a result, you've always had a drinking squad to share the victory with. When it's all gone up in smoke, that same squad comes out and commiserates with you. It's a bit like a family, only it's a family without the big brother that picks on you and the auntie that asks when you're going to get married.' He noted the nods and twinges of facial expression that indicated agreement. As he'd expected, there were fewer from the women than the men.

He paused for a moment and leaned forward. 'You've just been collectively bereaved. Your families are dead and you can never, never go home any more. This is the only home you have, this is your only family.' He had them now, gripped tighter than any thriller had ever held them. The Bowman woman's right eyebrow twitched up into an astonished arc, but other than that, they were motionless.

'The best profilers have probably got more in common with serial killers than with the rest of the human race. Because killers have to be good profilers, too. A killer profiles his victims. He has to learn how to look at a shopping precinct full of people and pick out the one person who will work as a victim for him. He picks the wrong person and it's good night, Vienna. So he can't afford to make mistakes any more than we can. Like us, he kicks off consciously sorting by set criteria, but gradually, if he's good, it gets to be an instinct. And that's how good I want you all to be.'

For a moment, his perfect control slipped as images crowded unbidden to the front of his mind. He was the best, he knew that now. But he'd paid a high price to discover that. The idea that payment might come due again was something he managed to reject as long as he was sober. It was no accident that Tony had scarcely had a drink for the best part of a year.

Collecting himself, Tony cleared his throat and straightened in his seat. 'Very soon, your lives are going to change. Your priorities will shift like Los Angeles in an earthquake. Believe me, when you spend your days and nights projecting yourself inside a mind that's programmed to kill until death or incarceration prevents it, you suddenly find a lot of things that used to seem important are completely irrelevant. It's hard to get worked up about the unemployment figures when you've been contemplating the activities of somebody who's taken more people off the register in the last six months than the government has.' His cynical smile gave them the cue to relax the muscles that had been taut for the past few minutes.

26

'People who have not done this kind of work have no notion of what it is like. Every day, you review the evidence, raking through it for that elusive clue you missed the last forty-seven times. You watch helplessly as your hot leads turn out colder than a junkie's heart. You want to shake the witnesses who saw the killer but don't remember anything about him because nobody told them in advance that one of the people who would fill up with petrol in their service station one night three months ago was a multiple murderer. Some detective who thinks what you're doing is a bag of crap sees no reason why your life shouldn't be as fucking miserable as his, so he gives out your phone number to husbands, wives, lovers, children, parents, siblings, all of them people who want a crumb of hope from you.

'And as if that isn't enough, the media gets on your back. And then the killer does it again.'

Leon Jackson, who'd made it out of Liverpool's black ghetto to the Met via an Oxford scholarship, lit a cigarette. The snap of his lighter had the other two smokers reaching for their own. 'Sounds cool,' he said, dropping one arm over the back of his chair. Tony couldn't help the pang of pity. Harder they come, the bigger the fall.

'Arctic,' Tony said. 'So, that's how people outside the Job see you. What about your former colleagues? When you come up against the ones you left behind, believe me, they're going to start noticing you've gone a bit weird. You're not one of the gang any more, and they'll start avoiding you because you smell wrong. Then when you're working a case, you're going to be transplanted into an alien environment and there will be people there who don't want you on the case. Inevitably.' He leaned forward again, hunched against the chill wind of memory. 'And they won't be afraid to let you know it.'

Tony read superiority in Leon's sneer. Being black, he

reasoned, Leon probably figured he'd had a taste of that already and rejection could therefore hold no fears for him. What he almost certainly didn't realize was that his bosses had needed a black success story. They'd have made that clear to the officers who controlled the culture, so the chances were that no one had really pushed Leon half as hard as he thought they had. 'And don't think the brass will back you when the shit comes down,' Tony continued. 'They won't. They'll love you for about two days, then when you haven't solved their headaches, they'll start to hate you. The longer it takes to resolve the serial offences, the worse it becomes. And the other detectives avoid you because you've got a contagious disease called failure. The truth might be out there, but you haven't got it, and until you do, you're a leper.

'Oh, and by the way,' he added, almost as an afterthought, 'when they do nail the bastard thanks to your hard work, they won't even invite you to the party.'

The silence was so intense he could hear the hiss of burning tobacco as Leon inhaled. Tony got to his feet and shoved his springy black hair back from his forehead. 'You probably think I'm exaggerating. Believe me, I'm barely scratching the surface of how bad this job will make you feel. If you don't think it's for you, if you're having doubts about your decision, now's the time to walk away. Nobody will reproach you. No blame, no shame. Just have a word with Commander Bishop.' He looked at his watch. 'Coffee break. Ten minutes.'

He picked up his folder and carefully didn't look at them as they pushed back chairs and made a ragged progress to the door and the coffee station in the largest of the three rooms they'd been grudgingly granted by a police service already strapped for accommodation for their own officers. When at last he looked up, Shaz Bowman stood leaning against the wall by the door, waiting.

'Second thoughts, Sharon?' he asked.

'I hate being called Sharon,' she said. 'People who want a response go for Shaz. I just wanted to say it's not only profilers that get treated like shit. There's nothing you said just now that sounds any worse than what women deal with all the time in this job.'

'So I've been told,' Tony said, thinking inevitably of Carol Jordan. 'If it's true, you lot should have a head start in this game.'

Shaz grinned and pushed off from the wall, satisfied. 'Just watch,' she said, swivelling on the balls of her feet and moving through the door on feet as silent and springy as a jungle cat.

Jacko Vance leaned forward across the flimsy table and frowned. He pointed to the open desk diary. 'You see, Bill? I'm already committed to running the half-marathon on the Sunday. And then after that, we're filming Monday and Tuesday, I'm doing a club opening in Lincoln on Tuesday night – you're coming to that, by the way, aren't you?' Bill nodded, and Jacko continued. 'I've got meetings lined up Wednesday back to back and I've got to drive back up to Northumberland for my volunteer shift. I just don't see how we can accommodate them.' He threw himself back against the striped tweed of the production caravan's comfortless sofa bench with a sigh.

'That's the whole point, Jacko,' his producer said calmly, stirring the skimmed milk into the two coffees he was making in the kitchen area. Bill Ritchie had been producing *Vance's Visits* for long enough to know there was little point in trying to change his star's mind once it was made up. But this time, he was under sufficient pressure from his bosses to try. 'This documentary short's *supposed* to make you look busy, to say,

"Here's this amazing guy, busy professional life, yet *he* finds time to work for charity, so why aren't you?"' He brought the coffees to the table.

'I'm sorry, Bill, but it's not on.' Jacko picked up his coffee and winced at its scalding heat. Hastily, he put it down again. 'When are we going to get a proper coffee maker in here?'

'If it's anything to do with me, never,' Bill said with a mock-severe scowl. 'The lousy coffee's the one thing guaranteed to divert you from whatever you're going on about.'

Jacko shook his head ruefully, acknowledging he'd been caught out. 'OK. But I'm still not doing it. For one, I don't want a camera crew dogging my heels any more than I already have to put up with. For two, I don't do charity work so I can show off about it on prime-time telethons. For three, the poor sick bastards I spend my nights with are terminally ill people who do not need a hand-held camera shoved down their emaciated throats. I'll happily do something else for the telethon, maybe something with Micky, but I'm not having the people I work with exploited just so we can guilt-trip a few more grand out of the viewers.'

Bill spread his hands in defeat. 'Fine by me. Do you want to tell them or will I?'

'Would you, Bill? Save me the aggravation?' Jacko's smile was bright as a shaft of sunlight from a thundercloud, promising as the hour before a first date. It was imprinted on his audience like a race memory. Women made love to their husbands with more gusto because Jacko's sexually inviting eyes and kissable mouth were flickering across the inside of their eyelids. Adolescent girls found their vague erotic longings suddenly focused. Old ladies doted on him, without connecting the subsequent feelings of unfulfilled sadness.

Men liked him too, but not because they found him sexy. Men liked Jacko Vance because he was, in spite of everything, one of the lads. A British, Commonwealth, and European gold medallist and holder of the world javelin record, Olympic gold had seemed like an inevitability for the darling of the back pages. Then one night, driving back from an athletics meeting in Gateshead, Jacko drove into a dense bank of fog on the A1. He wasn't the only one.

The morning news bulletins put the figures at between twenty-seven and thirty-five vehicles in the multiple pile-up. The big story wasn't the six dead, however. The big story was the tragic heroism of Jacko Vance, British athletics' golden boy. In spite of suffering multiple lacerations and three broken ribs in the initial impact, Jacko had crawled out of his mangled motor and rescued two children from the back of a car seconds before it burst into flames. Depositing them on the hard shoulder, he'd gone back into the tangled metal and attempted to free a lorry driver pinioned between his steering wheel and the buckled door of his cab.

The creaking of stressed metal turned to a shriek as accumulated pressures built up on the lorry and the roof caved in. The driver didn't stand a chance. Neither did Jacko Vance's throwing arm. It took the firemen three agonizing hours to cut him free from the crushing weight of metal that had smashed his flesh to raw meat and his bones to splinters. Worse, he was conscious for most of it. Trained athletes knew all about pushing through the pain barrier.

The news of his George Cross came the day after the medics fitted his first prosthesis. It was small consolation for the loss of the dream that had been the core of his life for a dozen years. But bitterness didn't cloud his natural shrewdness. He knew how fickle the media could be. He still smarted at the memory of the headlines when he'd blown his first attempt at the European title. JACK SPLAT! had been the kindest stab at the heart of the man who only the day before had been JACK OF HEARTS.

He knew he had to capitalize on his glory quickly or he'd soon be another yesterday's hero, early fodder for the 'Where Are They Now?' column. So he called in a few favours, renewed his acquaintance with Bill Ritchie and ended up commentating on the very Olympics where he should have mounted the rostrum. It had been a start. Simultaneously, he'd worked to establish his reputation as a tireless worker for charity, a man who would never allow his fame to stand in the way of helping people less fortunate than himself.

Now, he was bigger than all the fools who'd been so ready to write him off. He'd charmed and chatted his way to the front of the sports presenters' ranks in a slash and burn operation of such devious ruthlessness that some of his victims still didn't realize they'd been calculatedly chopped off at the knees. Once he'd consolidated that role, he'd presented a chat show that had topped the light entertainment ratings for three years. When the fourth year saw it drop to third place, he dumped the format and launched *Vance's Visits.*

The show claimed to be spontaneous. In fact, Jacko's arrival in the midst of what his publicity called 'ordinary people living ordinary lives' was invariably orchestrated with all the advance planning of a royal visit but none of the attendant publicity. Otherwise he'd have attracted bigger crowds than any of the discredited House of Windsor. Especially if he'd turned up with the wife.

And still it wasn't enough.

Carol bought the coffees. It was a privilege of rank. She thought about refusing to shell out for the chocolate biscuits on the basis that nobody needed three KitKats to get through a meeting with their DCI. But she knew it would be misinterpreted, so she grinned and bore the expense. She led the troops she'd chosen with care to a quiet corner cut off from the rest of the canteen by an array of plastic parlour palms. Detective Sergeant Tommy Taylor, Detective Constable Lee Whitbread and Detective Constable Di Earnshaw had all impressed her with their intelligence and determination. She might yet be proved wrong, but these three officers were her private bet for the pick of Seaford Central's CID.

'I'm not going to attempt to pretend this is a social chat so we can get to know each other better,' she announced, sharing the biscuits out among the three of them. Di Earnshaw watched her, eyes like currants in a suet pudding, hating the way her new boss managed to look elegant in a linen suit with more creases than a dosser's when she just looked lumpy in her perfectly pressed chain-store skirt and jacket.

'Thank Christ for that,' Tommy said, a grin slowly spreading. 'I was beginning to worry in case we'd got a guv'nor who didn't understand the importance of Tetley's Bitter to a well-run CID.'

Carol's answering smile was wry. 'It's Bradfield I came from, remember?'

'That's why we were worried, ma'am,' Tommy replied.

Lee snorted with suppressed laughter, turned it into a cough and spluttered, 'Sorry, ma'am.'

'You will be,' Carol said pleasantly. 'I've got a task for you three. I've been taking a good look at the overnights since I got here, and I'm a bit concerned about the high incidence of unexplained fires and query arsons that we've got on our ground. I spotted five query arsons in the last month and when I made some checks with uniform, I found out there have been another half-dozen unexplained outbreaks of fire.'

'You always get that kind of thing round the docks,' Tommy said, casually shrugging big shoulders inside a baggy silk blouson that had gone out of fashion a couple of years previously.

'I appreciate that, but I'm wondering if there's a bit more to it than that. Agreed, a couple of the smaller blazes are obvious routine cock-ups, but I'm wondering if there's something else going on here.' Carol left it dangling to see who would pick it up.

'A firebug, you mean, ma'am?' It was Di Earnshaw, the voice pleasant but the expression bordering on the insolent.

'A serial arsonist, yes.'

There was a momentary silence. Carol reckoned she knew what they were thinking. The East Yorkshire force might be a new entity, but these officers had worked this patch under the old regime. They were in with the bricks, whereas she was the new kid in town, desperate to shine at their expense. And they weren't sure whether to roll with it or try to derail her. Somehow she had to persuade them that she was the star they should be hitching their wagons to. 'There's a pattern,' she said. 'Empty premises, early hours of the morning. Schools, light industrial units, warehouses. Nothing too big, nowhere there might be a night watchman to put the mockers on it. But serious nevertheless. Big fires, all of them. They've caused a lot of damage and the insurance companies must be hurting more than they like.'

'Nobody's said owt about an arsonist on the rampage,' Tommy remarked calmly. 'Usually, the firemen tip us the wink if they think there's something a bit not right on the go.'

'Either that or the local rag gives us a load of earache,' Lee chipped in through a mouthful of his second KitKat. Lean as a whippet in spite of the biscuits and the three sugars in his coffee, Carol noted. One to watch for high-strung hyperactivity.

'Call me picky, but I prefer it when we're setting the agenda, not the local hacks or the fire service,' Carol said coolly. 'Arson isn't a Mickey Mouse crime. Like murder, it has terrible consequences. And like murder, you've got a stack of potential motives. Fraud, the destruction of evidence, the elimination of competition, revenge and cover-up, at the "logical" end of the spectrum. And at the screwed-up end, we have the ones who do it for kicks and sexual gratification. Like serial killers, they nearly always have their own internal logic that they mistake for something that makes sense to the rest of us.

'Fortunately for us, serial murder is a lot less common than serial arson. Insurers reckon a quarter of all the fires in the UK have been set deliberately. Imagine if a quarter of all deaths were murder.'

Taylor looked bored. Lee Whitbread stared blankly at her, his hand halfway to the cigarette packet in front of him. Di Earnshaw was the only one who appeared interested in making a contribution. 'I've heard it said that the incidence of arson is an index of the economic prosperity of a country. The more arson there is, the worse the economy is doing. Well, there's plenty unemployed round here,' she said with the air of someone who expects to be ignored.

'And that's something we should bear in mind,' Carol said, nodding with approval. 'Now, this is what I want. A careful trawl through the overnights for CID and uniform for the last six months to see what we come up with. I want the victims re-interviewed to check if there are any obvious common factors, like the same insurance company. Sort it out among yourselves. I'll be having a chat with the fire chief before the four of us reconvene in . . . shall we say three days? Fine. Any questions?'

'I could do the fire chief, ma'am,' Di Earnshaw said eagerly. 'I've had dealings with him before.'

'Thanks for the offer, Di, but the sooner I make his acquaintance, the happier I'll feel.'

Di Earnshaw's lips seemed to shrink inwards in disapproval, but she merely nodded.

'You want us to drop our other cases?' Tommy asked.

Carol's smile was sharp as an ice pick. She'd never had a soft spot for chancers. 'Oh, please, Sergeant,' she sighed. 'I know what your case-load is. Like I said at the start of this conversation, it's Bradfield I came from. Seaford might not be the big city, but that's no reason for us to operate at village bobby pace.'

She stood up, taking in the shock in their faces. 'I didn't come here to fall out with people. But I will if I have to. If you think I'm a hard bastard to work for, watch me. However hard you work, you'll see me matching it. I'd like us to be a team. But we have to play by my rules.'

Then she was gone. Tommy Taylor scratched his jaw. 'That's us told, then. Still think she's shaggable, Lee?'

Di Earnshaw's thin mouth pursed. 'Not unless you like singing falsetto.'

'I don't think you'd feel a lot like singing,' Lee said. 'Anybody want that last KitKat?'

Shaz rubbed her eyes and turned away from the computer screen. She'd come in early so she could squeeze in a quick revision of the previous day's software familiarization. Finding Tony at work on one of the other terminals had been a bonus. He'd looked astonished to see her walk through the door just after seven. 'I thought

I was the only workaholic insomniac around here,' he'd greeted her.

'I'm crap on computers,' she'd said gruffly, trying to cover her satisfaction at having him to herself. 'I've always needed to work twice as hard to keep up.'

Tony's eyebrows had jumped. Cops didn't generally admit weaknesses to an outsider. Either Shaz Bowman was even more unusual than he'd initially appreciated or else he was finally losing his alien status. 'I thought everybody under thirty was a wizard on these,' he said mildly.

'Sorry to disappoint you. I was behind the door when the anoraks were being handed out,' Shaz replied. She settled in front of her screen and pushed up the sleeves of her cotton sweater. 'First remember your password,' she muttered, wondering what he thought of her.

Two forces seethed under Shaz Bowman's calm surface, taking it in turns to drive her. On the one hand, fear of failure gnawed at her, undermining everything she was and all she achieved. When she looked in the mirror, she never saw her good points, only the thinness of her lips and the lack of definition in her nose. When she reviewed her accomplishments, she saw only the places where she had fallen short, the heights she had failed to scale. The countervailing force was her ambition. Somehow, ever since she'd first begun to formulate the ambitions that drove her, those goals had restored her damaged self-confidence and shored up her vulnerabilities before they could cripple her. When her ambition threatened to tip her over into arrogance, somehow the fear would kick in at the crucial point, keeping her human.

The setting up of the task force had coincided so perfectly with the direction of her dreams, she couldn't help but feel the hand of fate in it. That didn't mean that she could let up, however. Shaz's long-term career plan meant she had to shine brighter than anyone else in this task force. One of her tactics for achieving that was to pick Tony Hill's brains like a master locksmith, extracting every scrap of knowledge she could scavenge there while simultaneously worming her way inside his defences so that when she needed his help, he'd be willing to provide it. As part of her approach, and because she was terrified that otherwise she'd fall behind and make a fool of herself in a group that she was convinced were all better than her, she was covertly taping all the group sessions, listening to them over and over again whenever she could. And now, luck had dropped a bonus opportunity into her lap.

So Shaz frowned and stared at the screen, working her way through the lengthy process of filling out an offence report then setting in motion its comparison against the details of all the previous crimes held in the computer's memory banks. When Tony had slipped out of his seat, she'd vaguely registered the movement, but forced herself to carry on working. The last thing she wanted was for him to think she was trying to ingratiate herself.

The intensity of the concentration she imposed upon herself was sufficient for her not to notice when he came back in through the door behind her desk until her subconscious registered a faint masculine smell which it identified as his. It took all her willpower not to react. Instead, she carried on striking keys until his hand cleared the edge of her peripheral vision and placed a carton of coffee topped with a Danish on the desk beside her. 'Time for a break?'

So she'd rubbed her eyes and abandoned the screen. 'Thanks,' she said.

'You're welcome. Anything you're not clear about? I'll take you through it, if you want.'

Still she held back. Don't snatch at it, she cautioned herself. She didn't want to use up her credit with Tony Hill until she absolutely had to, and preferably not before she'd been able to offer him something helpful in return. 'It's not that I don't understand it,' she said. 'It's just that I don't trust it.'

Tony smiled, enjoying her defensive stubbornness. 'One of those kids who demanded empirical proof that two and two were always going to be four?'

A prick of delight that she'd entertained him, quickly stifled. Shaz moved the Danish and opened the coffee. 'I've always been in love with proof. Why do you think I became a cop?'

Tony's smile was lopsided and knowing. 'I could speculate. It's quite a proving ground you've chosen here.'

'Not really. The ground's already been broken. The Americans have been doing it for so long they've not only got manuals, they've got movies about it. It's just taken us forever to catch on, as per usual. But you're one of the ones who forced the issue, so there's nothing left for us to prove.' Shaz took a huge bite of her Danish, nodding in quiet approval as she tasted the apricot glaze on the flaky pastry.

'Don't you believe it,' Tony said wryly, moving back to his own terminal. 'The backlash has only just started. It's taken long enough to get the police to accept we can provide useful help, but already the media hacks who were treating us profilers like gods a couple of years ago are jumping all over our shortcomings. They oversold us, so now they have to blame us for not living up to a set of expectations they created in the first place.'

'I don't know,' Shaz said. 'The public only remember the big successes. That case you did in Bradfield last year. The profile was right on the button. The police knew exactly where to go looking when it came to the crunch.' Oblivious

39

to the permafrost that had settled over Tony's face, Shaz continued enthusiastically. 'Are you going to do a session on that? We've all heard the grapevine version, but there's next to nothing in the literature, even though it's obvious you did a textbook job on the profile.'

'We won't be covering that case,' he said flatly.

Shaz looked up sharply and realized where her eagerness had beached her. She'd blown it this time, in spades. 'I'm sorry,' she said quietly. 'I get carried away, and tact and diplomacy, they're history. I wasn't thinking.' Thick git, she berated herself silently. If he'd had the therapy he would have needed after that particular nightmare, the last thing he'd want would be to expose the details to avid prurience, even if it was masquerading as legitimate scientific interest.

'You don't have to apologize, Shaz,' Tony said wearily. 'You're right, it is a key case. The reason we won't be covering it is that I can't talk about it without feeling like a freak. You'll all have to forgive me. Maybe one day you'll catch a case that leaves you feeling the same way. For your sake, I sincerely hope not.' He looked down at his Danish as if it were an alien artefact and pushed it to one side, appetite dead as the past was supposed to be.

Shaz wished she could rerun the tape, pick up the conversation at the point where he'd put the coffee down on her desk and there was still the possibility of using the moment to build a bridge. 'I'm really sorry, Dr Hill,' she said inadequately.

He looked up and forced a thin smile. 'Truly, Shaz, there's no need. And can we drop the "Dr Hill" bit? I meant to bring it up during yesterday's session, but it slipped my mind. I don't want you all feeling that I'm the teacher and you're the class. At the moment, I'm the group leader simply because I've been doing this for a while. Before long, we'll all be working side by side, and there's no point in having barriers between us. So it's Tony from now on in, OK?'

'You got it, Tony.' Shaz searched for the message in his eyes and his words and, satisfied it contained genuine forgiveness, wolfed the rest of her Danish and returned to her screen. She couldn't do it while he was here, but next time she was in the computer room alone, she intended to use her Internet access to pull up the newspaper archives and check out all the reports of the Bradfield serial killer case. She'd read most of them at the time, but that had been before she'd met Tony Hill and everything had changed. Now, she had a special interest. By the time she was finished, she'd know enough about Tony Hill's most public profile to write the book that, for reasons she still couldn't understand, had never been written. After all, she was a detective, wasn't she?

Carol Jordan fiddled with the complicated chrome coffee maker, a housewarming present from her brother Michael when she'd moved to Seaford. She'd been luckier than most people caught in the housing market slump. She hadn't had far to look for a buyer for her half of the warehouse flat she and Michael owned; the barrister he'd recently been sharing his bedroom with had been so eager to buy her out that Carol had begun to wonder if she'd been even more of a gooseberry than she'd imagined.

Now she had this low stone cottage on the side of the hill that rose above the estuary almost directly opposite Seaford; a place of her own. Well, almost, she corrected herself, reminded by the hard skull head-butting her shin. 'OK, Nelson,' she said, stooping to scratch the black cat's ears. 'I hear what you're saying.' While the coffee brewed, she scooped out a bowl of cat food to a rapture of purring followed by the sloppy sound of Nelson inhaling his breakfast.

She walked through to the living room to enjoy the panorama of the estuary and the improbably slender arc of the suspension bridge. Gazing out across the misty river where the bridge appeared to float without connection to the land, she planned her coming encounter with the fire chief. Nelson walked in, tail erect, and jumped without pause straight on to the window sill where he stretched out, arching his head back towards Carol and demanding affection. Carol stroked his dense fur and said, 'I only get one chance to convince this guy that I know arse from elbow, Nelson. I need him on my side. God knows, I need somebody on my side.'

Nelson batted her hand with his paw, as if responding directly to her words. Carol swallowed the rest of her coffee and got to her feet in a movement as smooth as the cat's. One of the advantages she'd soon found with a DCI's office hours was that she actually managed to use her gym membership more than once a month, and she was already feeling the benefit in firmer muscle tone and better aerobic fitness. It would have been a bonus to have someone to share it with, but that wasn't why she did it. She did it for herself, because it made her feel good. She took pride in her body, revelling in its strength and mobility.

An hour later, enduring the tour of the central fire station, she was glad of her fitness as she struggled to keep pace with the long legs of the local chief of operations, Jim Pendlebury. 'You seem to be better organized here than CID ever manages,' Carol said, as they finally made it to his office. 'You'll have to share the secret of your efficiency.'

'We've had so much cost-cutting, we've really had to streamline everything we do,' he told her. 'We used to have all our stations staffed round the clock with a complement of full-time officers, but it really wasn't cost effective. I know a lot of the lads grumbled about it, but a couple of years back we shifted to a mix of part-time and full-time officers. It took a few months to shake down, but it's been a huge advantage to me in management terms.'

Carol pulled a face. 'Not a solution that would work for us.'

Pendlebury shrugged. 'I don't know. You could have a core staff who dealt with the routine stuff and a hit squad that you used as and when you needed them.'

'That's sort of what we have already,' Carol said drily. 'The core staff is called the night shift and the hit squad are the day teams. Unfortunately, it never gets quiet enough to stand any of them down.'

With part of her mind, Carol added to her mental profile of the fire chief as they spoke. In conversation, his straight dark eyebrows crinkled and jutted above his blue-grey eyes. Considering how much time he must spend flying a desk, his skin looked surprisingly weathered, the creases round his eyes showing white when he wasn't smiling or frowning. Probably a part-time sailor or estuary fisherman, she guessed. As he dipped his head to acknowledge something she'd said, she could see a few silver hairs straggling among his dark curls. So, probably a few years the far side of thirty, Carol thought, revising her initial estimate. She had a habit of analysing new acquaintances in terms of how their description would read on a police bulletin. She'd never actually had to produce a photofit of someone she'd encountered, but she was confident her practice would have made her the best possible witness for the police artist to work with.

'Now you've seen the operation, I take it you're a bit more willing to accept that when we say a fire's a query arson, we're not talking absolute rubbish?' Pendlebury's tone was light, but his eyes challenged hers.

'I never doubted what you were telling us,' she said calmly.

'What I doubted was whether we were taking it as seriously as we should.' She snapped open the locks on her briefcase and took out her file. 'I'd like to go through the details on these incidents with you, if you can spare me the time.'

He cocked his head to one side. 'Are you saying what I think you're saying?'

'Now that I've seen the way you run your operation, I can't believe the idea of a serial arsonist hasn't already crossed your mind.'

He tugged at the lobe of one ear, sizing her up. Finally, he said, 'I was wondering when one of your lot would notice.'

Carol breathed out hard through her nose. 'It might have been helpful if we'd been given a nudge in the right direction. You are the experts, after all.'

'Your predecessor didn't think so,' Pendlebury said. He might as well have been commenting on the price of fish. All of the enthusiasm he'd shown earlier for his job had vanished behind an impassive mask, leaving Carol to draw her own conclusions. They didn't make a pretty picture.

She placed the file on Pendlebury's desk and flipped it open. 'That was then. This is now. Are you telling me you've got query arsons that predate this one?'

He glanced down at the top sheet in the file and snorted. 'How far back would you like to start?'

Tony Hill sat alone at his desk, ostensibly preparing for the following day's seminar with the task force officers. But his thoughts were far away from those details. He was thinking about the psychopathic minds out there, already set in the moulds that would generate pain and misery for people they didn't even know yet.

There had long been a theory among psychologists that discounted the existence of evil, ascribing the worst excesses of the most sociopathic abductors, torturers and killers to a linked series of circumstances and events in their past that culminated in one final stress-laden event that catapulted them over the edge of what civilized society would tolerate. But that had never entirely satisfied Tony. It begged the question of why some people with almost identical backgrounds of abuse and deprivation went on not to become psychopaths but to lead useful, fruitful lives, integrated into society.

Now the scientists were talking about a genetic answer, a fracture in the DNA code that might explain this divergence. Somehow, Tony found that answer too pat. It seemed as much of a cop-out as the old-fashioned notion that some men were simply evil and that was that. It evaded responsibility in a way he found repugnant.

It was an issue that had always held particular resonance for him. He knew the reason he was so good at what he did. It was because for so many of the steps down the road that his prey had taken, he had walked in their footprints. But at some point he could never quite identify there had come a parting of the ways. Where they became hunters at first hand, he became a hunter at second hand, tracking them down once they had crossed the line. Yet his life still held echoes of theirs. The fantasies that drove them were about sex and death; his fantasies about sex and death were called profiling. They were chillingly close.

It sometimes seemed chicken and egg to Tony. Had his impotence started because he was afraid the unfettered expression of his sexuality might lead him to violence and death? Or had his knowledge of how often the sexual urge led to killing worked on his body to make him sexually inadequate? He doubted he would ever know. However the circuit worked, it was undeniable that his work had profoundly affected his life.

For no apparent reason, he recalled the spark of uncom-
plicated enthusiasm he'd seen in Shaz Bowman's eyes. He
could remember feeling that way too, before his fascination
had been tempered by exposure to the horrors humans could
inflict upon each other. Maybe he could use what he knew
to give his team better armour than he'd had. If he achieved
nothing else with them, that alone would be worthwhile.

In another part of the city, Shaz clicked her mouse button and
closed down her software. On autopilot, she switched off her
computer and stared unseeingly as the screen faded to black.
When she'd decided to explore the resources of the Internet
as her first stop on the road to disinterring Tony Hill's past,
she'd expected to come across a handful of references and,
if she was lucky, a set of cuttings in one of the newspaper
archives.

Instead, when she'd input 'Tony, Hill, Bradfield, killer'
as key words in the search engine, she'd stumbled upon a
darkside treasure trove of references to the case that had put
his face on the front pages a year before. There was a grisly
handful of websites entirely devoted to serial killers which
incorporated Tony's headline case. Elsewhere, journalists
and commentators had posted their articles on that specific
case on their personal websites. There was even a perverse
rogues' gallery, a montage of photographs of the faces of
the world's most notorious serial killers. Tony's target, the
so-called Queer Killer, featured in more than one guise in
the bizarre exhibit.

Shaz had downloaded everything she could find and had
spent the rest of the evening reading it. What had started out
as an academic exercise to figure out what made Tony Hill
tick had left her sick at heart.

The facts were not in dispute. The naked bodies of four

men had been dumped in gay cruising areas of Bradfield. The victims had been tortured before death with a cruelty that was almost beyond comprehension. After death, they had been sexually mutilated, washed clean and abandoned like trash.

As a last resort, Tony had been brought in as a consultant, working with Detective Inspector Carol Jordan to develop a profile. They were moving close to their target when hunter became hunted. The killer wanted Tony for a human sacrifice. Captured and trussed, he was on the point of becoming victim number five, the torture engine in place, his body screaming in pain. He was saved in the nick of time not by the arrival of the cavalry but by his own verbal skills, honed over years of working with mentally disturbed offenders. But to claim his life, he'd had to kill his captor.

As she'd read, Shaz's heart had filled with horror, her eyes with tears. Cursed with enough imagination to create a picture of the hell Tony had lived through, she found herself sucked into the nightmare of that final showdown where the roles of killer and victim were irrevocably reversed. The scenario made her shudder with fear and trepidation.

How had he begun to live with that? she marvelled. How did he sleep? How could he close his eyes and not be assailed with images beyond most people's imagination or tolerance? Little wonder that he wasn't prepared to use his own past to teach them how to manage their futures. The miracle was that he was still willing to practise a craft that must have pushed him to the edge of madness.

And how would she have coped if she'd been the one in his shoes? Shaz dropped her head into her hands and, for the first time since she'd heard of the task force, asked herself if she hadn't perhaps made a terrible mistake.

*   *   *

47

Betsy mixed a drink for the journalist. Heavy on the gin, light on the tonic, a quarter of a lemon squeezed so that the tartness of the juice would cut the oily sweetness of the gin and disguise its potency. One of the principal reasons that Micky's image had survived untainted by scandal was Betsy's insistence that they trust no one outside the trio that held their secret close. Suzy Joseph might be all smiles and charm, filling the airy sitting room with the tinkle of her laugh and the smoke from her menthol cigarettes, but she was still a journalist. Even if she represented the most accommodating and sycophantic of the colour magazines, Betsy knew that among her drinking cronies there would be more than one tabloid hack ready to dip a hand in a pocket for the right piece of gossip. So Suzy would be plied generously with drink today. By the time she came to sit down to lunch with Jacko and Micky, her sharp eyes would be blurred round the edges.

Betsy perched on the arm of a sofa whose squashy cushions engulfed the anorectically thin journalist. She could keep an eye on her easily from there, while Suzy would have to make a deliberate and obvious shift of position to get Betsy in her line of sight. That also made it possible for Betsy to signal caution to Micky without being seen. 'This is such a lovely room,' Suzy gushed. 'So light, so cool. You don't often see something so tasteful, so elegant, so – *appropriate*. And believe me, I've been in more of these Holland Park mansions than the local estate agents!' She twisted round awkwardly and said to Betsy in the same tones she'd have used to a waiter, 'You have made sure the caterers have all they need?'

Betsy nodded. 'Everything's under control. They were delighted with the kitchen.'

'I'm sure they were.' Suzy was back with Micky, Betsy dismissed again. 'Did you design the dining room yourself, Micky? So stylish! So very, very *you*! So perfect for *Junket with*

Joseph.' She leaned forward to stub out her cigarette, giving Betsy an unwanted view of a creped cleavage that fake tan and expensive body treatments couldn't entirely disguise.

Being commended on her taste by a woman who could without any indication of shame wear a brash scarlet and black Moschino suit designed for someone twenty years younger and an entirely different shape was a double-edged compliment, Micky felt. But she simply smiled again and said, 'Actually, it was mostly Betsy's inspiration. She's the one with the taste round here. I just tell her what I want the ambience to be like, and she sorts it out.'

Suzy's reflexive smile held no warmth. Another wasted opening; nothing quotable there, it seemed to say. Before she could try again, Jacko strode into the room, his broad shoulders in their perfect tailoring thrusting forward so he appeared like a flying wedge. He ignored Suzy's fluttering twitters and made straight for Micky, descending upon her with one enveloping arm, hugging her close, though not actually kissing. 'Sweetheart,' he said, his professional, public voice carrying the thrum of a cello chord. 'I'm sorry I'm late.' He half-turned and leaned back against the sofa, giving Suzy the full benefit of his perfectly groomed smile. 'You must be Suzy,' he said. 'We're thrilled to have you here with us today.'

Suzy lit up like Christmas. 'I'm thrilled to be here,' she gushed, her breathy voice losing its veneer and revealing the unmistakable West Midlands intonation she'd devoted herself to burying. The effect Jacko still had on women never ceased to astonish Betsy. He could turn the sourest bitch Barsac sweet. Even the tired cynicism of Suzy Joseph, a woman who had the same relationship to celebrity as beetles to dung, wasn't sufficient armour against his charm. '*Junket with Joseph* doesn't often give me the chance to spend time with people I genuinely admire,' she added.

49

'Thank you,' Jacko said, all smiles. 'Betsy, should we be heading through to the dining room?'

She glanced at the clock. 'That would be helpful,' she said. 'The caterer wants to start serving round about now.' Jacko jumped to his feet and waited attentively for Micky to get up and move towards the door. He ushered Suzy ahead of him too, turning back to roll his eyes upwards in an expression of bored horror for Betsy's benefit. Stifling a giggle, she followed them to the dining-room door, saw them seated and left them to it. Sometimes there were distinct benefits in not being the official consort, she reminded herself as she settled down with her bread and cheese and *The World at One*.

There was no such relief for Micky, who had to pretend she didn't even notice Suzy's vapid flirting with her husband. Micky tuned out the boring ritual dance going on next to her and concentrated on freeing the last morsels of lobster from a claw.

A change in Suzy's tone alerted her that the conversation had shifted a gear. Time for work, Micky realized. 'Of course, I've read in the cuttings how you two got together,' Suzy was saying, her hand covering Jacko's real one. She wouldn't have been so quick to pat the other, Micky reflected grimly. 'But I need to hear it from your own lips.'

Here we go, Micky thought. The first part of the recital was always hers. 'We met in hospital,' she began.

By the middle of the second week, the task force office felt like home to the entire team. It was no accident that all six of the junior officers chosen for the squad were single and unattached, according both to their records and the unofficial background checks that Commander Paul Bishop had pursued in canteens and police clubs up and down the country. Tony had deliberately wanted a group of people who, uprooted from their former lives, would be thrown together and forced to develop team spirit. That at least was something he seemed to have got right, he thought, looking around the seminar room where six heads were bowed over a set of photocopied police files he'd prepared for them.

Already, they had started to form alliances, and so far they'd done well to avoid the personality clashes that could split a group beyond salvaging. Interestingly, the associations were flexible, not fixed in rigid pairs. Although some affinities were stronger than others, there was no attempt to make any of them exclusive.

Shaz was the one exception, as far as Tony could tell. It wasn't that there was a problem between her and the others. It was more that she held herself apart from the easy intimacy that was growing between the rest. She joined in the jokes, took part in the communal brainstorming, but somehow there was always distance between her and her fellows. He sensed in her a passion for success that the rest of the squad lacked. They were ambitious, no denying that, but with Shaz it went deeper. She was driven, her need burning inside her and consuming any trace of frivolity. She was always first there in the mornings and last out at night, eagerly snatching any opportunity to get Tony to expand on whatever he'd been talking about last. But her very need for success made her correspondingly more vulnerable to failure. What he recognized as a desperate desire for approval was a blade that could be used against her with devastating effect. If she didn't learn to drop her defences so she could use her empathy, she'd never achieve her potential as a profiler. It was his job to find a way of making her feel she could relax her vigilance without risking too much damage.

At that moment, Shaz looked up, her eyes direct on his. There was no embarrassment, no awkwardness. She simply stared for a moment then returned to what she was reading. It was as if she had raided his memory banks for a missing piece of information and, having found it, had logged off again. Slightly unnerved, Tony cleared his throat. 'Four separate incidents of sexual assault and rape. Any comments?'

The group had moved beyond awkward silences and polite hanging back to give others a chance. In what was becoming an established pattern, Leon Jackson dived straight in. 'I think the strongest link is in the victims. I read somewhere that serial rapists tend to rape within their own age group, and all these women were in their mid-twenties. Plus they all have short blonde hair and they all took time and trouble to stay fit. You got two joggers, one hockey player, one rower. They all did sports where it wouldn't be hard for a weirdo stalker to watch them without attracting any attention.'

'Thanks, Leon. Any other comments?'

Simon, already the devil's advocate designate of the group, weighed in, his Glasgow accent and habit of staring out from under his heavy dark eyebrows multiplying the aggression factor. 'You could argue that that's because the kind of woman who indulges in these kind of sports is exactly the sort that's confident enough to be out in risky places on her own, convinced it's never going to happen to her. It could easily be two, three or even four attackers. In which case, bringing in a profiler is going to be a total waste of time.'

Shaz shook her head. 'It's not just the victims,' she stated firmly. 'If you read their evidence, in each case their eyes were covered during the attack. In each case, they mention that their assailant verbally abused them continually while he was actually assaulting them. That's more than sheer coincidence.'

Simon wasn't ready to give up. 'Come on, Shaz,' he protested. 'Any bloke who's so powerless he needs to resort

52

to rape to feel good about himself is going to need to talk himself up to it. And as for their eyes being covered – there's nothing in common there except with the first and third where he used their own headbands. Look –' he waved the papers – 'case number two, he pulled her T-shirt over her head and tied a knot in it. Case number four, the rapist had a roll of packing tape that he wound round her head. Way different.' He sat back, a good-natured grin defusing the force of his words.

Tony grinned. 'The perfectly contrived lead into the next subject. Thanks, Simon. Today, I'm going to hand out your first assignment, the preamble to which is the beginner's guide to signature versus MO. Anybody know what I'm talking about?'

Kay Hallam, the other woman on the team, raised her hand half a dozen inches and looked questioningly at Tony. He nodded. She tucked her light brown hair behind her ears in a gesture he'd come to recognize as Kay's keynote mechanism for looking feminine and vulnerable to defuse criticism, particularly when she was about to make a point she was absolutely sure of. 'MO is dynamic, signature is static,' she said.

'That's one way of putting it,' Tony said. 'However, it's probably a bit too technical for the plods among us,' he added with a grin, pointing his finger one by one at the other five. He pushed back his chair and started moving restlessly round the room as he talked. 'MO means *modus operandi*. Latin. The way of doing. When we use it in a criminal context, we mean the series of actions that the perpetrator committed in the process of achieving his goal, the crime. In the early days of profiling, police officers, and to a large degree psychologists, were very literal about their idea of a serial offender. It was somebody who did pretty much the same things every time to achieve pretty much the same results. Except that they usually showed escalation, moving, say, from assaulting a prostitute to beating a woman's brains out with a hammer.

'As we discovered more, though, we realized we weren't the only ones capable of learning from our mistakes. We were dealing with criminals who were intelligent and imaginative enough to do exactly the same. That meant we had to get our heads round the idea that the MO was something that could change quite drastically from one offence to the next because the offender found that a particular course of action wasn't very effective. So he'd adapt. His first murder could be a strangulation, but maybe our killer feels that took too long, was too noisy, frightened him too much, stressed him rather than allowing him to enjoy his fulfilment. Next time out, he smashes her skull in with a crowbar. Too messy. So number three, he stabs. And the investigators write them off as three separate killings because the MO looks so different.

'What doesn't change is what we call, for the sake of giving it a name, the signature. The sig, for short.' Tony stopped pacing and leaned against the window sill. 'The sig doesn't change because it's the *raison d'être* of the offence. It's what gives the perpetrator his sense of satisfaction.

'So what does this signature consist of? Well, it's all the bits of behaviour that exceed what is actually necessary to commit the crime. The ritual of the offence. To satisfy the perpetrator, the signature elements have to be acted out every time he goes out on a mission, and they have to be performed in the same style every time. Examples of signature in a killer might be things like: does he strip the victim? Does he make a neat pile of the victim's clothes? Does he use cosmetics on the victim after death? Is he having sex with the victim postmortem? Is he performing some kind of ritualistic mutilation like cutting off their breasts or penises or ears?'

54

Simon looked faintly queasy. Tony wondered how many murder victims he'd seen so far. He would have to grow a thicker skin or else be prepared to put up with the jibes of colleagues who would enjoy watching the profiler lose his lunch over another vitiated victim. 'A serial offender must accomplish signature activities to fulfil himself, to make the act meaningful,' Tony continued. 'It's about meeting a variety of needs – to dominate, to inflict pain, to provoke distinct responses, to achieve sexual release. The means can vary, but the end remains constant.'

He took a deep breath and tried to keep his mind off the very particular variations he'd seen at first hand. 'For a killer whose pleasure comes from inflicting pain and hearing victims scream, it's immaterial whether he . . .' his voice faltered as irresistible images climbed into his head. 'Whether he . . .' They were all looking at him now and he desperately struggled to look momentarily distracted rather than shipwrecked. 'Whether he . . . ties them up and cuts them, or whether he . . .'

'Whether he whips them with wire,' Shaz said, her voice casual, her expression reassuring.

'Exactly,' Tony said, recovering fast. 'Nice to see you've got such a tender imagination, Shaz.'

'Typical woman, eh?' Simon said with a grunt of laughter.

Shaz looked faintly embarrassed. Before the joke could escalate, Tony continued. 'So you might have two bodies whose physical conditions are very different. But when you examine the scenario, things have been done that were additional to the act of killing and the ultimate gratification has been the same. That's your signature.'

He paused, his control firmly in place again, and looked around, checking he was taking them all with him. One of the men looked dubious. 'At its most simplistic,' he said, 'think about petty criminals. You've got a burglar who steals videos. That's all he goes for, just videos, because he's got a fence who gives him a good deal. He robs terraced houses, going in through the back yard. But then he reads in the local paper that the police are warning people about the video thief who comes in through the back yard, and they're setting up neighbourhood watch teams to keep a special eye on back alleys. So he abandons his terraced houses and instead he goes for between-the-wars semis and gets in through the side windows in the downstairs hall. He's changed his MO. But he still only nicks the videos. That's his signature.'

The doubter's face cleared. Now he'd grasped it. Gratified, Tony picked up a stack of papers divided into six bundles. 'So we have to learn to be inclusive when we're considering the possibility of a serial offender. Think "linking through similarity", rather than "discounting through difference".'

He stood up again and walked around among their work tables, gearing himself up to the crucial part of the session. 'Some senior police officers and profilers have a hypothesis that's more confidential than the secrets of the Masonic square,' he said, capturing their attention again. 'We believe there could be as many as half a dozen undetected serial killers who have been operating in Britain over the past ten years. Some could have claimed upwards of ten victims. Thanks to the motorway network and the historic reluctance of police forces to exchange information, nobody has sat down and made the crucial connections. Once we're up and running, this will be something we'll be considering as and when we have time and staff available to look at it.' Raised eyebrows and muttering filled his momentary pause.

'So what we're doing here is a dummy run,' Tony explained. 'Thirty missing teenagers. They're all real cases, culled from a dozen forces over the last seven years. You've got a week to examine the cases in your spare time. Then you'll have the chance to present your own theories as to whether any of them have sufficient common factors to give us grounds for suspicion that they might be the work of a serial offender.' He handed them each a bundle of photostats, giving them a few moments to flick through.

'I should emphasize that this is merely an exercise,' he cautioned them, walking back to his seat. 'There's no reason to suppose that any of these girls or lads has been abducted or killed. Some of them may well be dead now, but that's probably got more to do with the attrition of life on the street than foul play. The common factor that links them is that none of these kids were regarded by their families as the kind who would run away. The families all claimed the missing teenagers were happy at home, there had been no serious arguments and there were no significant problems with school. Although one or two of them had some history of involvement with the police or social services, there weren't any current difficulties at the time of the disappearances. However, none of the missing kids subsequently made contact with home. In spite of that, it's likely that most of them made for London and the bright lights.'

He took a deep breath and turned to face them. 'But there could be another scenario lurking in there. If there is, it'll be our job to find it.'

Excitement started like a slow burn in Shaz's gut, powerful enough to dim the memories of what she'd read about Tony's last close encounter with a killer. This was her first chance. If there were undiscovered murder victims out there, she would find them. More than that, she would be their advocate. And their avenger.

Criminals are often caught by accident. He knew that; he'd seen programmes about it on the TV. Dennis Nilsen, killer of fifteen homeless young men, found out because human flesh blocked the drains; Peter Sutcliffe, the Yorkshire Ripper, despatcher of thirteen women, nicked because he'd stolen a set of number plates to disguise his car; Ted Bundy, necrophiliac murderer of as many as forty young women, finally arrested for speeding past a police car at night with no lights. This knowledge didn't frighten him, but it added an extra *frisson* to the adrenaline buzz that inevitably accompanied his fire-setting. His motives might be very different from theirs, but the risk was almost as great. The once soft leather driving gloves were always damp with his nervous sweat.

Somewhere around one in the morning, he parked his car in a carefully chosen spot. He never left it on a residential street, understanding the insomnia of the elderly and the late-night revels of the young. Instead, he chose the car parks of DIY stores, the waste ground beside factories, the forecourts of garages closed for the night. Secondhand car pitches were best; nobody noticed an extra car there for an hour or two in the small hours.

He never carried a holdall either, sensing it to be suspicious at that time of night. A policeman spotting him would have no cause to think he'd been out burgling. And even if a bored night-beat bobby fancied the diversion of getting him to turn out his pockets, there wouldn't be much to arouse suspicion. A length of string, an old-fashioned cigarette lighter with a brass case, a packet of cigarettes with two or three missing, a dog-eared book of matches with a couple remaining, yesterday's newspaper, a Swiss Army knife, a crumpled oil-stained handkerchief, a small but powerful torch. If that was grounds for arrest, the cells would be full every night.

He walked the route he'd memorized, staying close to the walls as he moved silently down empty streets, his blank-soled bowling shoes making no sound. After a few minutes, he came to a narrow alley which led to the blind side of a small industrial estate he'd had his eye on for a while. It had originally been a ropeworks and consisted of a group of four turn-of-the-century brick buildings which had recently been converted to their present uses. An auto electrician's sat next to an upholstery workshop, opposite a plumbing supplier and a bakery that made biscuits from a recipe allegedly as old as the York Mystery plays. He reckoned anyone who got away with charging such ridiculous prices for a poxy packet of gritty biscuits deserved to have their factory razed to the ground, but there wasn't enough flammable material there for his needs.

Tonight, the upholstery workshop was going to go up like a Roman candle.

Later, he'd thrill to the sight of yellow and crimson flames thrusting their long spikes into the plumes of grey and brown smoke billowing up from the blazing cloth and the wooden floors and beams of the elderly building. But, for now, he had to get inside.

He'd made his preparations earlier that day, dropping a carrier bag into a rubbish bin by the side door of the workshop. Now he retrieved it and took out the sink plunger and the tube of superglue. He walked round the outside of the building until he was outside the toilet window, where he stuck the plunger to the window. He waited a few minutes to be certain the contact adhesive had hardened, then he gripped the plunger with both hands, braced himself and gave a sharp tug. The glass broke with a tiny tinkle, the fragments falling on the outside of the window, just as they would if it had exploded from the heat. He tapped the plunger smartly against the wall to shatter the circle of glass, leaving only a thin ring still glued to the rubber. That didn't worry him; there would be no reason for any forensic expert to reconstruct the window and reveal a missing circle of glass at the heart of the shards. That done, he was inside within a few minutes. There was, he knew, no burglar alarm.

He took out the torch and flipped it quickly on and off to check his position, then emerged into the corridor that led along the back of the main work space. At the end, he recalled, were a couple of large cardboard boxes of scrap material that local handicraft hobbyists bought for coppers. No reason for fire investigators to doubt it was a place where workers might hang out for a sly fag.

It was a matter of moments to construct his incendiary device. First he opened up the cigarette lighter and rubbed the string with the wadding which he'd previously saturated with lighter fluid. Then he put the string at the centre of a bundle of half a dozen cigarettes held loosely together with an elastic band. He placed his incendiary so that the string fuse lay along the edge of the nearest cardboard box, then laid the oily handkerchief beside it with some crumpled newspaper. Finally, he lit the cigarettes. They would burn halfway down before the string ignited. That in its turn would take a little while to get the boxes of fabric smouldering. But by the time they'd caught hold, there wouldn't be any stopping his fire. It was going to be some blaze.

He'd been saving this one up, knowing it would be a beauty. Rewarding, in more ways than one.

Betsy checked her watch. Ten minutes more, then she would break up Suzy Joseph's junket with a fictitious appointment for Micky. If Jacko wanted to carry on charming, that was up to him. She suspected he'd rather seize the opportunity to escape. He'd have finished filming the latest *Vance's Visits* the night before, so he'd be off on one of his charity stints at one of the specialist hospitals where he worked as a volunteer counsellor and support worker. He'd be gone by mid-afternoon, leaving her and Micky to a peaceful house and a weekend alone.

'Between Jacko and the Princess of Wales, you get no peace these days when you've got a terminal illness,' she said out loud. 'I'm the lucky one,' she went on, moving from bureau to filing cabinet as she cleared her desk in preparation for a guilt-free weekend. 'I don't have to listen to the Authorized Version for the millionth time.' She imitated Jacko's upbeat, dramatic intonation. '"I was lying there, contemplating the wreck of my dreams, convinced I had nothing left to live for. Then, out of the depths of my depression, I saw a vision."' Betsy made the sweeping gesture she'd seen Jacko deploy so often with his living arm. '"This very vision of loveliness, in fact. There, by my hospital bed, stood the one thing I'd seen since the accident that made me realize life might be worth living."'

It was a tale that bore almost no relationship to the reality Betsy had lived through. She remembered Micky's first encounter with Jacko, but not because it had been the earth-shaking collision of two stars recognizing their counterparts. Betsy's memories were very different and far less romantic.

It was the first time Micky had been the lead outside broadcast reporter on the main evening news bulletin. She'd been bringing millions of eager viewers the first exclusive interview with Jacko Vance, hero of the hottest human story on the networks. Betsy had watched the broadcast at home alone, thrilled to see her lover the cynosure of ten million pairs of eyes, hugging herself in delight.

The exhilaration hadn't lasted long. They'd been celebrating together in the flickering glow of the video replay when the phone had interrupted their pleasure. Betsy had answered, her voice exuberant with happiness. The journalist who greeted her as Micky's girlfriend drained all the joy from her. In spite of Betsy's frostily vehement denials and Micky's scornful ridicule, both women knew their relationship was poised on the edge of the worst kind of tabloid exposure.

The patient campaign Micky had gone on to wage against the sneak tactics of the hacks was as carefully planned and as ruthlessly executed as any career move she'd ever made. Every night, two separate pairs of bedroom curtains would be closed and lights turned on behind them. The lamps would go off at staggered intervals, the one in the spare room controlled by a timer that Betsy adjusted to a different hour each night. Every morning, the curtains would be drawn back at diverse times, each pair by the same hands that had closed them. The only places the two women embraced were behind closed curtains out of the line of sight of the window, or in the hallway, which was invisible from outside. If both left the house at the same time, they parted at the bottom of the steps with a cheerful wave and no bodily contact.

Giving the presumed watchers nothing to chew on would have been enough to make most people feel secure. But Micky preferred a more proactive approach. If the tabloids wanted a story, she'd make sure they had one. It would simply have to be a more exciting, more credible and more sexy story than the one they thought they had. She cared far too much for Betsy to take chances with her lover's peace of mind or their relationship.

The morning after the ominous phone call, Micky had a spare hour. She drove to the hospital where Jacko was a patient and charmed her way past the nurses. Jacko seemed pleased to see her, and not only because she came armed with the gift of a miniature AM/FM radio complete with earphones. Although he was still taking strong medication for his pain, he was alert and receptive to any distraction from the tedium of life in his side ward. She spent half an hour chatting lightly about everything except the accident and the amputation, then left, leaning over to give him a friendly peck on the forehead. It had been no hardship; to her surprise, she'd found herself warming to Jacko. He wasn't the arrogant macho man she'd expected, based on her past experience with male sporting heroes. Nor, even more surprisingly, was he wallowing in self-pity. Micky's visits might have started out as cynical self-interest, but within a very short space of time she was sucked in, first by her respect for his stoicism, then by an unexpected pleasure in his company. He might be more interested in himself than in her, but at least he managed to be entertaining and witty with it.

Five days and four visits later, Jacko asked the question she'd been waiting for. 'Why do you keep visiting me?'

Micky shrugged. 'I like you?'

Jacko's eyebrows rose and fell, as if to say, 'That's not enough.'

She sighed and made a conscious effort to hold his speculative gaze. 'I have always been cursed with an imagination. And I understand the drive to be successful. I've worked my socks off to get where I am. I've made sacrifices and I've sometimes had to treat people in a way that, in other circumstances, I'd be ashamed of. But getting to where I want to be is the most important thing in my life. I can imagine how I would feel if a chain of circumstances outside my control cost me my goal. I guess what I feel for you is empathy.'

'Meaning what?' he asked, his face giving nothing away.

'Sympathy without pity?'

He nodded, as if satisfied. 'The nurse reckoned it was because you fancied me. I knew she was wrong.'

Micky shrugged. It was all going so much better than she'd anticipated. 'Don't disillusion her. People distrust motives they can't understand.'

'You're so right,' he said, an edge of bitterness in his voice that she hadn't heard there before, in spite of the ample reason. 'But understanding doesn't always make it possible to accept something.'

There was more, much more behind his words. But Micky knew when to leave well alone. There would be plenty of opportunity to broach that subject again. When she left that day, she was careful to make sure the nurse saw her kiss him goodbye. If this story was to be credible, it needed to leak out, not be broadcast. And from her own journalistic experience, gossip spread through a hospital faster than legionnaire's disease. From there to the wider community only took one carrier.

When she arrived a week later, Jacko seemed remote. Micky sensed violent emotions barely held in check, but couldn't be sure what those feelings were. Eventually, tired of conducting a monologue rather than a conversation, she said, 'Are you going to tell me or are you just going to let your blood pressure rise till you have a stroke?'

For the first time that afternoon, he looked directly into her face. Momentarily, she thought he was in the grip of fever, then she realized it was a fury so powerful that she couldn't imagine how he could contain it. He was so angry he could barely speak, she realized as she watched him struggle to find the words. At last, he conquered his rage by sheer effort of will and said, 'My fucking so-called fiancée,' he growled.

'Jillie?' Micky hoped she'd got the name right. They'd met briefly one afternoon as Micky had been leaving. She had the impression of a slender dark-haired beauty who managed sultry rather than tarty by an inch.

'Bitch,' he hissed, the tendons on his neck tensing like cords beneath the tanned skin.

'What's happened, Jacko?'

He closed his eyes and breathed deeply, his wide chest expanding and emphasizing the asymmetry of his once perfect upper body. 'Dumped me,' he managed at last, his voice thick with anger.

'No,' Micky breathed. 'Oh, Jacko.' She reached out and touched the tight fist with her fingers. She could actually feel the pulse beating in his flesh, so tightly was his hand clenched. His rage was phenomenal, Micky thought, yet his control seemed in no real danger of slipping.

'Says she can't cope with it.' He gave a grating bark of cynical laughter. 'She can't cope with it? How the fuck does she think it is for me?'

'I'm sorry,' Micky said inadequately.

'I saw it in her face, the first time she visited after the accident. No, I knew before that. I knew because she didn't come near me that first day. It took her two days to get her arse in here.' His voice was harsh and guttural, the heavy words falling like blocks of stone. 'When she did come, she couldn't stand the sight of me. It was all over her face. I repelled her. All she could see was what I wasn't any more.' He pulled his fist away and pounded it on the bed.

'More fool her.'

His eyes opened and he glared at her. 'Don't you start. All I need is one more silly bitch patronizing me. I've had that fucking nurse with her artificial cheerfulness all over me. Just don't!'

Micky didn't flinch. She'd won too many confrontations with news editors for that. 'You should learn to recognize respect when you see it,' she flared back at him. 'I'm sorry Jillie hasn't got what it takes to see you through, but you're better off finding that out now than further down the road.'

Jacko looked astonished. For years now, the only person who'd spoken to him with anything except nervous deference was his trainer. 'What?' he squawked, his anger displaced by baffled astonishment.

Micky continued regardless of his response. 'What you have to decide now is how you're going to play it.'

'What?'

'It's not going to stay a secret between the two of you, is it? From what you said, the nurse already knows. So by teatime, it's going to be, "Hold the front page." If you want, you can settle for being an object of pity – hero dumped by girlfriend because he's not a proper man any more. You'll get the sympathy vote, and a fair chunk of the Great British Public will spit on Jillie in the street. Alternatively, you can get your retaliation in first and come out on top.'

Jacko's mouth was open, but for a moment no words came. At last, he said in a low voice that fellow members of the Olympic squad would have recognized as a signal for flak jackets, 'Go on.'

'It's up to you. It depends whether you want people to see you as a victim or a victor.'

Micky's level stare felt as much of a challenge as anything that had ever faced him on the field of competition. 'What do you think?' he snarled.

'I'm telling you, man, this is the *sticks*,' Leon said, waving a chicken pakora in a sweeping gesture that seemed to include not only the restaurant but most of the West Riding of Yorkshire as well.

'You've obviously never been to Greenock on a Saturday

night,' Simon said drily. 'Believe me, Leon, that makes Leeds look positively cosmopolitan.'

'*Nothing* could make this place cosmopolitan,' Leon protested.

'It's not that bad,' Kay said. 'It's very good for shopping.' Even outside the classroom, Shaz noticed, Kay slipped straight into the conciliatory role, smoothing down her hair as she smoothed down the rough edges in the conversations.

Simon groaned theatrically. 'Oh please, Kay, don't feel you need to glide effortlessly into bland womanly stuff. Go on, make my night, tell me how terrific Leeds is for body-piercing.'

Kay poked her tongue out at him.

'If you don't leave Kay alone, us women might well consider piercing some treasured part of your anatomy with this beer bottle,' Shaz said sweetly, brandishing her Kingfisher.

Simon put his hands up. 'OK. I'll behave, just as long as you promise not to beat me with a chapati.'

There was a moment's silence while the four police officers attacked their starters. The Saturday night curry looked like becoming a regular feature for the quartet, the other two preferring to return to their former home turf rather than explore their new base. When Simon had first suggested it, Shaz hadn't been sure if she wanted to bond that closely with her colleagues. But Simon had been persuasive, and besides, Commander Bishop had been earwigging and she wanted to avoid a black mark for being unco-operative. So she'd agreed and, to her surprise, she'd enjoyed herself, even though she had made her excuses and left before the nightclub excursion that had followed. Now, three weeks into the Job, she found she was actually looking forward to their night out, and not just for the food.

Leon was first to clear his plate, as usual. 'What I'm saying is, it's primitive up here.'

'I don't know,' Shaz protested. 'They've got plenty of good curry houses, the property's cheap enough for me to afford something bigger than a rabbit hutch, and if you want to go from one part of the city centre to another, you can walk instead of sitting on the tube for an hour.'

'And the countryside. Don't forget how easy it is to get out into the countryside,' Kay added.

Leon leaned back in his seat, groaning and rolling his eyes extravagantly like a terrible caricature of a Black and White Minstrel. 'Heathcliff,' he warbled in falsetto.

'She's right,' Simon said. 'God, you're such a cliché, Leon. You should get off the city streets, get some fresh air into your lungs. What about coming out tomorrow for a walk? I really fancy seeing if Ilkley Moor lives up to the song.'

Shaz laughed. 'What? You want to walk about without a hat and see if you catch your death of cold?'

The others joined in her laughter. 'See, man, it's primitive, like I said. Nothing to do but walk about on your own two feet. And shit, Simon, I'm not the one that's a cliché. You know I've been stopped driving home three times since I moved here? Even the Met got a bit more racially enlightened than thinking every black man with a decent set of wheels has to be a drug dealer,' Leon said bitterly.

'They're not stopping you because you're black,' Shaz retorted as he paused to light a cigarette.

'No?' Leon exhaled.

'No, they're stopping you for being in possession of an offensive weapon.'

'What do you mean?'

'That suit, babe. Any sharper and you'd cut yourself getting dressed. You're wearing a blade, of course they're going to stop you.' Shaz held out her hand for Leon to give her five and, amid the hoots of laughter from the other two, he made a rueful face and hit her hand.

'Not as sharp as you, Shaz,' Simon said. She wondered if it was only the heat of the spices that was responsible for the scarlet flush across his normally pale cheekbones.

'Speaking of sharp,' Kay chipped in as their main courses arrived, 'you can't get anything past Tony Hill, can you?'

'He's smart, all right,' Simon agreed, sweeping his wavy dark hair back from his sweating forehead. 'I just wish he'd loosen up a bit. It's like there's a wall there that you get right up to but you can't see over.'

'I'll tell you why that is,' Shaz said, suddenly serious. 'Bradfield. The Queer Killer.'

'That's the one he did that went well and truly pear-shaped, yeah?' Leon asked.

'That's right.'

'It was all hushed up, wasn't it?' Kay said, her intent face reminding Shaz of a small furry animal, cute but with hidden teeth. 'The papers hinted at all sorts of stuff, but they never went into much detail.'

'Believe me,' Shaz said, looking at her half-chicken and wishing she'd gone for something vegetarian, 'you wouldn't want to know the details. If you want to know the whole story, check out the Internet. They weren't constrained by technicalities like good taste or requests from the authorities to keep things under wraps. I'm telling you, if you can read what Tony Hill went through without having second thoughts about what we're doing, you're a fuck of a sight braver than I am.'

There was a moment's silence. Then Simon leaned forward and said confidingly, 'You're going to tell us, aren't you, Shaz?'

69

He always arrived fifteen minutes ahead of the agreed time because he knew she'd be early. It didn't matter which she he'd chosen, she'd turn up ahead of schedule because she was convinced he was Rumpelstiltskin, the man who could spin twenty-four-carat gold out of the dry straw of her life.

Donna Doyle – no longer the next one but rather the latest one – was no different from the others. As her silhouette appeared against the dim light of the car park, he could hear the clumsy childish music crashing in his head. '*Jack and Jill went up the hill to fetch a pail of water . . .*'

He shook his head to clear his ears, like a snorkeller surfacing from a coral reef. He watched her approach, moving cautiously between the expensive cars, glancing from side to side, a slight frown creasing her forehead, as if she couldn't work out why her antennae weren't pointing her to his precise position. He could see she'd done her best to look good; the school skirt that had obviously been folded over at the waist to show off shapely legs, the school blouse open one button further than parent or teacher would ever have allowed in public, the blazer over one shoulder, hanging thus to obscure the backpack of school supplies. The make-up was heavier than the night before, its excess weight catapulting her straight into middle age. And her hair glinted glossy black, the swing of the short bob catching the dull gleam of the car park lights.

When Donna was almost level, he pushed open the passenger door of the car. The sudden interior light made her jump even as she registered his shockingly handsome profile cutting a dark line through the bright rectangle. He spoke through his already lowered window. 'Come and sit with me while I tell you what all this is about,' he said conversationally.

Donna hesitated fractionally, but she was too familiar with the open candour of his public face to pause properly for reflection. She slid into the seat next to him and he made sure she saw him carefully not looking at the expanse of thigh her moves had revealed. For the time being, chastity was the best policy. Her smile was coquettish yet innocent as she said, 'When I woke up this morning, I wondered if I'd dreamed it all.'

His answering smile was indulgent. 'I feel like that all the time,' he said, building another course of bricks on the false foundation of fake rapport. 'I wondered if you'd have second thoughts. There are so many things you could do with your life that would be a greater contribution to society than being on TV. Believe me, I know.'

'But you do those things too,' she said earnestly. 'All that charity work. It's being famous makes it possible for TV stars to raise so much money. People pay money to see them. They wouldn't be shelling out otherwise. I want to be able to do that. To be like them.'

The impossible dream. Or rather, nightmare. She could never have been like him, though she had no notion of the real reason why. People like him were so rare it was almost an argument for the existence of God. He smiled benevolently, like the Pope from the Vatican balcony. It pushed all the right buttons. 'Well, perhaps I can help you make a start,' he told her. And Donna believed him.

He had her there, alone, co-operative, in his car, in an underground car park. What could have been easier than to whisk her away to his destination?

Only a fool would think like that, he'd realized long ago, and he was no fool. For a start, the car park wasn't exactly empty. Businessmen and women were checking out of the hotel, stowing suit carriers into executive saloons and reversing out of tight spots. They noticed a lot more than anyone would expect. For another thing, it was broad daylight outside, a city centre festooned with traffic lights where people sat with nothing better to do than pick their noses and stare slack-jawed at the inhabitants of the next car. First, they'd register the car. A silver Mercedes, smart enough to catch the eye and the admiration. Or, of course, the envy. Then they'd clock the flowing letters along the front wing that announced, *Cars for Vance's Visits supplied by Morrigan Mercedes of Cheshire.* Alerted to the possible proximity of celebrity, they'd peer through the tinted windows, trying to identify the driver and passenger. They weren't going to forget that in a hurry, especially if they glimpsed an attractive teenager in the passenger seat. When her photograph appeared in the local paper, they'd remember, no question.

And finally, he'd got a busy day ahead. There was no space in his schedule for delivering her to a place where he could exact what was due. No point in drawing attention to himself by failing to keep appointments, not turning up for the public appearances that were so carefully constructed to give *Vance's Visits* maximum exposure for minimal effort. Donna would have to wait. For both of them, it would be the sweeter for the anticipation. Well, for him, at least. For her, it wouldn't be long before reality turned her breathless expectation into a sick joke.

So he whetted her appetite and kept her on the leash. 'I couldn't believe it when I saw you last night. You'd be absolutely perfect as the co-host. With a two-handed show, we need contrast. Dark-haired Donna, fair-haired Jacko. Petite Donna, hulking great brute Jacko.' He grinned, she giggled. 'What we're working on is a new game show involving parent and child teams. But the teams don't know they're in the show until we turn up to whisk them off. A total surprise, like *This is Your Life*. That's part of the reason why we need to be so sure that whoever I end up working with is absolutely trustworthy. Total discretion, that's the key.'

'I can keep my mouth shut,' Donna said earnestly. 'Honest. I never told a living soul about coming here to meet you. My mate that was at the opening last night with me, when she asked what we were talking about for so long, I just said I was asking whether you had any advice for me if I wanted to break into TV.'

'And did I?' he demanded.

She smiled, beguiling and seductive. 'I told her you said I should get some qualifications behind me before I made any decisions about a career. She doesn't know enough about you to realize you'd never come out with all that boring shit that I get off my mum.'

'Good thinking,' he told her appreciatively. 'I can promise you I'll never be boring, that's for sure. Now, the problem I've got is that I'm desperately busy for the next couple of days. But I've got Friday morning free, and I can easily set up some screen tests for you. We've got a rehearsal studio up in the north-east and we can work there.'

Her lips parted, her eyes glowed in the dimness of the car interior. 'You mean it? I can be on telly?'

'No promises, but you look the part and you've got a beautiful voice.' He shifted in his seat so he could fix her with a direct gaze. 'All I need to prove to myself is that you really can keep a secret.'

'I told you,' Donna replied, consternation on her face. 'I've said nothing to anybody.'

'But can you keep that up? Can you stay silent until Thursday night?' He put his hand inside his jacket and produced a rail ticket. 'This is a train ticket for Five Walls Halt in Northumberland. On Thursday, you catch the 3.25 Newcastle train from the station here, then at Newcastle, you change to the 7.50 for Carlisle. When you come out of the station, there's a car park on the left. I'll be waiting there in a Land Rover. I can't get out to meet you on the platform because of commercial confidentiality, but I'll be there in the car park, I promise. We'll put you up for the night, then first thing in the morning, you do the screen test.'

'But my mum'll panic if I stay out all night and she doesn't know where I am,' she protested reluctantly.

'You can phone her as soon as we get to the studio complex,' he told her, his voice rich in reassurance. 'Let's face it, she probably wouldn't let you take the screen test if she knew, would she? I bet she doesn't think working in TV is a proper job, does she?'

As usual, he'd calculated to perfection. Donna knew her ambitious mother wouldn't want her to throw her university prospects away to be a game-show bimbo. Her worried look disappeared and she peered up at him from under her eyebrows. 'I won't say a word,' she promised solemnly.

'Good girl. I hope you mean that. All it takes is one wrong word and a whole project can crash. That costs money, and it costs people's jobs too. You might say something in confidence to your best friend, but she'll tell her sister, and her sister will tell her boyfriend, and the boyfriend will tell his best mate over a frame of snooker, and the best mate's sister-in-law just happens to be a reporter. Or a rival TV company executive. And the show's dead. And your big chance goes with it. Let me tell you something. At the start of your career, you only get one bite of the cherry. You screw up, and no one will ever hire you again. You have to have a lot of success under your belt before the TV bosses forgive a bit of failure.' He leaned forward and rested a hand on her arm as he spoke, invading her space and making her feel the sexual thrill of his dangerous edge.

'I understand,' Donna said with all the intensity of a fourteen-year-old who thought she was really a grown-up and couldn't understand why the adults wouldn't admit her into their conspiracy. The promise of an entrée into that world was what made her so ready to swallow something as preposterous as his set-up.

'I can rely on you?'

She nodded. 'I won't let you down. Not with this or anything else.' The sexual innuendo was unmistakable. She was probably still a virgin, he reckoned. Something about her avidity told him so. She was offering herself up to him, a vestal sacrifice.

He leaned closer and kissed the soft, eager mouth that instantly opened under his primly closed lips. He drew back, smiling to soften her obvious disappointment. He always left them wanting more. It was the oldest showbiz cliché in the world. But it worked every time.

Carol wiped up the remaining traces of chicken jalfrezi with the last chunk of nan bread and savoured the final mouthful. 'That,' she said reverently, 'was to die for.'

'There's more,' Maggie Brandon said, pushing the heavy casserole dish towards her.

'I'd have to wear it,' Carol groaned. 'There's no room inside.'

'You can take some home with you,' Maggie told her. 'I know the kind of daft hours you'll be working. Cooking's the last thing you'll have time for. When John was made up to DCI, I considered asking his Chief Constable if the family could move into the cells at Scargill Street since that seemed to be the only way his kids would ever get to see him.'

John Brandon, Chief Constable of East Yorkshire Police, shook his head and said affectionately, 'She's a terrible liar, my wife. She only says these things to guilt-trip you into working so hard there'll be nothing left for me to worry about in your whole division.'

Maggie snorted. 'As if! How do you think he ended up looking like that, eh?'

Carol gave Brandon a shrewd look. It was a good question. If ever a man had been born with a graveyard face, it was Brandon. His countenance was all verticals, long and narrow; lines in his hollow cheeks, lines between his brows, aquiline

76

nose, iron-grey hair straight as the grid line on a map. Tall and thin, with the beginnings of a stoop, all he needed was a scythe to audition for Death. She considered her options. It might be 'John' tonight, but on Monday morning it would be back to, 'Mr Brandon, *sir*.' Better not push her informal relationship with the boss too far. 'And there was me thinking it was marriage,' she said innocently.

Maggie roared with laughter. 'Diplomatic as well as quick, eh?' she got out at last, reaching across to pat her husband's shoulder. 'You did well to get Carol to abandon the fleshpots of Bradfield for the back of beyond, my love.'

'Speaking of which, how are you settling in?' Carol asked.

'Well, this is a police house,' Maggie told her, waving a hand at the brilliant white walls and paintwork, a depressing contrast to the hand-marbled paintwork Carol remembered from their Bradfield dining room. 'But it'll have to do us. We've rented out the house in Bradfield, you know? John's only got another five years till he has his thirty in, and we want to go back there. It's where our roots are, where our friends are. And the kids will all be out of school by then, so it's not like they'll be uprooted again.'

'What Maggie isn't saying is that she feels a bit like a Victorian missionary among the Hottentots,' Brandon said.

'Well, you've got to admit, East Yorkshire's a bit different from Bradfield. Plenty of scenery, but there's not a decent theatre within half an hour's drive of here. There seems to be only one bookshop on the whole patch that sells more than the bestsellers. And as for opera – you can forget it!' Maggie protested, getting to her feet and gathering the empty plates.

'Don't you feel happier about the kids growing up away from the influence of the inner city? Out of the reaches of the drug lords?' Carol asked.

Maggie shook her head. 'They're so insular round here, Carol. Back in Bradfield, the kids had friends from all kinds of backgrounds – Asian, Chinese, Afro-Caribbean. Even one Vietnamese lad. Out here, you stick to your own. There's nothing to do except hang around on street corners. Frankly, I'd take a chance on them having the sense to stay out of trouble in the inner city as a trade-off for all the opportunities they had in Bradfield. This country living is well over-rated.' She marched through to the kitchen.

'Sorry,' Carol said. 'Didn't realize it was such a sore point.'

Brandon shrugged. 'You know Maggie. She likes to get it off her chest. Give it a few more months, she'll be running the village, happy as a pig. The kids like it well enough. How about you? What's the cottage like?'

'I love it. The couple I bought it from did an immaculate restoration job.'

'I'm surprised they were selling it, then.'

'Divorce,' Carol said succinctly.

'Ah.'

'I think they were both more upset about losing the cottage than the marriage. You and Maggie will have to come over for a meal.'

'If you ever find the time to shop,' Maggie said darkly, walking back in with a large cafetiere.

'Well, worst comes to worst, I'll send Nelson out to bring us a rabbit back.'

'He's enjoying the opportunities for murder that living in the country offers?' Maggie asked drily.

'He thinks he's died and gone to feline heaven. You might crave the inner city, but he's turned into a country boy overnight.'

Maggie poured coffee for John and Carol, then said, 'I'm

going to leave you pair to it, if you don't mind. I know you're dying to talk shop and I promised Karen I'd pick her up after the pictures in Seaford. There's enough coffee there to keep you both awake till dawn, and if you feel peckish in a bit, there's home-made cheesecake in the fridge. But Andy's due back around ten, so you'd better help yourself before then. I swear that lad's got worms. That or hollow legs.' She swooped down on Brandon and gave him an affectionate peck on the cheek. 'Enjoy yourselves.'

Unable to resist the feeling that she'd been set up by professionals, Carol took a sip of her coffee and waited. When it came, Brandon's question was hardly a surprise. 'So how are you settling in on the ground?' His voice was casual, but his eyes were watchful.

'Obviously, they're wary of me. Not only am I a woman, which on the evolutionary scale in East Yorkshire comes somewhere between a ferret and a whippet, but I'm also the Chief Constable's nark. Brought in from the big city to crack the whip,' she said ironically.

'I was afraid you'd get lumbered with that,' Brandon said. 'But you must have known how it would be when you took the job on.'

Carol shrugged. 'It's not come as a surprise. But there's been rather less of it than I anticipated. Maybe they're all still on their best behaviour, but I think the Seaford Central Division CID are not a bad crew. Because they were stuck out in the boondocks before the reorganization and nobody was paying much attention, they've got a bit lazy, a bit sloppy. I suspect one or two might be spending a bit more than they're earning, but I don't think there's any deep-rooted, systemic corruption.'

Brandon nodded, satisfied. Trusting Carol Jordan's judgement had been a steep learning curve for him, and he'd known instinctively she was the one senior officer he wanted to tempt away from Bradfield. With her setting the tone in Seaford, word would spread through other divisions and the CID culture would adapt accordingly, given time. Time and a certain amount of stick which Brandon wasn't afraid to apply. 'Anything on the books that's causing you a problem?'

Carol finished her coffee and poured herself another cup, offering the pot to Brandon, who refused with a shake of the head. She frowned in thought, gathering her arsenal of information. 'There is something,' she said. 'Since we're talking informally?'

Brandon nodded.

'Well, I noticed going through the overnights that there seemed to be a positive spate of unexplained fires and query arsons. All at night, all in unoccupied premises like schools, factories, cafés, warehouses. None of them very big in itself, but taken together, you're looking at a lot of damage. I put a team together to re-interview the previous victims, see if we could find any connection – financially or insurance-wise. Zilch. But I went myself to talk to the local fire chief, and he produced a series of incidents going back about four months. None of the fires could be absolutely, positively put down as arson, but circumstantially, he reckons there have been something between six and a dozen possible deliberate fires per month on his patch,' Carol said.

'A serial arsonist?' Brandon said softly.

'It's hard to imagine another interpretation,' Carol agreed.

'And you want to do what, exactly?'

'I want to catch him,' she said with a grin.

'Well, what else?' Brandon smiled. 'Did you have something specific in mind?' he continued mildly.

'I want to carry on working with the team I've already got on it, and I want to do a profile.'

Brandon frowned. 'Bring someone in?'

'No,' Carol said sharply. 'There's not really enough evidence to justify the expense. I think I can take a pretty good stab at it myself.'

Brandon looked impassively at Carol. 'You're not a psychologist.'

'No, but I learned a lot last year, working with Tony Hill. And since then, I've read everything about profiling I could find.'

'You should have applied for the National Task Force,' Brandon said, keeping his eyes fixed on her.

Carol felt her skin burn. She hoped the wine and the coffee would account for her heightened colour. 'I don't think they were looking for officers of my rank,' she said. 'Apart from Commander Bishop, there's no one above the rank of sergeant. Besides, I prefer to work a patch, get to know the people and the ground.'

'They're due to be up and running a full case-load in a few weeks,' Brandon continued implacably. 'Maybe they'd welcome something like this to cut their teeth on before then.'

'Maybe they would,' Carol said. 'But it's my case. And I'm not ready to let it go.'

'Fine,' Brandon said, interested that Carol had already developed such fierce possessiveness about the work of the East Yorkshire force. 'But keep me posted, yes?'

'Of course,' Carol said. Her sense of relief, she told herself, was entirely because she would now have the chance to cover herself and her team in glory when they cracked the case. Deep down, though, she knew she was lying.

Sleeping in what the estate agent had referred to as the guest bedroom of Shaz's flat would have been beyond most people, particularly if they were the sort who needed to read a few pages before they could nod off. While the bookcase in the living room contained an innocuous mix of middlebrow middle-of-the-road modern fiction, the shelves in the room Shaz thought of as her study held only hard-core horror, most of it masquerading as textbooks. There were a few novels by pathologists of psychopathy and anatomists of agony like Barbara Vine and Thomas Harris, but most of Shaz's working library was both stranger and more brutal than fiction ever dared to be. If there had been a vocational course for serial killers, her library would have comprised the set books.

The lowest shelves held those items which mildly embarrassed her – pulp true-crime biographies of notorious serial killers with lurid nicknames, sensational accounts of careers that had robbed hundreds of people of their trust and their lives. Arranged above these were the more respectable versions of those same lives, portentous renderings that provided thoughtful revelations and insights sociological, psychological and sometimes illogical.

Next, at eye-level for anyone sitting at the table that held Shaz's notepads and laptop, were the battle stories of the veterans of the war against serial offenders. Since it was the best part of twenty years since the infancy of offender profiling, the pioneers had been trickling into retirement for a few years now, each determined to augment his pension with graphic accounts of his contribution to the latest soft science with the case histories of his notable successes and a passing gloss over his failures. They were, thus far, all men.

Above these autobiographies was the serious stuff; books with titles like *The Psychopathology of Sexual Homicide, Crime Scene Analysis* and *Serial Rape: A Clinical Study*. The top shelf gave the only indications that she aspired to be hunter rather than hunted, with its selection of legal texts, including a couple of guides to the Police and Criminal Evidence Act. It was a comprehensive collection and Shaz hadn't amassed it in the mere couple of months since she'd won her place on the task force; it had been years in the building, helping her prepare for the day she'd always been convinced would come, when she'd be called upon to bring her very own notorious killer to book. If textual familiarity alone caught criminals, Shaz would have had the best arrest record in the country.

She had begged off the nightclub run following the curry in spite of the blandishments of the other three. It wasn't just that she had never been a great one for clubbing. Tonight, her spare room was infinitely more tempting than anything a DJ or a barman had to offer. The truth was, she'd been in a ferment all evening, eager to get back to her computer and to finish the comparisons she'd begun to run through her database that afternoon. In the three days since Tony had set their assignment, Shaz had spent every spare moment working her way through the thirty sketchy sets of case notes. At last, the opportunity had come to put into practice all the theories and tricks of the trade she'd picked up in her reading. She'd read the papers from start to finish, not once, but three times. Not until she was fairly sure she had them well differentiated in her head did she approach her computer.

The database Shaz used hadn't represented the leading edge of software development way back when she'd copied it from a fellow student, and now it was practically a candidate for display in a computing museum. But while it might not have all the latest bells and whistles, it was more than capable of performing what she needed. It displayed the material clearly, it allowed her to create her own categories and criteria for sorting the information, and she found its procedures in tune with her instincts and logic and thus easy to use. She'd been inputting data since early that morning, so focused on her work that she hadn't even left the screen to cook lunch, settling instead for a banana and half a packet of digestive biscuits, upending her laptop afterwards to remove the crumbs from the keyboard.

Now, back in front of her screen, stripped of her glad rags and scrubbed clean of her make-up, Shaz was happy. The mouse pointer flickered as fingers clicked on buttons, summoning up menus that interested her far more than anything on offer at the restaurant. She sorted the so-called runaways by age and printed out the results. She followed the same steps for geographical area, physical type, previous police contact, various permutations on their domestic situation, drink and drugs experience, known sexual contacts and interests. Not that the investigating officers had been much concerned with their hobbies.

Shaz pored over the print-outs, reading them individually then spreading them over the desktop so she could more readily compare notes. As she gazed at the printed lists, the slow burn of excitement began in the pit of her stomach. She scrutinized them one more time, double-checking against the photographs in the files to make sure she wasn't willing something into existence that wasn't there. 'Oh, you beauty,' Shaz exclaimed softly, letting out a long sigh.

She closed her eyes and took a deep breath. When she looked again, it was still there. A cluster of seven girls. First, the positive similarities. They all had bobbed dark hair and blue eyes. They were all fourteen or fifteen years old, between 5'2" and 5'4" tall. They had all lived at home with one or both parents. In each case, their friends and family had told the police they were baffled at the girl's disappearance, convinced that she had no real reason to run away. In every instance, the girls had taken almost nothing with them, though in each case, at least one change of clothes appeared to have gone missing with them, which was the main reason why the police hadn't seriously considered them as possible victims of abduction or murder. Reinforcing that view were the times of the disappearances. In each case, the girl concerned had set off for school as usual but had never arrived. She'd also given a false explanation of where she'd be spending the evening. And, although this couldn't be quantified in a way the computer could digest, they were all of a similar type. There was a flirtatious sensuality in their looks, a knowing quality in the way they embraced the camera that indicated they had left childhood innocence behind. They were sexy, whether they knew it or not.

Next, the negative similarities. None of the seven had ever been in care. None had ever been in trouble with the police. Friends admitted to a bit of recreational drinking, maybe even the occasional joint or even a dab of speed. But no significant drug usage. In none of the seven cases was there any hint that the girls might have been engaged in prostitution or the victims of sexual abuse.

There were problems with the cluster, of course. Three had current boyfriends, four did not. The geographical locations were unconnected – Sunderland was the furthest north, Exmouth the most southerly point. In between were Swindon, Grantham, Tamworth, Wigan and Halifax. The reports also spanned six years. The intervals between the disappearances were not constant, nor did they seem to diminish as time went by, which Shaz would have expected if she were really dealing with the victims of a serial killer.

On the other hand, there might be girls she didn't know about yet.

When Shaz woke early that Sunday morning, she tried to will herself back to sleep. She knew there was only one thing she could do that would advance her search for connections among her theoretical victim cluster and that single task wasn't one that could be hurried. When she'd gone to bed around midnight, she'd promised herself she would achieve it with a lunchtime phone call. But lying wide awake with a racing brain at quarter to seven, she knew she couldn't hold out that long.

Irritated by her inability to make progress except at someone else's hands, she threw back the covers. Half an hour later, she was accelerating up the long incline where the M1 began.

Showering, dressing and swallowing a coffee with the radio news in the background had kept thought at arm's length. Now that the empty black three-lane strip stretched out before her, she couldn't hide behind distraction. The radio presenter's voice wasn't enough on its own. Not even Tony Hill's words of wisdom could hold her today. Impatiently, Shaz pushed a cassette of operatic arias into the stereo and gave up the pretence of concentration. For the next two and a half hours, she had nothing to do but run memories through her mind like old movies on a rainy Sunday.

It was almost ten when she drove down the ramp to the Barbican complex's underground car park. She was pleased to see the car park attendant clearly remembered her, as she'd hoped, though he looked startled to see her face smiling uncertainly round the door of his office. 'Hello, stranger,' he said cheerfully. 'We've not seen you around for a long time.'

'I've moved up to Leeds,' she said, carefully avoiding any hint of how recent her move had been. It had been more than eighteen months since she'd last been here, but the reasons for that were nobody's business but hers.

'Chris didn't say to expect you,' the car park attendant

said, getting up from his seat and walking towards her. Shaz backed out of the booth and down the steps as he followed her.

'It was all a bit last-minute,' she said noncommittally, opening her car door.

That seemed to satisfy the attendant. 'Are you here overnight?' he asked, frowning as he scanned the car park for an appropriate space.

'No, I'm not planning on staying long,' Shaz said firmly, starting her engine and crawling down the aisles of cars, following the attendant and slotting the car into the space he indicated.

'I'll let you into the block,' he said as she joined him. 'What's it like up in the frozen north, then?'

Shaz smiled. 'The football's better,' was all she said as he pulled back the massive glass and metal door and waved her inside. Just as well I'm not a terrorist sleeper, she thought as she waited for the lift.

On the third floor, she stopped halfway along the carpeted corridor. Taking a deep breath, she pressed the doorbell. In the silence that followed, she breathed out through her nostrils in a slow steady stream, trying to contain the nervousness that was turning her stomach into a jacuzzi. When she'd almost given up hope, she heard the faint whisper of footfalls. Then the heavy door inched open.

Tousled chestnut hair, bleary brown eyes with dark smudges under them and frown lines between, a snub nose and a yawn half-stifled behind a square hand with blunt, well-manicured fingers appeared in the gap.

For once, Shaz's narrow smile made it as far as her eyes. The blaze of warmth melted Chris Devine, and not for the first time. The hand dropped away from the mouth, but the lips remained parted. Astonishment came first, then delight, then consternation. 'Any chance of a cup of coffee?' Shaz asked.

Chris stepped back uncertainly, pulling the door wide. 'You'd better come in,' she said.

Nothing worth having had ever come easy. He told himself that at regular intervals through two days of torment, though it was not a lesson he was ever likely to forget. His childhood had been scarred with oppressive discipline, any rebelliousness or frivolity stifled by force. He had learned not to show the currents that moved under the surface, to present a bland and acceptable face to whatever adversity people threw in his teeth. Other men might have revealed some traces of the seething excitement that swirled inside whenever he thought of Donna Doyle, but not him. He was too practised at dissemblement. No one ever noticed his mind was ranging through entirely different territory, detached from his surroundings, entirely elsewhere. It was a trait that in the past had saved him pain; now it kept him safe.

In his head he was with her, wondering if she was keeping her promise, imagining the excitement burning in her veins. He thought of her as a changed being, charged with the secret weapon of knowledge, convinced she had the edge on every tabloid astrologer because she knew for sure what her future held.

Of course, hers could not be the same vision as his, he realized that. It would have been hard to imagine two more disparate fantasies, so far apart on the continuum that there could exist no single uniting factor. Apart from orgasm.

Imagining her imagining a false future had its own *frisson* of delight that cohabited and alternated with the sliver of fear that she would not keep her word, that even as he played computer games with the stricken inhabitants of a children's cancer ward, Donna was huddled in a corner of the school cloakroom revealing her secret to her best friend. That was the gamble he took every time. And every time, he'd judged the roll of the dice perfectly. Not once had anyone come looking for him. Well, not in the investigative sense. There had been one time when the distraught parents of a missing teenage girl asked for a TV appeal because, wherever she'd run off to, their daughter would never miss her weekly fix of *Vance's Visits*. Sweet irony, so delicious he'd grown hard for months afterwards just thinking about it. He could hardly have told them that the only way they were ever going to talk to their daughter again was via a medium, could he?

For two nights running, he went to sleep in the early hours and woke at dawn tangled in damp sheets, his pulse racing and his eyes wide open. Whatever the evaporated dream, it robbed him of further sleep, leaving him to prowl the confined spaces of his hotel room, alternately exulting and fretting.

But nothing lasted forever. Thursday evening found him in his Northumberland retreat. Only fifteen minutes' drive from the centre of the city, it was nevertheless as isolated as a Highland croft. Formerly a tiny Methodist chapel that could never have held more than a couple of dozen, it had been bought when it was reduced to four bulging walls and a sagging roof. A team of local builders happy to have the cash in hand renovated it to very particular specifications, never doubting the reasons they were given for the desired features.

He savoured the preparations for his visitor. The sheets were clean, the clothes laid out. The phone was switched off, the answering machine turned down low, the fax shut away inside a drawer. The fibre optics might sing all night with calls for him, but he wouldn't be hearing them till morning. The table was covered with linen so white it seemed to glow in the dark. On it, crystal, silver and porcelain were arranged in traditional patterns. Red rosebuds in an engraved crystal vase, candles splendid in simple Georgian silver. Donna would be captivated. Of course, she wouldn't realize that it would be the last time she'd ever use cutlery.

He looked around, checking everything was as it should be. The chains and leather straps were all out of sight, the silken gag tucked away, the carpentry bench innocent of tools except for the permanently mounted vice. He had designed the workbench himself, all the tools arrayed on a solid piece of wood like the drop leaf of a table attached to the far end of the bench at ninety degrees to the work surface.

One last glance at his watch. Time to drive the Land Rover across the rutted field track to the empty B-road that would take him to Five Walls Halt with its isolated railway station. He lit the candles and smiled with sheer pleasure, confident now that she would have kept faith and silence alike.

Won't you come into my parlour? said the spider to the fly.

Tim Coughlan had finally had his prayers answered. He'd found the perfect spot. The loading bay was slightly less wide than the factory proper, leaving a recess about seven feet square at one end. At first glance, it looked as if the alcove was blocked off by flattened cardboard cartons stacked on their ends. If anyone had bothered to look more closely, they would have noticed that the cartons weren't tightly packed and that, with a little effort, it wouldn't be too hard to squeeze between them. Anyone inclined to investigate further would have found Tim Coughlan's bedsit, containing a stained and greasy sleeping bag and two carrier bags. The first bag contained one clean T-shirt, one clean pair of socks and one clean pair of underpants. The other held one dirty T-shirt, one dirty pair of socks, one dirty pair of boxer shorts and a pair of shapeless cords that might once have been dark brown but were now the colour of seabirds after the oil slick has trapped them.

Tim slouched in a corner of his space, the sleeping bag scrunched into a cushion beneath his bony buttocks. He was eating chips and curry sauce from a polystyrene container. He had the best part of a litre of cider left to wash it down and send him to sleep. He needed something on the cold nights to carry him forward into oblivion.

It had taken long months living rough on the streets

before he'd emerged on the other side of the heroin haze that had robbed him of his life. He'd dropped so low that even drugs were above his reach. That, ironically, was what had saved him. Shivering through cold turkey in a Christmas charity shelter, he'd finally turned the corner. He'd started selling the *Big Issue* on street corners. He'd managed to put together enough cash to buy clothes from charity shops that looked like poverty rather than hopeless homelessness. And he'd managed to find work on the docks. It was casual, poorly paid, cash in hand, the black economy at its gloomiest. But it was a start. And that was when he'd found his spot in the loading bay of an assembly plant too strapped for cash to afford a night watchman.

Since then, he'd managed to save nearly three hundred pounds, stashed in the building society account that was probably his only extant connection to his past. Soon, he'd have enough for the deposit and a month's rent on a proper place to live and enough to spare to feed himself while the dole dragged their feet over his claim.

Tim had hit bottom and nearly drowned. Soon, he was convinced, he'd be ready to swim back up to the daylight. He screwed up the chip container and tossed it into the corner. Then he opened the cider bottle and tipped the contents down his throat in a long series of quick gulps. The notion of savouring it never occurred to him. There was no reason why it should.

Opportunity had seldom knocked at Jacko Vance's door. Mostly, he'd gripped it by the throat and dragged it kicking and screaming to centre stage. He'd realized while he was still a child that the only way he was ever going to come by some luck was if he managed to make it himself. His mother, plagued by a kind of post-natal depression that had made him repugnant to her, had ignored him as far as possible. She hadn't actually been cruel, simply absent in any meaningful sense. His father had been the one who paid attention, most often of a negative sort.

He hadn't long been at school when the handsome child with the floppy blond hair, the hollow cheeks and the huge baffled eyes had realized that there was a point in having dreams, that things could be made to happen. His little-boy-lost appearance worked on some teachers like a blowtorch on an icicle. It didn't take him long to work out that he could manipulate them into playing accessories in his own particular power game. It didn't erase what happened at home, but it gave him an arena where he began to understand the pleasure of power.

Although he traded on his looks, Jacko never relied solely on the power of his charm. It was as if he had a built-in understanding that there would be those who needed different weaponry if they were to succumb. Since he'd had the work ethic instilled into him from the moment he had begun to comprehend the messages of speech, it was never a hardship to him to work for his effect. The sports field was the obvious place for him to focus, since he had a certain natural talent and it offered a wider arena to shine in than the narrow stage of the classroom. It was also an area where effort paid off visibly and spectacularly.

Inevitably, the elements of his behaviour that endeared him to those who had power alienated his contemporaries. Nobody ever loved a teacher's pet. He fought the obligatory fights, winning some and losing a few. When he did lose, he never forgot. Sometimes it took years, but he found ways to exact some sort of satisfactory revenge. Often, the victim of his vengeance never knew Jacko was behind his ultimate humiliation, but sometimes he did.

Everyone on the council estate where he'd grown up remembered how he'd got his own back on Danny Boy Ferguson. Danny Boy had been the bane of Jacko's life between the ages of ten and twelve, picking on him mercilessly. Finally, when Jacko had flown at him in a rage, Danny Boy had smashed him to the ground with one hand held ostentatiously above his head. Jacko's broken nose had healed without trace, but his black rage burned behind the charm that the adults saw.

When Jacko won his first junior British championship, he became an overnight hero on the estate. No one from there had ever had their picture in the national papers before, not even Liam Gascoigne when he dropped that concrete slab on Gladstone Sanders from the tenth floor. It wasn't hard to persuade Danny Boy's girlfriend Kimberley to come up west with him for a night on the town.

He'd wined and dined her for a week, then dumped her. That Sunday night in the local, just as Danny Boy was working up to his fifth pint, Jacko slipped the landlord fifty quid to broadcast over the pub's PA system the tape he'd secretly recorded of Kimberley telling him in graphic detail what a lousy fuck Danny Boy was.

When Micky Morgan had started visiting him in hospital, he'd recognized a kindred spirit. He wasn't sure what she wanted, but he had a strong feeling she wanted something. The day Jillie dumped him and Micky offered to help him out, he became certain.

Five minutes after she walked out of the ward, he hired the private eye. The man was good; the answers came even faster than he'd expected. By the time he read her handiwork in the headlines that screamed across all the tabloids, he understood Micky's motives and knew how best he could use her.

JACK THE LAD LETS LOVE GO! HEARTBREAK HERO!

He smiled and read on.

Britain's bravest man has revealed he's making the greatest sacrifice of all.

Days after he lost his Olympic dream saving the lives of two toddlers, Jacko Vance has broken his engagement to his childhood sweetheart Jillie Woodrow.

Heartbroken Jacko, speaking from the hospital bed where he is recovering from the amputation of his javelin-throwing arm, said, 'I'm setting her free. I'm no longer the man she agreed to marry. It's not fair to expect her to carry on as before. I can't offer her the life we'd expected to have, and the most important thing to me is her happiness.

'I know she's upset now, but in the long run, she'll come to see I'm doing the right thing.'

Now Jillie could never deny his version of events without making herself look a complete bitch.

Jacko bided his time, playing along with Micky's proffered friendship. Then, when he deemed the moment was right, he struck like a rattler. 'OK, so when's payback day?' he asked, his eyes holding hers.

'Payback day?' she echoed, puzzled.

'The story of my love sacrifice,' he said, larding his words with heavy irony. 'Don't they call tales like that a nine-day wonder?'

'They do,' Micky said, continuing to arrange the flowers she'd brought in the tall vase she'd charmed from the nurse.

'Well, it's ten days now since the media broke the news. Jacko and Jillie are officially no longer headline material. I was wondering when I'd get the account for payment due.'

His voice was mild, but looking into his eyes was like staring into a frozen puddle on high moorland.

Micky shook her head and perched on the edge of the bed, her face composed. But he knew her mind was racing, calculating how best to handle him. 'I'm not sure what you mean,' she stalled.

Jacko's smile was laced with condescension. 'Come on, Micky. I wasn't born yesterday. The world you work in, you've got to be a piranha. Favours don't get done in your circles without the full understanding that payback day is lurking somewhere in the background.'

He watched her consider lying and reject it; he waited while she considered the truth and rejected that, too. 'I'll settle for having one in the bank,' she tried.

'That's the way you want to play it, OK,' he said nonchalantly. His left hand suddenly snaked out and seized her wrist. 'But I'd have thought you and your girlfriend were in pretty dire need as of now.'

His large hand encircled her wrist. The sculpted muscles of his forearm stood out in strong relief, a shocking reminder of what he'd lost. The grip wasn't tight against her flesh, but she sensed it was unbreakable as the bracelet of a handcuff. Micky looked up from her wrist to his implacable face and he saw a momentary clutch of fear as she wondered what lay behind his impenetrable eyes. He made his face relax into a ghost of a smile and the instant passed. He saw himself reflected in her eyes, not a trace of sinister showing now. 'What a strange thing to say,' she said.

'It's not just journalists who have contacts,' Jacko said contemptuously. 'When you started taking an interest in me, I returned the compliment. Her name's Betsy Thorne, you've been together more than a year. She acts as your PA but she is also your lover. For Christmas you bought her a Bulova watch from a Bond Street jeweller's. Two weekends ago you shared a twin room overnight at a country house hotel near Oxford. You send her flowers on the twenty-third of each month. I could go on.'

'Circumstantial,' Micky said. Her voice was cool; the skin under his grip felt like a burning ring of flesh. 'And none of your business.'

'It's not the tabloids' business either, is it? But they're digging, Micky. It's only a matter of time. You know that.'

'They can't find what isn't there to be found,' she said, slipping into obstinacy as if it were a tailored blazer.

'They'll find it,' Jacko promised her. 'Which is where I might be able to help.'

'Supposing I did need help . . . what form would your help take?'

He released her wrist. Rather than pull her arm to her and rub it, Micky let it lie where he dropped it. 'Economists say good money drives out bad. It's like that with journalists. You should know. Give them a better story and they'll abandon their sordid little fishing expedition.'

'I won't argue with that. What did you have in mind?'

'What about, "Hospital romance for hero Jacko and TV journo"?' He raised one eyebrow. Micky wondered if he'd practised the gesture before the mirror in adolescence.

'What's in it for you?' she asked, after a moment when they'd each stared appraisingly at the other, as if measuring for romantic congruence.

'Peace and quiet,' Jacko said. 'You have no idea how many women there are out there who want to save me.'

'Maybe one of them would be the right one.'

Jacko laughed, a dry, bitter sound. 'It's the Groucho Marx principle, isn't it? Not wanting to be a member of any club that would let me in. A woman who's demented enough to think that, a) I need saving and b) that she's the person for the job is by definition the world's worst woman for me. No, Micky, what I need is camouflage. So that when I get out of here – which should be quite soon – I can go about my life without every brain-dead bimbo in Britain thinking I'm her chance at the big time. I don't want someone who feels sorry for me. Until somebody I choose comes along, I could use the erogenous equivalent of a bulletproof vest. Fancy the job?'

Now it was his turn to guess what was really happening behind her eyes. Micky was back in control of herself, maintaining the air of bland interest that would later stand her in good stead as the housebound nation's favourite interviewer. 'I don't do ironing,' was all she said.

'I've always wondered what a PA did,' Jacko said, his smile as wry as his tone.

'You better not let Betsy hear you say that.'

'Deal?'

Jacko covered her hand with his. 'Deal,' she said, turning her hand over and clasping his fingers in hers.

The stench hit Carol as soon as she opened her car door. There was nothing quite as disgusting as barbecued human flesh, and once smelled, it could never be erased from the memory. Trying not to gag too obviously, she walked the short distance to where Jim Pendlebury appeared to be conducting an impromptu press conference under the fire brigade's portable arc lights. She'd spotted the journalists as soon as her driver had turned into the car park, and she'd asked to be dropped nearby, well away from the phalanx of scarlet engines where fire officers were still spraying a smouldering warehouse with water. High above his colleagues, one man on a cherry picker sent a soaring arc of water above their heads on to the flaking remains of the roof. Milling around behind the fire brigade were half a dozen uniformed police officers. One or two watched Carol's arrival with vague interest, but soon turned back to the more absorbing vista of the fag end of the fire.

Carol hung back as Pendlebury gave brief and non-committal answers for the benefit of local radio and press. Once they realized they would get nothing much out of the fire chief at that stage, they dispersed. If any of them paid attention to the blonde in the trench coat, they probably assumed she was another reporter. Only the crime reporters had met Carol so far, and it was too early for this to have graduated from a news headline into a crime story. As soon as the night-shift news reporters called in that the factory fire was not only fatal but also suspected arson, the jackals on the crime beat would have their morning assignments on a plate. One or two of them might even be turfed out of bed as unceremoniously as she had been.

Pendlebury greeted Carol with a grim smile. 'The smell of hell,' he said.

'Unmistakably.'

'Thanks for turning out.'

'Thanks for tipping me off. Otherwise I'd have known nothing about it till I got into the office and read the overnights. And then I'd have missed the joys of a fresh crime scene,' she said wryly.

'Well, after our little chat the other day, I knew this one would be right up your street.'

'You think it's our serial arsonist?'

'I wouldn't have phoned you at home at half past three in the morning if I hadn't been pretty sure,' he said.

'So what have we got?'

'Want to have a look?'

'In a minute. First, I'd appreciate a verbal briefing while

I'm in a position to concentrate on what you're saying rather than on what my stomach's doing.'

Pendlebury looked slightly surprised, as if he expected her to take such horrors in her stride. 'Right,' he said, sounding disconcerted. 'We got the call just after two, from one of your patrol cars, actually. They'd been cruising and saw the flames. We had two units here within seven minutes, but the place was well ablaze. Another three tenders were here inside the half-hour, but there was no way we were going to save the building.'

'And the body?'

'As soon as they had the fire damped down at this end of the warehouse – which took about half an hour – the officers became aware of the smell. That was when they called me out. I'm on permanent stand-by for all fatal fires. Your lads called in CID, and I called you.'

'So where is the body?'

Pendlebury pointed to one side of the building. 'As far as we can tell, it was in the corner of the loading bay. There seems to have been a kind of alcove at one end. Looking at the ash, there was probably a load of cardboard stashed at the front of it. We've not been able to get in yet, it's still too hot and too chancy in terms of walls coming down, but from what we can see and what we can smell, I'd say the body's behind or underneath all that wet ash down the back of that recess.'

'There's no doubt in your mind that there's definitely a body in there?' Carol was grasping at straws, and she knew it.

'There's only one thing that smells like roast human, and that's roast human,' Pendlebury said bluntly. 'Besides, I think you can just about see the outline of the body. Come on, I'll show you.'

A couple of minutes later, Carol stood by Pendlebury's side at what he claimed was a safe distance from the smoking ruin. It felt uncomfortably warm to her, but she had learned when to trust the expertise of others during her years in the force. To have hung back would have been insulting. As Pendlebury pointed out the contours of the blackened form the fire and water had left at the end of the loading bay, she found herself irresistibly forming the same conclusion as the fire chief.

'When can the scene-of-crime people start work?' she asked dully.

Pendlebury pulled a face. 'Later this morning?'

She nodded. 'I'll make sure the team's on stand-by.' She turned away. 'This is exactly what I didn't want to happen,' she said, half to herself.

'It was bound to happen sooner or later. Law of averages,' Pendlebury said lightly, falling into step with her as she walked back towards her car.

'We should have been all over this arsonist ages ago,' Carol said, angrily searching through her pockets for a tissue to wipe the wet ash from her trainers. 'It's sloppy policing. He should have been nabbed by now. It's our fault that he's still on the loose to kill people.'

'You're not being fair on yourself,' Pendlebury protested. 'You've only been here five minutes, and you picked up on it right away. You mustn't blame yourself.'

Carol looked up from her attempts at cleaning her shoes and scowled. 'I'm not blaming myself, though maybe we could have put a bit more effort into the case. I'm saying that somewhere along the line the police on this patch have let down the people they're supposed to serve. And maybe you should have been a bit more forceful about making the point to my predecessor that you thought you had a firebug.'

Pendlebury looked shocked. He couldn't remember the last time he'd been criticized to his face by a member of another emergency service. 'I think you're a bit out of order, Chief Inspector,' he said, made pompous by his outrage.

'I'm sorry you feel like that,' Carol said stiffly, standing up and straightening her shoulders. 'But if we're going to have a productive working relationship, there's no room for cosiness at the expense of honesty. I expect you to tell me if we're not keeping our end of the deal. And when I see things I don't like, I'll call them. I don't want to fall out with you about this. I want to catch this guy. But we're not going to make any progress if we all stand around saying it can't be helped that some poor bastard is lying there dead.'

For a moment, they glared at each other, Pendlebury uncertain how to deal with her fiery determination. Then he spread his hands in a conciliatory gesture. 'I'm sorry. You're right. I shouldn't have taken no for an answer.'

Carol smiled and thrust out her hand. 'Let's both try and get it right from now on, OK?'

They shook on it. 'Deal,' he said. 'I'll talk to you later, when the forensics team have been all over it.'

As she drove off, Carol had room for only one thought. She had a serial arsonist who had now become a killer on her patch. Catching him was the only show in town. By the time the forensics team had something positive to tell her, she intended to have a draft profile. By the time the inquest opened, she meant to have a suspect in custody. If John Brandon had thought she was driven when they'd worked together in Bradfield, he was in for a surprise. Carol Jordan was out to prove a lot of points to a lot of people. And if she felt discouraged along the way, the stink that clung to her nostrils would be impetus enough to get her moving again.

*   *   *

Shaz turned over and looked at the clock. Twenty minutes to seven. Only ten minutes since she'd looked at it last. She wasn't going to fall asleep again, not now. If she was honest, she thought as she got out of bed and made for the bathroom, she probably wasn't going to sleep properly until Chris had delivered on her promise.

Asking the favour had been less awkward than she'd expected, Shaz reflected as she sat on the loo and leaned over to turn on the bath taps. Time seemed to have smoothed the rough edges of her relationship with Detective Sergeant Devine until it was back where it had been before misunderstandings and false moves had abraded it to a series of painful snags.

From the start of Shaz's career in the Met, Chris Devine had represented everything Shaz aspired to. There had been only two women in CID at the station where Shaz was based in West London, and Chris was the higher ranking. It was obvious why. She was a good cop with one of the best arrest records in the division. Rock solid in a crisis, hard working, imaginative and incorruptible, she also demonstrably possessed a brain and a sense of humour. Even more importantly, she could be one of the lads without ever letting anyone forget she was a woman.

Shaz had studied her like a specimen under a microscope. Where Chris was, she wanted to be, and she wanted that same respect. Already she'd seen too many women officers dismissed as plonks or slits, and she was determined that would never happen to her. Shaz knew that as a brand new uniformed constable, she was an insignificant dot somewhere in Chris's peripheral vision, but somehow she insinuated herself into the older woman's consciousness until, whenever they were in the station taking refs at the same time, they could invariably be found in a corner of the canteen drinking brutally strong tea and talking shop.

The very day Shaz became eligible for a CID aide posting, she'd submitted her name. Chris's recommendation was enough to swing it and, a few weeks later, Shaz found herself on her first night-shift stakeout with Chris. It took her rather longer to realize that Chris was gay, and had been working on the assumption that Shaz's hot pursuit was sexual rather than professional. The night her sergeant kissed her had been the worst moment of her police career.

For an instant, she'd almost gone along with it, so deep-rooted was her ambition. Then reality had clicked in. Shaz might not have been much good at forming relationships, but she knew enough about herself to be clear that it was very definitely men rather than women that she wasn't connecting with. She'd recoiled from Chris's embrace more vigorously than from a sawn-off shotgun. The aftermath was something neither Shaz nor Chris could recall without an uncomfortable mixture of emotions; humiliation, embarrassment, anger and betrayal. The sensible option would probably have been for one of them to seek a transfer, but Chris wasn't prepared to abandon a patch she knew like her own back garden, and Shaz was too stubborn to give up her first best chance at making it on to a permanent CID appointment.

So they'd established an awkward armistice that allowed them to stay on the same team, though whenever they could avoid working shift together, they did. Six months before Shaz's move to Leeds, Chris had been promoted and transferred to New Scotland Yard. They hadn't spoken from that day until Shaz had fetched up on Chris's doorstep looking for a favour.

Shaz chopped fresh fruit into her muesli and reflected that it had been easier than she'd expected to swallow her pride and ask Chris for help, possibly because Chris had been wrong-footed by the presence in her flat – and, clearly, her bed – of a fingerprint technician Shaz remembered from Notting Hill Gate. When Shaz had explained what she wanted, Chris had agreed immediately, understanding exactly why Shaz was so eager to push far beyond what her course leader expected from his officers. And, again as if fate had taken a hand in Shaz's life, it happened that Chris was off duty the following day, so garnering Shaz's information in the minimal time available would be simple.

As she absently shovelled breakfast into her mouth, she imagined Chris spending her day in the national newspaper archives at Colindale, copying page after page of local papers until she'd covered the period surrounding each of the seven disappearances that had captured Shaz's imagination. Shaz ran her empty cereal bowl under the hot tap with happy anticipation swelling inside. She couldn't say why she was so certain, but she was convinced that the first steps on her journey of proof would be waymarked in the local press.

She'd never been wrong so far. Except, of course, about Chris. But that, she told herself, had been different.

'The kind of cases we'll be working are the ones that leave most police officers feeling edgy. That's because the perpetrators are dancing to a different beat from the rest of us.' Tony looked around, double-checking that they were listening to him rather than shuffling through their papers. Leon looked as if he'd rather be somewhere else, but Tony had grown accustomed to his affectations and no longer took them at face value. Satisfied, he continued. 'Knowing you're dealing with someone who has manufactured their own set of rules is a very unsettling experience for anyone, even trained police officers. Because we come in from the outside to make sense of the bizarre, there's a tendency to lump us as part of the problem rather than the solution, so it's important that the first thing we concentrate on is building a rapport with the investigating officers. You've all come here from CID work – any ideas about the sort of thing that might work?'

Simon jumped straight in. 'Take them out for a pint?' he suggested. The others groaned and catcalled at his predictability.

Tony's smile came nowhere near his eyes. 'Chances are they'll have half a dozen good excuses why they can't come to the pub with you. Any other ideas?'

Shaz raised her pen. 'Work your socks off. If they see you're a grafter, they'll give you some respect.'

'Either that or think you're brown-nosing the bosses,' Leon sneered.

'It's not a bad idea,' Tony said, 'though Leon does have a point. If you're going to go down that road, you also need to demonstrate a complete contempt for everyone over the rank of DCI, which can be wearing, not to say counterproductive.' They laughed. 'What does the trick for me is incredibly simple.' He gave them a last questioning look. 'No? How about flattery?'

A couple nodded sagely. Leon's lip curled and he snorted. 'More brown-nosing.'

'I prefer to think of it as one technique among many in the arsenal of the profiler. I don't use it for personal advancement; I use it for the benefit of the casework,' Tony corrected him mildly. 'I have a mantra that I trot out at every available opportunity.' He shifted his position slightly, but that small change altered his body language from comfortable authority to subordinate. His smile was self-deprecating. 'Of course,' he said ingratiatingly, 'I don't solve murders. It's bobbies that do that.' Then, just as swiftly, he returned to his previous posture. 'It works for me. It might not work for you. But it's never going to do any harm to tell the investigating officers how much you respect their work and how you're just a tiny cog that might make their machine work better.' He paused for a moment. 'You have to tell them this at least five times a day.' They were all grinning now.

'Once you've done that, there's a reasonable chance they'll give you the information you need to draw up your profile. If you can't be bothered making the effort, they're likely to hold as much back as they can get away with because they see you as a rival for the glory of solving a high-profile case. So. You've got the investigating officers on your side, and you've got your evidence. It's time to work on the profile. First you assess probabilities.'

He stood up and began to prowl round the perimeter of the room, like a big cat checking the limits of its domain. 'Probability is the only god of the profiler. To abandon probability for the alternative demands the strongest evidence. The downside of that is that there will be times when you end up with so much egg on your face you'll look like an omelette on legs.'

Already, he could feel his heart rate increasing and still he hadn't said a word about the case. 'I had that experience myself on the last major case I worked. We were dealing with a serial killer of young men. I had all the information that was available to the police, thanks to a brilliant liaison officer. On the basis of the evidence, I drew up a profile. The liaison officer made a couple of suggestions based on her instincts. One of those suggestions was an interesting idea I hadn't thought of because I didn't know as much about information technology as she did. But equally, because it was something only a small proportion of the population would know about, I assigned it a moderately low probability.

Normally, that would mean the investigation team would assign it low priority, but they were stuck for leads, so they pursued it. It turned out she'd been right, but in itself it didn't move the investigation much further forward.'

His hands were clammy with perspiration, but now he was actually confronting the details that still shredded his nights, his stomach had stopped clenching. It was less effort than he'd expected to continue his analysis. 'Her other suggestion I discounted out of hand because it was completely off the wall. It ran counter to everything I knew about serial killers.' Tony met their curious stares. His tension had transmitted itself to the entire squad and they sat silent and motionless, waiting for what would come next.

'My disregard for her suggestion nearly cost me my life,' he said simply, reaching his seat and sitting down again. He looked around the room, surprised he could speak so levelly. 'And you know something? I was right to ignore her. Because, on a scale of one to a hundred, her proposition was so unlikely it wouldn't even register.'

As soon as the formal confirmation of the body in the blaze came through, Carol called a meeting of her team. This time, there were no chocolate biscuits. 'I expect you've all heard this morning's news,' she said flatly as they arranged themselves around her office, Tommy Taylor straddling the only chair apart from Carol's on the basis that he was the sergeant. He might have been brought up never to sit while women were standing, but he'd long since stopped thinking of Di Earnshaw as a woman.

'Aye,' he said.

'Poor bugger,' Lee Whitbread chimed in.

'Poor bugger nothing,' Tommy protested. 'He shouldn't have been there, should he?'

Repelled but not surprised, Carol said, 'Whether he should or shouldn't have been there, he's dead, and we're supposed to be looking for the person who killed him.' Tommy looked mutinous, folding his arms across the chair back and planting his feet more firmly on the floor, but Carol refused to respond to the challenge. 'Arson's always a time bomb,' she continued. 'And this time it's gone off right in our faces. Today has not been the proudest day of my career to date. So what have you got for me?'

Lee, leaning against the filing cabinet, shifted his shoulders. 'I went through all the back files for the last six months. Leastways, all I could get my hands on,' he corrected himself. 'I found quite a few incidents like you told us to look for, some off night-shift CID reports, some off the uniform lads. I was planning on getting them collated on paper today.'

'Di and me, we've been re-interviewing the victims, like you said. There doesn't seem to be any linking factor that we've come across so far,' Tommy said, his voice distant following Carol's snub.

'A variety of insurance companies, that kind of thing,' Di amplified.

'What about a racial motive?' Carol asked.

'Some Asian victims, but not what you'd call enough to make it look significant,' Di said.

'Have we spoken to the insurers themselves yet?'

Di looked at Tommy and Lee stared out of the window. Tommy cleared his throat. 'It was on Di's list for today. First chance she's had.'

Unimpressed, Carol shook her head. 'Right. Here's what we do next. I've had some experience in offender profiling . . .' She stopped when Tommy muttered something. 'I'm sorry, Sergeant Taylor, did you have a contribution?'

Confidence restored, Tommy grinned insolently back at Carol. 'I said, "We'd heard," ma'am.'

For a moment, Carol said nothing, merely staring him down. It was situations like this that could make the job degenerate into a misery if they weren't handled right. So far, it was only cheeky disrespect. But if she let it go, it would quickly slide into full-scale insubordination. When she spoke, her voice was quiet but chill. 'Sergeant, I can't think why you have this burning ambition to go back into uniform and play at community policing, but I'll be more than happy to oblige you if CID work continues not to be to your taste.'

Lee's mouth twitched in spite of himself; Di Earnshaw's dark eyes narrowed, waiting for the explosion that never came. Tommy pushed his shirtsleeves above his elbows, looked Carol straight in the eye and said, 'Reckon I'd better show you what I'm made of then, Guv.'

Carol nodded. 'You better had, Tommy. Now, I'm going to work on a profile, but to make that anything more than a bit of an academic exercise, I'm going to need a lot of raw data. Since we can't find any evidence of linkage between the victims, I'm going to stick my neck out and say we've got a thrill seeker rather than a torch for hire. Which means we're looking for a young adult male. He's probably unemployed, likely to be single and still living with his parents. I'm not going to go into all the psychobabble about social inadequacy and all that right now. What we need to look for is someone with a record of police contact for petty nuisance offences, vandalism, substance abuse, that sort of thing. Maybe minor sex offences. Peeping Tom, exposing himself. He's not going to be a mugger, a burglar, a thief, a fly boy. He's going to be a sad bastard. In and out of minor bother since he was a pre-teen. He probably doesn't have a car, so we need to look at the geography of the fires; chances are if you drew a line

111

linking the outermost fires, he'll live inside its boundaries. He'll probably have watched all the fires from a vantage point, so have a think about where that might have been and who might have witnessed him there.

'You know the ground. It's your job to bring me suspects that we can match against my profile. Lee, I want you to talk to the collator and see who uniform know that fits those criteria. I'll get going on a fuller profile and Tommy and Di will do the routine work-up on the crime itself, liaising with forensics and organizing a door-to-door in the area. Hell, I don't have to tell you how to run a murder inquiry . . .'

A knock at the door interrupted Carol's flow. 'Come in,' she called.

The door opened on John Brandon. It was, Carol realized, a measure of how far she had to go before she'd be accepted into the East Yorkshire force that no one had stuck a head round the door to warn her the chief was on his way. She jumped to her feet, Tommy nearly toppled in his hurry to get out of his chair and Lee cracked his elbow on the filing cabinet pushing himself upright. Only Di Earnshaw was already in place, standing against the back wall with her arms folded across her chest. 'Sorry to interrupt, DCI Jordan,' Brandon said pleasantly. 'A word?'

'Certainly, sir. We're pretty much finished here. You three know what we're after, I'll leave you to it.' Carol's smile managed to dismiss as well as encourage and the three junior officers edged out of the office with barely a backward glance.

Brandon waved Carol to her seat as he folded his long body into the guest chair. 'This fatal fire at Wardlaw's,' he began without formalities.

Carol nodded. 'I was out there earlier.'

'So I heard. One of your series then, I take it?'

'I think so. It's got all the hallmarks of it. I'm waiting to hear from the fire investigators, but Jim Pendlebury, the fire chief, reckons it's got generic similarities to the earlier incidents we'd identified.'

Brandon chewed one side of his lower lip. It was the first time Carol had ever seen him look anything other than completely composed. He breathed heavily through his nose and said, 'I know we talked about this before and you were convinced that you could handle it. I'm not saying that you can't, because I think you're a bloody good detective, Carol. But I want Tony Hill to take a look at this.'

'There's really no need,' Carol said, feeling heat spreading up her chest and into her neck. 'Certainly not at this stage.'

Brandon's gloomy bloodhound face seemed to grow even longer. 'It's no slur on your competence,' he said.

'I'm bound to say that's what it looks like from here,' Carol said, trying not to sound as mutinous as she felt, forcing herself to remember how angry Tommy Taylor's earlier impertinence had made her feel. 'Sir, we've barely started our own inquiries. It may well be that we'll have this whole thing wrapped up in a matter of days. There can't be that many potential suspects in Seaford who fit the serial arsonist profile.'

Brandon shifted in his chair, as if struggling to find an appropriate arrangement for his long legs. 'I find myself in a slightly awkward position here, Carol. I've never been happy with the "theirs not to reason why" approach to command. I've always thought things run better when my officers understand why I issue the orders I do rather than having to rely on blind obedience. On the other hand, for operational reasons, sometimes things have to be taken on trust. And when other units outside my command are involved, even when I think there's no earthly reason for confidentiality, I have to respect what they ask for. If you follow me?' He raised his eyebrows in an anxious question. If any of his officers could read between so oblique a set of lines, it would be Carol Jordan.

Carol frowned as she digested Brandon's words. 'So, hypothetically,' she eventually said, taking her time to think through what she was saying, 'if a new unit was being set up with a specialist area of responsibility, and they wanted a sympathetic force to let them use one of their cases as a sort of guinea pig, even if you thought the officer in charge had a right to know what the score was, you'd be obliged to go along with their demand for confidentiality as to the real reason why they were being handed the case? That sort of thing, sir?'

Brandon smiled gratefully. 'Speaking purely hypothetically, yes.'

There was no answering smile. 'This wouldn't be an appropriate occasion for such an experiment, in my opinion.' She paused. 'Sir.'

Brandon looked surprised. 'Why not?' he asked.

Carol thought for a moment. Few fast-track graduates climbed the greasy pole as fast as she'd done, particularly women. John Brandon's patronage had given her more than she could ever have expected. And she couldn't even be certain if her real reasons for reluctance were the ones she was about to voice. Nevertheless, she'd stuck her neck out this far and she'd never been a quitter. 'We're a new force,' she said carefully. 'I've only just arrived to work with a group of people who have been a team for a long time. I'm trying to build up a working relationship that will allow us to protect and serve our community. I can't do that if I'm stripped of the first major case that's crossed my desk since I got here.'

'No one's talking about taking the case away from you,

114

Chief Inspector,' Brandon said, reflecting Carol's formality. 'We're talking about using the new task force on a consultancy basis.'

'It'll look like you've no confidence in me,' Carol insisted.

'That's nonsense. If I had no confidence in your abilities, why on earth would I have appointed you to a promoted post?'

Carol shook her head in disbelief. He really didn't get it. 'I'm sure the canteen cowboys won't have any trouble coming up with ideas on that score, sir,' she said bitterly.

Brandon's eyes widened as he grasped her meaning. 'You think they . . . That can't be . . . It's ridiculous! I never heard anything so absurd!'

'If you say so, sir.' Carol managed a twisted smile and ran a hand through her shaggy blonde hair. 'I didn't think I looked that rough.'

Brandon shook his head in disbelief. 'It never occurred to me that people would misinterpret your promotion. You're self-evidently such a good copper.' He sighed and chewed his lip again. 'Now I'm in an even worse position than I was when I walked in.' He looked up at her and made a decision.

'I'm going to speak off the record. Paul Bishop has been having liaison problems with the local brass in Leeds. They've made it clear they don't want his team on their ground and they won't let him near any of their crimes. He needs a real case for his officers to learn their trade, and for obvious reasons, he doesn't want some high-profile serial killer or rapist. He rang me because we're next door to him and he asked me to keep an eye out for something that might do for his squad to cut their teeth on before they're officially available to catch cases from every Tom, Dick and Harry. To be perfectly honest, I was going to offer them your serial arsonist even before it turned fatal.'

Carol tried to keep her anger out of her face. It was always the way. Just when you thought you'd got them house-trained, they reverted to Neanderthal. 'It's a murder now. You don't get much more high profile than that,' she said. 'For my own self-respect, never mind the respect of my team, I need to head the investigation. I do not need to be seen to be hanging on the coat-tails of the National Offender Profiling Task Force,' she continued coldly. 'If I'd thought sending in visiting firemen was the best way to police serious crime, I'd have applied to join them. I can't believe you'd undermine me like this. Sir.' The last word came out like a expletive.

Brandon's method of dealing with threatened insubordination was very different from Carol's. A man in his position had little need of veiled threats; he could afford to be more creative. 'I have no intention of undermining any of my officers, DCI Jordan. That's why you will be the only officer who has direct dealings with the task force. You will go to them in Leeds, they will not come on our ground. I will make it clear to Commander Bishop that his officers will discuss the case with no other officer of the East Yorkshire force. I trust you will find that satisfactory?'

Carol couldn't help feeling a grudging respect for the speed with which her chief had thought on his feet. 'You've made your orders perfectly clear,' she said, leaning back in resignation.

Relieved that the crisis had been resolved without anything that would have been embarrassing to report back to Maggie, Brandon got to his feet with a relaxed smile. 'Thanks, Carol. I appreciate it. Funny, I could have sworn you'd have jumped at the chance to work with Tony Hill again. The two of you hit it off so well when you worked liaison on the Bradfield murders.'

She coaxed her muscles to conjure up a smile from memory and hoped it would pass for the real thing. 'My reluctance was nothing to do with Dr Hill,' she said, wondering whether Brandon would believe her when she couldn't even convince herself.

'I'll let them know you'll be in touch.' Brandon closed the door on his way out, a courtesy Carol was profoundly grateful for.

'I can hardly wait,' she said grimly to the empty room.

Shaz bounced through the door of the police station where the task force was based and grinned at the uniformed officer behind the desk with cheerful expectation. 'DC Bowman,' she said. 'NOP task force. There should be a package for me?'

The constable looked sceptical. 'Here?'

'That's right.' She glanced at her watch. 'It was supposed to be sent by overnight courier. For delivery by nine a.m. And since my watch says it's ten past . . .'

'Then you owe somebody a bollocking, because there's nowt here for you, love,' the constable said, incapable of keeping the satisfaction out of his voice. It wasn't often he had the chance to score a point against a task force outsider *and* patronize a woman in a single go.

'You sure?' Shaz asked, trying not to show the consternation that she knew would only increase his smugness.

'I've got my reading badge, love. Trust me, I'm a bobby. There's no package here for you.' Bored now, he ostentatiously turned away and pretended to be interested in a pile of paperwork.

Fizzing with frustration, her good mood history, Shaz bypassed the bank of lifts and jogged up the five flights of stairs to the task force operations room. 'Never trust someone else, never trust someone else,' pounded in her head in sync with her feet on the stairs and the blood in her ears. She marched straight into the room that held their computer terminals and threw herself into her chair, barely managing to grunt a greeting to Simon, the only other occupant of the room. Shaz grabbed her phone and punched in Chris's home number. 'Bugger!' she muttered when the answering machine picked up. She yanked her personal organizer out of her bag and keyed in Chris's name. Her index finger stabbed out the direct line at New Scotland Yard. The phone was answered on the second ring. 'Devine.'

'It's Shaz.'

'Whatever it is you're after, the answer's no, doll. I don't think I'm ever going to get the dust and ink out from under my fingernails after yesterday's little exercise. Definitely a non-starter on the "fun things to do with your day off" list.'

'I really appreciate it, you know that. Only . . .'

Chris groaned. 'What, Shaz?'

'The stuff hasn't arrived.'

Chris snorted. 'That all? Listen, by the time I'd got finished – which I have to tell you I only managed by flashing the old warrant card and roping the staff in – it was too late to get an overnight delivery. Best they could do was by noon. So you should get it some time this morning. All right?'

'It'll have to be,' Shaz said, aware she was being ungracious, but unable to care.

'Relax, doll. It's never the end of the world. You're going to give yourself an ulcer,' Chris told her.

'I've got to present my case tomorrow afternoon,' Shaz pointed out.

Chris laughed. 'So what's the problem? 'King hell, Shaz, that Yorkshire air's slowing you up. Time was, you were greased lightning. You got a whole night to turn it around. Don't tell me you're getting soft.'

'I do like the odd bit of sleep between dusk and dawn,' Shaz said.

'Just as well you and me never got it together, then, isn't it? Gimme a call if you haven't got the stuff by the middle of the afternoon, all right, doll? Just hang loose. Nobody's going to die.'

'I flaming hope not,' Shaz said to a dead line.

'Problems?' Simon asked, plonking himself down next to her and pushing a mug of coffee towards her.

Shaz shrugged, reaching for the brew. 'Just some stuff I wanted to check out before we report back on the exercise tomorrow.'

Simon's interest suddenly expanded beyond the erotic possibilities of a fling with Shaz. 'You on to something?' he asked, trying for nonchalant and failing.

Shaz's grin was evil. 'You mean you haven't spotted the cluster?'

'Course I have. Saw it right away, no messing,' he said, clearly blustering.

'Right. So you also found the external link?' Shaz enjoyed the momentary blankness that crossed Simon's milk-pale face before he regained command. She snorted with laughter. 'Good try, Simon.'

He shook his head. 'All right, Shaz, you win. Will you tell me what you've got if I buy you dinner tonight?'

'I'll tell you what I've got tomorrow afternoon, same time as I tell everybody else. But if the offer's genuine and not just a bribe, I'd say yes to a drink before we go for the curry on Saturday night.'

Simon thrust out his hand. 'Deal, DC Bowman.' Shaz took his hand and matched his grip.

119

The prospect of a pre-dinner drink with Simon, enticing though it was, couldn't distract Shaz from the anticipation of her parcel. At coffee break, she was at the front counter before the others had even brewed up. For the rest of the morning, as Paul Bishop took them through the application of a profile to a suspect list, Shaz, normally the most attentive of students, fidgeted like a four-year-old at the opera. As soon as they broke for lunch, Shaz was off down the stairs like a greyhound out of a trap.

This time, her prayers were answered. A cardboard archive box sealed with what looked like an entire roll of packing tape sat on the front counter. 'Any longer and I'd have phoned the bomb disposal squad to get rid of it,' the desk officer said. 'We're a police station, not a post office.'

'Just as well. You'd never stand the pace.' Shaz swept the box off the counter and marched out to the car park with it. She opened the boot of her car and snatched a quick look at her watch. She reckoned she had about ten minutes to spare before her absence from the communal lunch table would excite comment. Hastily, she ripped at the packing tape with her fingernails, managing to unpick it enough to force the lid open.

Her heart sank. The box was almost brimful of photocopies. For a brief moment, she wondered if she couldn't just ignore her hunch. Then she thought of the seven teenage girls, their faces smiling up at her with all the expectation that, however many disappointments life might hold, at least they'd have a life. This wasn't just an exercise. Somewhere out there was a cold-hearted killer. And the only person who seemed to be aware of it was Shaz Bowman. Even if it did take all night, she owed them that effort at the very least.

*   *   *

Seeing him again face to face, Carol was struck by the realization that it was pain that lurked behind Tony Hill's face. All the time she'd known him, she'd never recognized what underpinned his intensity. She'd always assumed that he was like her, driven only by the desire to capture and understand, fired by a passion to elucidate, haunted by the things he'd seen, heard and done. Now, distance had allowed her to comprehend what she had failed to see before, and she found herself wondering how different her behaviour towards him would have been had she really grasped what was going on behind his dark and troubled eyes.

Of course, he'd arranged it so that they would not be alone when they first encountered each other after the intervening months. Paul Bishop had been despatched to greet her when she'd arrived at the task force base in Leeds, smothering her in the charm that had made him such a media darling. His gallantry didn't extend to offering to carry her two briefcases heavy with case files, and Carol noticed with amusement that he couldn't pass a reflective surface without checking his appearance for imperfection, now smoothing an eyebrow, now straightening broad shoulders in a uniform that had plainly been made to measure. 'I can't tell you how thrilled I am to meet you,' he said. 'John Brandon's best and brightest. Some accolade in itself, never mind your track record. That speaks for itself, of course. Did John mention we'd been at staff college together? What a copper that man is, and what a talent spotter.' His enthusiasm was infectious and Carol found herself responding to his flattery in spite of her best intentions.

'I've always enjoyed working with Mr Brandon,' she said. 'How are things bedding down with the task force?'

'Oh, you'll see all that for yourself,' he said dismissively, ushering her into the lift. 'Of course, Tony's been singing your praises to the heavens. What a joy you are to work with, what a delightful colleague, how bright, how easy to deal with.' He grinned down at her. 'And the rest.'

Now Carol knew he was a bullshitter. She had no doubt as to Tony's professional respect for her, but she knew him well enough to be certain he would never have spoken about her in personal terms. His ingrained reticence would have taken far greater subtlety and skill to penetrate than Paul Bishop clearly possessed. Tony would never talk about Carol because to do so, he'd have to talk about the case that had brought them together. And that would mean revealing far more about both of them than any stranger had a right to know. He'd have had to explain how she'd fallen for him and how his sexual inadequacies forced him to reject her, how any hope of them ever getting together had been the last victim of the murderous psychopath they'd tracked. She felt in her bones that he would never have told another living soul these things, and if there was one thing that raised her above her colleagues, it was her instinct. 'Mmm,' she said noncommittally. 'I've always admired Dr Hill's professionalism.' Bishop brushed against her hip as he pushed the button for the fifth floor. If I'd been a man, Carol thought, he'd just have told me which floor to go for.

'It's a real bonus for us that you've worked with Tony before,' Bishop continued, eyeing his hair in the brushed metal doors. 'Our new trainees will be able to learn a lot from watching how you divide up the process, how you communicate, what you both need from each other.'

'"You know my methods, Watson,"' Carol parodied wryly.

Bishop looked momentarily puzzled, then his face cleared. 'Ah, yes.' The lift opened. 'This way. We're going to have coffee together, just the three of us, then you and Tony can work through the initial contact interview with the students looking on.' He strode down the corridor and held a door open for her, standing back while she entered what looked like a scaled-down scruffy school staff-room.

Across the room, Tony Hill swung round, coffee filter in one hand, spoon in the other. His eyes widened at the sight of Carol and she felt a slow smile spread irresistibly across her face. 'Tony,' she said, managing to keep her voice formal. 'How nice to see you.'

'Carol,' he greeted her, dropping the teaspoon on the table with a clatter. 'You look . . . well. You look well.'

She'd have been lying if she'd said the same to him. He was still pale, though she'd seen him paler. The dark smudges under his eyes were less like bruises than they'd been the last time the two of them had stared at each other, but they were still the badges of someone to whom eight hours' sleep was the impossible dream. His eyes had lost some of the strain she'd grown accustomed to seeing there after their one memorable case had finally been resolved, but he still looked tense. Regardless, she wanted to kiss him.

Instead, she placed her briefcases on the long coffee table and said, 'Any chance of a brew, then?'

'Strong, black, no sugar?' Tony checked with the hint of a smile.

'You must have made an impression,' Bishop said, striding past Carol and dropping into one of the sagging chairs, carefully lifting the knees of his trousers to avoid bagging them. 'He can't remember from one day to the next how I like mine.'

'When we worked together before, it was the kind of situation where every detail is engraved on your brain forever,' Carol said repressively.

Tony flashed her a quick look of gratitude then turned away to brew up. 'Thanks for sending the case files over,' he said against the wheezing of the elderly electric kettle. 'I've had them copied and the team have had them to study overnight.'

'Fine. How do you want to play this?' Carol asked.

'I thought we could go into live role-play,' Tony said, still with his back to them as he made the coffee. 'Sit across a table from each other and run through the case file exactly the way we would do it for real.' He half-turned with a tentative smile and a spasm ran across Carol's stomach.

Get a grip, she told herself angrily. Even if he could, he wouldn't want you. Remember? 'That sounds fine,' she heard herself say. 'How were you planning on involving the trainees?'

Tony juggled the three hot mugs in his broad square hands and managed to get them on to the coffee table without spilling much on the tobacco brown carpet. 'Specially chosen to hide the stains,' he muttered, frowning in concentration.

'There's half a dozen of them,' Bishop said. 'So it's not feasible to let them each have a crack at you, even if you were willing to give up that much of your time. They'll watch you and Tony work through the case files. Then, if they have any questions about that part of the process, they'll ask them. After you've gone, Tony will work with them on the drawing up of a profile, which will be passed back to you in a matter of days. What we're hoping is that when you develop a suspect to the point of arresting and charging, you'll liaise with Tony on interview strategies and allow us access to the taped interviews afterwards.' His smile said he wasn't accustomed to being refused.

'That may not be possible,' Carol said cautiously, not completely sure of her position. 'You may have to wait until after a trial to have access to the interview tapes, and then only if the interviewee agrees. I'll need to take advice on that.'

Tiny movements of muscle beneath the skin stripped Bishop's face of its bonhomie. 'My impression from Mr Brandon was that we weren't being slavish about formalities on this one,' he said briskly.

'I'm the investigating officer here, Commander. This is not a classroom exercise. It's an inquiry into an unlawful death and it's my intention to get a conviction if that's appropriate. I will take absolutely no risk that could cost me a successful prosecution. I don't leave windows open for smart defence counsel.'

'She's right,' Tony said unexpectedly. 'We get carried away with ourselves here. It's heady stuff, you know, Paul. The bottom line is, Carol has to make the case against this arsonist stand up in court, and we can't expect her to go along with anything that might interfere with that.'

'Fine,' Bishop said curtly. Ignoring his coffee, he stood up and headed for the door. 'I'll leave you to it. I've got some phone calls I need to get out of the way if I'm going to sit in on your session. See you later, DCI Jordan.'

Carol grinned. 'Would five get me ten that he'll be on the phone to John Brandon before his backside hits the chair?'

Tony shook his head, eyes glinting with amusement. 'Probably not, actually. Paul doesn't like being crossed, but he keeps his powder dry for the battles that matter.'

'Not like me, rushing in where angels fear to tread, eh?'

Tony met her gaze and recognized the goodwill there. 'Nobody's quite like you, Carol. I was genuinely sorry that you didn't want to join the team here.'

She twitched one shoulder in a shrug. 'Not my kind of policing, Tony. Sure, I like the big cases, but I don't like living in limbo.'

Her words hung between them, freighted with more meaning than any casual bystander could have read. Tony looked away and cleared his throat. 'All the more reason why I'm pleased to have the chance to work this case with you. If we'd already been up and running, I don't expect you'd have come running to us with what looks on the face of it to be a fairly straightforward serial arson that's turned nasty almost by accident. So it's a bonus for the squad that they're going to get to see someone as good as you at work.'

'You know, all I've had since this task force was mentioned in connection with my case is enough flattery to choke a politician,' Carol said, trying to cover her gratification with a sardonic tone.

'When did I ever offer you flattery?' Tony said simply.

Again, Carol's stomach clenched. 'Maybe it's not such a good idea,' she said. 'Having an officer like me along, I mean. You should have given them a reality check and wheeled in one of the cavemen,' she added, struggling to keep her smile in place.

Tony laughed in delight. 'Can you imagine? Great session that would be.' He dropped his voice and broadened his Yorkshire accent. 'Right bloody load of crap this is. You want me to go round asking me suspects if they pissed the bed when they were kids?'

'I'd forgotten you were from round here,' Carol said.

'I hadn't,' Tony said. 'Back in the West Riding, last place on earth I ever wanted to be. But I wanted the task force, and the Home Office were adamant we had to be based outside London. God forbid we should do anything sensible like billet the profiling squad with the intelligence unit. How are you finding it out in the primeval ooze of Seaford?'

Carol shrugged. 'Life among the dinosaurs? Ask me in six months.' She glanced at her watch. 'What time are we due to kick off?'

'Couple of minutes.'

'Fancy catching up over lunch?' She'd practised the casual tone half a hundred times on the motorway coming over to Leeds.

'I can't.' He looked genuinely sorry. 'We eat together in the squad. But I was going to ask you . . .'

'Yes?' Careful, Carol, not too eager!

'Are you in a hurry to get back?'

'No, no rush.' Her heart singing, yes, yes, he's going to ask me to dinner.

'Only, I wondered if you'd like to sit in on the afternoon session?'

'Right.' Her voice bright, her hopes squashed, the light in her eyes dulled. 'Any particular reason?'

'I set them an exercise last week. They're supposed to produce their conclusions today and I thought it might be helpful to have your response to their analyses.'

'Fine.'

Tony took a shallow breath and said, 'Plus, I thought we could maybe have a drink afterwards?'

Apprehension and anticipation had pitched Shaz on an adrenaline high. Even though she'd only squeezed three hours' sleep out of the night, she was buzzing like a raver on an amphetamine high. She'd attacked the photocopied newspapers the minute she'd got home, laying them out in piles on her living-room carpet and pausing only to phone for a pizza. So engrossed was she that she didn't even notice when they sent her a ten-inch Margarita and charged her for a twelve-inch with everything on.

By one in the morning, she'd eliminated everything except the entertainments ads and the sports pages. Her earlier conviction that the external link that would prove her contention was lurking in the local papers was starting to look less like a solid hunch than a desperate clutching at straws. Stretching her stiff back and rubbing her gritty eyes, Shaz got to her feet and staggered through to the kitchen to brew another Thermos of coffee.

Refuelled, she returned to her task, deciding to go for the sports pages first. Maybe the same visiting football team with its loyal supporters? Or a player who had moved from club to club and then become a manager? Maybe a local golf championship that attracted outsiders, or a series of bridge trophies? Eliminating all the sporting possibilities took another couple of hours, and left Shaz jittery with exhaustion, caffeine and a looming fear of failure.

When the connection finally emerged, her first response was that she was hallucinating. It was so outrageous an idea she couldn't take it seriously. She caught herself giggling nervously, like a child who hasn't yet learned the appropriate response to the pain of others. 'This is crazy,' she said softly, double-checking through all seven sets of newspapers to confirm she wasn't seeing things. She lurched stiffly to her feet, trying to loosen her cramped muscles, and staggered through to the bedroom, stripping her clothes off as she went. It was too much to take in at half past three in the morning. Setting her alarm for half past six, Shaz fell face down on the bed where sleep hit her like a truck colliding with a motorway bridge.

Shaz dreamed about television game shows where the winner got to choose how they'd be killed. When the alarm clock went off, she dreamed it was a buzzer on an electric chair. Still groggy from sleep, her memory of what she'd unearthed in the newspapers felt like an extension of the nightmare. She pushed the duvet back and tiptoed through to the living room as if normal footfalls would scare her discovery away.

There were seven ragged piles of photocopies. On the top of each pile was a page from the entertainment section. Each page contained either an advertisement for a personal appearance or a featured interview with the same man. However she cut it, it looked as if one of the nation's darlings was somehow tied in to the disappearance and presumed murder of at least seven teenage girls.

And now she was going to have to share her revelation.

It wasn't difficult to set tongues wagging, Micky had soon discovered. Whenever she visited the rehabilitation unit where Jacko was learning how to use his artificial arm, they made a point of closing the door of his room and sitting close together so that when they were interrupted by a physio or a nurse, they could spring apart and appear embarrassed.

At work, she would phone him when the surrounding desks were occupied and she was almost certain to be overheard. The conversations would swing between animated hilarity, with his name dropped in at regular intervals, and the low, intimate tones her colleagues would unimaginatively associate only with lovers.

Finally, to move things up a gear, it was time for scandal and drama. Micky chose a friend on a middle-market tabloid. Three days later, the paper splashed with PERVERT TARGETS JACKO'S NEW LOVE.

Lifesaving hero Jacko Vance's new girlfriend has become the target of a terrifying campaign of vandalism and hate mail.

Since the start of their whirlwind romance, TV journalist Micky Morgan has had
* paint thrown over her car
* dead mice and birds posted through her letter box
* a vicious series of poison pen letters sent to her home.

129

The couple met when she interviewed the world record-holding javelin star in hospital after the motorway pile-up where Jacko's tragic heroism cost him his lower right arm and his Olympic dream. They had been trying to keep their affair under wraps.

But we can exclusively reveal that their secret has leaked to someone who bears a grudge against attractive blonde Micky, 25, a popular reporter on *Six O'Clock World*.

Last night, at her West London home, Micky said, 'It's been a nightmare. We've no idea who's behind it. I just wish they'd stop.

'We've been keeping our relationship to ourselves because we wanted to get to know each other better without the glare of publicity. We're very much in love. The private man is even more exciting than the person the public sees.

'He's brave and he's beautiful. How could I not be madly in love? All we want now is for this heartless campaign to end.'

A spokesman for Jacko, who is undergoing intensive rehabilitation and physiotherapy at London's exclusive Martingale Clinic, said, 'Jacko is obviously disgusted that anyone should treat Micky like this. She's the most wonderful woman he's ever met. Whoever is behind this better hope the police catch them before he does.'

Jacko, who ended his engagement to (*Continued on page 4*)

The press coverage was hectic for a couple of weeks, then it slowly died away, resurfacing every now and again whenever something happened to either of the alleged lovers. Jacko's emergence from rehab into his old life; his hiring as a

TV sports presenter; Micky's new job as an interviewer on breakfast television; Jacko's voluntary work with the terminally ill; all of these and more refreshed interest in their supposed affair. They soon learned it was necessary for them to be seen together somewhere public and high profile at least once a week to avoid speculation in the gossip columns. Often, knowing they were being followed, Jacko ended up spending the night under the same roof as the two women after he and Micky had been clubbing or charity working. After nearly a year of this, Micky summoned Jacko to a powwow over dinner with Betsy.

Her lover's culinary skills had not deserted her since the years she had spent catering for boardroom lunches. As he swallowed the last morsel, Jacko gave the two women his most wolfish grin. 'It must be bad,' he said, 'if it took something that good to soften me up.'

Betsy smiled demurely. 'You haven't had the sticky toffee pudding with home-made hazelnut ice cream yet.'

Jacko pretended to be shocked. 'If I was a police officer, you could be arrested for an offer like that.'

'We do have a proposition for you,' Micky said.

'Something tells me you're not talking three in a bed,' he said, rocking gently on the back legs of the chair.

'You might try and sound a little disappointed,' Betsy said drily. 'The idea that we're so unappealing is bad for what the Americans so charmingly call our self-esteem.'

Jacko's smile reminded Micky disturbingly of Jack Nicholson. 'Betsy, my dear, if you knew what I like to do with my women, you'd be profoundly grateful for my lack of interest.'

'Actually, our ignorance on that very point is one of the factors that has made us reluctant to put our proposal to you before now,' Betsy said, briskly clearing the plates and carrying them through to the small kitchen.

'I'm intrigued now,' Jacko said, tipping forward with a slight thump and leaning his prosthetic arm on the table. He held Micky's eyes in a glittering stare. 'Spill the beans, Micky.'

Betsy appeared in the kitchen doorway and leaned against the jamb. 'It's awfully time consuming, this silly business of you and Micky having to go out enjoying yourselves. I don't mind in the slightest that she's out with you. It's just that we'd both rather spend what limited time we can spare together.'

'You want to call the whole thing off?' Jacko frowned.

'Quite the opposite,' Betsy said, sitting down at the table again and placing her hand over Micky's. 'We rather thought it might be a good idea if the two of you were to get married.'

He looked astonished. Micky thought she had never seen a more genuine expression cross Jacko Vance's carefully controlled features. 'Married,' he echoed. It wasn't a question.

Shaz looked around the seminar room again, assessing her audience, hoping she wasn't about to make a complete fool of herself. She tried to second-guess where the objections would come from and what they'd be. Simon would pick holes on principle, she knew that. Leon would tilt his chair back and smoke, the ghost of a sneer on his mouth, then find some load-bearing prop in her argument and demolish it. Kay would cavil and quibble over details, never seeing the big picture. Tony, she hoped, would be quietly impressed with her brilliance in spotting the cluster and her diligence in pursuing it to a demonstrable external connection. Her groundwork would be the trigger for a major inquiry and when the dust finally settled, her future would be sealed. The woman who nailed the celebrity serial killer. She'd be a legend in squad rooms up and down the country. She'd be in a position to pick her billet.

Carol Jordan was the wild card. A morning watching her work with Tony hadn't provided nearly enough raw material for accurate conjecture about her response to Shaz's theory. To leave as little to chance as possible, she'd have to hang back and let a couple of her colleagues go first so she could watch Carol carefully while they presented their reports.

Leon went first. Shaz was surprised by the brevity of his report, and she didn't think she was the only one. He said that while there were clearly similarities between certain of the cases, given the number of teenage runaways recorded annually it was hard to argue that there was any statistical significance in that. He had, seemingly grudgingly, chosen four girls from the West Country, including one of Shaz's cluster. The connecting factor he'd identified was that all four were reported to have harboured ambitions to become models. He suggested they might have been abducted by one or more pornographers under the pretext of offering them the opportunity to become photographers' models then suckered into a life of blue movies and sex for sale.

A short silence was followed by a few apathetic comments from the room. Then Carol said coolly, 'And how long did you spend on this analysis, Mr Jackson?'

Leon's eyebrows descended. 'There wasn't a lot to analyse,' he said belligerently. 'I did what it took.'

'If I were the investigating officer who had handed this material to you, I would be rather underwhelmed by something so superficial,' Carol said. 'I'd feel disappointed, short-changed, and I'd have a pretty low opinion of a specialist unit which produced nothing of more significance than one of my own officers could have provided in an afternoon's work.'

Leon's mouth opened in astonishment. Neither Tony nor

Bishop had ever been so openly critical of anyone's work. Before he could respond, Tony cut in. 'DCI Jordan's right, Leon. It's not good enough. We're supposed to be an elite squad, and we're not going to make any friends if we don't treat every assignment as something serious and worthy of our attention. It doesn't matter if we think a group of cases are Mickey Mouse. To the investigating officers, they're important. To the victims, they're important.'

'This was just an exercise,' Leon protested. 'There isn't an investigating officer. It's just playtime. You can't get worked up about that!' The whine in his voice said, 'It's not fair!' louder than the actual words.

'As I understand it, every one of these cases is real,' Carol said quietly. 'Every one of those kids is on the missing list. Some of them are almost certainly dead. The pain of uncertainty can often be more damaging than knowledge of the truth. If we ignore people's pain, we deserve their contempt.'

Shaz watched Tony's impassive face incline in a tiny acknowledgement of Carol's words, then followed his eyes across to Leon, who had compressed his mouth into a thin line, half-turning in his seat so he didn't have to look at Carol. 'Right,' said Tony. 'We've established that DCI Jordan doesn't do polite. Who's next for the high jump?'

Shaz could barely contain her impatience during Kay's report, a pedestrian but painstakingly thorough analysis that forged several possible groups with an assortment of linkages. One was identical to Shaz's own cluster, but it was given no extra weight compared to the others. When the recital drew to a close, Tony looked happier. 'A thorough piece of work,' he said, the unspoken 'but' hanging in the air like a relay baton.

Carol picked up the challenge. 'Yes, but it sounds like

134

you're sitting on the fence. An investigating officer wants information presented in a way that underpins specific initiatives. So you need to prioritize your conclusions. "This is quite likely, this is less likely, this is tenuous, this is frankly improbable." That lets the officers on the ground structure their inquiries in the most productive way.'

'In fairness, it's hard to do that in the vacuum of a classroom exercise,' Tony added. 'But we should always attempt to do it. Any ideas regarding the order of priority we should be looking at here?'

Shaz barely contributed to the vigorous discussion that followed. She was too nervous about what lay ahead to care about the impression she might be making. A couple of times, she caught a stray look of inquiry from Carol Jordan, and responded with some innocuous comment.

Then, suddenly, it was her turn. Shaz cleared her throat and assembled her papers in front of her. 'Although there are several superficial similarities that pull together a variety of potential groupings, closer analysis reveals that there is one strong cluster linked by a nexus of common factors,' she began firmly. 'What I intend to show this afternoon is that this cluster is further linked by a significant common external factor and the irresistible conclusion is that the members of this cluster are the victims of a single serial killer.'

She looked up, hearing a gasp from Kay and a guffaw from Leon. Tony looked startled, but Carol Jordan was leaning forward, chin on her fists, gripped. Shaz allowed a small smile to twitch one corner of her mouth. 'I'm not making this up, I promise you,' she said, distributing stapled pages of photocopies around the table.

'Seven cases,' she said. 'The first page you have in front of you is a table listing the common features in these seven disappearances. One of those key connections, in my view, is that all seven girls took a change of clothes with them. But they didn't go for the kind of things you'd choose if you were planning on running away and living on the streets. In every case, what they went missing with was their "best" gear, the fashion outfits they'd have worn if they were going out on a special date, not trainers for walking the streets and ski jackets for staying warm at night. I know teenagers aren't always sensible when it comes to what they wear, but remember, our sample weren't irresponsible, out of control, wild-child girls.'

She glanced up and was gratified to see that Tony was now as rapt as Carol Jordan. 'In each case, they didn't turn up for school and had lied in advance about what they were doing afterwards to give themselves a clear run of about twelve hours. Only one of them had ever come to the notice of the police or social services and that was for shoplifting when she was twelve. They weren't delinquent, they didn't do drink or drugs to any significant degree.

'Now, if you turn to page two, you'll see I've laid out their photographs scaled down to the same size. Don't you think there's a remarkable physical similarity?' Shaz paused for effect.

'That's eerie,' Simon muttered. 'I can't believe I didn't see that.'

'It's more than physical,' Carol said, sounding faintly bemused. 'There's a look they've all got. Something ... almost sexual.'

'They're dying to become former virgins,' Leon told the room. 'That's what it is. Unmistakable.'

'Whatever it is,' Shaz interrupted, 'they've all got it. The cases are geographically scattered, the time frame is six years at irregular intervals, but the victims look practically interchangeable. Now, that's strong evidence in itself.

But Tony's taught us that we should also be looking for external connectors; factors outside the victim's control or influence that are common. Factors that link to the killer, not the victim.

'I asked myself where I might find the relevant external link that would tie together my cluster of putative victims.' Shaz picked up another pile of stapled photocopies and passed them round. 'Local newspapers. I trawled the local papers for two weeks either side of each disappearance. And in the early hours of this morning, I found what I was looking for. You've got it in front of you. Just before each one of these girls died, the same very public personality was in their home town. And each and every one of them, let's not forget, went off with the one and only outfit they'd have chosen from their wardrobes if they were planning on impressing a man.'

The murmur of disbelief was already rising around her as the enormity of Shaz's suggestion hit them. 'That's right,' she said. 'I couldn't believe it either. I mean, who's going to believe the nation's favourite sporting hero and TV personality is a serial killer? And who's going to authorize an investigation of Jacko Vance?'

The soft whimper seemed to be swallowed by the chill darkness. Donna Doyle had never felt more frightened in her short life. She'd never realized that fear could act like an anaesthetic, apprehension dulling excruciating agony to a throbbing ache. What had already happened had been terrible enough. But not knowing what the future held was almost worse.

It had all started so well. She'd kept the secret, in spite of the way it kept bubbling up inside her, almost seeming to press against her lips and demand release. But she knew he'd meant what he'd said about the importance of confidentiality, and this was too good a chance to miss. Excitement at her new prospects had buoyed her up, allowing her to stifle her awareness that what she was doing would cause uproar at home. She rationalized her failure to inform her mother of her plans by telling herself that when everything worked out as she dreamed, there would be so much joy that the trouble would be forgotten. Deep down, she knew that was a lie, but she couldn't bear to let that knowledge interfere with her elation.

Bunking off school had been easy. She'd set off as usual, then, instead of turning in down the road leading to school, she'd carried on into the town centre where she'd dodged into the public lavatories and changed into the clothes she'd carefully folded into her school backpack instead of books. Her best outfit, she knew, making her look older than she was, making her look like the young women she saw on MTV, cool as fuck. In the dim light of the toilet, she applied her make-up and pouted at the mirror. God, she looked good. But would it be good enough for him?

He'd picked her out when she wasn't even dressed up to the nines, she reminded herself. He'd seen her star quality. Dressed like this, she'd knock him dead. Wouldn't she?

The memory of that nonchalant self-confidence was like a sick joke to Donna now, lying in pain and fear in the dark. But at the time it had been more than enough to get her through the day. She'd caught a bus into Manchester, hanging back until it was about to leave, making sure there wasn't one of the neighbours or her mother's boring friends on board. Then she'd run upstairs, sitting at the back so she could see who got on and off.

Having a few hours in Manchester on a weekday on her own was almost adventure enough in itself. She browsed the department stores, played the fruit machines in the video arcades, bought a couple of lottery scratch cards in a newsagent near the station and told herself that winning ten straight off wasn't just a result, it was an omen. By the time she boarded the train, she was irrepressibly high, more than capable of ignoring the nerves that still fluttered annoyingly in her stomach when she thought of what her mum was going to say.

Changing trains wasn't quite so much fun. It was growing dark, and she couldn't understand a word anyone on Newcastle station tannoy said. They didn't sound like Jimmy Nail or Kevin Whately off the telly. They sounded like aliens. Somehow, she managed to find the right platform for Five Walls Halt and nervously boarded the train, aware that she was among strangers with curious faces who eyed her short skirt and dramatic make-up with predatory eyes. Donna's imagination began to work overtime, translating weary commuters into stalkers and mad axemen.

It had been a relief to get off the train and find him waiting in the car park, just like he'd said. And it had been lovely. He'd said all the right things, reassuring her and convincing her she'd done the right thing. He was lovely, she told herself, not a bit like she expected someone off the telly to be.

As they'd driven down narrow country roads, he'd explained that they wouldn't be able to do the screen test until morning, but that he hoped she'd have dinner with him. He said he had a cottage, that she could stay overnight, there was a spare room, which would save him having to drive after he'd had a glass or two of wine. If she didn't mind, of course. Otherwise, he could take her to a hotel.

The part of her that had been well brought up and drilled to wariness wanted to go instantly to a hotel where she could phone her mother and reveal that she was safe and well. But it wasn't an enticing prospect, a night in a lonely room in a strange place where she knew no one, with no company except the TV and her mum complaining down the phone line. The other voice in her head, the tempting adventurous voice, told her she'd never have a chance like this to make her mark. Having him to herself for a whole evening would be the perfect opportunity to impress him so much that the screen test would be a formality.

The voice she stifled through a mixture of apprehension and anticipation pointed out that there might never be a more propitious time to lose her virginity.

'Staying with you'd be great,' she said.

He smiled, briefly turning his eyes away from the road. 'I promise we'll have fun,' he said.

And he hadn't been lying. Not to begin with, anyway. The food had been wonderful, like the really expensive stuff from Marks and Spencer that her mum always said they couldn't afford. And they'd had wine. Lots of different kinds. Champagne to start with, then white wine with the starters, then red with the main course and a sticky aromatic golden one with the pudding. She'd had no idea there were so many different-tasting ones. He'd been lovely, all through dinner. He'd been funny and flirty and full of stories that made her smile and hug herself inside because she was learning all these secrets about telly people.

And he seemed to find her entertaining, too. He was always asking her what she thought, what she felt, who she liked on TV and who she hated. He was interested, staring deep into her eyes and really paying attention, like men were supposed to when they fancied you, not like the lads she'd gone out with from school who were only interested in football and how far you'd let them go. It was obvious he fancied her. But he wasn't slobbering all over her like some dirty old man. He was considerate, treating her like she was a person. With all the conversation, phoning her mum had been the last thing on her mind.

By the end of the meal, she'd been pleasantly woozy. Not drunk, not like at Emma Lomas's party when she'd had five bottles of extra-strong cider and thrown up for hours. Just a bit blurred round the edges, filled with happiness and desire to feel his warm flesh against hers, to bury her face in the citrus and woody smell of his cologne, to make her fantasies reality.

When he got up to make coffee, she followed, a little unsteady on her feet, conscious of the giddiness that made the room sway gently but not unpleasantly. She came up behind him and slipped her arms round his waist. 'I think you're gorgeous,' she said. 'Fantastic.'

He'd turned and let her lean into him, burying his face in her hair and nuzzling her ear. 'You're very special,' he murmured. 'Very special.'

She felt his erection hard against her stomach. For a moment, a thrill of fear squirmed through her, then his lips were on hers and she was lost to the sensation of what felt like her first kiss. They kissed for what seemed like a lifetime, a dizzying parade of colours spinning behind her eyes as arousal sent her blood charging through her veins.

Almost without her realizing, he moved her gradually round so that her back was against the workbench and he was facing her, still kissing, his tongue darting in and out of her mouth. Suddenly, without warning, his hand clamped over her wrist and yanked her arm to one side. Donna felt cold metal against her flesh and her eyes jerked open. At the same moment, their mouths parted.

Baffled, she looked at her arm, not understanding why it was pinned between the two faces of a big steel vice. He stepped back and quickly spun the handle so the jaws closed on the flushed flesh of her naked arm. Vainly, she tried to pull away. But there was no escape. She was trapped by the arm, pinioned to the workbench vice. 'What are you doing?' she squealed. All her face revealed was hurt puzzlement. It was too soon for fear.

His face was blank. An impassive mask had replaced the interest and affection she'd seen there all evening. 'You're all the same, aren't you?' he said dispassionately. 'You're all out for what you can get.'

'What are you talking about?' Donna entreated him. 'Let me go, this isn't funny. It hurts.' With her free arm, she reached across her body towards the handle of the vice. He raised his arm and smashed her in the face with a backhanded swipe that sent her reeling.

'You do as you're told, you treacherous bitch,' he said, still sounding calm.

Donna tasted blood. A rending sob broke from her throat. 'I don't understand,' she stuttered. 'What did I do wrong?'

'You throw yourself at me because you think I'll get you what you want. You tell me you love me. But if you woke up tomorrow and I couldn't give you what you wanted, you'd throw yourself at the next meal ticket that walked past.' He leaned against her, pressing his body to hers, his weight preventing her from making another attempt at releasing the vice.

'I don't know what you're on about,' Donna whined. 'I never . . . Aagh!' Her voice rose in a yell of pain as he turned the vice tighter. Pain shot up her arm as muscle and bone were compacted, the edges of the vice cutting deep and cruel into the tissue of her arm. As her scream subsided into tearful entreaty, he half-turned so that his weight was still on her free arm and tore her dress from top to bottom with one powerful wrench.

Now she was really afraid. She couldn't understand why he was doing this. All she'd wanted was to love him, to be chosen by him to appear on the telly. It wasn't supposed to be like this. It was supposed to be romantic and tender and beautiful, but this was senseless and stupid and she couldn't believe how much her arm was hurting and all she wanted was for it to stop.

He'd barely begun. Within moments, her knickers were in a torn heap at her feet, deep welts in her side where the fabric had bitten into her skin before the seams had finally yielded to his force. Shaking with sobs, her voice a mumbling of meaningless pleadings, she had no resources left to resist as he unzipped his trousers and thrust his cock into her.

It wasn't the pain of losing her virginity that Donna remembered. It was the agony that coursed through her when he bore down on the vice in rhythm with the thrusting of his hips into hers. The breaking of her hymen went unnoticed among the splintering of the bones of her wrist and forearm and the pulverizing of her flesh between the blank metal plates.

As she lay in the dark, she was glad only that she'd passed out then. She didn't know where she was or how she'd got there. All she knew was that she was blessedly alone. And that was enough. For now, that was enough.

Tony walked down Briggate, hands thrust deep into his jacket pockets against the cold, swerving to avoid the last straggles of shoppers and the weary-footed sales assistants making for the bus stops. He deserved a drink. It had been a difficult afternoon. For a time it had looked as if the group spirit nurtured from day one was about to become a memory as differences of opinion escalated into argument then teetered on the edge of hurling abuse.

The first response to Shaz's dramatic hypothesis had been stunned silence. Then Leon had slapped his leg and rocked to and fro on his chair. 'Shazza, baby,' he yelled. 'You are more full of shit than a sewage farm, but you are the best value in town! All right, baby, way to go!'

'Hang on a minute, Leon,' Simon objected. 'You're quick off the mark to slap the girl down. What if she's right?'

'Oh, yeah,' Leon drawled contemptuously. 'Like Jacko Vance is *obviously* a psychopathic serial killer. You've only got to watch him on the telly. Or read about him in the tabloids. Yeah, Jack the Lad, marriage made in heaven, England's glory, the hero who sacrificed his arm and his Olympic medal so that others might live. Very Jeffrey Dahmer, very Peter Sutcliffe. Not.'

Tony had kept half an eye on Shaz during Leon's outburst, noticing the apparent darkening of her eyes and the tense line of her mouth. She couldn't handle mockery the way she dealt with straightforward criticism, he realized. As Leon paused for breath, Tony jumped in with a dose of irony. 'I just love the cut and thrust of intellectual debate,' he said. 'So, Leon, how about you stop showing off and provide us with some cogent argument against the case that Shaz is making?'

Leon scowled, unable as usual to disguise his emotions. Hiding behind the lighting of a cigarette, he mumbled something.

'Can you let us have that again?' Carol interjected sweetly.

'I said, I didn't think Jacko Vance's personality fit our general terms of reference for serial offenders,' he repeated.

'How do you know that?' Kay cut in. 'All we ever see of Jacko Vance is the image manufactured by the media. Some serial killers have been superficially charming and manipulative. Like Ted Bundy. If you're going to be a top athlete, you have to develop phenomenal self-control. Maybe that's what we're seeing with Jacko Vance. A totally synthetic front covering up a psychopathic personality.'

'Spot on,' Simon said vigorously.

'But he's been married a dozen years or more. Would his wife have stayed with him if he was a psychopath? I mean, he couldn't maintain the mask permanently,' someone objected.

'Sonia Sutcliffe always asserted she was totally unaware that her husband went out topping prostitutes the way some men go to football matches. And Rosemary West still claims she had no idea Fred was using bodies for foundations under their patio extension,' Carol pointed out.

'Yeah, and think about it,' Simon urged, 'couples with jobs like Micky Morgan and Jacko Vance, they're not like the rest of us. Half the time Jacko's on the road doing *Vance's Visits*.

Then there's all his hospital voluntary work. And Micky must be in the studio at the crack of sparrowfart getting prepared for her programme. They probably see less of each other than coppers see of their kids.'

'It's an interesting point,' Tony said, cutting across a couple of loud interjections. 'What do you think, Shaz? It's your theory, after all.'

Shaz's jaw was set mutinously. 'I don't hear anybody arguing against my identification of the cluster as a significant entity,' she started.

'We-ell,' Kay said. 'I'm wondering how significant it really is. I mean, I pulled together several clusters that maybe are just as validly connected. The girls who the police thought might have been sexually abused, for example.'

'No,' Shaz said firmly. 'Not with as many linking factors as this group. It's worth saying again that some of the things that connect them are unusual features, unusual enough for investigating officers to make a particular note of them. Like taking their best clothes with them.' Tony was pleased to see she was undaunted by this latest example of Kay's constant nit-picking.

Her rebuttal didn't win her a reprieve, however. 'Of course you'd note that,' Leon chipped in, never squashed for long. 'It's the single factor that indicates you're looking at a runaway rather than the victim of a serial killer. You didn't make a note of it, you'd be a pretty crap detective.'

'Like the one who didn't even notice the cluster in the first place?' Shaz demanded belligerently.

Leon cast his eyes upwards and stubbed out his cigarette. 'You women, when you get an idea in your heads . . .'

'Christ, you talk shite sometimes,' Simon said. 'If we could just get back to what this is supposed to be about . . . I'm wondering how much of a coincidence it is that Vance visited those towns. I mean, we don't know how many public appearances he does in the average week. It may be that he's constantly on the road, in which case it wouldn't mean a lot.'

'Exactly,' Kay backed him up. 'Did you check the local newspapers for the missing kids who aren't in your cluster to see if Vance turned up there as well?'

Shaz's pursed lips gave the answer before she even opened her mouth. 'I didn't have the chance,' she admitted reluctantly. 'Maybe you'd like to take on that little task, Kay?'

'If it was a real operation, you'd have to follow up Kay's suggestion,' Carol pointed out. 'But you would have the bodies and time to do it, which you didn't have here. I must say, I'm impressed with what you have achieved with the limited time and resources available.' Shaz's shoulders squared at Carol's praise, but as the DCI continued, she looked wary. 'However, even if it's a genuine connection, it's too much of a leap in the dark to point the finger straight at Jacko Vance. If these disappearances and presumed murders are connected to his appearances, it's much more likely that the perpetrator is a member of Jacko's entourage or even a member of the public who has an initiating stressor in his past that connects to Vance. At its most obvious, perhaps he was rejected by a woman who was a big fan of Jacko's. These would be my first areas of interest, before I came to the assumption that Jacko himself was involved.'

'It's a point of view,' Shaz said, momentarily mortified that she'd been so carried away with her headline-grabbing theory that she hadn't considered that possibility. It was the nearest Tony had ever seen her come to a concession. 'But you think the cluster is worth pursuing?'

Carol had looked desperately at Tony. 'I . . . uh . . .'

Coming to her rescue, he'd said, 'This was only ever going

148

to be an exercise, Shaz. We've got no authority to take any of these cases any further.'

She looked devastated. 'But there's a cluster heré. Seven suspicious disappearances. Those girls, they've got families.'

Leon butted in again, sarcasm back in full working order. 'C'mon, Shazza. Get them synapses working. We're supposed to be clearing things up for the plods on the street, not finding more work for them to do. D'you really think anybody's going to thank us for stirring up a load of aggro over a theory that's dead easy to dismiss out of hand as the product of the fevered minds of a bunch of rookies on a special squad that nobody much wants on the job anyway?'

'Fine,' Shaz said bitterly. 'Let's just forget I spoke, eh? So whose turn is it to be shot down in flames next? Simon? We going to get the benefit of your words of wisdom now?'

Tony had taken Shaz's seeming capitulation as a signal to move on. The other team members' analyses had been considerably less controversial, which had allowed him to demonstrate useful tips and pitfalls in data sifting and the developing of conclusions from raw material. As the afternoon had worn on, he'd noticed Shaz slowly recover from the combative reception her ideas had been given. Gradually, she had ceased to look desolate, moving through crestfallen to an air of stubborn determination that he found slightly worrying. Some time in the next few days, he'd have to make time to have a word with her, to point out the quality of much of her analysis and explain the importance of keeping apparently wild conclusions private until she could back them up with something more solid than a hunch.

He turned off the main street into the narrow alley that housed Whitelocks pub, an old-fashioned relic that had somehow survived the years when the city centre died at half past five. If he was honest, the last thing he felt like was a drink with Carol. The history between them meant theirs could never be entirely easy encounters, and tonight he had something he ought to tell her that she wouldn't want to hear.

At the bar, he ordered a pint of bitter and found a quiet table in the far corner. He'd never been one to shirk his obligations. But Shaz's failure to consider one of Jacko Vance's fans or a member of his entourage as a possibility had reminded him of the importance of waiting for data before exposing theories to the harsh scrutiny of others. Just for once, Tony thought he'd take his own mental advice to Shaz and say nothing of his ideas until he too had more evidence.

It had taken Carol half an hour to escape from the probing questions of the two women task force officers. She had the distinct feeling that if she hadn't taken so very definite a leave, the one with the eyes, Shaz, would have pinned her to the wall until she'd sucked her dry of every piece of pertinent information, and a fair amount of impertinent. By the time she pushed open the etched glass door of the pub, she was convinced he'd have given up on her and left.

She saw his wave of greeting as soon as she approached the bar. He was sitting in a wood-panelled nook at the far end of the room, the remains of a pint of bitter in front of him. 'Same again?' she mouthed, making the universal gesture of a hand tipping a glass.

Tony placed one index finger across the top of the other to form a T. Carol grinned. Moments later, she placed a straight glass of Tetley's in front of Tony and sat down opposite him with her own half-pint. 'Driving,' she said succinctly.

'I took the bus. Cheers,' he added, raising his glass.

'Cheers. It's good to see you.'

'And you.'

Carol's answering smile was wry. 'I wonder if there'll ever come a time when you and I can sit opposite each other and not feel there's a third person at the table?' She couldn't help it. It was like a scab she was impelled to pick, always convinced that this time it wouldn't draw blood.

He looked away. 'Actually,' he said, 'you're about the only person who doesn't make me feel like that. Thanks for coming today. I know it probably wasn't the way you would have chosen to reopen our . . .'

'Acquaintance?' Carol said, unable to avoid a sour note.

'Friendship?'

It was her turn to look away. 'I hope so,' she said. 'I hope friendship.' It was less than the truth and they both knew it, but it served its purpose. Carol found a frail smile. 'An interesting bunch, your baby profilers.'

'They are, aren't they? I suppose you saw what they've all got in common?'

'If ambition was illegal they'd all be doing life. In the next cell to Paul Bishop.'

Tony nearly choked on his mouthful of beer, spraying the table and narrowly missing Carol's cream twill jacket. 'I see you haven't lost your killer instinct,' he spluttered.

'What's to be coy about? You can't miss it. High octane aspiration. It fills the room like testosterone in a nightclub. Doesn't it worry you that they all see the task force as a stepping stone in their brilliant careers?'

Tony shook his head. 'No. Maybe half of them will use it as a springboard to what they perceive as greater things. The other half think that's what they're doing, but actually they're going to fall in love with profiling and they're never going to want to do anything else.'

'Name names.'

'Simon, the lad from Glasgow. He's got that sceptical turn of mind that takes nothing on trust. Dave, the sergeant. He likes the idea that it's methodical and logical yet it still has space for flair. But the real star is going to be Shaz. She doesn't know it yet, but she's been bitten by the bug. Don't you think?'

She nodded. 'She's an obsessive workaholic and she can't wait to get to grips with the screwed-up minds out there on the street.' She cocked her head to one side. 'Know what?'

'What?'

'She reminded me of you.'

Tony looked like he couldn't decide whether to be offended or amused and settled for puzzled. 'How odd,' he said. 'She reminded *me* of you.'

'What!' Carol exclaimed, startled.

'This afternoon's presentation. The basic work was solid. The cluster she'd identified is definitely worth consideration as a phenomenon.' He spread his hands and opened his eyes wide. 'To jump from that to the conclusion that Jacko Vance is a serial killer was a leap of imagination unrivalled since your virtuoso performance in the Bradfield case!'

Carol couldn't help laughing at his histrionics. 'But I was right,' she protested.

'You may have been right in *fact*, but you broke all the laws of logic and probability to get there.'

'Maybe Shaz is right. And maybe we're just better at profiling than the boys,' Carol teased.

Tony grunted. 'I wouldn't deny the possibility that girls are better at this,' he said. 'But I can't believe you think Shaz is right.'

Carol pulled a face. 'Six months down the road, she'll be mortified she even suggested it.'

'Knowing cops, one of that bunch will probably set her up with a face-to-face on *Vance's Visits*.'

Carol shuddered. 'I can see it now. Jacko Vance nailed to the wall by those extraordinary eyes, Shaz saying, "And where were you on the night of 17th January 1993?"' When they'd both stopped laughing, she added, 'I'll be fascinated to see what she comes up with for my serial arsonist.'

'Mmm,' Tony said.

She raised her glass in a toast. 'To the mumbo jumbo squad.'

'May we be a long time in heaven before the devil notices we're gone,' he responded wryly and drained his glass. 'Another?'

Carol looked at her watch consideringly. It wasn't that she had to be anywhere; she wanted a moment to decide whether it was better to leave things on this pleasant footing or stay for another drink with the risk they might end up putting the distance back between each other. Deciding not to chance it, she shook her head regretfully. 'No can do, I'm afraid. I want to catch the night-shift CID team before they all disappear into the twilight zone.' She swallowed the last half-inch of beer and stood up. 'I'm glad we had the chance for a chat.'

'Me too. Come back on Monday, we'll have something for you then.'

'Great.'

'Drive safely,' he said as she turned to go.

She half-turned. 'I will. And you take care.'

Then she was gone. Tony sat for a while staring into his empty glass considering why someone might set fires without the pay-off of a sexual thrill. When the glimmer of an idea crept into his mind, he got up and walked alone through the echoing streets.

*   *   *

153

It wasn't the laughter of Shaz's colleagues that smarted like shampoo in her eyes. It wasn't even Carol Jordan's metaphorical pat on the head. It was Tony's sympathy. Instead of being bowled over by the quality of her work and the incisiveness of her insights, Tony had been kind. She hadn't wanted to hear that it took courage to stick her neck out, that she'd shown real initiative but that she'd fallen into the trap of getting carried away by coincidence. It would have been easier if he'd been dismissive or even patronizing, but the fellow-feeling in his compassion was too obvious for her to hide her crushing disappointment in anger. He'd even told a couple of stories against himself about mistaken conclusions he'd leapt to in his early efforts at profiling.

It was a generosity of spirit that Shaz had no equipment to deal with. The only, and accidental, child of a couple so devoted to each other that the emotional needs of their daughter barely impinged, she had learned to get by without expectations of tenderness or indulgence. She'd been told off for misbehaving, praised absent-mindedly for success, but mostly, she'd been ignored. Her driven ambition had its roots in a childhood where she'd worked desperately hard to win the recognition from her parents that she craved. Instead, her teachers had offered approval, and their off-handed professional assessments had been the only generosity she'd learned to feel at ease with. Now, genuine personal kindness left her baffled and uncomfortable. She could handle Carol Jordan's businesslike appreciation of her work, but Tony's sympathy unsettled her and fired her to do something that would render it redundant.

The morning after the debacle, she endured the chaffing of her colleagues, even managing to join in their banter rather than fixing them with her chill blue stare and stripping their self-confidence to the bone. Underneath the affable

154

surface, though, her mind was churning, thoughts revolving in an attempt to find a way forward that would show she was right.

Trawling the missing persons records in a bid to find other cases that fitted the pattern was out of the question. Shaz knew from her days on the beat that somewhere in the region of a quarter of a million people went missing every year, nearly a hundred thousand of them under eighteen. Many of them simply walked away from the pressures of jobs they hated and families who offered them nothing. Others ran from lives grown intolerable. Some were seduced by promises of streets paved with gold. And a few were snatched unwilling from their familiar worlds and plunged into hell. But it was almost impossible to tell which category individuals fell into by a swift scrutiny of the report summary. Even if she could have persuaded her doubting colleagues to join the search, to unearth other possible victims of Shaz's serial killer would take far more resources than they had available.

When Tony announced that the afternoon would be devoted to private study, Shaz felt the itch of her impatience ease. Now she could at least *do* something. Rejecting Simon's suggestion of a pub lunch, she made straight for the city's biggest bookshop. Minutes later, she was standing by the till with a copy of *Jack on the Box: the Unauthorized Version* by Tosh Barnes, a Fleet Street columnist known for his vitriolic pen, and *Lionheart: the True Story of a Hero* by Micky Morgan, an updated version of the account she'd first written shortly after their marriage. Tony had suggested that even if Shaz was right about the link, the killer would be more likely to be one of Vance's entourage than the man himself. The books might help either to eliminate him or to provide corroborative support for her theory.

A short bus ride and she was home. Popping the top on

a can of Diet Coke, she sat down at her desk and plunged straight into his wife's adoring take on Jacko Vance's brilliant career. Great athlete, selfless hero, indomitable fighter, peerless broadcaster, tireless charity worker and sublime husband. As she forced herself through the hagiography, Shaz started to think it might actually be a pleasure to demolish so revoltingly perfect a figure. If her first assumption was right, he didn't so much have feet of clay as an entirely false facade.

It was a relief to reach the end, even though that meant facing the question she'd been pushing to the back of her mind. It was the classic misgiving of serial killer inquiries: how could the wife not know? Even leading such busy lives independent of each other, how could Micky Morgan share her bed and her existence with an abductor and murderer of adolescent girls and not sense something in his head was twisted out of true? And if she knew, or even suspected, how could she sit in front of the cameras day after day interviewing life's victims and victors without a flicker of anything other than professional compassion and composure?

It was a question that had no answer. Unless Tony had been right and it wasn't Jacko himself but a fan or a team member. Suppressing these misgivings, Shaz turned to *Jack on the Box* which proved to be merely an irreverent version of the same myth. Only the anecdotes were different, revealing nothing more sinister than that when he was wearing his professional hat, Jacko Vance was a perfectionist with a corrosive line in invective that could strip even TV's hardest cases of their protective armour. It was hardly a signpost to a homicidal maniac.

But for someone searching for elements that would fit the identikit notion of a serial killer, there were hints and clues that suggested she might not be completely deluded. There were certainly more factors than the average person would exhibit and, in her book, that kept Jacko Vance in the prime suspect slot thus far. It might well be someone else around him, but so far the research she had done had provided nothing to contradict her original theory.

Shaz had made notes as she worked her way through both books. At the end of her initial research, she booted up the laptop and opened a file she'd developed earlier in the profiling course. Headed *Organized Offender Checklist*, it was exactly what it said: a list of potential indicators to reveal to an investigator whether a suspect was a serious contender. She made a copy of the file; then, using her notes for guidance, occasionally referring back to the books, Shaz worked her way down the inventory. When she'd finished, she almost purred with satisfaction. She wasn't crazy after all. This was something Tony Hill wouldn't be able to ignore when it formed Part One of the new dossier she planned to present him with. She printed it out and smiled in satisfaction as she double-checked it.

Shaz was particularly pleased with the concluding para-graph. Concise, to the point, but telling the readers who knew what to look for all they needed to know, she thought. She wished she could get her hands on the newspaper cuttings about Vance and Micky Morgan, particularly the tabloids and the gossip columns. But to put in a formal request to any of the newspaper libraries would set too many alarm bells ringing. On a story this big, she couldn't even dare trust a personal contact.

She considered whether to present Tony with this fresh analysis. In her heart, she knew there wasn't enough to change his mind. But someone was killing young girls and on the balance of probabilities, given how long it had been going on and how many indicators lurked in his background, she reckoned Jacko Vance was her man. Somewhere, there was something that would expose his weakness, and she was going to find it.

The desk sergeant tipped the second spoonful of sugar into his mug of black tea and stirred it languidly, staring at the sluggish whirlpool it produced as if willing it to do something interesting enough to divert him from the pile of paperwork stacked beside him on the desk. The swirling slowed then stilled. Nothing else happened. With a sigh that started in the pit of his stomach, he picked up the first file and opened it.

The reprieve came two pages into the report. His hand shot out to the phone as if it was attached by elastic suddenly released. 'Glossop Police, Sergeant Stone,' he said cheerfully.

The voice on the phone was staccato with nerves, control barely in place. It was a woman, not young, not old, Peter Stone registered automatically as he pulled a pile of scrap paper towards him. 'It's my daughter,' the woman said. 'Donna. She's not come home. She's only fourteen. She never went to her friend's. I don't know where she is. Help me! You've got to help me!' The pitch rose to a frightened squeak.

'I understand how upsetting this is for you,' Stone said stolidly. Himself a father of daughters, he refused to allow his imagination to run riot over the possible disasters that could befall them. Otherwise he'd never have slept again. 'I'll need a few details so we can set about being of some assistance.' His formality was deliberate, a calculated attempt to slow things down and instil calmness in his frantic caller. 'Your name is . . . ?'

'Doyle. Pauline Doyle. My daughter's Donna. Donna Theresa Doyle. We live up Corunna Street. Number 15 Corunna Street. Just the two of us. Her dad's dead, see? He took a brain haemorrhage three years ago, dropped down dead, just like that. What's happened to my Donna?' Tears shook her voice. Stone could hear sniffs and sobs despite her best efforts to stay coherent.

'What I'm going to do, Mrs Doyle, I'm going to send somebody round to take a statement from you. Meantime, can you just tell me how long Donna's been missing?'

'I don't know,' Pauline Doyle wailed. 'She left the house this morning to go to school and said she was going for her tea to her pal Dawn's house. They had some science project they were working on together. When she wasn't home by ten, I rang Dawn's mum and she told me Donna hadn't been there and Dawn said she wasn't in school all day.'

Stone glanced at the clock. Quarter past eleven. That meant the girl had been somewhere other than where she was supposed to be for the best part of fifteen hours. Not officially time to worry yet, but a dozen years in the Job had given him an instinct for the significant. 'You hadn't had words, had you?' he asked gently.

'No-o-o-o,' Mrs Doyle wept. She hiccupped and Stone could hear her breathe deeply to calm her voice. 'She's all I've got,' she said, her voice soft and piteous.

'There could be a simple explanation. It's not uncommon with young girls, going missing overnight. Now, I want you to put the kettle on and brew a pot of tea, because there'll be a couple of officers with you within ten minutes, OK?'

'Thank you.' Forlorn, Pauline Doyle replaced the phone

and stared bleakly at the photograph on top of the television set. Donna smiled back at her, a flirtatious, knowing smile that said she was nudging the borderline between child and woman. Her mother stuffed her hand between her teeth to avoid crying out, then stumbled to her feet and went through to the fluorescent brilliance of the kitchen.

At that point, Donna Doyle had been alive and well and slightly drunk.

Once the decision had been taken, all that remained were details. First, the official proposal, arranged for maximum effect during the annual fund-raising telethon that garnered millions for children's charities. Jacko went down on one knee in front of eight million viewers and asked Micky to marry him. She looked suitably stunned, then moved. With tears in her eyes, she said yes. Like every other aspect of their marriage, there was nothing about the whole process that couldn't be screened before the watershed.

The wedding took place in a register office, of course, but that was no reason not to splurge on a party that would keep the gossip column inches flowing for days. Jacko's agent and Betsy were the witnesses, each acting as a kind of unofficial minder to make sure neither member of the wedding drank champagne to the destruction of discretion. Then, afterwards, the honeymoon. A private island in the Seychelles, Betsy and Micky in one cottage, Jacko in the other. On several occasions they spotted him on the beach, with a different woman each time, but no one apart from Jacko himself ever joined them for a meal and they were never introduced to any of his partners.

On the last night, the three had dinner together under the Indian Ocean moon. 'Your friends gone, then?' Betsy had asked, emboldened by the fifth glass of champagne.

'Not friends,' Jacko said carefully. His mouth twisted in a strange smile. 'Not even personal assistants, I'm afraid. I don't sleep with friends. Sex is something I keep in the realm of transactions. After the accident, after Jillie, I told myself I was never ever going to put myself in a position where anybody could take anything that mattered from me again.'

'That's sad,' Micky said. 'You lose a lot by not being prepared to take risks.'

His eyes seemed to glaze over, like a tinted-glass limo window rising to obscure its inhabitant. It was a look she was certain was never seen by his public, nor even the terminally ill and permanently damaged that he gave his time and energy to reassure so potently. If the powers that be had ever seen that darkness behind his eyes, they'd have made sure he never came within a hundred miles of the sick and dying. All the world got was the charm. Come to that, it was mostly all she ever got. But either he willingly let her see more, or else he wasn't aware that she knew him so well. Even Betsy told her she was exaggerating when she spoke of the darkness battened down inside her husband. Only Micky knew she wasn't.

Jacko looked unsmiling into his wife's eyes and said, 'I take plenty of risks, Micky. I just minimize the possibility of damage. Take this marriage. It's a risk, but I wouldn't have taken it unless I'd been certain it was safer for me because you have a lot more to lose than I do if it's ever exposed as a sham.'

'Maybe so,' Micky acknowledged with a tip of her glass. 'But I think it's sad to cut yourself off from the possibility of love, which is what you've done ever since you split with Jillie and started playing games with me.'

'This isn't a game,' Jacko said, his face closed and intense. 'But if you're worried about me lacking nourishment, don't be. I take responsibility for my own needs. And I promise my solutions will never embarrass you. I am the king of deniability.' He put his left hand over his heart and smiled solemnly.

The words had always haunted Micky, though he had never given her reason to throw them in his face. But sometimes, when she saw expressions cross his eyes that reminded her of the first time she'd seen his contained fury in that sterile hospital room, she wondered what exactly there might be lurking in Jacko's secret world that would require denial. Murder, however, would never have made it to the list.

The trouble with working alone was that you just couldn't cover the ground, Shaz had realized after a fitful night's sleep. There weren't enough hours in the day, she didn't have the authority to make full background inquiries, she had no access to the information network of the bobbies who worked the patches where Jacko Vance had grown up or lived since. There was no one to gossip with. If she was going to make any progress worth speaking of, there was only one possible route to go.

She'd have to stir things up. And that meant calling in more favours. She picked up the phone and rang Chris Devine's number. The answering machine picked up on the third ring. It was a relief not to have to explain the whole seemingly insane enterprise to Chris. When she heard the beep, she said, 'Chris? It's Shaz. Thanks for your help the other day. It was so useful, I need another favour. Any chance you could get me a home number for Jacko Vance? I'll be at home all evening. You're a star, thanks.'

'Hang on,' Chris's voice cut across hers. Shaz jumped and almost knocked her coffee cup to the floor. 'Hello?' she said. 'Chris?'

'I was in the shower. What are you up to?' Chris's voice was more affectionate than Shaz reckoned she deserved.

'I want to set up an interview with Jacko Vance, and I haven't got a number for him.'

'Is there some problem with official channels, doll?'

Shaz cleared her throat. 'It's not exactly an official inquiry.'

'You're going to have to do better than that. Has this got something to do with the half-dozen trees I had to murder to do the last favour you asked for?'

'Sort of. The exercise I told you about? Well, it's thrown up what looks like a genuine cluster. I think there's a real serial killer out there doing teenage girls. And it's connected to Jacko Vance.'

'Jacko Vance? *The* Jacko Vance? *Vance's Visits* Jacko Vance? What's he got to do with a serial killer?'

'That's what I'm trying to find out. Only we're not supposed to be doing this for real yet, so nobody's prepared to take any action unless I can come up with something more concrete.'

'Hang on a minute, doll. Back up a bit, to where you said it's connected to Jacko. How d'you mean, "connected"?' Chris was starting to sound worried, Shaz thought. Time for a bit of back-pedalling. Time also to adopt the less dramatic suggestion of her colleagues.

'It could be something and nothing. Only, this cluster I spotted: he was doing a personal appearance in each of the girls' home towns a couple of days before they went walkabout. It's an odd coincidence, and I'm thinking maybe it's someone in his entourage or some psycho fan of his who has it in for girls who maybe come on too strong to Jacko or something.'

'So, let me get this right. You want to front up Jacko Vance to see if he's noticed any revolving-eyed maniacs hanging around his gigs? And you want to do this unofficial?' Chris's voice mixed incredulity and concern.

'That's about the size of it, yeah.'

'You're off your head, Bowman.'

'I thought that was part of my charm.'

''King hell, doll, charm won't get you out of the shit if you put a foot wrong on this one.'

'Tell me something I don't know. Are you going to help me or not?'

There was a long silence. Shaz let it stretch, even though her nerves were stretching to breaking point with it. Finally, Chris caved in. 'If I don't, you'll just go somewhere else, won't you?'

'I have to, Chris. If I'm right, somebody's killing kids. I can't ignore that.'

'It's if you're wrong I'm worried about, doll. You want me to come with you, give you a bit of back-up, make it look more official?'

It was tempting. 'I don't think so,' Shaz said slowly. 'If I end up going down in flames, I don't want to take you with me. But there is something you could do.'

Chris groaned. 'Not if it involves a library.'

'You could cover my back. I'll probably need to give a ring-back number. People like him, they don't take anything on trust. Only, we can't take phone calls on the course because we're always in lectures or group sessions or whatever. If I could use your office number, at least he's going to be getting a police phone if he calls back to check me out.'

'You got it,' Chris sighed. 'Give me five minutes.'

Shaz endured the wait stoically. There were times when she envied smokers, though not enough to start. She stared at the second hand of her watch, tightening her lips as it swept into the sixth minute. When the phone rang, she grabbed it before the end of the first peal.

'Got a pen?' Chris said.

'Yeah.'

'Here you go, then.' She recited the supposedly secret unlisted number she'd wheedled out of the desk officer at Notting Hill police station. 'You didn't get it from me.'

'Thanks, Chris. I owe you.'

'More than you'll ever pay, unfortunately,' Chris said ruefully. 'Hang loose, doll. Talk to you soon.'

'I'll keep you posted. Bye.' Shaz contemplated the piece of paper with a quiet smile of triumph. Here I come, ready or not, she thought, reaching for the phone again. Half past eight wasn't too early to call.

The number rang out a couple of times, then an automated voice told Shaz, 'Your call is being diverted.' A series of clicks, a hollow sound, then the distinctive warble of a mobile phone ringing. 'Hello?' The answering voice was instantly recognizable. Shaz found it disconcerting to have what normally came from the TV issuing from her phone, especially since it wasn't the voice she expected.

'Ms Morgan?' she asked tentatively.

'Speaking. Who is this?'

'I'm Detective Constable Sharon Bowman of the Metropolitan Police. I'm sorry to trouble you, but I need to speak to your husband.'

'I'm afraid he's not at home just now. Nor am I. You've actually come through on the wrong line. This is my personal line. His is a different number.'

Shaz felt a blush creeping up her neck. 'I'm sorry to have disturbed you.'

'No problem. Is it something I can help you with, officer?'

167

'I don't think so, Ms Morgan. Unless you could possibly give me a number where I can reach him?'

Micky hesitated. 'I'd rather not, if you don't mind. I could pass a message on, if that would do?'

It would have to, Shaz thought grimly. The rich really did do things differently. Just 'as well she'd already made the arrangement with Chris. 'I think he might have some background information' relating to an inquiry we're pursuing. I realize he's a very busy man, but I can meet him any time tomorrow, wherever and whenever suits him. Now, I'm going to be out of the office for the rest of the day, so if he could ring this number . . .' she dictated Chris's direct line. 'And ask to speak to Sergeant Devine. He can make the arrangements with her.'

Micky read the number back to her. 'That right? Tomorrow? Fine, DC Bowman, I'll pass the message on to him.'

'Sorry to have intruded,' Shaz said gruffly.

The familiar chuckle came down the line. 'Think nothing of it. I'm always delighted to help the police. But you'll know that, if you ever see the programme.'

It was so obviously an opening that Shaz couldn't resist. 'It's a terrific show. I watch you whenever I can.'

'Flattery will always get your messages delivered,' Micky said, her voice as seductive as it always managed to be at noon.

'I look forward to hearing from Mr Vance,' Shaz said. She'd never meant anything more in her life.

Pauline Doyle stared at the empty frame on top of the television. The officers who had visited her the night of Donna's disappearance had taken the photograph to have some copies made. They'd seemed concerned about Donna, asking a lot of questions about her friends and her school, whether she had a boyfriend, what she liked to do on a weekend. When they'd eventually left with the photo and a description of Donna, she felt they'd helped her keep hysteria at bay. All her instincts were to run through the midnight streets crying her daughter's name, but the composed responses of the two uniformed officers who had filled her kitchen had soothed her, made her understand this was not the time to act on irrational impulses. 'Best stop here,' the older man had said. 'If she tries to phone home, you don't want her missing you. Leave it to us to look for her. We're the experts, we know what we're about.'

The woman who'd come the following morning had undermined those reassurances. She'd persuaded Pauline to do a detailed audit of Donna's possessions. When they'd established the absence of Donna's favourite dance outfit – a short black Lycra skirt, a body-hugging black-and-white striped T-shirt with a scoop neck and black patent leather Doc Martens – the detective had visibly relaxed. Pauline understood why. In the eyes of the police, the missing clothes meant just another teenage runaway. They could relax now, stop worrying about their earlier assumption that they might well be looking for a body.

How could she explain in a way that they'd understand? How could she make them see that Donna had neither need nor reason to run away? She hadn't fallen out with Pauline. Quite the opposite. They were close, closer than most women managed to stay to their teenage daughters. Bernard's death had driven them to each other for comfort and they'd continued to share their confidences. Pauline clenched her eyes shut and sent a fierce supplication to the Virgin she'd lost faith in years before. The police wouldn't listen; what harm could it do to pray?

The dawn came up on her left-hand side to road noise and the sound of her own voice. All the way down the M1, Shaz practised the interview. She'd always envied lawyers the comfort of only asking questions to which they knew the answers. To face a professional without role-playing and exploring every possible response would have been madness, so she drove on automatic pilot, rehearsing her questions and the imagined replies. By the time she arrived in West London, she was as ready as she'd ever be. Either he'd let something slip, which she doubted he'd be amateur enough to do, or else she'd panic him into some subsequent action that would confirm everything she'd worked out for herself. Or she might be wrong and the others right and he might simply point her in the direction of a fanatical devotee that he'd spotted with the putative victims. It would be an anti-climax, but one she could live with if it saved lives and put a killer behind bars.

That she might be putting herself at risk never seriously occurred to her in spite of Chris Devine's warnings. At twenty-four, Shaz had no intimations of mortality. Even three years in the police, with the occasional assaults and regular dangers, hadn't dented her sense of invincibility. Besides, people who lived in Holland Park mansions didn't attack police officers. Especially not when it was their wife who'd made the appointment.

Early as usual, Shaz ignored the instructions to park on their drive that had been passed on to her. Instead, she found a meter in Notting Hill and walked down into Holland Park, strolling down the street where they lived. Carefully counting the numbers, Shaz identified the house belonging to Jacko and Micky. It was hard to believe that somewhere so huge in the heart of Central London was still dedicated to only one household, but Shaz knew from her background reading that this was no mansion split into flats. It was all for Jacko and Micky, the only live-in staff, Micky's long-standing personal assistant Betsy Thorne. Gobsmacking, Shaz thought as she passed the wedding cake white house with its flawless facade. She couldn't see much of the garden, shielded from the world by tall, clipped variegated laurel hedges, but the section beyond the electronic gates appeared to be as immaculate as an exhibit at the Chelsea Flower Show. Shaz felt a momentary doubt in the pit of her stomach. How could she suspect the tenant of such a jewel of the hideous crimes her imagination had constructed? People like this didn't do things like that, did they?

Biting her lip in anger at her lack of self-belief, Shaz turned on her heel and marched back to her car, determination building with the very rhythm of her stride. He was a criminal and when she'd finished with him, the whole world would know it. It took her less than five minutes to drive back to the house and turn into the gateway. She wound down her window and pressed the speaker box. 'DC Bowman to see Mr Vance,' she said firmly.

The gates swung open with a low electric hum and Shaz advanced into what she couldn't help thinking of as enemy territory. Not sure where to leave her car, she opted to avoid blocking the double garage and followed the drive round to the other side of the house, past a Range Rover parked by the front steps, and stopped alongside a silver Mercedes convertible. She turned off the engine and sat for a moment, gathering her energies and focusing on her objective. 'Just do it,' she finally said, her voice low and tough.

She ran up the steps to the front door and pushed the bell. Almost instantaneously, the door swung open and Micky Morgan's face smiled down at her, familiar as family. 'Detective Constable Bowman,' she said, stepping back and waving Shaz inside. 'Come in. I was just leaving.' Micky extended an arm to one side, indicating a middle-aged woman with grey-streaked hair pulled loosely back in a heavy plait. 'This is Betsy Thorne, my PA. We're off to catch Le Shuttle.'

'An overnight break in Le Touquet,' Betsy amplified.

'Lots of seafood and a flutter in the casino,' Micky added, reaching over to take a leather holdall from Betsy. 'Jacko's expecting you. He's just finishing a phone call. If you take that first door on the left, he'll be with you in a minute.'

Shaz finally managed to get a word in. 'Thanks,' she said. Micky and Betsy hovered on the doorstep, till Shaz realized they weren't going to close the door until they were certain she was in the correct place. With an awkward smile, Shaz nodded and walked through the open door Micky had indicated. Only when she'd disappeared from sight did she hear the front door closing. Moving to the window, she saw the women climb into the Range Rover.

'DC Bowman?'

Shaz whirled around. She hadn't heard anyone enter. Across the room, smaller in life than he appeared on TV, Jacko Vance smiled. Fuelled by her imagination, Shaz saw the grin of the panther just before its prey becomes a carcass. She wondered if she was face to face with her first serial killer. If so, she hoped he didn't realize he was seeing Nemesis.

* * *

Her eyes were extraordinary. From behind, she'd looked so average. Brown hair brushing the collar of a tailored dark navy blazer over blue jeans and tan deck shoes. Nothing you'd glance at twice in a crowded bar. But when he startled her into turning round, the blaze of her blue eyes converted her into an entirely different creature. Vance felt a tingle of apprehension coupled with a strange sense of satisfaction. Whatever she was after, this woman wasn't a nobody. She was an adversary. 'Sorry to keep you waiting,' he said, his voice the familiar TV caress.

'I was early,' she said neutrally.

Vance walked towards her, stopping when there was about six feet between them. 'Have a seat, officer,' he said, indicating the sofa behind her.

'Thanks,' Shaz said, ignoring his instruction and moving instead to the very armchair he'd planned to occupy. He'd chosen it because the seat was higher and the light was behind it. He'd intended to place her at a disadvantage, but she'd turned the tables. Irritation stung him like an insect bite and rather than sitting down himself, he moved over to the fireplace and leaned against the ornately carved overmantel. He stared across at her, his silence demanding that she open the bidding.

'I appreciate you making the time to see me,' she said after a long moment. 'I realize how busy you are.'

'You didn't leave me much option. Besides, I'm always happy to be of assistance to the police. Your Deputy Commissioner could fill you in on the details of the number of times I've helped police charities.' The smile never left his voice but didn't make it to his eyes.

The blue stare didn't blink. 'I'm sure he could, sir.'

'Which reminds me. Your warrant card?' Vance didn't move, forcing Shaz to get up and cross the room once she'd taken out the wallet that contained her police credentials. 'I can't believe we'd be so careless,' Vance said conversationally as she approached. 'Letting a stranger across the door without checking she was who she claimed to be.' He gave her Metropolitan Police warrant card a perfunctory glance. 'There's another one, isn't there?'

'I'm sorry? This is the only card Metropolitan Police officers are issued with. It's our ID,' Shaz said, face giving nothing away of the alarm bells ringing in her head, telling her he knew too much and she should clear out while the going was good.

Vance's lips seemed to shrink as his smile became more vulpine. Time to show her who held the cards, he decided. 'But you're not with the Met any longer, are you, DC Bowman? You see, you're not the only one who's done their homework. You have done your homework?'

'I am still an officer of the Metropolitan Police,' Shaz said firmly. 'Anyone who has told you different is mistaken, sir.'

He pounced. 'But you're not based in the Met's area, are you? You're on attachment to a special unit. Why don't you show me your current ID so that I know you are who you say you are and we can get down to business?' Careful, he told himself, don't get carried away just because you're so much smarter than her. You don't know yet what she's doing here. He shrugged winningly, his eyebrows lifting. 'I don't mean to be difficult, but a man in my position can't be too careful.'

Shaz looked him up and down, her face a mask. 'That's very true,' she said, producing her National Profiling Task Force ID, complete with photograph. He reached out for it, but she moved it out of his grasp.

'I've not seen one of those before,' he said chattily, hiding his frustration at not being able to glimpse more than a logo and the word 'profiling', which had leapt out like a burning brand. 'The profiling task force we've all read so much about, eh? Once you're actually up and running, you should get one of your experienced officers to go on my wife's programme, tell the people what's being done to protect them.' Now she'd know he knew she was an absolute beginner.

'That wouldn't be my decision, sir.' Shaz deliberately turned her back on him and walked back to the chair. 'Now, if we could get down to business?'

'Of course.' He spread his left arm in an expansive gesture without making a move towards a chair. 'I'm at your disposal, DC Bowman. Perhaps we could start with you telling me exactly what this is all about.'

'We've reopened the cases of a group of missing teenage girls,' Shaz said, opening the folder she was carrying. 'Initially, we have identified seven cases with strong similarities. The cases cover a period of six years, and we will be expanding our inquiries to see whether there are other cases with common features that we haven't pinpointed yet.'

'I don't quite see what I . . .' Vance frowned convincingly. 'Teenage girls?'

'Fourteen- and fifteen-year-olds,' Shaz said firmly. 'I can't go into the precise details that have linked these cases, but we have grounds for believing they may be connected.'

'You mean, they're not just run-of-the-mill runaways?' he asked, sounding perplexed.

'We have reason to believe their disappearances were planned by a third party,' Shaz said cautiously, never shifting her eyes from his face. The intensity of her gaze made him uncomfortable. He wanted to edge away from her stare, to fidget his way out of her eyeline. But he forced himself to keep his pose casual.

'Kidnapped, is that what you're saying?'

Her eyebrows and a slight movement of her head indicated a shrug. 'I'm not in a position to release any more information,' she said with a sudden smile.

'Fine, but you're still not making much sense. What has a bunch of missing teenagers got to do with me?' He made his voice sound a little edgy. It wasn't hard to do; there was plenty of nervous tension buzzing in his veins to draw on.

Shaz flipped open her folder and drew out a sheaf of photocopied photographs. 'In every case, a couple of days before the girls disappeared, you'd made a public appearance or taken part in a charity event in the towns where they lived. We have reason to believe that each of the girls attended the occasion.'

He could feel the red tide rising up his neck. He was powerless to stop the flush of anger as it climbed into his face. It was an effort to keep himself calm and his voice level. 'Hundreds of people come to my events,' he said evenly, his voice a fraction husky to his ears. 'Statistically, some of them must go missing. All the time.'

Shaz cocked her head, as if she'd also picked up on a change in his tone. She looked like a hunting dog who's just had the faintest whiff of what might possibly be a rabbit. 'I know. I'm sorry we have to bother you with this. It's just that my boss thinks there's an outside possibility that either someone in your entourage or possibly someone who's got an unhealthy interest in you might conceivably be involved in the disappearance of those girls.'

'You mean, you think I've got a stalker who's capturing my fans?' This time, he found it wasn't hard to sound incredulous. As a cover story, it was ridiculous. An imbecile could see that the person she was really interested in wasn't some crazy, nor a member of his entourage. It was him. He could tell by her eyes, obsessively fixed on him, recording

177

his every move, noticing the faint sheen of sweat he could feel on his forehead. And her talk of a boss was just as evidently a bluff. She was a lone wolf, like him. He could smell it on her.

Shaz nodded. 'It could be. Transference, the psychologists call it. Like John Hinckley. Remember him? The guy who shot Ronald Reagan because he wanted Jodie Foster to take notice of him?' Her voice was pleasant, friendly, carefully pitched so he wouldn't feel threatened. He hated her for thinking so simple a technique would slip past him unnoticed.

'This is bizarre,' he said, pushing off from the mantelpiece and striding to and fro on the hearth rug, a hand-knotted silk Bokhara that he'd chosen himself. Staring down at the grey and cream intricacies under his feet calmed him until he was able to meet the woman's intense eyes again. 'It's absurd. If it wasn't so appalling a suggestion, it would be funny. And I still don't see what it has to do with me.'

'It's simple, sir,' Shaz said soothingly.

Feeling patronized, Vance stopped in his tracks and scowled. 'What?' he demanded, charm disintegrating by the second.

'All I want you to do is to look at some photographs and tell me if you noticed the girls for any reason. Maybe they were particularly pushy with you, and someone wanted to punish them. Maybe you noticed one of your staff chatting them up. Or maybe you never spotted any of them. Just a couple of minutes of your time, then I'm out of here,' Shaz coaxed. She leaned forward and spread the photocopies over a kilim-covered footstool the size of a coffee table.

He moved towards her, transfixed by the photographs that she'd arranged to face him. Only a fraction of his work, that was all she'd captured. But every single smiling stare was one he'd destroyed.

Vance forced a laugh. 'Seven faces out of thousands? Sorry, DC Bowman, you've been wasting your time. I've never seen any of them before.'

'Look again,' she said. 'Are you absolutely certain?' There was an edge in her voice that hadn't been there before, sharp and excited. He dragged his eyes away from the pale reflections of the living flesh he'd punished and met Shaz Bowman's implacable eyes. She knew. She might not have the proof yet, but he knew she knew now. He also knew she wouldn't stop until she had destroyed him. It had come down to dog eat dog, and she had no chance. Not handicapped by the law.

He shook his head, a sorrowful smile on his lips. 'I'm positive. I've never clapped eyes on any of them before.'

Without even looking, Shaz pushed the middle picture closer to him. 'You made an appeal in a national tabloid for Tiffany Thompson to call her parents,' she said without inflexion.

'My God,' he exclaimed, forcing his features into an expression of happy astonishment. 'Do you know, I'd completely forgotten about that? You're right, of course, I see it now.'

Her attention was all on his face as he spoke. In a swift movement, he swung his prosthesis round in a short arc and smashed it violently into the side of her head. Her eyes showed a momentary shock, then panic. As she fell out of the chair, her forehead smacked into the footstool. By the time she crashed to the floor, she was unconscious.

Vance wasted no time. He raced down to the cellar where he grabbed a reel of hi-fi speaker wire and a pack of latex gloves. Within minutes, Shaz was trussed like a hog-tied steer on the polished parquet. Then he ran up to the top floor and opened his wardrobe, scrabbling around on the floor until he found what he was looking for. Back downstairs, he covered Shaz's head with the soft flannel bag that his new leather briefcase had come in. Then he wrapped a few lengths of wire round her neck, tight enough to be uncomfortable but not so that it would constrict her breathing. He wanted her dead, but not yet. Not here, and not accidentally.

As soon as he was sure that she wasn't going to be able to break free, he picked up her shoulder bag and sat down with it on the sofa, gathering the photocopies and the file they'd come from on the way. Meticulously, he began to go through everything, starting with the file. The abstracts of the police reports he skimmed over, knowing he would have the opportunity to look at them in more detail later. When he came to the analysis Shaz had presented to her colleagues, he took his time, weighing and calculating how dangerous to him it might prove. Not very, he decided. The photocopies of the newspaper clippings about his visits to the places in question were meaningless; for every one connected to a disappearance, he could produce twenty that weren't. Putting that aside, he picked up the organized offender checklist. Reading her conclusion so angered him that he jumped to his feet and gave the unconscious detective a couple of savage kicks in the stomach. 'Fuck do you know, bitch?' he shouted angrily. He wished he could see her eyes now. They wouldn't be judging him, they'd be begging him for mercy.

Furious, he stuffed the papers back in the file along with the photocopies. He'd have to study them more carefully, but there wasn't time now. He'd been right to nip this in the bud before anyone else paid attention to this bitch's allegations. He turned to her roomy shoulder bag and pulled out a spiral-bound notebook. A quick flick through the pages revealed nothing of interest except Micky's phone number and their address. Since he wasn't going to be able to deny she'd been here, that had better stay. But he tore out a handful of pages after the last entry, making it look as if someone had ripped out details pertaining to a subsequent appointment, then replaced it in the bag.

Next out was the microcassette recorder, the tape still turning. He stopped the machine and removed the tape, placing it with the blank sheets of paper on one side. He ignored the Ian Rankin paperback and pulled out a filofax. Under that day's date, the only entry read, 'JV 9.30'. He considered adding another cryptic entry and settled for the single letter 'T' underneath her appointment with him. Let them think about that. Inside the front cover, he found what he was looking for. 'If found, return to S. Bowman, Flat 1, 17 Hyde Park Hill, Headingley, Leeds. REWARD.' His fingers groped around the bottom of the bag. No keys.

Vance stuffed everything back into the shoulder bag, picked up the file and crossed to Shaz. He patted her down until he found a bunch of keys in her trouser pocket. Smiling, he went upstairs to his office and found a padded envelope big enough for the file. He addressed it to his Northumberland retreat, stamped it and sealed Shaz's research inside.

A quick glance at his watch told him it was barely half past ten. He went through to his bedroom and changed into jeans, one of the few short-sleeved T-shirts he possessed, and a denim jacket. He picked up a holdall from the back of the fitted wardrobes that ran deep under the eaves. He took out a Nike baseball cap that was attached to a professional quality wig of collar-length salt-and-pepper hair and put it on. The effect was remarkable. When he added a pair of aviator glasses with clear lenses and a pair of foam pads to fill out his hollow cheeks, the transformation was complete. The only giveaway was his prosthetic arm. And Jacko had the perfect answer to that.

He let himself out of the house, careful to lock up behind himself, and opened Shaz's car. He took a careful note of the seat position, then climbed in and adjusted it to suit his longer legs. He spent a few minutes familiarizing himself with the controls, making sure he was going to be able to manage the stick shift and steer at the same time. Then he set off, stopping only to drop the padded envelope in a pillar box in Ladbroke Grove. As he hit the approach ramp to the M1 shortly after eleven o'clock, he allowed himself a small, private smile. Shaz Bowman was going to be very sorry she'd ever crossed him. But not for long.

The first pain was a scream of cramp in her left leg, penetrating her muzzy unconsciousness like a serrated knife across a knuckle. The instinctive attempt at stretching and flexing the muscle triggered a slash of agony around her wrists. It made no sense to a disorientated mind that had started to throb like a thumb hit with a hammer. Shaz forced her eyes open, but the blackness didn't go away. Then she registered the damp material against her face. It was some sort of hood, made of thick fabric with a soft nap. It covered her whole head, fastening tightly round her throat, making it hard to swallow.

Gradually, she made sense of her position. She was lying on her side on a hard surface, her hands fastened behind her back with some sort of ligature that bit cruelly into the flesh of her wrists. Her feet were also fastened at the ankle, and both sets of bonds were linked to allow minimal movement. Anything adventurous like stretching her legs or trying to shift her spot cost too much in pain. She had no idea how small or how large her area of confinement was, nor any desire to explore once she had experienced the torment of attempting to turn over.

She had no idea how long she'd been unconscious. The last thing she could remember was Jacko Vance's laughing face looming over her, as if he didn't have a care in the world, secure in the certainty that no one would ever take this pipsqueak detective seriously. No, that wasn't quite right. Something else tugged at her memory. Shaz tried the deep breathing of relaxation techniques and tried to picture what she'd seen. The memory stirred and took shape. Out on the edge of her peripheral vision, his right arm rising, then swinging down savagely like a club. That was the last thing she could remember.

With the memory came terror, sharper than any of her physical afflictions. Nobody knew where she was except Chris, who wasn't expecting to hear from her anyway. She hadn't told anyone else, not even Simon. She hadn't been able to face their mockery, however friendly. Now the fear of being laughed at was going to cost her her life. Shaz was under no illusion about that. She'd asked Jacko Vance questions that made him realize she knew he was a serial killer and he hadn't panicked as she'd believed he would. Instead, he'd worked out for himself that she was a maverick. That although her deductions were a threat to him, he could win himself a stay of execution by getting rid of her, the renegade cop in hot pursuit of a solo hunch. Removing Shaz would, at worst, buy him time to cover his tracks or even leave the country.

Shaz felt a wave of sweat drench her skin. There was no question about it. She was going to die. The only question was how.

She'd been right. And being right was going to kill her.

Pauline Doyle was desperate. The police refused to regard Donna's disappearance as anything other than a typical teenage runaway. 'She'll have gone to London, probably. There's no point in us looking for her round here,' one of the uniformed officers she'd mithered at the counter of the police station had said in exasperation one night.

Pauline might shout from the rooftops that someone had stolen her daughter, but the evidence of the missing outfit was more than enough to convince overworked cops that Donna Doyle was just another teenager bored with home and convinced the streets somewhere were paved with gold. You only had to look at her photograph, that knowing smile, to understand she was nothing like as innocent as her poor misguided mother wanted to believe.

With the police showing no interest beyond a routine posting of Donna on the missing list, Pauline was stymied. Not for her the passionate television appeals for the missing daughter, not with the absence of official backing. Even the local paper wasn't interested, though the women's editor toyed with the idea of running a feature on teenage runaways. But like the police, when she saw Donna's photograph, she thought again. There was something about Donna that defied any attempt to portray her as an innocent abroad, seduced by chaste dreams. Something about the line of her mouth, the tilt of her chin said that she had crossed the line. The women's editor reckoned Donna Doyle was the sort of Lolita that would make most women want to put blinkers on their husbands.

Her frustration spilling over into nightly storms of tears, Pauline decided the time had come to take matters into her own hands. Her job in the estate agency wasn't particularly well paid. It was enough to feed and clothe her and Donna and to keep a roof over their heads, but not much more than that. There was still a couple of thousand left over from Bernard's insurance. Pauline had been saving that for when Donna went off to university, knowing how tight things would be then.

But if Donna didn't come back, there would be no point in saving it for university, Pauline reasoned. Better then to spend the money to try and get her home and let higher education fend for itself. So Pauline took Donna's photograph to the local print shop and had them make up thousands of flyers with her daughter's image occupying the whole of one side. The text on the reverse read, 'HAVE YOU SEEN THIS GIRL? Donna Doyle went missing on Thursday 11th October. She was last seen at quarter past eight in the morning, on her way to Glossop Girls Grammar. She was wearing school uniform of maroon skirt, maroon cardigan, white open-necked blouse. Her shoes were black Kickers, and she had a black anorak. She was carrying a black Nike backpack. If you saw her at any time after that, please contact her mother, Pauline Doyle.' It gave the address in Corunna Street, and telephone numbers at home and the agency.

Pauline took a week off work and stuffed the leaflets through letterboxes from dawn till dusk. She started in the town centre, thrusting the reproductions of Donna's face at anyone who would take them, and gradually worked her way out into suburban streets, not noticing the steepness of the hills she climbed or the blisters that swelled inside her shoes.

No one phoned.

While Shaz Bowman was lying on his hard floor in London, conscious only of fear and pain, Jacko Vance was exploring her domain. He'd made good time to Leeds, stopping only to fill up with petrol and visit the disabled toilet at the motorway services. He'd wanted to use its sanitary disposal unit to get rid of the tape he'd unravelled from Shaz's microcassette. In the car park, he'd crushed the casing underfoot, leaving the fragments to scatter in the blustery wind that swept across the Midlands.

Finding Shaz's home had been made even easier by her recently purchased *A to Z*, which conveniently had the street circled in blue biro. He parked the car round the corner and forced himself to combat his twitching nerves by strolling slowly down the street, empty except for a couple of small boys playing cricket on the opposite pavement. He turned in at the gate of number 17 and tried one of the two Yale keys in the heavy Victorian front door. That he got it right first time convinced him that the gods really were on his side.

He found himself in a gloomy hallway, lit only by two thin lancet windows on either side of the door. Peering into the murk, he saw a wide and graceful staircase rising ahead of him. There seemed to be one ground-floor flat on either side. He chose the left-hand side, and was proved right again. Breathing more easily now, convinced everything was going his way, Vance let himself into the flat. He wasn't planning on staying long, just enough to scout out the lie of the land, so he moved swiftly through the rooms. As soon as he saw the living room, he realized that Shaz could not possibly have chosen a flat better suited to his purpose. The French windows led out on to a garden surrounded by high walls, shaded by tall fruit trees. At the end, he could discern the outlines of a wooden door in the brick wall.

Only one thing remained to be done. He slipped off his jacket and unfastened his prosthesis. From the holdall, he took an object he'd persuaded the props department to make for him a couple of years back, supposedly as a practical joke. Using the fittings from one of his previous artificial arms, an earlier model now discarded, they'd built a plaster cast with disturbingly realistic fingertips protruding from the end. Once it was fitted, especially with a jacket over it and a sling holding it in place, it looked exactly like a broken arm. When he was satisfied he'd arranged it correctly, Vance re-packed the holdall, took a deep breath and decided it was time to go.

He let himself out of the French windows, pushing them to behind him, then strode confidently down the gravel path to the gate. He could feel the hair on his neck prickling under the wig, wondering if there were eyes behind any of the windows at his back, eyes that would remember what they'd seen once his handiwork was over and exposed to the public gaze. In a bid for reassurance, he reminded himself that any description they could come up with would sound nothing like Jacko Vance.

He unbolted the back gate, convinced that no one would fasten it again before he returned. He found himself in a narrow lane that ran between two sets of walled back gardens and led out on to one of the main roads that ran down towards the city centre. Walking to the station took the best part of an hour, but he had barely ten minutes to wait for a London train. He was back in Holland Park and restored to Jacko Vance by half past seven.

Before he made his final preparations, he slammed a twelve-inch pizza into the oven. It wasn't his usual idea of Saturday night dinner, but the carbohydrate should stop his stomach turning somersaults. Tension always hit him in the gut. Whenever the fever of anticipation had him in its grasp, he'd have to endure cramps and clenches, knots and nausea. He'd learned early on in his days as a live sports commentator that the only way to stop the churning and grumbling was to stodge out in advance. What worked for TV worked just as well for murder, he'd soon discovered. Now, he always ate before he picked up his targets. And of course, he always ate with them before the act itself.

While the pizza was cooking, he loaded his Mercedes. Exertion was easier on an empty stomach. Now everything was ready for Shaz Bowman's final performance. All he had to do was get her on stage.

Donna Doyle was also alone. But, deranged by agony, she lacked the luxury of introspection. The first time she'd woken from broken sleep, she'd felt strong enough to explore her prison. Her fear was still overwhelming, but it was no longer paralysing. Wherever she was, it was dark as a grave and had the dank smell of the tiny coal cellar at home. She used her good arm to help her gain a sense of where she was and what was around her. She was, she realized, lying on a plastic-covered mattress. Her fingers explored the edges and felt cold tiles. Not as smooth as the ceramic ones in the bathroom at home, more like the glazed terracotta on Sarah Dyson's mum's conservatory steps.

The wall behind her was rough stone. She struggled to her feet, realizing properly for the first time that her legs were shackled. She bent and let her fingers trace the outline of an iron cuff round each ankle. They were attached to a heavy chain. One-handed, it was impossible to gauge how long it was. Four hesitant steps along one wall brought her to a corner. She turned through ninety degrees and moved on. Two steps and her shin crashed painfully against something solid. It didn't take long both by touch and smell to identify it as a chemical toilet. Pathetically grateful, Donna subsided on to it and emptied her bladder.

That only reminded her of how thirsty she was. Hunger she

wasn't too sure about, but thirst was definitely a problem. She stood up and carried on along the wall for another few feet before the chain round her ankles brought her up short. The jerk sent a spasm of pain shooting from her arm into her neck and head, and she gasped. Slowly, bent like an old woman, she retraced her steps and moved past the other end of the mattress, her hand brushing the wall.

Within a few feet, the questions of food and drink were answered. A stiff metal tap produced a surge of icy water which she drank thirstily, falling to her knees to get her head right underneath the flow. As she did, she knocked something over beyond her. Her thirst slaked, she groped blindly for whatever she'd bumped into. Probing fingers found four boxes, all large and light. She shook them and heard the familiar rustle of cornflakes.

An hour of investigation later and she was forced to realize that was it. Four boxes of cornflakes – she'd tested each one – and as much freezing water as she could drink. She'd tried running the water over her shattered arm, but the pain had made her head reel. This was it. The bastard had left her chained up like a dog. Left her to die?

She sat back on her heels and keened like a bereft mother.

But that had been a couple of endless days ago. Now, delirious with pain, she moaned and gibbered, occasionally passing out, occasionally drifting exhausted into tormented sleep. If she'd been able to comprehend the state she was in, Donna wouldn't have wanted to live.

The car stopped. Shaz slid irresistibly forward into the bulwark separating the narrow confines of the boot from the back seat, crushing her wrists and shoulders again. She tried to strain upwards to bang her head on the lid in a desperate bid to attract someone's attention, but all she achieved was a fresh wave of pain. She tried not to sob, afraid that if mucus blocked her nose, she'd suffocate, unable to breathe through the gag that Vance had tied over the hood before he'd rolled her agonizingly across hard floors, over a carpeted area and down a short flight of steps, then hoisted her into the boot of the car. She had been horribly amazed at the strength and dexterity of this one-armed man.

Shaz breathed as deeply as she could; too far and her chest expansion made her stiff shoulder muscles protest. Only sheer willpower kept her from gagging at the stench of her own urine. Let's see you get rid of that from your boot carpet, she thought triumphantly; she couldn't do anything to save her life, but she was still determined to seize every opportunity to prevent Jacko Vance from walking away from his crimes. If SOCO ever got this far, a piss-stained carpet would make their day.

Abruptly the muffled music stopped. Ever since they'd set off, he'd listened to hits of the sixties. Shaz had forced herself to pay attention and had counted the tracks. At an average of three minutes a song, she reckoned they'd been driving for somewhere around three hours of what had felt like motorway after the first twenty minutes or so. That probably meant the north; heading west would have taken them on to the motorway more quickly. Of course, it was possible that he could have confused her by driving a circuit round the M25, orbiting London until he'd laid a completely false trail. Shaz didn't think so; she doubted whether he felt any need to mislead her. She wasn't going to be alive to tell anyone, after all.

It was probably dark by now; she'd lain bound in the house for what felt like several hours before Vance had returned to deal with her. If they were in the depths of the country, there would be no one to see or hear her. Somehow, she thought that was probably Vance's plan. He must have taken his victims somewhere isolated to escape detection. She could think of no reason why he'd treat her differently.

A car door closed with a soft thud and a faint click. Then a metallic sound closer to hand and the soft hydraulic sigh of a boot opening. 'God, you stink,' Vance said contemptuously, dragging her carelessly forward.

'Listen,' he continued, sounding closer. 'I'm going to free your feet. I'm going to cut them free. The knife is very, very sharp. Mostly I use it to joint meat. If you take my meaning.' His voice was almost a whisper, his hot breath penetrating the hood next to her ear. Shaz felt another ripple of nausea. 'If you try to run, I'll gut you like a pig on a butcher's hook. There's nowhere to run to, see? We're in the middle of nowhere.'

Shaz's ears told her different. To her surprise, there was the rumble of traffic not far off, the underlying mutter of city life. If she had half a chance, she'd take it.

She felt the cold blade of the knife briefly against the skin of her ankle, then her feet were miraculously free. For a second, she thought she could kick out then make a run for it. Then her circulation reasserted itself and spasms of excruciating pins and needles squeezed a moan from the dry mouth behind the unyielding gag. Before the cramp could pass, Shaz felt herself hauled over the edge of the boot. She collapsed in an uncoordinated heap before he slammed the boot shut and yanked her to her feet. He half-dragged, half-carried her through a gap or a gateway where she bashed her shoulder on the wall, then down a path and up a couple of steps. Then he pushed her sharply and she crashed to a carpeted floor, her legs still useless rubbery handicaps.

Even through the haze of disorientation and pain, the closing of the door and the rattle of curtains being drawn sounded strangely familiar to Shaz. A fresh dread seized her and she began to shiver uncontrollably, losing control of her bladder for the second time in the past hour.

'God, you're a disgusting bitch,' Vance sneered. Again she felt herself irresistibly hauled upwards. This time she was dumped unceremoniously in a hard, upright chair. Before she could adjust to the fresh pain in her shoulders and arms, she felt a new restraint being fastened to her leg, attaching it to the chair like a broken limb to a splint. In a desperate bid for freedom, she forced her other leg to kick out, rejoicing in the jarring connection with Vance's body, exulting in his cry of surprised pain.

The blow to her jaw snapped her head back with a crack that sent waves of sick pain down her spine. 'You fucking stupid cow,' was all he said before he grabbed her other leg and forced it against the chair while he bound them tightly together.

She felt his legs between her knees. The warmth of his body was almost the worst suffering she'd had to endure so far. He raised her arms agonizingly and forced them back down

194

over the back of the chair to hold her irresistibly upright. Then the hood was pulled away from her flesh and she heard the whisper of a razor-sharp blade through cloth. Blinking at the sudden appalling brightness, Shaz's stomach was gripped with a cold cramp as she discovered her worst fear was a reality. She was sitting in her own living room, strapped to one of the four dining chairs she'd bought only ten days before in Ikea.

Vance pressed his body against hers as he cut the hood away just above the gag, leaving her able to see and hear properly, but incapable of any noise other than a muffled grunt. He stepped back, giving her breast a cruel tweak with his artificial hand as he went.

He stood staring at her, flicking the blade of the butcher's filleting knife against the table edge. Shaz thought she had never seen a more arrogant human being. His pose, his expression, everything reeked of self-important righteousness. 'You really fucked up my weekend,' he said witheringly. 'Believe me, this is not how I planned to spend Saturday night. Dressing up in fucking surgical greens and latex in some shitty flat in Leeds is not my idea of a good time, bitch.' He shook his head pityingly. 'You're going to pay, Detective Bowman. You're going to pay for being a stupid little fuck.'

He put the knife down and fumbled under his top. Shaz glimpsed a bum bag as he unzipped it and took out a CD-ROM. Without another word he walked out of the room. Shaz heard the familiar hum then clatter as first her computer then her printer were switched on. Straining her ears, she fancied she heard the clicking of the mouse and the sound of keys being struck. Then, unmistakably, the vibrating thrum of paper loading and printing.

When he returned, he carried a single sheet of paper which he held in front of her face. She recognized the print-out of an illustrated encyclopaedia article. She didn't have to read the words to understand the symbolism of the line drawing at the top of the page. 'You know what this is?' he demanded.

Shaz just stared at him, her eyes bloodshot but still arresting. She was determined not to give in to him on any level.

'It's a teaching aid, student detective Bowman. It's the three wise monkeys. See no evil, hear no evil, speak no evil. You should have taken that as your class motto. You should have stayed away from me. You should have kept your nose out of my business. You won't be doing that again.'

He let the paper flutter to the floor. Suddenly he lunged forward, hands pushing her head back. Then his prosthetic thumb was over her eyeball, pushing down and out, rending muscles, ripping the hollow globe free from its moorings. The scream was only inside Shaz's head. But it was loud enough to carry her over into blessed unconsciousness.

Jacko Vance studied his handiwork and saw that it was good. Because his usual killings were fuelled by a completely different set of needs, he'd never contemplated them in a purely aesthetic light before. But this was a work of art, laden with symbolism. He wondered if anyone would be smart enough to read the message he'd left and, having read it, to heed it. Somehow, he doubted it.

He leaned forward and made a slight adjustment to the angle of the sheet of paper in her lap. Then, satisfied, he allowed himself the luxury of a smile. All he had to do now was to make sure she'd left no messages behind. He began to search the flat methodically, inch by inch, including the waste bins. He was used to the company of corpses, so the presence of Shaz's remains caused him no stress. He was so relaxed as he meticulously searched her kitchen that he actually caught himself singing softly as he worked.

In the room she'd made her office, he found more than he'd bargained for. A box of photocopies of newspapers, a pad of rough notes, files on the hard disk of her laptop and back-ups on floppy disk, print-outs of various drafts of the analysis he'd found earlier in the file she'd brought to his house. What was even worse was that much of the print-out didn't seem to have any matching files on the computer. There were copies on floppy disk, but not on the hard disk. It was a nightmare. When he spotted the modem, he almost panicked. The reason the files weren't on her hard disk was that they were somewhere else, presumably on some National Profiling Task Force computer. And there was no way he could access that. His only hope was that Shaz Bowman had been as paranoid with her computer files as she seemed to have been about sharing her showdown with a colleague. Either way, there was nothing he could do about it now. He'd get rid of every trace there was here and just have to hope that nobody would go looking in her computer files at work. If the Luddite cops he knew were anything to judge by, it would never occur to them that she might have techie tendencies. Besides, she wasn't supposed to be working cases, was she? Not according to the contacts he'd so cautiously and entirely naturally exploited to find out what he had about her before their meeting. There was no reason why anyone should connect so bizarre a death to her profiling training.

But how was he going to deal with all this *stuff*? He couldn't take the material with him in case a chance encounter with a traffic cop led to a search of his car. Equally, he couldn't leave it behind, pointing a giant finger of blame in his direction. He wasn't singing now.

He crouched in one corner of the office, thinking furiously.

He couldn't burn it. It would take too long and the smell would be bound to attract the attention of her neighbours. The last thing he needed was the fire brigade. He couldn't flush it down the toilet; it would block the drains in no time at all unless he tore it into tiny fragments, and that would take till dawn and beyond. He couldn't even dig a hole in the garden and bury it, since the discovery of the bitch's body would only be the starting point for a massively thorough investigation, beginning with the immediate environs of the body.

In the end, the only solution he could come up with left no choice but to take all the incriminating evidence with him. It was a scary thought, but he kept telling himself that luck and the gods were with him, that he'd been untouchable up to now because he took every precaution humanly possible and left only a fraction of the risk to a benevolent fate.

Vance loaded a couple of bin liners with the material and staggered out to the car with them, every step an effort. He had been working on ditching Detective Constable Shaz Bowman for something like fifteen or sixteen hours, and he was running out of mental and physical energy. He never used drugs when he was working; the false sense of power and capability they induced were certain steps to fallibility and stupid mistakes. But just this once, he wished he had a neatly folded paper packet of cocaine in his pocket. A couple of lines of charlie and he'd be flying through the tasks that remained instead of dragging his weary body down this bloody gravel path through the arse end of Leeds.

With a small groan of relief, he dropped the second bin liner in the boot. He paused momentarily, wrinkling his nose in disgust. Leaning forward and sniffing, he confirmed his suspicion. The bitch had pissed in his car, soaking the carpet. One more item to dispose of, he thought, glad he had a ready solution to the problem. He stripped off his surgical greens and gloves and pushed them into the spare-tyre well then gently closed the lid with a soft snap of metal. 'Goodbye, DC Bowman,' he muttered as he lowered himself wearily into the driving seat. The clock on the dashboard told him it was nearly half past two. Provided he wasn't stopped by the cops for being in possession of a smart motor in the small hours of the morning, he'd be at his destination by half past four. The only difficulty would be fighting his instinct to hammer the pedal to the metal so he could put as much distance between him and his achievement as possible. With one hand sweating and the other as cool as the night air, he drove out of the city and headed north.

He made it ten minutes ahead of schedule. The maintenance area of the Royal Newcastle Infirmary was deserted, as he knew it would be until the Sunday morning skeleton shift arrived at six. Vance backed his car into a space in the service bay right next to the double doors that led through to the incinerators that dealt with the hospital's surgical waste. Often when he'd finished his voluntary work with the patients, he'd come down here to have a brew and a gossip with the service staff. They were proud to count a celebrity like Jacko Vance as a friend, and they'd been more than honoured to provide him with his own smart card to admit him to the maintenance sectors so he could come and go at will. They'd even known him to come down on his own in the middle of the night when there was no one else around and help them out by getting stuck in to the incineration work himself, stoking the furnace with the sealed bags of waste that came down from clinics, wards and operating theatres.

It never occurred to them that he added his own fuel to the flames.

That was one of the many reasons why Jacko Vance never

feared discovery. He was no Fred West with bodies underpinning the foundations of his home. When he'd finished taking his pleasure with his victims, they disappeared forever in the fierce disintegrating heat of the RNI's incinerator. For an appliance that routinely swallowed the waste of an entire city hospital, two bin bags full of Shaz Bowman's research would be a mere *amuse bouche*. He'd be in and out in twenty minutes. Then the end would be in sight. He could fall into his favourite bed, the one at the heart of his killing floor, ignore all the other distractions and sleep the sleep of the just.

PART TWO

'Anybody know where Bowman is?' Paul Bishop asked impatiently, looking at his watch for the fifth time in two minutes. Five blank faces stared back at him.

'Gotta be dead, hasn't she?' Leon grinned. 'Never late, not Shazza baby.'

'Ha ha, Jackson,' Bishop said sarcastically. 'Be a good boy and call down to the front desk, see if they've taken a message from her.'

Leon tipped his chair forward on to all four feet and slouched out of the door, the wide shoulders of his sharply tapering jacket managing to make his six feet of skinniness look challenging. Bishop started drumming his fingers on the edge of the video remote control. If he didn't get this session kicked off soon, he'd be running late. He had a series of scene-of-crime videos to get through then a meeting with a Home Office minister scheduled for lunch. Bloody Bowman. Why did she have to be late today of all days? He'd give her till Jackson got back and then he was forging ahead with the session. Too bad if she missed something crucial.

Simon spoke softly to Kay. 'Have you spoken to Shaz since Friday?'

Kay shook her head, her light brown hair falling like a curtain across one cheek to create the image of a fieldmouse peering through winter grasses. 'I left a message when she didn't turn up for the curry, but she didn't get back to me. I was half-expecting to see her at the women's swim last night, but she wasn't there either. Mind, it wasn't a firm arrangement or anything.'

Before Simon could say anything more, Leon returned. 'Not a dicky bird from her,' he announced. 'She's not rung in sick or anything.'

Bishop tutted. 'Well, we'll just have to manage without her.' He briefed them on the morning's programme, then pressed 'play' on the video.

The aftermath of uncontrolled violence and viciousness that unfolded before them made little impact on Simon. Nor did he have much to contribute to the discussion afterwards. He couldn't get Shaz's absence out of his head. He'd gone round to her flat to pick her up on Saturday night for their pre-curry drink, as they'd agreed. But when he'd rung the bell, there had been no reply. He'd been early, admittedly, so, thinking she might have been deafened by the shower or the hair dryer, he'd walked back to the main road and found a phone box. He'd let her number ring out until the call was automatically disconnected, then he'd tried twice more. Unable to believe she'd stood him up without a word, he'd walked back up the hill to the flat and tried the doorbell again.

He knew which ground-floor flat was Shaz's – he'd given her a lift home after they'd all been out for a drink one evening and, already wistfully hoping he might pluck up the courage to ask her out, he'd lingered long enough to see which set of lights came on. So, just by looking, he could see that the curtains were closed across the deep bay of the master bedroom at the front of the house although it wasn't long dark. As far as he was concerned, that meant she'd been getting ready to go out. Though not, it appeared, with him.

He was about to give up and go to the pub alone to drown his humiliation in Tetley's when he noticed the narrow passage running down the side of the house. Not giving himself time to wonder whether he was either justified or wise, he slipped down the ginnel, through the wrought-iron gate and into the gloomy darkness of the back garden.

He rounded the corner of the house and almost tripped over a short flight of steps leading up from the garden to a pair of French windows. 'For fuck's sake,' he muttered angrily, catching himself before he pitched headlong. He peered through the glass, cupping his hand round his eyes against the stray beams of light from the next-door house. He could see dim shapes of furniture against a faint glow that appeared to be coming from another room opening off the hall. But there was no sign of life. Suddenly a light snapped on from the floor above, casting an irregular rectangle of light right next to Simon.

Instantly aware that he must appear more like burglar than policeman to any casual observer, he'd slid back into the darkness against the wall and returned to the street, hoping he'd managed to avoid anyone's attention. The last thing he needed were jibes from the local uniforms about the Peeping Toms of the profiling squad. Baffled by Shaz's apparent rebuff, he'd walked miserably down to the Sheesh Mahal to meet Leon and Kay for the agreed meal. He wasn't in the mood to join in their speculation that Shaz had had a better offer, concentrating instead on getting as much Kingfisher lager down his throat as he could.

Now, on Monday morning, he was seriously worried. It was one thing standing him up. Let's face it, she could probably do a lot better than him without trying too hard. But to miss a training session was completely out of character. Oblivious to Paul Bishop's words of wisdom, Simon sat and fretted, a pair of frown lines dividing his dark brows. As soon as the screech of chairs on floor announced the end of the session, he went in search of Tony Hill.

He found the psychologist in the canteen, sitting at the table the profiling squad had made their own. 'Can you spare a minute, Tony?' he asked, his dark intense expression almost a mirror image of his tutor's.

'Sure. Pull up a coffee and join me.'

Simon looked uncertainly over his shoulder. 'It's just that the others'll be down any minute, and ... well, it's a bit ... you know, sort of private.'

Tony picked up his own coffee and the file he'd been reading. 'We'll grab one of the interview rooms for a minute.'

Simon followed him down the corridor to the first witness interview room without a red light showing. The air smelled of sweat, stale cigarettes and, obscurely, burnt sugar. Tony straddled one of the chairs and watched Simon pace for a moment before he leaned into one corner of the room. 'It's Shaz,' Simon said. 'I'm worried about her. She didn't turn up this morning and she didn't phone in or anything.'

Tony knew without being told there was more to it than that. It was his job to find out what. 'I agree, it's not like her. She's very conscientious. But something could have come up unexpectedly. A family problem, perhaps?'

One corner of Simon's mouth twitched downwards. 'I suppose so,' he conceded reluctantly. 'But she would have phoned somebody if that's what it was. She's not just conscientious, she's obsessive. You know that.'

'Maybe she's had an accident.'

Simon pounced. 'Exactly. My point exactly. We should be worried about her, shouldn't we?'

Tony shrugged. 'If she has had an accident, we'll hear about it soon enough. Either she'll call us or else someone else will.'

Simon clenched his teeth. He was going to have to explain why it was more urgent than that. 'If she's had an accident, I don't think it was this morning. We had a sort of date on Saturday night. Leon and Kay and me and Shaz, we've taken to going out on a Saturday night for a curry and a few bevvies. But I'd arranged to have a drink with Shaz first, just the two of us. I was supposed to meet her at her flat.' Once he'd started, the words poured out of him. 'When I turned up, there was no sign of her. I thought she'd had second thoughts. Bottled out, whatever. But now it's Monday, and she's not turned up. I think something's happened to her, and whatever it is, it's not trivial. She could have had an accident at home. She could have slipped in the shower and hit her head. Or outside. She could be lying in hospital somewhere and nobody knows who she is. Don't you think we should do something about it? We're supposed to be a team, are we not?'

A dreadful premonition shimmered at the edge of Tony's mind. Simon was right. Two days was too long for a woman like Shaz Bowman to drop out of sight when that meant letting down a colleague and missing work. He got to his feet. 'Have you tried ringing her?' he asked.

'Loads of times. Her answering machine's not on, either. That's why I thought maybe she'd had an accident in the house. You know? I thought, she might've switched the machine off when she came in, and then something happened and . . . I don't know,' he added impatiently. 'This is really embarrassing, you know? I feel like a teenager. Making a fuss about nothing.' He shrugged away from the wall and crossed to the door.

Tony put a hand on Simon's arm. 'I think you're right. You've got a policeman's instinct for when something doesn't smell right. It's one of the reasons you're on this squad. Come on, let's go round to Shaz's flat and see what we can see.'

In the car, Simon leaned forward in his seat as if willing them forward. Realizing any attempt at conversation would be futile, Tony concentrated on following the young officer's terse directions. They pulled up outside Shaz's flat and Simon was on the pavement before Tony could even turn off the engine. 'The curtains are still drawn,' Simon said urgently as soon as Tony joined him on the doorstep. 'That's her bedroom on the left. The curtains were drawn on Saturday night when I was here.' He pushed the bell marked 'Flat 1: Bowman'. They could both hear the irritating buzz from within.

'At least we know the bell's working,' Tony said. He stepped back and looked up at the imposing villa, its York stone blackened by a century of the internal combustion engine.

'You can get round the back,' Simon said, finally releasing the bell push. Without waiting for a response, he was off down the ginnel. Tony followed him, but not quickly enough. As he reached the corner, he heard a wail like an agonized cat in the night. He emerged in time to see Simon reel back from a pair of French windows like a man struck in the face. The young policeman sank to his knees and emptied his guts on the grass, groaning incoherently.

Shocked, Tony took a few hesitant steps forward. As he came level with the steps leading up to the windows, the sight that had stripped Simon McNeill of his manhood turned his stomach to ice. Beyond thought, beyond emotion, Tony stared through the glass at something that looked more like a pastiche of a Bacon painting executed by a psychopath than it did a human being. At first, it was more than he could grasp.

When realization came a moment later, he'd have sold his soul for that previous incomprehension.

It was not the first mutilated corpse Tony had ever faced.

But it was the first time he'd had any personal connection to a victim. Momentarily, he put a hand over his eyes, massaging his eyebrows with thumb and forefinger. This wasn't the time to mourn. There were things he could do for Shaz Bowman that no one else was capable of, and crawling round on the grass like a wounded puppy wasn't one of them.

Taking a deep breath, he turned to Simon and said, 'Call this in. Then go round the front and secure the scene there.'

Simon looked up at him beseechingly, his baffled pain impossible to ignore. 'That's Shaz?'

Tony nodded. 'That's Shaz. Simon, do as I say. Call this in. Go round the front. It's important. We need to get other officers here, now. Do it.' He waited until Simon stumbled to his feet and reeled towards the ginnel like a drunk. Then he turned back and stared through the glass at the ruination of Shaz Bowman. He longed to be closer, to move round her body and take in the horrific details of what had been done to her. But he knew too much about crime scene contamination even to consider it.

He made do with what he could see. It would have been more than enough for most people, but for Tony it was a tantalizing partial picture. The first thing he had to do was to stop thinking of this shell as Shaz Bowman. He must be detached, analytical and clear-headed if he was to be any use at all to the investigating officers. Looking again at the body in the chair, he found it wasn't so hard to distance himself from memories of Shaz. The deformed freakish head that faced him bore so little resemblance to anything human.

He could see dark holes where her startling eyes had last looked out at him. Gouged out, he guessed, judging by what looked like threads and strings trailing from the wounds. Blood had flowed and dried round the black orifices, making the hideous mask of her face even more grotesque. Her mouth looked like a mass of plastic in a dozen hues of purple and pink.

There were no ears. Her hair stuck out in spikes above and behind where the ears should have been, held in place by the dried blood that had sprayed and flowed over them.

His eyes moved down to her lap. A sheet of paper was propped up against her chest. Tony was too far away to make out the words, but he could distinguish the line drawing easily. The three wise monkeys. A shiver shook him from head to foot. It was too early to tell, but from what he could see, there was no sign of any sexual assault. Coupled with the deadly calculation of the three wise monkeys, Tony read the scene. This was no sex killing. Shaz hadn't caught the chance attention of some psychopathic stranger. This was an execution.

'You didn't do this for pleasure,' he said softly to himself. 'You wanted to teach her a lesson. You wanted to teach all of us a lesson. You're telling us you're better than us. You're showing off, thumbing your nose at us because you're convinced we'll never find anything to incriminate you. And you're telling us to keep our noses out of your business. You're an arrogant bastard, aren't you?'

The scene before him told Tony things it would never reveal to a police officer trained to look only for the physical clues. To the psychologist, it revealed a mind that was incisive and decisive. This was a cold-blooded killing, not a frenzied, sexually motivated attack. To Tony, that suggested that the killer had identified Shaz Bowman as a threat. Then he'd acted on it. Brutally, coldly and methodically. Even before the SOCOs arrived, Tony could have told them they would find no significant material clues to the identity of this perpetrator. The solution to this crime lay in the mind, not the forensic lab. 'You're good,' Tony murmured. 'But I'm going to be better.'

When the sirens tore the silence into shreds and uniformed feet pounded down the ginnel, Tony was still standing at the windows, memorizing the scene, drinking in every detail so it would be there later when he needed it. Then and only then he walked round to the front of the house to offer what consolation he could to Simon.

'Hardly bloody urgent,' the police surgeon grumbled, opening his bag and pulling out a pair of latex gloves. 'State she's in, an hour's neither here nor there. Not like doctoring the living, is it? Bloody pager, bane of my bloody life.'

Tony resisted the impulse to hit the chubby doctor. 'She was a police officer,' he said sharply.

The doctor flashed him a shrewd look. 'We've not met, have we? You new here?'

'Dr Hill works for the Home Office,' the local DI said. Tony had already forgotten the man's name. 'He runs this new profiling task force you'll have heard about. The lass was one of his trainees.'

'Aye, well, she'll get the same treatment from me as a Yorkshire lass would,' the doctor said drily, turning back to his grim task.

Tony was standing outside the now open French windows, looking in on the crime scene where a photographer and a team of SOCOs worked their way round the room. He could not take his eyes off the wreckage of Shaz Bowman. No matter how hard he tried, he could not avoid the occasional flashback image of what she had been. It heightened his resolve, but it was a provocation he could well have done without.

Worse for Simon, he thought bitterly. He'd been taken,

putty-skinned and trembling, back to police HQ to give a statement about Saturday night. Tony knew enough about the workings of the official mind to realize that the murder squad were probably treating him as their current prime suspect. He was going to have to do something about that sooner rather than later.

The DI whose name he couldn't remember walked down the steps and stood behind him. 'Helluva mess,' he said.

'She was a good officer,' Tony told him.

'We'll get the bastard,' the DI said confidently. 'Don't you worry about that.'

'I want to help.'

The DI raised one eyebrow. 'Not my decision,' he said. 'It's not a serial killer, you know. We've never seen owt like this on our patch.'

Tony fought to suppress his frustration. 'Inspector, this is not a first-time killing. Whoever did this is an expert. He might not have killed on your patch or used this precise method before, but this is not the product of amateur night out.'

Before the inspector could respond, they were interrupted. The police surgeon had finished his grisly work. 'Well, Colin,' he said, walking over to them, 'she's definitely dead.'

With a quick sidelong glance, the policeman said, 'Spare us the gallows humour for once, Doc. Any idea when?'

'Ask your pathologist, Inspector Wharton,' the doctor said huffily.

'I will. But in the meantime, can you give me a ball-park figure?'

The doctor peeled off his gloves with a snap of latex. 'Monday lunchtime . . . let me see . . . Some time between seven o'clock Saturday night and four o'clock Sunday morning, depending on whether the heating was on and how long for.'

DI Colin Wharton sighed. 'That's a bloody big window of opportunity. Can't you get it tighter than that?'

'I'm a doctor, not bloody Mystic Meg,' he said caustically. 'And I'm going back to my game of golf, if you don't mind. You'll have my report in the morning.'

Tony impulsively put a hand on his arm. 'Doctor, I could use some help here. I know it's not really your place to say, but you've obviously developed a lot of expertise in this kind of thing.' When in doubt, flatter. 'The injuries . . . Do you know if she was still alive, or are they postmortem?'

The doctor pursed full red lips and stared back consideringly at Shaz's body. He looked like a small boy puckering up for his maiden aunt, calculating how much of a tip it was going to earn him. 'A mixture of both,' he said finally. 'I reckon the eyes both went while she was still alive. I think she must have been gagged or she'd have screamed the place down. She probably passed out then, a combination of shock and pain. Whatever was poured down her throat was very caustic and that's what killed her. The total disintegration of her respiratory tract, that's what they'll find when they open her up. I'd stake my pension on it. Looking at the amount of blood, I'd reckon the ears came off more or less as she was dying. They're neatly cut off, though. No trial attempts like you usually get with any kind of mutilation. He must have one hell of a sharp knife and a lot of nerve. If he was trying to make sure she'd end up like them three wise monkeys, he went the right way about it.' He nodded to the two men. 'I'll be off, then. Leave you to it. Good luck finding him. You've got a right nutter here.' He waddled off round the side of the house.

'That bastard's got the worst bedside manner in the whole West Riding,' Colin Wharton said in disgust. 'Sorry about that.'

Tony shook his head. 'What's the point in dressing up something as brutal as that in fancy words? Nothing alters the fact that somebody took Shaz Bowman apart and made sure we knew why.'

'What?' Wharton demanded. 'Have I missed something here? What d'you mean, we know why? I don't bloody know why.'

'You saw the drawing, didn't you? The three wise monkeys. See no evil, hear no evil, speak no evil. The killer destroyed her eyes, her ears, her mouth. Doesn't that say something to you?'

Wharton shrugged. 'Either the boyfriend's the killer, in which case he's a certifiable nutter and it doesn't matter what screwed-up shite was going round his head. Or else it was some other nutter who's got it in for coppers because he thinks we stick our noses into things that we'd be better off leaving alone.'

'You don't think it could be a killer who specifically had it in for Shaz because she was sticking her nose in somewhere it didn't belong?' Tony suggested.

'I don't see how it could be,' Wharton said dismissively. 'She's never worked any cases up here, has she? You lot aren't catching live ones yet, so she's not had the chance to get up some local nutter's nose.'

'Even though we're not catching new cases, we've been working on some genuine old ones. Shaz came up with a theory the other day about a previously unidentified serial killer . . .'

'The Jacko Vance story?' Wharton couldn't stop the snigger. 'We've all had a good laugh about that one.'

Tony's face tightened. 'You shouldn't have heard anything about it. Who let that out of the bag?'

'Nay, Doc, I'm not for dropping anybody else in it. Besides, you know there are no secrets in a nick. That were too good a joke to keep a secret. Jacko Vance, serial killer. It'll be the Queen Mum next!' He spluttered with laughter and clapped Tony indulgently on the shoulder. 'Face it, Doc, chances are you picked a wrong 'un when you co-opted the boyfriend. You don't need me to tell you that nine times out of ten we never end up looking beyond whoever the stiff's been shagging.' He raised a speculative eyebrow. 'Not to mention the person who finds the body.'

Tony snorted derisively. 'You'll be wasting your time if you try pinning it on Simon McNeill. He hasn't done this.'

Wharton turned to face Tony, pulling a Marlboro out of its pack with his teeth. He caught it in his lips and lit it with a throwaway lighter. 'I heard you lecture once, Doc,' he said. 'Over in Manchester. You said the best hunters were the ones who were most like the prey. Two sides of the same coin, you said. I reckon you were right. Only, one of your hunters has gone native on you.'

Jacko flapped a dismissive hand at his PA and hit a button on the remote control. His wife's face filled the king-size TV screen as she handed her audience over to the newsroom for the midday headlines. Still nothing. The longer the better, he couldn't help thinking. The less accurate the pathologist could be about the time of death, the further it could be distanced from the stupid cow's visit to his home. As he killed the TV picture and turned to the script in front of him, he wondered momentarily what it must be like to have the sort of life where no one would notice you'd been lying dead for a couple of days. It was never likely to happen to him, he thought, self-satisfied as ever. It had been a very long time since he'd been that insignificant in anyone's life.

Even his mother would have noticed if he'd disappeared. She might well have been delighted at the prospect, but she'd have at least noticed. He wondered how Donna Doyle's mother was reacting to the disappearance of her daughter. He'd seen nothing on the news, but there was no reason why she should cause more of a stir than any of the others.

He'd made them pay, all of them, for what had been done to him. He knew he couldn't take it out on the one who deserved it; it would be too obvious, the finger pointing straight at him. But he could find surrogate Jillies all over the place, looking just as ripe and delicious as she'd been when he'd first pinned her to the ground and felt her virginity surrender to his power. He could make them understand what he'd been through, feel what he'd felt in ways that the treacherous bitch had never comprehended. His girls could never abandon him; he was the one with power over life and death. And he could make them discharge her debt over and over again.

Once, he had believed that there would come an occasion when these surrogate deaths would have purged him for good. But the catharsis never lasted. Always, the need came creeping back.

Lucky he'd got it off to such a fine art, really. All those years, all those deaths, and only one off-the-wall maverick cop had ever suspected.

Jacko smiled a very private smile, one his fans never saw. The means of payment had had to be different for Shaz Bowman. But they'd been satisfying, nonetheless. It made him wonder if it might not be the time to ring a few changes.

It never did to become a slave to routine.

Frustration drove Tony up the stairs two at a time. No one would let him near Simon. Colin Wharton was stone-walling, claiming he didn't have the authority to allow Tony to collaborate on the investigation. Paul Bishop was out of the building at one of his interminable and ever-convenient meetings, and the Divisional Chief Superintendent was allegedly too busy to see Tony.

He threw open the door of the seminar room, expecting to see the four remaining members of his task force engaged in some meaningful activity. Instead, Carol Jordan looked up from the file of papers in front of her. 'I was beginning to think I'd got the day wrong,' she said.

'Ah, Carol,' Tony sighed, subsiding into the nearest chair. 'I completely forgot you were coming back this afternoon.'

'Looks like you weren't the only one,' she said drily, gesturing at the remaining empty seats. 'Where's the rest of the team? Playing truant?'

'Nobody's told you, have they?' Tony said, looking up at her with angry eyes in a pained face.

'What's happened?' she asked, her chest constricting. What had happened now to drill more anguish into him?

'You remember Shaz Bowman?'

Carol nodded with a rueful smile. 'Ambition on legs. Blazing blue eyes, uses her ears and mouth in the correct proportion of two to one.'

Tony winced. 'Not any more she doesn't.'

'What's happened to her?' The concern in Carol's voice was still more for Tony than for Shaz.

He swallowed and closed his eyes, summoning the picture of her death and forcing all emotion out of his voice. 'A psychopath happened to her. Somebody who thought it would be entertaining to gouge out those blazing blue eyes and chop off those wide-open ears and pour something so corrosive into that smart mouth that it ended up looking like multicoloured bubble gum. She's dead, Carol. Shaz Bowman is dead.'

Carol's face opened in incredulous horror. 'No,' she

217

breathed. She was silent for a long moment. 'That's terrible,' she finally said. 'So much life in her.'

'She was the best of the bunch. Desperate to be the best. And she wasn't arrogant with it. She could work with the others without making it obvious that she was the racehorse among the donkeys. What he did to her, it went straight to the heart of who she was.'

'Why?' As she had done so often in their previous case, Carol picked the important question.

'He left her with a computer print-out. A drawing and an encyclopaedia entry about the three wise monkeys,' Tony said.

Understanding flashed into Carol's eyes, followed swiftly by a confused frown. 'You don't seriously think ... That theory she came out with the other day? It can't be anything to do with that, can it?'

Tony rubbed his forehead with his fingertips. 'I keep coming back to it. What else is there? The only live case we've had anything to do with is your arsonist, and none of them came up with enough to threaten anyone.'

'But Jacko Vance?' Carol shook her head. 'Surely you can't believe that? Grannies from Land's End to John O'Groats dote on him. Half the women I know think he's as sexy as Sean Connery.'

'And you? What do you think?' Tony asked. There was no innuendo in the question.

Carol turned the question over in her mind, making sure she had the right words before she spoke. 'I wouldn't trust him,' she eventually said. 'He's too glossy. Non-stick. Nothing leaves a lasting impact. He'll be charming, sympathetic, warm, understanding. But as soon as he moves on to the next interview, it's like the previous encounter never happened. Having said that ...'

'You'd never have thought of him as a serial killer,' Tony said flatly. 'Me neither. There are some people in public life that you wouldn't feel overly surprised to see on a fistful of murder charges. Jacko Vance isn't one of them.'

They sat in silence facing each other across the room. 'It might not be him,' Carol said at last. 'What about somebody in his entourage? A driver, a minder, a researcher. One of those hangers-on, what do they call them?'

'Go-fers.'

'Yeah, go-fers, right.'

'But that still doesn't answer your question. Why?' Tony pushed himself to his feet and started pacing out the perimeter of the room. 'I don't see how anything she said in here could conceivably have made it into Jacko Vance's circles. So how did our theoretical killer know she was on to him?'

Carol swung round awkwardly in her chair so she could watch him as he crossed behind her. 'She wanted to be a glory girl, Tony. I don't think she was ready to let it drop. I think she decided to follow up her idea. And one way or another, she alerted the killer.'

Tony reached the corner and stopped. 'Do you know . . .' was all he had time for before the door opened on Detective Chief Superintendent Dougal McCormick. His bulky shoulders almost filled the frame.

An Aberdonian, he resembled one of the black Aberdeen Angus cattle from his native territory: black curls tumbling over a broad forehead, liquid dark eyes always on the lookout for the red rag, wide cheekbones seeming to drag his fleshy nose across his face, full lips always moist. The only incongruity was his voice. Where a deep roar should have rumbled in his chest, a melodious light tenor emerged. 'Dr Hill,' he said, closing the door behind him without looking at it. His eyes flickered in Carol's direction then looked a question at Tony.

'DCS McCormick, this is DCI Carol Jordan from the East Yorkshire force. We're helping her with an arson inquiry,' Tony said.

Carol stood up. 'Pleased to meet you, sir.'

McCormick's nod was almost imperceptible. 'If you'd excuse us, I need a moment with Dr Hill,' he said.

Carol knew when she was being dismissed. 'I'll wait down in the canteen.'

'Dr Hill won't be staying on the premises,' McCormick said. 'You'd do better to wait in the car park.'

Carol's eyes widened, but she simply said, 'Very well, sir. I'll see you outside, Tony.'

As soon as Carol had closed the door behind her, Tony rounded on McCormick. 'And what exactly do you mean by that, Mr McCormick?'

'What I said. This is my division and I'm running a murder inquiry. A police officer has been . . . destroyed, and it's my job to find out who's responsible. There's no sign of forcible entry in Sharon Bowman's flat and, by all accounts, she was no fool. So the chances are she knew her killer. And as far as I know at this point in time, the only people Sharon Bowman knew in Leeds were her fellow officers in the task force, and you, Dr Hill.'

'Shaz,' Tony interrupted. 'She hated being called Sharon. Shaz, that's what she was called.'

'Shaz, Sharon, whatever, it makes little difference now.' McCormick brushed the objection aside with all the casual grace of a bull flicking its tail at a fly. 'The point is that you people are the only ones she'd have let in. So I don't want you talking to each other until my murder squad officers have had a chance to interview each and every one of you. Until further notice, this task force is suspended. You will not be authorized to occupy police premises and you are not to communicate with each other. I've already discussed this with Commander Bishop and the Home Office, and we're all agreed that's the appropriate path to go down. Is that clear?'

Tony shook his head. It was all too much. Shaz was dead, horribly dead. And now McCormick wanted to arrest one of the handful of people who might actually be able to provide a way through to her killer. 'You might, by some stretch of the imagination, have authority over the officers in my squad. But I'm not a police officer, McCormick. I don't answer to you. You should be using our talents, not pissing on us. We can help, man, can't you understand that?'

'Help?' McCormick's voice was scornful. 'Help? What were you planning on doing? I've heard some of the daft ideas your lot have come up with. My men are going to be chasing leads, not jokes. Jacko Vance, for heaven's sake. You'll be asking us to arrest Sooty next.'

'We're on the same side,' Tony said, smudges of scarlet rising across his cheekbones.

'Maybe so, but some kinds of help turn out to be more of a hindrance. I want you out of here now, and I don't want you bothering my men. You will report back to this station at ten tomorrow morning so that my officers can interview you formally about Sharon Bowman. Have I made myself clear, Dr Hill?'

'Listen, I can help you here. I understand killers; I know why they do the things they do.'

'It's not hard to work that out. They're sick in the head, that's why.'

'Granted, but they're all sick in the head in their own particular ways,' Tony said. 'This one, for example. I bet he didn't assault her sexually, did he?'

McCormick frowned. 'How did you know about that?'

Tony ran a hand through his hair and spoke passionately.

'I didn't know in the sense of being told. I know because I can read things in a crime scene that your men can't. This wasn't a run-of-the-mill sexual homicide, Superintendent, this was a deliberate message to us that this killer thinks he's so far ahead of us he's never going to be caught. I can help you catch him.'

'Sounds to me like you're more interested in covering up for your own,' McCormick said, shaking his head. 'You've picked up some information at the scene of the crime and turned it into some fancy theory. It'll take more than that to convince me. And I haven't got time to wait till you pick up the next bit of gossip. As far as this station's concerned, you're history. And your bosses at the Home Office agree with me.'

Fury drove Tony's normal tools of flattery and appeasement underground. 'You are making one hell of a mistake, McCormick,' he said, his voice rough with anger.

The big detective gave a snort of laughter, 'I'll take that risk, son.' He gestured with his thumb towards the door. 'Away you go, now.'

Realizing he couldn't win on this battleground, Tony bit down hard on the flesh of his cheek. The flavour of humiliation was the coppery taste of fresh blood. Defiantly, he walked over to his locker and pulled out his briefcase, filling it with the missing person files and the squad's analyses. Snapping the lock shut, he turned on his heel and walked out. On his way through the police station, officers fell silent as he passed. He was thankful that Carol wasn't there to witness his rout. She would never have been able to keep the silence that was his only remaining weapon.

As the front door swung shut behind him, he heard an unidentifiable voice behind him call out, 'Bloody good riddance.'

In a rare moment of lucidity in the ocean of pain, Donna Doyle contemplated her brief life and the foolish trust that had brought her to this place. Regret swelled inside her like a strange tumour, devouring everything it encountered. One mistake, one attempt to follow the rainbow to the pot of gold, one act of faith that was no more preposterous than the one the priest talked about every Sunday, and here she was. Once upon a time, she'd have said she'd do anything for a chance at stardom. Now she knew it wasn't true.

It wasn't fair. It wasn't as if she'd just wanted to be famous for herself. With the fame would have come money, so her mum wouldn't have had to scrimp and save and worry about every penny like she'd had to all the time since Dad had died. Donna had wanted it to be a surprise, a wonderful, wicked, exciting surprise. Now it would never happen. Even if she got out of here, she knew she wasn't going to be a star, not ever. She might be famous for fifteen minutes, like the song said, but not for being a one-armed TV star like Jacko Vance. Even if they found her, she was finished.

They could still find her, she told herself. She wasn't just whistling in the dark, she thought defiantly. They'd be looking for her by now, surely. Her mum would have gone to the police, her picture would be in the papers, maybe even on the telly. People all over the country would see her and search their memory. Somebody would remember her. There had been loads of people on the trains. Half a dozen other passengers had got off with her at Five Walls Halt. At least one of them *must* have noticed her. All dolled up in her best outfit, she knew she looked tasty. Surely the police would be asking questions, working out whose Land Rover she'd got into? Wouldn't they?

She groaned. In her heart, she knew this would be the last place she would lie. Alone in her tomb, Donna Doyle wept.

Tony sat hunched forward in the armchair, staring into the flickering gas flames of the fake hearth. He was still nursing the same glass of Theakston's he'd had since they'd arrived back at Carol's cottage. She'd refused to take no for an answer. He'd had a shock, he needed someone to discuss the case with, and she needed his input on her arsonist. She had a cat to feed, he had none, so logically their destination should be an hour down the motorway to the outskirts of Seaford.

Since they'd arrived, he'd said barely a word. He'd sat with his eyes on the fire and his mind projecting the film of Shaz Bowman's death. Carol had left him alone, taking the chance to throw together a packet of chicken breasts from the freezer, a couple of chopped onions and a jar of ready-made cider and apple sauce. She'd put the result into the oven with a couple of baking potatoes and left it on a low heat while she made up the guest bedroom. She knew there was little point in expecting anything more or less from Tony.

She poured herself a large gin and tonic, adding a couple of chunks of frozen lemon, and returned to the living room. Without saying anything, she tucked her legs under her and let the armchair opposite his swallow her up. Between them, Nelson lay stretched out like a long black hearth rug.

Tony looked up at Carol and managed a faint smile.

'Thanks for the peace and quiet,' he said. 'It has a very welcoming ambience, your cottage.'

'That's one of the reasons why I bought it. That and the view. I'm glad you like it.'

'I ... I keep imagining it,' he said. 'The process. Tying her up, gagging her. Torturing her with the knowledge that she wasn't going to get out of it alive, not knowing what she knew.'

'Whatever that was.'

He nodded. 'Whatever that was.'

'I suppose it brings it all back to you?' Carol said softly.

He let out a long breath. 'Inevitably,' he said through tight lips. He looked up at her, his keen eyes shining under the jut of his frowning eyebrows. When he spoke again, his voice was a brisk contrast, indicating he wanted to escape the memories that were sometimes almost as bad as the experience itself. 'Carol, you're a detective. You heard Shaz's presentation, you were one of the ones who passed judgement on it. Imagine you'd been on the other end of our criticisms. Imagine you're back at the start of your career, with it all to prove. Don't think too hard about this. Give me your gut reaction. What would you do?'

'I'd want to prove you were wrong and I was right.'

'Yes, yes,' Tony acknowledged impatiently. 'That's a given. But what would you *do*? How would you go about it?'

Carol sipped her drink and considered. 'I know what I'd do now. I'd put a small team together – just a sergeant and a couple of DCs – and blitz every one of those cases. I'd go back and talk to friends, family. Check out whether the missing girls were Jacko Vance fans, whether they'd gone to the event he was appearing at. If they did, who they went with. What their companions noticed.'

'Shaz didn't have either the time or the team for that kind

of operation. Think back to what it was like when you were young and hungry,' Tony urged.

'As to what I'd have done then ... Given no resources, you have to fall back on your own assets.'

Tony gave her an encouraging nod. 'Meaning?'

'Smart mouth, fancy footwork. You know you're right, that's the bottom line. You know the truth is out there waiting for the proof to go round it. Me? I'd shake the tree and see what falls out.'

'So you'd do what, specifically?'

'These days, I'd probably drop some poison in the ear of a friendly journalist and plant a story that would mean something more to our killer than it would to the casual reader. But I haven't seen any signs that Shaz had those kind of contacts or, if she did, that she used them. What I'd probably have done in her shoes, if I'd had the bottle, would have been to set up a meeting with the man himself.'

Tony sat back in his chair and took a long swallow of beer. 'I'm glad you said that. It's the sort of idea I'm always reluctant to bring out into the open in case your lot starts laughing because no self-respecting police officer would dream of doing something so risky either to life or career.'

'You think she made contact with Jacko Vance?'

He nodded.

'And you think that whatever she said to him ...'

'Or to someone around him,' Tony interrupted. 'It might not be Vance. It might be his manager or his minder or even his wife. But yes, I think she said something to someone in that group of people and she made a killer afraid.'

'Whoever it was didn't waste much time.'

'He didn't waste time and he's clearly got a lot of nerve to kill her in her own living room. To risk a cry, a scream, the noise of furniture being knocked over, anything untoward in a house split into flats.'

Carol sipped her drink, savouring the growing edge of lemon as the frozen fruit thawed completely. 'And he had to get her there in the first place.'

Tony looked puzzled. 'What makes you say that?'

'She'd never have agreed to meet someone she suspected was a serial killer in her own home. Not even with the hubris of youth. That would be like inviting a fox into the henhouse. And if he turned up there later, after the official interview, she'd hit the panic button, not let him in. No, Tony, she was already his prisoner by the time she got home.'

It was such flashes of insight backed with impeccable logic that had made Carol Jordan such a joy to work with before, Tony remembered. 'You're right, of course. Thank you.' He toasted her mutely with his glass. Now he knew where to start. He finished his beer and said, 'Any chance of another one? Then I think we need to talk about your little problem.'

Carol uncurled herself from the chair and stretched like Nelson. 'You sure you don't want to talk some more about Shaz?' Tony's expression of distaste told her all she needed to know. She went through to the kitchen for another beer.

'I'll save it for your West Yorkshire colleagues tomorrow morning. If you haven't heard from me by teatime, you'd better make sure I've got a decent brief,' he called after her.

When she was settled again in the armchair, he dragged his brooding eyes away from the fire and pulled a couple of sheets of lined paper from his briefcase. 'At the tail end of the week, I got the squad to work on their idea of a profile for you. They had a day to work up an individual profile, then on Friday, they collaborated on a joint effort. I've got a copy of it with me, I'll show you later.'

'Terrific. I didn't want to say anything before, but I've been

228

working on a profile of my own. It'll be interesting to see how they compare.' She tried to keep her voice light, but Tony heard the desire for his praise, nevertheless. It made what he had to say all the more awkward. Sometimes he wished he smoked. It would give him something to do with his hands and mouth at times like this.

Instead, he ran a hand over his face. 'Carol, I have to tell you that I suspect you've all been wasting your time.'

Unconsciously, her chin jutted forward. 'Meaning what?' The words were more aggressive than the tone.

'Meaning that I don't think your fires fit into any known category.'

'You mean they're not arson?'

Before he could answer, a heavy knock reverberated through the cottage. Startled, Carol spilled a few drops of her drink. 'Are you expecting visitors?' Tony asked, turning to the dark window behind him to see if anything penetrated the darkness outside.

'No,' she said, jumping to her feet and moving across the room to the heavy wooden door that opened into the small stone porch. As she unlatched the door, a chill gust of wind filled the room with a cold waft of estuary silt. Carol looked surprised. Beyond her, Tony glimpsed the outline of a large male shape. 'Jim,' she exclaimed. 'I wasn't expecting you.'

'I tried to ring you this afternoon and I kept getting the runaround from Sergeant Taylor. So I thought I might as well head on up here and see if I could run you to earth.' As Carol stepped back, Pendlebury followed her in. 'Oh, I'm sorry – you've got company.'

'No, your timing couldn't be better,' she said, waving him towards the fire. 'This is Dr Tony Hill from the Home Office. We're just talking about the arson case. Tony, this is Jim Pendlebury, the fire chief in Seaford.'

Tony ceded his hand into the bone-grinding grip of a competitive handshake. 'Pleased to meet you,' he said mildly, refusing the invitation to joust.

'Tony is in charge of the new National Offender Profiling Task Force in Leeds,' Carol said.

'Tough job.' Pendlebury thrust his hands into the deep pockets of the fashionably oversized mac he was wearing. They emerged with a bottle of Australian Shiraz on the end of each. 'Housewarming present. Now we can all discuss our firebug with a bit of lubrication.'

Carol fetched glasses and corkscrew and poured wine for herself and Pendlebury, Tony waving his glass to indicate he'd stick with the beer. 'So, Tony, what have your baby boffins got to tell us?' Pendlebury asked, stretching his long legs out in front of him, forcing Nelson to move to one side. The cat gave him a malevolent glare and curled into a ball beside Carol's chair.

'Nothing Carol couldn't work out for herself, I imagine. The problem is that I suspect what they've done is irrelevant.'

Pendlebury's laugh sounded too loud in the confines of the cottage. 'Am I hearing things?' he said. 'A profiler admitting it's all a load of bollocks? Carol, have you got the tape running?'

Wondering how many more times he would have to smile politely while his life's work was denigrated, Tony let Pendlebury wind down before he spoke. 'Would you use a screwdriver to drive a fence post into the ground?'

Pendlebury cocked his head to one side. 'You're saying profiling is the wrong tool for the job?'

'That's exactly what I'm saying. Profiling works on certain crimes where the motivation is psychopathic to some degree.'

'Meaning?' Pendlebury asked, drawing his legs up and leaning forward, his interest wholly engaged, his face sceptical.

'Do you want the thirty-second version or the full lecture?'

'You'd better give me the idiot's guide, me being a mere fireman.'

Tony ran a hand through his thick dark hair, a reflex that always left him looking like a cartoon mad scientist. 'OK. Most crimes in this country are committed either for gain or in the heat of the moment, or under the influence of drink or drugs. Or a combination of all of the above. The crime is a means to an end – acquiring cash or drugs, gaining revenge, putting a halt to unacceptable behaviour.

'A handful of crimes have their roots in stranger soil. They grow from an inner psychological compulsion on the part of the criminal. Something drives him – and it's almost always a him – to perform certain acts that are an end in themselves. The criminal act can be as petty as stealing women's underwear from washing lines. It can be as serious as serial murder. Serial arson is one such crime.

'And if what we were dealing with here was serial arson, I'd be the first to defend the value of a psychological profile. But as I was saying to Carol just before you arrived, I don't think you've got your common or garden thrill-seeking firebug in Seaford. It's not a torch for hire either. What you've got here is a beast of a different colour altogether. More of a hybrid.'

Pendlebury looked unconvinced. 'Want to tell us what you mean by that?'

'I'd be happy to,' Tony said, leaning back and cradling his glass in his linked fingers. 'Let's eliminate the hired arsonist for a start. While it's true that a handful of the fires have probably been an answer to the building owner's prayers, in the vast majority of cases, there seems to be no financial gain. Mostly, we're looking at massive inconvenience and, in a few cases, positive damage to the businesses or sections of the community affected. They're not grudge fires either – different insurance companies, no reason why anyone would have it in for such a wide spectrum of buildings. There's no common link at all, except that the fires were all set at night and up until the last one, they took place in deserted premises. So, no reason to think there is a professional torch for hire behind the blazes. Agreed?'

Carol bent over to pick up the wine and refill her glass. 'You'll get no argument from me.'

'What if there was a mixture of motives behind the hiring? What if he was hired sometimes for gain, sometimes for grudge?' Pendlebury stubbornly asked.

'Still leaves too many unaccounted for,' Carol said. 'My team ruled out a torch for hire almost from the start. So, Tony, why isn't it some emotional retard doing it for kicks?'

'I could be wrong,' he said.

'Oh, yeah. Your track record is littered with mistakes,' Carol said ironically.

'Thank you. Here's why I don't think it's some nutter. All these fires have been carefully set. In most cases, there have been almost no forensic traces, just the identification of the seat of the fire and some indication of lighter fuel and ignition trails. Mostly there's no sign of forced entry either. If there hadn't been such a spate of these fires over a relatively short period of time, chances are most of them would have been written off as accidents or carelessness. That would point to a professional torch, except that we've already written that off for other reasons.' He picked up the papers he'd dropped by his chair earlier and gave his notes a quick glance.

'So we've got someone who's controlled and organized,

which firebugs almost never are. He brings stuff with him and also uses available materials. He knows what he's doing, yet there's no sign of him having graduated to this from small-scale fires in rubbish tips, garden sheds, building sites.

'Then you've got to consider that most firebugs are sexually motivated. When they set fires, they often masturbate or urinate or defecate at the sites. There have been no traces of that, nor of any pornographic materials. If he doesn't wank at the fire site, he probably does it at the vantage point where he watches the fire from. Again, there are no reports from outraged members of the public of anyone exposing themselves in the vicinities of the fires. So, another negative.'

'What about timing?' Carol interrupted. 'He's doing it more often than he was when he started out. Isn't that typical of a serial offender?'

'Yeah, it's in all the books about serial killers,' Pendlebury added.

'It's less true of firebugs,' Tony said. 'Especially the ones who go in for the more serious arson attacks like this. The gaps are unpredictable. They can go weeks, months or even years without a big blaze. But within the series, you do get sprees, so yes, the timing of these fires might support the idea that you're looking at a serial offender. But I'm not trying to suggest that these fires are the work of several individuals. I think it's one person. I just don't believe he's a thrill seeker.'

'So what are you saying?' Carol said.

'Whoever is setting these fires is not a psychopath. I believe he has a conventional criminal motive for what he's doing.'

'So what is this so-called motive?' Pendlebury asked suspiciously.

'That's what we don't know yet.'

Pendlebury snorted. 'Minor detail.'

'Actually, in a sense it is, Jim,' Carol chipped in. 'Because once we've established that it's not a psychopath operating on unique and personal logic, we should be able to apply reasoning to uncover what's behind the fires. And once we've done that ... well, it's just a matter of solid coppering.'

A look of disgruntled annoyance had settled over Jim Pendlebury's face like an occluded cold front on the weather map. 'Well, I can't think of any reason for setting these fires unless you get a kick out of them.'

'Oh, I don't know,' Tony said casually, starting almost to enjoy himself.

'Share it then, Sherlock,' Carol urged him.

'Could be a security firm coming round in the wake of the fires offering cut-rate night watchmen. Could be a fire-alarm or sprinkler-system company facing hard times. Or ...' his voice tailed off and he cast a look of speculation at the fire chief.

'What?'

'Jim, do you employ any part-time firemen?'

Pendlebury looked horrified. Then he took in the half-smile twitching the corner of Tony's mouth and misread it completely. The fire chief visibly relaxed and grinned. 'You're at the wind-up,' he said, wagging a finger at Tony.

'If you say so,' Tony said. 'But do you? Just as a matter of curiosity?'

The fireman's eyes showed uncertainty and suspicion. 'We do, yes.'

'Maybe tomorrow you could let me have their names?' Carol asked.

Pendlebury's head thrust forward and he stared intently into Carol's closed face. His broad shoulders seemed to expand as he clenched his fists. 'My God,' he said wonderingly. 'You really mean it, don't you, Carol?'

'We can't afford to ignore any possibilities,' she said calmly. 'This is not personal, Jim. But Tony has opened up a valid line of inquiry. I'd be derelict in my duty if I didn't follow it through.'

'Derelict in your duty?' Pendlebury got to his feet. 'If my fire crews were derelict in their duty, there wouldn't be a building in this city left standing. My people put their lives on the line every time this nutter has a night on the town. And you sit there and suggest one of them might be behind it?'

Carol stood up and faced him. 'I'd feel just the same if it was a question of a bent copper. No one's accusing anyone at this stage. I've worked with Tony before, and I'd stake my career that he doesn't make mischievous or ill-considered suggestions. Why don't you sit down and have another glass of wine?' She put a hand on his arm and smiled. 'Come on, there's no need for us to fall out.'

Slowly Pendlebury relaxed and gingerly lowered himself back into his chair. He allowed Carol to top up his glass and even managed a half-smile at Tony. 'I'm very protective of my officers,' he said.

Tony, impressed at Carol's smooth handling of a potentially explosive situation, had shrugged. 'They're lucky to have you,' was all he said.

Somehow, the three of them managed to shift the conversation on to the more neutral territory of how Carol was settling in at East Yorkshire. The fire chief slipped into professional Yorkshireman mode, keeping everyone happy with a series of anecdotes. For Tony, it was a blessed rescue from thoughts of Shaz Bowman's last hours.

Later, in the small hours and the loneliness of Carol's spare room, there was no distraction to damp down the flames of imagination. As he pushed away the nightmare vision of her distorted and devastated face, he promised Shaz Bowman that he would expose the man who had done this to her. No matter what the price.

And Tony Hill was a man who knew all about paying the ferryman.

Jacko Vance sat in his soundproofed and electronically shielded projection room at the top of the house, behind locked doors. Obsessively, he replayed the tape he'd spliced together from his recordings of the late evening news bulletins on a variety of channels, terrestrial and satellite. What they all had in common was the news of Shaz Bowman's death. Her blue eyes blazed at him again from the screen time after time, an exciting contrast to his last memory of her.

They wouldn't be showing pictures of her like that. Not even after the watershed. Not even with an X-certificate.

He wondered how Donna Doyle was feeling. There had been nothing on TV about her. They all thought they had star quality, but the truth was none of them raised the faintest flicker of interest in anyone except him. For him, they were perfect, the ultimate representation of his ideal woman. He loved their pliancy, their willingness to believe exactly what he wanted them to believe. And the perfection of the moment when they realized this encounter was not about sex and fame but pain and death. He loved that look in their eyes.

When he saw that translation from adoration to alarm, their faces seemed to lose all individuality. They no longer merely resembled Jillie, they became her. It made the punishment so easy and so perfectly right.

What also made it appropriate was the unfairness. Almost all of his girls spoke about their families with affection. It might be shrouded behind a veil of adolescent frustration and exasperation, but it was obvious as he listened to them that their mothers or fathers or siblings cared about them even though their sluttish readiness to do whatever he wanted demonstrated they didn't merit that concern. He'd deserved their lives, and what had he got?

Anger surged through him, but like a thermostat, self-control cut in and tamped the fires down. This was not an appropriate time or place for that energy, he reminded himself. His anger could be channelled in a variety of useful directions; ranting pointlessly about what he had been deprived of wasn't one of them.

He took a series of deep breaths and forced his emotions into another mould. Satisfaction. That's what he ought to be feeling. Satisfaction at a job well done, a danger neutralized.

> *Little Jack Horner*
> *Sat in the corner*
> *Eating his pudding and pie.*
> *He put in his thumb*
> *And pulled out a plum*
> *And said, 'What a good boy am I!'*

Vance giggled softly. He'd put in his thumbs and pulled out the glistening plum of Shaz Bowman's eyes and felt the silent scream vibrating in his very core. It had been easier than he'd expected. It took surprisingly little force to pop an eye free from its roots.

The only pity of it was that you couldn't then see her expression when you poured the acid in or sliced the ears off. He didn't anticipate any need for there to be a next time, but if there were, he'd have to think carefully about the order of the ceremony.

Sighing with satisfaction, he rewound the tape.

*   *   *

If Micky hadn't been such a purist about her morning routine, they might have heard about Shaz's death on the radio news or seen it on satellite TV. But Micky insisted on no exposure to the day's news until she was behind the closed door of her office at the studios. So they breakfasted to Mozart and drove in to Wagner. No one from the programme was ever foolish enough to thrust a tabloid at Micky as she strode from car parking slot to her desk. Not twice, anyway.

So, because their early morning start forced them to bed before the late bulletins that had alerted Jacko, it was Betsy who had the first shock of recognition at Shaz's picture. Even dulled by newsprint, her blue eyes were still the first thing that demanded notice. 'My God,' Betsy breathed, moving round behind Micky's desk the better to examine the front pages.

'What is it?' Micky said without pausing in the habitual process of removing her jacket, placing it on a hanger and checking it critically for creases.

'Look, Micky.' Betsy thrust the *Daily Mail* towards her. 'Isn't that the policewoman who came to the house on Saturday? Just as we were leaving?'

Micky registered the thick black type before she took in the photograph. SLAUGHTERED, it read. Her eyes moved to Shaz Bowman's smiling face underneath the peak of a Metropolitan Police cap. 'There can't be two of them,' she said. She sat down heavily on one of the visitors' armchairs that faced her desk and read the melodramatic copy that provided Shaz's epitaph. Words like 'nightmare', 'gory', 'blood-soaked', 'agony' and 'gruesome' leapt out to ambush her. She felt strangely queasy.

In a television career that had spanned war zones, massacres and individual tragedy, no one in Micky's life had ever been touched personally by any of the catastrophes she had reported. Even a connection as tangential as hers to Shaz Bowman was all the more shocking because it had no precedent. 'Jesus,' she said, stretching the syllables. She looked up at Betsy, who read the shock in her face. 'She was in our house on Saturday morning. According to this, they think she was murdered late Saturday or early Sunday. We spoke to her. And within hours, she was dead. What are we going to do, Bets?'

Betsy moved round the desk and crouched beside Micky, hands flat on her thighs, staring up into her face. 'We're going to do nothing,' she said. 'It's not up to us to do anything. She came to see Jacko, not us. She's nothing to do with us.'

Micky looked appalled. 'We can't do *nothing*,' she protested. 'Whoever killed her, they must have hooked up with her after she left our house. At the very least, it lets the police know she was alive and well and walking around of her own free will in London on Saturday morning. We can't ignore it, Bets.'

'Sweetheart, take a deep breath and think about what you're saying. This isn't any old murder victim. She was a police officer. That means her colleagues are not going to be satisfied with a one-page statement saying she came to the house and we left. They're going to be stripping our lives down to the bone, on the off chance that there's something there they should know about. You know and I know that we just won't stand up to that kind of scrutiny. I say, leave it to Jacko. I'll give him a call and tell him to say we'd gone before she arrived. It's simplest that way.'

Micky pushed herself back violently. The chair slid along the carpet and Betsy almost toppled forward. Micky jumped to her feet and started pacing agitatedly. 'And what happens if they start questioning the neighbours and there's some nosy old biddy who remembers DC Bowman arriving and then us leaving? Anyway, I was the one who spoke to her in the first place. I made the appointment. What if she jotted that down in her notebook? What if she even taped the call, for God's sake? I can't believe you think we should just shut up about it.'

Betsy struggled to her feet, her chin tipped back to reveal a stubborn set to her firm jaw. 'If you'd stop being such a bloody drama queen, you'd see I'm talking sense,' she said in a low, angry voice. She'd spent too long providing the advice that Micky routinely acted upon to abandon the role now it had become so crucial. 'No good will come of it,' she added ominously.

Micky stopped by the desk and picked up the phone. 'I'm ringing Jacko,' she said, glancing at her watch. 'He won't be up yet. At least I can break the news more gently than the tabloids.'

'Good. Maybe he'll talk some sense into you,' Betsy said caustically.

'I'm not calling for permission, Betsy. I'm calling to tell him I'm about to phone the police.' As she punched in her husband's private number, Micky looked sadly at her lover. 'God, I can't believe you're running so scared that you'd kid yourself you can walk away from doing the right thing.'

'It's called love,' Betsy said bitterly, turning away to hide the tears of anger and humiliation that had sprung without warning.

'No, Betsy. It's called fear . . . Hello, Jacko? It's me. Listen, I've got some terrible news for you . . .'

Betsy turned her head and watched Micky's mobile face with its frame of silky blonde hair. It was a sight that had given her pleasure beyond dreams of avarice over the years. All she felt now was an unreasonable, unfathomable sense of impending disaster.

*   *   *

Jacko leaned back on his pillows and considered what he'd just heard. He'd been in two minds whether to call the police himself. On the one hand, it argued for his innocence, since, for all he knew, nobody outside his household knew DC Bowman had been anywhere near him. On the other hand, it made him look a little too eager to be involved in a high-profile murder inquiry. And one of the things everyone who had read a book on psychopathic killers knew was that the murderer often tried to insert himself into the investigation.

Leaving it to Micky was somehow much safer. It demonstrated his innocence at second hand; she was his devoted wife, crammed with public probity and therefore to be trusted in her account of events. He knew it was safe to assume she'd go straight to the police as soon as she saw Shaz's picture, which would be well before his normal rising time, so there would be no question of him having known and said nothing. Because, of course, officer, he'd been too busy to watch the evening news the previous day. Why, sometimes he barely had time to watch his own show, never mind his wife's!

What he had to do now was to work out his strategy. There would be no question of him having to schlepp up to Leeds to talk to the investigating plods; the police would come to him, he felt sure. If he was proved wrong, he wouldn't call in any favours just yet. He'd play along, the magnanimous man with nothing to hide. Of course you can have an autograph for your wife, officer.

The important thing now was to plan. Imagine every contingency and work out in advance how best to deal with it. Planning was the secret of his success. It was a lesson he'd almost had to learn the hard way. The first time, he'd not really worked out the eventualities ahead of time. He'd been intoxicated by the possibilities he saw opening in front of him, and he'd not realized how necessary it was to project all the conceivable outcomes and work out how to deal with them. He'd not had the Northumberland cottage then, relying foolishly on a tumbledown walkers' hut that he remembered from hill-walking expeditions in his youth.

He'd thought no one would be using the place in the dead of winter and knew he could drive right up to it on an old drovers' track. Because he dared not leave her alive, he'd had to finish her off the night he'd taken her there. But it had been almost dawn by the time she'd taken her last breath. Shaken and exhausted by the effort of confining her, carrying the heavy vice that would crush her arm to a bloody pulp, then killing her with a wicked ligature made from a guitar string (symbolic, if he'd but considered it, of another of the accomplishments he'd lost), the planned burial had been beyond him. He decided to leave her where she was and come back the following night to deal with the carcass.

Jacko sucked his breath in at the memory. He'd been on the main road, only a couple of miles from the turn-off to the track, when the local news bulletin announced that the body of a young woman had been discovered by a group of ramblers within the past hour. The shock had nearly sent the Land Rover off the road.

Somehow, he'd controlled himself and driven home in a lather of clammy sweat. Amazingly, he hadn't left sufficient forensic traces for there to be any trail leading back to him. He was never questioned. As far as he knew, he was never even considered. The previous connection was so minimal as to be insignificant.

He'd learned three crucial things from that experience. Firstly, he needed to find a way to make it last so he could savour her suffering as she went through what he'd endured.

Secondly, he didn't actually enjoy the act of killing. He liked what led up to it, the agony and the terror, and he loved the sense of control that having been responsible for taking a life gave him, but despatching a strong, healthy young woman was no fun. Far too much like hard work, he had decided. He didn't much mind whether they died of septicaemia or despair, he preferred it when he didn't have to do it himself.

And thirdly, he needed a place of safety, both metaphorically and literally. Micky, Northumberland and the voluntary work with the terminally ill had been the tripartite answer. For the six months it had taken to put that answer together, he'd simply had to be patient. It hadn't been easy, but it had made the next one all the more sweet.

He wasn't about to give up on that sweet and secret pleasure just because Shaz Bowman had thought she was smarter than him. All it would take was a little bit of planning.

Jacko closed his eyes and considered.

Carol took a deep breath and knocked on the door. A familiar voice told her to come in and she walked into Jim Pendlebury's office as if there had never been a moment's tension between them. 'Morning, Jim,' she said briskly.

'Carol,' he said. 'Come with some news for me?'

She sat down opposite him, shaking her head. 'I've come for the list of part-time firemen we spoke about last night.'

His eyes widened. 'You're not still entertaining that daft idea in the cold light of morning?' he said scornfully. 'I thought you must just be humouring your guest.'

'When it comes to criminal investigation, I'd back Tony Hill's ideas over yours any time.'

'You expect me to sit back and help you turn my men into

scapegoats?' he said, his voice low. 'When they're the ones who stand at risk every time we get a call-out?'

Carol sighed in vexation. 'I'm trying to put an end to that risk. Not just for your firefighters, but for the poor sods like Tim Coughlan who don't even know they're taking a chance. Don't you understand that? This isn't a witch-hunt. I'm not out to frame the innocent. If you think that's what I'm about, then you certainly don't know enough about me to have the right to turn up at my home unannounced and uninvited and expect to cross the threshold ever again.'

Long seconds dragged past while they stared each other down. Finally, Pendlebury shook his head in resignation, his mouth a thin line. 'I'll give you the list,' he said, loathing every word. 'But you won't find your arsonist on it.'

'I hope not,' she said calmly. 'I know you don't believe me, but I don't want this to be one of yours, any more than I enjoy the prospect of uncovering police corruption. It undermines all of us. But I can't ignore the possibility now it's been pointed out to me so convincingly.'

He turned away and walked his chair over to a filing cabinet. He pulled out the bottom drawer and took out a sheet of paper. With a flick of the wrist, he floated it across the desk to her. All it contained were the names, addresses and telephone numbers of Seaford's twelve part-time fire officers.

'Thank you,' Carol said. 'I appreciate this.' She half-turned to go, then looked back as if struck by an afterthought. 'One thing, Jim. These fires. Do they all come under one division or are they more spread out?'

He pursed his lips. 'They're all on Seaford Central's patch. If they hadn't been, you wouldn't be walking out the door with that bit of paper.'

It confirmed what she'd already thought. 'I figured it might be something like that,' she said, her voice offering armistice. 'Believe me, Jim, there'd be nobody happier than me if all your lads check out.'

He looked away. 'They will do. I know those lads. I've trusted my life to them. Your psychologist – he knows nothing about it.'

Carol walked to the door. As she opened it, she looked back. He was staring intensely at her. 'We'll see, Jim.'

The steel-capped heels of her brown boots clattered on the stairs as she ran down to the anonymous security of her car. The pain of Jim Pendlebury's conviction that she would scapegoat a fellow member of the emergency services cut deep. 'Damn it,' Carol said, slamming the door closed behind her and jabbing the key angrily at the ignition. 'Damn it all to hell.'

Working on the principle that any psychologist worth his salt would see straight through any attempts at manipulation, they'd clearly decided to dispense with finesse. They had, however, paid Tony the compliment of rank. Detective Chief Superintendent McCormick and Detective Inspector Colin Wharton rubbed shoulders at the narrow table in the inter-view room. The tape was running. They hadn't even bothered with the spurious reassurance that it was for his benefit.

They'd run through the discovery of the body first, their questions clearly directed at tripping him up in his assertion that he'd never been to Shaz's flat before and had no idea which windows were hers. Now they were moving into areas for which there was less obvious justification. Tony was not unprepared. He'd fully expected to be given a hard time. For one thing, he wasn't actually a cop, so if they were looking for a scapegoat, he'd be a preferable choice to one of his team. Add to that the local force's resentment at having to hand over space and resources to a bunch of outsiders led by a Home Office boffin they regarded as one step away from a leader of Satanic rituals, and he was inevitably on a hiding to nothing. With this in mind, he'd been running alternative scenarios on the projection screen inside his head almost before his eyes had opened. Concern about the interview had preoccupied him through breakfast, in spite of Carol's best efforts to reassure him that it would be no more than routine.

On the train back to Leeds he had stared out of the window without registering anything except that he had to find a way to convince his interrogators that they should be looking outside Shaz's circle of friends and colleagues for whoever had done this to her. Now he was faced with the reality, he wished he'd caught a train to London instead. Already the muscles in his shoulders were cramped into tight knots. He could actually feel the creeping rigidity climbing up the back of his neck and into his scalp. He was going to have one hell of a headache.

'Take us right back to the beginning,' McCormick said brusquely.

'When did you first meet DC Bowman?' Wharton demanded. At least they weren't playing 'nice cop, nasty cop'. They were both comfortably displaying their true colours as oppressive aggressors.

'Commander Bishop and I interviewed her in London about eight weeks ago. The exact date is in our office diary.' His voice was blank and even, kept so by willpower alone. Only a Voice Stress Analyser could have detected the micro-tremors skittering beneath the surface. Luckily for Tony, the technology hadn't penetrated that far.

'You interviewed her together?' McCormick with the question this time.

'Yes. Following the interview, Commander Bishop withdrew and I administered some psychological tests. Then DC Bowman left and I did not see her again until the start of the task force's training period.'

'How long were you alone with Bowman?' McCormick again. Wharton was leaning back in his seat, fixing Tony with a professional blend of speculation, contempt and suspicion.

'It takes about an hour to carry out the tests.'

'Long enough to get to know somebody, then.'

Tony shook his head. 'There's no time for casual conversation. In fact, that would be counterproductive. We were aiming to keep the selection process as objective as possible.'

'And the decision to take Bowman on the squad was unanimous?'

Tony hesitated for a moment. If they hadn't already talked to Paul Bishop, they would. There was no point in any diversion from the truth. 'Paul had some reservations. He thought she was too intense. I argued that we needed some diversity on the team. So he agreed to Shaz and I conceded on one of his choices that I was less enthusiastic about.'

'Which one was that?' McCormick asked.

Tony was too smart to walk into that one. 'You'd better ask Paul about that.'

Wharton suddenly leaned forward, thrusting his heavy blunt features towards Tony. 'Find her attractive, did you?'

'What kind of question is that?'

'About as straightforward as you can get. Yes or no. Did you find the lass attractive? Did you fancy her?'

Tony paused momentarily, assembling his careful response. 'I registered that her looks would have made her appealing to a lot of men, yes. I was not myself sexually attracted to her.'

Wharton sneered. 'How could you tell? From what I've heard, you don't respond like most red-blooded blokes, do you?'

Tony flinched as if he'd been struck. A tremor ran through his taut muscles and his stomach grew turbulent. The inquiry that had inevitably followed the case he'd worked with Carol Jordan the year before had had to be told of his sexual problems. He had been promised absolute confidentiality, and if the reactions of the police officers he had encountered since were anything to go by, he had been granted that. Now, overnight, Shaz Bowman's death seemed to have stripped him of that right. He wondered momentarily where they'd gained their information, hoping this didn't mean his impotence would now be common gossip. 'My relationship with Shaz Bowman was purely professional,' he said, forcing his voice to stay calm. 'My personal life has nothing to do with this inquiry whatsoever.'

'That's for us to decide,' McCormick stated baldly.

Without pausing, Wharton continued. 'You say your relationship was purely professional. But we have statements that indicate you spent more time with Bowman than you did with other members of the squad. Officers would arrive of a morning to find the two of you deep in conversation. She would stay behind at the end of group sessions for a word in private. A very close relationship seems to have sprung up between you.'

'There was nothing untoward between Shaz and me. I've always been an early starter in the morning. Check it out with anyone who's ever worked with me. Shaz was having some problems mastering the computer software we're using so she came in beforehand to put in some extra time. And yes, she did stay behind after group sessions with questions, but that was because she was fascinated with the work, not for any seedy ulterior motive. If your murder inquiry had taught you anything at all about Shaz Bowman, you'd know the only thing she was in love with was the Job.' He took a deep breath.

There was a long moment's silence. Then McCormick said, 'Where were you on Saturday?'

Tony shook his head, mystified. 'You're wasting your time with this. You should be using us to catch the killer, not trying to make it look like one of us is guilty. We should be talking about the meaning of what this killer did to Shaz, why he left the picture of the three wise monkeys on the body, why there was no sexual interference with the body nor any forensic traces.'

McCormick's eyes narrowed. 'I'm interested that you're so definite about the absence of forensic traces. Now how would you happen to know that?'

Tony groaned. 'I don't *know* it. But I did see the body and the scene of crime. From my experience of psychopathic killers, I reckoned it was the most likely scenario.'

'A police officer or someone who works closely with the police would recognize the significance of forensic evidence,' McCormick said cannily.

'Everybody who has a TV set or who can read recognizes the significance of forensic evidence,' Tony countered.

'But they don't all know how to erase all traces of their presence like people who are accustomed to watching SOCOs avoiding the contamination of evidence at a crime scene, do they?'

'So you're saying there was no forensic evidence?' Tony challenged, latching on to the one piece of information that seemed significant.

'I didn't say that, no,' McCormick retorted triumphantly. 'Whoever killed Sharon Bowman probably thinks they didn't leave a trace. But they'd be wrong.'

Tony's mind raced. It couldn't be finger or shoe prints; that would be completely at odds with the organized precision of this killer. It might be hairs or fibres. Hair would only be useful if they had a serious suspect to match it against. Fibres, on the other hand, could be tracked down by a forensic expert. He hoped West Yorkshire used the best. 'Good,' was all he said. McCormick scowled.

Wharton opened a folder and placed a sheet of paper in front of Tony. 'For the tape, I am showing Dr Hill a photostat of DC Bowman's diary for the week of her death. There are two entries for the day she was murdered. JV, nine thirty. And the letter T. I put it to you, Dr Hill, that you had arranged to meet Shaz Bowman on Saturday. That you did in fact meet her on Saturday.'

Tony ran a hand through his hair. The confirmation of Carol's idea that Shaz would have confronted Vance with what she knew gave him no satisfaction. 'Inspector, I made no such arrangement. The last time I saw Shaz alive was at the end of the working day on Friday. What I was doing on Saturday could not be less relevant to this inquiry.'

McCormick leaned forward and spoke softly. 'I'm not so sure about that. T for Tony. She could have been meeting you. She could have met you out of office hours away from the squad room, and the boyfriend could have found out about it and let it wind him up. Maybe he confronted her with it and she admitted she fancied you more than she fancied him?'

Tony's lip twitched in contempt. 'Is that the best you can come up with? That's pathetic, McCormick. I've had patients who came up with more credible fantasies. Surely you must recognize that the crucial thing here is the diary entry that says JV, nine thirty? Shaz may have *intended* talking to me after that interview, but she never made it. If you're interested in what the killer was doing on Saturday, you really should be checking out Jacko Vance and his entourage.' As soon as the name was out of his mouth, Tony knew he'd blown it. McCormick shook his head pityingly and Wharton jumped to his feet, his chair shrieking on the cheap vinyl flooring.

'Jacko Vance tries to *save* lives, not take them. You're the one with the track record here,' Wharton shouted. 'You've already killed somebody, haven't you, Dr Hill? And as you psychologists are always telling us, once the taboo's breached, it's gone for good. Once a killer . . . Fill in the blanks, Doctor. Fill in the fucking blanks.'

Tony closed his eyes. His chest hurt, as if a punch to the diaphragm had robbed him of air. All the progress he'd made over the past year was stripped away and again he smelled sweat and blood, felt them slick on his hands, heard the screams ripped from his own throat, tasted the Judas kiss. His eyes snapped open and he looked at Wharton and McCormick with a hatred he'd forgotten he was capable of. 'That's it,' he said, standing up. 'Next time you want to talk to me, you'll have to arrest me. And you'd better make sure my lawyer's on the premises when you do.'

Only his desire not to give them the satisfaction held him together as he marched out of the interview room, through the police station and out into the fresh air. No one made any move to stop him. He set off across the car park, desperate to make it to the street before his stomach lost its battle with breakfast. Just as he reached the kerb, a car pulled up beside him and the passenger window descended. Simon McNeill's dark head loomed towards him. 'Want a lift?'

Tony recoiled as if from a blow. 'No . . . I . . . No thanks.'

'Come on,' Simon urged. 'I've been waiting for you. They

kept me in half the night. They'll try and pin this on me given half a chance. We need to find out who killed Shaz before they decide it's time to make an arrest.'

Tony leaned into the car. 'Simon, listen very carefully to me. You're right that they want it to be one of us. I'm not sure they'd go so far as to manufacture evidence against anybody. But I don't intend to sit back and wait and see if that happens. I intend to find out who's behind this, and I can't have you along. It's dangerous enough going up against a man who's capable of what this guy did to Shaz. It'll be hard enough for me to watch my own back without having to watch yours as well. You might be a great detective, but when it comes to going head to head with psychopaths like this, you're an absolute beginner. So do us both a favour. Please. Go home. Deal with your loss. Don't try to be a hero, Simon. I don't want to bury another one of you.'

Simon looked as if he wanted to burst into tears and thump Tony. 'I'm not a child. I'm a trained detective. I've worked on murder squads. I cared about her. You can't shut me out. You can't stop me nailing this bastard.'

A long sigh. 'No, I can't. But Shaz was a trained detective. She'd worked on murders. She knew she was rattling a killer's cage. And she still got demolished. Not just killed, but annihilated. It's not conventional police methods that are going to sort this out, Simon. I've done this once before. Believe me, I know what it's like and I wouldn't wish it on another living soul. Go home, Simon.'

With a screech of rubber on asphalt, Simon's car streaked away from the kerb. Tony watched it take the next left far too fast, the rear spoiler fishtailing out of sight. He hoped it would be the biggest risk Simon had to take until Shaz's killer was dealt with. He knew a traffic accident would be the least of his own worries.

There was something to be said for delirium. When feverish sweat ran down her face and added another layer to the sour staleness that covered her sticky skin, it meant she could escape into hallucinations that were infinitely preferable to reality.

Donna Doyle lay huddled against the wall, holding on to the chimeras of childhood memory as if they could somehow save her. One year, her mum and dad had taken her to the Valentine Fair at Leeds. Candyfloss, hot dogs and onions, the blurry kaleidoscope of lights on the waltzer, the sparkling jeweller's window of the city spread beneath her from the top of the Ferris wheel as they swung gently in the cold night air, the neon glow of the fair like a carpet at their feet.

Her dad had won her a big teddy bear, electric pink fun fur with a goofy grin stitched across its white face. It had been the last present he'd given her before he died. It was all his fault, Donna thought, snivelling. If he hadn't gone and died, none of this would have happened. They wouldn't have been poor and she wouldn't have had to think about being a telly star, she could have listened to her mum and stuck in at school and gone to university.

Tears crept out of the corners of her eyes and she beat her left fist against the wall. 'I hate you,' she cried, screaming at the wavering image of a thin-faced man who had adored his daughter. 'I hate you, you bastard!'

At least the incoherent sobs tired her out, letting her consciousness slide mercifully from her again.

The brashness that characterized Leon's performance among his peers was gone. Instead, he was locked behind the blank insolent face he'd seen on too many young blacks, both in custody and on the street. His street. He might have the warrant card that said he was one of them, but he had enough smarts to know that the two Yorkshiremen sitting across the interview room table were still The Man.

'So, Leon,' Wharton was saying in seemingly expansive mode, 'what you're telling us squares with what we've already heard from DC Hallam. The pair of you met at four o'clock and went tenpin bowling. Then you went for a drink in the Cardigan Arms, after which you met Simon McNeill for a curry.' He smiled encouragingly.

'So neither of you two killed Shaz Bowman,' McCormick said. Leon had him figured for a racist, his pink slab of a face showing no rapport, his eyes hard and cold, his wet mouth permanently a mere twitch away from a sneer.

'None of us killed Shaz, man,' Leon said, deliberately drawing out the last word. 'She was one of us. Maybe we've not been a team for long, but we know how to stick together. You're wasting your time on us.'

'We've got to go through the motions, lad, you know that,' Wharton said. 'You're going to be a profiler, you know that over ninety per cent of murders are committed by families or lovers. Now, when Simon turned up, how did he seem?'

'I don't know what you mean.'

'OK. Did he seem agitated, wound up, in a state?'

Leon shook his head. 'None of that, no. He was a bit quiet, but I put that down to Shaz not being there. I reckoned he fancied her, and he was disappointed when she didn't show.'

'What made you think he fancied her?'

Leon spread his hands. 'Stuff. You know? The way he tried to impress her. The way he was always checking her out. The way he'd always be bringing her into the conversation. The way a man does when he's interested, know what I mean?'

'Did you think she was interested in him?'

'I don't reckon Shaz was too interested in anybody. Not in the shagging sense. She was too obsessed with the Job to be bothered with it, if you ask me. I don't think Simon was going to drop lucky and get his leg over. Not unless he had something she wanted bad, like the inside track on a serial killer.'

'Did he say he'd been round her house?' McCormick interjected.

'He never mentioned it, no. But you wouldn't, would you? I mean, if you thought a woman had just stood you up, you wouldn't be telling people about it. Not saying anything isn't strange behaviour. Saying something, setting yourself up for having the piss taken out of you all round the squad room, now that would be strange.' Leon lit a cigarette and gave McCormick the blank-eyed stare again.

'What was he wearing?' Wharton asked.

Leon frowned with the effort of recollection. 'Leather jacket, bottle green polo shirt, black jeans, black Docs.'

'Not a flannel shirt?'

Leon shook his head. 'Not when we met him. Why? You found some flannel fibres on her clothes?'

'Not her clothes,' Wharton said. 'We think she was –'

'I don't think we'll be going into details about the forensic evidence just now,' McCormick interrupted firmly. 'Weren't you worried when DC Bowman didn't show up for this big night out?'

Leon shrugged and blew out a stream of smoke. 'Not worried, no. Kay figured she'd got a better offer. Me, I thought she probably had her head in her computer, doing her homework.'

'Bit of a teacher's pet, was she?' Wharton asked, sympathy to the fore again.

'Nah. She was just a grafter, that's all. Look, shouldn't you be out there catching the bastard who did this, instead of wasting your time with us? You're not going to find her killer in the task force. We signed up to solve shit like this, not commit it, man.'

Wharton nodded. 'So the sooner we get this over, the better. We need your help here, Leon. You're a trained detective, but you've also got trained instincts, or else you wouldn't be on this task force. Give us the benefit of your insights. What do you make of Tony Hill? I mean, you do know that he didn't want you on the task force, don't you?'

Tony stared at the dark blue screen. McCormick and Wharton might have barred him from the task squad offices, but either they didn't know about the group's networked computer system or they had no idea how to exclude him from it. The set-up was straightforward. It had to be; the people using it were less computer literate than the average seven-year-old. All the PCs in the office were linked via a central processing and storage unit. A modem connection made it possible for any of the team who was working off site to plug straight into their personal data store as well as any of the general material that was available to everyone. For security reasons, they each had personal logins as well as individual passwords. The trainees had all been instructed to change their passwords weekly to avoid possible leaks. Whether any of them bothered was a moot point.

What none of the squad knew was that Tony had a list of every individual login. In effect, he could dial up the office computer and pretend to be any of them, with the machine none the wiser. Of course, without the password, he wouldn't get very far with the private material, but he'd be in the system.

As soon as he'd returned home from his interview, he'd switched on his home computer. First, he'd called up Shaz's application form and test responses, all scanned in as soon as she'd been accepted for the squad. He printed them out, along with the progress reports that both he and Paul Bishop had compiled.

Then he signed off as himself and signed in as Shaz. Now, the best part of two hours and a pot of coffee later, he was no further forward. He'd tried everything he could think of. SHAZ, SHARON, BOWMAN, ROBIN, HOOD, WILLIAM, TELL, ARCHER, AMBRIDGE ... He'd run through every character he could think of from the eponymous radio soap opera. He'd tried her parents' names, every town, city, institution and street name mentioned in her CV. He'd even attempted the obvious JACKO, VANCE and the less obvious MICKY, MORGAN. And still he was staring at a screen that said, 'Welcome to the National Offender Profiling Task Force. Please type in your password now: –'. The cursor had been flashing so long the only thing he could say with total certainty was that he had no epileptic tendencies.

He stood up and prowled round the room. He didn't have an idea to bless himself with. 'Enough,' he muttered in exasperation. He lifted his jacket from the chair where he'd thrown it and shrugged it on. A walk down to the shop for the evening paper, that might clear his head. 'Don't fool yourself,' he muttered as he opened his front door. 'You just want to see what those pillocks have told the latest press conference.'

He walked down the path bisecting two flower beds where grimy rose bushes fought a rearguard action against urban enemies both human and industrial. As he turned into the street, he noticed a couple of men in a nondescript saloon car opposite. One was scrambling out of the passenger seat to the accompaniment of the engine being over-enthusiastically started. Shocked, Tony recognized all the hallmarks of an amateurish stakeout. Surely they couldn't be wasting their human resources keeping tabs on him?

At the corner, he stopped to look in the window of Bric'n'Brac, a junk shop with sad pretensions. Its proud owner kept the glass clean, which allowed Tony to take a look over his shoulder and across the street. The man who'd jumped out of the car was over there, loitering by the bus stop, pretending to read the timetable. It was an activity that marked him out as a stranger more than almost anything else could have done; the locals knew the anarchic practices of the rival bus companies too well to regard the timetable as anything other than a bad joke.

Tony walked on to the corner. Under the cloak of crossing the road, he threw a look over his shoulder. The car had turned round and was creeping down his street about fifty yards behind him. There was no doubt about it. If these were the best the local force had to offer, Shaz Bowman's killer didn't have much to worry about.

Despairing of his supposed colleagues, Tony bought an

evening paper from the local newsagent and walked slowly home, reading as he went. At least the police weren't publicly saying anything to attract ridicule. In fact, they weren't saying anything much at all. Either they were playing things very close to their chest, or they had nothing to play with. He knew which he believed was the case.

Once inside, under the guise of drawing a curtain across to protect his computer screen from the bright sun, he checked for his watchers. They were both back in the car, parked in the same spot as before. What were they waiting for? What did they expect him to do?

If it wasn't so appalling in its potential consequences, it would be funny, he thought as he grabbed the phone and dialled Paul Bishop's mobile. When Bishop answered, Tony dived straight in. 'Paul? You're not going to believe this. McCormick and Wharton have got it into their heads that someone connected to the task force killed Shaz, since we're the only people up here she knew.'

'I know,' Bishop said, sounding depressed. 'But what can I do? It's their inquiry. If it makes you feel any better, I do know they've been in touch with her old division, asking them to check out if there were any villains down there who might have had enough of a grudge against her to follow her up here. So far, no joy. But her old CID sergeant has apparently been in touch to say she acted as intermediary to set up a meeting between Jacko Vance and Bowman on Saturday morning. It looks as if she was determined to pursue that wild idea of hers about the teenage girls.'

Tony let out a sigh of relief. 'Well, thank God for that. Now maybe they'll begin to take us seriously. I mean, they have to be asking at the very least why Vance hasn't come forward and revealed this himself, given that Shaz's picture has been all over the papers.'

'It's not quite that simple,' Bishop said. 'Vance's wife actually rang in within minutes of the other call to say Bowman had come to the house on Saturday morning. She said her husband hadn't seen the papers yet. So no one's actually hiding anything.'

'But they are at least going to talk to him?'

'I'm sure they will.'

'So they'll have to treat him as a suspect.'

Tony heard Bishop exhale. 'Who knows? The trouble is, Tony, I can make gentle suggestions, but I've no authority to stop them running this their own sweet way.'

'I was told that you'd agreed with them that the squad should effectively be suspended,' Tony pointed out. 'You didn't have to go along with that, surely.'

'Come on, Tony, you know how difficult the politics of the task force are. The Home Office is adamant that we don't cause problems on the ground. It was a small concession. The squad hasn't been disbanded. Nobody's being reassigned to their old units. We're just out of the operational loop until this case is either resolved or out of the headlines. Try and treat it like a sabbatical.'

Exasperated, Tony got to the initial point of his call. 'It's a pretty strange sabbatical that includes a stakeout straight out of the Keystone Cops on my doorstep.'

'You're joking?'

'I wish I was. I walked out of my interview with them this morning after they accused me of being their best bet because I'm already a killer. And now I've got Beavis and Butthead on my tail. This is intolerable, Paul.'

He could hear Bishop take a deep breath. 'I agree, but we're just going to have to roll with the punches until they get bored with us and start running a proper investigation.'

'I don't think so, Paul,' Tony said, his voice clipped and

authoritative. 'One of my team is dead and they won't let us help find out who killed her. They're quick enough to remind me that I'm not one of them, I'm an outsider. Well, that cuts both ways. If you can't persuade them to get out of my face, I will be holding a press conference of my own tomorrow. And I promise, you won't like it any more than Wharton and McCormick will. It's time to pull some strings, Paul.'

'I hear you, Tony,' Bishop sighed. 'Leave it with me.'

Tony dropped the phone back into its cradle and pulled the curtain back. He switched on his desk lamp and stood in front of the window staring mutinously out at his watchers. He reviewed the information Paul Bishop had given him and related it to what he had learned at the crime scene. This killer was angry because Shaz had stuck her nose into his business. That indicated that she had been right in her supposition that there was at large a serial killer of teenage girls. Something she had done had panicked the murderer into making her his next target. The only thing she had apparently done that was connected to her theory was to visit Jacko Vance within hours of her death.

He knew now that Shaz Bowman's killer could not be some crazed fan of Vance's. There was no way for even the most dedicated stalker to find out in the short interval before her murder who Shaz was or the reason for her visit to Vance's house.

He had to find out more about the encounter between Shaz and Vance. If the killer was one of his entourage, it was possible he'd been present. But if Vance had been alone when Shaz confronted him, the finger pointed only at him. Even if he'd picked up the phone the minute she'd left and reported her suspicions to someone else, there was no way such a third party could have picked up Shaz's trail, discovered where she lived, or persuaded her to open her door to him in the time available.

As he reached this conclusion, his watchers departed. Tony threw his jacket down and dropped like a stone into the chair facing the screen. It was a small victory, but it renewed his appetite for the struggle. Now he had to find the proof to demonstrate that Shaz had been right and it had killed her. What would Shaz Bowman have used as a password? A fictional hero? Warshawski and Scarpetta were too long. KINSEY, MILLHONE, MORSE, WEXFORD, DALZIEL, HOLMES, MARPLE, POIROT all failed. A fictional villain? MORIARTY, HANNIBAL, LECTER. Still nothing.

Normally, the sound of a car pulling up outside wouldn't have penetrated his concentration. But after the day he'd had, the stilling of the engine sounded louder than an alarm buzzer. He looked out and his heart sank again. The last three people he wanted to see piled out of a familiar scarlet Ford. Mob-handed, Leon Jackson, Kay Hallam and Simon McNeill crowded up the path, sheepishly acknowledging his scowl through the window. With a groan, he got up and unlocked the door, turning straight on his heel and walking back down the hall to his study.

They followed him, crowding into the small room and, without waiting to be asked, finding places to settle; Simon on the window sill, Leon leaning elegantly against a filing cupboard, Kay in the armchair in the opposite corner. Tony swivelled round in his chair and glared, trying not to acknowledge the resignation he felt. 'Now I understand why people confess to crimes they haven't committed,' he said, only half-joking. They were impressive in spite of their youth and their uncertainty.

'You wouldn't take me seriously, so I brought in reinforcements,' Simon said. He looked too pale to be conscious, Tony

263

registered, noticing for the first time a dusting of freckles across the bridge of his nose.

'That McCormick and Wharton, they've got it in for us,' Leon burst out. 'I've been in there all afternoon, with them doing kissy faces, "Come on, Leon, you can tell us what you really think about Tony Hill and Simon McNeill." Man, they are two sick fuckers, let me tell you. "McNeill fancied Bowman, but she was in love with Hill, so he killed her out of jealousy, what do you reckon? Or Hill wanted to get into Bowman's knickers but she was more interested in a date with McNeill and he killed her in a fit of jealous rage." More bullshit than a farmyard, made me sick.' He pulled his cigarettes out, then paused. 'Is this OK?'

Tony nodded, pointing to a lopsided Christmas cactus on a shelf. 'Just use the saucer.'

Kay leaned forward in her chair, elbows on knees. 'It's like they can't see past the end of their noses. And while they're trying to find evidence against you, they're not looking anywhere else. Least of all at what Shaz was digging into. They think her theory about a serial killer preying on teenagers is the sort of stupid thing us girls come up with because we've got our hormones in a twist. Well, we figured that if they won't do what needs to be done, we better had.'

'Do I get a word in edgeways?' Tony said.

'Be our guest,' Leon said, with an expansive gesture.

'I appreciate how you feel. And it does you credit. But this isn't a classroom exercise. It's not, "Five Go Hunting a Psychopath". This is the most dangerous game, in both senses of the word. The last time I got involved with a serial killer, it nearly cost me my own life. And, with great respect to your talents as police officers, I knew a hell of a lot more than all three of you rolled into one. I'm not prepared to take the responsibility of having you working with me off the books.' He ran a hand through his hair.

'We know it's the real thing, Tony,' Kay protested. 'And we know you're the best. That's why we've come to you. But we can do stuff you can't. We've got warrant cards. You don't. Strange cops only trust other cops. They won't trust you.'

'So if you won't help us, we'll just have to do the best we can without you,' Simon said, his mouth set in a stubborn line.

The shrill insistence of the phone came as a relief. Tony's hand closed over the receiver. 'Hello?' he said cautiously, eyeing the other three as if they were an unexploded bomb.

'It's me,' Carol said. 'I just called to see how you'd got on.'

'I'd rather tell you face to face,' he said briskly.

'You can't talk just now?'

'I'm in the middle of something. Can we meet later?'

'My cottage? Half past six?'

'Better make it seven,' he said. 'I've got a lot to do here before I can get away.'

'I'll be there. Safe journey.'

'Thanks.' He gently replaced the phone. He closed his eyes momentarily. He hadn't realized how isolated he'd been feeling. It was the existence of police officers like Carol, and the stubborn belief that one day they'd be in the majority, that made his job bearable. He opened his eyes again to find the three junior members of his squad staring avidly at him. The ghost of an idea was taking shape at the back of his mind. 'What about the other two?' he stalled. 'Saw sense, did they?'

Leon breathed smoke. 'Got no bottle. They're frightened to rock the boat in case their promotion prospects get drowned.'

'Who gives a shit about promotion when someone like

Shaz gets killed and nobody cares enough to catch the killer? Who'd want to be a copper on that kind of force?' Simon spat.

'I'm sorry,' Tony said. 'The answer's still no.'

'Fine,' Kay said. Her smile could have cut steak. 'In that case, we'll move on to Plan B. The sit-in. We're staying on your case till you come on board. Where you go, we go. Twenty-four hours a day. Three of us, one of you.'

'Not good odds.' Leon lit a fresh cigarette while the embers of the previous stub still glowed.

Tony sighed. 'OK. You won't listen to me. Maybe you'll listen to somebody who really knows the score.'

The dashboard clock said it was just after seven; the radio played the theme from *The Archers*, revealing the clock was three minutes slow. Tony's car jounced up the rough track from the road, his suspension giving its age away. He rounded the last bend and saw with satisfaction that the lights were on in Carol's cottage.

She was framed in the doorway as he closed the car door behind himself. He couldn't remember the last time he'd felt so glad to be walking into someone else's company, someone else's territory. The only sign that his companions were completely unexpected was the slight lift of her eyebrows.

'Kettle's on, beer's cold,' she greeted them, offering Tony a gentle squeeze of the arm. 'Is this your bodyguard?'

'Not as such. I am currently being held hostage,' he said drily, following her indoors. His squad didn't wait for an invitation. They were right there on his heels. 'You remember Kay, Leon and Simon? They're going to hang round my neck like millstones until I agree to work with them on uncovering who killed Shaz.' In the living room, he gestured with his thumb towards the sofa and chairs. The threesome sat. 'I was hoping you would help me talk them out of it.'

Carol shook her head, acting bemused. 'They *want* to work with you on a live case? God, the rumour mill must have deteriorated one hell of a lot recently.'

'Coffee first,' Tony said, lifting a hand and placing it lightly on her shoulder, steering her towards the kitchen.

'Coming up.'

He closed the door behind them. 'I'm sorry for landing you with this. But they wouldn't listen to me. The problem is that West Yorkshire are acting like Simon's the prime suspect and I'm a close second. And this lot are not going to lie down and take that. But you know what it's like when you're working a serial killer case and it gets personal. They don't have the experience to handle this. Vance or someone close to him has already killed the best and brightest of them. I don't want any more deaths on my conscience.'

Carol spooned coffee into the filter and switched it on as he spoke. 'You're absolutely right,' she said. 'However . . . unless I misjudge them completely, they're going to pursue this anyway. The best way to make sure you don't lose another one is to take control. And the way to do that is to work with them. Set them all the drudge jobs, the runaround background inquiries that baby detectives cut their teeth on. Anything dodgy, anything we think is dangerous or needs expert interrogation techniques, we'll sort out.'

'"We"?'

Carol clapped the palm of her hand to her forehead and grimaced. 'Why do I feel like I've just been suckered?' She punched his arm. 'Put some sugar and milk and mugs on a tray and take it through before I get seriously cross.'

He did as he was told, feeling strangely gratified that he had moved from the Lone Ranger to team captain in the space of a few hours. By the time Carol brought the coffee through, he'd shared the new deal with a self-satisfied team.

He opened his laptop on the stripped pine dining table, jacked the modem into the phone line, and plugged the transformer into the nearest power point. As the others arranged themselves so they could see the screen, Carol asked Tony, 'How bad was the interview?'

'I walked out in the end,' he said succinctly as he watched the machine boot up. 'It was what you might call hostile. When it comes to, "Hey, lads, hey," they don't really think I'm on the same side, you see. But they're saving the prime suspect slot for Simon. He had the bad luck to get Shaz to agree to a date on the very night she was killed. But I'm probably second favourite in the book that some smart-arse on the murder team will be running.' He looked up and Carol could see the hurt behind the assumed self-possession.

'Stupid bastards,' Carol said, putting his mug of coffee next to the computer. 'But then, they are Yorkshiremen. I can't believe they're not using you lot.'

Leon gave a bark of mirthless laughter. 'Tell us about it. You let people smoke in here?'

Carol glanced at him, taking in the fingers beating a silent tattoo on his thigh. Better that the tobacco combusted than he did. 'You'll find a saucer in the cupboard above the kettle,' she said. 'Only in this room, please.' As he left, she took over his chair and settled down next to Tony, watching the screen change as his fingers hit the keys.

Tony worked his way into the task force computer system with Shaz's login. He pointed to the flashing cursor. 'This is what I've been racking my brains over all afternoon. I can get on to the system as Shaz, but I can't figure out her password.' He ran through the attempts he'd made, ticking the categories off on his fingers. Leon, Kay and Simon started throwing out their own suggestions based on what they knew of their late colleague.

Carol listened carefully, left hand teasing the tendrils of blonde hair on the back of her neck. When Tony and the other three had run out of steam and ideas, she said, 'Missed the obvious, didn't you? Who did Shaz look up to? What did she want to be?'

'Running Scotland Yard? You think I should try famous Met Commissioners?'

Carol reached over and pulled the laptop within touch-typing range. 'Famous profilers.' She typed in RESSLER, DOUGLAS, LEYTON. Nothing happened. A rueful quirk of the lips, then she typed TONYHILL. The screen went momentarily blank, then a menu appeared. 'Fuck, I wish I'd taken a bet on it,' she said wryly. Around her, the trainee profilers applauded, Leon wolf-whistling and whooping.

Tony shook his head, astonished. 'What do I have to do to get you on the national squad?' he asked. 'You're wasted in ordinary CID work at your rank. All that admin when you should be harnessing that inspiration to catch psychopaths.'

'Right,' Carol said sarcastically, pushing the laptop back towards him. 'If I'm so good, how come I didn't work out that my arsonist was a crook, not a crazy?'

'Because you were working alone. That's never the best way to operate when you're dealing with psychological analysis. I think profilers should work in pairs, detective and psychologist, complementary skills.' He took the cursor down to the 'File directory' option and hit ENTER.

The quality of their meeting of minds was not a conversation Carol wanted to have, especially not in company as sharp as the present one. Deftly, she moved the subject forward, bringing Leon, Kay and Simon up to speed with

Tony's theory that the arsonist was a part-time fireman with a conventional criminal motive.

'But what *is* the motive?' Kay asked. 'That's the important bit, isn't it?'

'If it's criminal, you always want to know who benefits,' Leon pointed out. 'And since there's no common ownership or insurance, maybe it's somebody high up in the fire service who doesn't want any more cutbacks.'

Tony looked up from the file names he was scrolling through. 'Nice idea,' he said. 'Devious, though. And as a proponent of Occam's Razor, I'm going to go for the most straightforward theory. Debt,' he said and turned his eyes back to the screen.

'Debt?' Carol's voice was full of doubt.

'That's right.' He swung round to face her. 'Somebody who owes money all over the place, somebody with a credit rating that's fallen through the floor. His house has been repossessed or it's on the point of it, he's got a stack of county court judgements against him and he's robbing Peter to pay Paul.'

'But a night call-out is, what? Fifty, a hundred quid max, depending on how long they're out there? You surely don't think somebody would put his liberty, his mates' lives, at risk for that sort of cash!' Simon protested.

Tony shrugged. 'If you're up against the wall, perpetually juggling creditors, an extra hundred quid a week can make all the difference to staying in one piece and having your legs broken, your car snatched, your electricity cut off, the bank putting you into bankruptcy. You pay twenty quid off one debt, fifty off another, a tenner here, a fiver there. You show willing. It keeps everybody off your back. The courts are reluctant to take drastic steps if you can show you're really trying. Any sensible person knows that it's only postponing the evil hour, but when you're in debt up to your eyeballs, you stop thinking straight. You get into this self-deluding fantasy that if you can just get over this hump, you'll be heading towards getting straight again. Nobody cons themselves better than a bad debtor. I've seen pathetic idiots who owe the best part of twenty grand to a loan shark still employing a cleaning lady and a gardener because getting rid of them would be an admission that their lives were totally out of control. Look for somebody who's teetering on the brink of insolvency, Carol.'

Already back in communion with the computer screen, he muttered, 'Let me see . . . MISPER.001. That'll be the report she did for the squad, wouldn't you think?'

'Seems likely. And MISPERJV.001 could be her Jacko Vance inquiries.'

'Let's take a look.' Tony opened the file. Shaz's words spilled down the screen, giving him a strange sense of communing with the dead. It was as if those extraordinary blue eyes were hovering behind his head, fixing him with their inexorable stare. 'My God,' he whispered. 'She wasn't playing games.'

Leon peered over his shoulder. 'Fuck,' he breathed. 'You fucking witch, Shazza.' It summed up everyone's feelings perfectly as they stared at Shaz's briefing from beyond the grave.

ORGANIZED OFFENDER CHECKLIST

Jacko Vance
Re: MISPER cluster

High birth order
    Only child.

Father's work stable
   Civil engineer – often away from home for prolonged
   periods on long-term contracts.

Absent father
   See above.

Parental discipline perceived as inconsistent
   See above; also, mother appears to have suffered
   post-natal depression, rejected JV and later treated
   v. strictly.

Higher than average IQ
   Regarded as bright by teachers but never did as well
   as expected academically; poor exam performer.

Skilled occupation, work history uneven
   First as a champion javelin thrower then as TV
   presenter; perfectionist, prone to temper tantrums
   and firing junior members of team; if not for medal-
   winning prowess/popularity with TV audience, would
   have lost several contracts over the years because of
   arrogant and overbearing behaviour.

*Socially adept; may be gregarious and good talker, but
can't connect emotionally*
   See above; relates very well to members of the public
   on superficial level; however, one of reasons why
   his marriage is perceived as so successful is that he
   appears to have no intimate relationships with either
   gender outside that relationship.

Living with partner
Wife, Micky, been together for twelve years. A very public marriage, the golden couple of UK TV. However, often away from home both on business and on extensive charity work.

Controlled mood during commission of crime
Unknown: but Vance is known in the business for coolness under pressure.

Use of alcohol or drugs during commission of crime
Unknown. No history of drink problem, some hint that there may have been a problem with painkiller addiction following accident in which Vance lost his arm.

Mobile; car in good condition
Vance has a silver Mercedes convertible and a Land Rover. Both are automatics and have been adapted for his disability.

Follows crimes in the media
He's perfectly placed to do this – he has direct access to all areas of the media. He numbers many journalists among his circle of acquaintance.

Victims share common characteristics
Yes – see appendix A on original cluster of seven victims.

Unsuspicious demeanour
Millions of people would trust him with their lives or their daughters. In a poll four years ago, he was

voted the third most trustworthy person in Britain after the Queen and the Bishop of Liverpool.

Looks average
Impossible to comment objectively. The gloss of celebrity, grooming and an expensive wardrobe makes it hard to judge beyond the facade.

Mental illness in immediate family
Nothing known; mother died eight years ago, cancer.

Alcohol or drugs problem in immediate family
Nothing known.

Parents with criminal records
Nothing known.

Emotional abuse
Mother reportedly told him he was ugly and clumsy, 'just like your father'. Mother appeared to blame him for his father's absences.

Sexually dysfunctional – incapable of mature, consensual relationship with another adult
Nothing to support this: marriage very public. No indications that MM unhappy with marriage or has lover. ??? Check newspaper gossip columns ??? Check with uniforms on local patrol – any signs ???

Cool, distant mother; very little touching or emotional warmth as child
Implied in both books.

Egocentric world view
All the evidence – even from MM's adoring account – supports this.

Beaten as child
MM recalls him speaking of his father coming home from trip and thrashing him for failing eleven-plus; otherwise, nothing known.

Witnessed sexually stressful situation as child, e.g. marital rape, mother engaged in prostitution
Nothing known.

Parents separated in childhood or early adolescence
Parents divorced when he was twelve.
According to MM book, his obsession with athletics was bid to gain father's attention.

Autoerotic adolescence
Nothing known.

Rape fantasies
Nothing known.

Obsession with pornography
Nothing known.

Voyeuristic tendencies
Nothing specific known; but cf. *Vance's Visits*, the ultimate poke-your-nose-in television.

Aware his sexual/emotional relationships are abnormal and resents it
Nothing known.

Obsessive
   Attested to by work colleagues and rivals alike.

Irrational phobias
   Nothing known.

Chronic liar
   Several instances of him 'remaking' past incidents;
   compare two books.

Initiating stressor?
   Jacko Vance's first girlfriend was Jillie Woodrow.
   He was unsuccessful with girls before her, and by
   the time they got together, he was almost sixteen
   and she was just fourteen. Apart from his obsessive
   sports training, she was his only interest. They had
   a relationship that was exclusive, compulsive and
   consuming. He appears to have been a dominating
   influence upon her. They were engaged as soon as
   she turned sixteen, opposed by her parents and his
   mother; he was no longer in touch with his father
   by this time. After the accident when he lost his
   arm, MM's account claims he set Jillie free since he
   was no longer the man she'd contracted to marry;
   TB's version is that she had been looking for a way
   out of the claustrophobic relationship for some time
   and fixed on his accident as a way out, claiming she
   was repelled by his injury and the prospect of living
   with a man with a prosthesis. MM and Vance got
   together shortly afterwards. Just before they married,
   Jillie did a 'kiss and tell' with the *News of the World*

revealing that Vance had forced her to indulge in sadomasochistic rituals, tying her up to have sex in spite of her protests that it frightened her. Vance tried to prevent the story's publication, denying it vigorously. He failed to get an injunction, but never sued for libel, claiming that he couldn't afford the legal process. (Probably true at that stage in career.) Either the end of the relationship with Jillie in such stressful circumstances or her subsequent revelations could have been a powerful enough stressor to trigger off the first in Vance's series of crimes.

'Oh, shit,' Carol said as she reached the end of Shaz's analysis. 'You really have to wonder, don't you?'

'You think Jacko Vance could be a serial killer?' Kay asked.

'Shaz thought so. And I think she might have been right,' Tony said grimly.

'There's something bothering me about this,' Simon said. Encouraged by a questioning look from Tony he continued. 'If Vance is a sociopath, how come he saved those kids and tried to rescue that lorry driver in the accident where he lost his arm? Why did he not just leave them to it?'

'Good point,' Tony said. 'You know I hate to theorize ahead of the data, but looking at what we know so far, I'd say Jacko spent most of his formative years desperate for attention and approval. When the accident happened, he automatically went down the road that would make him look good in other people's eyes. It's not uncommon for what looks like heroism to be a desperate craving for glory. I think that's what happened there. If you still think we're barking up the wrong tree, let me tell you about a conversation I had with Commander Bishop this afternoon.' He told them about Shaz's appointment with Vance and the conclusions he'd drawn from that.

'You're going to have to let McCormick and Wharton know about this file,' Carol said.

'I don't feel much like it, the way they treated me.'

'You want them to put Shaz's killer away, don't you?'

'I want Shaz's killer put away,' Tony said firmly. 'I just don't think those two have the imagination to deal with the information. Think about it, Carol. If I tell them what we've found here, first off, they won't want to believe it. They'll think we've tinkered with her files. I can just imagine the interview with Vance. He slipped effortlessly into the broad Yorkshire of his childhood. 'A'right, Mr Vance, we're sorry to trouble tha, but we think the lass here last Saturday thought tha were a serial killer. Daft, tha knows, but seeing as 'ow she got herself murdered that night, we thought we'd better come and 'ave a word. 'Appen tha might've seen summat, some weirdo following her, like.'

'They're not that bad, surely,' Carol protested, spluttering with laughter in spite of herself.

'You ask me, he's being generous,' Leon muttered.

'They're not going to go in and *interrogate* Jacko Vance,' Simon said. 'They're going to be overawed, they're going to be on his side. All they'll do is mark his card.'

'And Jack the Lad is a clever bastard,' Tony continued. 'Now he knows they know about Shaz's visit, he'll be the biggest Goody Two Shoes on legs. So there's part of me that thinks, no, don't tell them.'

There was a long silence. Then Simon said, 'So what now?'

Tony had taken a notepad from the laptop bag and started scribbling. 'If we're going to do this, we've got to do it right. Which means I act as controller and coordinator. Carol, is there a local takeaway that delivers?'

She snorted with derision. 'Out here? Do me a favour. There's bread, cheese, salami, tuna, salad stuff. Give me a hand, team. We'll throw some butties together while our leader cogitates.'

When they returned fifteen minutes later with mounds of sandwiches and a mixing bowl filled with crisps, Tony was ready for them. Sprawled round the room with bottles of beer and plates of food, they listened while he explained what he wanted them to do.

'I think we're all agreed that on the balance of probabilities, Shaz was killed because of the work she'd done since she came to Leeds. There's no indication that she had any kind of personally threatening experiences up to that point. So we take as our starting point the assumption that Shaz Bowman correctly identified the existence of an as yet unknown serial killer of teenage girls.' He raised his eyebrows in a question and noted four nods.

'The external connector in these cases concerned Jacko Vance. Shaz assumed him to be the killer, though we shouldn't fail to consider that our target could conceivably be someone in his entourage. Me, I'm inclined to go for Vance.'

'Good old Occam,' Simon muttered wryly.

'Not just on the least complicated principle,' Tony said. 'My view is coloured by the length of time these killings apparently cover. I don't know if there's anyone who has been professionally close to Vance for that long. Even if they had, I'm not convinced that they would have the charisma to lure young women into what looks superficially like a runaway bid.

'So, we've got Shaz's profile of Vance. It's inevitably superficial. She only had access to what was in the public domain that she could get her hands on readily. That seems to have consisted mainly of two biographies, one written by his wife, the other by a showbiz hack. We need to dig a lot deeper than that before we can check whether this man is a serious possible for the series of killings we're postulating. This is an unusual job for us profilers. Usually we're making deductions from crime to offender. This time, we're going from putative offender to hypothetical murders. I don't feel entirely confident about it, if I'm honest. It's fresh territory for me. So we need to be very careful before we put our heads anywhere near the parapet.' More nods. Leon stood up and moved across to the doorway so he could smoke without polluting everyone else's food.

'We get the message,' Leon drawled. 'Our missions, should we choose to accept them, are . . . ?'

'We need to track down his fiancée, Jillie Woodrow. The person responsible for interviewing Jillie should also carry out a general investigation into his early life – family, neighbours, school friends, teachers, any local bobbies still on the payroll or recently retired. Simon, are you up for that?'

Simon looked apprehensive. 'What exactly do I do?'

Tony signalled to Carol with his eyes. 'Find out everything you possibly can about Jacko,' she said. 'Deep background. If you want a cover story for everyone except Jillie, say we're investigating threats against him and we think the reason may lie deep in his past. People love a bit of melodrama. With Jillie, that won't work. It might be worth hinting that you're investigating allegations made against Jacko by a prostitute, perhaps imply that you suspect they're malicious lies?'

'OK. Any ideas how I find her, given that I haven't got access to the PNC?'

'I'll get to that in a minute,' Tony said. 'Leon, I want you to start digging into what was going on in his life around the time of the accident where he lost his arm. That and his early TV career. See if you can find his old trainer, the first people he worked with when he was starting out in sports' broadcasting. Athletes on the British team with him, that sort of thing. OK?'

'Just watch me,' Leon said, cold and serious for once. 'You won't be sorry you asked me, man.'

'Kay, your job is to go round the parents of the girls Shaz identified in her cluster and re-interview them. All the usual misper stuff, plus anything and everything you can pull out about Jacko Vance.'

'The local lads should be more than happy to hand off their case files to you,' Carol put in. 'They'll be so delighted that somebody else is prepared to take responsibility for such a no-hoper, they'll probably give you the freedom of the nick.'

'All of which DCI Jordan here will set up for you in advance,' Tony continued. 'She will be your facilitator, the one who speaks to ranking officers in other police stations around the country and gets you the information that will kick-start your inquiries. Stuff like where Jillie Woodrow is now, what happened to Vance's coach, which victim's parents have moved to Scunthorpe.'

Carol stared open-mouthed for a long moment. Leon, Simon and Kay looked on with the delight of adolescents watching grown-ups on the verge of behaving badly. 'Fine,' she eventually said, her voice loaded with sarcasm. 'I have so little to do at work, it'll be a pleasure fitting it in. So, Tony, what are you going to be up to while the rest of the squad are doing all the hard graft?'

He reached for a sandwich, checked the filling, then looked up with a smile that appeared entirely free from guile. 'I'm going to shake the tree,' he said.

Detective Inspector Colin Wharton looked like a refugee from one of those dreadfully predictable gritty northern cops-and-robbers dramas that the networks churned out to fill the gap between the late news and bedtime, Micky thought. Once handsome in a craggy way, too much drink and junk food had blurred his features and shrouded his blue eyes in heavy pouches. She imagined him on a second marriage which would be in trouble; the kids from his first marriage would be the teenagers from hell; and he'd have a vague but worrying recurring pain somewhere in his internal organs. She crossed her legs demurely and gave him the smile that had reassured a thousand studio guests. She just knew he'd be a complete sucker for it. Him and Detective Constable Sidekick, who looked one step away from asking for her autograph.

She glanced at her watch. 'Jacko should be back any minute. It'll be the traffic. Same with Betsy. My personal assistant.'

'You mentioned that,' Wharton said. 'If it's all the same to you, we might as well get started. We can talk to Ms Thorne and Mr Vance when they get here.' He consulted a folder spread across his tightly trousered lap. 'I'm told you spoke to DC Bowman the day before she died. How did that come about?'

'We've got two phone lines – one for me and one for Jacko. They're ex-directory, very private. Only a handful of people have the numbers. I switch mine over to the mobile when I'm out and DC Bowman came through on that. It must have been about half past eight on Friday morning – I was with one of my researchers at the time, she could probably confirm that.' Realizing she was wallowing in inconsequentiality, too obvious a marker for nervousness, Micky paused for a moment.

'But it wasn't your researcher?' Wharton prompted her.

'No. It was a voice I didn't recognize. She said she was

Detective Constable Sharon Bowman from the Metropolitan Police and she wanted to arrange an appointment with Jacko. My husband.'

Wharton nodded encouragingly. 'And you said?'

'I told her she'd come through on my line and she apologized and said she'd been told this was his private number. She asked if he was there, and when I said he was away she said could she leave a message. I don't normally act as Jacko's secretary, but since she was with the police and I didn't know what it was about, I thought it would be best just to make a note of what she wanted and pass it on to him.' She smiled, aiming for the self-deprecating air of a woman unsure of herself faced with authority. It was a blatant performance, but Wharton didn't seem to notice.

'Sensible approach, Ms Morgan,' he said. 'What was the message?'

'She said it was merely a formality, a routine matter, but she'd like to interview him in connection with a case she was working on. Because of her other commitments, she said it would have to be Saturday, but she'd happily fit in with his arrangements. The time and place would be up to him. And she left a number where he could get back to her.'

'Do you still have that number?' Wharton asked, just another standard question.

Micky picked up a notepad and held it out to him. 'As you see, we start a fresh page for each day. It's a catch-all – phone messages, programme ideas, domestic bits and pieces.' She handed it over, pointing to a few lines near the top of the page.

Wharton read, 'Det. Con. Sharon Bowman. Jacko. i/v ???Saturday??? you name time + place. 307 4676 Sgt Devine.' That confirmed the telephone statement Chris Devine had already given them, but Wharton wanted to double-check. 'This number . . . is it London?'

Micky nodded. 'Yes. 0171. Same code as ours, that's why I didn't bother writing it down. Well, it would be, wouldn't it? She was with the Met.'

'She was on secondment to a unit in Leeds,' he said heavily. 'That's why she was living there, Ms Morgan.'

'Oh God, of course,' she said hollowly. 'Do you know, for some reason that just hadn't registered. How odd.'

'Indeed,' Wharton said. 'So, you passed the message on to your husband and that was that?' he said.

'I left the message on his voice mail. He mentioned later that he'd arranged for her to come to the house on Saturday morning. He knew I wouldn't mind since Betsy and I were going off on Le Shuttle on a freebie. Perks of the job.' She gave him the full-beam smile again. Wharton wondered sourly why the women in his life never managed to look so gratified when they spoke to him.

Before he could ask the next question, he heard footfalls on the parquet floor of the hall. He half-turned as the door opened behind him. His first impression of Jacko Vance was a sense of tremendous energy contained within expensive tailoring. There was something irresistibly watchable about him, even doing something as banal as crossing the room and extending his left hand in a gesture of welcome. 'Inspector Wharton, I presume,' Vance said warmly, affecting not to notice the policeman's fluster as he half-rose, reached out with the wrong hand then clumsily shifted his papers and grabbed at the proffered hand in an awkward shake. 'I'm Jacko Vance,' he said, pretending a humility Micky recognized as false as her own. 'Desperate business, this.' Vance turned away from the detective, nodding a friendly greeting at the hovering constable and dropped on to the sofa next to his wife. He patted her thigh. 'All right, Micky?' His voice dripped the same concern he always showed the terminally ill.

'We've just been going over DC Bowman's phone call,' she said.

'Right. Sorry I'm late. Got held up in traffic in the West End,' he said, his mouth curling upwards in a familiar self-deprecating smile. 'So, what can I tell you, officer?'

'Ms Morgan passed a message on to you from DC Bowman, is that right?'

'Absolutely,' Vance said confidently. 'I called the number she'd left and spoke to a detective sergeant whose name I have completely forgotten. I said that if DC Bowman came to the house on Saturday morning between half past nine and noon, I would see her then.'

'Very generous, a busy man like yourself,' Wharton said.

Vance raised his eyebrows. 'I always try to help the authorities when I can. It didn't inconvenience me in any way. All I had planned for the day was to catch up on some personal paperwork then drive up to my cottage in Northumberland in time for an early night. I was running a charity half-marathon at Sunderland on Sunday, you see.' He leaned back negligently, fully expecting his throwaway line to be noted, believed and filed away in support of his innocence.

'What time did DC Bowman arrive?' Wharton asked.

Vance pulled a face and turned to Micky. 'What time was it? You were just leaving, weren't you?'

'That's right,' she confirmed. 'Must have been around half past nine. Betsy could probably tell you more exactly. She's the only one in the house with any sense of time.' She smiled wryly, amazed at how ready this policeman was to accept that two major TV personalities who anchored key programmes couldn't measure time instinctively to the last half-minute. 'We more or less passed on the doorstep. Jacko was on the phone upstairs, so I pointed her in here, and we were off.'

'I didn't keep her waiting more than a couple of minutes,' Vance continued seamlessly. 'She apologized for interrupting my weekend, but I explained that in this job, we don't really have weekends. We take time for ourselves when we can, don't we, darling?' He gazed adoringly at her, slipping his arm round her shoulders.

'Not often enough,' Micky sighed.

Wharton cleared his throat and said, 'Can you tell me what it was DC Bowman wanted to talk to you about?'

'You mean, you don't know?' Micky demanded, the dormant news reporter inside her springing into action. 'A police officer comes all the way from Yorkshire to London to interview someone with as high a profile as Jacko, and you don't know what it was in aid of?' She looked astonished, leaning forward, forearms on thighs, hands spread open.

Wharton shifted in his seat and stared fixedly at a point on the wall between the two long windows. 'DC Bowman was attached to a new unit. Strictly speaking, she should not have been on operational duties at present. We think we know what she was working on, but as yet we have no independent corroboration of that. It'd help us a lot if Mr Vance could just tell us what transpired between the two of them on Saturday morning.' He breathed out heavily through his nose and shot them a quick look that mingled embarrassment and pleading.

'No problem,' Vance said easily. 'DC Bowman was very apologetic about invading my privacy with her questions, but she said she was working on a series of missing teenage girls. She thought they had been lured away from home by the same individual. It appeared that some of these girls had

286

been at one of my public appearances shortly before they dropped out of sight and she wondered if some nutter was targeting my fans. She said she wanted to show me pictures of the girls, just in case I'd noticed them talking to a particular person.'

'One of your entourage, you mean?' Wharton prompted, proud of knowing the right word.

Vance laughed, a rich baritone laugh. 'I'm sorry to disappoint you, Inspector, but I don't exactly have an entourage. When I'm doing the programme, I have a team who work very closely with me. Sometimes when I'm doing PAs – public appearances, that is – my producer or my researcher will come along to keep me company and provide a bit of back-up. But that apart, anything I spend on minders or whatever comes out of my pocket. And since most of the work I do involves earning cash for charities as well, it seems crazy to spend any more than is absolutely necessary. So, as I explained to DC Bowman, there are no loyal retainers. What there is, however, is a hard core of devotees. There are, I suppose, a couple of dozen fans who turn up regularly at virtually every event I do. Strange people, but I'd always considered them harmless.'

'It's a mark of celebrity,' Micky said matter-of-factly. 'If you don't have your retinue of attendant weirdos, you're nobody. Badly dressed men in anoraks and women in polyester slacks and acrylic cardies. All of them with dreadful haircuts. Not the sort your average teenage girl would run off with, take it from me.'

'Which is pretty much what I told DC Bowman,' Vance continued. They were so smooth, so natural, he thought. Maybe it was about time they made some programmes together. He made a mental note to explore the idea with his producer. 'She showed me a few photographs of the girls she was concerned about, but none of them rang any bells.' His shrug was disarming. 'Not surprising. I can sign upwards of three hundred autographs at a PA. Well, I say sign . . . scrawl would be more like it.' He looked ruefully at his prosthetic hand. 'Writing's one of the many things I can't do properly any more.'

There was a moment's silence. To Wharton it felt as long as Remembrance Sunday. He searched around for a meaningful question. 'How did DC Bowman respond, sir? To your lack of recognition, I mean.'

'She seemed disappointed,' Vance said. 'But she admitted it had always been a long shot. I said I was sorry not to have been more help, and she left. That must have been around . . . oh, half past ten, thereabouts?'

'So she was here for about an hour? That seems quite a long time for a few questions,' Wharton said, punctilious rather than suspicious.

'It does, doesn't it?' Vance agreed. 'But I did keep her waiting a few minutes, then I made us both some coffee, we did the usual small talk. People always want to know behind-the-scenes gossip about *Vance's Visits*. Then I had to go through all the photographs. I took my time. Missing girls is too serious a subject to take lightly. I mean, no contact with their families after all this time – years, in some cases, according to DC Bowman – chances are they could have been murdered. It merited my attention.'

'Quite so, sir,' Wharton said heavily, wishing he hadn't bothered asking. 'I don't suppose she mentioned any plans she might have for the rest of the day?'

Vance shook his head. 'Sorry, Inspector. I had the impression she had another appointment, but she didn't say where or with whom.'

'What gave you that impression, sir?' Wharton looked up,

for the first time feeling he might be doing more than going through the motions.

Vance frowned for a moment, as if thinking. 'After I'd finished with the photographs, I offered to make fresh coffee. But she looked at her watch and seemed startled. As if she hadn't realized the time. She said she had to be going, she'd no idea we'd been talking for so long. She was out the door within minutes.'

Wharton closed his notebook. 'As I think I should be too, sir. I very much appreciate both of you taking the time to talk to me. If there's anything else, which I very much doubt, I'll be in touch.' He rose and gave his junior officer a 'let's go' jerk of the head.

'You don't need to speak to Betsy?' Micky asked. 'She shouldn't be long.'

'I don't think that'll be necessary,' Wharton said. 'Frankly, I think DC Bowman's visit here was almost certainly nothing to do with her death. We just have to tie up the loose ends.'

Vance crossed to the door and opened it to usher them out. 'A shame you have to be dragged down here when the real work's waiting for you in Yorkshire,' he said, his sympathetic smile adding weight to the commiseration in his voice.

Micky said goodbye and watched from the window as Vance saw the police officers off the premises. She wasn't sure what her husband was hiding. But she knew him well enough to know that what she had just heard was only a distant relative of the truth, the whole truth and nothing but the truth.

When he walked back into the room, she was leaning against the fireplace. 'Are you going to tell me what you didn't tell them?' she asked, her eyes giving him the shrewd appraisal that could always penetrate his glossy surface.

Vance grinned. 'You're a witch, Micky. Yes, I'll tell you

what I didn't tell them. I did recognize one of the girls whose picture Bowman showed me.'

Micky's eyes widened. 'You did? How come? Where from?'

'No need to panic,' he said scornfully. 'It's perfectly innocent. When she went missing, her parents contacted us. Said she was my biggest fan, blah, blah, blah, never missed a show, blah, blah, blah. Wanted us to put out an appeal for her to contact them.'

'And did you?'

'Course not. It wouldn't fit the format of the programme at all. Somebody from the office sent them a sympathetic letter and we got one of the tabloids to run a story saying, "Jacko begs runaway to phone home".'

'So why didn't you tell Wharton? If you did something for the press, there'll be cuttings somewhere! They could dig them out and then you'll be in deep shit.'

'How? They don't even know what Bowman was doing, which doesn't sound like they've got her files, does it? Look, Mick, I never met the girl. I never spoke to her. But if I tell DI Plod I recognized her . . . shit, Mick, you know the police are the leakiest sieve in town. Next thing you know, it'll be "Jacko in murder quiz" splashed all over the front pages. No thanks. I can do without it. They can't connect me to a single one of Bowman's runaways. The king of deniability, remember?'

Micky shook her head, admiring his chutzpah in spite of herself. 'More like Teflon Man,' she said. 'I've got to hand it to you, Jacko. When it comes to playing the audience like a fiddle, even I can't hold a candle to you.'

He crossed to her and kissed her cheek. 'Never try to bullshit a bullshitter.'

Carol walked next morning into her office to find her crew had wrong-footed her by being there ahead of her. Tommy

Taylor sprawled in the chair opposite hers, legs wide apart to emphasize his masculinity. Lee had the window cracked open, blowing his smoke out to join the traffic fumes. Di was in her usual position leaning against the wall, arms folded over her badly fitting suit. Carol itched to drag her kicking and screaming to the January sales to kit the woman out in clothes that would both fit and flatter her instead of the expensive and nasty stuff she chose now.

Carol made straight for her bastion behind the desk, flipping open her briefcase as she sat. 'Right,' she said. 'Our serial arsonist.'

'Crunchy nut cornflake,' Lee said.

'Actually, not,' Carol said. 'Apparently, our firebug is as sane as you or me. Well, me, anyway, since I can't speak for you three. According to a psychologist whose judgement I trust implicitly, we're not dealing with a psychopath. The man who's setting these fires has a straightforward criminal motive. And that points to Jim Pendlebury's part-timers.' The three stared at her as if she'd suddenly slipped into Swedish.

'You what?' Lee managed to speak first.

Carol distributed copies of the list the fire chief had given her. 'I want deep background checks into these men. Particular attention to financial details. And I don't want them to get so much as a sniff that we're interested.'

Tommy Taylor found his voice. 'You're accusing *firemen*?'

'I think you'll find we're supposed to call them firefighters these days,' Carol said mildly. 'I'm not accusing anybody yet, Sergeant. I'm trying to gather enough information on which we can base a decision.'

'Firemen *die* in fires,' Di Earnshaw sniped mutinously. 'They get injured, they inhale smoke. Why would a fireman set fires? He'd have to be a real sicko, and you just said this bloke isn't. Surely that's a contradiction in terms?'

'He's not sick,' Carol said firmly. 'Desperate, maybe, but he's not suffering from a mental illness. We're looking for someone who's so deep in debt he's lost sight of anything except how to get out of it. It's not that he wants to put his mates at risk; he's just not allowing himself to include them in the equation.'

Taylor shook his head sceptically. 'It's a helluva slur on the fire service,' he protested.

'No more so than outside inquiries into allegations of police corruption. And we all know that happens.' Carol's voice was dry. She shuffled the case papers back into her briefcase then looked up at them. 'You lot still here?'

Lee tossed his cigarette into the street below in an eloquent gesture and pushed himself into a slouching walk to the door. 'I'm on it,' he said.

Taylor stood up and ostentatiously rearranged the outward evidence of his gender. 'Aye,' he said, following Lee and indicating to Di Earnshaw that she should follow.

'Softly, softly,' Carol said to the retreating backs.

If spines could speak, Di Earnshaw's would have uttered a fluent 'Fuck off.' The door closed behind them and Carol leaned back in her chair, one hand massaging the tight knots at the base of her skull. It was going to be a very long day.

Tony reached for the phone automatically, mumbling, 'Tony Hill here, can you hang on a minute,' before finishing the sentence he was typing into his computer. He looked at the receiver in his hand as if not quite certain how it had arrived there. 'Yes, sorry, Tony Hill speaking.'

'This is DI Wharton.' His voice was neutral.

'Why?' Tony asked.

'What?' Wharton stumbled, wrong-footed.

'I asked why you were calling. What's so strange about that?'

'Aye, right. Well, I'm calling out of courtesy,' Wharton said with a brusqueness that contradicted his words.

'That's novel.'

'There's no need to get clever. My boss would have no problem with bringing you in for another visit.'

'He'd have to take that up with my lawyer. You've had your one free shot. So what was this courtesy you wanted to extend me?'

'We had a telephone call from Micky Morgan, the TV presenter who, as you may or may not know, is Mrs Jacko Vance. She volunteered the information that Bowman visited their house in London on Saturday morning to interview her husband. So we took a trip down there and spoke to Mr Vance ourselves. And he's in the clear. Bowman might have made a fool of herself in front of your little clique, but she wasn't daft enough to repeat her nonsense to the man himself. Turns out all she wanted to ask was if he'd seen anybody at his events stalking these missing girls. And he hadn't. Not surprising, when you consider how many faces pass his in a week. So you see, Dr Hill, he's clean. They came to us, we didn't go to them.'

'And that's it? Jacko Vance told you he'd waved goodbye to Shaz Bowman on the doorstep and that's good enough for you?'

'We've no reason to think otherwise,' Wharton said stiffly.

'The last person to see her alive? Aren't they usually worth a look?'

'Not when they have no known connection to the victim, a reputation for probity that's never been challenged and they said goodbye twelve hours before the crime was committed,' Wharton said, his voice laced with acid. 'Especially when they're a registered disabled, one-armed person who's supposed to have overwhelmed a highly trained, able-bodied police officer.'

'Can I ask one question?'

'You can ask.'

'Was there a witness to this interview or did Vance see Shaz alone?'

'His wife let her into the house, but she left them to it. Bowman saw him alone. But that doesn't automatically mean he's lying, you know. I've been in this game a long time. I can tell when folk are telling me lies. Face it, Doctor, you're well off target. I can't say I blame you for trying to divert us, but we're sticking with the people that she knew.'

'Thanks for letting me know.' Not trusting himself to say more, Tony dropped the phone back into its cradle. The blindness of the human animal never ceased to amaze him. It wasn't that Wharton was a stupid man; he was simply, in spite of years in the police service, conditioned to the belief that men like Jacko Vance could not be violent criminals.

In a way, Wharton's call was what he had been waiting for. The police could not avenge Shaz Bowman and vindicate his own work. It was up to him now, and there was a mordant satisfaction in that. Besides, Wharton's answer to his question had confirmed Vance as prime suspect in Tony's eyes. It had to be him. Tony had already eliminated a psychotic fan; now he could eliminate the members of Vance's entourage. If no one else had witnessed the interview, no one else could have picked up Shaz's trail after she left the house.

Picking up the phone again, Tony called the number he'd

obtained earlier from Directory Enquiries, anticipating this moment. When the switchboard answered, he said, "Can you put me through to the *Midday with Morgan* production office?' Then he leaned back to wait, a grim little smile curving his lips.

John Brandon fiddled with the handle of his coffee cup. 'I don't like it, Carol,' he admitted. She opened her mouth to respond and he lifted a finger to silence her. 'Oh, I know you're no more fond of the idea than I am. It's still a big step, pointing the finger at the fire service. I only hope we're not making a terrible mistake here.'

'Tony Hill's been right before,' she reminded him. 'And when you look at his analysis, it makes sense the way nothing else does.'

Brandon shook his head despairingly, looking more like a world-weary undertaker than ever. 'I know. It's such a depressing thought, though. To put so many lives at risk for so little. At least when coppers go bent, people don't usually end up dead.' He sipped his coffee. The aroma wafted across the desk to Carol, making her mouth water. Normally he offered her a cup; it was a measure of how shocked he was by her report that she wasn't sharing the fragrant brew. 'Ah well,' he said. 'Keep me informed of what your team comes up with. I'd appreciate advance notice of an arrest.'

'No problem. There was one other thing, sir?'

'Was that the bad news or the good news?'

'I think it was the bad news. Depending on what you think of the other matter, sir.' Carol's smile held no cheer.

The Chief Constable sighed and half-turned in his swivel chair to stare out across the estuary. As usual, the boss had the best view, Carol thought irrelevantly as an ocean-going trawler slid from one window to the next. 'Let's hear it, then,' he said.

'It also concerns Tony Hill,' she said. 'You know about the murder on his squad?'

'Hellish business,' Brandon said accurately. 'The worst thing that can happen in this job is losing an officer. But losing one like that . . . It's your biggest nightmare.'

'Especially if you've got memories like Tony Hill's to draw on.'

'You're not wrong.' He looked shrewdly across at her. 'Apart from our natural compassion, how does this engage us?'

'Officially, not at all.'

'But unofficially?'

'Tony's having some problems with West Yorkshire. They appear to be treating him and his profiling trainees as their principal suspects instead of an effective resource. Tony feels they've dismissed other avenues for arbitrary reasons, and he's determined that Shaz Bowman's killer shouldn't escape simply because the investigating officers are taking a blinkered approach.'

A smile escaped and spread across Brandon's face. 'Those his words?'

Carol's answering smile was complicit. 'Not verbatim, sir. I didn't take a contemporaneous note.'

'I can see why he feels the need to take action,' Brandon said cautiously. 'Any investigator would have the same reaction. But we have rules in the police service that prevent officers investigating crimes where they have a personal interest. Those rules exist for the very good reason that crimes close to home distort an officer's judgement. Are you sure it wouldn't be best to let West Yorkshire get on with this in their own way?'

'Not if it means leaving a psychopath on the streets,' Carol said firmly. 'There's nothing wrong that I can see with the way Tony's mind's working.'

'You still haven't explained what this has to do with us.'

'He needs help. He's working with some of his task force officers, but they're all currently on suspension, so they don't have access to any official channels. Plus he needs input from an experienced police officer to counterbalance his viewpoint. He can't get that from West Yorkshire. All they want to do is find a reason to stick him or one of his team behind bars.'

'They never wanted to host that unit in the first place,' Brandon said. 'It's not surprising they see this as an excuse to shoot it down in flames. Nevertheless, it is their case and they're not looking to us for assistance.'

'No, but Tony is. And I feel I owe him, sir. All I'd be doing is a little background digging to provide his team with raw materials like names and addresses. I intend to give him what help I can. I'd prefer to do it with your blessing.'

'When you say help . . . ?'

'I won't be treading on West Yorkshire's heels. The angle Tony's interested in is miles away from their inquiries. They won't know I'm there. I'm not going to drop you in a jurisdictional wrangle.'

Brandon swallowed the last of his coffee and pushed the cup away from him. 'Damn right, you're not. Carol, do what you've got to do. But you're doing it off the books. This conversation never happened, and if it all comes on top, I never met you before.'

She grinned and got to her feet. 'Thank you, sir.'

'Stay out of trouble, Chief Inspector,' he said gruffly, dismissing her with a flutter of his fingers. As she opened the door to leave, he added, 'If you need my help, you have my number.'

It was a promise Carol hoped she'd never have to collect on.

Sunderland was the furthest north, Exmouth the most southerly point. In between were Swindon, Grantham, Tamworth, Wigan and Halifax. In each place, a teenage girl's disappearance had snagged Shaz Bowman's attention. Kay Hallam knew that somehow she had to squeeze fresh juice from those investigations that would shore up the edifice of circumstantial evidence Tony was building against Jacko Vance. It wasn't an easy assignment. Years had passed and with them the sharpness of memory. Doing it single-handed wasn't the best option either. In an ideal world, there would be two of them, taking a couple of weeks to complete the task, conducting interviews with brains that weren't exhausted from driving the length and breadth of the country.

No such luxury. Not that she wanted to hang around. Whoever had killed Shaz didn't deserve a minute longer at liberty than they'd already had. It was tough enough sitting on her hands while she waited for the results of DCI Jordan hammering the phones. Now there was a role model, Kay thought as she prowled from room to room of her terraced Victorian artisan's cottage. Whatever Carol Jordan had done, she'd obviously done it right. 'If you want to be successful, hang around with successful people and copy what they do,' Kay recited, a familiar mantra from one of her American self-improvement tapes.

The call came at lunchtime. Carol had spoken to all of the CID divisions who had dealt with the missing girls. In three cases, she'd even managed to contact the investigating officer, though investigation was probably too exalted a word for the cursory inquiries into missing teenage girls who didn't appear to want to be found. She had arranged for Kay to survey the slender files, and she'd contrived to elicit addresses and phone numbers for the distraught parents.

Kay put the phone down and studied a road atlas. She reckoned she could do Halifax in the afternoon and Wigan that evening. Then down the motorway to the Midlands and an overnight motel. Breakfast at Tamworth then hammer down to Exmouth for late afternoon. Back up the motorway to overnight at Swindon, then cross-country to Grantham. A stop the following day in Leeds to report to Tony, then she could finish off in Sunderland. It sounded like the road movie from hell. Even Thelma and Louise got it more glamorous than this, she thought.

But then, unlike some of her colleagues, she'd never expected it to be glamorous. Hard graft, job security and a decent pay cheque were all Kay had ever supposed she'd get from the police. The gratification of detective work had come as a surprise. And she was good at it, thanks to an eye for detail that her less appreciative colleagues called anal. Profiling seemed like the ideal area for using her observational skills to the full. She hadn't imagined her first case would be so close to home, or how personal it would feel. Nobody deserved what Shaz Bowman had endured, and nobody deserved to get away with it.

That was the thought Kay held on to as she hacked her way round the network of motorways that crisscrossed England. She noticed that all of her destinations were either close by one of those motorways or to one of the other major arterial roads peppered with fast-food joints tacked on to petrol stations. She wondered if there were any significance in that. Did Vance arrange to meet his victims at service areas they could easily scrounge a lift to? It was almost the only fresh thing to come out of two days' work, she thought grimly. That and the faintest ghostly glimmering of a pattern.

But the stories of the parents were depressingly similar, and distressingly short on significant detail, certainly where Vance was concerned. She'd managed to talk to a couple of friends of missing girls, and they'd been scarcely more helpful. It wasn't that they didn't want to help; Kay was the sort of interviewer people always talked to. Her mousey insignificance belied her intelligence; she was no threat to women and made men feel protective. No, it wasn't that they were holding back, it was simply that there wasn't much to be said. Yes, the missing girls were daft on Jacko, yes, they'd been to events where he was present and yes, they were really excited about it. But nothing more than that flimsy gleaning.

By Grantham, she was operating on automatic pilot. Two nights in motels with the beds too soft and the constant high zip, zing and zoom of all-night traffic diluted but not deleted by double glazing was no recipe for a productive interview, but it was better than no sleep at all, she scolded herself as she yawned expansively before ringing the doorbell.

Kenny and Denise Burton didn't seem to notice her exhaustion. It had been two years, seven months and three days since Stacey had walked out of the front door and never returned and the shadows under their eyes indicated neither had had a decent night's sleep since. They were like twins; both short, burly with pale, indoor skin and puffy fingers. Looking at the wall of photographs of their slim, bright-eyed daughter, it was hard to believe in genetics as a science. They sat in a living room that was a monument to the expression 'a place for everything and everything in its place'. There were a lot of places in the cramped room; corner display cabinets, alcoves shelved to accommodate knickknacks without number, a feature fireplace with built-in niches. It was a claustrophobic, timidly conventional room. With the two bars of the electric fire throwing out dusty heat, Kay could hardly breathe. It was no wonder Stacey hadn't been reluctant to leave.

'She was a lovely girl,' Denise said wistfully. It was a refrain Kay had come to hate, hiding as it did every useful element of an adolescent girl's personality. It also reminded her discouragingly of her own mother, forever obliterating the reality of Kay's identity behind the anodyne phrase.

'Not like some,' Kenny said darkly, smoothing his greying hair back over the bald patch threatening to burst through like a cartoon bump on the head. 'She was told to be in by ten, by ten she'd be in.'

'She'd never have gone off of her own free will,' Denise said, the next line in the litany perfectly timed, perfectly placed. 'She had no reason to. She must have been abducted. There's no other explanation.'

Kay avoided the painfully obvious one. 'I'd like to ask some questions about the days before Stacey disappeared,' she said. 'Apart from going to school, did she go out at all that week?'

Kenny and Denise didn't pause for thought. In counterpoint, they said, 'She went to the pictures.'

'With Kerry.'

'The weekend before she was taken.'

'Tom Cruise.'

'She loves Tom Cruise.' The defiant present tense.

'She went out on the Monday as well.'

'We wouldn't normally allow her out on a school night.'

'But this was special.'

'Jacko Vance.'

'Her hero, he is.'

'Opening a fun pub in town, he was.'

'We wouldn't normally have allowed her into a pub.'

'What with her only being fourteen.'

'But Kerry's mum was taking them, so we thought it would be all right.'

'And it was.'

'She was home right on time, right when Kerry's mum said they'd be.'

'Full of it, our Stacey was. She got a signed photo.'

'Personally signed. To her personally.'

'She had that with her. When she went.' There was a pause while Kenny and Denise swallowed their grief.

Kay took advantage. 'How did she seem after their night out?'

'She was very excited, wasn't she, Kenny? It was like a dream come true to her, talking to Jacko Vance.'

'She actually got to talk to him?' Kay forced herself to sound nonchalant. The faint pattern she'd discerned was growing stronger with each interview.

'Like a moonstruck calf she was, after,' Stacey's father confirmed.

'She'd always wanted to go on the television.' The counterpoint was back.

'Your people reckoned she'd run off to London to try and break into showbiz,' Kenny said contemptuously. 'No way. Not Stacey. She was far too sensible. She agreed with us. Stay at school, get her A-levels, then we'd see.'

'She could have been on the television,' Denise wistful now.

'She had the looks.'

Kay cut in before they could get off and running again. 'Did she say what she'd talked about with Jacko Vance?'

'Just that he was really friendly,' Denise said. 'I don't think he said anything in particular to her, did he, Kenny?'

'He hasn't got time to take a personal interest. A busy man. Dozens of people, no, hundreds of people want him to sign an autograph, exchange a few words, pose for a picture.'

The words hung in the air like the afterimage of sparklers. 'Pose for a picture?' Kay said faintly. 'Did Stacey have her picture taken with him?'

They nodded in sync. 'Kerry's mum took it.'

'Could I see it?' Kay's heart was suddenly thudding like a drum, her palms sweating in the stuffy room.

Kenny pulled an embossed album from under a coffee table stained a colour unknown in nature. With practised hand, he turned swiftly to the last page. There, blown up to ten by eight was a fuzzy snapshot of a cluster of people surrounding Jacko Vance. The angle was skewed, the faces blurred, as if seen through a heat haze. But the girl standing next to Jacko Vance, the one he was unquestionably talking to, his hand on her shoulder, his head inclined towards her, the girl looking up with the adoring look of a new puppy was without a shadow of a doubt Stacey Burton.

It had been harder than Wharton had expected to talk to Detective Sergeant Chris Devine. When he'd rung her office, he'd discovered she'd signed up for a couple of days' compassionate leave following her initial telephone statement to the murder inquiry. It was the first time Wharton had encountered anyone who seemed to be genuinely grieving for Shaz Bowman; he'd not been the officer charged with breaking the news to her devastated parents.

By the time Chris had returned the message on her answering machine, Wharton was already in London interviewing Vance and his wife. It had been easy to arrange to meet at her flat afterwards.

The hard-nosed copper in him had warmed to Chris Devine immediately she'd opened her door and greeted them with, 'I sincerely hope you're going to nail the bastard who did this.' He wasn't bothered by the array of artistic photographs of beautiful women that covered the walls of her flat. He'd worked with dykes before and on balance he thought they were a damn sight less disruptive than most of the straight women on the force. His sidekick was less sanguine, carefully choosing to sit facing the wall of glass that looked out from the modern block of flats to the ancient church left incongruously standing at the heart of the Barbican complex.

'I hope so, too,' he'd said, perching on the lumpy futon sofa and wondering fleetingly how people ever slept on the things.

'You've been to see Jacko Vance?' Chris said almost before she was settled in the big wing chair opposite him.

'We interviewed him and his wife yesterday. He confirmed what you'd already told us about the appointment DC Bowman kept with him on the day she died.'

She nodded, pushing her thick chestnut hair away from her face. 'I had Vance down as the type that would keep a note of everything.'

'So what was all that about?' Wharton asked. 'Why were you helping DC Bowman maintain the illusion that she was a Met officer?'

The frown line between her eyes deepened. 'I'm sorry?'

'Your direct line in the CID office was left as a contact number for DC Bowman. The impression it gave was that she was still a Met officer.'

'She *was* still a Met officer,' Chris pointed out. 'But there was nothing sinister in giving my number as a contact. During their training period, the profiling squad officers can't take phone calls in working hours. Shaz asked if I'd sort it, that's all.'

'Why you, Sergeant? Why not the desk officer where she was stationed? Why not leave her home number and ask him to call in the evening?' There was nothing hostile in Wharton's manner; he was genuinely interested in the answer.

'I suppose because we were already in contact over the case,' Chris said, feeling irritation rise inside her but giving no outward sign. Her years in the police had left her with the tendency to see innuendo in everything and the ability not to show her reaction.

'You were? In what respect?'

Chris turned her head and her dark eyes looked over Wharton's shoulder to the sky beyond. 'She'd already asked for my help. She needed some newspapers photocopied and I went out to Colindale to do it for her.'

'You were responsible for that parcel?'

'I was, yes.'

'I've heard about that. Must have been hundreds of pages, box that size and weight. That's a lot of work for an officer as busy as you must be,' Wharton said, starting to lean a little now he suspected there might be more going on here than met the eye.

'I did it in my own time. OK, Inspector?'

'That's a lot of time to give up for a junior officer,' Wharton suggested.

Chris's mouth tightened momentarily. With her snub nose, she had more than a passing resemblance to Grumpy from the Seven Dwarves. 'Shaz and I were partners on the night shift for a long time. We were friends as well as colleagues. She was probably the most talented young officer I've ever worked with and frankly, Mr Wharton, I don't see how questioning why I was happy to give up my day off to help her is going to help you put her killer away.'

Wharton shrugged. 'Background. You never know.'

'I know, believe me. You should be asking about Jacko Vance.'

In spite of himself, Wharton couldn't help an ironic grin. 'Don't tell me you fell for that as well?'

'If you mean, do I go along with Shaz's theory that Jacko Vance was killing teenage girls, the answer is, I don't know. I've not had the chance to review her evidence. But what I do know is that Vance arranged with me that she should come to his house early on Saturday and she was dead by the next morning. Now, the way we work things down here is we get very interested in the last known person to see a murder victim alive, and according to Shaz's mum, you don't seem to have any record of anyone seeing her after she left Vance's house. That would make me very interested in Jacko Vance. What are the profiling squad saying about it?'

'I'm sure you'll appreciate that until we can conclusively rule out her immediate colleagues from our inquiries, we can't use them to investigate the case.'

Chris's mouth fell open. 'You're not using Tony Hill?'

'We think she may have known her killer, and the only people she knew in Leeds were the ones she was working with. You're an experienced detective. You must see that we can't risk contaminating the inquiry by taking any of them into our confidence.'

'You've got the most talented profiler in the country in the palm of your hand, a man who actually knew the victim and knew what she was working on, and you're ignoring him? Is there some reason you don't want to catch Shaz's killer? I bet Tony Hill doesn't think you should be letting Jacko Vance off the hook.'

Wharton smiled indulgently. 'I can understand you getting a bit emotional about this case.' Chris seethed inside but said nothing as he continued. 'But I can assure you, I've spoken to Mr Vance and there's nothing to suggest that he had anything to do with the murder. According to him, all DC Bowman was interested in was whether he'd spotted any of her so-called cluster of missing girls in the company of any regular attenders at his events. He said he hadn't and that was that.'

'And you take his word for it? Just like that?'

Wharton shrugged. 'Like I said, why wouldn't we? Where's the evidence to suggest anything suspicious?'

Chris stood up abruptly and picked up a packet of cigarettes from a corner table. She lit up and turned back to face Wharton. 'He is the last person that we know who saw her,' she said, her voice harsh.

Wharton's smile was meant to placate but only enraged. 'We don't know that, with respect. She'd written the letter "T" in her diary beneath the appointment with Vance. As if she was going on somewhere else. You wouldn't know who "T" is, would you, Sergeant?'

A deep inhalation of smoke, a long exhalation, then Chris said, 'I can't think of anyone. Sorry.'

'You don't think it might refer to Tony Hill?'

She shrugged. 'It could, I suppose. It could mean almost anything. She could have been going to the Trocadero to play laser games, for all I know. She never said anything about any other plans to me.'

'She didn't come here?'

Chris frowned. 'Why would she?'

'You said you were friends. She was in London. I'd have thought she'd have popped in, especially with you being so helpful and all.' There was a tougher element in Wharton's voice and his jaw thrust outward.

'She didn't come here.' Chris's mouth clamped shut.

Sensing a weak spot, Wharton pushed harder. 'Why was

that, Sergeant? Did she prefer to keep a bit of distance between you? Especially now she'd got herself a boyfriend?'

Chris walked briskly to the door and opened it. 'Goodbye, Inspector Wharton.'

'That's a very interesting response, Sergeant Devine,' Wharton said, taking his time getting to his feet and checking that his junior officer was still taking notes.

'If you want to insult Shaz's memory and my intelligence, you're not doing it in my home. Next time, make it formal. Sir.' She leaned against the door, watching them walk down the hall to the lifts. 'Arsehole,' she muttered under her breath. Then she let the heavy door swing shut and crossed to the phone where she rang an old flame in the Home Office. 'Dee? It's Chris. Hey, doll, I need a favour. You've got a psychologist on the payroll, geezer called Tony Hill. I need a personal number . . .'

Jimmy Linden had noticed the young black man even before he'd reached his seat in the sixth row of the empty stand. Years of working with promising young athletes had developed his instinct for spotting strangers. It wasn't only sex perverts you had to be on the lookout for. The drug pushers were just as dangerous with their promises of steroid magic. And Jimmy's youngsters were the very ones most prone to falling for their promises. Anyone who wanted to be the best at javelin, hammer, shot or discus needed the kind of muscle that anabolic steroids could provide a lot more easily than training.

No, it never hurt to keep a weather eye out for strangers, especially here at Meadowbank Stadium where he coached the Scottish junior squad, the pick of the bunch, all of them desperate for that edge that would make them a champion. Jimmy looked up again at the stranger. He looked in pretty good shape, though if he'd ever had dreams of being a contender, he should have knocked those fags on the head a long time ago.

As the session drew to a close and the young athletes climbed into their tracksuits, Jimmy spotted the stranger getting up and disappearing down the stairway. When he emerged trackside moments later, demonstrating he had some official reason for being there, Jimmy felt the muscles in the back of his neck relax slightly, the first sign he'd had that they'd been tense. Old age was creeping up at a gallop, he thought wryly. Used to be he was that close to his body that not a nerve fluttered without him knowing about it.

Before he could follow the sweating bodies into the changing rooms, the stranger stepped in front of him and flashed a warrant card. It was too fast for Jimmy to suss which force he belonged to, but he knew what the card was. 'Detective Constable Jackson,' the man said. 'I'm sorry to bother you at work, but I could use half an hour of your time.'

Jimmy tutted, his whippet face narrowing in displeasure. 'You'll not find any drugs with this lot,' he said. 'I run a clean team, and they all know it.'

Leon shook his head and smiled. 'It's nothing to do with your squad. I just need to pick your brains about some ancient history, that's all.' There was no trace of the smart-mouthed jive talk he used on his fellow profilers.

'What kind of ancient history?'

Leon noticed Jimmy's eyes flickering after his disciples and realized the trainer still had things he wanted to say to them. Hastily, he said, 'It's nothing to worry about, honestly. Look, I noticed a half-decent café just down the road. Why don't you meet me there when you're done here and we can have a chat?'

'Aye, OK,' Jimmy said grudgingly. Half an hour later he was

facing Leon over a mug of tea and a plate piled with the sort of bakery products that earned Scotland its nickname of the Land O'Cakes. He must be one hell of a coach, Leon thought as the little man wolfed down a coconut-covered snowball. All the successful throwing jocks Leon had ever known were big blokes, broad in the shoulder and heavy through the thighs. But Jimmy Linden resembled a medieval ascetic, the classic long-distance runner, one of those creatures of bone and sinew who stride easily across the finishing line at marathons, eyes on the middle distance, looking as if the only thing they could want was the next twenty-six miles.

'So what's this all about?' Jimmy said, wiping his mouth with surprising daintiness on a proper monogrammed cotton handkerchief pulled from the sleeve of his sweatshirt.

'For reasons that will become obvious, I can't go into too much detail. We're investigating a case that may have its roots deep in the past. I thought you might be able to give me some pointers.'

'About what? All I know anything about is athletics, son.'

Leon nodded and watched a meringue disappear. 'I'm going back now a dozen or more years ago.'

'When I was based down south? Before I came back up here?'

'That's right. You coached Jacko Vance,' Leon said.

A shadow passed across Jimmy's face. Then he cocked his head to one side and said, 'You're not telling me somebody's putting the black on Jacko and thinking they'll get away with it?' Amusement lit up his watery blue eyes.

Leon winked. 'You didn't hear that from me, Mr Linden.'

'It's Jimmy, son, everybody calls me Jimmy. So, Jacko Vance, eh? What can I tell you about the boy wonder?'

'Anything you can remember.'

'How long have you got?'

310

Leon's smile was tinged with grimness. He hadn't forgotten why he was in Edinburgh. 'As long as it takes, Jimmy.'

'Let me see. He won the British under-fifteen title when he was only thirteen. I was coaching the national squad at the time and I said as soon as I saw him throw that he was the best chance of an Olympic gold that we'd had in a generation.' He shook his head. 'I wasn't wrong. Poor bugger. Nobody deserves to watch the event they should be winning when they're trying to learn how to use an artificial limb.' Leon understood the implied but unspoken, 'not even Jacko Vance'.

'He never considered doing the disabled games?' Leon asked.

Jimmy snorted derisively. 'Jacko? That would have meant admitting he was disabled.'

'So you became his coach when he was thirteen?'

'That's right. He was a worker, I'll say that for him. He was lucky, living in London, because he had good access to me and to the facilities, and by Christ, he made the most of it. I used to ask him, did he not have a home to go to?'

'And what did he say to that?'

'Ach, he'd just shrug. I got the impression that his mother wasn't bothered what he was doing as long as he was out from under her feet. She was away from his father by then, of course. Separated, divorced, whatever.'

'Did his parents not come along, then?'

Jimmy shook his head. 'Never saw the mother. Not a once. His dad came to one meeting. I think it was the time he was going for the British junior record, but he blew it. I mind his dad took the piss out of him good style. I took him to one side and told him if he couldn't back his boy up, he wasn't welcome.'

'How did he take that?'

Jimmy took a gulp of tea and said, 'Ach, stupid bastard called me a bum boy. I just told him to fuck right off, and that was the last we saw of him.'

Leon made a mental note. He knew Tony would be interested in this. As he saw it, the young Jacko had been desperate for attention. His mother was indifferent, his father absent and his whole being was focused on his sporting achievement in the hope that somehow that would win him approval. 'So, was he lonely, Jacko?' He lit a cigarette, ignoring the disapproving look on the coach's narrow face.

Jimmy considered the question. 'He could mess about with the best of them, but he wasn't really one of the lads, know what I mean? He was too dedicated. He couldn't loosen up enough. Not that he was a loner. No, he always had Jillie in tow, hanging around him, telling him he was wonderful.'

'So they were devoted to each other?'

'She was devoted to him. He was devoted to himself, but he liked the adoration. Unconditional, like you get from a collie dog. Mind you, even Jillie got the hump sometimes. I moved heaven and earth to keep that pair together. Whenever she got fed up with taking the back seat to his training or competitions, I used to bolster her up with how great she'd feel when he stood there on the Olympic rostrum picking up the gold. I'd say, most girls, the only gold they ever got was a poxy wedding ring, but she was going to get a gold medal.'

'And that was enough, was it?'

Jimmy shrugged, wafting Leon's smoke away with one hand. 'To be honest, it got so that was the only thing that kept her going. When he started competing on the senior circuit, and Jillie was that wee bit older, she started taking notice of the way the other lads treated their girls. And Jacko didn't stand up too well to the comparison. If he hadn't have lost his arm, she might just have put up with it for the

312

acclaim and the cash that went with it, because athletes were just about starting to make megabucks around then and the writing was on the wall for more to come. But as soon as she decided he wasn't going to be a cash machine or a household name, she got shot of him.'

Leon was on full alert. 'I thought he dumped her? Didn't I read at the time that he broke off the engagement because he wasn't the man she'd signed up for and it wasn't fair to tie her down? Something like that?'

Jimmy's mouth curled into a contemptuous smile. 'So you fell for that load of toffee? That was just the story Jacko leaked to the press, to make him look like the big man instead of the sad bastard who'd been dumped.'

So Shaz might well have been right, Leon thought. Circumstance had piled two traumatic stressors right on top of each other. First Vance had lost his arm and his future. Then he had lost the one person who had believed in him as a human being rather than as a throwing machine. It would take a strong man to survive that unscathed; a warped one would need to take revenge against a world that had done this to him. Leon stubbed out his cigarette and said, 'Did he tell you the truth?'

'No. Jillie did. I was the one drove her to the hospital that day. And I saw Jacko after she told him.'

'How did he take it?'

Jimmy's eyes dripped contempt. 'Oh, just like a man. He told me she was a heartless bitch who was only after one thing. I told him he didn't have to give in to his injuries, that he could train for the disabled games and that it was just as well he found out the truth about Jillie now. He told me to fuck off and never come near him again. And that was the last time I saw him.'

'You didn't go back to the hospital?'

The trainer's face was bleak. 'I went every day for a week. He wouldn't see me. Refused point-blank. He didn't seem to realize I had lost my dreams, too. Anyway, I got the chance of this job back in Scotland round about then, so I came back here and started all over again.'

'Were you surprised when he popped up as a television celebrity?'

'I can't say I was, no. He needs somebody telling him he's wonderful, that one. I've often wondered if all those millions of viewers are ever enough, if he's still as desperate to be adored as he was back then. He could never see any value in himself that wasn't reflected in other folks' eyes.' Jimmy shook his head and signalled for another cup of tea. 'I suppose you want to know if he had any enemies and what his deep dark secrets were?'

An hour later, Leon knew that what Jimmy Linden had told him at the start of their conversation was the stuff that had mattered. Just as well, he realized as he sat in the car afterwards. For some reason, his miniature tape recorder had failed to turn over automatically and had only recorded the first half of their chat. Feeling well pleased with himself nevertheless, Leon set out on the long journey south, wondering who'd done best so far. He knew it wasn't a competition. He'd liked Shaz enough to do it for her sake. But he was sufficiently human to realize that if he performed well out on the street, it would do him no harm. Especially since he now understood that as far as Tony Hill was concerned, he had more than a little to prove.

It wasn't difficult to spot the sports stadium and leisure-centre complex. Spotlit against the dark Malvern Hills, it was visible for miles from the motorway. Once he'd turned off on to minor roads and a rash of mini-roundabouts, however,

Tony was glad he'd called in advance for directions. The centre was too recently built for most locals to know where it was, so the anonymous voice that had given explicit guidance over the phone was clearly used to the process.

As it turned out, he'd have arrived safely if he'd simply followed any other car heading in the same direction. The car park was already crowded when he reached it, and he had to park a few hundred yards away from the main entrance with its banner proclaiming, 'Grand Opening Gala – with Special Guests Jacko Vance and Stars from the England Squad'. Footballers for the lads, Jacko for the women, he thought as he walked briskly across the Tarmac, grateful for the bulk of the stadium acting as a buffer against the chill night wind.

He joined the throng of eager people thrusting through the turnstiles, casting a practised eye along the staff checking tickets. He chose a middle-aged woman who looked competent and motherly, and squeezed through the press of bodies to present himself at her window. He slipped his Home Office credentials out of his pocket and showed them to her, arranging his face into a rueful, harried expression. 'Dr Hill, Home Office, sports research group. I was supposed to have a VIP pass, but it didn't arrive. I don't suppose ... ?'

The woman frowned momentarily. She gave him a swift appraisal, reckoning whether he was up to something, realizing the queue behind him was building up, finally deciding it was someone else's problem if he was, she pressed the release button to let him through. 'You want the directors' suite. Round to the right, second floor.'

Tony let the natural movement of the crowd carry him forward into the vast echoing area under the grandstand, then edged to one side to study the giant map of the stadium cunningly laid out on the underside of the tiered seating. Whoever had designed it had been aware of the three-dimensional surface it would be reproduced on, and it somehow managed to be clear from whatever angle it was viewed. According to the programme he'd just bought, there would be live music in the main arena, followed by a demonstration five-a-side football match featuring England squad players, then an Irish dance spectacular. For those who had shelled out an extra fifty pounds or won one of the contests run by the local TV, radio and newspapers, there would be a chance to meet the celebrities. And that was where he needed to be.

He slid through the crowd, calculating his moves so he upset no one on his route to the executive lift. The lobby was cordoned off with heavy crimson ropes. A security guard wearing a belt loaded with enough equipment to stock a hardware store stared balefully out from under a cap worn low like a guardsman. Tony knew it was nothing more than bravado. He flashed his credentials at the guard, moving purposefully as if the last thing he expected was to be challenged. The man took a step backwards and said, 'Wait a minute.'

Tony was already at the lift, pressing the call button. 'It's OK,' he said. 'Home Office. We like to turn up when they least expect us. Got to keep an eye on things, you know.' He winked and stepped into the car. 'Don't want another Hillsborough, do we?' The doors slid closed on the bemused face of the guard.

After that, it was easy. Out of the lifts, down the hall, in through the open double doors, a glass of something straw-coloured and fizzy from the nearest waistcoated flunkey and he was established. Tony took in the long windows that ran the length of the opposite wall, looking down on the all-weather pitch. He could just see a team of majorettes strutting their stuff down below. A thin crowd bunched around the edges of the room. At the far end, over by the window, Jacko Vance stood at the centre of a cluster of middle-aged women and a few men. His hair gleamed in the refracted light from the spotlights over the pitch, his eyes shone in the soft lighting of the executive suite. Even though he'd already glad-handed his way through two charity appearances that day, his body language was still warm, welcoming, his smile treating everyone as a welcome equal. He looked like a god dealing with his worshippers without condescension. Tony gave a thin smile. The third event since he'd gone out on the prowl for Jacko, and every time he'd struck gold. It was almost as if there were a connection, an invisible fibre optic linking the hunter and the prey. This time, though, he'd make certain those roles were never reversed. Once had been enough for that.

Tony moved to one side and made his way up the room, using the legitimate guests as cover. After a few minutes, he had travelled the length of the room, occupying a corner opposite Vance but slightly behind him. His eyes moved regularly from side to side, scanning the area immediately around the TV star, never lingering for long, but never leaving Vance unattended for more than a moment.

He didn't have long to wait. A young woman with slicked back blonde hair, John Lennon glasses and a scarlet cupid's bow bounced into the room clutching a bag emblazoned with SHOUT! FM, checking over her shoulder to see that her charges were still firmly in tow. Following in a ragged line came three adolescent girls overdressed and overpainted, a couple of youths with more spots than charm and an elderly woman whose hair was so rigidly set it appeared the rollers were still bound into it. Three paces behind slouched a nerd in a gilet with a dozen bulging pockets, a pair of battered

SLR cameras hanging negligently round his neck. The winners of some moronic phone-in competition, Tony guessed. He could think of one question they wouldn't have been asked: How many teenagers has Jacko Vance murdered? It would take a year or two after he'd finished his work for that to filter down into the trivia quiz books.

The bouncy blonde approached where Vance was holding court. Tony could see Vance look up at her then dismissively abandon her for the middle-aged woman in the turquoise sari he'd been charming previously. The blonde lunged through the inner circle round Jacko, only to be headed off by the woman Tony had noticed running interference for Jacko the first time he'd staked him out. Their heads huddled together, then the PA nodded and touched Vance on the elbow. As he turned, his professional gaze slid round the room and caught Tony. The sweep of his eyes paused momentarily, then continued, nothing else in his expression changing.

The blonde's competition winners were ushered into the presence of their idol. He smiled down on them, charm personified. He chatted, signed autographs, shook hands, pecked cheeks and posed for photographs. Every thirty seconds, his eyes lost their focus and glanced unerringly at where Tony stood leaning against the wall, sipping fake champagne, his pose and his expression reeking assurance and confidence.

As the competition winners reached the end of their audience, Tony moved away from his vantage point and headed for the little group, still standing near Vance, their expressions ranging from ecstasy to an affected nonchalance, depending on how cool they felt the need to be. All bonhomie, Tony insinuated himself into their group, his expression a model of openness and geniality. 'I'm sorry to butt in on you,' he said. 'But I think you might be able to help me. My name's Tony Hill and I'm a psychological profiler. You know how stars like Jacko are always being plagued by stalkers? Well, I'm working with a team of crack police officers on ways to find out who those stalkers are before they start causing real problems. What we're trying to do is to come up with a psychological profile of the perfect fan, the good supporter. Someone like you, the sort of fan any celebrity would be glad to have on their side. We need to do this so we can get what's called a control profile. All we need is a short interview with you. Half an hour, tops. We come to your place or you come to us, we pay you £25, and you get the comfort of knowing you might have stopped the next Mark Chapman.' He loved the way their faces always changed when he mentioned the money.

Tony took out the pre-printed name and address slips from his inside pocket. 'How about it? Painless anonymous questionnaire, you help us save a life and you earn yourself £25. Just fill in your name and address on one of these and one of my researchers will be in touch.' Out came the handsome embossed National Offender Profiling Task Force business cards. 'This is who I am.' He handed them out. By now, all except one of the youths had their hands out for a form. 'There we go,' he said, providing them with pens.

He looked across at Vance. His face was still smiling, his mouth forming words, his hands patting an elbow here, a shoulder there. But his eyes were on Tony; dark, questioning, hostile.

The house was nothing special, Simon thought as he parked the car. A three-bedroomed dormer bungalow on a thirty-year-old development that was well on course to disprove the adage that life begins at forty. She'd have done a lot better if she and Jacko had stayed together. She certainly wouldn't have ended up in a town like Wellingborough where a night out at the DIY superstore was most people's idea of a good time.

He was amazed at the speed with which Carol Jordan had come up with Jillie Woodrow's whereabouts, particularly since she was three years into her second marriage. 'Don't ask,' Carol had said when he'd complimented her, admitting it would have taken him days to make that much progress. He remembered Tony Hill mentioning something to Carol about her brother in the computer industry and wondered if their shoestring task force had just added data burglary to its irregularities.

He sat in the car and looked across the narrow street at the house belonging to Jillie and Jeff Lewis. It looked spick and span and relentlessly suburban with its perfectly trimmed lawn and borders filled with neatly equidistant hebes and heathers. There was a year-old Metro on the drive and net curtains across the picture window. If Jillie Lewis's attention had been caught by the sound of his engine, she could be watching him and he'd have no idea at all.

This was almost certainly going to be the most crucial interview of his career to date, Simon thought, gearing himself up for the task. He had no clear idea of what he was going to ask, but if Jillie Lewis had information that would nail Jacko Vance for the murder of Shaz Bowman, he was determined to prise it out of her, one way or another. He hadn't had the chance to find out whether he would ever have been allowed to owe Shaz more than a colleague would. But even that was more than debt enough for him. Simon got out of the car and pulled on the jacket of his Marks and Spencer suit. Straightening his tie and his shoulders, he took a deep breath and walked up the path.

The door opened seconds after his ring, stopped short by a flimsy chain that he could have been past in seconds if he'd had a mind to. For a brief, mad moment, he wondered whether this was the cleaner or the nanny. The woman who faced him across the doorstep bore no superficial resemblance to the old newspaper photographs of Jillie Woodrow, nor to the teenage girls on the missing list. Her hair was a streaked blonde urchin cut rather than the dark bob he'd expected, and she'd lost every vestige of puppy fat, being skinny to the point where, if he were her husband, Simon would be surreptitiously reading up on anorexia. He was about to make his apologies when he recognized the eyes. The expression had hardened, there were lines starting to show at the edges, but these were Jillie Woodrow's dark blue soulful eyes. 'Mrs Lewis?' he asked.

The woman nodded. 'Who are you?' Simon presented his warrant card and she gasped, 'Jeff?'

Quickly Simon reassured her. 'It's nothing to do with your husband. I'm currently attached to a special investigations unit in Leeds, but my home force is Strathclyde. I don't have any local connection.'

'Leeds? I've never been to Leeds.' When she frowned, discontent was written across her face like an advertising hoarding.

Simon smiled. 'Lucky you. There have been times lately when I've wished I could say the same thing. Mrs Lewis, this is a very awkward situation and it would be a lot easier for me to explain it inside with a cup of coffee than it is on the doorstep. Can I come in?'

She looked uncertain, making a show of checking her watch. 'I'm supposed to be at work,' she said, carefully not saying when.

'I wouldn't be here if it wasn't important,' Simon said, his apologetic smile displaying the charm that had been one of the assets that had taken him this far in his career.

'I suppose you'd better come in, then,' she said, slipping the chain off and stepping back. He walked into a hall that looked as if it belonged to a show house. Spotless, tasteless and immaculate, it led into a kitchen that no one appeared ever to have cooked in. Jillie led the way and gestured to the circular table crammed into one corner. 'You better have a seat,' she muttered as she picked up a kettle, dark green to match the tiles along the splashback of the sink. 'Coffee, then?'

'Please,' Simon said, wedging himself behind the table. 'Milk, no sugar.'

'I suppose you think you're sweet enough,' Jillie said sourly, taking a jar of cheap instant from the cupboard and spooning it into two china mugs. 'I suppose this is something to do with Jacko Vance, is it?'

Simon tried not to reveal how taken aback he was. 'What makes you say that?'

Jillie turned and leaned against the worktop, crossing her jean-clad legs and folding her arms protectively over her chest. 'What else would it be? Jeff's an honest hard-working salesman, I'm a part-time data processor. We don't know any criminals. The only thing I've ever done that anybody outside these four walls would be interested in was being Jacko Vance's girlfriend. The only person I've ever had anything to do with who would interest some special investigation unit is Jacko bloody Vance, come back to flaming haunt me again.' It was a defiant outburst and she concluded it by turning her back on him and managing to make vicious the act of pouring two coffees.

Not quite sure where to go next, Simon said, 'I'm sorry. It's clearly a sensitive subject.'

Jillie dumped the coffee in front of him. Given the pristine kitchen, he was surprised she didn't run for a cloth when

322

it slopped on the pine tabletop. Instead, she retreated back against the worktop, clutching her coffee like a child with a hot-water bottle. 'I've got nothing to say about Jacko Vance. You've had a wasted journey from Leeds. Still, I suppose you get good mileage since it's the taxpayers that foot the bill and not some skinflint company.'

Her bitterness seemed to have infected the coffee, Simon thought ruefully, sipping the brew to give himself time to think of a reply. 'It's a serious inquiry,' he said. 'We could use your help.'

She banged her mug down on the worktop. 'Look. I don't care what he says. It's not me that's pestering him. I had this up to the back teeth just after I first married Jeff. I had cops round half a dozen times. Was I sending Jacko anonymous letters? Was I making abusive phone calls to his wife? Did I parcel up dog turds and post them to his office? Well, the answer's the same now as it was then. If you think I'm the only person Jacko Vance has upset in his selfish journey to the top of the greasy pole, you have got a serious imagination deficiency.' She stopped short and glared at him. 'I don't do blackmail, either. You can check. Every penny in and out of this house is accounted for. I've had that accusation to contend with, and that's a load of flaming rubbish as well.' She shook her head. 'I can't believe that *pig*,' she fumed.

Simon held his hands up in a placatory gesture. 'Whoa, wait a minute. I think you've got hold of the wrong end of the stick here. I didn't come to see you because Jacko made a complaint. Sure, I want to talk to you about Jacko, but I'm only interested in what he's done, not what he says you've done. Honest!'

She gave him a sharp look. 'What?'

Uneasy that he might have gone too far, Simon said, 'As I said, this is all very sensitive. Jacko Vance's name has come

323

up in an inquiry and my job is to make some background checks. Without alerting Mr Vance to our interest, if you take my point.' He hoped he didn't look as nervous as he felt. Whatever he'd expected, it hadn't been this.

'You're investigating Jacko?' Jillie sounded incredulous but had started to look almost cheerful.

Simon shifted in his chair. 'Like I said, his name has come up in connection with a serious matter . . .'

Jillie punched her thigh. 'Yes! And not before bloody time. Don't tell me, let me guess. He hurt some poor bloody woman too much and didn't terrify her enough to make her keep her mouth shut, is that it?'

Simon sensed the interview spiralling out of his control. All he could do was cling on with his fingernails and hope he wouldn't get shaken off somewhere along the way. 'What makes you say that?' he asked.

'It was bound to happen some day,' she said, all but gleeful. 'So, what do you want to know?'

By the time he got home, Tony's eyes were gritty with staring at too many night motorway miles. He hadn't intended to check his answering machine, but the flashing light caught his eye as he passed the door of his study. Wearily, he hit the playback button. 'Hi. My name's Chris Devine. Detective Sergeant Chris Devine. I was Shaz Bowman's CID partner in London for a while. She used me to set up her appointment with Jacko Vance. Give me a call whenever you get in. Doesn't matter how late it is.'

He grabbed a pen and scribbled the number, reaching for the phone as soon as the message clicked off. The phone rang half a dozen times, then was picked up. 'Is that Chris Devine?' he said to the silence.

'Is that Tony Hill?' The voice was pure South London.

'You left a message on my machine. About Shaz?'

'Yeah. Listen, I've had them turnips from West Yorkshire down here, and they told me they're not working with you. Is that right?'

He liked a person who didn't waste time. 'They feel it would compromise the integrity of their investigation to involve me or any of Shaz's other immediate colleagues,' he said caustically.

'Bollocks,' she said in disgust. 'They haven't got a fucking clue, pardon my French. So are you running your own investigation, or what?'

It was like being pinned to the wall by a very large weight, Tony thought. 'I'm obviously very keen to see Shaz's killer caught,' he tried.

'So what are you doing about it?'

'Why do you ask?' he parried.

'To see if you need an extra pair of hands, of course,' she said, exasperated. 'Shaz was a great kid, and she was gonna be a great cop. Now, either Jacko Vance topped her for reasons we don't entirely know yet, or somebody else did. Either way, the trail starts at his front door, no?'

'You're right,' Tony said. Now he knew what cement felt like under a steamroller.

'And you're working the case?'

'In a manner of speaking.'

Her sigh sounded like something from the Shipping Forecast. 'Well, in a manner of speaking, I could help. What do you need from me?'

Tony's mind raced. 'I'm a bit stalled on leverage where Vance and his wife are concerned. Something that might help me put a bit of a wedge between them might help.'

'Like, Micky Morgan's really a dyke?'

'That sort of thing, yes.'

325

'You mean that's not enough?' Chris demanded.
'That's for real?'

She snorted. 'Course it's for real. They're so far in the closet you'd take them for a pair of winter coats, but they're coke.'

'Coke?'

'The real thing. She's been with Betsy for donkey's years. Way before she even met Jacko.'

'Betsy Thorne? Her PA?'

'PA, bollocks. Lover, more like. Betsy had a good little catering business with her ex, then she met Micky Morgan and it was wham, bam, thank you, ma'am. They used to go to a couple of very discreet places in the early days. Then they disappeared off the scene and, next thing you know, she pops up as Jacko Vance's tottie. But Betsy's still right there in the picture. See, Micky was on the up and up, and there were rumours that the tabloids were going to nail her for being a dyke.'

'How do you know all this?' Tony said faintly.

'How do you think? Christ, twelve, fifteen years ago, you didn't stay in this job if you were out. We used to go to the same places. Places where everybody was in the same boat so nobody ever shopped anybody else. Take it from me, whoever Jacko Vance is shagging, it's not his wife. Tell you the truth, that's what made me think Shaz was maybe on to something.'

'Did you tell Shaz about this?'

'I hadn't thought about Micky Morgan from one year's end to the next. It only came to me after I set up the interview. I was gonna let Shaz know when she belled me to tell me how she'd got on with Jacko. So no, I never got round to telling her. Is this any use to you?'

'Chris, it's fabulous. You're fabulous.'

326

'That's what they all say, babe. So, you want me to help, or what?'

'I think you already have.'

When Carol walked into her domain, the threesome were already there in their accustomed places, a trickle of smoke curling out of the corner of her window from Lee's cigarette. She sensed the smoking was meant as a challenge. But although she'd never smoked – or perhaps for that very reason – the faint tang of cigarettes was something that seldom troubled her. Carol found the energy for a smile and tried not to slump when her backside hit the chair. 'So, what have we got?'

Tommy Taylor rested his left ankle on his right knee and squirmed lower in the chair. Carol didn't envy him the lower back pain he was storing up for later years. He tossed a file negligently on to her desk. As it slithered towards her, the edges of the papers inside spilled out. 'We know more about this lot's finances than their wives do.'

'From what I hear about Yorkshire, that's not saying much,' Carol said. Tommy and Lee Whitbread grinned. Di Earnshaw's dour expression didn't crack.

'By heck, ma'am, I think that might just be a sexist remark,' Lee said.

'So sue me. What have we got?'

'It's all in the file,' Tommy said, jerking a thumb towards her.

'Summarize.'

'Di?' Tommy said. 'You're the wizard with words.'

Di unfolded her arms and thrust her hands into the pockets of an olive green jacket that made her look ripe for throwing up. 'Mr Pendlebury wasn't very keen, but he did authorize us to gain access to payroll information which provided us with bank details, addresses and dates of birth for our suspects. With that information we were able to check county court judgements . . .'

'And a little bird helped us with some commercial credit checking,' Lee chipped in.

'But we don't talk about that,' Tommy said repressively.

Carol said, 'Can we edit out the stand-up and cut to the chase?'

Di's lips pursed in their now familiar disapproval. 'Two candidates stand out. Alan Brinkley and Raymond Watson. They're both heavily in debt, as you'll see. Both local men. Watson's single, Brinkley's wed about a year since. They're both on the edge of having their houses repossessed, both got CCJs against them, both juggling Peter to pay Paul. These fires have been a bit of a blessing for the pair of them.'

'It's an ill wind,' Taylor added.

Carol opened the file and took out the sheets relating to the two men. 'Good work. You did well to get this much detail.'

Lee shrugged. 'When you get down to it, Seaford's a big village. Favours owed, favours paid.'

'As long as we don't cross the line when it comes to wages day,' Carol said.

'Don't you trust us, ma'am?' Tommy drawled.

'Give me five good reasons why I should.'

'So, d'you want us to pull them in for questioning?' Lee asked.

Carol considered for a moment. What she actually wanted was to consult with Tony, but she didn't want them to know their guv'nor wasn't able to make her own decisions. 'I'll get back to you when I've had a chance to go through these in more detail. There might be more fruitful options than trying to sweat it out of them.'

'We could try for a search warrant.' Lee again, the eager beaver of the team.

'We'll discuss it again in the morning,' Carol promised. She watched them leave, then shoved the file into her bulging briefcase. Time for a quick tour of the squad room, making sure the rest of the CID were doing what they were supposed to be doing with the cases dominating the stacks of paper on their desks. She hoped no one expected inspiration. Perspiration was about all she had left to offer.

She was about to walk through the door when the phone rang. 'DCI Jordan,' she said.

'Brandon here.'

'Sir?'

'I've just been speaking to a colleague over in West Yorkshire. In the course of our chat, we got round to talking about their officer murder. He mentioned that their prime suspect seems to have done a runner. Some chap called Simon McNeill. He said they'd probably be putting out an internal bulletin tomorrow morning asking other forces to keep a lookout for McNeill and detain him if they find him.'

'Ah.'

'I thought you might be interested,' Brandon said airily. 'With our patch being next door to theirs.'

'Absolutely, sir. As soon as I get the official notice, I'll be sure to mention it to the squad.'

'Not that I expect he'll turn up here.'

'Mmm. Thank you, sir.' Carol gingerly replaced the receiver. 'Oh, shit,' she said softly.

Tony licked his finger and smoothed down a couple of unruly hairs in his left eyebrow. He studied himself critically in the mirror that was, apart from a pair of orange polypropylene bucket chairs, the only furnishing in a room little bigger than a cupboard where he had been asked to wait. He thought he looked appropriately serious in his one decent suit even if Carol had told him it made him look like a time-warped professional footballer. But not even she could fault his dove grey shirt and dark magenta tie, he decided.

The door opened to reveal the calm-faced woman who had introduced herself as Micky's PA but whom he'd identified, thanks to Chris, as Micky's lover Betsy. 'Everything all right?' she asked.

'I'm fine.'

'Good.' Her voice was warm and encouraging, like the best type of primary school teacher. Her smile, however, was perfunctory, Tony realized, her mind clearly elsewhere. 'Now, this is quite unusual for us, because normally Micky likes to come completely fresh to her guests. But because . . . well, because she feels *involved*, however tangentially, with your tragic loss, she wants to have a few words with you ahead of time. I take it you have no objection?'

There was something about that steely upper class voice that left no possible room for demurral. Lucky Micky, he thought, to have such a lioness at the gates. 'I'd be delighted,' he said, quite truthfully.

'Good. She'll be along in a few minutes. Is there anything you need? Some coffee? Mineral water?'

'Does the coffee come from a machine?' he asked.

The smile this time was genuine. 'I'm afraid so. Indistinguishable from the tea, the hot chocolate and the chicken soup.'

'I'll pass, then.'

The head disappeared and the door snicked shut. His stomach fluttered apprehensively. Public displays always stressed him. But today there was the additional tension of his campaign to unsettle Jacko Vance to the point where he would make a mistake. Staking out Vance's personal appearances was only the opening shot across the bows. Insinuating himself into the heart of Vance's wife's TV programme was an incremental upping of the stakes. There was no point in trying to kid himself otherwise.

He cleared his throat nervously and compulsively rechecked his appearance in the mirror. The door opened without warning and suddenly Micky Morgan was in the room. Tony forced himself to turn slowly to face her. 'Hello, Ms Morgan,' he said, extending a hand.

'Dr Hill,' Micky said. Her handshake was swift, cool and firm. 'Thanks for coming on the programme.'

'My pleasure. There's so much misunderstanding about what we do, I always welcome the chance to set the record straight. Especially since we're in the news again for all the wrong reasons.' He deliberately dropped his eyes momentarily.

'Quite. I was genuinely sorry to hear about Detective Constable Bowman. I only met her very briefly, but she struck me as being very sharp, very focused. As well as being very beautiful, of course.'

Tony nodded. 'She'll be missed. She was one of the best young officers I've ever had the privilege of working with.'

'I can imagine that. It's a terrible thing for police officers to lose one of their own.'

'There's always a lot of anger flying around, covering up for the fact that they tend to feel a death in the family is a reflection of their competence, that somehow they should have been able to prevent it if they'd only been doing their jobs properly. And in this instance, I share that guilt.'

'I'm sure there was nothing you could have done to prevent it,' Micky said, impulsively putting a hand on his arm. 'When I told my husband you were coming on the programme, he said the same thing, and he's got even less reason to feel responsible.'

'No reason at all,' Tony said, surprised he could sound so sincere. 'Even though we're now coming round to thinking that her killer may have made contact with her in London rather than in Leeds. In fact, I was hoping you might give me the chance to put out an appeal for witnesses?'

Micky's hand flew to her throat in a curiously vulnerable gesture. 'You don't think she was stalked from our house, do you?'

'There's no reason to think that,' he said hastily.

'No?'

'No.'

'Thanks for the reassurance.' She took a deep breath and pushed her blonde hair back from her face. 'Now, the interview. I'm going to ask about why the unit was set up, how it's constituted, what sort of offences you'll be covering and when the task force will go into action. Then I'll move on to Sharon . . .'

'Shaz,' Tony interrupted. 'Call her Shaz. She hated being called Sharon.'

Micky nodded. 'Shaz. I'll move on to Shaz, which will give you the chance to ask for any help you want to solicit. Is that OK? Is there anything else you particularly want the opportunity to say?'

'I'm sure I'll be able to get the message across,' he said.

She reached for the door handle. 'Betsy, my PA – you spoke to her earlier – she'll come and fetch you shortly before we go on air. You'll be the last item before we break for the news bulletin.'

'Thanks,' he said, wanting to say something to build a bridge between them but not knowing what that might be. She would be his best way under Jacko Vance's defences if he could only find a way to manipulate her into unconsciously helping him.

'You're welcome,' Micky said. Then she was gone, leaving nothing behind her but the faint scent of cosmetics. He'd only have one more chance to get her on his side. He hoped he'd make a better job of it.

It had better be worth it, Vance thought. He'd cancelled lunch cooked personally by Marco Pierre White for this, and the notoriously temperamental chef would make him suffer for it. He locked his office door and closed the blinds. His secretary knew better than to put any calls through, and neither his producer nor his PA knew he was still in the building. Whatever *Midday with Morgan* revealed, there would be no one to see his reaction.

He threw himself on to the long leather sofa that dominated one side of the room and put his feet up. His face a mask of petulance, he turned on the giant TV screen with the remote control just as the familiar titles started to roll. He had nothing to fear, he knew that. Whatever Shaz Bowman had thought she'd known, she hadn't been able to convince her colleagues. He'd already dealt with the police. They'd eaten out of his hand, and rightly so. Some academic psychologist doling out half-baked theories could hardly threaten him without the backing of the plod. Nevertheless, being careful had kept him safe until now, and he wasn't about to give in to the temptation towards arrogance that such a successful career might breed.

He'd been able to glean some information about Tony Hill from his sources, though not as much as he would have liked. Again, he had been careful to keep the questions casual, taking pains not to have his inquiries arouse curiosity. What he'd learned had pricked his interest. He'd been behind the controversial Home Office study that had led to the setting up of the profiling task force that Shaz Bowman had aspired to. He'd been involved in a serial killer hunt in Bradfield where he'd ended up with blood on his hands because he hadn't been smart enough. And there were murmurings that there was something borderline perverse about his sexuality. That had really got Vance's adrenaline pumping, but it was the one angle he simply had to leave alone or risk his source wondering exactly what his concern was with the psychologist.

Fascinated though Vance was with his speculations about Tony, his thoughts were no competition for the TV screen. His attraction to the glamour of television had never waned in all his years on the performing end of the camera. He loved the medium, but most of all, he loved live TV with all its high-wire risks. Even though he ought to have been wondering how to neutralize Tony Hill if that became necessary, he couldn't resist Micky. Familiarity had bred respect rather than contempt for her professional skills and her talent. She really was one of the best. He'd spotted that right from the word go, recognized that she was one to have on his side. That he'd been able to keep her there so effectively had been a huge bonus.

She'd been good back then, but she'd improved, no doubt about that. Confidence had been part of that, Betsy another part. Her lover had shown her how to submerge the rougher edges of aggression beneath a surface of unruffled, gently probing interest. Most of Micky Morgan's victims didn't even realize how effectively they'd been filleted till someone played the tape back to them afterwards. If there was any ruffling of Tony Hill's surface to be done, a live interview with Micky would do it. He'd hinted to her that there might be darkness lurking behind her guest's facade. Now it was up to her.

He watched the first fifty minutes of the programme with a connoisseur's eye, assessing and appraising the performance of his wife and her colleagues. That Midlands reporter was going to have to go, he decided. He'd have to tell Micky. Vance hated journalists who brought the same breathless urgency to stories of distant wars, cabinet reshuffles and soap opera plots. It revealed a lack of empathy most successful hacks learned to hide early on.

It was strange, he thought, how he'd never felt the slightest twinge of sexual desire for his wife. True, she wasn't his type, but even so, he'd periodically found women attractive who didn't conform to his blueprint of desire. Never Micky, however. Not even on those rare occasions when he'd glimpsed her naked. It was probably as well, given the basis of their relationship. One glimmer of what he really wanted from the female of the species and Micky would be history. And he definitely didn't want that. Particularly not now.

'And after the break,' Micky said with that intimate warmth he suspected of causing erections among unemployed youths throughout the land, 'I'll be talking to a man who spends his days inside the heads of serial offenders. Psychological profiler Dr Tony Hill reveals the inside secrets of the new national police task force. And we pay tribute to the officer who has already tragically lost her life in that battle. All that, and the news on the hour, after the break.'

As the adverts took over, Vance pressed the record button on the video remote. He swung his feet to the floor and leaned forward, intent on the screen. The last commercial faded to the logo of *Midday with Morgan* and his wife was smiling out at him as if he were the only light of her life. 'Welcome back,' Micky said. 'My guest now is the distinguished clinical psychologist Dr Tony Hill. Nice to have you with us, Tony.'

The director switched to a two-shot, giving Vance his first

sight of Shaz Bowman's boss. The colour drained from his cheeks then raced back in a dark flush. He'd thought Tony Hill was going to be a stranger. But he knew the man on the screen. He'd spotted him first three gigs ago at the sponsored sequence dancing competition. Lurking on the fringes, talking to some of the regulars. He'd initially written him off as the latest addition to the sad squad of his camp followers. But the night before, at the sports centre, when he'd spotted him handing business cards out to the others, he'd wondered. He'd planned to send someone over to check him out, but it had slipped his mind. Now, here was the stranger, sitting on a sofa talking to Vance's wife in front of millions of viewers.

This was no routine nutter. This was no dumbshit plod. This was Shaz Bowman's boss. This might just also be an adversary.

'How has the tragic death of one of your trainees affected the squad?' Micky asked solicitously, her eyes glistening perfectly to convey heartfelt sympathy as she leaned forward.

Tony's eyes slid away from hers, the pain obvious. 'It's been a shocking blow,' he said. 'Shaz Bowman was one of the brightest officers it's ever been my privilege to work with. She had a real flair for offender profiling work, and she'll be impossible to replace. But we're determined that her killer will be caught.'

'Are you working closely with the investigating officers on the case?' Micky asked. His response to what she'd thought was a routine question was interesting. His eyebrows flashed up and his eyes widened momentarily.

'Everyone on the profiling task force is doing all they can to help,' he said quickly. 'And it's possible that your viewers could also help us.'

She was impressed with the speed of his recovery. She doubted if one in a thousand of her viewers had even noticed the blip. 'How is that, Tony?'

'As you know, Shaz Bowman was murdered in her flat in Leeds. However, we have reason to believe this wasn't a random killing. Indeed, her murderer may not even be a local man. Shaz was in London on Saturday morning, about twelve hours before she was murdered. We don't know where she went or who she saw after about ten thirty on Saturday morning. It's possible that her killer made contact with her that early in the day.'

'You mean it could have been a stalker?'

'I think it's possible that she was followed back to Leeds from London.'

That wasn't quite the same thing, but Micky knew she didn't have time to quibble. 'And you hope someone witnessed this?'

Tony nodded and stared directly into the camera with the red light showing. She could see his sincerity on the monitor in front of her. God, he was a natural, all nervousness gone as he made his impassioned appeal. 'We're looking for anyone who saw Shaz Bowman after half past ten on Saturday morning. She was very distinctive-looking. She had particularly bright blue eyes, very noticeable. You may have seen her alone or with her killer, perhaps filling her car with petrol – she drove a black Volkswagen Golf. Or possibly in one of the motorway service areas between London and Leeds. You may have noticed someone taking an unusual amount of interest in her. If so, we need to hear from you.'

'We have the number of the Leeds incident room,' Micky cut in as it appeared on a ribbon across the foot of the monitor screen. She and Tony disappeared to be replaced by a head and shoulders shot of Shaz grinning at the camera. 'If you saw Shaz Bowman on Saturday, no matter how briefly, call the police and let them know.'

'We want to catch him before he kills again,' Tony added.

'So don't be afraid to call West Yorkshire Police or even your local police station if you can help. Tony, thanks for coming in and talking to us.' Her smile shifted to the camera because her director was bellowing from the control room. 'And now, over to the newsroom for the lunchtime bulletin.'

Micky leaned back and let out her breath in an explosive sigh. 'Thanks, Tony,' she said, unclipping her mike and leaning forward so their knees touched in the angle of the sofa.

'It's me that should be thanking you,' he said in a rush as Betsy strode efficiently towards them. She reached over his shoulder to unfasten his mike.

'I'll see you out,' Betsy said.

Micky jumped to her feet. 'It's been fascinating,' she said. 'I wish we could have had longer.'

Grabbing the chance, Tony said, 'We could have dinner.'

'Yes, I'd like that,' Micky said, sounding surprised at herself. 'Are you free this evening?'

'Yes. Yes, I am.'

'Let's make it this evening, then. Is six thirty OK? I need to eat early, working this show.'

'I'll book a table.'

'No need. Betsy'll see to it, won't you, Bets?'

There was a flicker of indulgent amusement in the woman's face, Tony thought. Almost immediately, the professional mask was back. 'No problem. But I need to get Dr Hill off set, Micky,' she said, with an apologetic smile at him.

'OK. See you later, Tony.' She watched Betsy hustle him away, savouring the anticipation of picking the brains of someone really interesting for a change. The demented bleating in her earpiece brought her back to the cold reality of getting the rest of the programme out of the way. 'We go straight to the classroom anarchy piece, yeah?' she said peering up at the control booth, her mind back on her job, Shaz Bowman already a memory.

Carol stared out of her office window at the port below. It was cold enough to get rid of the casual strollers. Everyone out there was brisk, even the dog walkers. She hoped her detectives were following their example. She dialled the hotel number Tony had left her. She was as eager to hear about his TV appearance as she was to pass on her own news. She didn't have to listen to the 'Cuckoo Waltz' for long. 'Hello?' she heard him say.

'*Midday with Morgan* was great, Tony. What did you think? Did you see Jack the Lad?'

'No, I didn't see him, but I liked her more than I expected to. She's a good interviewer. Lulls you into a false sense of security then sticks in a couple of awkward questions. I managed to make the points I wanted to make, though.'

'So Vance wasn't around?'

'Not at the studios, no. But she said she'd told him I was going to be on, so I wouldn't take any bets on Jack the Lad having missed today's programme.'

'Do you think she has any idea?'

'That we suspect her husband?' He sounded surprised at the question.

'That her husband's a serial killer.' He was a little slow tonight, Carol thought. Normally he read any conversation as if he'd seen the script in advance.

'I don't think she has the faintest notion. I doubt she'd be with him if she did.' He sounded unusually positive. It wasn't like Tony to categorize things as black or white.

'He really is a smooth operator.'

'As silk. Now we have to sit back and see how much more it takes to unsettle him. Starting with tonight. I'm taking his wife out to dinner.'

Carol couldn't help the pang of jealousy, but she kept her voice even. She'd had plenty of practice with Tony. 'Really? How did you manage that?'

'I think she's genuinely interested in the profiling,' he said. 'Let's hope I can dig some information out of her that we can use.'

'If anyone can, you can. Tony, I think we've got a problem. With Simon.' Briefly, she relayed her conversation with John Brandon. 'What do you think? Should we persuade him to turn himself in?'

'I think we leave it up to him. If you're comfortable with that? Given that he might well be sitting in your living room again before all of this is over.'

'I don't expect it to be a problem,' Carol said slowly. 'It's only an internal bulletin we're talking about here. It's not as if there's going to be a nationwide manhunt with his picture splashed across the papers. Well, not for a couple of days yet, anyway. If it runs into next week and he's not been home or in contact with his friends and family, it might get more serious, in which case we'd have to persuade him to come in from the cold.'

'You're assuming he won't meekly walk into police HQ in Leeds?'

Carol snorted derisively. 'What do you think?'

'I think he's got too much invested in what we're doing. And speaking of which, how have the team been doing?'

She filled him in on Kay's grand tour of the grieving. When she came to the photograph she'd prised from the unwilling hands of Kenny and Denise Burton, Carol heard a sharp intake of breath.

'The zealots,' he said.

'I'm sorry?'

'Zealots. Fanatics. Jacko Vance's disciples. I've been to three of his public appearances so far, and there's a few obsessives who show up every time. Just three or four of them. I noticed them right away.'

'You ever end up on the dole, you could get a job as a spotter for Neighbourhood Watch,' she said. 'You could call it Nutter Watch.'

He laughed. 'The point is, two of them were taking photos.'

'Gotcha?'

'Could be. Could very well be. This is very, very good. This might just give us the edge. He's clever, Carol. He's the best I've ever seen, ever heard about, ever read about. Somehow, we've got to be better.' His voice was soft but keen, charged with determination.

'We are. There are five of us. He only ever sees things from one angle.'

'You're so right. I'll talk to you tomorrow, OK?'

She could sense his eagerness to be active, to be gone. She couldn't blame him. Micky Morgan would be a real challenge to his skills and Tony was a man who adored a challenge. Whether he obtained fresh information from her or merely used their dinner date to set the cat among Jacko Vance's pigeons, he would be more effective than anyone else she could think of. But she couldn't let him go just yet. 'There's one more thing . . . the arsonist?'

'Oh God, yes, of course, I'm sorry. Any progress?'

341

She outlined the discoveries of her team, giving a thumb-nail sketch of the two suspects. 'I'm not sure at this stage whether to bring them both in for questioning and try for a search warrant for their homes, or set up surveillance. I thought I'd run it past you.'

'How do they spend their money?'

'Brinkley and his wife go in for conspicuous consumption. New cars, household goods, store credit cards. Watson looks like a gambler. He raises cash any way he can and passes it on to the bookies.'

Tony said nothing for a moment. She pictured him frowning, a hand running through his thick black hair, his deep-set eyes dark and distant as his mind moved over the question. 'If I was Watson, I'd bet on Brinkley,' he said eventually.

'How so?'

'If Watson is truly a compulsive gambler, he's convinced it's the next bet, the next lottery ticket that will solve all his problems. He's a believer. Brinkley hasn't got that conviction. He thinks if he can just keep ahead of the game, cut down on spending, find some extra cash, he can get out of this mess by some conventional route. That's my reading of it. But whether I'm right or wrong, bringing them in for questioning isn't going to get you a result. It might stop the fires, but nobody will ever be charged with them. A search warrant won't help either, from what you've told me about how the fires are started. I know it's not the answer you want to hear, but surveillance is your best chance of a conviction. And you need to cover both of them in case I've got it wrong.'

Carol groaned. 'I knew you were going to say that,' she complained. 'Surveillance. A copper's favourite job. A budgetary nightmare.'

'At least you only have to cover the hours of darkness. And he's operating frequently, so it's not going to last for long.'

'That's supposed to make me feel better?'

'It's the best I can manage.'

'OK. Not your fault. Thanks for your help, Tony. Off you go and enjoy dinner. I'm going home to a frozen pizza and, hopefully, updates from Simon and Leon. And, please God, an early night. Sleep . . .' The last word sounded like a caress.

Tony laughed. 'Enjoy it.'

'Oh, I will,' she promised fervently. 'And Tony – good luck.'

'In the absence of miracles, I'll settle for that.'

The click of his receiver going down sliced off any chance of her telling him the other thing she'd initiated that day. She couldn't work out exactly why she'd felt impelled to do it, but her instinct told her it was important. And past experience had taught her painfully that her instinct was sometimes far more reliable than logic. Something had niggled at the back of her mind until, in the midst of all the other tasks for the day, she'd found time to send a query out to all the other police forces in the country. Detective Chief Inspector Carol Jordan of East Yorkshire Police wanted to hear about any recent reports of teenage girls inexplicably missing from home.

'Mike McGowan? That's him, over in the corner booth, duck,' the barmaid said, gesturing with her thumb.

'What does he drink?' Leon asked. But the barmaid had already moved on to another customer. The pub was moderately busy, occupied almost completely by men. In a small East Midlands town like this, there were clear distinctions between pubs where men went to spend their time with women and ones where they went to avoid that necessity. The giveaway here was the large board outside advertising 'All day satellite sport, giant screens'.

Leon sipped his lager shandy and took a moment to watch Mike McGowan. Jimmy Linden had offered his name as the media expert on Jacko Vance. 'Like me, Mike spotted him early on and he wrote a lot about him over the years,' he'd said. When Leon had contacted McGowan's old paper in London, he'd discovered that the journalist had been made redundant three years before. Divorced, his children grown and scattered round the country, there had been nothing to keep McGowan in the expensive capital, so he'd returned to the Nottinghamshire town where he'd grown up.

The ex-reporter looked more like a caricature of an Oxbridge don than any national newspaperman Leon had ever seen. Even sitting down, he was clearly tall. A mop of grey-blond hair cut in a heavy fringe that flopped over his eyes, big tortoiseshell glasses and pink and white skin gave him the same boyish looks that Alan Bennett and David Hockney turned into trademarks. His jacket was the sort of ancient tweed that takes fifteen years to look wearable then lasts another twenty without any sign of attrition. Beneath it he wore a grey flannel shirt and a striped tie with a narrow tight knot. He sat alone in the narrow corner booth, staring up studiously at a 56-inch TV screen where two teams were playing basketball. As Leon watched, McGowan tapped the bowl of a pipe against the ashtray, automatically cleaning and filling it without taking his eyes from the screen.

When Leon loomed up next to him, he still didn't take his eyes off the basketball. 'Mike McGowan?'

'That's me. And who are you?' he said, local vowels as distinctive as the barmaid's shattering the illusion of lofty academe.

'Leon Jackson.'

McGowan threw him a quick look of assessment. 'Any relation to Billy Boy Jackson?'

Astounded, Leon almost crossed himself. 'He was my uncle,' he blurted out.

'You've got the same shaped head. I should know. I was ringside the night Marty Pyeman fractured your uncle's skull. That's not what you've come to see me about, though, is it?' The quick glance this time was shrewd.

'Can I get you a drink, Mr McGowan?'

The journalist shook his head. 'I don't come here for the drink. I come for the sport. My pension's crap. I can't afford a satellite subscription or a screen like this. I was at school with the landlord's dad, so he doesn't bother that I make a single pint last the best part of the day. Sit down and tell me what you're after.'

Leon obeyed, taking out his warrant card. He tried to snap it shut and away, but McGowan was faster. 'Metropolitan Police,' he mused. 'Now what would a London bobby with a Liverpool accent be doing with a retired hack in darkest Nottinghamshire?'

'Jimmy Linden said you might be able to help me,' Leon said.

'Jimmy Linden? Now there's a name from the past.' He closed the warrant card and slid it across to Leon. 'So what's your interest in Jacko Vance?'

Leon shook his head admiringly. 'I never said I had an interest in the man. But if that's who you want to talk about, be my guest.'

'My, they're teaching them subtlety these days,' McGowan said acidly, striking a match and applying it to his pipe. He sucked and expelled a cloud of blue smoke that swallowed whole the feeble spiral from Leon's cigarette. 'What's Jacko supposed to have done? Whatever it is, I bet you never manage to nick him for it.'

Leon remained silent. It nearly killed him, but he managed

345

it. This clever old bastard wasn't going to put one over on him, he thought, almost convincing himself.

'I haven't seen Jacko in years,' McGowan finally said. 'He's not that keen on faces who remember what he was like when he had all his limbs. He hates being reminded of what he lost.'

'You'd think what he's got now would be compensation,' Leon said. 'Great job, more money than any reasonable geezer could spend, gorgeous wife, house the size of a stately home. I mean, how many Olympic gold medallists got a better deal than that?'

McGowan slowly shook his head. 'Nothing can compensate a man who thinks he's a god for the discovery of his vulnerability. That lass of his was lucky she got out from under. She'd have been the obvious choice when it came to making somebody pay for what the gods had done to Jacko Vance.'

'Jimmy said you knew more about Jacko than anybody else.'

'Only superficially. I followed his career, I interviewed him. I probably caught a few glimpses behind the mask, but I wouldn't say I knew him. I can't think of anybody that did. Really, there's nothing I want to say about Jacko Vance that I haven't already put in writing.'

McGowan breathed out another plume of smoke. Leon thought it smelled like Black Forest gateau, all cherries and chocolate. He couldn't imagine wanting to smoke a pudding. 'Jimmy also said that you kept cuttings files on the athletes that really interested you.'

'My, you did get a lot out of old Jimmy. He must have taken to you in a big way. Mind you, he's always had a lot of respect for black athletes. He reckoned they had to work twice as hard as anybody else to get their start. I

346

suppose he reckoned it was probably much the same in the police.'

'Or maybe I'm just a good interviewer,' Leon said drily. 'Any chance of you letting me take a look at your cuttings?'

'Any in particular, Detective?' McGowan teased.

'I'd be guided by you as to what was interesting, sir.'

McGowan, his eyes firmly on the basketball, said, 'A career as long as mine, it'd be hard to pick out particular highlights.'

'I'm sure you could manage it.'

'This finishes in ten minutes. Perhaps you'd care to come back and look at my files?'

Half an hour later, Leon was sitting in a room in McGowan's two-bedroomed terrace that managed to be both spartan and cluttered. The only furniture was a battered leather swivel chair that looked as if it had seen service in the Spanish Civil War, and a scarred and scratched gun-metal grey desk. All four walls were covered with industrial metal shelving and packed with shoeboxes, each with a label stuck to the outer edge. 'This is incredible,' he said.

'I always promised myself that when I retired, I'd write a book,' McGowan said. 'Amazing how we delude ourselves. I used to travel the world covering the top sporting events. Now my world's shrunk to the satellite screens in the Dog and Gun. You'd think I'd be depressed. But the funny thing is, I'm not. I've never been so bloody contented all my born days. It's reminded me that what I always liked best about sport was watching it. Freedom without responsibility, that's what I've got now.'

'A dangerous mixture,' Leon said.

'A liberating mixture. Three years ago, you turning up would have had me sniffing a story. I'd not have rested until I'd found out what was going on. Now, it's hard to imagine how I could care less. I'm more excited about the Vegas fight on Saturday than I could ever be about anything Jacko Vance has said or done.' He pointed to a shelf. 'Jacko Vance. Fifteen shoeboxes full. Enjoy yourself, lad. I've got an appointment with a tennis match at the Dog and Gun. If you're gone before I get back, just pull the front door closed behind you.'

When Mike McGowan returned just before midnight, Leon was still working his way systematically through the cuttings. The journalist brought him a mug of instant coffee and said, 'I hope they're paying you overtime, lad.'

'More of a labour of love, you might say,' Leon said wryly.

'Yours or your boss's?'

Leon thought for a moment. 'One of my mates. Call it a debt of honour.'

'The only kind worth paying. I'll leave you to it. Try not to slam the door behind you when you go.'

Leon was half aware of the sounds of someone getting ready for bed: floorboards creaking, plumbing grumbling, a toilet flushing. Then silence apart from the whisper of yellowed newsprint.

It was almost two when he found what he thought he might just be looking for. There was only one cutting, a fleeting mention. But it was a start. When he let himself out into the dark and empty street, Leon Jackson was whistling.

Her eyes were as candid as any he could remember. She pushed the last morsel of the smoked duck on to her fork, speared a final mangetout and said, 'But surely it has an effect on you, spending so much time and energy getting inside such twisted logic?'

Tony took longer than he needed to finish his mouthful

of polenta. 'You learn to build Chinese walls,' he said at last. 'You know but you don't know. You feel but you don't feel. I imagine it's similar to being a news journalist. How do you sleep at night after you've been out reporting on something like the Dunblane massacre or the Lockerbie bombing?'

'Yes, but we're always outside the event. You have to get inside or you fail, surely?'

'You're not always outside the event, though, are you? When you met Jacko, the story invaded your life. You must have had to build walls between what you knew of the man personally and what you reported to the world. When his ex-girlfriend was doing her kiss-and-tell revelations with the tabloids, you can't have looked at that as just another story. Didn't it affect the way you viewed your world?' he said, seizing the first chance he'd had to get her talking about her husband.

Micky pushed her hair back from her face. Twelve years on, he could see the contempt for Jillie Woodrow hadn't grown less. 'What a bitch,' she muttered. 'But Jacko said it was mostly fiction, and I believe him. So it didn't really get under my defences.'

The arrival of the waiter let her off the hook and he cleared their plates in silence. Then, alone again, Tony repeated the question.

'You're the psychologist,' she parried, reaching into her bag and producing a pack of Marlboro. 'Do you mind if I . . . ?'

He shook his head. 'I didn't realize you did.'

'Only after dinner. A maximum of five a day,' she said, a droll twist to her mouth. 'The control freak's control freak, that's me.'

The expression gave him a jolt. The one and only time he'd used the expression, he'd been talking about a compulsive killer who had almost robbed him of his own life. To hear it from her lips was dislocating and strange.

'You look like you've seen a ghost,' she said, inhaling her first mouthful of smoke with an air of sensuous pleasure.

'Just a stray memory,' he said. 'There are a lot of very bizarre resonances kicking around inside my head.'

'I bet. Something I've always wondered is how you *know* when you're getting it right in a profile.' She inhaled deeply and blew pale filtered smoke down her nostrils, an expression of interest on her face.

He gave her an appraising look. It was now or never. 'The same way any of us work out anything about people. A mixture of knowledge and experience. Plus knowing the right question to ask.'

'Such as?'

The interest was so genuine he almost felt guilty for what he was about to do to their pleasant evening. 'Doesn't Jacko mind that Betsy's in love with you?'

Her face froze and her pupils dilated in a panic reflex. After a long moment she swallowed and managed a faint laugh. 'If you were trying to wrong-foot me, you certainly succeeded.' It was one of the best recoveries he'd ever seen, but he hadn't imagined the confession in her eyes.

'I'm no danger to you,' he said softly. 'Confidentiality is second nature to me. But I'm not a fool either. You and Jacko, it's as fake as a nine-bob note. Betsy was there first. Oh, there were rumours. But you and Jacko had the most public courtship since Charles and Diana. It killed the gossip.'

'Why are you bringing this up?' she asked.

'We're both here because we're curious. I've answered all the questions you asked me. You can return the compliment, or not.' His smile was, he hoped, warm.

'God,' she said wonderingly. 'You have got a nerve.'

'How do you think I got to be the best?'

Micky looked speculatively at him, waving away the waiter who was approaching with the dessert menus. 'Bring us another bottle of the Zinfandel,' she said as an afterthought. She leaned forward and spoke softly. 'What do you want to ask?'

'What's in it for Jacko? Surely he's not gay?'

Micky shook her head emphatically. 'Jillie dumped Jacko after his accident because she didn't want to be with a man who wasn't perfect. He swore he would never enter into another sexual relationship where his emotions were engaged. He needed a decoy to keep the women away from him, I needed a man to hide Betsy behind.'

'Mutual benefit.'

'Oh, yes, mutual benefit. And to be fair to Jacko, he's never tried to renege on the deal. I don't know what he does for sex, though I suspect well-paid call girls come into it. Frankly, I don't care as long as he never embarrasses me.' She stubbed out her cigarette and gave him the accomplished frank gaze she normally directed at the camera.

'I'm amazed that someone who's paid to be curious about other people is so lacking in curiosity about her own husband.'

Her smile was ironic. 'If there's one thing that eleven years of marriage to Jacko has taught me, it's that nobody gets to know Jacko. It's not that I think he tells lies,' she said consideringly, 'just that I don't think he tells very much of the truth. Different people get little bits of Jacko's truth, but I don't think anybody gets it all.'

'How do you mean?' Tony picked up the discreetly delivered bottle of wine, refilling Micky's glass and topping up his almost full one.

'I get to see Jacko behaving in public like the perfect,

solicitous husband, but I know that's an act. When there's only the three of us around, he's so distant it's hard to believe we've all lived under the same roof for the last dozen years. When he's working he acts like people expect a TV celeb to behave – perfectionist, a bit OTT, yelling at the crew and his PA when things don't get done just so. But with the public, he's Mr Charm. Then, when it comes to raising money, he's a hard-headed businessman. Do you know that for every pound he makes for charity, he earns two for himself?'

Tony shook his head. 'I suppose he'd argue that he's generating funds for the charity they wouldn't get otherwise.'

'And why should he work for free? Right. Me, when I do charity events, I don't even take my expenses. But then there's the other side, the volunteer work he does with people who are terminally ill or severely damaged after accidents. He spends hours by their bedsides, listening, talking, and nobody knows what goes on between them. One time a journalist tried to sneak in a tape recorder to reveal "the secret heart of Jacko Vance". Jacko found out about it and he smashed the tape recorder. He literally stamped it to pieces. They thought he was going to do the same to the journalist, but the guy had the good sense to make his legs do the walking.'

'A man who likes his privacy,' Tony said.

'Oh, he gets plenty of that. He's got a house in Northumberland, out in the middle of nowhere. I've seen it once in twelve years and that was only because Bets and I were driving up to Scotland and we decided to drop in on him. I practically had to force him to make us a cup of tea. I've never felt less welcome in my whole life.' Micky smiled indulgently. 'Yes, you could say that Jacko likes his privacy. But that's OK with me. Better that than hanging around in my face all the time.'

'He can't have been very pleased to have the police poking

their noses in, then,' Tony said. 'After Shaz Bowman's visit, I mean.'

'You're not kidding. It was actually me who called the police, you know. The way Betsy and Jacko reacted, you'd think I'd shopped them on a murder rap. It was a nightmare, trying to make the pair of them see that we couldn't ignore the fact that this poor woman had been at the house not long before she was murdered.'

'Just as well one of you has a sense of duty,' Tony said drily.

'Well, yes. Besides, at least one other person knew she was coming to the house – that other police officer that Jacko spoke to. It wasn't as if we could hope to keep it to ourselves.'

'I feel so guilty about Shaz,' Tony said, half-turning away. 'I knew she was worrying away at some theory of her own, but I didn't think she'd take action on it without clearing it with me.'

'You mean you don't know what she was working on either?' Micky said incredulously. 'The cops who came to the house didn't seem to have much of a clue, but I thought you'd be sure to know.'

Tony shrugged. 'Not really. I know she had some idea that there was a serial killer preying on teenage girls and that he might be a celebrity stalker as well. But I didn't have the details. It was only supposed to be a training exercise, not the real thing.'

Micky shivered and emptied her glass. 'Can we change the subject? It's bad for the digestion, talking about murder.'

For once, he wasn't about to argue. The gamble had paid off handsomely. And he'd never been greedy. 'OK. Tell me how you got the Agriculture Minister to admit his involvement with that biotechnology company.'

*   *   *

Carol stared down the three mutinous faces opposite her. 'I know nobody likes stakeout work. But that's the way we're going to catch our man. At least the intervals between his outings are pretty short, so the chances are we're going to get lucky within a few days. Now, this is the way I want it to work. We're going to do it single-handed. I realize that makes it tougher, but you know what budgets are like. I've spoken to uniform and they've agreed to let us have some bodies to cover during daylight hours. Each night at ten, two of you will pick up the surveillance. You'll each work two nights on and one off. You will each use the other as back-up if it looks like we've got something going off. We start today. The first watchers are out there now. Any questions?'

'What if we get clocked?' Lee asked.

'We don't get clocked,' Carol said. 'But if the unthinkable happens, you pull off, call your oppo and swap targets at the first opportune moment. I appreciate this is a tough operation with such a low body count. But I have every confidence that you can pull this off. Don't disappoint me, please.'

'Ma'am?' Di said.

'Yes?'

'If we're really that tight on staffing levels, why don't we prioritize our two suspects and focus on the most likely with all our resources?'

It was an awkward question, and an intelligent one. It was one Carol herself had debated with Nelson over breakfast that morning. It had taken her mind off a growing fear that was coming to obsess her. 'Good question,' she said now. 'I considered it myself. Then I thought, what if we go for the wrong candidate and we only find that out after another fatal fire?' She let the question hang in the air. 'So I decided it was probably better in terms of public policy to opt for thin cover over both suspects.'

Di nodded. 'Fair enough. I just wondered.'

'Right. Sort out the rota among yourselves, and knock off now until ten. Keep me posted. Anything happens, I'm only a phone call away. Don't keep me in the dark.'

'When you say only a phone call away, ma'am . . .' Tommy drawled suggestively.

'I want to be there when you make an arrest.'

'Aye, that's what I thought you meant.'

His feigned disappointment was aimed at annoying her, she knew. Determined not to show he'd succeeded, Carol smiled sweetly. 'Believe me, Tommy, you should be grateful for that. Now get out of here and let me get some work done.' Her hand was on the phone before she'd finished speaking. She hit the first number on a list in front of her, tapping her pad with a pencil as Seaford's finest trooped out with all the brio of a snail on Valium. 'Close the door behind you, please,' she called. 'Hello? Force control? This is DCI Jordan from East Yorkshire. I need to talk to someone about Mispers . . . I sent out an information request about teenage girls . . .'

Tony eased the car on to the slip road, wondering whether he'd enjoy driving more if he had one of those ultimate driving machines he saw in all the glossy adverts instead of a clapped out old Vauxhall. Somehow, he doubted it. But that wasn't what he was supposed to be thinking about as his windscreen wipers slapped the slanting Yorkshire rain away to reveal a distant prospect of Bradford. At the ring road, he followed the achingly precise instructions he'd been given and eventually pulled up outside a terraced house whose obsessive neatness was matched only by the military precision of its single flower bed. Even the curtains appeared to have been drawn back so that exactly the same amount of lining showed at each side of the window.

The doorbell was a nasty insistent buzz. It opened to reveal a man Tony had spotted at every Jacko Vance event he'd attended. He'd persuaded him and a couple of other camera-toting enthusiasts to part with names and addresses on the pretext that he was doing a study of the phenomenon of fame as seen through the eyes of the fans rather than the famous. It was meaningless drivel, but it made them feel important enough to be co-operative.

Philip Hawsley was first, for no better reason than living nearest. As he followed him into a preternaturally tidy front room that smelled of furniture polish and air freshener, and looked like a heritage museum recreation of lower middle class life in 1962, Tony registered all the signs of the obsessive compulsive. Hawsley, who could have been any age between thirty and fifty, constantly ran his fingers over the buttons of his beige cardigan to check they were all in place. He studied his fingernails at least once a minute to ensure they hadn't grown dirty since he last looked. His greying hair was cropped in a short, military style and his shoes were polished to mirror radiance. He invited Tony to sit, pointing out the chair he wanted him to occupy, and offered no refreshment, sitting down very precisely opposite the psychologist, ankles and knees pressed firmly together.

'Quite a collection,' Tony said, glancing round the room. An entire wall was given over to shelves of video tapes, each labelled with a date and name of a programme. Even from where he was sitting, he could see the vast majority were *Vance's Visits*. A laminated wall unit held a series of albums and scrapbooks. Half a dozen books sat on a shelf above the unit. Pride of place went to a large framed colour photograph sitting on the wall-mounted gas fire. It showed Hawsley shaking hands with Jacko Vance.

'A small tribute, but mine own,' Hawsley said in a prissily camp voice. Tony could imagine all too vividly how he would have been teased as an adolescent. 'We're the same age, you know. To the very day. I feel our fates are inextricably linked. We're like two sides of the same coin. Jacko is the public face and I am the private.'

'It must have taken years to amass all this material,' Tony said.

'I've dedicated myself to maintaining the archive,' Hawsley said primly. 'I like to think I have a better overview of Jacko's life than he does himself. When you're so busy living it, you don't have time to sit and reflect on it the way I do. His bravery, his common touch, his warmth, his compassion. He's the complete man of our time. It's one of life's little paradoxes that he had to lose part of himself to gain that pre-eminence.'

'I couldn't agree more,' Tony said, naturally falling back into the conversational techniques that years of working with the mentally ill had delivered into his repertoire. 'He's an inspiration, is Jacko.' He sat back and let Hawsley's adulation flow over him, pretending to fascination when what he felt was disgust for this killer who disguised himself so well that the innocent and ill fell for his every pretence. Eventually, after Hawsley had relaxed enough to inch back from the edge of his chair into an approximation of comfort, Tony said, 'I'd love to see your photograph albums.'

The crucial dates were carved on his memory. 'For the purposes of our study, we're going to be looking at precise points in people's careers,' Tony said as Hawsley opened the cabinet and started taking down albums. Every time Tony mentioned a month and year, Hawsley chose a particular volume and laid it on the coffee table in front of Tony, open at the appropriate pages. Jacko Vance was clearly a busy man, doing between five and twenty appearances a month, many of them related to charity fund-raising, often for the hospital in Newcastle where he did volunteer work.

Hawsley's memory for detail when it related to his idol was phenomenal, a mixed blessing for Tony. On the plus side, it gave him plenty of time to scrutinize the images before him; the minus side of the equation was that his droning voice came close to sending Tony into a hypnotic trance. Soon, however, Tony felt a quiver of excitement that snapped him back to full attentiveness. There, just two days before the first of Shaz Bowman's cluster of teenage girls had disappeared for good, was Jacko Vance opening a hospice in Swindon. In the second of Hawsley's four photographs of the event, Tony saw a face he'd memorized, right next to Jacko Vance's gleaming head. Debra Cressey. Fourteen when she vanished. Two days earlier, gazing up adoringly at Jacko Vance as he signed an autograph, she'd looked like a girl in paradise.

Two hours later, Tony had identified another missing girl next to Vance, this time apparently in conversation with her. A third possibility was straining upwards on tiptoe to steal a kiss from a laughing Vance. But her head was half-turned from the camera, making it hard to be certain. Now all he had to do was to extract the photographs from Hawsley. 'I wonder if I could borrow some of these photographs?' he asked.

Hawsley shook his head vigorously, looking deeply shocked. 'Of course not,' he said. 'It's vital that the integrity of the archive is maintained. What if I were called on and there were missing items from the inventory? No, Dr Hill, I'm afraid that's completely out of the question.'

'What about negatives? Do you still have them?'

Clearly offended, Hawsley said, 'Of course I do. What

kind of sloppy operation do you think I'm running here?' He rose and opened the cupboard in the wall unit. Negative storage boxes were stacked on the shelves, each as obsessively labelled as the videos. Tony shuddered inwardly, imagining the painstaking listing of every negative in the box. Not so much anal retentive as banal retentive.

'Well, could I borrow the negatives so I can have them copied?' he asked, determinedly keeping the edge of exasperation out of his voice.

'I can't let them out of my possession,' Hawsley said stubbornly. 'They're significant.'

It took another fifteen minutes to find the acceptable compromise. He drove Philip Hawsley and his precious negatives to the local photographic shop where Tony paid an extortionate sum to have prints made of the relevant photographs while they waited. Then he drove Philip Hawsley home so he could replace the negatives in their proper place before their companions noticed they'd gone.

Driving down the motorway to the next name on his list, he allowed himself a short moment of triumphalism. 'We're going to get you, Jack the Lad,' he said. 'We are going to get you.'

All Simon McNeill really knew about Tottenham was that they had a second-rate football team and they killed a copper during a riot some time in the eighties when he'd still been at school. He didn't expect the natives to be friendly, so it was no surprise when his appearance at the local electoral roll office was greeted with less than rapture. When he explained what he wanted, the stick insect in a suit behind the counter cast his eyes heavenwards and sighed. 'You'll have to do it yourself,' he said grudgingly. 'I haven't the staff to spare, especially with no notice at all.' He showed Simon into the dusty archives, gave him a ten second run-down on the filing system and left him to it.

The results of his search were not encouraging. The street where Jacko Vance had grown up had consisted of about forty houses back in the sixties. By 1975, twenty-two of the houses had disappeared, replaced, presumably, by a block of flats called Shirley Williams House. The eighteen remaining houses revealed a steady turnover of registered electors, few people seeming to remain for more than a couple of years, particularly during the grim poll tax years of the mid-eighties. Only one name remained constant throughout. Simon pinched the bridge of his nose to ease the beginning headache. He hoped Tony Hill was right, that all this would bring them closer to nailing Shaz's killer. The image of her face rose painfully before him, her startling blue eyes bright with laughter. It was almost more than he could bear. No time to brood, he told himself as he shrugged back into his leather jacket and set off to find Harold Adams.

Number 9 Jimson Street was a tiny terraced house in dirty yellow London brick. The little oblong of garden that separated it from the street was choked with empty beer cans, crisp packets and takeaway food containers. A scrawny black cat stared up malevolently as he opened the gate, then sprang for freedom with a chicken bone in its teeth. The street smelled of decay. The desiccated shell who opened the door after much rattling of bolts and turning of locks looked as if he must have already been an old man when Jacko Vance was a boy. Simon's heart sank. 'Mr Adams?' he asked, without much hope of intelligent response.

The old man cocked his head in an effort to defeat his stoop and look Simon in the eye. 'You from the council? I told that woman already, I don't need a home help and I don't want meals on wheels.' His voice sounded like a hinge in desperate need of oil.

'I'm from the police.'

'I never saw anything,' Adams said swiftly, moving to close the door.

'No, wait. It's nothing like that. I want to talk about somebody who lived here years ago: Jacko Vance. I want to talk about Jacko Vance.'

Adams paused. 'You're one of them journalists, aren't you? You're trying to con an old man. I'm going to call the police.'

'I *am* the police,' Simon said, waving his open warrant card in front of faded grey eyes. 'Look.'

'All right, all right, I'm not blind. You lot are always telling us, you can't be too careful. What d'you want to talk about Jacko Vance for? He hasn't lived here for . . . let me see, must be seventeen, eighteen years now.'

'Could I come in and have a chat, maybe?' Simon said, half-hoping Adams would send him off with a flea in his ear.

'I suppose so.' Adams pulled the door wide and stood back to let Simon enter. He caught a whiff of the old man smell of spilled urine and stale biscuits before he turned into the living room. To his surprise, the place was spotless. There wasn't a speck of dust on the screen of the huge TV set, not a mark on the lace-edged arm protectors on the easy chairs, not a smear on the glass of the framed photographs that lined the mantelpiece. Harold Adams was right; he didn't need a home help. Simon waited for the old man to settle in his own chair before he sat down.

'I'm the last one left,' Adams said proudly. 'When we came here in 1947, it was like a big family, this street. Everybody knew everybody's business and, just like a family, they was always falling out. Now, nobody knows anybody, but they still fall out just the same.' When he grinned, Simon thought, his face looked like the skull of a predatory bird whose eyes had somehow survived.

'I bet they do. So you knew the Vance family pretty well?'

Adams sniggered. 'Not much of a family, you ask me. His dad, called himself an engineer, but as far as I could see, all that meant was he had an excuse for disappearing at the drop of a hat for weeks on end. Mind you, it wouldn't surprise me if he earned a bob or two. He was always dressed better than the street, if you get my meaning. Never spent a shilling on the house or the wife and kid that he didn't have to, though.'

'What was she like?'

'Off her head. She had no time for that lad, not even when he was a babe in arms. She'd stick him out the front in his pram and just leave him there for hours. Sometimes she even forgot to take him in when it started raining and my Joan or one of the other women would have to go and knock on her door and tell her. My Joan used to say that some days she was still in her dressing gown at dinner time.'

'Did she drink, then?'

'I never heard that, no. She just didn't like the kid. Cramped her style, I suppose. When he got older, she just let him run wild, then when people went to complain, she'd come down on him like a ton of bricks. I don't know what went on behind closed doors, but sometimes you'd hear that kid sobbing his heart out. Never did no good, mind.'

'How do you mean?'

'He was a nasty piece of work, that Jacko Vance. I don't care what they say about him being a hero and sportsman, he had a nasty streak a mile wide. Oh, he could be all charm when he thought it would get him somewhere. He had all the wives in this street wrapped round his little finger. They were always giving him little treats, letting him watch telly round their house when his mum locked him out.' Adams was enjoying himself. Simon suspected it wasn't often these days that his malice was allowed free rein. He was determined to make the most of it.

'But you knew different?'

Adams sniggered again. 'I knew everything that went on in this street. I caught that little bugger Vance once round the back of the lock-up garages off Boulmer Street. He had a cat by the scruff, you know, so it couldn't fight him off. He was dipping its tail in a jar of petrol when I came round the corner. And there was a box of matches on the ground beside him.' The momentary silence was eloquent. 'I made him let the cat go, then I kicked his arse for him, good and proper. I shouldn't think I stopped him, though. Cats were always going missing round here. People used to comment on it. Me, I had my own ideas.'

'Like you said, a nasty piece of work.' It was almost too good to be true. Simon had spent too much time preparing for his assignment in Leeds not to recognize the accepted markers for psychopathy in a background history. Torturing animals was textbook stuff. And this man had seen it first hand. He couldn't have found a better source if he'd searched for weeks.

'He was a bully, an' all. Always picking on the little kids, daring them to do dangerous things, getting them hurt, but he never laid a finger on them himself. It was like he set it up to happen and then stood back and watched. Me and Joan, we were glad our two were grown and gone by then. And by the time the grandkids came along, Vance had discovered he could throw a silly spear further than anybody else. We hardly saw him after that, and good riddance to bad rubbish, if you ask me.'

'You'll not find many people with a bad word to say about that man,' Simon said mildly. 'He saved some lives, you can't argue with that. He does a lot of work for charity. And he gives up his time to work with the terminally ill.'

Adams screwed up his face in a sneer. 'I told you, he likes watching. He probably gets a kick out of knowing they'll be dead soon and he'll still be strutting around like Lord Muck on the telly. I'm telling you, sonny, Jacko Vance is a nasty piece of work. So, what are you after him for?'

Simon smiled. 'I never said I was after him.'

'So what d'you want to go around talking about him for, then?'

Simon winked. 'Now, you know I can't reveal the details of a police investigation, sir. You've been extremely helpful, I will say that much. If I was you, I'd keep an eye on the television for the next few days. With a bit of luck, you'll find out exactly why I came here.' He got to his feet. 'And now, I think I'd better be on my way. My senior officer will be very interested in what you have to say, Mr Adams.'

'I've been waiting years to say it, sonny. Years, I've been waiting.'

Barbara Fenwick had been killed six days before her fifteenth birthday. If she'd lived, she'd have been almost twenty-seven. Her mutilated body had been found in a walker's hut on the moors above the city, strangled. There were signs that she had had sexual intercourse against her will, though there had been no trace of sperm either inside or outside her body. What made the crime unusual was the nature of her injuries. Where most psychopathic killers disfigured the sexual organs of their victims, this killer had crushed the girl's right arm to a bloody pulp, shattering bones and tearing muscle till it was difficult to reconstruct which fragment went where. Even more interestingly, the pathologist had been insistent that the injuries were consistent with the application of increasing pressure rather than a single, terrible impact.

It had made no sense to the investigating officers.

The finders of Barbara's body were in the clear, having been camping and hiking together for the previous six days. Her parents, who had been distraught since her disappearance five days previously, were also under no suspicion. The girl had been alive and well for a couple of days after they had reported her missing and her stepfather had been in the company of his wife and at least one police officer ever since. The parents had said all along that their daughter was happy at home, that she would never have run away, that she must have been abducted. The police had been sceptical, pointing out that Barbara's best clothes were missing and that she had told her parents a lie about her movements following school the day she disappeared. Added to that, she'd bunked off school, and not for the first time.

It had made no sense to the investigating officers.

Barbara Fenwick hadn't been a wild, troublesome teenager. She wasn't known to the police, her friends denied she drank more than the occasional can of sweet cider and no one thought she'd ever experimented with drugs or sex. Her last boyfriend, who had chucked her a month before to go out with someone else, said they'd never gone all the way and he thought in spite of her sexy looks she was probably, like him, a virgin. She'd been doing reasonably well at school and had ambitions to train as a nursery nurse. The last reliable sighting of her had been on the local bus to Manchester on the morning of her disappearance. She'd told the neighbour who had spotted her that she was going to the Dental Hospital for an appointment to do with her wisdom teeth. Her mother said Barbara didn't have any sign of wisdom teeth, a fact borne out by the pathologist.

It had made no sense to the investigating officers.

There had been nothing in her behaviour to suggest a girl about to go off the rails. She'd been out to a disco with a bunch of friends on the Saturday night before her disappearance. Jacko Vance had been there, making a celebrity appearance, signing autographs for charity. Her friends said she'd had a great night.

None of this had made any sense to the investigating officers.

But it made a lot of sense to Leon Jackson.

The stone slab was so well engineered that it didn't even make the sinister grating sound of a horror film. When a small electrical current applied pressure to a particular, precise point, it simply pivoted silently through 180 degrees to reveal the steps that led to the small crypt that no one would any longer suspect existed beneath the converted chapel. Jacko Vance flipped the switch that flooded the crypt with harsh fluorescent light and descended.

The first thing he noticed was the smell, hitting him before his head was far enough underground to be able to see the creature that had once been Donna Doyle. The putrefaction of pulverized flesh mingled with the stale smell of unwashed fevered skin and the acrid reek of the chemical toilet. He felt his stomach turn, but told himself he'd smelled worse in the terminal ward as gangrene devoured the bodies of people who had already had as much amputated as could reasonably be excised. It was a lie, but one that stiffened his sinews.

At the bottom of the steps, he stood and stared at the pathetic creature pressing herself against the cold stone wall as if she expected to be able to push her way through it and so escape him. 'God, you're disgusting,' he said contemptuously, taking in her matted hair, foul wounds and the dirt she'd gathered bumping into things in the dark.

He'd left her boxes of breakfast cereal and she had water

from the tap on the rising main. There was no excuse for her to be in this state; she could have made an effort to clean herself up instead of sitting on the mattress in her own filth, he thought. The leg irons allowed her enough freedom of movement for that, and the pain from her arm hadn't been enough to stop her from eating, judging by the open packets lying around her. He was glad he'd opted for a plastic-covered mattress so he could hose off her disgusting presence when he'd finished with her.

'Look at yourself,' he sneered, swaggering across the room towards her, unbuttoning his jacket and tossing it over a chair that was well out of her reach. 'Why should I want anything to do with a mess like you?'

The whimpering noise that came from Donna's bruised lips was wordless. With her undamaged hand, she grabbed at the blanket in a poignant attempt to cover her nakedness. In one swift step, Jacko was towering over her, yanking the rough woollen cover away from her. With his prosthetic arm, he smashed her across the face and she fell back on the mattress, tears spilling and mingling with the blood and mucus from her nose.

Vance stepped back and spat at her. Coolly, he stripped himself, folding his clothes and placing them neatly on the chair. He was hot and hard, ready for what he'd come there for. He'd had to wait longer than usual, longer than he'd wanted because of that inconvenient bitch Bowman. After the discovery of her body he hadn't dared come near the place until he'd seen off the police, wary of attracting their notice. And even if Tony Hill thought he had something on him, there was no proof and no one to pay him any attention. It was safe to come back for another dose of what made life worth living, the sweet allotment of vengeance, the savour of suffering.

He dropped to his knees on the mattress, forcing the teenager's legs apart with a rough hand, relishing her protests, her futile attempts at prevention, her sad little cries of repudiation. As he thrust into her, he let his full weight fall on her injured arm.

Donna Doyle finally produced a coherent sound. The scream that echoed round the grim little crypt was, unequivocally, 'No!'

Carol yanked open the door and practically dragged Tony into the cottage. 'We were beginning to wonder if you'd got lost,' she said, marching ahead of him to the dining table where a wide-mouthed Thermos of soup sat next to a couple of loaves of olive bread and a selection of cheeses.

'Accident on the motorway,' he said, dropping a folder on to the table and sinking into a chair. He looked disorientated and sounded preoccupied.

Carol poured two mugs of soup and passed one to Tony. 'I need to talk to you before the others get here. Tony, this isn't just an academic exercise any more. I think he took another one a few days before he killed Shaz.'

Suddenly she had all his attention. Whatever had been on his mind when he'd walked through the door was thrust aside and his dark blue eyes burned into hers. 'Evidence?' he demanded.

'I had a hunch, so I put out a Misper request nationwide. I got a call this afternoon from Derbyshire. Donna Doyle. Aged fourteen. From Glossop. About five miles from the end of the M67.' Carol gave him a copy of the fax the local CID had sent her. 'The mother put this flyer together because the police weren't terribly worried. The usual pattern, you see. She left the house to go to school in the morning, with an excuse for not being home until late. Her best clothes were missing.

Premeditated runaway, case not so much closed as discreetly ignored. But I had a chat with the WPC who interviewed the mother before they lost interest. I didn't lead her; she volunteered that a couple of nights before she went missing, Donna had been out with one of her friends at a charity do where Jacko Vance was the guest of honour.'

'Shit,' Tony exhaled. 'Carol, depending on what he does with them, she could still be alive.'

'I didn't even want to think it.'

'It's possible. If he keeps them before he kills them – and we know a lot of serial offenders do that for the power charge it gives them – chances are he won't have risked going near her since he murdered Shaz. Christ, we've got to find a way to locate his killing ground. And soon.' They looked at each other with the constricting realization that another life could depend on how well they did their jobs. 'He's got a cottage in Northumberland,' Tony said.

'He's not going to be doing it on his own doorstep,' Carol objected.

'Probably not, but I wouldn't mind betting that his killing ground is a short drive from there. What have the team got?' he said grimly.

Carol glanced up at the clock. 'I don't know. They're due here any minute. They were meeting in Leeds and coming on together. They've all checked in, and it sounds like we've hit a lot of pay dirt.'

'Good.' Before he could say more, they both heard the sound of an engine labouring up the hill to the cottage. 'Here comes the cavalry, by the sounds of it.'

Carol opened the door and the trio trooped in, all looking remarkably pleased with themselves. They piled into chairs round the table, pulling off jackets and coats and dumping them on the floor, eager to begin. Tony ran a hand through his hair and said, 'We think he took a girl just before he killed Shaz. She could still be alive.' It gave him no pleasure to watch the light bleed out of their eyes, to see their faces change from the glow of satisfaction to the pinched pale of anxiety. 'Carol?'

Carol relayed the information she'd already given Tony, while he went to the kitchen and poured out the coffee he'd smelled brewing. When he returned, he said, 'We're not going to have the luxury of time to draw out a detailed profile and brainstorm all the elements of it. We're going to have to go hell for leather to get evidence and do what we can to save another life. So. Let's hear how we've all been doing. Kay, why don't you kick off?'

Succinctly, Kay reported on her interviews with the bereft parents. 'The bottom line is that they're all telling the same story. There are no significant discrepancies, either with what they originally told the police, or with each other's version of events. I managed to pick up a photograph of one of the girls with Jacko Vance, and I have established that they all went to events in their local area within a few days of their disappearance. But no stronger connection than that. Sorry.'

'You've nothing to apologize for,' Tony said. 'You did a great job. It can't have been easy, getting this much out of people who are still suffering because their child is on the missing list. The picture is helpful, too, because we can tie that down very specifically. Good job, Kay. Simon?'

'Thanks to Carol, I was able to track down the fiancée who chucked Jacko after his accident. If you remember, Shaz put forward the theory it was that emotional event, coupled with the shock of his accident, that tipped him over the edge into killing. Well, from what I heard, he maybe didn't have that far to fall.

'According to Jillie Woodrow, there was nothing normal about Jacko's bedroom habits. Right from the start of their sex life, he had to be in control. She was supposed to be passive and adoring. He hated her touching him sexually and, on occasion, he actually slapped her for laying hands on him. He became more interested in S&M pornography and wanted her to act out fantasies from magazines and books and from his own imagination. She didn't mind being tied up, she says, and she didn't much mind the spanking or the whipping, but when he started on the hot candle wax and the nipple clamps and the outsize vibrators, she drew the line.' He glanced down at the brief notes he'd made to ensure he got through his report without missing out anything crucial.

'She reckons that somewhere around the time his athletics career took off and he started banking big money, he began going to prostitutes. Nothing seedy, nothing low rent or street corner. From what he let slip, she thinks he had a couple of expensive call girls that he used, women who would either go along with the more extreme stuff that he wanted, or else they'd lay on the kind of lassies that it didn't matter if he messed up. Junkies, that sort of thing. According to Jillie, she was desperate to get out, but she was terrified of how he'd react. Outside the bedroom, he was the perfect partner. Solicitous, kind, generous, but incredibly possessive. So, after the accident, she grabbed the chance with both hands. She figured if she told him while he was in the hospital, he wouldn't be able to react. And he'd be stuck in there long enough to cool down and get over her.' Simon looked up and was surprised by how grim Tony looked.

'And we all know what happened next, don't we?' Tony said. 'Micky Morgan. The marriage of convenience.'

The faces around the table went from incomprehension to shocked amazement as he filled them in on what he'd heard first from Chris Devine and then from Micky herself. 'So we're seeing some fascinatingly aberrant behaviour here,' he said. 'Still hard to stand anything up that a senior officer would stake his arrest record on, but we know now, don't we?' They didn't have to say anything. The answer was in their eyes.

'There's more,' Simon said, launching into Harold Adams's tale.

'Man, the more we find out, the more incredible it is that Jack the Lad is still walking the streets,' Leon sighed, lighting his third cigarette since he'd walked in. 'Wait till you hear what I've dug up.' He passed on the meagre information he'd obtained from Jimmy Linden in a matter of minutes. 'Then he told me about this retired journo, Mike McGowan. This guy has forgotten more about sport than we'll ever know. He's got archives the British Library would kill for. I tell you, it took me half the night to get through the stuff he's got on Jack the Lad. And then I found this.'

With a flourish, Leon produced a brittle clipping and five photocopies of the article. It came from the *Manchester Evening News* and dealt with the murder of Barbara Fenwick. Emphasized in yellow highlighter, one paragraph stood out. '"Barbara was no party girl, according to her friends. Her last Saturday night out was typical. She was one of a group who went to a disco where sports hero Jacko Vance was making a charity appearance." This was just fourteen weeks after the accident,' Leon pointed out.

'He didn't hang about, did he? Got stuck right into the charity work,' Simon said.

'Well, we never doubted that he was driven,' Tony commented. 'So, is there any evidence that Vance actually met this girl?'

'The high point of her night out was getting his autograph.'

Leon passed round copies of the summary he'd prepared from the police evidence store. 'They wouldn't let me photocopy the files, so I had to do this. I reckon she was his first victim,' he said confidently.

'And I reckon you're right,' Tony breathed. 'Oh, this is good, Leon, this is really good. He got better after this. My God, those hillwalkers must practically have stumbled over him. Look, it says they saw what they thought was a Land Rover heading off down the track just after they came over the ridge. Jack the Lad got a fright. He realized he needed a proper killing ground, a place where he wasn't going to be disturbed. We think that might be in Northumberland, by the way. Near his cottage. But without more information . . .' He rubbed his hands over his face. 'A twelve-year-old case, though. Where's the evidence?'

Leon looked slightly downcast. 'They don't know. They moved all the unsolved stuff to a new location about five years ago, and all the forensics on this case have either got lost or misfiled. Not that there was much, according to the abstract. No prints, no body fluids. Some tyre tracks, but that's no use a dozen years on.'

'The investigating officers. That's who we need to talk to. But before we discuss what comes next, I'd better tell you what I've come up with. It's pretty meagre compared to the huge strides you three have taken, but it does give us a handy chunk of circumstantial evidence.' Tony opened his folder and fanned out an array of photographs. 'I've done the rounds of the zealots. I have to say it was very like being back working in a secure mental hospital. At the risk of baffling you with professional jargon, they're all a few bricks short of a wall. However, after enduring the histories of their assorted obsessions with Jacko Vance, what we've got is a selection of photographs of Jacko taken at events where we know our putative victims were also present. Four of the pics put him next or near to one of our missing girls. In another five or six, it's possible that the girl in the picture is one of ours, but by no means certain without computer enhancement.' He leaned over and began carving himself a chunk of bread.

'With Kay's pick-ups, that makes five. We've got an overlap,' Carol said.

'I don't suppose it's enough to start an official investigation?' Tony asked without hope. He started to slice some cheese.

Carol pulled a face. 'The trouble is, there's no connection to my patch. If one of these girls had disappeared from East Yorkshire, I'd be willing to have a go at getting something moving, but I can't find one. Even so, I don't know where we could take any investigation. All we've got is highly circumstantial; it's nowhere near enough to bring him in for questioning, never mind a search warrant.'

'So you don't reckon we could convince West Yorkshire to take another look at Vance, even with this much?' Kay asked.

Simon snorted. 'Are you kidding? Given what they think about me? Every time I see a cop car on the road, I start sweating. Anything we come up with is tainted because they're convinced I'm the killer and you're protecting me. I don't think they're going to believe a word we say.'

'Point taken,' Kay said.

'What we need is a witness who saw him with Shaz after she's supposed to have left his house. Ideally, someone who saw them in Leeds,' Leon suggested.

'Ideally, a bishop of the Church of England,' Carol said cynically. 'Don't forget, it has to be somebody whose word would stand up against the people's champion.'

The hand that was cutting the cheese slipped and Tony sliced the edge off his index finger. He jumped to his feet, blood dripping from the wound. 'Shit, fuck and God damn it,' he exploded. He thrust his finger into his mouth and sucked.

Carol grabbed the paper napkin wrapped round the Thermos to catch drips and bandaged it round his finger, gripping it tightly. 'Klutz,' she said briskly.

'It was your fault,' he said, subsiding into the chair.

'My fault?'

'What you said. About unimpeachable witnesses.'

'Yes?'

'The camera doesn't lie, right?'

'Depends if it's digital or not,' Carol said ironically.

'Don't be difficult. I'm talking cameras that are already used to convict criminals.'

'What?'

'Motorway cameras, Carol. Motorway cameras.'

Leon snorted in derision. 'Don't tell us you've fallen for that one?'

'What?' Tony said, puzzled.

'Great myths of our time number forty-seven. Motorway cameras catch villains. Not.' Leon leaned back in his chair, his cynical swagger full on.

'What do you mean? I've seen those programmes on TV, police videos of car chases. And what about all those speeding convictions on the back of still photographs from the motorway cameras?' Tony demanded indignantly.

Carol sighed. 'The cameras operate perfectly. But only in certain situations. That's what Leon's getting at. The still cameras only snap vehicles travelling well in excess of the speed limit. They're not going to flicker a shutter at much under ninety. And the videos are only actually turned on if there's an incident in progress or a traffic-flow problem. The rest of the time, they're just not running. And even when they are, you'd need state-of-the-art enhancement software to get anything convincing from them.'

'Wouldn't your brother know somebody?' Simon asked. 'I thought he was some sort of computer whizz kid.'

'Well, yes, but we haven't got anything to show him yet, and we're not likely to have,' Carol objected.

'But I thought when Manchester city centre got blown to bits by the IRA, the police backtracked the route the bombers' van took using the motorway cameras?' Tony said persistent to the last.

Kay shook her head. 'They thought they might have been able to pick it up on the photos of the speeders, but there wasn't enough detail . . .' Her voice tailed off and her face lit up.

'What is it?' Carol asked.

'Private CCTV videos,' she breathed. 'Remember? Greater Manchester Police put out an appeal for any garages or food outlets with CCTV surveillance on possible routes to submit their recordings. We won't get Vance or Shaz on motorway surveillance, but we'll get them wherever they stopped for petrol. Logically, Shaz would have filled up before she left Leeds. She'd have got all the way to London, but she'd not have made it all the way back on a single tank. And the chances are, she would have used a motorway service area rather than come off the motorway just for petrol.'

'And you lot can get access to these tapes?'

Carol groaned. 'It won't be access that's the problem. Most companies are happy to co-operate. Usually they don't even bother asking what it's all in aid of. It's the prospect of all those hours of jerky video. I'm getting a migraine just at the thought of it.'

Tony cleared his throat. 'Actually, Carol, I was going to suggest that you come with me to talk to the police officers who investigated Barbara Fenwick's murder.' He gave an apologetic smile to the other three. Simon and Kay looked merely disappointed, but Leon looked mutinous. 'I'm sorry, but this needs a senior officer to look good. And it needs to be small scale. We don't want to give these guys the hump. We want to avoid giving the impression that they did a lousy job and we're the crack troops coming in to clear up the mess. This is one for me and Carol. What I'd like you to do is divide up the motorway and check out all these service station cameras.' Now all three looked deeply fed up. 'I'd do it myself if I could,' Tony said sympathetically. 'But this is one for the warrant card.'

Inarticulate grumbling came from round the table. 'We know,' Simon said scathingly.

'And Donna Doyle might still be alive,' Carol pointed out.

The trio of detective constables stared at each other, eyes dark and serious. Leon nodded slowly. 'And even if she isn't, the next one is.'

One of the first lessons Tony Hill had learned as a profiler was that preparation was never wasted. It was hard for him and Carol to work up enthusiasm in the stacks of a dusty police document store, but they both knew how important it was to stay alert as they combed the files. The drudgery of poring over every available piece of information was as vital to painting an accurate picture of a killer as the flair that some people seemed naturally to bring to the job. Plodding alone never made a good profiler, but neither did flashy charisma. He'd been happy to be proved wrong about Leon. His superficial approach to the training exercise had confirmed all Tony's prejudices about his peacock display. But either he'd learned from the humiliation of being shown up in front of the rest of the team or else he was one of the ones who could only ever do it for real. Either way, Tony thought as he and Carol ploughed the identical furrow a day later, he couldn't fault the job he'd done.

At the end of a couple of hours, they leaned back in their seats almost simultaneously. 'Looks like Leon didn't miss a thing,' Tony said.

'Looks that way. But if we're going to talk to the man who ran the case, we needed to know that for ourselves.'

'I really appreciate your help in this, Carol,' he said quietly, knocking the papers into a neat pile. 'You didn't have to stick your neck out.'

One corner of her mouth twisted in what might have been a smile or a trace of pain. 'I did, you know,' was all she said. What she didn't say was that they both knew she would never be able to turn her back on his need, personal or professional. And that she also knew the feeling was mutual, provided they both stayed within the limits they seemed to have evolved to keep themselves whole.

'You're sure you can spare the time away from your arson investigation?' he asked, understanding what lay unspoken.

She stacked papers in a file box. 'If anything's going to happen, it'll happen at night. That may be the price you have to pay for crashing in my spare room.'

'I think I can just about afford that,' he said wryly. He followed her back to the counter where they returned the files to a uniformed PC who looked like his thirty was approaching but not fast enough for him.

Carol gave him her best smile. 'The officer in charge of this inquiry – Detective Superintendent Scott? I take it he's retired now?'

'Finished up ten years ago,' the man said, hefting the heavy boxes and heading for the distant shelves where they had come from.

'I don't suppose you know where I could find him?' Carol called to his retreating back.

His voice floated back, muffled by the shelves. 'He lives out Buxton way. Place called Countess Sterndale. There's only three houses.'

It took a few minutes to obtain directions to Countess Sterndale, which didn't appear on their map, and another thirty-five to drive there. 'He wasn't lying, then,' Tony said at the end of the single-track road that concluded in a tree-lined loop round a circle of grass. A battered Queen Anne manor house faced them and over to their left was a pair of long, low cottages with heavy slate roofs and thick limestone walls. 'Which one, d'you reckon?'

Carol shrugged. 'Not the manor, unless he was on the take. Eeny meeny, miny mo . . .' She pointed to the right-hand cottage.

As they walked across the grass, Tony said, 'You take the lead. He'll open up more easily to a copper than a mumbo jumbo man.'

'Even though I'm a woman?' Carol asked ironically.

'You have a point. Play it as it lays.' He opened a smartly painted gate which swung back silently. The path was herringbone brick, not a single weed in the interstices. Tony raised the black iron knocker and let it fall. The sound echoed behind the door. As it died away, heavy footsteps approached and the door opened to reveal a broad man with iron grey hair brilliantined in a side parting and a toothbrush moustache. He looked like a forties matinee idol put out to grass, Carol thought, stifling a smile. 'I'm sorry to trouble you, but we're looking for ex-Detective Superintendent Scott,' she said.

'I'm Gordon Scott,' he said. 'And you are?'

This was where it got difficult. 'DCI Carol Jordan, sir. East Yorkshire Police. And this is Dr Tony Hill from the National Profiling Task Force.' To her surprise, Scott's face lit up with delight.

'Is this to do with Barbara Fenwick?' he said eagerly.

Dismayed, Carol looked helplessly at Tony. 'What makes you say that?' he asked.

A laugh rumbled in his chest. 'I might have been out of the game for ten years, but when three people in two days turn up to look at the files of my only unsolved murder, somebody picks up the phone. Come in, come in.' He ushered them into a comfortable sitting room, ducking to avoid cracking his head on the door frame. The room felt lived in, with magazines and books in unruly piles by the pair of armchairs that faced each other across the beamed fireplace. Scott waved them into the chairs. 'How about a drink? My wife's off doing the shopping in Buxton, but I can just about manage tea. Or a beer?'

'A beer would be great,' Tony said, reluctant to wait while Scott brewed tea. Carol nodded agreement and moments later he returned with three cans of Boddington's.

Scott moved a large ginger cat and settled his bulky frame in the window seat, reducing the light in the room by at least half. He popped the top of his beer, but before he drank, he launched into speech. 'I was that glad when I heard you were looking at Barbara Fenwick's murder. I worried at that case for the best part of two years. It kept me awake nights. I'll never forget the look on her mother's face when I arrived with the news we'd found the body. It still haunts me. I always thought the answer was out there, we just didn't have what it took to get it. So when I got the call and I heard it was the profiling task force ... well, I have to say, my hopes have been raised. What's drawn you to Barbara?'

Tony decided to take advantage of Scott's enthusiasm and offer him frankness. 'This is a somewhat unorthodox investigation,' he began. 'You may have read about the murder of one of my squad.'

Scott nodded his big head sadly. 'Aye, I saw. You have my sympathies.'

'What you won't have read is that she was working on a theory that there is an unsuspected serial killer of teenage girls on the loose and that he's been doing it for a long time. It started off as a classroom exercise, but Shaz couldn't sit on it. My team and I think that's why she was killed. Unfortunately, West Yorkshire Police don't agree. The main reason for that is the person Shaz put in the frame.' He glanced at Carol, ready for some seemingly official back-up.

'There is a significant amount of circumstantial evidence that points to Jacko Vance,' she said baldly.

Scott's eyebrows climbed. 'The telly man?' He let out a soft whistle and his hand went automatically to the cat, stroking its head rhythmically. 'I'm not surprised they didn't want to know. So how does this connect to Barbara Fenwick?'

Carol outlined how Leon's researches had turned up the clipping that had brought them to Gordon Scott's case files. When she had finished, Tony said, 'What we hoped was that there was stuff that never made it on to paper. I know from working with Carol what it's like on a murder squad. You have a feeling in your water, hunches that you never confide to anybody except your partner, never mind put in a memo. We wondered what the gut feelings were among the officers who actually worked the case.'

Scott took a long draught of beer. 'Of course you did. And quite right, too. The trouble is, there's bugger all I can tell you. A couple of times, we got the wrong smell off some of the nonces we had in for questioning, but it was always something else that they were wound up about. To be honest, the gut feeling on our team was total frustration. We just could not get a handle on the bugger. He seemed to have come out of nowhere and vanished the same way. We ended up convinced it was someone from off our patch who'd stumbled across the girl when she was doing a routine bunk off school. And that would sort of fit in with your idea, wouldn't it?'

'Broadly, except that we think he sets it up a lot more carefully than that,' Tony said. 'Oh well, it was worth a try.'

'Sir, there didn't seem to be a lot of forensic evidence,' Carol prompted.

'No. That set us back a bit. Truth to tell, I'd no experience of a sex offender who took that kind of forensic care. Mostly they're hot-headed, spur of the moment, leave all sorts of traces, go home covered in mud and blood. But there was almost nothing to work off. The only distinctive thing was the crushed arm, according to the pathologist. She wouldn't stick her neck out on paper, but she had this notion that the girl's arm had been crushed in a vice.'

The thought of such cold-blooded torture sent a shiver of unwelcome echoes through Tony's stomach. 'Ah,' he said.

Scott struck his forehead with the heel of his hand. 'Of course! Vance lost his arm, didn't he? He was going for the Olympics and he lost his arm. Perfect sense, why didn't we think of something like that at the time? God, what an idiot I am!'

'There's no reason why you should have considered it,' Tony said, wishing he meant it, wondering how many lives might have been saved if a psychologist had been brought in all those years ago.

'Is the pathologist still working?' Carol asked, as ever straight to the point.

'She's a professor now at one of the London teaching hospitals. I've got her card somewhere,' Scott said, getting to his feet and lumbering out of the room. 'God, why didn't I think more about the arm?'

'It's not his fault, Tony,' Carol said.

'I know. I sometimes wonder how many more people have to die before everybody recognizes psychologists aren't just witch doctors,' he said. 'Listen, Carol, in the interests of speed, I think we should get Chris Devine to follow up on this pathologist. She's desperate to help, and she's got the experience to know the kind of things she should be looking for. What do you say?'

'I think that's a good idea. To tell you the truth, I was dreading telling you that I couldn't go to London now. I need to be around tonight in case the arsonist decides to have a go.'

He smiled. 'I remembered.' It was probably the first time in his career as a profiler that something outside the case obsessing him had impinged. That was the trouble with working with Carol Jordan. She affected him in ways no one else ever had. When he didn't see her, he could conveniently forget that. Working this closely, it was impossible to ignore. He gave her a grave smile. 'I'm too scared of upsetting John Brandon to let you chance blowing the arson collar,' he lied.

'I know.' She detected the lie, but did not show it. It was neither the time nor the place for some kinds of truth.

Kay had lost count. She couldn't remember if this was the seventh or the eighth set of videos she'd inspected. Having drawn the short straw in the division of the sites, she'd set

385

off on the M1 from Leeds before dawn and driven all the way to London. Then she turned the car round and retraced her journey, stopping at every service area she came to. Now it was late afternoon and she was sitting in yet another scruffy office, stuffy with stale sweat and smoke, watching jerky images dancing in front of her as she fast-forwarded through the tapes. She was awash with bad coffee, her mouth still slimy and fat-flavoured from the long ago breakfast at Scratchwood Services. Her eyes were gritty and tired, and she wished she was anywhere else.

At least they'd managed to narrow the time frame down. They reckoned the earliest Shaz or Vance could possibly have hit the first northbound services on the motorway was eleven in the morning, the latest seven at night. Adjusting the times forward for each service area wasn't difficult.

The tapes took much less running time than real time, since, rather than taping continuously, the cameras only took a certain number of still frames per second. Even so, she'd spent hours working her way through the recordings, fast-forwarding until she saw either a black Volkswagen Golf or one of the cars registered to Jacko Vance – a silver Mercedes convertible or a Land Rover. The Golf was common enough to cause frequent pauses, the other cars turning up less often.

She thought she was faster now than when she'd started. Her eyes were in tune with what she was searching for, though she feared she was beginning to flag and worried that might make her miss something crucial. Forcing herself to concentrate, Kay flicked forward until the familiar black pram-like shape of another Golf appeared. She slowed to normal speed, then almost at once she registered that the driver was a male with grey hair sticking out from under a baseball cap rather than either of her expected targets so her finger moved towards the fast-forward button. Then, suddenly, it swerved to the pause button as she noticed that there was something odd about the man.

But the first thing that struck her on closer scrutiny had nothing to do with the person who'd climbed out of the driver's seat and headed for the petrol pump. What Kay spotted was quite different. Although the car was sitting at an awkward angle to the pumps, she could make out the last two letters of the number plate. They were identical to the final digits of Shaz's registration.

'Ah, shit,' she breathed softly. She rewound the tape and watched it again. This time she identified what had caught her eye about the driver. He was awkwardly left-handed, to the point where he hardly used his right arm at all. Just as Jacko Vance would inevitably be if he were using equipment that wasn't specially designed to accommodate his disability.

Kay studied the tape a few more times. It wasn't easy to make out the man's features, but she wouldn't mind betting that Carol Jordan would know someone who could help them over that particular hurdle. Before the night was over, they'd have something on Jacko Vance that even a team of highly paid defence lawyers wouldn't be able to get him out of. And it would be down to her, the best tribute she could pay to a woman who had been on the way to becoming a friend.

She flipped open her mobile phone and called Carol. 'Carol? It's Kay. I think I might have something your brother would like to see . . .'

It wasn't that Chris Devine objected to pathologists having a day off. What pissed her off royally was that this particular pathologist spent her free time sitting in the pouring rain in the middle of nowhere waiting for a glimpse of some bloody stupid bird that was supposed to be in Norway but had managed to get lost. There was nothing clever about getting lost, Chris muttered as she felt more rain slide between her neck and her collar. Bloody Essex, she thought bitterly.

She sheltered from the gusting easterly so she could take another look at the rough map the bird warden had sketched out for her. She couldn't be far away now. Why did these bloody hides have to be so inconspicuous? Why didn't they just make them look like her nan's house? She had more bloody birds in her back garden than Chris had seen all afternoon on the marshes. The birds were too flaming sensible to come out on a day like this, she grumbled as she stuffed the map back in her pocket and set off round the edge of the copse.

She almost missed the hide, so well was it camouflaged. Chris pulled back the wooden door and forced the scowl from her face. 'Sorry to butt in,' she said to the three people cramped inside, grateful that her head at least was out of the wind. 'Is one of you Professor Stewart?' She hoped she was in the right place; it was impossible to tell even genders inside waxed jackets, woolly scarves and thermal hats.

A gloved hand rose. 'I'm Liz Stewart,' one of the figures said. 'What's going on?'

Chris sighed with relief. 'Detective Sergeant Devine, Metropolitan Police. I wonder if I could have a word?'

The woman shook her head. 'I'm not on call,' she said, her Scottish accent growing stronger in indignation.

'I appreciate that. But it is rather urgent.' Chris unobtrusively edged the door wider so the wind could whip inside the rickety structure.

'Oh, for God's sake, Liz, go and see what the woman wants,' an irritated male voice said from under one of the other hats. 'We're not going to see anything worthwhile at all if you two stand there screaming like fishwives.'

The grudging professor squeezed past the other two and followed Chris outside. 'There's some shelter under the trees,' Professor Stewart said, pushing past her and scrambling through the undergrowth until they were out of reach of most of the weather. In the clearing, Chris could see she was a sharp-featured forty-something with clear amber eyes like a hawk. 'Now, what is all this about?' she demanded.

'You worked a case twelve years ago. An unsolved murder of a teenage girl in Manchester, Barbara Fenwick. Do you remember it?'

'The girl with the crushed arm?'

'That's the one. The case has cropped up in connection with another investigation. We think we're looking at a serial killer, and it's possible that Barbara Fenwick is the only one of his victims where the body's turned up. Which makes your postmortem pretty significant.'

'Which it will still be on Monday morning,' the professor said briskly.

'Yeah, but the girl we think he's holding might not make it that long,' Chris said.

'Ah. You'd better fire away then, Sergeant.'

'Retired Superintendent Scott told my colleagues that you had thought, but didn't put in your report, that the arm looked like it might have been crushed deliberately in something like a vice rather than accidentally, is that right?'

'That was my opinion, but it was only speculation. Not the sort of fanciful thing I'd put in a formal postmortem report unless I had considerably stronger grounds for my belief,' she said repressively.

'But if you were pressed, you'd say that?'

'If I were asked directly if it were possible, yes, I'd have to agree.'

'Was there anything else you didn't write down because it was "fanciful"?' Chris asked.

'Not that I can think of.'

'I know you said you didn't put it in your formal report, but would you have put something in your notes to that effect?'

'Oh yes,' the professor said, as if it were the most natural thing in the world. 'That way, if it became important later, the prosecution could introduce it more readily.'

Chris closed her eyes momentarily in a short prayer. 'And have you still got your notes?'

'Of course. In fact, I've got something even better than that.'

The café of the motorway services at Hartshead Moor on the M62 had never been anyone's idea of a good Saturday night out, which made it perfect for their purposes. The ad hoc investigative team was now augmented by Chris Devine, who had slotted in as if she'd always been there. Already, it seemed she and Carol were about to sign up as blood sisters, both because of their common experiences in the Job and because they were the nearest thing the team had to senior officers.

The group had colonized a distant corner with no prospect of being overheard or disturbed since it was right on the border of the smoking area. Leon, dispirited at drawing a blank, was buoyed up by Kay's results. But Simon's face was showing signs of strain inevitable in a man whose name was on the wanted list, turned on by the very group who had given him a sense of community. Tony wondered how long the younger man could stand it without his judgement slipping dangerously.

Carol cut into his thoughts. 'I've arranged for Kay to meet a friend of my brother who can enhance these pictures for us, to cut the margin of doubt to the bone.'

'You're not coming along?' Kay asked, looking slightly worried.

'Carol has responsibilities in East Yorkshire tonight,' Tony said. 'Is that a problem, Kay?'

She looked embarrassed. 'Not a problem, not as such. It's just . . . well, I don't know this bloke, and he's doing this as a favour, right?'

'That's right,' Carol said. 'Michael says he owes him.'

'It's just that . . . well, if I want to push a bit harder, you know, if I don't think he's going to the max because he can't be bothered, or it's going to cost too much, I can't actually lean on him the way Carol could.'

'She's got a point,' Chris affirmed from the smoking table she was occupying with Leon. 'She's not even the one who's asked for the favour. And it's Saturday night. Even computer nerds must have something better to do than a favour for somebody who can't be bothered to turn up in person. That'll be how it looks. I think Carol should be there.'

Carol stirred her sludgy coffee. 'You're right. I can't fault your logic. But I can't afford to be off my patch tonight.' She glanced at her watch and made rapid calculations.

'No, Carol,' Tony said hopelessly, knowing already he was wasting his breath.

'If we left now . . . we could be there by nine . . . I could be back in Seaford by one at the latest. And nothing ever happens before then . . .' Coming to a decision, Carol grabbed her coat and bag. 'All right. Come on, Kay, we're off.' As they walked towards the door with Kay scrambling to catch up, Carol turned. 'Chris – good hunting.'

'So what do we do now?' Leon demanded aggressively, lighting another cigarette from the butt of the one he'd been smoking. 'I feel like I've wasted a whole day fucking about with motorway cameras. I want to be doing something worthwhile, you know?'

Tony was glad Chris Devine had come to join them; he had a feeling he was going to have to rely on her experience now the others were starting to fray round the edges. 'Nobody's been wasting their time, Leon. We've come a long way today,' he said calmly. 'We need to build on that. The information Chris has got from the pathologist is a big step forward. But on its own, it's still not worth a whole lot. He profiles right. Everything we learn about him puts another tick in the box. But we're still in the realms of supposition.'

'Even with a victim with a crushed right arm?' Simon asked incredulously. 'Come on, that's got to be a clincher. What more do we need, for God's sake?'

'Given the kind of lawyers Jack the Lad is going to be able to afford, we'd be laughed out of court – always supposing we got that far,' Tony said. 'I'm sorry, but that's the way it is.'

'The crushed arm is good stuff,' Chris said. 'But it's not a lot of use as an isolated case. What we need is something to compare it with. Only so far there haven't been any bodies, right?' The others nodded. 'But you reckon he'd got another one just before Shaz fronted him up? Well then, chances are he'd started on her but he hadn't finished. So we find her, we tie her to him, and we've got him. Anything wrong with that?'

'No, except we don't know where he keeps them before he kills them,' Tony said.

'Course we don't. Or do we?'

If they'd been dogs, their ears would have pricked up. 'Go on,' Tony encouraged her.

'The great thing about being a dyke my age is that when I was getting into the scene, everyone who had a job was in the closet. Now, half the women I used to drink with are bosses all over the shop. One of them just happens to be a partner in the agency that handles Jacko's publicity.' She pulled out a sheaf of fax paper from inside her jacket. 'Jacko's schedule for the last six weeks. Now, unless he's Superman or his wife is in on this, there's only one area of the country he could possibly be keeping this kid.' She leaned back and watched them cotton on to what had leapt out at her.

Tony ran his hand through his hair. 'I know he's got a cottage up there. But it's a huge area. How can we narrow it down?'

'He could be using his own place,' Leon said.

'Yeah,' Simon butted in eagerly. 'Let's get up there, take a look at this hideaway.'

'I don't know,' Chris said. 'He's been so careful about everything else, I can't believe he'd do something so risky.'

'Where's the risk?' Tony demanded. 'He brings the girls there under cover of darkness, they're never seen or heard from again. There's never a trace of the bodies. But Jack the Lad does volunteer work at the hospital in Newcastle. They must have an incinerator. He's always pushing the image of himself as being a man with the common touch. I'd guess he regularly pops down to the boiler room, having a natter with the lads. And if he helps them load the incinerator from time to time, well, who's going to notice the extra bag of body parts?'

A chilled silence fell over the group. Tony scratched the stubble on his chin. 'I should have worked this out before now. He's a control freak. The only killing ground he'd trust would be one he had total control over.'

'So let's go,' Simon said, pushing his cup away and reaching for his jacket.

'No,' Tony said firmly. 'Simon, this is not the time for Action Man tactics. We need to plan carefully here. We can't just go charging in mob-handed and hope what we find justifies the action. His lawyers would make mincemeat of us. We need to have a strategy.'

'That's easy for you to say, man,' Leon said. 'You're not the one the cops are looking to arrest. You can sleep in your own bed at night. Simon needs this to be sorted.'

'All right, all right,' Chris said mildly. 'It wouldn't hurt to do a trawl locally with pictures of Donna Doyle. Looking at his timetable, she must have got there under her own steam. I bet he sends them up on the train or the coach. We need to blitz the bus terminal and the train station, talk to the staff. And the locals. If there's a small local station near to Jack the Lad's hideaway, somebody might have seen her getting off the train.'

Simon stood up, dark eyes burning. 'So what are we waiting for?'

'No point in hitting it before morning,' Chris said.

'It's a two-and-a-half-hour drive from here. We're not doing anything better, are we? Let's go now, find a cheap hotel and get cracking first thing in the morning. You up for it, Leon?'

Leon stubbed out his cigarette. 'Long as I don't have to go in your car. What're you driving, Chris?'

'You wouldn't like my music. We'll take all the cars. OK, Tony?'

'OK. Provided you stay well away from his house. I have your word on that, Chris?'

'You got my word, Tony.'

'That go for you two? Bearing in mind Chris is technically your senior officer?'

Leon scowled but gave a grudging nod. Simon, too, conceded. 'OK. I probably shouldn't be making the decisions anyway.'

'What've you got planned, Tony?' Chris asked.

'I'm going home to draw up a full profile based on all we know now. I can't say I blame you for wanting to hare off up the A1, but if Carol and Kay come back with the goods, I'm proposing we go to West Yorkshire first thing in the morning and persuade them to make this official. So, nothing except local inquiries until we've spoken. OK?'

Chris nodded sombrely. 'Trust me, Tony. Shaz meant too much to me to risk fucking this up.'

If she'd been trying to take the gung-ho madness out of the two male officers' eyes, she succeeded. Even Leon stopped bouncing on the balls of his feet. 'I hadn't forgotten that,' Tony said. 'Or how much she wanted to catch Jack the Lad.'

'I know,' Chris said. 'Fucking mad bitch, she'd have loved this.'

Once upon a time she'd understood most of what there was to know about computers, Carol thought wistfully. Back around 1989, she was almost as much of a whizz with CP/M and DOS as her brother. But she'd gone into the police force and it had eaten up her life. While she'd been getting to grips with the Police and Criminal Evidence Act, Michael had been assimilating software and hardware that often moved forward on a daily basis. Now she was the one-eyed woman in the kingdom of 20/20 vision. She knew enough to crunch numbers and process words, to retrieve lost files from limbo and to rewrite boot files so that a reluctant machine could be persuaded to talk to its user. But ten minutes with her brother and his mate Donny and she knew that, these days, this was the culinary equivalent of being able to boil a kettle. From the look on Kay's face, it wasn't any better for her. It was just as well she'd come along, Carol thought. At least she had enough knowledge to know when the boys were spinning off into a world of their own and the authority to drag them back to the job in hand.

The two men sitting in front of a computer screen the size of a pub TV muttered to each other incomprehensibly about video drivers, local buses and smart caches. Carol knew what the words meant, but she couldn't connect them to anything they were doing with keyboard and mouse. Donny, Michael had told her, was the best man in the north when it came to computer-enhancing photographs or video stills. And he just happened to work in the same building where Michael's software company had its suite of offices. And, in spite of Chris's convictions, he was so devoid of a life that he was thrilled to be dragged away from *The X Files* and a microwave dinner to show off his toys.

Carol and Kay looked over their shoulders at the screen. Donny had already done everything he could with the number plate, yielding confirmation of the last two letters and a strong probability of a match with the third. Now he was working on the driver. He'd already tweaked and twiddled with some full-length shots of the man, pronouncing himself finally satisfied with one and printing out a couple of colour copies for the two women to pore over. The more Carol looked, the more convinced she was that under the Nike baseball cap and behind the aviator glasses, Jacko Vance was peeking out at her. 'What do you think?' she asked Kay.

'I don't know if you'd pick him out of a line-up, but if you know who you're looking for, I think you can tell it's him.'

Now, without any prompting from them, Donny was working on a head and shoulders of the man who'd filled the Golf with petrol at lunchtime on the Saturday Shaz Bowman died. It was hard to find a good shot to work with because the peak of the cap shaded his face most of the time when he wasn't actually bending over the fuel tank. Only by advancing one frame at a time did Donny finally come up with a single shot where the man in the cap glanced swiftly up at the pump to check how much petrol he'd taken.

Watching Donny painstakingly improve the quality of the picture was agonizing. Carol couldn't keep her eyes off her watch, gripped with the knowledge that she should be elsewhere and if anything happened in Seaford she'd be in deep shit. The minutes crawled by while the powerful processor drove a search through the computer's massive memory for the next best alternative to the pixels on the screen. Although it was making more calculations per second than the human brain could comfortably comprehend, the computer seemed to Carol to take forever. At last, Donny turned away from the screen and pushed his own baseball cap back on his head. 'Best you're going to get,' he said. 'Funny, he looks familiar. Is he supposed to?'

'Can you print me off half a dozen copies?' Carol said. She felt mean ignoring his good-natured question, but it wasn't the time or place to tell Donny that, apart from cheeks that were undeniably too chubby, the face he'd recreated was that of the nation's favourite TV personality.

Michael was either quicker on the uptake or more familiar with the medium. 'He looks like Jacko Vance, that's what's got you confused, Donny,' he said innocently.

'Yeah, right, that dickhead,' Donny said, swinging round in his chair and blinking at the women. 'Fucking hell, shame it's not him you're going to arrest. You'd be doing the world a favour, getting that shit he does off the box. Sorry I couldn't get a better head shot, but there wasn't a lot to go on. Where did you say you got the tape from?'

'M1 services. Watford Gap,' Kay said.

'Yeah, right. Pity you weren't looking for your man in Leeds.'

'Leeds?' Carol leapt on the word. 'Why Leeds?'

'Cos that's where the state-of-the-art CCTV development company is. Seesee Vision. They are the total business. They think civil liberties is that posh but polite department store in London.' He laughed at his own bad joke. 'Double wicked fuckers, they are. You can't miss them. That sodding great smoked glass monolith just after the end of the motorway. You want somebody coming off the M1 at Leeds, they've got it taped.'

'What do you mean, somebody coming off at Leeds?' Carol's fingers were twitching with the desire to grab Donny by the shirt and make him get to the point.

Donny cast his eyes upwards as if he were tired of dealing with mental defectives. 'Right. History lesson. Nineteenth-century Britain. Little pockets of mains water supply, gas providers, railway companies. Gradually, they all linked up to make national utilities. With me so far?'

'And there's me thinking nerds knew nothing about the Victorian era apart from Charles Babbage,' Carol snapped. 'OK, Donny, we did the Industrial Revolution at school. Can we get to CCTV?'

'OK, OK, be chill. CCTV is kind of like the baby utilities were then. But soon it won't be. Soon we're going to have all these inner-city systems linking up with private security systems and motorway cameras and we're going to have a national network of CCTV. And these systems will be so finely tuned that they can recognize you or your wheels and if you're not supposed to be some place, then the big fuck-off security guards are gonna remove you. Like if you're a convicted shoplifter and Marks and Sparks don't want you hanging out in their food hall, or you're a known perv and your local launderette doesn't want you in there ogling the knickers –' He made a throat-cutting gesture.

'So what exactly has all this got to do with the M1?'

'Seesee Vision are the masters of the universe when it comes to leading-edge techno. And they test all their new gear on the traffic flow off the M1. Their stuff is so well developed they can give you a high-res picture of the drivers and the front-seat passengers, never mind baby stuff like number plates.' Donny shook his head in wonder. 'I went for a job there, but I didn't like it. You could tell it was seagull city.'

'Seagull city?' Carol asked faintly.

'The bosses fly in, do a lot of screaming, grab everything worth having, crap over everybody and fly out again. Not my scene.'

'Do you think they'd co-operate with me?'

'They'd wet their pants. They're desperate to make a big impression on your lot. When this national network finally creaks into being, they want to be in the driving seat. The company of choice.'

Carol looked at her watch. It was after ten. She should be heading back to Seaford, on the spot if her team had to swing into action. Besides, no one in authority would be at Seesee Vision at this time of night.

Donny spotted her glance and read her mind. 'There'll be somebody there this time of night, if that's what you're wondering. Give them a bell. You got nothing to lose.'

But Donna Doyle might, Carol thought, catching Kay's pleading look. And besides, Leeds was halfway between Manchester and Seaford. Her team were grown-ups. It wouldn't be the first time they'd had to think for themselves.

First, the victims. It was always the place to start. The problem here was to convince anyone that there were victims. It was

399

always possible that they were wrong, Tony realized. They so badly wanted Shaz to have been right, they so desperately needed to be instrumental in putting a stop to the person who had killed her that they might all be deluding themselves about the value of the material they had uncovered. It was almost conceivable that the circumstantial evidence piling up against Jacko Vance was just that and no more.

But that way madness lay. Madness and the prospect of poor Simon being arrested as soon as he crossed the threshold of his own home. 'The victims,' Tony said. He stared at the laptop screen and started to type.

THE CASE FOR A SERIAL OFFENDER

The first known victim in this putative cluster is Barbara Fenwick whose murder took place twelve years ago (see attached summary prepared by DC Leon Jackson for crime details). We can say with some degree of certainty that this was the first killing by this perpetrator since there is no previous record of this signature behaviour, namely the pulverizing of the lower right arm. This is clearly signature behaviour; there is no need to inflict such an injury in order to commit sexual assault and murder. It is extraneous, it is ritualistic and therefore it is safe to assume that it has particular significance for this offender. Given the ceremonial nature of this signature behaviour, it is likely that he has used the same implement to produce these injuries in all his killings; other victims could therefore be expected to display very similar disfigurement.

There is at least one other indication that this was a first murder. The killer had chosen what he thought was a sufficiently isolated and safe place to carry out his crime undisturbed, but he was in fact almost caught in the act. This will have frightened him considerably and he will have taken immediate steps to secure his future killing grounds. That he was successful in this is shown by the fact that no bodies have been recovered from his subsequent victims.

In the absence of bodies, what possible grounds can there be for assuming a serial offender?

He paused and referred back to the list of common features that Shaz had presented to the profiling team what felt like an age ago. The least he could do was make sure the work she'd left wasn't wasted. With a few changes and additions, he typed in the list then continued.

While two or three common features are to be expected with any such grouping, the number and congruence we can identify here is of far too high a level to be coincidental. Of particular importance is the degree of physical similarity between the victims. They could be sisters.

Perhaps more significantly, they could also be sisters of a woman called Jillie Woodrow as she looked fifteen or sixteen years ago, when she first became the earliest known lover of Jacko Vance, our prime suspect. It is not coincidence, in my opinion, that Vance was robbed of a brilliant athletic career when he lost his lower right arm in an accident that crushed it beyond hope of restoration.

Further, the date of the killing of Barbara Fenwick was a mere fourteen weeks after Jacko Vance's accident. For much of that time, he was in hospital recovering from his injuries and subsequently undergoing extensive physiotherapy. It was during this hospitalization that

Jillie Woodrow took the opportunity to terminate what had become an increasingly oppressive and unwelcome relationship (see appended notes of interview with JW, conducted by DC Simon McNeill). The combined stress of these two events would be sufficient to trigger a sexual homicide in one who was predisposed to realize his sociopathic responses in violent behaviour.

He has never released his sexual impulses in a normal fashion since. His extremely high-profile marriage is a sham, his wife being a lesbian whose 'personal assistant' is in fact her lover and has been since before the wedding took place. Vance and his wife have never had sexual intercourse and his wife assumes he uses 'high-class call girls' to provide him with a sexual outlet. There is no suggestion that she has any suspicion of his homicidal activities.

When Vance's early life is set against the criteria that experience has demonstrated are common features among homicidally active sociopaths, a remarkable degree of commonality is obvious. We have witness interviews that attest to a difficult relationship with a rejecting mother, an often absent father whom the subject was desperate to impress, bullying of younger children, cruelty to animals and sadistic, controlling sexual behaviour, and evidence of powerful and perverse sexual fantasies. His sporting prowess can be identified as a massive overcompensation for the worthlessness he felt in every other area of his life, and the loss of that prowess as a devastating blow to his extremely fragile self-esteem.

In those circumstances, women would be the obvious victim gender. He would perceive his mother and subsequently his fiancée as having emasculated him. But he is far too intelligent to vent his rage on the obvious targets, and so he has assumed a series of surrogates. These are girls who bear a strong resemblance to Jillie Woodrow at the age when he first seduced her.

It should be borne in mind that captured serial killers have in the main been above average intelligence, in some cases well above. We should not therefore be surprised that uncaught and unsuspected serial offenders exist who are using their greater intelligence more effectively. Jacko Vance is, in my opinion, an example of this principle in action.

He leaned back in his chair. So much for the psychology. He'd have to draw up a more detailed table of corresponding preconditions, but that wouldn't take long. Added to the hard evidence he hoped Carol and Kay would produce that night, he felt sure that there was enough material to make certain that within twelve hours, West Yorkshire would have started to take Jacko Vance seriously.

Detective Sergeant Tommy Taylor knew a pile of crap when he saw it. And surveilling part-time firemen was the biggest pile of crap he'd seen in a very long time. He'd spent the night before watching Raymond Watson, which in effect meant watching Raymond Watson's house. It wasn't as if it was packed with architectural detail to keep the mind active. A bog-standard terraced house with a pocket handkerchief front garden that boasted a tired rose bush contorted by the north-east winds into a shape some modern sculptors would have given their eye teeth to achieve. Flaked paintwork, scabby varnish on the front door.

Watson had come home at eleven the night before, after the last race at the dog track. There was no meeting tonight, so he'd arrived home just after seven, according to the seconded uniforms who'd been keeping an eye out in their mufti. Since then, nothing. Unless you counted putting out the milk bottles as a major event.

The lights had gone off about ten minutes after that. An hour later, there was no sign of life anywhere. The back streets of Seaford weren't noted for their liveliness after midnight. The only thing that was going to get Raymond Watson out of his kip now was a major fire, Taylor reckoned. He grunted and shifted in the car seat, scratching his balls and sniffing his fingers afterwards. Bored shitless, he flicked the switch on his personal radio and called Di Earnshaw. 'Owt happening your end?' he asked.

'Negative,' came the reply.

'If Control come through to you with news of a fire that our lads are getting called out on, give me a shout on the PR, OK?'

'Why? Are you leaving the car on foot pursuit?' She sounded eager. Probably as bored as him, excited by the thought of some action even at second hand.

'Negative,' Taylor said. 'I need to stretch my legs. These fucking sardine tins weren't built for the likes of me. Like I said, anything doing, give me a shout. Over and out.'

He turned the key in the ignition. The engine coughed to life, sounding freakishly noisy in the quiet side street. Bollocks to Carol Jordan's daft ideas. Less than a mile away there was a club that kept late doors, catering mainly for the sailors off the foreign ships. There was a pint there with Tommy Taylor's name on it, unless he was very much mistaken. It was time he checked out the possibility.

Carol and Kay followed the security guard down blindingly white corridors. He opened a door and stood back, waving them into a large, dimly lit room. Computer monitors occupied almost every horizontal surface. A young woman in jeans and a polo shirt, hair dyed platinum blonde and cut flat to her head, glanced over her shoulder, registered the new arrivals and turned back to the screen she'd been engrossed in. Fingers tapped keys and the display changed. Carol caught movement in her peripheral vision and turned her head. A tall man in a suit that screamed money was perched on the edge of a computer desk over to one side. What she'd caught was him unfolding his arms and dropping his hands in preparation for rising to greet them.

He took a step towards them, pushing a persistent cowlick of mid-brown hair out of his eyes. If he was going for boyish, Carol thought, he'd missed it by about a generation. 'Detective Chief Inspector Jordan,' he said, clearly relishing the bass resonance of his voice. 'And Detective Constable Hallam. Welcome to the future.'

God help me, Carol thought. 'You must be Philip Jarvis,' she said, forcing a smile. 'I'm impressed and grateful that you were prepared to help me out at this time of night.'

'Time waits for no man,' he said, as proudly as if he'd coined the phrase. 'Or woman, come to that. We recognize the importance of your work and, like you, we operate twenty-four hours a day. We are, after all, in the same business, the business of crime prevention and, when that fails us, catching those responsible.'

'Mmm,' Carol murmured noncommittally. It was clearly a prepared speech that placed no reliance on a response.

Jarvis smiled benevolently, revealing the sort of brilliant white dental work more common in New York than Yorkshire. 'This is the viewing room,' he said with a sweep of his arm, undaunted by the obviousness of his statement. 'It's fed either from our fully automated library or by live feeds from the many cameras we have being road-tested on the site. The

405

operator chooses the source and summons the images he or she wants to look at.'

He ushered Carol and Kay forward until they were standing behind the woman. Close up, Carol could see her skin was older than her face, faded to unhealthy by the lack of natural light and the radiation from the monitors. 'This is Gina,' Jarvis announced. He made her sound like royalty. 'When you told me the date and time period you were interested in and the vehicle index numbers that you wanted to know about, I got Gina on to it right away.'

'As I said, I really appreciate this. Have you had any luck?'

'Luck doesn't enter into it, Chief Inspector,' Jarvis said with throwaway arrogance. 'Not with a leading-edge system like ours. Gina?'

Gina tore her eyes from the screen and pushed off with her feet, spinning round to face them, grabbing a sheet of paper from the desk. 'Seventeen minutes past two on the afternoon in question.' Her voice was clipped and efficient. 'The black Volkswagen Golf left the M1 heading for the city centre. Then, at eleven thirty-two p.m., the silver Mercedes convertible did exactly the same thing. We can supply timed and dated tapes and still photographs of both events.'

'Is it possible to identify the drivers of either vehicle?' Kay asked, trying to keep the excitement out of her voice and failing. Gina flicked an interested eyebrow upwards and stared.

'Obviously, the daytime shots pose fewer problems in that respect,' Jarvis butted in. 'But we're using very high-end experimental media with the night filming at present, and with our computer enhancement technology, it would be possible to come up with surprisingly good images.'

'If you knew who it was you were looking at, you would

be able to recognize them. If you were planning on doing a "does anyone know this man" on *Crimewatch UK*, you might have one or two problems,' Gina qualified.

'You say this system's experimental. How well do you think this evidence would stand up in court?' Carol asked.

'One hundred per cent on the vehicles. More like a seventy-five per cent chance on the drivers,' Gina said.

'Come on now, Gina, let's not be so pessimistic. It depends, like so much evidence, on how it's presented to the jury,' Jarvis protested. 'I'd happily testify that I'd stake my reputation on the reliability of the system.'

'And you're a qualified expert witness, are you, sir?' Carol asked. She wasn't trying to put him on the spot, but time was short and she needed to know how firm was her ground.

'I'm not, no, but some of my colleagues are.'

'Like me,' Gina said. 'Look, Ms Jordan, why don't you look at what we've got and see if that isn't enough to help you get the corroborative evidence so it won't depend on what a jury thinks about our technology?'

When she left half an hour later, Kay was clutching a bundle of video tape and laser-printed stills that both women knew in their bones would corner Jacko Vance. If Donna Doyle remained alive, they were her last best hope. Carol could hardly wait to tell Tony. She looked at her watch when she got back to the car. Half past midnight. She knew he'd want to see what she had, but she needed to get back to Seaford. And Kay could always take the material over to him now. Carol stood by her car, undecided.

To hell with it, she thought. She really wanted to talk over the evidence with Tony. He'd only get one shot at McCormick and Wharton and she needed to make sure he'd prepared a case that would speak directly to a copper's idea of evidence.

She had her mobile if they really needed her, after all.

Detective Constable Di Earnshaw pushed her shoulders hard back against the car seat, thrusting her pelvis forward in a vain attempt to loosen her stiff spine and find a comfortable position in the unmarked CID car. She wished she'd been able to bring her own little Citroën whose seat seemed moulded to her contours. Whoever had designed the police Vauxhall had obviously been a hell of a lot narrower in the hips and longer in the leg than she had any hope of ever achieving.

At least the discomfort kept her awake. There was a kind of spiteful pride in Di's determination to stay on the job. She was as convinced as Tommy Taylor that these stakeouts were a total waste of time and money, but she reckoned there were more subtle and effective ways of demonstrating that to the powers that be than skiving off. She knew her sergeant well enough by now to have a pretty shrewd idea of how he was passing the weary hours as night crawled relentlessly towards dawn. If Carol Jordan found out, he'd be back in uniform so fast he wouldn't know what had hit him. CID was such a gossip factory, she was bound to find out sooner or later. If not on this job, then on another, perhaps one that actually counted.

Di wouldn't dream of doing anything so obvious to undermine Jordan's authority. More in sorrow than in anger, that would be her line. The pitying smiles behind Jordan's back, the back-stabbing, 'I shouldn't really say this, but ...' at every opportunity. Make it look like every cock-up emanated from Jordan's orders, every success from the troops' initiatives. There was almost nothing as destructive as constant undermining. She should know. She'd experienced plenty of it in her years with the East Yorkshire Police.

She yawned. Nothing was going to happen. Alan Brinkley

was tucked up in bed with his wife inside their pretentious modern box on a so-called executive development with ideas above its station. Never mind that it would be easier to keep clean and maintained, Di preferred her little trawlerman's terraced cottage down by the old docks, even though they were now a tourist trap heritage centre. She loved the cobbled streets and the salt on the air, the sense that generations of Yorkshirewomen had stood on those doorsteps and scanned the horizon for their men. She should be so lucky, she thought with a moment's self-hatred.

She checked her watch against the clock on the dashboard. In the ten minutes that had passed since she'd last done it, the two had managed to remain precisely five seconds out of sync. Yawning, she switched on her small portable radio. Hopefully the phone-in she personally called prole-speak would be over and the DJ would be playing some decent sounds. Just as Gloria Gaynor stridently revealed that as long as she knew how to love, she knew she'd stay alive, soft light abruptly appeared behind the four frosted glass panels of the mock-Georgian fanlight in the Brinkleys' front door. Di grabbed the steering wheel tightly and sat up hurriedly. Was this it? Or was it insomnia pushing someone towards a cup of tea?

Just as suddenly as it had appeared, the light vanished. Di slumped back with a sigh, then from under the garage door, a thin rope of brightness stretched across the driveway. Startled, she punched the off button on the radio and wound down the car window, letting the raw night air flood her airways and sharpen her senses. Yes, there it was. The unmistakable cough of a car engine.

Within moments, the garage door shuddered upwards and the car rolled forward on to the drive. It was Brinkley's car, no mistake. Or rather, it was the car on which Brinkley had

409

only ever paid three hire-purchase instalments and which would be snatched back just as soon as the repo men figured out how to grab it without actually breaking into Brinkley's garage. As she watched, Brinkley himself got out of the car and walked back to the garage, reaching inside presumably to hit the button that closed the door behind him.

'Oh boy,' Di Earnshaw said, winding up her window. She pressed the record button on her personal microcassette recorder and said excitedly, 'Alan Brinkley is now leaving his home by car at one twenty-seven a.m.' Dropping the tape machine on the seat beside her, she grabbed the personal radio that was meant to keep her in close touch with Tommy Taylor. 'This is Tango Charlie. Tango Alpha, do you read me? Over.' She started her engine, careful to avoid the reflex of turning on her lights. Brinkley had pulled off the drive now and was driving out of the cul-de-sac, signalling a right turn. She eased her foot off the clutch, still driving without lights, and picked him up on the winding avenue that ran through the housing development and out to the main road.

She clicked the radio as she drove, repeating her message to her sergeant. 'Tango Charlie to Tango Alpha. Subject on the move, do you read me? Tango Alpha, do you read me? Over.' At the main road, Brinkley turned left. She counted to five, then switched on her lights and turned after him. He was heading for the city centre three miles away, keeping his speed steady, just above the limit. Not so careful he'd be pulled on suspicion of over-cautious drunk driving, not so fast he'd attract a tug for speeding. 'Tango Charlie to Tango Alpha.' She swore silently at her errant boss. She needed back-up and he wasn't there. She thought about calling in to control, but they'd only send a troop of patrol cars that would scare off any arsonist for three counties.

'Oh, shit,' she complained as Brinkley turned off the main

road into the dimly lit streets of a small industrial estate. It looked very much as if this was it. Turning off her lights again, she followed cautiously. As the high walls of the units closed around her, she decided she had to call for uniformed back-up. She turned up the volume on her police radio and picked up the mike. 'Delta Three to control, over?'

There was a crackle of static, then nothing. Her heart sank as she realized she was in one of a handful of radio shadows that peppered the city centre. She might as well have been in a black hole for all the chance she had of raising back-up. There was nothing else for it. She was on her own.

Donna Doyle no longer felt any pain. She was swimming through a warm soup of delirium, revisiting memories through a distorting lens. Her dad was still alive, alive and throwing her up into the air in the park where the trees waved at her. Their branches turned into arms and Donna was in the centre of a ring of friends playing party games. Everything was bigger than usual, because she was only six and things always loomed larger when you were little. The colours bled into each other and it was Well Dressing week, the carnival floats melting over the streets like jellies left out in the sun.

And there she was at the heart of the parade, on a dais in a pick-up truck covered in crepe-paper flowers that swelled big as cabbage roses in her fevered derangement. She was the Rose Princess, radiant in layers of stiff petticoat, the glory of the occasion cancelling out the discomfort of the itchy fabric on the warm summer afternoon and the plastic tiara cutting into the soft flesh behind her ears. Through the misty dislocation between dream and reality Donna wondered why the sun was burning with such tropical fervour that it made her sweat and then shiver.

Outside her consciousness, the swollen, discoloured meat that hung uselessly down by her side continued to decay, sending more poisons into her body, continually shifting the balance between toxicity and survival. The rotting stink and the corrupt flesh were only the outward signs of a deeper putrefaction.

Her eager body couldn't wait for death to begin the business of decomposition.

Getting out of the car to close the garage door, Alan Brinkley had noticed his breath puff white on the night air. It was a bitter one, all right. Winter was gripping tight. Just as well he'd got one earmarked that didn't involve a long walk. The last thing he needed was fingers numbed with cold fumbling about their work. But there was nothing like a good fire to warm a man to the bone, he'd thought with an ironic smile as he revved the car engine to encourage the heater to deliver its scarlet promise of warmth.

His target was a specialist paint factory at the far end of a small industrial estate on the edge of town. For once, he could avoid the walk from his chosen parking spot because the unit next to his goal was a body shop. There were always half a dozen cars parked outside in varying stages of being resprayed or restored after an accident. One more wouldn't be noticeable. Not that there was anyone to notice. He happened to know for a fact that the guard employed to patrol the estate was never there between two and three thirty. Brinkley had watched him often enough to know that the guy was a victim of greedy bosses. He had too many premises to protect and not enough time to keep an eye on them properly.

He turned into the narrow canyon between tall warehouses that led into the estate and nosed slowly down the access road that led to the body shop. He killed the engine and lights then double-checked that none of the items in his kit had slipped out of his pocket. They were all there: the string, the brass cigarette lighter smelling of petrol, the packet of seventeen cigarettes, the dog-eared book of matches, last night's evening paper, his seven-bladed Swiss Army knife and a crumpled oil-stained handkerchief. He leaned across and took the small but powerful torch out of the glovebox. Three deep breaths with eyes closed and he was ready.

He got out of the car and glanced quickly around. His gaze swept over the cars surrounding the body shop. He saw without seeing the nose of a Vauxhall sitting in the shadow of a warehouse just on the curve of the access road. He failed to register that he hadn't passed it moments before since there was no thrum of an engine or blur of lights to alert him. Certain there was nothing else moving in the landscape, he cut across the Tarmac apron to the paint factory. God, this was going to be one hell of a display, he thought with satisfaction. He wouldn't mind betting that when this went, it would take one or two other buildings with it. Another couple of conflagrations like this and Jim Pendlebury was going to have to say, 'Bugger the budget,' and take him on full-time. It wouldn't be enough even to pay off the interest on the debts he and Maureen seemed to have accumulated like fleas on a cat, but it would keep the creditors at bay while he could work out a way to get their heads above water once and for all.

Brinkley shook his head to clear away the clutter of worry and dread that engulfed him whenever he allowed their mountain of debt to cast its shadow over him. He couldn't do this unless his mind was focused, and whenever he thought about the amount he owed, his head swam and he couldn't imagine ever making it out the other side in one piece. He kept telling himself that what he was doing was the only way he had to survive. The dosser who had died had already given up on that struggle long before Brinkley had come on the scene. He would be different. He would survive. So now he had to stifle distractions and concentrate on achieving the right result without getting caught.

Getting caught would defeat the whole purpose. He'd never get the debts paid off then. Maureen would never forgive him getting caught.

Brinkley thrust his hand between the industrial-sized rubbish skip and the wall of the factory, his fingers closing on the bag he'd stowed there earlier. This time, the office window was his best bet for entry. The fact that it was wide open to the eyes of anyone who happened to walk or drive down the access road didn't worry him. None of the units worked a night shift, the security guard wasn't due for another hour and the paint factory was the last building before the dead end of a seven-foot security fence. Nobody would be taking a short cut down here.

It took less than five minutes to get inside, and only another seven for his practised hands to set his standard fuse. The cigarette smoke billowed upwards, to his nostrils the most fragrant aroma around, its sweetness mingling with the chemical smells of the paint that permeated the air of the factory. The paint would go up like a pillar of flame in the desert, Brinkley thought with satisfaction as he backed down the dark corridor, his eyes never leaving the smouldering fuse.

He felt behind him for the open doorway of the office where he'd come in. Instead of empty space, his fingers brushed against warm fabric. Startled, he whirled in his tracks and the glare of a torch hit his eyes like a thrown glass of wine. Blinded, he tried to blink the light away. He struggled to back through the doorway, but, disorientated, stumbled sideways into the wall. The light moved and he heard the door snick shut.

'You're fucking nicked,' a woman's voice said. 'Alan Brinkley, I am arresting you on suspicion of arson ...'

'No!' he roared like a cornered animal, throwing himself forward at the light. They collided and crashed to the ground in a tangle of limbs and a crash of office furniture. The woman beneath him struggled and wriggled like a furious kitten, but he was heavier and stronger, his upper body developed through years of fire officer's training.

She tried to hit him with the torch, but he easily fended off the blow with his shoulder, sending the light rolling across the floor where it came to rest against a filing cabinet, rocking slightly and throwing a seasick light on the struggle. He could see her face now, her mouth screwed open in a rictus of determination as she tried to break free. If he could see her, she could see him, his panicking mind screamed.

Getting caught would defeat the whole purpose. He'd never get the debts paid off then. Maureen would never forgive him getting caught.

He brought one knee up over her abdomen and leaned on it to crush the air from her lungs. He pushed his forearm against her throat, pinning her to the floor. As her tongue thrust out in a desperate fight for air, he grabbed her hair with his free hand and yanked her head forward against the brace of his forearm. He felt rather than heard something snap. Suddenly she was limp. The fight was over.

He fell away from her, curling on the floor in a foetal crouch. A sob rose in his throat. What had he done? He knew the answer well enough, but he had to repeat the question continually inside his head. He rolled on to his knees, head hanging like a disgraced dog. He couldn't leave her there. They'd find her too soon. She needed to be somewhere else.

A groan dragged from his lips. He forced himself to touch flesh that already felt dead and cold in his imagination. Somehow he hauled the woman's body over his shoulders in the traditional fireman's lift. Staggering to his feet, he lurched through the doorway and back towards the seat of the fire. He carried on beyond the fuse that now smelled harsh, on to where cases of paint tins stood on pallets waiting to be loaded on lorries. The fire would burn hot here, leaving the forensic people little to go on. There would certainly be nothing left to connect him to her. He let the body fall loose-limbed to the floor.

Wiping tears from his eyes, Brinkley turned and ran into the welcoming cold of the night. How had it come to this? How had a few good times, a taste for the good life, brought him to this place? He wanted to fall to the ground and howl like a wolf. But he had to get to his feet, get to the car, answer his pager when it summoned him to the fire station. He had to get through this. Not for his sake but for Maureen's.

Because getting caught would defeat the whole purpose. He'd never get the debts paid off then. Maureen would never forgive him getting caught.

'Shouldn't you be in Seaford?' he'd asked.

'I've got my phone with me. It'll only take me half an hour longer on the motorway than it does from the cottage. And we need to sort out what we've got and what comes next.'

'You'd better come in, then.'

It took Carol longer to read Tony's report than he needed to scan the photographs and watch the videos she'd brought, but he didn't mind that. He kept replaying the tape and shuffling the date-stamped photographs, a tight smile on his lips, fire in his eyes. Eventually, Carol reached the end. The look of complicity they shared told them both that they had been right, and now they could demonstrate a case that could no longer be ignored. 'Good work, Doctor,' Carol said.

'Good work, Detective Chief Inspector,' he echoed.

'Vengeance is mine, saith the profiler.'

He bowed his head in acknowledgement. 'I wish I'd paid more attention when Shaz first raised it. Maybe we could have achieved this without such a high price then.'

Carol reached out impulsively and covered his hand with hers. 'That's ridiculous, Tony. No one would have mounted an investigation on the basis of what she came up with at that classroom session.'

'I didn't mean that, exactly.' He ran his fingers through his hair. 'I meant that I'm supposed to be a psychologist. I should have seen that she wasn't going to let it go. I should have discussed it with her, made her feel that she wasn't being discounted, explored ways we could have taken the matter further without putting her at risk.'

'You might as well say it's Chris Devine's fault,' Carol said briskly. 'She knew Shaz was going to interview him and she let her go alone.'

'And why do you think Chris is spending her valuable time off tearing round Northumberland with Leon and Simon? It's not out of a sense of duty. It's out of a sense of guilt.'

'You can't take responsibility for them all. Shaz was a copper. She should have considered the risk. There was no need for her to go in like she did, so even if you had tried to stop her, she probably wouldn't have paid any attention. Let it go, Tony.'

He lifted his head and read the compassion in her eyes. He gave a rueful nod. 'We need to go official on this now, if we're going to avoid accusations that we're as out of control as Shaz was.'

Carol slipped her hand away from his. 'I'm glad you said that, because I'm starting to feel really edgy about uncovering hard evidence like this without any formal relationship to the investigation and no chain of custody on any of the physical evidence apart from "It was in my handbag, Guv." I keep thinking about the defence counsel making mincement out of me on the witness stand. "And so, DCI Jordan, you expect the jury to believe that on this maverick quest for justice – that only you, as opposed to the entire West Yorkshire force, could conduct – you just happened upon the one piece of evidence that links my client to the murder of DC Bowman, a woman he met once for less than an hour? And what is it your brother does again, Ms Jordan? Computer wizard, would that be a fair description? The sort of whizz kid who can make a digital image say anything he wants it to say?" We need to get this under West Yorkshire's umbrella so they can construct the case properly.'

'I know. There comes a point where you have to stop playing at being the Lone Ranger and we're there now. We need to cover your back as well. In the morning, I'll go straight over to the murder room. How does that sound?'

'It's not that I want to wash my hands of this, Tony,' she said plaintively. 'It's just that we're going to lose it if we don't bring it in.'

He felt a rush of warmth towards her. 'I couldn't have achieved any of this alone. When Jacko Vance faces a jury, it'll be thanks to you coming on·board.'

Before she could reply, her phone rang, splitting the closeness between them like an axe in wood. 'Oh, shit,' she said, grabbing the handset and hitting the button. 'DCI Jordan.'

The familiar voice of Jim Pendlebury came down the line. 'We've got what looks like another one, Carol. Paint factory. It's gone up like a torch.'

'I'll be there as soon as I can, Jim. Can you give me a locus?' Without being asked, Tony shoved pencil and paper across to her and she scribbled down directions. 'Thanks,' she said. She ended the call and closed her eyes momentarily. Then she hit the memory buttons and was connected to her communications room. 'This is DCI Jordan. Has there been anything from DS Taylor or DC Earnshaw?'

'Negative, ma'am,' came the anonymous voice. 'They were supposed to be maintaining radio silence unless they had something specific to their stakeouts.'

'Will you see if you can raise them and get them to meet me at the site of the paint factory fire on the Holt Industrial Estate. Thanks. Good night.' She looked at Tony, perplexed. 'It seems we were wrong,' she said.

'The arsonist?'

'He's struck again. But neither Tommy Taylor nor Di Earnshaw radioed in, so it looks as if it was neither of our suspects.' She shook her head. 'Back to square one, I guess. I'd better get over there and see what's going on.'

'Good luck,' Tony said as she pulled on her mac.

'It's you that'll need the luck, talking round Wharton and McCormick,' she said as he followed her down the hall. On the doorstep, she turned and impulsively put a hand on his arm. 'Don't beat yourself up about Shaz.' She leaned into him and kissed his cheek. 'Concentrate on beating up Jack the Lad.'

Then she was gone, leaving nothing behind but a shiver of her scent in the night air.

Above the blur of sodium and neon, it was a clear, starry night. From his eyrie on top of the Holland Park house, Jacko

Vance stared out across the London night and imagined the Northumberland stars. There was a loose end, the only possible strand that could unravel and leave him stripped of his protective colouring. It was time for Donna Doyle to die.

He hadn't actually had to kill one for a long time now. It wasn't the killing he enjoyed. It was the process. The disintegration of a human being through the degradation of pain and infection. One had been defiant. She had refused to eat or drink or to use the chemical toilet. She'd been a challenge, but she hadn't lasted long. She had failed to consider the infective possibilities of piss and shit all over the floor. All she'd been thinking about was making herself too disgusting for him to touch, and she'd failed in that, too.

But he'd have to get rid of this particular Jillie soon. Her existence had been worrying him, a constant itch like a fleabite under a waistband. But while the police had been sniffing around after Shaz Bowman's death, he hadn't wanted to make an untoward move. An unscheduled dash for Northumberland would have been suspicious. The swift visit he had made hadn't been long enough to deal with the bitch properly. Then there had been Tony Hill's involvement to consider. Did the man have anything or was he just trying to rattle him into doing precisely the one thing that would expose him?

Either way, she had to go. That she might still be alive was a possibility that put him in mortal danger. He should have disposed of her on the night he killed Bowman, but he'd been afraid that his movements might come under too close scrutiny for comfort. Besides, he'd been too exhausted to have been certain of making a proper job of it.

He'd just have to rely on the invisibility of her hiding place, entombed beneath the stone flags. The only people who knew about the old crypt were the two builders he'd hired to install the perfectly engineered opening. Twelve years before, people had still believed in the nuclear threat. His talk of wanting to create a bomb shelter had gone down as merely eccentric among the locals. It would, he felt certain, be long forgotten.

Nevertheless, she had to go. Not tonight. He was filming early in the morning and he needed what sleep his apprehensions would allow him. But in a day or two, he could slip away overnight and see to the girl.

He'd have to make the most of it. It would have to be a little while before he could indulge himself again. A thought flickered into his mind. If he was ever going to feel safe again, perhaps Tony Hill needed to be taught a lesson more personal than Shaz Bowman. Jacko Vance gazed across the city and wondered if there was a woman in his life. He'd remember to ask his wife in the morning if Hill had said anything over dinner about a partner.

It had been no hardship killing Shaz Bowman. A repetition with Tony Hill's girlfriend could only be easier.

Hands thrust deep into the pockets of her mac, collar turned up against the harsh estuary wind, Carol Jordan stared stonily at the still smoking ruin of the paint factory. Her vigil was already three hours old, but she wasn't ready to leave yet. Fire officers, their distinctive yellow helmets smudged with greasy residue, moved in and out of the fringes of the building. Somewhere inside that creaking shell, some of them were trying to penetrate to the seat of the fire. Carol was beginning to accept that she didn't need the evidence of their eyes to know why Di Earnshaw hadn't responded to the control room's radio messages telling her to come to the fire site.

Di Earnshaw had been there already.

Carol heard a car draw to a halt behind her, but she didn't turn her head. A rustle of the crime scene tapes, then Lee Whitbread moved into her line of sight, proffering a carton of burger joint coffee. 'I thought you could probably do with this,' he said.

She nodded and took the brew wordlessly. 'No news, then?' he asked, his normally eager expression apprehensive.

'Nothing,' she said. She flipped off the polystyrene lid and raised the cup to her lips. The coffee was strong and hot, surprisingly good.

'There's been nothing at the station, neither,' Lee said, cupping his hands round his mouth to light a cigarette. 'I bobbed round her house, just to check, like, that she hadn't knocked off and gone home, but there's no sign. Bedroom curtains are still shut, so maybe she's got her head down and earplugs in?' Like every cop, his occupational pessimism was always tempered with hope when it appeared that a colleague was in line for a police funeral.

Carol couldn't bring herself to share even the fragile hope of earplugs. And if she knew Di Earnshaw wasn't the sort to go on the missing list, Lee must be doubly sure that his fellow DC was out of action for good. 'Have you seen DS Taylor?' she asked.

Lee hid his expression behind his hand as he smoked furiously. 'He says she never called in. He's back at the station, seeing if anything comes up there.'

'I hope he's coming up with something a little more imaginative than that,' Carol said grimly.

Three figures emerged from the dark hulk of the factory and pulled the breathing apparatus from their mouths. One detached himself from the other two and walked towards them. A few feet away from her, Jim Pendlebury came to a halt and pulled off his helmet. 'I can't tell you how sorry I am, Carol.'

Carol's head tilted back, then dropped in a tired nod. 'No doubt, I suppose?'

'There's always room for doubt until they've done the business down the path. lab. But we reckon it's a female, and there's what looks like a melted down radio next to the body.' His voice was soft with sympathy.

She looked up at his compassionate expression. He knew what it was like to lose people he was nominally responsible for. She wished he could tell her how long it would take before she could look herself in the mirror again. 'Can I see her?'

He shook his head. 'It's still too hot in there.'

Carol exhaled, a short, sharp sigh. 'I'll be in my office if anyone wants me.' She dropped the carton of coffee, turned away and ducked under the tapes, hurrying blindly in the direction of her car. Behind her, the coffee pooled on the Tarmac. Lee Whitbread flicked his cigarette butt into it, watching it fizz depressingly before dying. He looked up at Jim Pendlebury. 'Me too. We've got a fucking cop killer to nail now.'

Colin Wharton shuffled the pile of video stills together then leaned across and ejected the tape from the video recorder in the training suite that Tony's team had abandoned what felt like half a lifetime ago. Avoiding Tony's eye, he said, 'It proves nothing. OK, somebody else was driving Shaz Bowman's car back from London. It could be anybody behind that disguise. You hardly see anything of the guy's face, and these computer enhancements . . . *I* don't trust them, and juries are worse. By the time fucking Rumpole the defence brief's finished, they assume anything that's come from a computer's been doctored to make it show what we want it to show.'

'What about the arm? You can't doctor that. Jacko Vance has a prosthesis on his right arm. The man putting the petrol in never uses that arm at all. It's really noticeable,' Tony pressed.

Wharton shrugged. 'There could be all sorts of reasons for that. Could be that the man in question is left-handed. It could be that he'd hurt his arm in a struggle to overpower Bowman. It could even be that he knew about that daft bee Bowman had in her bonnet about Jacko Vance, and he decided to play on that. *Punters* know about video cameras now, Dr Hill. Vance *works* in the business – do you really think he's not going to have thought about cameras?'

Tony ran a hand through his hair, gripping the ends as if he were holding on to his temper. 'You've got Vance coming off the motorway at Leeds in his own wheels at the crucial time. Surely that's too much of a coincidence?'

Wharton shook his head. 'I don't think so. The man has a cottage in Northumberland. He does all that volunteer work up there. OK, the A1 might be the more direct route, but the M1's a faster road, and it's easy enough to pick up the A1 north of the city. He might even have decided he wanted fish and chips at Bryan's on the road,' he added with a pale attempt to lighten the atmosphere.

Tony folded his arms as if this would hold his dark anger inside. 'Why won't you take this seriously?' he asked.

'If Simon McNeill wasn't on the run, we might not assume everything you produce is tainted,' Wharton said angrily.

'Simon has nothing to do with this. He did not murder Shaz Bowman. Jacko Vance did. He is a cold-blooded killer. Everything I know about psychology tells me he killed Shaz Bowman because she threatened to bring his playhouse down about his ears. We've got pictures of him driving her car, she's nowhere in sight. Then in his car, covering the same ground.

You've seen the psychological profile I prepared. What more do we have to do to persuade you to at least take a serious look at the man?'

The door behind him opened. DCS Dougal McCormick thrust his massive torso into the room. His face was the dark red of a man who'd had too much drink at lunchtime, a sheen of sweat gleaming on his fleshy cheeks. His light voice had dropped half an octave with the alcohol. 'I thought you were barred from here unless we came for you?' he said, stabbing a finger at Tony.

'I brought you the evidence to make a case against Shaz Bowman's killer,' Tony said, his voice weary now. 'Only Mr Wharton doesn't seem to be able to grasp its significance.'

McCormick shouldered his way into the room. 'Is that right? What have you got to say to that, Colin?'

'There's some very interesting motorway petrol station footage that's been computer-enhanced to show someone else driving Shaz Bowman's motor the afternoon she was killed.' Silently, he spread the pictures out for McCormick to check. The Chief Superintendent screwed up his dark eyes and studied them closely.

'It's Jacko Vance,' Tony insisted. 'He took her car back to Leeds, then made his way back to London before driving north again, presumably with Shaz in the boot.'

'Never mind Jacko Vance,' McCormick said dismissively. 'We've got a witness.'

'A witness?'

'Aye, a witness.'

'A witness to what, exactly?'

'A neighbour who saw your blue-eyed boy Simon McNeill going round the back of Sharon Bowman's flat the night she was killed and didn't see him come back out front again. I've got a team taking his place apart even as we speak. We were looking for him already, but now there'll be a public announcement. Maybe you'd know where we could find him, eh, Dr Hill?'

'You're the ones who disbanded my squad. How would I know where Simon is now?' Tony said, his voice a cold disguise for the frustration boiling inside.

'Ach, well, never mind. We'll be able to put our hand on him sooner or later. I've no doubt my boys will end up with something better to show a court than some videos your girlfriend's brother's tarted up.' Seeing Tony's startled expression, he nodded grimly. 'That's right, we know all about you and DCI Jordan. Do you really think we don't talk to each other in this job?'

'You keep telling me you're interested in evidence, not supposition,' Tony said, hanging on to his self-possession by sheer force of will. 'For the record, DCI Jordan is not now nor has she ever been my girlfriend. And my contention that Vance is the killer does not rely solely on the video evidence. I'm really not trying to teach you how to suck eggs, but at least look at the report I've drawn up. There's solid evidence there.'

McCormick picked the folder up from the table and flicked through it. 'A psychological profile is not what I'd call evidence. Rumour, innuendo, jealous people getting their own back. That's what you're relying on here.'

'His own wife says he's never slept with her. You're not telling me that's regarded as normal behaviour in West Yorkshire?'

'She might have all sorts of reasons for lying to you,' McCormick said dismissively, dropping the report with a soft rustle.

'He met Barbara Fenwick a couple of days before she was abducted and murdered. It's there, in Greater Manchester

428

Police's murder file. One of his first ever charity events after the accident that destroyed his dream. We have photographs of him at later events with other girls who have disappeared and never been heard from again.' Tony's voice was discouraged now. He'd failed to establish a rapport that would have allowed the two policemen to back down and consider what he had to say. Worse than that, he seemed to have alienated McCormick to the point where if he said 'black', McCormick would retort, 'white'.

'A man like that meets hundreds of lassies a week and nothing ever happens to them,' McCormick said, sinking into a chair. 'Look, Dr Hill, I know it's hard to accept that you've had the wool pulled over your eyes, with you being a senior Home Office psychologist. But look at your man McNeill. He was in love with the lassie, and she doesn't seem to have felt the same about him. We've only got his word for it that she was supposed to be meeting him for a drink in advance of their night out with the other two. He was seen going round the back of the house at about the time she could have died. We've got his fingerprints on the glass of the French windows. And now he's done a disappearing act. You've got to admit, it's a hell of a lot more persuasive than a stack of circumstantial evidence against a man who's a national hero. What you're trying to do, Dr Hill, it's understandable. I'd probably feel the same as you if it was one of my officers in the frame. But face it, you made a mistake. You picked a bad apple.'

Tony stood up. 'I'm sorry we can't see eye to eye on this. I'm particularly sorry because I think Jacko Vance is holding another teenage girl prisoner, and she might still be alive. Gentlemen, there are none so blind as those who will not see. I sincerely hope your blindness doesn't cost Donna Doyle her life. Now, if you'll excuse me, I have work to do.'

Wharton and McCormick made no attempt to prevent him leaving. As he reached the door, Wharton said, 'It would be better for McNeill if he didn't wait to be arrested.'

'I don't think so, somehow,' Tony said. Out in the car park, he leaned against the car door, head on folded arms. What the hell was left to do? The only senior police officer who believed his flimsy evidence was Carol, and she had no clout with West Yorkshire Police now, that much was clear. The evidence they still needed was the sort that came from TV reconstructions and nationwide press appeals; not resources available to a discredited psychologist, a pair of maverick cops from opposite ends of the country and a ragbag of junior detectives.

Conventional means had failed them. Now it was time to throw away the rule book. He'd done it before and it had saved his life. This time, it might just save someone else's.

Carol stood in the doorway of the squad room, fists on hips, glaring down the room. The news had travelled ahead of her and the only two detectives on the premises were clearly downcast by it. One was typing up notes, the other working bleakly through a wad of paperwork. Neither moved more than their eyes, a quick sidelong glance to register her arrival.

'Where is he?' Carol demanded.

The two detectives flicked their eyes towards each other, mutual understanding and decisions passing instantly between them. The one at the keyboard spoke, keeping his eyes on his work. 'DS Taylor, ma'am?'

'Who else? Where is he? I know he was here earlier, but I want to know where he is now.'

'He went out just after the news came through about Di,' the other man said.

'And where will he be?' Carol wasn't giving an inch. She couldn't afford to. Not for the sake of her future authority, but for her own self-respect. The buck stopped with her, and she had no wish to evade that responsibility. But she needed to understand how her operation had gone so disastrously wrong. Only one man might be able to tell her, and she was determined to find him. 'Come on,' she urged. 'Where?'

The two detectives exchanged another look. This time resignation was the key component. 'Harbourmaster's Club,' the typist said.

'He's in a drinking den at this time of the morning?' she demanded angrily.

'It's not just a bar, it's a club, ma'am. Originally for officers on merchant ships. You can get meals there, or just go in and read the papers and have a cup of coffee.' Carol turned to leave, but the typist continued. 'Ma'am, you can't go there,' he said, his voice urgent.

The look she gave him had induced rapists to confess. 'It's men only,' the young detective stammered. 'They won't let you in.'

'Jesus Christ!' Carol exploded. 'God forbid we should disturb the native customs. All right, Beckham, stop what you're doing and get down the Harbourmaster's Club. I want you and DS Taylor back here within half an hour, or I'll have your warrant card as well as his. Do I make myself clear?'

The file folder closed and Beckham jumped to his feet, brushing past her with an apology as he hurried out. 'I'll be in my office,' Carol growled at the remaining detective. She tried to slam the door behind her, but the hinges were too stiff.

Carol flopped into her chair, not even taking off her mac. Bleak self-reproach settled oppressively, immobilizing her. She stared emptily at the back wall where Di Earnshaw had stood during their briefing, remembering the dead fish stare, the badly fitting suit, the pug-nosed face. They'd never have been friends, Carol knew that instinctively, and in a way that made what had happened worse. Coupled with the guilt of Di Earnshaw's death in her own botched operation, Carol had the guilt of knowing she hadn't liked the woman very much, that if she'd been forced under duress to choose a victim from her command, Di wouldn't have been last on the list.

Carol ran through the case history again, wondering what she could have, should have done differently. Which was the decision that got Di Earnshaw killed? However she cut it, she came back to the same thing every time. She'd not kept a tight enough grip on the investigation, or a close enough eye on junior officers who weren't worried about discrediting her with their sloppy policing. She'd been too busy playing knight-in-shining-armour games with Tony Hill. Not for the first time, she'd let her emotional response to him interfere with her judgement. This time, the consequences had been fatal.

The peal of her phone cut across her self-flagellation and she grabbed it in the middle of the second ring. Not even a major guilt-trip could stifle her instincts to the point where she could ignore a ringing phone on her office desk. 'DCI Jordan,' she said, her voice dull.

'Guv, it's Lee.' His voice sounded brighter than it had any right to be. Even as negative a personality as Di Earnshaw had the right to a little more sorrow from her immediate colleagues.

'What have you got?' Carol asked brusquely, swivelling round in her chair to stare out of the window at the deserted windswept quay.

'I found her car. Tucked away down the side of one of the other warehouses, well out of sight. Guv, she had this little tape recorder. It was lying on the passenger seat, so I got one of the traffic lads to get me into the car. It's all there, name, time, route, destination, the lot. There's more than enough there to nail Brinkley!'

'Good work,' she said dully. Better than nothing, it still wasn't enough to assuage the guilt. Somehow, she knew that when she told Tony that, after all, he'd been right, he wouldn't consider it an acceptable trade-off either. 'Bring it in, Lee.'

She turned to replace the handset to find John Brandon standing in the doorway. Wearily, she started to get up, but he motioned her to stay seated, folding his long limbs into one of the comfortless visitor's chairs. 'A bad business,' he said.

'No one to blame but me,' Carol said. 'I took my eye off the ball. I left my officers to their own devices on an operation they all thought was a waste of time. They weren't taking it seriously, and now Di Earnshaw's dead. I should have stayed on their tails.'

'I'm surprised she was out there without back-up,' Brandon said. The words were censure enough without the look of reproach on his face.

'That wasn't the intention,' Carol said flatly.

'For both our sakes, I hope you can substantiate that.' It wasn't a threat, Carol realized, seeing the warmth of regret in his eyes.

Carol stared unseeing at the scarred wood of her desk top. 'Somehow, I can't get worked up about that now, sir.'

Brandon's voice hardened. 'Well, I suggest you do, Chief Inspector. Di Earnshaw doesn't have the luxury of feeling sorry for herself. All we can do for her now is take her killer off the streets. When can I expect an arrest?'

Stung, Carol jerked her head up and glared at Brandon.

'Just as soon as DC Whitbread gets back here with the evidence, sir.'

'Good.' Brandon got to his feet. 'Once you have a clearer idea what happened out there last night, we'll talk.' The ghost of a smile crossed his eyes. 'You're not to blame, Carol. You can't be on duty twenty-four hours a day.'

Carol stared at the empty doorway after he'd gone, wondering how many years it had taken John Brandon to learn how to let go. Then, weighing up what she knew of the man, she wondered if he ever had, or if he'd simply learned to hide it better.

Leon looked around, bemused. 'I thought Newcastle was supposed to be the last place on earth where men were men and sheep ran scared?'

'You got a problem with a vegetarian pub?' Chris Devine asked mildly.

Simon grinned. 'He only pretends he likes his meat raw.' He sipped his pint experimentally. 'Nothing wrong with the bevvy, though. How did you find out about this place?'

'Don't ask and you won't be embarrassed, babe. Just trust your senior officer, especially when she's a woman. So, how are we doing?' Chris asked. 'I got nowhere showing her picture round the station. Nobody in the buffet or the ticket office or the bookstall remembered seeing her.'

'The bus station was the same,' Simon reported. 'Not a sausage. Except that one of the drivers said, was it not that lass that went missing in Sunderland a couple of years back?' They contemplated the irony glumly.

'I got a sniff,' Leon said. 'I talked to one of the train guards, and he put me on to a café where all the drivers and guards go for a brew and a bacon butty on their breaks. I sat down with the guys and flashed the photos. One of them reckoned he was pretty sure he'd seen her on the Carlisle train. He remembered because she double-checked with him what time the train got into Five Walls Halt and that they were running on time.'

'When was this?' Chris asked, offering him an encouraging cigarette.

'He couldn't be sure. But he reckoned it was the week before last.' Leon didn't have to remind them that timetable would fit perfectly with Donna Doyle's disappearance.

'Where's Five Walls Halt?' Simon asked.

'It's somewhere in the middle of nowhere this side of Hexham,' Chris informed him. 'Near Hadrian's Wall. And presumably another four. And don't ask how I know that either, right?'

'So what's at Five Walls Halt that she'd want to get off there?'

Leon looked at Chris. She shrugged. 'I'm only guessing, but I'd say it might be somewhere near Jacko Vance's place in the country. Which, I don't have to tell you, we're not supposed to be going anywhere near.'

'We could go to Five Walls Halt, though,' Leon said.

'Not until you finish that pint, we can't,' Simon prompted.

'Leave the pint,' Chris instructed him. 'She can't have been the only one who got off the train there. If we're going knocking on doors, we don't want to smell like a brewery.' She got to her feet. 'Let's go and discover the beauties of the Northumberland countryside. Did you bring your wellies?'

Leon and Simon exchanged a look of panic. 'Thanks, Chris,' Leon muttered sarcastically as they trailed after her into the soft rain.

Alan Brinkley stood under the shower, the cascade of water almost scalding. The man who made the decisions had finally decreed that the officers who had fought the fierce fire at the paint factory could be stood down and replaced by a smaller crew who would damp down the hot spots and keep their fresh eyes peeled for anything significant among the wreckage. No one in authority was taking any chances now the body had been found.

At the thought of the body, a shudder convulsed Brinkley from head to foot. In spite of the steaming heat, his teeth chattered involuntarily. He wasn't going to think about the body. Normal, he had to be normal. But what was normal? How did he usually behave when there had been a fatal fire? What did he say to Maureen? How many beers did he drink the night after? What did his mates see in his face?

He slumped against the streaming tiles of the shower cubicle, tears falling invisibly from his eyes. Thank God for the privacy of the new fire station, not like the old communal showers they'd had when he'd learned his trade. In the shower now, no one could see him weep.

He couldn't get the smell out of his nostrils, the taste out of his mouth. He knew it was imagination; the chemicals in the paint factory overlaid any hint of incinerated flesh. But it was as real as it had ever been. He didn't even know her name, but he knew what she smelled like, what she tasted like now.

His mouth opened in a silent scream and he pounded with the sides of his fists against the solid wall, making no sound. Behind him, the shower curtain rattled back on its metal hoops. He turned slowly, pressing himself into the corner of the cubicle. He'd seen the man and the woman before, inside the scene-of-crime tapes at the fires. He watched the woman's lips move, heard her voice, but could not process what she was saying.

It didn't matter. He suddenly knew this was the only relief.

He slid down the wall into a foetal crouch. He found his voice and started to sob like a damaged child.

Chris Devine was only a few miles out of Newcastle when her mobile rang. 'It's me, Tony. Any joy?'

She filled him in on the limited success of their morning, and in turn he told her about his failure to convince Wharton and McCormick to take him seriously. 'It's a nightmare,' he said. 'We can't afford to hang around indefinitely on this. If Donna Doyle is still alive, every hour could count. Chris, I think the only thing to do is for me to confront him with the evidence and hope we can panic him into a confession or an incriminating move.'

'That's what killed Shaz,' Chris said. Mentioning her name brought the grief back like a physical blow. If she could ignore the bright presence Shaz had been in her life and the darkness of her absence, she could get through this in a fair simulacrum of the normal breezy Chris Devine. But every time Shaz was mentioned by name, it knocked the breath from her. She suspected she wasn't the only one who suffered a reaction; it would explain why Shaz was seldom spoken of directly.

'I wasn't planning on going it alone. I need back-up.'

'What about Carol?'

There was a long silence. 'Carol lost an officer in the night.'

'Ah, shit. Her arsonist?'

'Her arsonist. She's beating herself up because she thinks her involvement in this made her derelict in her duty. She's wrong, as it happens, but there's no way she can walk away from her responsibilities in Seaford today.'

'Sounds like she's got more shit on her plate right now than anyone should ever have to eat. Yeah, forget Carol.'

'I'm going to need you down there, Chris. Can you bear to pull out and go back to London? Now?'

She didn't have to hesitate for a moment. When it came to catching the man who brutalized Shaz Bowman's beautiful face before destroying her soul, there wasn't much Chris would have refused. 'No problem. I'll flag the lads down and tell them.'

'You can tell them Kay's on her way, too. She was waiting for me when I got back from Leeds HQ this morning. I'll call her and tell her to head for Five Walls Halt station. She can meet Simon and Leon there.'

'Thank God there'll be one person there with a bit of common sense,' she said ironically. 'She can keep the lid on Die Hard one and two.'

'Getting a bit gung-ho, are they?'

'There's nothing they'd love more than kicking Jacko Vance's head in. Failing that, they'd settle for his front door.' She spotted a lay-by on the fast dual carriageway and indicated she was going to pull over, checking in her mirror that Simon and Leon were following.

'I was thinking of reserving that pleasure for myself.'

Chris gave a grunt of sardonic laughter. 'Join the queue, babe. I'll call you when I hit the M25.'

The officers in the canteen broke into a ragged round of applause as Carol and Lee Whitbread walked in. Carol nodded a distant acknowledgement, Lee doing better with a wan smile. Two coffees, two doughnuts, her treat, then they were out of there and heading back to the CID room. It would be at least an hour before Alan Brinkley's solicitor could get there, and till then, he was off limits.

Halfway up the stairs, she turned and blocked Lee's way. 'Where was he?'

Lee looked shifty. 'I don't know,' he mumbled. 'Must have been in a radio black spot.'

'Bollocks,' Carol said. 'Come on, Lee. This isn't the time for false loyalty. Di Earnshaw would probably still be alive if Taylor had been watching her back like he was supposed to. It could have been you. Next time it could be. So where was he? Over the side?'

Lee scratched his eyebrow. 'The nights we were on together, he stuck with it till gone midnight. Then he called in and said he were going for a bevvy to Corcoran's.'

'If he'd done that with Di, why would she have been shouting for back-up over the radio?' Carol demanded.

Lee squirmed, his mouth twisting awkwardly. 'He wouldn't have told Di. Not one of the lads, was she?'

Carol closed her eyes momentarily. 'You're telling me I've lost one of my officers because of traditional Yorkshire male chauvinism?' she said incredulously.

Lee dropped his eyes and studied the step he stood on. 'None of us thought owt would happen.'

Carol turned on her heel and marched upstairs, leaving Lee to trail in her wake. This time when she shouldered open the squad-room door, Tommy Taylor jumped to his feet. 'Guv,' he began.

'Chief Inspector to you. My office. Now.' She waited for him to move ahead of her. 'You know something, Taylor? I'm ashamed to work in the same squad as you.' The other detectives in the room suddenly developed total fascination with their routine tasks.

Carol kicked the door shut behind her. 'Don't bother sitting down,' she said, moving behind her desk and dropping into her chair. For this interview, she didn't need artificial aids like standing while her junior officer sat. 'DC Earnshaw is lying in the morgue incinerated because you went on the piss while you were supposed to be working.'

'I never . . .' he began.

Carol simply raised her voice and continued. 'There will be an official inquiry where you can bullshit all you like about radio black spots. By that time, I'll have statements from every drunk in Corcoran's. I am going to bury you, Taylor. Until you're officially drummed out of this force, you're on suspension. Now get out of my squad room and stay away from my officers.'

'I never thought she were at risk,' he said pathetically.

'The reason we get our wages is that we're always at risk,' Carol snapped. 'Now get out of my sight and pray you don't get reinstated because there isn't a cop in East Yorkshire who would piss on you if you were on fire.'

Taylor backed out, carefully closing the door behind him. 'Feel better now?' Carol said under her breath. 'And you're the woman who said she'd never pass the buck.' Her head dropped into her hands. She knew any inquiry would lay little blame at her door. It didn't stop her feeling that Di Earnshaw's blood stained her hands as much as Taylor's. And once the identification was official, she was the one who'd have to break the news to her parents.

At least she wouldn't have to worry about Jacko Vance and Donna Doyle any more. That, thank God, must be someone else's problem by now.

When Chris Devine had talked about knocking on doors, Simon and Leon had pictured a neat little village with two or three streets. Neither of them had considered the area served by a small station halfway between Carlisle and Hexham. Apart from the straggle of houses that made up Five Walls Halt itself, there were farms, smallholdings, outlying pockets of agricultural cottages now colonized by city commuters, holiday homes and cramped council estates snagged improbably in the distant corners of narrow valleys.

They'd ended up in a tourist information office buying Ordnance Survey maps.

Once Kay arrived, they split the area among themselves, agreeing to meet back at the station at the end of the afternoon. It was a thankless task, but one that Kay was more successful with than the others. People always talked more to a woman on their doorstep than they ever would to a man. By late afternoon, she'd got two possible sightings of Donna Doyle. Both put her on their regular evening train home, but neither could be certain of the day.

She'd also discovered the location of Jacko Vance's hideaway. One of the doors she'd knocked on had belonged to the roofer who'd replaced the black slate roof of the former chapel only five years before. Her oblique raising of the subject and her gossipy questioning about Vance had left him unsuspicious. He would merely mention down the pub that night that women coppers were just like any other women when it came to being pushovers for a famous name with a nice smile and a big bank balance.

By the time the three reconvened, she had added a few more bits and pieces to her store of knowledge. Vance had bought the place a dozen years before, maybe six months or so after his accident. It hadn't been much more than four walls and a roof, and he'd spent a fair whack of cash on doing it up. When he'd married Micky, the locals had expected them to use it as a weekend cottage, but instead he'd used it more as a retreat; a useful base for the voluntary work he did at the hospital in Newcastle. No one knew why he'd chosen the area. He had no roots or connections to it as far as anyone knew.

Leon and Simon were excited by her information. They had little to offer themselves apart from a couple of dubious sightings of Donna. One put her in the station car park,

441

getting into a vehicle. But the witness couldn't remember the day, the time or the make of the wheels. 'It's no coincidence that witness sounds very like witless,' Leon said. 'We're not getting anywhere with this shit. Let's go over Vance's place.'

'Tony said to stay away,' Simon objected.

'I'm not sure it's a good idea,' Kay agreed.

'What harm can it do? Listen, if he picked up the kid here and took her back to his gaff, chances are somebody local might have seen him. We can't just go back to Leeds now, not knowing this much.'

'We should call Tony first,' Simon said stubbornly.

Leon cast his eyes heavenwards. 'OK,' he sighed. He made great play of getting his phone out and tapping in a number. Neither of the others thought to check it was Tony's number. As the ringing tone continued without interruption, Leon said triumphantly, 'He's not answering, right? So what harm can it do if we go and check it out? Shit, that kid could still be alive, and we're talking about sitting on our butts till Christmas? Come on, we got to *do* something.'

Kay and Simon exchanged a look. Neither wanted to contradict Tony's orders. But equally, they were too infected with the glory of the chase to bear sitting around doing nothing while a young woman's life might be on the line. 'All right,' Kay said. 'But all we do is take a look around. Right?'

'Right,' said Leon enthusiastically.

'I hope so,' Simon said wearily. 'I really hope so.'

Chris Devine sipped a double espresso and drew deeply on another cigarette in an attempt to keep her tiredness at bay. At teatime on a Sunday, the Shepherd's Bush diner was less lively than a funeral parlour. 'Run it past me again,' she commanded Tony.

'I go to the house. According to your contact's schedule for him, Vance was supposed to be compering a charity fashion show in Kensington this afternoon, so he's not going to be in Northumberland.'

'Are you sure we shouldn't be hitting his place up there first?' Chris interrupted. 'If Donna Doyle's still alive . . .'

'And if she's not there? We couldn't start poking around without the locals noticing and probably getting straight on the phone to Vance. And then we're completely blown. At the moment, he doesn't know for sure that anybody's close to him. All he knows is that I've been sticking my nose in. That's the only advantage we've got. We have to go straight for the direct confrontation.'

'What if his wife's there? He's not going to risk her hearing anything you might have to say to him about Shaz.'

'If Micky and Betsy are there, he'll make damn sure he gets me out of their way before I get the chance to say a word. In a way, it's safer for me if they are around, since I'm more likely to get out in one piece.'

'I suppose so. You better take me through it, then,' she said, exhaling a cloud of smoke.

'I tell Jacko I've been working independently of the police and I've uncovered important video evidence relating to Shaz Bowman's death that I think he might be able to help us with. He'll let me in because I'm alone and he'll figure he can dispose of me the same way he got rid of Shaz if it emerges that I really am a lone maverick. I show him the enhanced video and the stills and accuse him. You are sitting outside in your car with a radio receiver and a tape recorder picking up everything that's transmitted from the mike in this natty little pen I bought in Tottenham Court Road on the way here.' Tony wiggled the pen in front of Chris's nose.

'You don't seriously think he's going to roll over?'

Tony shook his head. 'I think if he's alone, he'll try to kill me. And that's where you come in like the cavalry, leaping tall buildings with one mighty bound.' His words were light, but his tone was sombre. They looked bleakly at each other.

'So let's do it,' Chris said. 'Let's nail the fucker to a tree.'

It had taken them less than ten minutes to discover it was impossible to stake out Jacko Vance's converted chapel without being as obvious as a wolfhound in a flock of sheep. 'Fuck,' Leon said.

'I don't think he picked somewhere like this by chance,' Simon said, looking around at the bleak hillside opposite the hideaway. On either side of the gravel circle in front of the tall narrow building were fields of sheep held at bay by wire fences. Even in the thickening dusk, it was obvious there was neither human being nor habitation within sight.

'It's funny,' Kay mused. 'Normally, celebs like a bit of privacy. Gates, walls, high hedges. But you must be able to see this place for miles if you walked over the moors.'

'Cuts both ways, man,' Leon said. 'They can see you, but you get plenty of warning when anybody approaches you. Look at that road. Them fucking Romans didn't mess about, did they? Any Picts came looking for trouble, you'd see them soon as they hit the horizon.'

'He likes the kind of privacy where you can't be spied on,' Simon said. 'I reckon that means he's got a lot more to hide than some starlet sucking his toes.'

'And I reckon we ought to check out what it is,' Leon said.

They looked at each other for a long moment. Kay shook her head. Simon said, 'There is no way I'm going to be party to kicking Jacko Vance's door in.'

'Who said anything about kicking his door in?' Leon said. 'Kay, you talked to the guy that put the roof on this place. He

444

say anything about locals that work here? Gardener, cleaner, cook? Anything like that?'

'Oh, yeah, like he's going to have a cleaner in premises where he's stashing murder victims,' Simon scoffed scornfully.

'This guy loves the double bluff,' Leon said. 'He loves putting one over on the stupid old plod. There's nothing would appeal to him more than having some old dear polishing the secret panel when he's got some kid chained up behind it. What did the guy say, Kay?'

'He didn't say anything,' she said. 'But if anybody knows that, chances are it's the nearest neighbour.'

'So who does the best Geordie accent?' Leon demanded, pointing directly at Simon.

'This is not a good idea,' he protested. Ten minutes later, he was knocking at the door of the first dwelling they came to, a large square farmhouse that faced out over the moorland towards Hadrian's Wall less than a mile away. He shifted from one foot to the other.

'Calm down,' Kay said. 'Just flash the warrant card dead fast. They'll never examine it closely.'

'We're going to lose our careers over this,' Simon muttered through clenched teeth.

'I'd rather chance that than let Shaz's killer walk.' Kay's frown changed to a radiant smile as the door opened on a small dark scowling man. It wasn't hard to imagine his Pictish ancestors making Roman lives a misery.

'Aye? What is it?'

They flipped their warrant cards open and closed in unison. The man looked momentarily confused, then resumed his glower. 'DC McNeill from Northumbria Police,' Simon gabbled. 'We've had a report of intruders at Mr Vance's place down the road. We can't obtain entry to the property, and we wondered whether you knew if there was a local keyholder?'

'Did the local man not tell you?' he demanded in an accent Kay found almost incomprehensible.

'Why no,' Simon said, laying on the Newcastle accent. 'We cannot get hold of him, with it being Sunday, like.'

'You want Doreen Elliott. Back down the road past Vance's place, gan down the first turning on the left and her cottage is down the dip. She keeps an eye on the place for him.' The door began to close.

'Thanks,' Simon said weakly.

'Aye,' the man said, shutting the door firmly in their faces.

Half an hour later, they had the keys to Jacko Vance's pied-à-terre in their possession. Unfortunately for them, they also had Mrs Doreen Elliott in the passenger seat of Kay's car, determined to make sure Jacko's precious property didn't come to harm in the clumsy hands of the police. Kay could only hope for the older woman's sake that they didn't find what she feared behind Jacko Vance's heavy wooden front door.

The gate had been released at the mention of his name and Tony walked up the drive, with each step becoming more immersed in the persona he had chosen for the encounter. He wanted Vance to think he was uncertain and capable of being outwitted. He would take control by appearing to be the weaker of the two. It was a risky strategy, but one he felt confident he could handle.

Vance had opened the door wreathed in smiles, greeting him by his first name. Tony could only allow himself to be swept inside, assuming a faintly confused look. 'I'm so sorry, you've missed Micky,' Vance said. 'She's spending the weekend with some friends in the country. But I didn't want you to go off without taking the opportunity to meet you face to face,' he continued as he ushered Tony in. 'Of course, I saw you on my wife's programme the other day, but I've been noticing you at all my events lately. You should have come over and introduced yourself, we could have had a chat before now, saved you coming all the way to London.' He was the model of charm and suavity, his words flowing calm and mollifying.

'Actually, it wasn't Micky I came to see. I wanted to talk to you about Shaz Bowman,' Tony said, trying to appear stiff and awkward.

A momentary look of puzzlement. Then Vance said, 'Ah, yes, the detective who was killed so tragically. Right. I had it in mind that it was something altogether other that you wanted to ... Are you actually working with the police on the case, then?'

'As you'll recall from the interview I did with your wife, I was in charge of the unit Shaz was on attachment to. So, naturally, I have taken a role in the investigation,' Tony said. Hiding behind formality would make Vance feel he was uncomfortable.

Vance's eyebrows rose, his dancing blue eyes teasing as they always seemed to on TV. 'I heard your role in the investigation was on the opposite side of the fence,' he said mildly. 'That you were answering questions rather than asking.'

Vance's inside information, however gleaned, could be turned to his own advantage, Tony realized. In a way, it actually played into the strategy he'd outlined to Chris. 'You have good sources,' he said, trying to sound grudging. 'But I can assure you that although I'm working independently of the police, the evidence I have uncovered will be placed in their hands at the appropriate time.' That planted the idea he was working solo.

'And what has all of this to do with me?' Vance leaned casually against the newel post of the staircase that curved upwards.

'I have some video footage that I think you might be able to cast some light on,' Tony said, patting his jacket pocket.

For the first time since his greeting, Vance looked slightly disconcerted. His face cleared momentarily and the golden boy smile was back. 'Then I suggest you come upstairs with me. I have a room on the top floor that I use for screenings for small and select audiences.' He stepped to one side and with a graceful sweep of his real arm indicated that Tony should climb ahead of him.

Tony mounted the stairs. He told himself it didn't matter which room they were in; Chris could still hear him, and if things turned dangerous, she'd have time enough to mount a rescue. He hoped.

He paused at the landing, but Vance silently directed him up the next flight. 'First door on the right,' he said as they emerged on the top landing, an astonishingly bright area lit by a four-sided pyramid skylight.

The room Tony entered was long and narrow. The far wall was mostly occupied by a video screen. To his left, bolted to the floor, was a tall trolley holding a video recorder and a film projector. Behind it, shelves built round an editing desk were crammed with video tapes and film canisters. A cluster of comfy-looking leather slings on wooden frames completed the furnishings.

The window was what should have made Tony's heart sink. Although it was transparent, it had clearly had some sort of coating applied to it. Had he paid the same attention to his surroundings as he did to their occupants, he'd have noticed the precaution previously in government buildings where things went on that officials didn't want to become common knowledge. The coating made the windows impervious to radio signals, preventing electronic eavesdropping. This, added to the baffles that covered the walls, ensured that the room was to all intents and purposes sealed to the outside world. He could scream all he liked. Chris Devine would no longer be able to hear him.

Chris stared at the Holland Park mansion, wondering what the hell to do. Tony and Vance's voices had been coming through loud and clear then suddenly, nothing. The last thing she'd heard had been Vance saying, 'First door on the right.' It wasn't even enough information to work out which room they were in, since she had no idea which way the staircase turned.

- At first, she'd thought there was something wrong with the equipment – a loose wire, a dislodged battery. Terrible seconds raced past as Chris quickly checked what she could. But the reels of tape were still turning, although nothing was coming through on the receiver. She clutched her forehead, trying to figure out what was happening. Certainly there had been no sound of a struggle, no indication that the transmitter had been spotted. It could even be that Tony had turned it off. If, for example, he'd found himself in the kind of environment where electronic feedback might betray him. Vance had spoken of a special viewing room, the kind of place that might just house that sort of sensitive electronic gear.

She could feel herself dithering and hated herself for it. Anything could be happening to Tony. He was in a house with a killer, a man he fully expected to try to murder him.

She could, she supposed, try his mobile. They had agreed

she would only use the phone as a last resort. Well, there was nothing else she could attempt in the face of radio silence. She hit the memory button that summoned his number and hit 'send'. Moments of nothing then the familiar three tones followed by the infuriatingly calm female voice intoning, 'I'm sorry. The Vodaphone you are calling has not responded. Please try later.'

'Shit, shit, shit,' Chris hissed. There was nothing else for it. She might blow Tony out of the water, but better that than cost him his life by wavering like this. Chris jumped out of her car and ran up the road towards the Vance mansion.

Oblivious to the danger he had walked into, Tony turned to face Vance. 'Smart set-up,' he said.

Vance couldn't help preening. 'The best money can buy. So, what was it you wanted me to look at?'

Tony handed him the video cassette and watched him slot it into the machine, noticing that here on his home ground Vance's handicap was almost unnoticeable. A jury might find it hard to believe that he could be as awkward as he appeared when filling Shaz Bowman's car with petrol. Tony made a mental note to suggest a restaging of the event for the court's benefit.

'Grab a seat,' Vance said.

Tony chose a chair where he could just see Vance in his peripheral vision. As the tape started to play, Vance used a remote control to dim the lights. Tony readied himself for the next stage of the confrontation. The first section showed the unenhanced sequence of the disguised Vance at the motorway filling station. Barely thirty seconds into the film, Vance made a low sound in the bottom of his throat, almost a growl. As it continued to play, the sound grew in volume and rose in pitch. Tony realized the man was laughing. 'Is that meant to be me?' he eventually squeezed out between laughter, turning his grinning face to Tony.

'It is you. You know it, I know it. And soon the rest of the world will know it.' Tony hoped he'd struck the right note, somewhere between bravado and whingeing. As long as Vance was confident he was in control, there was the chance he might make a mistake.

Vance's eyes flicked past him to the screen. In slo-mo, the enhanced video was playing. To anyone who knew who they were looking for, it was hard to resist the resemblance between the man on the video and the one with the remote control. 'Dear, oh dear,' he said sardonically. 'You think anyone's going to build a case on something as obviously doctored as that?'

'There's not just that,' Tony said mildly. 'Keep watching. I like the footage of you arriving back in Leeds to finish the job off.'

Ignoring him, Vance hit the button that stopped the tape. He flipped it out of the player and tossed it back to Tony, all with single-handed smoothness. 'I don't move like that,' he said contemptuously. 'I'd be ashamed of myself if I'd adapted that poorly to my disability.'

'It was an unfamiliar car, a strange situation.'

'You'll have to do better than that.'

Tony threw a copy of his report at Vance. His left hand shot out in a trained reflex and caught it. He opened it at the first page and glanced at it. For a moment, the skin round his mouth and eyes tightened. Tony could sense the sheer force of will that stopped him from a more powerful reaction. 'It's all there,' Tony said. 'A selection of your victims. Photographs of you with them. Their astonishing resemblance to Jillie. The mutilation of Barbara Fenwick. It's all tied in to you.'

Vance lifted his handsome face and shook his head pityingly. 'You haven't got a hope,' he said contemptuously. 'Circumstantial trash. A load of doctored photographs. Have you any idea how many people have their photographs taken with me in a year? The only surprising thing in statistical terms is that more of them don't end up murdered. You're wasting your time, Dr Hill. Just like DC Bowman before you.'

'You can't talk your way out of this, Vance,' Tony said. 'This goes way beyond coincidence. There isn't a jury in the land will fall for that.'

'There isn't a jury in the land that won't contain half a dozen of my fans. If they're told this is a witch-hunt, they'll believe me. If I hear another word of this, I will not only set my lawyers on you but I will also go to the press and tell them about this sad little man who works for the Home Office and is obsessed with my wife. He's deluded, of course, just like all the sad little men who fall in love with an image on the TV screen. He thinks just because she had dinner with him that she'd fall into his arms if I was out of the picture. So he's trying to frame me for a bunch of non-existent serial killings. Let's see who ends up looking like a fool then, Dr Hill.' Gripping the folder under his right upper arm, Vance ripped it across.

'You killed Shaz Bowman,' Tony said. 'You've killed a lot of other girls, but you killed Shaz Bowman and you are not going to walk away from that. You can tear up my report as many times as you like, but we are going to get you.'

'I don't think so. If there was anything like evidence in this folder, there would be a team of senior police officers here. This is fantasy, Dr Hill. You need help.'

Before Tony could respond, a green light started flashing on the wall near the door. Vance strode over and picked up a handset. 'Who is it?' He listened for a moment. 'There's no need for you to come in, Detective. Dr Hill is just leaving.' He replaced the receiver and gave Tony a measured look. 'Well, Dr Hill? Are you? Or do I have to call police officers who will be rather more rational on the subject of DC Bowman than Sergeant Devine?'

Tony got to his feet. 'I'm not giving up on this,' he said.

Vance gave a shout of laughter. 'And my friends at the Home Office thought you had such a promising career. Take my advice, Dr Hill. Go on holiday. Forget about Bowman. Get a life. You've obviously been working too hard.' But his eyes were not laughing. In spite of his experience at presenting a facade for the world, even Jacko Vance could not prevent apprehension leaking out from behind his genial expression.

Tony resisted the impulse to show the jubilation he felt and began to descend the stairs with the air of a man drowned in defeat. He'd achieved almost exactly what he'd expected. It wasn't quite the same goal as he'd revealed to Chris Devine, since he hadn't been sure he could carry it off. Well satisfied, Tony plodded down the hall and through Jacko Vance's front door.

The chapel had been built for a small but passionately devout congregation. It was simple but genuinely beautiful in its proportions, Kay thought as she stood in the doorway. The conversion to living space had been done tastefully, retaining the sense of airiness. Vance had chosen furnishings with simple, uncluttered lines, the only ornamentation a series of bright gabbeh rugs scattered over the stone flags of the floor. The single room had a galley kitchen, a small dining area and a sitting space with a couple of sofas angled round a big low slate table. At the far end, a raised sleeping gallery had been built. Underneath was what looked like a workbench fitted out with tools. Kay felt the clench of excitement in her stomach as she watched Simon and Leon range through the room, ostensibly looking for signs of the fictitious intruder.

By her side, Doreen Elliott stood foursquare and firm, a squat blunt obelisk of a woman in her fifties with a face as impassive as the massive stones of Hadrian's Wall itself. 'Who did you say reported the intruder?' she demanded, jealously guarding her rights as custodian of Jacko Vance's privacy.

'I don't know exactly,' Kay said. 'I think the call came from a car phone. Someone driving past saw a flickering light inside, like a torch.'

'Must be a quiet night for three of you to come out on something like this.' Her acerbic tone indicated that the local police generally failed to meet her exacting standards.

'We were in the area,' Kay said. 'It was easier to divert us than to send out other officers. Besides,' she added with a confiding smile, 'when it's someone like Jacko Vance involved, well, I suppose we try a bit harder.'

'Hmmph. What do they think they're looking for, that pair?'

Kay looked down the room where Simon seemed to be scanning the floor, lifting the corners of rugs with his toe and peering underneath. Leon was methodically opening kitchen cupboards and drawers, looking, she knew, for any indication that Donna Doyle might have been here.

'Just checking nothing obvious is missing, and there's nowhere for anyone to hide,' she said. Simon had given up on the rugs and moved on to the workbench. She saw his back stiffen as he got closer. His steps changed almost to a prowl and he angled his head all the better to study whatever had caught his attention. He turned to face them, and Kay saw the brightness of discovery in his eyes.

'Looks like Mr Vance is quite into woodwork,' Simon said, gesturing with his head to Leon.

'He makes wooden toys for the bairns in the hospital,' Mrs Elliott said, as proudly as if he were her own son. 'He cannot do enough for them. Never mind the George Cross, they should give him a medal for the hours he puts in with people at death's door. You cannot measure the comfort he gives folk.'

Leon had joined Simon at the workbench. 'Some serious kit here,' he said. 'Man, these chisels are sharp as razors.' His face was sombre and grim. 'And you want to see this vice, Kay. I've never seen anything like it.'

'He needs that to hold the wood,' Mrs Elliott said firmly. 'With his arm the way it is, he cannot manage without it. He calls it his extra pair of hands.'

Tony trudged down Vance's drive, head down, the sound of the slamming door still ringing in his ears. He raised his eyes and caught Chris's anxious look. Giving her a broad wink, he maintained his dejected body language until he was through the electronic gates and back on the street, hidden from the house by the high hedge.

'What the fuck happened in there?' Chris demanded.

'What do you mean? I was just getting into my stride when you butted in,' Tony protested.

'You went off the air. I didn't know what the hell was going on.'

'What do you mean, I went off the air?'

'It just went dead. He said, "First on the right," then total silence. For all I knew, he'd topped you.'

Tony frowned, trying to work out what had happened. 'He must have that room electronically shielded,' he eventually said. 'Of course. The last thing he'd want is anyone doing any snooping round him that he didn't know about. It never crossed my mind.'

Chris cupped her hands against the wind and lit a cigarette. 'Jesus,' she exploded softly in a long stream of smoke. 'Don't ever give me a fright like that again. So what happened? Did he cough? Don't tell me he coughed and we didn't get it on tape?'

Tony shook his head, walking her across the street to where he'd parked his car in full view of Vance's house. He glanced back and was pleased to see his target standing at a window on the top floor looking down at them. 'Get in my car for now, I'll explain,' he said.

He started the engine and drove round the corner. 'He poured scorn on the evidence,' Tony said as he turned into another street, doubling back to get behind where Chris was parked a couple of hundred yards from Vance's gate, out of the line of sight from the house. 'He made it plain that he thought we had nothing on him and that if we didn't call off the dogs he'd come after me.'

'He threatened to kill you?'

'No, he threatened to go to the papers and make an idiot of me.'

'You sound pretty pleased with yourself for somebody that just blew their big showdown,' Chris said. 'I thought he was supposed to either roll over and spill his guts or else try to top you?'

Tony shrugged. 'I didn't really expect him to confess. And if he was going to kill me, I don't think he'd have done it on the spot. He might have convinced Wharton and McCormick that there was nothing sinister about Shaz visiting him before she died, but I think even they would have to pay attention if I was killed after I'd just been to Vance's house. No, what I wanted to do was unsettle him to the point where he starts to worry how well he's covered his tracks.'

'And what good does that do?' She wound the window down an inch to flick her ash clear.

'With a bit of luck, it sets him off like a clockwork mouse, straight for his killing ground. He needs to make sure there's nothing that can incriminate him in the unlikely event that I could ever persuade the police to apply for a search warrant.'

'You think he'll go now?'

'I'm banking on it. According to his schedule, he's got nothing on tomorrow until a meeting at three. After that, the week starts looking horrendous. He's got to go for it now.'

Chris groaned. 'Not the M1 *again*.'

'You up for it?'

'I'm up for it,' she said wearily. 'What's the plan?'

'I go now. He's seen me drive off with you, so he should think the coast's clear. I'll head on up to Northumberland and you try to stay with him when he emerges. We can keep in touch by phone.'

'At least it's dark,' she said. 'Hopefully he won't notice the same headlights in his rear-view mirror.' She opened the door and got out, leaning back in to speak. 'I can't believe I'm doing this. All the bloody way down from Northumberland to London just to turn round and go back there again. We must be demented.'

'No. Just determined.'

He was that, all right, Chris thought as she walked to her car and watched Tony do a three-point turn and return the way he'd come. God, she thought. It was already seven. Five, six hours back to Northumberland. She hoped there wasn't going to be too much action at the other end of the trip because she would be dead on her feet.

She tuned the radio to a golden oldies station and settled down to sing along with the sixties. She didn't have long to harmonize before the gates of Vance's house slid back and the long silver nose of his Mercedes appeared. 'You fucking beauty,' she said, turning on her ignition and rolling forward to keep him in her sights. Holland Park Avenue, then up to join the A40. As they headed out through Acton and Ealing, Chris felt a vague sense of uneasiness. This wasn't just the pretty way to Northumberland. It was perverse. She couldn't believe he was going to drive all the way out west to the orbital M25 just to circle round to the northbound M1.

She stayed close enough not to lose him at the lights, always managing to keep a single car between them. It was hard driving, but at least the streetlights helped. Eventually, the signs for the M25 appeared and Chris prepared to take the slip road even though Vance showed no signs of leaving the carriageway. Probably do a last-minute lane change, she thought, if he thinks he might have a tail.

But he didn't move and it was she who had to do the last-minute rescue, stamping on the accelerator to keep in touch with his tail lights. She only made it because he was driving a scant handful of miles above the limit, like a man who absolutely doesn't want to be stopped for speeding. She grabbed her phone and hit the recall button for Tony's number.

'Tony? It's Chris. Listen, I'm on the M40 heading west tight on Jack the Lad's tail. Wherever he's going, it's not Northumberland.'

The discovery of the vice injected a new urgency into the search. Acutely aware of how bizarre this must seem to Doreen Elliott, Kay desperately tried to distract her with conversation. 'They made a lovely job of converting this place,' she said brightly.

It was clearly the right thing. Mrs Elliott turned to the kitchen and ran a hand along the polished smoothness of the solid wood. 'Our Derek did the kitchen. He wanted no expense spared, like. Everything you could possibly want, all the latest stuff.' She pointed to the cupboard fronts. 'Washer-dryer, dishwasher, fridge, freezer, all tucked away.'

'I'd have thought he'd have brought his wife up with him more often,' Kay tried.

It was clearly the wrong thing. Mrs Elliott frowned. 'Well, he told us they'd be using it as a weekend place. But in the end, she never came. He said she was too much of a city girl. She doesn't like the country, you see. Well, you only have to look at her on that TV programme to see she'd not fit in with the likes of us. Not like Mr Vance.'

'What, she's never been here at all?' Kay tried to sound as if this was news to her. She had half her attention on Simon and Leon, but she was still keeping watch on Mrs Elliott's reactions. 'We're just trying to work out who else might have a key. For security reasons,' she added hastily as the older woman's face grew more slab-like.

'Never seen hide nor hair of her.' Then a smirk. 'That's not to say there's never been a woman's hand on the place. Well, a man's entitled to his compensations if his wife cannot bring herself to share his interests.'

'You've seen him here with other women, then?' Kay asked, aiming for casual.

'Not actually seen him, no, but I come in once a fortnight to give the place a clean, and there's been a couple of times I've unloaded the dishwasher and there's been glasses with lipstick traces. It doesn't always come off in the machine, you see. So putting two and two together, I suppose he's got a girlfriend. But he knows he can rely on us to keep our mouths shut.'

Only because no one's ever asked you, Kay thought cynically. 'As you say, if his wife won't come to a place like this ...'

'It's a palace,' Mrs Elliott said, doubtless comparing it to the dark kitchen of her own cottage. 'I tell you something: I bet it's the only house in Northumberland with its own private nuclear shelter.'

The words fell into the conversation like a bomb.

'A nuclear shelter?' Kay asked faintly. Simon and Leon froze where they stood like gun dogs on point.

She mistook the stillness of their surprise for doubt. 'Right under our feet,' Mrs Elliott said. 'I'm not making this up, pet.'

Chris had barely finished the call to Tony when she saw the tail lights ahead of her wink to indicate that Vance was about to take the next slip road. Chris followed, leaving her move to the last possible moment. They turned north then, a couple of miles from the motorway, Vance signalled a left turn. At the junction, Chris slowed down and saw something that made her swear like a football supporter.

She switched off her main lights and drove cautiously down the narrow lane on sidelights only. She rounded a bend and there on her left was Jacko Vance's destination.

The private airfield was floodlit. Parked on a strip of Tarmac, Chris saw a dozen small planes standing in front of four hangars. She watched Vance's headlamps cut twin cones through the darkness round the perimeter then be swallowed up in the greater brightness as he drew up behind one of the planes. A man jumped out of the cockpit and waved. Vance got out of his car and walked to the plane, greeting the pilot with a clap on the shoulder.

'Oh, fuck,' Chris said. For the second time in the space

of an hour, she had no idea what to do. Vance could have chartered the plane to get him to Northumberland ahead of any possible pursuit. Or he could have chartered it to get him out of the country. A quick flight across the Channel into the open borders of Europe and he could be anywhere by morning. Should she opt for dramatic intervention or leave him to take off?

It was a gamble, and one she didn't want to take responsibility for. Her eyes scanned the airfield, settling on the small control tower that jutted out beyond the furthest hangar. Then she saw Vance and the pilot disappear aboard. Seconds later, the propellers stuttered into life. 'Fuck it,' Chris said and put the car in gear. She raced round the airport perimeter fence and reached the control tower just as the small plane taxied out on to the runway.

She raced inside, startling the man who sat at a plotting desk beside a computer. Chris thrust her warrant card in his face. 'That plane on the runway. Has it filed a flight plan?'

'Yeah, yeah, he has,' the man stammered. 'He's going to Newcastle. Is there some sort of a problem? I mean, I can tell him to abort his take-off if there's a problem. We're always keen to help the police ...'

'No problem,' Chris said grimly. 'Just forget you ever saw me, OK? No little radio messages saying anybody was interested, OK?'

'No, I mean yes, whatever you say, officer. No messages.'

'And just to make sure,' Chris said, pulling up a chair and giving him the predatory smile that sucked confessions from hard men, 'I'm staying right here.' She pulled out her phone and called Tony. 'Sergeant Devine,' she said. 'Subject is aboard private plane, destination Newcastle. You're going to have to deal with it from here on in. Suggest you organize

461

a reception committee with the troops on the ground at his ultimate destination. OK?'

A bemused Tony stared at the shifting lights ahead of him on the motorway and said, 'Oh, shit, a plane? I take it you can't speak freely?'

'Correct. I'm staying here to make sure subject isn't given a warning by the control tower.'

'Ask him how long it'll take to Newcastle.'

There was a muffled conversation, then Chris came back on the line. 'He says they're flying an Aztec, which should do it in about two and a half to three hours. No chance you can beat the clock.'

'I'll do what I can. And, Chris – thanks.' He ended the call and carried on driving on automatic pilot. So, somewhere between two and a half and three hours? Then he'd have to find his way to Five Walls Halt, either by taxi or by hiring a car, which wouldn't be easy at ten o'clock on a Sunday night. Even so, Tony realized Chris was right. There was no way he could possibly arrive at Vance's bolt hole ahead of him.

'Which is why he did it, of course,' he said aloud. Vance was no fool. He would expect Tony to know about his other home and to make for there once he'd stirred things up. What Vance hadn't known was that Tony already had three police profilers in Northumberland. At least, he presumed they were still making inquiries up there, since he'd heard nothing to the contrary. Come to that, he'd heard nothing since mid-afternoon, when he'd checked in with Simon to discover that they were going door-to-door in a bid to trace any sightings of Donna Doyle.

It wasn't enough, though. Three junior CID officers, none from the local force, none with any experience of command. They'd be uncertain, not knowing when or whether to challenge Vance. They wouldn't know when to hang back and when to move. It needed more than any of them had to give. There was only one person who could get there in time and keep Leon, Simon and Kay in check.

She answered on the second ring. 'DCI Jordan.'

'Carol? It's me. How are you doing?'

'Not good. To be honest, I'm grateful for the human contact. I've been feeling like a leper. I'm an outcast from the infantry because they think I'm partly responsible for Di Earnshaw's death. I'm isolated from John Brandon because there will have to be an inquiry which he can't be seen to influence. And I'm out of the loop when it comes to questioning Alan Brinkley in case I compromise the interrogation for personal reasons. And I have to tell you that breaking the news to her parents left me feeling that the Ancient Greeks' method of dealing with bad news must sometimes have been a relief to the messenger.'

'I'm sorry. You must wish now I hadn't dragged you into this Vance business,' he said.

'I don't,' she said firmly. 'Somebody's got to put a stop to Vance, and nobody else would listen to you. I don't blame you for what went wrong in Seaford. That's my responsibility. I shouldn't have tried to do surveillance on a shoestring. I knew you were right and I should have carried that conviction through and demanded the bodies to do the job properly instead of settling for a skeleton crew. If I had, Di Earnshaw would still be alive.'

'You can't know that for sure,' Tony protested. 'Anything could have happened. Her partner could have gone for a piss at the crucial moment, they could have separated to circle the building. If anyone's to blame, it's the sergeant. Not only were they supposed to look out for each other, he was her immediate boss. He owed her a duty of care and he failed her.'

'And what about my duty of care?'

Tony shook his head. 'Oh, Carol, ease up on yourself.'

'I can't. But enough of that. Where are you? And what's happening with Vance?'

'I'm on the M1. It's been a complicated day.' As he hammered on in the outside lane oblivious to anything but the traffic and the woman on the end of the phone, he brought Carol up to speed.

'So now he's somewhere between London and Newcastle?' Carol asked.

'That's right.'

'You're not going to make it in time, are you?'

'No.'

'But I could?'

'Possibly. Probably, if you stuck the blue light on. I can't ask you to, but I . . .'

'There's nothing for me to do here. I'm off duty, and nobody's going to call out the CID leper tonight. I'm better off doing this than sitting here feeling sorry for myself. Get me some directions. I'll call you when I get near Newcastle.' Her voice was stronger and firmer than it had been at the start of the call. Even if he'd wanted to argue, he realized it would have been pointless. She was the woman he'd taken her for, and she wouldn't walk away from a challenge.

'Thanks,' he said simply.

'We're wasting time talking.' Abruptly, the line went dead.

The price of Tony's skill was the empathy he brought to situations like this. He understood precisely what Carol was going through. Very few people ever experienced a justified sense of responsibility for the death of another human being. Everything Carol had been certain of had suddenly shifted on to shaky ground and no one who had not shared a similar experience could help her back to terra firma. But he understood and he cared enough to try. He suspected that his phone call had, serendipitously, been the first step in the right direction. Hoping he was correct, Tony stared into the narrowing tunnel of red lights and carried on driving north.

On the exact location of the entrance to the basement shelter, Mrs Elliott was rather more vague. 'It's under the flags somewhere. He had a couple of lads from Newcastle over to install it so that you cannot see it just by looking.'

The three police officers glared in frustration at the metre-square stone slabs that made up the floor. Then Simon said, 'If you can't see it, how do you get down there?'

'Our Derek said they'd installed an electric motor,' Mrs Elliott said.

'Well, if there's a motor, there's gotta be a switch,' Leon muttered. 'Si, you start on the right-hand side of the door. Kay, you start on the left. I'll go up to the sleeping gallery.' The two men moved away and started flicking switches, but Kay was held back by Mrs Elliott's hand on her sleeve.

'What do you need to find the shelter for?' she asked. 'I thought you said there was supposed to be a prowler? They're not going to be down there.'

Kay dug out her most reassuring smile. 'When we're dealing with a celebrity like Mr Vance, we have to be especially careful. A prowler in his house could be a lot more serious than a straightforward burglar. If someone was stalking him, for example, they could be hiding in waiting for him. So we have to take this extremely seriously.' She covered the woman's hand with her own. 'Why don't we wait outside?'

'What for?'

'If there is someone down there, it could be very danger-ous.' Kay's smile felt strained. If Donna Doyle was trapped in the cellar, discovering her would be a revelation that would give even the stolid Doreen Elliott nightmares for the rest of her life, Kay knew. 'It's our job to protect members of the public, you know. How do you think my boss would react if I let you be taken hostage by some nutter with a knife?'

Mrs Elliott let herself be led into the tiny porch with only a single backward glance at Simon and Leon moving round the room snapping switches on and off. 'You think it's a stalker, then?' she asked avidly. 'Up here?'

'It wouldn't necessarily be someone from around here,' Kay said. 'These people are obsessive. They'll follow a celebrity for weeks, months, learning every detail of their life and routine. Have you seen any strangers hanging around?'

'Well, we get the tourists and the hikers, but mostly they're only here for the wall. They don't hang about.'

Before Kay could say more, her phone rang. 'Will you excuse me? I'll only be a minute,' she said, slipping back inside to take the call. 'Hello?'

'Kay? It's Tony. Where are you?'

Oh, shit, she thought. Why me? Why couldn't he have phoned Leon? 'Er . . . we're inside Jacko Vance's house in Northumberland,' she said. Simon glanced across at her, but she waved to him to continue his search.

'What?' Tony exclaimed, outraged.

'I know you said to wait, but we kept thinking about Donna Doyle . . .'

'You broke in?'

'No. We're perfectly entitled to be here. A local woman has a key. We informed her there had been reports of a prowler and she let us in.'

'Well, you'd better get out asap.'

'Tony, she could be here. This place has got a sealed basement. Vance told the builders he wanted a nuclear shelter.'

'A nuclear shelter?' His incredulity was palpable.

'It was a dozen years ago. People still believed Russia was going to nuke us,' Kay reminded him plaintively. 'The point is, she could be down there and we wouldn't hear her, not even standing right above her. We've got to find the door.'

'No. You've got to leave it. He's on his way there. He's chartered a plane, Kay. He's probably coming up there to make sure he's not left any loose ends. Kay, we need to catch him in the act. We need to stake the place out and watch him go down there to an untouched crime scene.'

As he spoke, Kay looked on in amazement as the ground moved only feet away from her. Silently, a single slab tilted and swung open in response to a switch flicked by Simon. As the fetid air escaped, Kay gagged. Recovering herself, she said, 'It's too late for that. We've found the door.'

Simon was already at the opening in the floor, peering down a set of stone steps. His groping hands found a switch and flooded the area with light. A long moment passed then he turned to Kay, his face the colour of putty. 'If that's Tony, you better tell him we've found Donna Doyle, as well.'

He drummed his fingers gently against the arm rest, the only movement in a body still as a lion preparing for the pounce. He didn't even brace himself against the jolts of the pockets of turbulence the small twin-engined plane hit occasionally, but let his body shift with the movement. Once upon a time, he used to bite the nails of his right hand when he was nervous. Losing his arm had been an extreme cure for a bad habit, he was fond of saying wryly in public. Now, he had cultivated stillness, understanding that nervous tics made nothing happen faster or easier. Besides, stillness was much more unsettling for everyone else.

The engine note changed as the pilot prepared to land.

Jacko peered out of the window, staring down at the smudge of suburban streetlights through the fine rain. He'd left Tony Hill standing. There was no way he could have beaten the aircraft. And he had no back-up, Jacko knew from his own discreet inquiries, confirmed by what both Micky and Tony himself had admitted.

The wheels hit the runway and jolted him against his seatbelt. A slight swerve, a correction, then they were heading for the flying club hangars at a gentle taxi. They had barely come to a standstill when Jacko had the door open. He jumped to the Tarmac and looked around, his eyes searching for the familiar shape of his Land Rover. Sam Foxwell and his brother were always glad to earn the twenty quid he paid them whenever he needed the Land Rover brought to the airport and when he'd spoken to them from the car phone, they'd promised to have it there for him.

When he couldn't spot it, he felt a shiver of panic. They couldn't have let him down, not tonight of all nights. The pilot interrupted his thoughts, pointing to the side of the hangar in deep shadow. 'If you're looking for your Land Rover, I think it's tucked round there. I noticed it when I was taxi-ing.'

'Cheers.' Jacko dug into his pocket and took a twenty-pound note from his money clip. 'Have a beer on me. See you soon, Keith.'

As he thundered along the narrow Northumberland side roads that were the quickest route to the place he considered his real home, he reviewed what he had to do in the couple of hours' grace he had before Tony Hill could possibly arrive. First, check if the bitch was still alive and if she was, see she didn't stay that way. Then, take the chain saw to her, get her bagged and into the Land Rover. Clean the basement with the high-pressure hose and set off for the hospital. Would he have time? Or should he simply disable the motor that opened the door on its swivel? After all, Hill had no way of knowing about the basement shelter and the local police were not going to mount a search on his say-so, not when it would offend an upstanding local taxpayer like Jacko Vance. And there was no guarantee that Tony Hill would even show up.

Maybe he should just settle for making sure she was dead and leave the clearing up for later. There would be a certain delight in entertaining Tony Hill only feet away from his latest victim. His mouth twisted in an ugly snarl. Donna Doyle would have to be his last victim for a while. Damn the man. Tony Hill should have let sleeping bitches lie. Jacko had plans for Tony Hill, though. One day, when it had all gone quiet and Tony Hill had resigned himself to the fact that he'd failed, that plan would go into action and he'd wish he'd never stuck his nose into someone else's business.

The headlights sliced through the deep darkness of the countryside, breasting the hill that rolled down to his sanctuary. Where there should have been nothing but blackness, light spilled out over the cropped moorland grass and the grey gravel of his drive. Jacko stamped on the brakes and the Land Rover screamed to a jittering halt. What the fuck?

As he sat there, mind racing, adrenaline pumping, a pair of headlights on full beam crept up behind him, angling across the narrow road so there was no possibility of going backwards. Slowly, Vance took his foot off the brake and let the Land Rover cruise down the hill towards his home. The lights shifted and fell into convoy behind him. As he grew closer, he saw a second car parked diagonally just beyond his gateway, effectively blocking the road beyond.

Vance drove on to his property, the cold grip of fear in his stomach focusing his mind. When he rolled to a halt he jumped out of his vehicle, every inch the outraged householder, and confronted the young black man standing in his doorway. 'What the hell's going on?' he demanded.

'I'm afraid I'm going to have to ask you to wait outside, sir,' Leon said deferentially.

'What do you mean? This is my house. Has there been a burglary or what? What's going on? And who the hell are you?'

'I'm Detective Constable Leon Jackson of the Metropolitan Police.' He held out his warrant card for inspection.

Vance switched the charm on. 'You're a long way from home.'

'Pursuing an investigation, sir. It's amazing where a line of inquiry can take us in these days of electronic communications and efficient travel networks.' Leon's voice was impassive, but his eyes never left Vance.

'Look, you know who I am, obviously. You know this is my place. Can't you at least tell me what the hell is going on?'

A horn beeped and Vance turned to see the car that had followed him down the hill stop just outside the gate, blocking the road in the opposite direction. He was hemmed in completely. Jesus, he hoped the bitch was dead. Another young man got out of the car and walked across the gravel. 'Are you from the Metropolitan Police as well?' Vance asked, forcing himself to maintain his professionally beguiling mode.

'No,' Simon said. 'I'm from Strathclyde.'

'*Strathclyde?*' Vance was momentarily confused. He'd taken someone from London a few years ago, but he'd never brought anyone down from Scotland. He hated the accent. It reminded him of Jimmy Linden and all that meant to him. So if there was a cop here from Scotland, they couldn't be tracking the girls. It was going to be fine, he told himself. He could walk away from this.

'That's right, sir. DC Jackson and myself have been working

470

on different aspects of the same case. We were in the area and we had a report from a passing motorist of a prowler here. So we thought we'd better check it out.'

'That's very commendable, officers. Perhaps I could go inside and check to see if anything's missing or broken?' He moved to edge around Leon, but the policeman was too fast for him. He extended his arm, blocking Vance, and shook his head.

'I'm afraid not, sir. It's a crime scene, you see. We need to make sure nothing interferes with it.'

'A crime scene? What on earth has happened?' Concerned, try to sound concerned, he warned himself. This is your house, you're an innocent man and you want to know what's happened on your property.

'I'm afraid there's been a suspicious death,' Simon said coldly.

Jacko made himself take what looked like an involuntary step backwards, covering his face with his hands to make sure no sign of the relief that flooded him was visible to the police. She was dead, hallelujah. A dead woman could never testify. He pasted an expression of worried anxiety on his face and looked up. 'But that's terrible. A death? Here? But who . . . How? This is my home. Nobody comes here except me. How can there be someone dead here?'

'That's what we're trying to establish, sir,' Leon said.

'But who is it? A burglar? What?'

'We don't think it was a burglar,' Simon said, trying to keep the lid on the rage he felt face to face with the man who had killed Shaz and who was trying to pretend he had nothing to do with the putrefying mess in his cellar.

'But . . . the only person who has keys is Mrs Elliott. Doreen Elliott at Dene Cottage. It's not . . . It's not her?'

'No, sir. Mrs Elliott is in excellent health. It was Mrs Elliott

471

who let us in to the property and gave us permission to search. One of our colleagues has taken her home.' There was something in the way the black cop held his stare when he said this that sent a tremor of fear skittering round Vance's nerves. The message coming through loud and clear between the spoken words was the unspoken warning that his first line of defence had crumbled. This was not an illegal entry and search.

'Thank God for that. So who is it?'

'We can't speculate at this point, sir.'

'But you must be able to tell me if it's a man or a woman, surely?'

Simon's lip curled. He could hold back no longer. 'As if you didn't know,' he said, his voice thick with angry contempt. 'You think our heads button up the back?' He turned away, his hands balling into fists.

'What is he talking about?' Vance demanded, moving into the angry mode of the innocent bystander who senses they're about to become snagged up in someone else's trouble.

Leon shrugged and lit a cigarette. 'You tell me,' he said negligently. 'Oh good,' he said, looking over Vance's shoulder. 'Looks like the cavalry.'

The woman emerging from the car that had drawn up behind Simon's didn't look much like the cavalry to Vance. She couldn't have been more than thirty. Even shrugged into an oversized mac, she was clearly slim and pretty, with short blonde hair cut thick and shaggy. 'Good evening, gentlemen,' she said briskly. 'Mr Vance, I'm Detective Chief Inspector Carol Jordan. Would you excuse me for a moment, while I confer with one of my colleagues. Leon, can you keep Mr Vance company for a minute? I want to take a look inside. Simon, a word, please?'

Before he had the chance to say anything, she'd swept

472

Simon inside, managing to open the door so narrowly that Vance had no chance to see within. 'I don't understand what's going on,' Vance said. 'Shouldn't there be scene-of-crimes people here? And uniformed officers?'

Again, Leon shrugged. 'It's not very like the telly, life.' He continued smoking down to the tip then threw his cigarette on the porch step and ground it out.

'Do you mind?' Vance said, pointing. 'This is my house. My doorstep. Just because somebody got themselves killed inside doesn't mean the police can vandalize the place, too.'

Leon raised an eyebrow. 'Frankly, sir, I think that's the least. of your worries right now.'

'This is outrageous,' Vance said.

'Me, I find suspicious death enough outrage for one night.'

The door inched open and Simon and Carol re-emerged. The woman looked sombre, the man faintly sick, Vance thought. Good. She didn't deserve to die pretty, the bitch. 'Chief Inspector, when is someone going to tell me what is going on here?'

He'd been so busy watching her, he hadn't noticed the two men had moved to either side of him in a flanking movement. Carol locked eyes with him, her cold blue stare a match for his. 'Jacko Vance, I am arresting you on suspicion of murder. You do not need to say anything, but I must warn you that it may harm your defence if you do not mention when questioned something which you later rely upon in court. Anything you do say may be given in evidence.'

Disbelief blazed across his face as Simon and Leon closed in on him. Before it had really sunk in that not only was this woman arresting him but these idiots were laying hands on him, a cuff of steel clamped hard over his left wrist. He recovered himself as they tried to manhandle him back

473

towards the Land Rover, convulsing beneath their hands in a desperate attempt to free himself by sheer superiority of strength. But he was off balance, and his feet went from under him on the gravel.

'Don't let him fall,' Carol yelled, and somehow, Leon managed to get under Vance as he hit the ground. Simon hung on grimly to the other end of the handcuffs, yanking Vance's arm back, making him squeal.

'Make my day, shithead,' Simon shouted. 'Give me a reason to give you a taste of what you gave Shaz.' He hauled upwards on Vance's arm, forcing him to struggle to his feet.

Leon scrambled back upright and pushed Vance in the chest. 'You know what would really make me happy? You trying to leg it, that would make me fucking delirious, because then I'd have an excuse for kicking seven colours of shit out of your scumbag body.' He pushed him in the chest again. 'Go on, go for it. Go on, do one.'

Vance stumbled back, as much to escape the venom in Leon's voice as to ease the pain on his arm. He hit the Land Rover with a thud. Simon yanked his arm down and fastened the other end of the handcuffs to the bull bar. He took a deep breath then spat in Vance's face. When he turned to face Carol, there were tears in his eyes. 'He'll not be going anywhere in a hurry,' he croaked.

'You are going to regret this night,' Vance said, his voice low and dangerous.

Carol stepped forward and put a hand on Simon's arm. 'You did well, Simon. Now, unless anybody's got any better ideas, I think it's about time we called the police.'

There was something generic about police stations, Tony thought. The canteens never served salad, the waiting areas always smelled of stale cigarettes in spite of smoking having been banned for years, and the decor never varied. Looking round the interview room in Hexham police station at three in the morning, he realized he could be anywhere from Penzance to Perth. On that gloomy thought, the door opened and Carol came in with two mugs of coffee. 'Strong, black and brewed some time in the last week,' she said, dropping into the chair opposite him.

'What's happening?'

She snorted. 'He's still screaming about wrongful arrest and false imprisonment. I've just given a statement of explanation.'

He stirred his coffee and took in the signs of strain round her eyes. 'Which was?'

'In the area on inquiries, the lads got a report of a possible prowler. They thought it would be quicker to check it out themselves – being into inter-force co-operation – so they found a keyholder who was happy to let them in and gave permission to search,' Carol recited, leaning back and staring sightlessly at the ceiling. 'Concerned about the possibility of a hidden stalker, they opened the basement where they found the dead body of a young white female who answered the description of Donna Doyle, whom they knew to be on the missing list. Since Mr Vance is the only person known to frequent the house, it was clear he must be a suspect in what was obviously a suspicious death. I considered he was a fugitive risk. He was at the scene with a vehicle capable of leaving the road and avoiding pursuit.

'Although my authority does not extend into the force area of Northumbria Police, I am empowered to effect a citizen's arrest. Placing Mr Vance in restraints which caused him minimal discomfort seemed a better alternative than leaving him at large where any movement towards his vehicle might have led to an over-reaction on the part of the officers I was working with. Cuffing him to the Land Rover was, in effect, for his own protection.'

By the time she ended her recital, they were both grinning. 'Anyway, the local lads did me the favour of re-arresting him when they got there.'

'What about charging him?'

Carol looked depressed. 'They're waiting for Vance's brief to arrive. But they're running very scared. They've seen your dossier and they've interviewed Kay and Simon and Leon, but they're still wary. It's not over, Tony. Not by a long way. The fat lady hasn't even arrived yet.'

'I just wish that they hadn't opened that cellar. That they'd staked the place out and witnessed him opening it and going down there with Donna's body.'

Carol sighed. 'She hadn't been dead long, did you know?'

'No.'

'The police surgeon thought less than twenty-four hours.' They sat in silence, each wondering what they could have done better or faster, whether more or less orthodoxy could have won them a faster response. Carol broke the uneasy stillness. 'If we can't put Vance away, I don't think I want to be a copper any more.'

'You feel like that because of what happened to Di Earnshaw,' Tony said, laying his hand on her arm.

'I feel like that because Vance is a lethal weapon and if we can't neutralize the likes of him, we're nothing more than glorified traffic wardens,' she said bitterly.

'And if we can?'

She shrugged. 'Then maybe we redeem ourselves for the ones we lose.'

They sat in silence, sipping coffee. Then Tony ran a hand through his hair and said, 'Have they got a good pathologist?'

'I've no idea. Why?'

Before he could answer, the door opened on the worried face of Phil Marshall, the superintendent in charge of the division. 'Dr Hill? Could I have a word?'

'Come in, it's a shop,' Carol muttered.

Marshall closed the door behind him. 'Vance wants to talk to you. Alone. He's happy for the conversation to be taped, but he wants it to be just you and him.'

'What about his brief?' Carol asked.

'He says he just wants Dr Hill and himself. What do you say, Doc? Will you talk to him?'

'We've got nothing to lose, have we?'

Marshall winced. 'From where I'm standing, we've got quite a lot to lose, actually. Frankly, I want evidence to charge Vance with or else I want him out of here within the day. I'm going to no magistrate to ask if I can keep Jacko Vance under lock and key on the basis of what you've given me so far.'

Tony took out his notebook and tore out a sheet of paper, scribbling down a name and number. He handed it to Carol. 'This is who we need to get up here. Can you explain to them while I'm in with Jack the Lad?'

Carol read what he'd written and comprehension lit up her tired eyes. 'Of course.' She reached out and squeezed his hand. 'Good luck.'

Tony nodded, then followed Marshall down the corridor. 'We'll be taping it, of course,' Marshall said. 'We've got to be squeaky clean on this one. He's already talking about suing DCI Jordan.' He stopped outside an interview room and opened the door. He nodded to the uniformed officer in the corner and the man left.

Tony stepped into the room and stared at his adversary. He couldn't believe that there was still no dent in that arrogant exterior, no crack in the charming facade. 'Dr Hill,' Vance said, not a tremor in the professionally smooth voice. 'I wish I could say it was a pleasure, but that would be too much of a lie for anyone to swallow. A bit like your insane accusations.'

'Dr Hill has agreed to talk to you,' Marshall interrupted. 'We will be taping the conversation. I'll leave you now.'

He backed out and Vance waved Tony to a chair. The psychologist shook his head and leaned against the wall, arms folded. 'What did you want me for?' Tony asked. 'A confession?'

'If I wanted confession, I'd have asked for a priest. I wanted to see you face to face to tell you that as soon as I get out of here I will be suing you and DCI Jordan for slander.'

Tony laughed. 'Go ahead. We're neither of us worth a fraction of your annual earnings. You'll be the one who ends up shelling out a fortune in legal costs. Me, I'd relish the opportunity to get you on a witness stand under oath.'

'That's something you'll never achieve.' Vance leaned back in his chair. His eyes were cold, his smile reptilian. 'These trumped-up accusations won't stand up in the cold light of day. What have you got? This dossier of yours with its doctored photographs and circumstantial coincidences. "Here's Jacko Vance on the M1 at Leeds the night Shaz Bowman died." Well, yes, that's because my second home is in Northumberland and that's the best way to get there.' His sonorous voice dripped sarcasm.

'What about, "Here's Jacko Vance with a body in the cellar"? Or, "Here's a photo of Jacko Vance with the dead girl from his cellar when she was still living, breathing and laughing"?' Tony asked, keeping his voice level and mild. Let Vance get worked up, let him be the one to strain at the leash of his self-control.

Vance's response was a sardonic smile. 'It was your officers

478

who provided the answer to that,' he said. 'They were the ones who raised the possibility of a stalker. It's not so unlikely. Stalkers become obsessed with their targets. I don't find it too hard to imagine a stalker tracking me back to Northumberland. Everybody locally knows Doreen Elliott keeps a set of my keys and, like most of the people round here, she never locks her door if she's only popping next door for a cup of tea, or down to her vegetable garden to dig some potatoes. Child's play to borrow the keys and have a set made.'

As he warmed to his theme, his smile broadened and his body language grew more relaxed. 'It's also common knowledge that I had a nuclear shelter built in the chapel crypt. Slightly embarrassing in these days of détente, but I can live with that,' Vance continued, leaning forward now, his prosthesis resting on the table, his other arm hooked over the back of the chair. 'And let's not forget the very public vendetta with my ex-fiancée who, as you rightly pointed out, bears a strong resemblance to these poor missing girls. I mean, wouldn't you think you were doing me a favour by killing her image if you were obsessed with me?' His grin was positively triumphal.

'And you are, aren't you, Dr Hill? Or rather, as I will take great pleasure in explaining to the world's press, you're obsessed with my wife, I believe. Shaz Bowman's tragic death gave you the opportunity to force your way into our lives and when dear, sweet Micky agreed to have dinner with you, you formed the view that without me, she'd fall into your arms. And your sad delusion has brought us to this point.' He shook his confident head pityingly.

Tony lifted his head and stared into a pair of eyes that could have come from Mars for all the humanity they contained. 'You killed Shaz Bowman. You killed Donna Doyle.'

'You'll never prove that. Since it's a complete fabrication, you'll never prove it,' Vance said with an air of nonchalance. Then he raised one arm and covered first his eyes, then his mouth and finally, stroked his ear. To a casual observer, it was merely the gesture of a tired man. Tony read it instantly as the taunt it was.

He pushed off from the wall and took two long steps across the room. Leaning on his fists, he thrust his face into Vance's personal space. In spite of himself, the TV star craned his head back like a tortoise retreating into its shell. 'You may be right,' Tony said. 'It is entirely possible that we will never nail you for Shaz Bowman or Donna Doyle. But I'll tell you something, Jacko. You weren't always this good. We'll get you for Barbara Fenwick.'

'I have no idea what you're talking about,' Vance said contemptuously.

Tony stood up and slowly began to stroll around the confined space as leisurely as if it were the local park. 'Twelve years ago when you killed Barbara Fenwick there were a lot of things forensic science couldn't do. Take toolmarks, for example. Pretty crude, the comparisons they made back then. But these days, they've got scanning electron microscopes and back-scatter electron microscopes. Don't ask me how they work, but they can compare an injury to an implement and say whether the two match up. Within the next few days, they'll be matching the bones in Donna Doyle's damaged arm to the vice in your house.' He glanced at his watch. 'With a bit of luck, the pathologist will be on her way now. Professor Elizabeth Stewart. I don't know if you've heard of her, but she has a terrific reputation in forensic anthropology as well as pathology. If anyone can find the match between your vice and Donna's injuries, it's Liz Stewart. Now, I realize that doesn't implicate you if we accept the fantasy you've been spinning here.'

He turned slowly to face Vance. 'But it would if the vice matched Barbara Fenwick's bone injuries, wouldn't it? Serial killers often like to use the same weapon for all their murders. But it's hard to imagine a stalker who's followed you around on a killing spree for twelve years and never put a foot wrong, don't you think?'

This time, he saw a flicker of uncertainty in Vance's confident mask. 'What utter rubbish. Just for the sake of argument, even if you got an exhumation order, no Crown Prosecutor is going to push a case that depends on a mark on a piece of bone that's been in the ground for twelve years.'

'I couldn't agree more,' Tony said. 'But you see, the pathologist who did the postmortem on Barbara Fenwick had never seen injuries quite like that. They intrigued her. And she is a university professor. Professor Elizabeth Stewart, actually. She applied to the Home Office to retain Barbara Fenwick's arm so she could use it as a teaching aid. To illustrate the effect on bone and flesh of blunt trauma from compression. Funnily enough, she noticed that there was a slight imperfection on the bottom edge of the implement that inflicted the injuries. A tiny projection of metal that made a mark in bone as distinctive as a fingerprint.' He let the words hang in the air. Vance's eyes never left his face.

'When Professor Stewart moved to London, she left the arm behind. For the last twelve years, Barbara Fenwick's arm has been perfectly preserved in the anatomy department of Manchester University.' Tony smiled gently. 'One solid piece of irrefutable evidence tying you to a weapon used on a murder victim, and suddenly the circumstantial looks very different, don't you think?'

He walked to the door and opened it. 'And by the way –

I don't fancy your wife in the slightest. *I've* never been so inadequate that I had to hide behind a lesbian.'

In the corridor, Tony signalled to the uniformed officer by the door that he should go back into the interview room. Then, exhausted by the effort of confronting Vance, he leaned against the wall, sliding down into a squat, elbows on knees and hands over his face.

He was still there ten minutes later when Carol Jordan emerged from the viewing room where she and Marshall had watched the encounter between the hunter and the killer. She crouched in front of him and took his head between her hands. He looked into her face. 'What do you think?' he said anxiously.

'You convinced Phil Marshall,' she said. 'He's spoken to Professor Stewart. She wasn't too thrilled at being woken in the middle of the night, but when Marshall explained what was what, she got really excited. There's a train gets in from London around nine. She'll be on it, with her famous slides of the injury. Marshall's organized someone to go over and collect Barbara Fenwick's arm from Manchester University first thing. If it looks like a match, they'll charge him.'

Tony closed his eyes. 'I just hope he's still using the same vice.'

'Oh, I think you'll find he is,' Carol said eagerly. 'We were watching. You couldn't see from where you were, but when you hit him with Professor Stewart and her pre-served arm, his right leg started jittering up and down. He couldn't control it. He's still got the same vice. I'd stake my life on it.'

Tony felt a smile gather the corners of his mouth. 'I think the fat lady just landed.' He put his arms round Carol and stood up, bringing her with him. He held her at arm's length and grinned down at her.

'You did a great job in there. I'm really proud to be on your team.' Her face was solemn, her eyes grave.

Tony dropped his arms and took a deep breath. 'Carol, I've been running away from you for a long time,' he said.

Carol nodded. 'I think I understand why.' She looked down, reluctant to meet his eyes now they were finally having this conversation.

'Oh?'

The muscles along her jaw tightened, then she looked up at him. 'I didn't have blood on my hands. So I could never understand what it feels like to be you. Di Earnshaw's death changed that. And the fact that neither of us could save Donna . . .'

Tony nodded bleakly. 'It's not a comfortable thing to have in common.'

Carol had often visualized a moment like this between them. She had thought she knew what she wanted to happen. Now, she was taken aback to find her responses so different from what she had imagined. She put a hand on his forearm and said, 'It's easier for friends to share than lovers, Tony.'

He gazed at her for a long moment, frowning. He thought of the bodies Jacko Vance had incinerated in the hospital where he gave his time to sit with the dying. He thought of the loss of what Shaz Bowman could have achieved. He thought of all the other deaths that still lay ahead of them both. And he thought of redemption, not through work, but through friendship. His face cleared and he smiled. 'You know, I think you could be right.'

EPILOGUE

Murder was like magic, he thought. The quickness of his hand had always deceived the eye, and that was how it was going to stay. They thought they had him trapped, sewn into a bag and wrapped with chains of guilt. They thought they were lowering him into a tank of proof that would drown him. But he was Houdini. He would burst free when they least expected it.

Jacko Vance lay on the narrow police cell bed, the real arm tucked behind his head. He stared at the ceiling, remembering how he had felt in hospital, the only other place where he'd had no choice about staying put. There had been pockets of despair and impotent anger and he knew those would probably afflict him again before he was free of this place and others like it. But when he'd been in hospital, he'd known he would be free of it all one day and he'd focused all his powerful intelligence on shaping that moment.

True, he'd had Micky's help then. He wondered if he could still rely on her. He thought that as long as he could cast credible doubt, she would stand by him. As soon as it looked like he was going under, she'd be gone. Since he had no intention of letting that happen, he thought he could probably be sure of her.

The evidence was flimsy. But he couldn't deny that Tony Hill was impressive in his command of it. He would be hard to discredit in a courtroom, even if Vance succeeded in planting advance press stories accusing the psychologist of being obsessed with Micky. And there was a risk there. Hill had somehow discovered that Micky was a lesbian. If he leaked that in response to an accusation against him, it would do serious damage both to Micky's credibility and his own image as a man who needed no other woman but his adorable wife.

No, if it came to a court battle, even with a jury of telly addicts, Vance would be at risk. He had to make certain it never went past a preliminary hearing. He had to destroy the evidence against him, to demonstrate there was no case to answer.

The greatest threat came from the pathologist and her reading of the toolmarks. If he could discredit that, there were only circumstantial details. Together, they weighed heavy, but individually, they could be undermined. The vice was too solid a piece of substantiation to submit to that.

The first step was to cast doubt on whether the arm from the university really belonged to Barbara Fenwick. In a university pathology department, it could not be held under the sort of security of a police evidence room. Anyone could have had access to it over the years. It could even have been replaced with another arm deliberately crushed in his vice by, say, a police officer determined to frame him. Or students could have swapped it in some macabre prank. Yes, a little work there could force a few cracks into the reliability of the preserved arm.

The second step was to prove the vice had not belonged to him when Barbara Fenwick had died. He lay on the hard mattress and racked his brains to find an answer. 'Phyllis,' he eventually murmured, a sly smile creeping across his face. 'Phyllis Gates.'

She'd had terminal cancer. It had started in her left breast then worked its way through her lymphatic system and finally, agonizingly, into her spine. He'd spent several nights by her bedside, sometimes talking, sometimes simply holding her hand in silence. He loved the sense of power that working with the virtual dead gave him. They'd be gone, and he would still be here, on top of the world. Phyllis Gates was long gone, but her twin brother Terry was alive and well. Presumably he was still running his market stall.

Terry sold tools. New and second-hand. Terry credited Vance with the only happiness his sister had known in the last weeks of her life. Terry would walk on hot coals for Vance. Terry would think telling a jury he'd sold the vice to Vance only a couple of years previously was the least he could do to repay the debt.

Vance sat upright, stretching out his arms like a hero accepting the adulation of the crowd. He'd worked it out. He was as good as a free man. Murder was indeed like magic. And one day soon, Tony Hill would find that out for himself. Vance could hardly wait.